IRRESISTIBLE BILLIONAIRES

A Second Chance Romance Box Set

SCARLETT KING

MICHELLE LOVE

CONTENTS

1. The Billionaire's Forbidden Desires	1
Blurb	3
Coy	4
Collin	9
Fiona	15
Collin	21
Coy	28
Fiona	33
Collin	38
Fiona	42
Collin	48
Lila	54
Fiona	60
Collin	67
Fiona	73
Collin	77
Fiona	84
Coy	90
Lila	96
Coy	102
Lila	108
Coy	114
Lila	120
Coy	126
Lila	132
Coy	138
Lila	144
Epilogue	151
2. Make Her Mine	155
Blurb	157
Tyrell	158
Ella	165
Tyrell	170

Ella	176
Tyrell	182
Ella	187
Tyrell	193
Ella	198
Tyrell	204
Ella	210
Tyrell	215
Ella	221
Tyrell	226
Ella	232
Tyrell	237
Ella	243
Tyrell	248
Ella	253
Tyrell	259
Ella	264
Tyrell	269
Ella	274
Tyrell	280
Ella	285
Tyrell	290
Ella	295
Tyrell	300
Ella	305
Tyrell	310
3. Make Her Mine Extended Epilogue	320
4. Collin's Curse	334
Collin	335
Hilda	339
Collin	343
Hilda	347
Collin	351
5. His Revenge	354
Blurb	355
Jasper	357
Tiffany	364
Jasper	370
Tiffany	376

Jasper	382
Tiffany	388
Jasper	394
Tiffany	399
Jasper	405
Tiffany	411
Jasper	416
Tiffany	422
Jasper	427
Tiffany	433
Jasper	439
Tiffany	445
Jasper	451
Tiffany	456
Jasper	462
Tiffany	468
Jasper	474
Tiffany	480
Jasper	486
Tiffany	492
Jasper	498
Tiffany	504
Jasper	510
Tiffany	516
Jasper	522
6. His Revenge Extended Epilogue	533
7. Fiona's Catch	548
Fiona	553
Collin	557
Fiona	561
Collin	565
8. Stealing His Heart	569
Blurb	571
Cash	572
Bobbi Jo	579
Cash	584
Bobbi Jo	590
Cash	596
Bobbi Jo	602

Cash 608
Bobbi Jo 614
Cash 620
Bobbi Jo 626
Cash 632
Bobbi Jo 638
Cash 644
Bobbi Jo 650
Cash 656
Bobbi Jo 662
Cash 668
Bobbi Jo 674
Cash 680
Bobbi Jo 686
Cash 692
Bobbi Jo 698
Cash 704
Bobbi Jo 710
Cash 716
Bobbi Jo 722
Cash 728
Bobbi Jo 733
Cash 738
Bobbi Jo 743
Epilogue 747

Cash 749

Published in the USA by Scarlett King & Michelle Love

©Copyright 2021

ISBN-13: 978-1-63970-078-3

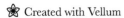 Created with Vellum

1. THE BILLIONAIRE'S FORBIDDEN DESIRES

A Second Chance Baby Romance
(The Irresistible Brothers Prequel)

BLURB

**I've bent her near to the breaking point for
what she's stolen from me—my heart.**
But she will never carry my name.
Only a woman of integrity can have that
— only integrity isn't my cup of tea.
It's time to grow up and be responsible.
Leave the past where it belongs.
Leave my sinful ways behind and find a good woman.
A woman that my family will accept.
She'll have to stay with me—in secret—feeding my darkest
desires.

COY

May 1988 – Carthage, Texas

My high school graduation party, meant to reacquaint me with those I'd attended kindergarten with, had me nearly as nervous as the day my parents dropped me off at boarding school in Dallas when I was just six years old. "This is surreal."

My mother patted me on the back as she smiled. "I know it feels that way to you. I want you to have a good time, though. So, don't let nerves get the best of you, son."

Nodding, I sipped on some punch as people began showing up. At first, I stayed seated, but then I got up and went to the door to welcome everyone and introduce myself to those I'd known back when I was young. "Coy Gentry." I shook a guy's hand as he came in.

"Yeah, I know." Freckles speckled his face as he smiled at me. "Tanner Richardson — I sat behind you in our kindergarten class."

"Wow, you remember that?" I couldn't believe it. "It's great to see you again, Tanner."

"Yeah, you too, Coy."

I pointed to the refreshments. "Go grab something to eat and drink, and we'll catch up later on."

As soon as he walked away, another guy I recognized from

school entered, and then more and more of my old classmates followed. In no time, I felt as comfortable as I'd felt at boarding school with the kids I'd grown up with.

Chatting with a group of guys as we hung out on the outer edge of the dancefloor, the band playing a slow country song, I caught something out of the corner of my eye. When I turned to see what had captured my attention, I was left breathless.

She had long, dark hair that shone in the twinkling lights. Her dark eyes reminded me of those of a doe's, and her caramel complexion, flawless. My eyes moved down her body, finding curves that some might find to be on the dangerous side — I found them delightful.

Scanning back up her body, I realized that her eyes were on mine and that a smile was curving her plump lips. I moved toward her, pulled in like a magnet. "Wanna dance?"

"Okay." She held her hand out, and I took it.

For a moment, I had no idea what was happening. My head felt light, my heart sped up as sparks of electricity shot all through me, and my manhood tingled. "Thanks."

Pulling her into my arms, making sure to leave some respectful distance between our bodies, I began to move slowly back and forth. "So, your name is?"

"Oh, yeah. I forgot to introduce myself. I'm Coy Gentry. And you are?"

"Lila Stevens." Pink filled her cheeks as her eyes darted away from mine. "So, I'm dancing with the guy who's throwing this party."

"You are." I pulled her a bit closer, inhaling her scent. Baby powder and the slightest hint of lemons made me heady for some reason. "Did you graduate this year too?"

"I did. I wasn't in your kindergarten class, though. But the ad in the newspaper said this party was for the entire graduating class of Carthage High." Her hand moved across my shoulder as she got more comfortable in my arms. "I heard you went to an all-boys school. So, where'd you learn how to dance?"

"We had socials with all-girls schools." I liked the way she moved. "You dance well. Where'd you learn how to dance?"

"At local dances. So, I guess you'll be leaving to go to college at the end of the summer."

"Yeah. Lubbock to Texas Tech. That's where both my parents went."

"Your mom was my third-grade teacher. She talked about you, and there were pictures of you on her desk too. You were a cute kid." She ducked her head as if feeling shy. "You've grown into a handsome young man, Coy Gentry."

My body heated. "You're a beautiful young woman, Lila Stevens."

"I bet you say that to all girls." She laughed a little. I loved the way it sounded.

"I do not." I hadn't dated anyone. My studies were too important to let romance interfere. At least, that's what my father and grandfather had shoved down my throat since I'd hit puberty. "I haven't talked to many girls."

Her dark eyes widened. "So, am I to believe that I'm the first girl you've called beautiful?"

It was the truth. "You are."

The band switched to another song, this one on the faster side, so we had to move around the dancefloor, dancing the Texas two-step. With the music loud and the movement fast, we didn't talk; we just danced and laughed.

This is nice.

I couldn't seem to let her go, and before I knew it, we'd danced until we were out of breath. I didn't let go of her hand as I led her off the dancefloor. "Come on, let's get a drink."

"I'm with ya, Coy. Whew! You can sure tear up a dancefloor."

"So can you." I picked up a cup that was already filled with fruit punch and handed it to her. "Here ya go."

After we took a few gulps of the cold beverage, she asked, "When do you have to take off to Lubbock?"

"At the end of the summer. Are you heading out to college then too?"

"No. I'd go if I could. My family doesn't have the money to send any of us to school. It's just the way it is. I'll probably get a job at the grocery store or something like that. You can work your way up there. Start out sacking groceries, move up to cashier, then up to head cashier, and maybe even assistant manager a few years later."

She looked smarter than that. "Well, I bet you move up to a manager in no time, Lila."

Laughter peeled through the air as she must've thought it to be a crazy notion. "You've got faith in me that my family doesn't."

I didn't like to hear that. "I'm not trying to pry, but how were your grades in school?"

"A's and B's. I'm not dumb. It's complicated, but my family kind of keeps us all grounded, and we tend to stay in the same lane they walked in. Do you know what I mean?" She sipped the punch, then licked the red off of her lips.

A tremble ran through me as I watched her tongue graze over her lips. "Uh, yeah." I'd lost my train of thought as my manhood stirred. "Are you doing anything tomorrow?"

"Depends." Placing one hand on her hip, she cocked her head to one side.

"Depends on what?"

"What you're about to ask me to do with you."

"I thought I might take you up to Dallas and show you where I went to school, and then I'd take you to this fancy restaurant that's shaped like a huge sphere and is way up in the sky. It turns around in slow circles so you can see the entire downtown skyline too. Some of us went this one time, and I thought it would be the perfect place to take a date."

"How many dates have you taken there?"

I didn't want her to know how inexperienced I was. But then again, I didn't want to lie either. "Lila, I feel like I can be honest with you, and you won't make fun of me."

Her eyes drooped a little as she put the drink down and took my hand. "I promise you that I won't."

Relief spread through me. "Well, Lila, you're the first girl I've asked out."

Blinking a few times, she asked, "Are you serious right now?"

"I am." Butterflies began to swarm inside my stomach as I anticipated her walking away from me.

"Wow." She smiled and squeezed my hand. "What an honor. I would love to go on a date with you tomorrow, Coy."

"So, that's a yes, then?" I had to ask to be sure there wasn't a but that was still coming.

"That is a yes."

I've got a feeling this is going to turn out great!

COLLIN

September 1966 – Lubbock, Texas

"Guns up!" I held my hands up, pointing my finger to the sky, just like the rest of the people in the crowded stadium as the Red Riders took the football field. My last year at Texas Tech University would be one to remember, I'd make damn sure of that.

One year away from earning a bachelor's degree in Agriculture, I was well on my way to making my father proud. That was the mission—make Daddy proud.

My father was very exacting—he demanded certain things of me. And if I failed him, I got my ass handed to me. He'd taught me to be tough and unrelenting in anything I did. And so far, it had paid off.

I'd made good grades and got my name on the Dean's list. That had earned me a nice new truck from my father. When I went back home at the end of the school year and handed him my diploma, I knew I'd earn even more.

Managing the ranch my grandfather had built was my ultimate goal. My father would finally show me how everything worked. I'd been taught how to take care of the cattle, but I hadn't been taught the business part of the ranch. I was eager to get to that.

During the summer break, my parents had spoken a lot about

my future—about how it was time for me to find a good woman from a good family and settle down.

There was a girl back home who'd taken my heart. But she wasn't marriage material in my father's eyes. She came from the wrong side of town. Her family was poor, and her father a drunk. Not the kind of people my father wanted attached to the Gentry family name.

It wasn't easy to find the right woman to marry when I still had that girl on my mind. But I knew I had to get on the ball, or my father would be disappointed. And when Daddy was disappointed, things got really hard for me.

"Excuse me, please," a feminine voice spoke up beside me, making me look away from the football game. She moved to the seat on my other side, a smile on her pretty face. She had a creamy ivory complexion, bright blue eyes, and blonde hair pulled back into a high ponytail. "Don't worry, I won't bother you by asking lots of questions about the game. Even though I don't understand it at all." She smoothed out her denim skirt, running her hands along her bottom to tuck it under before sitting down.

A white, button-down shirt, starched and ironed, was tucked into the waistline of a skirt that fell down past her knees, even when she sat down. She looked the part of a college girl. She looked the part of a nice girl from a nice family.

I didn't say anything to her, though, just gave her a nod, then looked back to the football field. A breeze blew past her, sending a fresh scent to my nose. She smelled nice too. A nice girl from a nice family, who smelled nice.

"I haven't seen you around here before." I looked at her for only a moments and then quickly looked back at the field.

"I've just transferred here. I've been going to the University of Texas in Austin. But my father's company moved him to the Lubbock office. My parents haven't allowed me to live on campus, so I had to come with them up here. Daddy told me to go to a football game, so I could get to know people."

I hadn't asked for her life story. But I wasn't going to say that to her. "I'm Collin Gentry, from Carthage."

"Oh, how silly of me." She held out her hand as if she wanted to shake mine.

I looked at her hand, then took it, shaking it. "Why's that?"

"I haven't told you *my* name yet," she said as she laughed a little. "I'm Fiona Walton, currently from Lubbock, formerly from Austin. Isn't Carthage around the Dallas area?"

"It's about two and a half hours from Dallas, but it's the nearest big city. We've got a ranch. That's why I'm going to school here. I'm getting a bachelor's in ag."

"Well, that makes perfect sense if you're a rancher. I'm getting a bachelor's in education so I can become a teacher."

She looked like someone who'd become a teacher. And teaching was a noble profession. "I think you'd make an excellent teacher."

"Thank you. I think I will too. I adore children." She ran her hand over her ponytail. The sunlight made the golden strands sparkle.

"I've never been around children to know if I like them or not."

She laughed, and the sound made me smile. "You're funny."

I wasn't trying to be funny. But I liked her laugh. "Am I?"

A kid came into the stands with a box hanging around his neck filled with sodas, popcorn, and hotdogs. I held up two fingers, and he came my way. "What can I get ya, mister?"

"Two dogs, a bag of that popcorn, and a couple of sodas." I took the first soda he handed me and gave it to Fiona.

"Oh, for me?" She took the drink as she smiled. "Well, thank you, Collin Gentry."

I handed her one of the hotdogs too, and then put the popcorn bag in her lap. "Don't mention it, Fiona."

Biting into the warm hotdog, I realized I liked the way I felt with her. It was an easy feeling. We sat there, watching the game and eating without saying a word for a long time. And that was okay.

Our team was losing pretty badly when the quarterback caught the ball and ran for a touchdown. Everyone stood up, cheering him on—even Fiona. "Go, go, go!"

For a girl who didn't understand the game, she'd caught on quickly. When our team scored the touchdown, the crowd went wild. There was no way they could win the game, but at least now there would be a number on the scoreboard instead of a big fat goose egg.

As we sat back down, I opened my mouth, and out came words I hadn't thought of saying. "Wanna go get a chocolate malt and some fries when this is over?"

"Sure." Her cheeks went a nice shade of pink. "That sounds yummy."

"There's this little hole-in-the-wall café. It's got good cheeseburgers too. If you're hungry."

"I'm sure I will be by the time the game is over." The stadium lights came on as the sun had almost set, making her blue eyes sparkle.

Mom would like her.

Seeing as I wasn't into wasting my time on any woman, I had a few things I had to know about Fiona before I went any further. "You goin' to church in the morning?"

"With my family, yes." She winked at me. "The First Baptist Church downtown."

She's passed the religion test.

"That's nice."

"Will you be there?" she asked.

"Me?" I didn't go to church unless my parents made me.

"Yes, you."

"Well, no."

"I see."

On to the next one. It wasn't easy to ask a question about one's political choice, so coming up with that wasn't easy. After a few minutes of thinking hard about it, I finally said, "So, a Texan in the White House."

Her eyes cut to me as her lips pulled up to one side. "You're referring to President Lyndon B. Johnson?"

"Yes." I didn't exactly know how to say it, but knew I had to figure that out. "What do you think about him?"

"I think he's done a wonderful job. I voted for him over Barry Goldwater in the sixty-four election."

Another correct answer.

She was nearing a perfect score. "You said you moved here

because of your father's job. What does he do?"

"My father's an investment banker."

Score!

"Good job."

"It is a pretty good job." She smiled at me as her eyes twinkled. "You're a rancher, which is a good job as well. How'd you vote in the last election?"

"For the man who won." I knew she was onto me. I grinned at her. "And I'm a Baptist too. Christmas and Easter, I take the back pew while Momma and Daddy take their seats up front, as usual."

"Yes, my family likes to sit up front too. I sit with them." She looked at me for a long moment as I kept staring straight ahead. "It would be nice to see you in church tomorrow, Collin. I'll save you a seat right next to me—just in case you decide to come."

She seemed to be checking off boxes the same way I was. I knew if I didn't go to church the next day, she'd never give me the time of day again. If I went to church, she'd probably give me all the attention I could handle.

"Who knows, you might just see me there, sittin' next to you tomorrow morning. I assume services start at ten and end around noon? We could get lunch afterward."

"My mother always puts a roast on before we leave for church. So, you could come to our home for lunch."

We were setting up dates left and right. And, for once, no one would be angry or upset with me over who I was dating. For once, I could take my girl out in public without fear of my father finding out and tanning my hide. For once, I wouldn't have to hide my relationship. "It's been a while since I had a good home-cooked meal."

"My mother is a wonderful cook. I'm not too bad myself either."

And she can cook too?

"I bet you are. What'll you be making for tomorrow's lunch?"

"I think I'll make some black-eyed peas and a pan of cornbread."

I have hit the jackpot!

But there was one thing I had to know first. "Do you add sugar to your cornbread?"

"Never."

And we have a winner!

"Good. I hate when people make the cornbread sweet. It makes it taste like cake, and who wants to have cake with their meal? Not me."

"I hope you like sweet tea. Mom always makes that. She serves it over plenty of ice, too."

This girl is almost too good to be true.

"What's a meal without ice-cold sweet tea?"

"I know." She laughed again.

I couldn't help but smile at her. She was perfect. She'd make any man proud to call her his.

My father would be proud if I brought this little filly home to the ranch. Momma would adore her too. And me—well, I would like her. She was nice. Pretty. Wholesome.

Those weren't things I particularly looked for in a woman. I usually liked a bit more excitement—some darkness instead of pure-white purity. But my father wouldn't allow that. So, I would give him what he wanted. And I could be happy enough with a woman like Fiona.

Happy enough was better than nothing. Happy enough was something I could build a life around.

Maybe I wasn't meant to have it all. Maybe no one was. But I could have a nice life with this nice girl. We'd have some nice-looking kids, too. Kids that our families would accept.

The girl I had left behind had given up so much for me, and here I was, looking at this pretty young woman with thoughts of marriage and raising a family with her. Guilt wasn't a thing I often felt, but as I thought about how hurt she'd be when I went back to Carthage with a wife, guilt welled up inside of me.

My father's voice echoed in my brain, "Time to grow up and do the responsible adult thing, Collin. Leave the past where it belongs. Leave your sinful ways behind you, and go into the future with a good woman. A woman the whole family will proudly call a Gentry."

I can do wholesome—I think. df

14

FIONA

Collin Gentry wasn't the most polite man, nor was he the most talkative. He was very handsome, though, and that made up for the things he lacked.

I blamed it on him being raised on a ranch with cattle and other animals instead of plenty of people. It was clear that he liked his solitude, never staying out past ten on none of the nights we had a date. He'd tell me that he had to get back to his dorm so he could wind down before going to sleep.

I'd had a couple of boyfriends before. They'd both had a hard time leaving me after they'd taken me out. Collin had no trouble leaving me at all.

We'd been dating for three months, and he'd never done more than kiss my cheek. He rarely held my hand, and he never told me how pretty I was or how happy I made him feel.

Somehow, I knew he did like me, though. He kept making time to see me—that let me know that I was special to him. Collin didn't care to spend time with anyone other than me. That had to mean something.

He'd met my parents, of course, as he joined us for lunch after church every Sunday. That was another reason I knew that he liked me. He'd come to church each Sunday since we'd met, sitting next to me in the front row, despite what he'd said when we'd first talked at the football game. No man would do a thing like that unless they actually liked a woman.

I'd never known a guy like Collin. Quiet, not in a rush to get to the first kiss or second or third base. My father told me he suspected Collin was looking at me as wife material. And he'd asked me what I thought about that, should the time come that Collin went to my father to ask for my hand in marriage.

Although I couldn't exactly explain why I felt the way I did, I still felt it. "I think I would like to be Collin Gentry's wife. He's a man who isn't into things most guys his age are into. He's rock-solid, too. Plus, he's nice to look at."

My father had given me a nod, and I knew that meant he'd tell Collin that he could marry me—if he ever asked.

Parents' weekend had come at the university, and Collin had told me that his parents would be coming to Lubbock to spend the weekend there. But he hadn't asked me if I wanted to meet them yet —which I did, of course.

Saturday morning turned into afternoon, and still no call from Collin. I tried to keep myself occupied by writing an essay for my biology class, but my head wasn't in it. I kept looking out the window, hoping to find Collin driving his truck into the driveway.

A knock came on my bedroom door, making me jump. "Honey, you've got a phone call in your father's office."

Springing to my feet, I ran to the door, throwing it open and running right past my mother. "Thanks, Mom."

My bare feet pounded against the wood floor as I sprinted to my father's office at the far end of the house. There was only one phone, and my father thought it should be in his office in case he had to take calls from his work while at home. He smiled at me as I came in, and I skidded to a stop. Pointing to the phone, which lay on his desk, he said, "I'll give you some privacy, dear."

"Thank you, Daddy." I picked up the phone just as my father closed the door. "Hello?"

"Hello, Fiona. This is Collin Gentry."

I tried not to laugh, as I'd easily recognized his deep voice. "Hello, Collin. How are you doing this afternoon?"

"I'm doing well. My parents arrived a short time ago, and they would like to invite you and your parents to join us for dinner at a restaurant in town. Would you like that?"

"I would love to. Can you hang on a moment while I ask my parents if they're free to go to dinner?"

"I can wait."

Putting the phone down, I raced out of my father's office. "Mom, Dad! Mom, Dad!"

My mother came out of the living room and into the hallway as I ran along it. "For goodness sakes, why are you shouting, dear?"

I stopped running and tried to control my voice. "Mom, do you and Dad have any plans for dinner tonight?"

She folded her arms and cocked her head. "Why do you ask?"

"Because Collin's parents are in town for parents' weekend, and they've invited all of us to go out to dinner with them somewhere here in town."

"Let me ask your father." She walked back into the living room. "Darling, your daughter would like it if we could go to dinner with Collin's parents this evening."

"I heard her talking to you in the hallway." He smiled at me. "And you look as if you'd love us to go."

Clapping my hands, I jumped up and down. "I would adore it if you would go."

"We're free, dear. Tell them we'd love to join them. Get the details, and I'll get us there on time."

Spinning around, I hurried back to the phone, nearly out of breath from all the running. "They said yes, Collin. We would love to meet you for dinner this evening." I sat in Dad's chair, trying to catch my breath as quietly as I could.

"Good. We'll see you at seven at the Fiesta Grill, then. Bye." And then he hung up, Collin-style. No sweet words of how he'd miss me until he saw me again, nothing but a solid 'bye.'

"Mexican food," I said quietly as I began nibbling my fingernail.

Spicy food and my tummy didn't get along well. And pinto beans gave me gas. But I was sure I could find something on the menu that wouldn't end up making my tummy rumble.

My parents, like most parents, had a steadfast rule—eat

everything on your plate. That meant I would have my work cut out for me, finding something to order.

Hours later, with my hair teased so that it stood high and pulled away from my face with a black headband and my bangs pulled forward, I put on a modest amount of makeup. My blue dress made my eyes pop, and pair of black flats finished my ensemble. Mom had put her strand of pearls around my neck to make me look even better.

My parents were dressed nicely as well. We all wanted to make a good first impression on Collin's parents. I'd never been so nervous in my life. "I'm shaking." I held out my hand, and my mother took it into hers.

She held it as we walked into the restaurant. "There's absolutely nothing to be nervous about, Fiona."

She could say that all she wanted, but it didn't make the butterflies inside my stomach swarm any less. "There they are." I spotted Collin, who had just sat down with his parents at a table for six.

Gulping, I looked at the back of his father's head. Dark hair, thick and wavy. I could easily see from where Collin had gotten his. And his mother had a sharply pointed nose—Collin had inherited a male version of it.

As soon as Collin saw us, he stood up and walked to us, shaking my father's hand. "Thank you for coming, Mr. Walton." He nodded at my mother. "Mrs. Walton, thank you for coming."

I waited for him to say something about how nice I looked. "Do you think this dress is okay, Collin?"

He smiled and nodded, then took the hand my mother had just released. "Come, let me introduce you to my parents."

After the introductions were over and done with, Collin pulled out the chair next to his, and I sat down. "Thank you, Collin."

He wasn't always such a gentleman. Often, he'd forget to open the door of his truck for me to get in. He rarely opened doors for me. But he didn't seem to think of doing such things, so I hadn't been completely offended.

He sat down next to me, and the smile he wore told me he was incredibly happy. Collin didn't smile often. And he never smiled for no reason at all. "Fiona is going to become a teacher."

"Is that so?" his mother asked me.

"Yes, ma'am," I said as I smiled at her. "I love children and can't wait to begin my teaching career."

Collin looked at me with a bit of confusion in his dark eyes. "Well, I'm sure you won't always teach. I wouldn't call it a career, Fiona. Someday, you'll have a family to take care of, and you won't be able to work and do that at the same time."

Although what he said bothered me a bit, I was sort of thrilled he was talking about this. "Well, of course my family would always come before anything else. When I have one. If I have one."

My mother laughed. "Certainly, you will have a family someday, Fiona."

My response pleased Collin, and his smile grew even bigger. "Certainly, you will. You would be a great mother."

My cheeks heated with embarrassment as I ducked my head. "Thank you."

His fingers touched my chin, lifting up my face to look at him. "And you'd make a great wife too, Fiona."

My heart stopped. *Is he going to ask me to marry him right here—right now?*

His father spoke, pulling my attention, "In the future. She must finish college and get her degree first."

"Of course," Collin said as he removed his hand from my face.

My flesh burned where he'd touched me. The touch was the most intimate thing he'd ever given me thus far. It felt more intimate than even his chaste kisses on my cheek.

I'd been much closer with the boyfriends I'd had in the past, especially after seeing them for as long as I'd been seeing Collin. I'd talked to them tons in the first few months. But Collin and I didn't talk a whole lot.

When we had a date, we spent the entire time eating, sitting out on the porch swing, listening to the chirping sound of birds, and watching the sun setting in the evening sky. And then he'd bid me goodnight and leave.

All Collin really needed was someone to show him tenderness. I could do that. I could bring out the caring, sensual man in him. If only he'd let me.

As I sat there, talking to his parents and feeling at ease with them in record time, I knew this was something special. This was meant to last. Things like this didn't happen all the time.

It almost felt as if we were already family. Collin's parents were happy we'd found each other, and mine were too. Everyone agreed that Collin and I were a good match for each other. And that made me incredibly happy.

And the way Collin's smile hardly left his face told me that having both of our parents agree on our relationship meant the world to him.

And it meant the world to me too.

COLLIN

May 1967 – Lubbock, Texas

The end of the school year had come, and I knew it was time to do what I needed to do—even if my heart wasn't entirely in it. Guilt still plagued me whenever I thought about how hurt the girl I'd left behind would feel when she found out about this.

Fiona was everything a wife was supposed to be — in my parents' eyes, at least. My mother did love her, and my father kept telling me how lucky I was that she'd stumbled upon me that fateful evening at the football game. He also kept telling me not to let her get away.

I liked Fiona. I liked her a lot. But love?

Well, love wasn't all it was cracked up to be anyway. My heart still belonged to someone else. But my brain knew that could never be. It kept nagging me to hurry up and make Fiona my wife before someone else swooped in and took her away from me.

I saw other guys looking at her, wondering why she was with me, I was sure. I didn't wine and dine her. I didn't fawn all over her. And I didn't compliment her the way other guys did with their girls. That just wasn't me.

Fiona never complained about that, not even once. She

accepted me for who I was. Don't ask me why, because I do not know. But she did, and that was all I needed.

The last day of classes saw me fingering an engagement ring in my pocket as I made my way to her house. I knew Fiona wasn't home yet, but I wasn't going there to see her anyway.

My heart pounded as I got out of my truck and walked to the front door. *This is it. If her father says yes, then I'll soon be a married man. And that will be that.*

Closing my eyes, I saw the woman I'd left behind. Her dark eyes drooped with sadness as she held her hands out to me. I opened my eyes, knowing that I couldn't take her hands, even if they were real and right in front of me.

She wasn't meant for me.

Fiona would make a good wife; I was sure of it. So, I knocked on the door and waited, shifting my weight from one leg to the other, trying not to seem as nervous as I was.

Mrs. Walton answered the door. "Hello, Collin. I'm afraid that Fiona hasn't made it home yet. But come on in and wait for her."

"Mrs. Walton, I'm not here to see Fiona. I'd like to speak with Mr. Walton if that's okay." It felt like a herd of cattle was stampeding around inside my stomach.

Her blue eyes matched her daughter's, and they went wide as she looked at me with a smile on her lips. "You want to speak with Mr. Walton?"

"Yes, please." My head felt light. I'd never passed out before, but I was sure this was what occurred prior to that.

"Follow me. He's in his office." She led me down the hallway, then tapped on the door to his office. "Honey, Collin's here, and he'd like to speak with you."

"Well, send him in then."

My throat closed up, and I saw black at the edges of my vision as she opened the door and gently pushed me inside. I heard the door close behind me, leaving me and Mr. Walton alone. "Hello, sir."

"Hello, Collin. Have a seat." He gestured to the chair on the other side of the desk he was sitting at.

I shook my head. "I should stand."

With a smile, he winked at me. "Okay then. Why don't you tell me what you came here to talk to me about?"

I pulled the ring out of my pocket and held it up. "I'd like to know if you would give me your permission to ask Fiona to marry me."

He clasped his hands, resting them on his desk. "You'd like to marry my daughter, Collin?"

"Yes, I would like that very much, sir." My mouth was as dry as a cotton ball.

"And if she says yes to your proposal, then would you two be living at the ranch in Carthage?"

I nodded. "Yes, sir."

"Would you two have your own home, or would you be living with your parents?"

"The ranch house is big enough for all of us to live there without getting in each other's way."

"What about Fiona being able to keep her own house? A woman likes to do that. And what about the cooking?"

"We have a cook and maids. Fiona wouldn't have to do any of those things."

"I'm not sure she would like that." He chuckled. "You know, being waited on hand and foot."

"It's not like that. It's just that our house is kept clean, and our laundry is done by the maids. And our meals are cooked by the cook. But we're not ones to ask people to wait on us hand and foot, sir. There are lots to do at the ranch—that's why we have the staff to keep the house and cook for us."

His green eyes narrowed. "Do you love my daughter, Collin?"

Oh, shit!

I had to tell her father that I did love Fiona, or he'd surely say no. So, I opened my mouth, and the lie popped out. "Yes, sir."

The smile he gave me told me he was happy with my answer. "Then I would love to give you my permission to ask Fiona to marry you."

Just then, the door flew open, and there stood Fiona with her mouth gaping. "Collin?"

I tried to shove the ring back into my pocket, but her eyes were already glued on it. "Fiona!"

Moving fast, she came right up to me. "I overheard you talking, Collin." She reached out, wiggling her fingers. "Can I see what you have in your fist?"

I opened my hand, the ring sitting on my palm. "It's for you."

She picked it up off my hand. "It's very pretty."

"I'm glad you like it." I wasn't sure what to say.

Her father cleared his throat. "I'll get out of here and leave you two alone."

With him gone, I felt more comfortable saying what I had to say. "Fiona, your father gave me his blessing, so would you marry me?"

She put the ring on her finger — it was a little big on her. Looking at the ring, she smiled and then looked into my eyes. "I would love to marry you, Collin Gentry."

Relieved that she'd said yes, I let out a long sigh. "Ah, good. We can go see the jeweler and get it fitted properly."

"Good. And while we're there, we can pick out our wedding rings." She reached up, cradling my face between her hands. "Thank you."

Her lips trembled as if she was waiting for a kiss. And I knew it was time to give her a proper one. So, I took her hands, moving them away from my face as I leaned in and pressed my lips to hers.

There was no zing, no electricity. But there wasn't repulsion either, so I thought that a good sign.

A month later, we got married at Whisper Ranch with our families in attendance. Our mothers cried, and our fathers beamed with pride. Fiona looked beautiful in her white wedding gown. And for the first time, I let her know that. "White suits you, Fiona."

We'd come to my bedroom to spend the first night of our marriage. She turned her back to me. "Can you unzip this for me?"

My hand shook as I gently pulled down the zipper, not wanting to mess up the dress in any way. It was as perfect as she was. "Are you ready for this?"

She nodded. "Yes. Are you?"

I was a man, so I was always ready for sex. "I am."

It had been years since I'd had sex, so I was more than ready for it. But things weren't exactly right yet, even though we were now legally married.

After unzipping her dress, I turned off the light so the dark could hide us from each other. Undressing, I got into bed and soon felt her getting under the blanket with me.

I had thought that when this time would come, I would find it hard not to pounce on my wife. That wasn't happening, though. Instead, I found myself thinking about another woman—one I thought I'd left behind.

Fiona's hand moved slowly across my chest. "It's okay, Collin. I'm ready for this. I've saved my virginity all these years for the man I would marry—for you. What I have is yours now. Take it."

My heart ached as I turned over and put my body on top of hers. Closing my eyes, I went back in time, and suddenly I was with her again—with my Hilda.

With one hard thrust, I broke through the barrier. "Yes," I moaned.

Nails bit into my back as she whimpered, "Oh, God."

Moving, I knew the pain would fade. "You're going to be okay."

"You've done this before?" Fiona asked with surprise, pulling me out of my fantasy.

I wasn't sure what to say. So, I lied. "No. I've just been told that the pain goes away."

"Oh, I see. I like that we're each other's first." She lay with her legs flat against the bed, not moving at all.

I didn't agree since it wasn't true. "Maybe bend your knees. That might help." I knew it would help but didn't want to give my sexual knowledge away.

"I'd rather not."

Doing my best to make some friction between us, I moved faster, not wanting to take too long, as she seemed uncomfortable. "I'll try to hurry."

"Please do."

This wasn't how it was supposed to go. She wasn't supposed to act as if having sex with me was simply another one of her wifely duties—another chore to get through. "I think you're supposed to enjoy this, Fiona."

"At this point, that's impossible. But please enjoy yourself."

Perfect to the point of madness.

"You're too tense, that's why it keeps hurting. You need to relax."

"I can't."

Her body was like a vise, and that made me feel uncomfortable too. "I need you to." I tried to appeal to her need to be a good wife. "Can you try for me?"

With a soft sigh, she whispered, "Collin, it burns like fire between my legs right now. I'm doing my best not to cry. Can you please just do your business so this can be over?"

All I wanted to do was roll off her and get the hell out of that bed. But I didn't do that. I kept moving as she lay stiff as a board under me. I kept going until my body gave in, giving her the ending she wanted so badly. "Ugh!" I grunted as I came.

"Oh, God!" she cried out. But it wasn't with desire or ecstasy. Pure repulsion filled her voice as she whispered, "That feels so—so…" she seemed unable to find the right word, but then she found it, "…disgusting."

Rolling off her, I got up and went to get a wet washcloth. "I'll get something so you can clean yourself."

"Thank you," came her tear-soaked words. She tried to cry quietly, but I could still hear her.

Disappointment, frustration, and even anger filled me. If she would've just tried to relax and tried to enjoy it, things would've been so different.

I washed my face, which was hot with emotion. Then I wet a washcloth and went back to her, handing it to her. "Here, wash yourself."

"I'm sorry, Collin. I had no idea it would feel so painful and end with such a smelly liquid. I know I'm naïve in the ways of love, but that wasn't at all what I'd expected."

I got into bed feeling completely frustrated with her. "That smelly liquid is called semen, and it makes babies. You do want babies, don't you?"

"Yes." She got out of bed, and when she came back, she had on a nightgown. "Aren't you going to put on something to sleep in?"

"No." I turned over and closed my eyes, trying to push that horrible experience out of my mind.

"I'll wash the bed linens tomorrow. I don't want the maids to have to deal with this disgusting mess."

My teeth ground together as my jaws clenched. She might be naïve to the ways of love, but I wasn't. And this wasn't the way it was supposed to be.

COY

July 1988 – Carthage, Texas – Whisper Ranch

Lila and I laid on a pallet on the ground beneath a blanket of stars in one of the back pastures of the ranch. No one came out here, as the cattle had been moved to another pasture to let this one recover for a few months.

We'd seen each other every day since the night we met at my graduation party. And we'd both found that neither one of our families wanted us together. Both her father and mine had forbidden it.

Dad had this archaic notion that our family was better than others in the small town. "When your last name is Gentry, you're expected to live your life a certain way," he'd said, "and you only fraternize with people within your class. And you only date the best young ladies."

My mother wasn't even standing up for me, which I found strange. But she wasn't in good condition at the time, and I thought her weakened state must've been why she didn't have my back.

Lila and I weren't without ideas, though—and we certainly weren't going to let our families get in the way of us being together. We decided to see each other in secret. And when the time would come for me to go away to Lubbock, I'd take her with me.

I wasn't going to be living in the dorms anyway. My father had already bought a house up there for me to live in for the next four years.

Sure, there were still some things to hammer out. Like what I would do with Lila when my parents came to visit. But we'd figure it out. And my father had already promised me a hefty allowance, so I wouldn't have to work and could focus on my classes.

I figured I'd put Lila up in a hotel when my family came to visit. And she was down with that, so things were cool. Eventually, we'd come out with our relationship. But for now, we were keeping it under wraps.

And I was keeping her wrapped in my arms as much as I possibly could. "How come you're so damn easy to love, baby?"

"I could ask you the same thing." She put her hands on my face, then pulled me towards her for a kiss.

Before I knew it, I was on top of her, trying to rid her of her clothes so I could get to that soft and creamy flesh of hers. Nothing had ever felt as right as being with Lila did. I knew she was it for me. I knew it—without a doubt.

What I didn't understand was why our families were so against us. Sure, my father had given me his reasons—that our family was better than Lila's—that we were above them. But that was bullshit.

I was more curious about why Lila's family was also so against us being together. I thought they might be upset that my family were assholes. But that wasn't reason enough to hate me.

And they did hate me.

Lila had taken me to meet her family the day after the party. She'd had no idea they would react negatively. And I hadn't told her a thing about what my father had said to me that first night either.

Everyone was all smiles until I told them my last name. Her father had immediately asked the name of my father, and I told him, never thinking that he would have an issue with him. But he did.

I had no idea what it was because he wouldn't tell me or Lila. He just told me that I wasn't welcome in his home and that I was forbidden to speak to his daughter.

Lila and I knew one thing—our families were both hiding

something. And it seemed to be a deep, dark secret. There was no other reason for them to forbid a relationship between us.

But that was something to worry about later. Despite the problems we faced with our families, everything felt easy—and right —when we were together. We tried our best not to let those worries intrude.

Lila unbuttoned my shirt, moving her hands over my chest as she pushed me off her, only to climb on top of me and sitting up. Her breasts looked gorgeous in the moonlight—full, supple, and juicy.

She smiled down at me as her long, dark hair cascaded around her shoulders. "Coy, what will you do if our families find out about us?"

"I'll do whatever I have to do to keep you." I wasn't about to let them get in our way. "I know it's only been a little over a month since we met, but I love you."

"Me too." She sighed and looked up at the sky. "Can't you give us a break, God?"

I took her by the wrists, pulling her down to me until our lips met. I knew God had already given us so much, allowing us to meet. I wasn't going to ask him for more than what he'd already given.

I rolled back over, pinning her to the ground beneath me. "Lila, my father can take away everything, and I still wouldn't let you go. I never want you to worry about my commitment to you."

"My father hasn't ever given me anything he can take away. About all he can do is disown me and tell me to leave his home. But that's not really such a threat." She laughed. "I know it's different for you, though. You stand to inherit all of Whisper Ranch. And you'd be giving up so much more."

"I. Love. You," I reiterated, emphasizing each word with a kiss. "You are all I want in this world. Money isn't worth losing you over."

She stared into my eyes, looking into them in a way I was sure was meant to find the truth. "You would give it all up for me?"

"I would." I hoped it wouldn't come to that, but I wouldn't be bullied by money. "You know, the only thing that really bothers me is that I'd lose my parents. Mom, especially. Dad's always been a hard ass. But I've always thought that he did what he thought was best for me. Now, I'm not so sure."

"He sent you away to go to school. I think that was harsh."

"Yeah. I was only six."

"I can't imagine being away from my mother and father when I was that age. You must've been afraid when they left you there—that school looks so big and impersonal."

I'd taken her to see the place where I'd lived for so long. She'd compared it to growing up in an orphanage. It wasn't quite that bad, but it wasn't like growing up at home, with my family.

"I was afraid. I cried every night for the first month. And then, when I realized that my father wasn't going to let me come back home for anything more than brief visits, I stopped crying. I accepted it." And I knew that I could live my life without my parents being a part of it—if it came to that. My father had made sure I knew how to live without them.

"I'll never leave you, Coy." The way her hands moved over my back comforted me. No one had ever comforted me the way Lila could. Not even my mother.

I'd always felt closer to Mom. Growing up, I'd watched as she was forced to accept my father's will over and over again. She was as much a victim as I was. But she was strong in many ways, and he didn't run over her nearly as much as he did over me. I'd been a kid then, though. Now, at eighteen, I was considered a man. My father couldn't rule over me any longer.

Pushing her silky hair away from her face, I looked at her. She was worth losing everything—even my parents. "I will never leave you, Lila. And one day, we will make this official. I can't wait to marry you, you know."

Lila had two more weeks before she turned eighteen. "I can't wait to marry you, Coy. I would be more than happy to go down to the courthouse and file our marriage license the day I turn eighteen."

I wondered what our families would do if we just ran off, gotten married, and then went back home. They couldn't do much, I thought. It would be a done deal, and they would just have to get over themselves.

"I don't want to hide you away any longer. And I don't want to hide you away in Lubbock either. I think we should get married before the summer is over. That way, I can take you to Lubbock with me as my wife. It makes me feel bad that we have to hide things, even now. I don't want to keep doing it."

"People will call us crazy," she told me.

"Well, I *am* crazy. Over you." I smiled, then kissed her. Her kisses transported me to a place beyond earthly understanding. And I knew I wanted to go everywhere with her from now on.

To hell with our families. All that really matters is the two of us.

FIONA

December 1967 – Carthage, Texas – Whisper Ranch

Six months into our marriage, Collin began disappearing at night. Not every night, though. About every third or fourth night, I'd wake, and he'd be gone. Not wanting to wander around the huge house and risk waking people up, I'd stay in bed, awake, wondering where he'd gone.

He stayed away so long that I would eventually fall asleep, only to wake with him sleeping soundly in our bed. He'd always be naked and would reek of sexual activity.

My hopes were that he was somewhere pleasing himself and not having relations with someone else. Thus far, I hadn't been able to bring myself to talk to him about what he was doing.

I didn't find sex comfortable in the least. I could feel his frustration with me each time we had sex, which was once a week on Sunday nights.

I'd go to church each Sunday morning with his mother—Collin and his father never joined us. I found that odd since he'd come to church with me and my parents the entire year we were in Lubbock. But once we'd gotten back to his home, things changed.

I was the one who had made Sunday nights the night we'd have sex. And it was purely to make a baby and nothing else. I had no idea why I found sex to be so disgusting, but I did.

I hated the heat of his semen when it flushed into my body. And I found the smell so foul that it always made my stomach hurl, and I had to try my best not to gag.

So when he came back to bed, stinking of the stuff, I would always sleep with my head under the pillow to block the stench.

After a month of him leaving our bed, I finally felt I should ask him what was going on. I woke up to find him gone again, but this time I stayed up until he came back into the bedroom.

When he opened the door and found me sitting up in bed with the lamp on, he looked like a deer in the headlights. "What are you doing awake, Fiona?"

"I think it's time you tell me what has you getting out of bed in the dead of night only to return hours later smelling of semen." I crossed my arms over my chest and waited for his answer.

In an instant, his face turned red. "None of your damn business." He strode to the bathroom, turning on the shower. I found that odd, as he'd never done that before.

I sat in bed, tears stinging the backs of my eyes as thoughts filled my mind. There were some young maids who worked and lived in the house. *Is he sneaking out to have sex with one of them?*

Getting out of bed, I went to the bathroom. Opening the door, I found the glass shower door covered in steam so thick that I could barely make out his silhouette. "Collin, I know that I don't please you when we have sex. Are you sleeping with one of the maids?"

"No," he barked. "And you don't even *try* to please me."

"I'm sorry. I don't know how to make myself feel differently."

"You just lay there, stiff as a board. It's not easy for me to even have an orgasm. And then you make that horrible sound every time I ejaculate."

I hadn't realized that he'd heard my gagging. I'd tried hard not to do it, but it must've been escaping my mouth without my knowledge. "I'm sorry. I really am. And I'll try harder not to do that."

He'd said he hadn't been sleeping with one of the maids, and that made me feel better. But not by much.

"Why can't you at least bend your knees?" He turned the water off, and I turned my back to him so I wouldn't see him naked.

I hadn't liked the few glimpses I'd gotten of his manhood hanging between his legs. "It feels awkward when you make me try that."

"Why are you turning away from me?"

"Because you're naked, and I don't want to make you feel self-conscious." I thought it was a nice thing for me to do.

But he obviously didn't. "Turn around and look at your husband, Fiona Gentry."

Taking a deep breath, I did as he asked, making sure to keep my eyes above his waistline. "There, are you happy now?"

He moved his hand to hold his penis. "Look at this."

I didn't want to look at it. "Collin, stop."

"No," he shouted. "Look at this." He moved his hand, shaking his manhood as if trying to taunt me with it.

"You're being disgusting." I walked back to the bed and got under the blanket. "Have you been drinking?" I thought he must have been downstairs, getting drunk, and probably playing with himself—which made me sick.

"A bit." He came towards the bed, naked.

I turned the lamp off so I didn't have to witness his penis swinging around between his legs. "Let's just go to sleep. I'm tired."

"You shouldn't have stayed up waiting for me to come back to bed. *Our* bed." He flopped down onto the bed, making the springs moan under his weight. And then he moved some more, making them squeak and squeak.

"What are you doing?"

"This is what it's supposed to sound like when two people have sex on a bed."

"Please go to sleep. You're inebriated."

"You know, if it makes you so sick to have sex with me, maybe you should just get on your hands and knees so you don't have to face me when we do it."

Picturing what he'd suggested, I felt as if I might throw up. "You want to mount me like an animal?"

35

"That's one way of putting it. We should try that right now. Get on your knees."

I wasn't about to have sex with him. "It's Tuesday, not Sunday. Perhaps I'll want to try that horrible position then. I doubt it, though. Missionary is the best way. Sex is to make babies, and nothing else."

"You're wrong. And you're even wrong about that position. In the pictures, the woman bends her knees," he let me know.

"In the pictures?" I got the idea that he was looking at some pornographic magazines while playing with himself.

"Yes. There are pictures of people having sex. And in all the pictures I've seen, the woman is bending her knees. And guess what —there are many more positions. That's not the only one."

I didn't want to talk about this any longer. "Can we just go to sleep now?"

He turned to face me, leaning his head on his hand as he raised his upper body to look down at me. "Why does talking about sex with your husband disturb you so much?"

"It's not appropriate." I felt my cheeks heat with embarrassment.

"If it's not appropriate to talk with *me* about sex, then *who* is it appropriate for you to talk about this with? Because you need to talk to someone about your problem." His chest rose and fell as he sighed.

One tear escaped me, slowly sliding down my cheek. He made me feel like I was on trial. "It's *not* a problem, Collin. We have sex. If you want me to bend my knees, then I will."

"Good, let's try that now." He threw the blanket off me, then pulled at the hem of my gown to rid me of it.

But I wasn't having any of that. Instead, I held the gown tightly in my hands. "Not tonight."

"Why not?" He smiled at me. "Sunday isn't the only night we can do this."

"We're not doing this tonight because you are clearly drunk." I could smell the slight scent of whiskey on his hot breath. And I felt sure he'd already given himself an orgasm. "Plus, you've already spent yourself."

"I've got plenty left for you." He ran his hand over my shoulder as if trying to seduce me.

"Collin, please stop. I want to sleep."

"Come on," he said with a chuckle as if he thought himself funny. "Let's just get crazy and wild."

"I feel as if you aren't listening to me. I'm not going to have sex with you tonight. End of discussion. Go to sleep." Rolling onto my side, I turned my back to him.

"Fine." The bed creaked as he moved to lie on his side, turning his back to me as well.

This isn't the way I pictured our marriage at all.

COLLIN

I had no idea Fiona would turn out to be such a damn prude. If I had, I wouldn't have married her. I was a man, after all. A man with the same needs as any other man.

It was now obvious to me that Fiona wasn't ever going to like sex.

I'd tried for months—for years—to forget about Hilda. But when Fiona proved to be more than a disappointment in the bedroom, I found myself driving to Hilda's small apartment on the other side of town—the wrong side of town.

She didn't ask me a thing when I first went to her. She just opened the door and let me take her into my arms as if no time had passed at all.

Hilda didn't care that I would come to her late at night. We'd have amazing, insane sex, and then I'd leave. And Hilda never complained, not even once.

She saw the wedding ring on my finger, and I saw the pained look in her dark eyes. But she didn't ask me anything.

I hadn't meant for things to keep going between us. I knew it was selfish of me, but I thought I'd only need Hilda until my wife found her sexual footing. Once that happened, I thought I would stop going to her. I'd be able to get everything a man needed at home.

I liked to get rough with Hilda, but I knew better than to think I could ever do that with a good woman like my wife. All I'd wanted from her was some okay sex. But it seemed as if that was a pipe dream.

It also seemed that seeing Hilda wasn't going to end. I wasn't sure how to feel about that either. It had been much different, sneaking around to see Hilda when I was young and single. Now that I was older and married, it lacked the thrill it did before. Now it seemed downright dangerous.

If I was caught having an affair with another woman, it wouldn't be good. If I was caught having an affair with Hilda, a woman my family considered beneath me, it meant that I should expect the worst.

My father might well disown me if this ever came out. I might end up on the streets with nothing, and Fiona would end up getting all my inheritance. I knew my father well enough to know that he would add insult to injury if I defied his wishes. He'd throw me to the wolves before he'd listen to why I'd gone to her in the first place.

Fiona lived up to the role expected of my wife in every way, except where sex was concerned. She was devoted to me in every way, save one. She had no interest in pleasing me in bed nor in allowing me to please her.

Is there something wrong with Fiona?

I laid there with my back to her, trying to figure out what I'd done wrong, and began to switch gears. Maybe Fiona needed to see a doctor. Perhaps if a doctor told her it was okay to enjoy having sex with her husband, then she'd look at it in a different light.

I knew one thing for certain. I wanted an heir. I wanted children. And I knew I had to make things better between us.

Flipping over, I ran my hand over her shoulder, trying to be comforting. "Fiona, I think you need to see a doctor."

"What?" She turned to lie on her back, looking at me with wide eyes.

"You need to see a doctor. Sex should feel good for you. I don't think things are working right for you. Were you ever injured in that area?" There had to be some scientific explanation for her frigidity.

"No!" She shook her head indignantly. "I really don't want to have this conversation." She closed her eyes, her cheeks turning scarlet.

"I know you don't. But you're going to have this conversation with a doctor. You'll need to get examined thoroughly by a doctor to make sure nothing is wrong." I didn't know what else to do—I figured it was time for professional help.

"You mean that I *have* to go see a doctor and let him look at my privates?" Another shake of her head sent her blonde hair flying around her face. "No! Never!"

"Fiona, what do you think is going to happen to you when you get pregnant?" I had to wonder how she thought things like that worked. It was now clear to me that she was very naïve about all of this.

"I don't know. I don't care either. All I know is that I will deal with that when the time comes. For now, I *don't* have to deal with that. Nothing is wrong with me."

I went to put on some pajamas, as I no longer wished to be naked anywhere near my wife. "I'm not going to beg you to let me please you."

"Good." She turned back on her side and pulled up the blanket to cover all but her head. "I'm going to sleep."

After putting on my pajamas, I got into bed and tried not to think of the events of the night. I'd had such a good time before I came back home. Hilda had gone down on me, and I'd exploded in her mouth. And she'd loved it as much as I had.

Hilda let me do anything I wanted to her, and she loved everything I did to her, including whipping her sweet ass until it turned a rosy red.

If I ever even said a thing to Fiona about spanking her sweet ass, she'd chew me up and spit me out. She and I were not compatible as lovers, that was for sure.

Fiona sighed as I got back into bed, then turned to face me. "I know you expect me to be more daring in the bedroom. So, I will

40

try. I'll bend my knees. I'll even let you take me from behind. But I don't want to do anything else. It...doesn't feel right to me."

"You're missing out." I thought she should know that. "You really should see a doctor."

"I will see a doctor when I'm pregnant, but not before that. You can have me more than one way now, so be satisfied with that."

"I want to have sex with you three times a week, or even more. If you say that sex is only to make babies, then I want to make sure we make some. As your husband, I expect you to participate in this."

She made a loud sigh. "Fine. You can have sex with me every night if you feel it will help us conceive. But only in the ways I've stated."

"Foreplay will help stimulate you—help you enjoy it more." She didn't seem to know the basics about sex and conception. "I've been raising cattle and horses for quite a while now. When one cow comes into season, it forces the others to join in as well. The bull changes how he acts with them too. He's more playful with the cows, and there's plenty more physical contact before he actually mounts them."

"I've been at the ranch long enough to have witnessed that. And what I've seen is that the cows try to get away from the bull. It seems to me that his attention is more of a bother to them than anything." She wasn't going to budge.

"Fine, Fiona. But don't be surprised when I let myself go and let out a moan or two when we're doing it doggy-style."

"Please, don't call it that. This is already hard enough for me."

Why does she have to be such a fucking prude?

FIONA

1969 – Carthage, Texas – Whisper Ranch

Two years went by with no pregnancy. I'd gotten used to the sex. It never got to the point where I liked it, but I'd gotten used to it. Collin had gone from wanting sex every night for the first month of us trying to have a baby to being fine with twice a week. Sunday nights and Wednesday nights, we'd have sex twice, once when going to bed and once in the middle of the night when he'd wake me up by climbing on top of me.

It seemed as if he had a mission, and finally, the mission was accomplished. I came into the living room, where Collin and his parents were sitting after dinner. I'd gone to the doctor a week before and had gone back that day to find out what the test results were. I had the paper in my hand and hoped the news would be joyful for everyone.

Collin didn't even look up at me as I walked into the room. His mother did, though, shifting her attention away from the knitting in her lap. "Hello, dear." Her eyes went to the paper in my hand. "What do you have there?"

"I have something that will change our lives around here a little." I knew a baby would make quite a difference in the house; there hadn't been a little one in it since Collin was a baby.

Mother Gentry looked at her son. "Listen up, Collin. It seems that your wife has something to show us."

He raised his eyes from the book he'd been reading. "And what's that?"

I held the paper out as I went towards him, handing it to him. "Here you go. Read it yourself."

He looked the page over as his dark brows rose. "You've gone to see a doctor."

"I have." I couldn't wipe the smile off my face.

He smiled too. "And this says that you had a pregnancy test done last week."

"I did." I swayed back and forth as I waited for him to say the words I'd been waiting to hear.

"And this says that the test results were positive." He put the paper down as he looked at me. "We're having a baby?"

Nodding, I said, "We are."

Suddenly his mother was behind me, hugging me, and his father stood up, his eyes shining. Collin was the only one who didn't get up. Instead, he put the paper down and nodded. "Good. You've finally done what a wife is supposed to do."

His mother let me go as we both stared at Collin with gaping mouths. She finally asked, "Aren't you going to get up and give your wife a hug?"

"Why?" He picked the book back up. "For doing what God made her to do?"

His dispassionate reaction wasn't something I'd been prepared for; I ran out of the room as my eyes clouded with tears. I went right up the stairs, straight to our bedroom.

I slammed the door behind me, then ran to the bed and crashed onto it, sobbing into my pillow. "How can he be so mean?"

I'd given my husband the best news a wife could possibly give her husband, and he had acted as if it meant nothing to him. I didn't understand the man at all.

I hadn't heard him come into our bedroom with all my crying, but a hand on my shoulder let me know he had. "Fiona, why in the world are you crying?"

Sitting up, I had to restrain myself from slapping him—I wanted to so badly. "How can you ask me such a thing? I told you that we're going to have a baby, and you don't seem to care at all. It's been two years since we began trying so hard to make this baby. Two years, Collin! And you can't muster enough emotion to even give me a hug and tell me that you're happy."

"Of course I'm happy. You know I want kids. I don't understand why you would think otherwise." He sat on the bed beside me, running his hand through my hair. "I just meant that your body finally decided to do what it was made to do, bear children."

"And why is it that you think this long wait was due to *my* body and not *your* sperm?" I knew he was still pleasuring himself at least once or twice a week. Countless nights I'd woken to find him gone, coming back before sunrise. "You haven't been storing it up, after all."

He cocked his head. "What do you mean by that?"

"I mean that you've been playing with yourself—no doubt looking at porno magazines and ejaculating. That could well be the reason why it took us so long to conceive, rather than it being any fault of mine. The doctor performed an exam on me, and he found nothing wrong."

His brows shot up. "He did?" His jaws tightened. "And how did this exam go, exactly?"

I was immensely proud of myself for how trusting I'd been with the doctor. "Last week, when I went for the pregnancy test, he asked me if I'd ever had a pelvic exam, and I told him that I hadn't. He replied that I would need one to make sure my reproductive system was in good working order."

"And he found that it is?" he asked.

"He did." But I'd told my doctor more. "Once he told me that everything looked great, I told him about my lack of enthusiasm where sex is concerned, and he asked me to lie back and close my eyes while he did some tests."

With narrowed eyes, he asked, "What kinds of tests did he do?"

"Professional ones." I didn't like the way he looked at me. "Anyway, he used this instrument to stimulate a sexual organ he called a clitoris, and it worked."

"He gave you an orgasm?" shock filled his voice, and anger filled his eyes.

"Yes." I didn't understand why he was so angry. "Look, he said that the reason I probably don't like having sex with you has something to do with your attitude toward me. So, you might want to see what you can do about that." He had to realize that, as a woman, I needed more than he was giving—and not just physically. "You don't compliment me." The doctor had asked me a lot of questions about our relationship and how we communicated. He had been very kind and attentive, and he said that my aversion to having sex with Collin could have lots to do with how we treated each other outside of the bedroom.

"Never have," he agreed. "That never bothered you when we dated."

"Well, we weren't having sex then. I suppose a girl needs to hear nice things from her husband now and then if she's to enjoy having sex with him." And there'd been more the doctor had told me. "I also told him about how you're pleasuring yourself at least twice a week, and he said that's like a slap in the face to a woman. So there's another reason why I might not enjoy having sex with you."

"I didn't do that at the beginning of our marriage, and you know it." He got off the bed and went to stand at its end, seemingly to get away from me.

"Look, you're taking this all wrong. I'm just telling you these things so we can change them. So we can try to change our love-life. That's what the doctor said. He said that we have to be honest with each other if we want a happy marriage and a healthy sex-life. Don't you want that with me?"

"Take your clothes off." He folded his arms over his chest.

I wasn't sure what he was getting at. "Why?"

"Because you let that man play with you, but you won't let me do that. You told me that you don't like being touched down there. But you clearly do. Just not by your husband—the *one* man who is *supposed* to touch you there."

"You're jealous?" I asked with confusion. "Of a doctor?"

"A doctor who gave my wife her first and only orgasm. And furthermore, you did this a week ago, so you've been hiding it from

45

me this whole time. How many times have we had sex since this doctor diddled you?"

"Don't say it like that. He didn't use his fingers. He used a machine. A medical device." I hated how ugly he was making this.

"That machine is called a vibrator, Fiona. And it's not just a medical device. Answer my question."

"Twice. You and I have had sex twice since my appointment." I didn't see why that mattered.

"So, you had two chances to tell me what went on between you and this doctor—who, by the way, you are never to see again."

I didn't like his tone—or what he was saying—but I was still stuck on something he'd said earlier. "How do you know that the medical device is called a vibrator?"

"Everyone knows that, Fiona. Lots of people use them. Not just doctors. To be honest with you, I had no idea that they used them to give their patients orgasms. What's next, more appointments to get orgasms?"

"I don't think so. I didn't get one today if that's what you're thinking." But the doctor had told me that I might think about getting myself an auto-stimulator. Not that I was about to tell my incredibly angry husband about that.

"How come you still have your clothes on?" He looked at me up and down. "I want you naked right now."

We both knew he couldn't give me an orgasm. "And what do you want to do to me?"

"You don't trust me."

"I know."

Pain filled his dark eyes. "Why don't you trust me? Have I ever hurt you?"

"I don't think you do it on purpose, but yes. You've hurt me almost every time we've had sex. You're too rough." I had never meant to tell him that, but he had asked.

His jaw clenched, and his hands fisted at his sides. "I'm not rough with you. You have no idea what rough sex is. I would show you, but you obviously are much too fragile for that."

"Reading all that nasty pornography has warped your mind, Collin. You should stop doing that. I've seen some of them, you know. And no one in real life does all the things those nasty people in those horrible magazines do."

"How do I hurt you?"

"You push too hard. You just shove your penis into me, and it hurts right from the beginning, and it keeps hurting until the end."

"I tried to get your juices flowing before inserting myself into you, but you said you hated it. And yet, you allowed some other man to do so. You let him have your only orgasm." He thumbed his chest. "That belonged to me, and you gave it away like it was nothing. That thing between your legs is mine and only mine. Do you understand me? You will never allow anyone—not even a fucking doctor—to stimulate anything on your body ever again. That is *mine*, and only *I* will be stimulating you. Now take your fucking clothes off so I can show you what I can do for you."

"No." I wasn't about to let him touch me. "I don't like your attitude about this, Collin. And I'm not about to give myself to you when you're so angry. Maybe when you calm down—but not right now."

"Because I've hurt you before."

"Yes."

Turning away from me, he walked to the door. "I'm going to go have some drinks."

"Great." I was far from happy about that. It meant he'd come home drunk and try to have sex with me. He was always rougher with me after he'd been drinking. But I was happy for him to be gone for a while. "I'll be right here."

"Where a wife belongs." And with that, he closed the door, leaving me alone.

COLLIN

The day I learned I was going to be a father should've been the happiest day of my life. Only it wasn't, because my frigid wife had let her doctor give her her first orgasm.

I poured another shot of whisky down my throat before getting off the barstool. "That's it. I'm going to show her."

As I drove out of the parking lot, I took a left instead of the right that would take me back to the ranch and back to my wife. I didn't want to see her yet. I was still too angry.

So I drove to Hilda's. I'd bought her a small house, still on the wrong side of town. If I'd put her up in a house on the right side of town, people would've started asking questions.

Not only was the house on the wrong side of town, but it was out of the city limits too. The driveway had huge salt cedar trees that flanked it, hiding the house and the parking area from prying eyes. That way, no one would accidentally find me at her place.

As soon as I drove up, the front door opened, and there she stood, waiting for me as always. Hilda never complained—even though she had every right to.

I got out of my truck and went to her. She stepped back to let me inside. "You seem upset, Collin."

"That's because I am." I'd never talked to Hilda about my wife or marriage. It didn't seem like a thing to talk to a mistress about. But I had to talk to someone. "She said I hurt her when we have sex. She let a fucking doctor give her an orgasm last week. I haven't even gotten one out of the frigid bitch, and she let some other man take what is mine!"

"I see." She went to pour me a drink.

"I know how to give a woman an orgasm."

"Yes, you do." She handed me the glass.

I took a sip. The hot whisky burned as it went down my throat. "She's too fragile, that's what she is. She'd rather someone use a vibrator on her than their mouth."

"She's a fool." She took a seat on the sofa, curling her legs underneath her.

Hilda was thick and curvy, her caramel skin supple and shining under the minimal light that came from the kitchen behind her.

Hilda was like home to me. She was easy to be with. She was easy to fuck. And she never complained.

"What she really needs is a firm hand." I put the glass down as I went to Hilda. "Like the one I give you."

"You're right." She ducked her head. "If you need to take out your anger for her on me, then I am yours to do with as you please, Master."

My body heated with her selfless words. Hilda accepted her role as my submissive with so much ease and pleasure. Fiona would never accept this part of me. I would never even let my wife see this side of me. I was dark as night — something Fiona had no inkling of.

But there was a part of me that wondered if the dominant in me could actually bend my wife's will to make it suit me. "If only I could whip her just once, then she'd watch the words that roll off her tongue far too easily."

"You're right."

I ran my hand over her bowed head. "If I could go down on her only once, she'd bend to my will."

"You're right."

"I own you."

"You do."

"And I own her as well."

"You do."

"So why can't I do to her the things I do to you?"

"Because she's not your submissive, Master. She is your wife."

She was right about that. Fiona was an educated woman who had opinions on everything. She knew what she wanted and how she wanted them. And she wanted as little to do with my dick as possible.

"I shouldn't have let her get that teaching job at the elementary school." I'd never allowed Hilda to work since I came back to Carthage. Why I'd let my wife work was beyond me. "She was already too headstrong, and the job has made her even more so."

As I stood in front of Hilda, she knew just what to do. She began undoing my jeans, pushing them down so that they pooled around my ankles. She took my cock in her very capable hands before looking up at me. "May I suck your cock, Master?"

Looking down at her soulful eyes, I nodded. "You may."

A soft smile curled her lips, and she licked them before setting to work. As always, she took me away from my thoughts, and everything became good again.

I smoothed my hand over her silky dark hair, loving the way it felt beneath my palm. Everything about Hilda did something for me; from her unending devotion to the way she took care of my every sexual need.

Society had rules that I didn't seem to be able to live by for long periods. I had always found my way back to Hilda and the decadent life we had.

After she'd done her job and drank down my juices, she stood up as I sat down, trying to catch my breath. She left me only for a moment and then returned with a leather belt in her hand and nothing on her body.

Handing me the belt, she lay over my lap, presenting her bare ass to me. "Whip her, Master. Whip your wife for her betrayal."

I bent the supple leather in half, then pulled it up high, letting it fall against her caramel-colored flesh. "Count your lashes."

"One," she whispered.

"Do you know why I am punishing you?" I raised the belt again.

"Because I allowed another man to take what was yours and yours alone."

I whipped her again. "Yes."

"Two."

Raising the belt once more, I asked, "Did you enjoy what that man did to you?"

"I did."

I whipped her again as anger ripped through me. "Ten more lashes then."

"Three."

I gave her three more in rapid succession. "Am I not enough for you?"

"You are," she said. "Four, five, six."

I hit her three more times. "How could you do that to me?"

"Seven, eight, nine," she said quietly. "I was thoughtless."

"Five more lashes then." I quickly gave them to her.

"Ten, eleven, twelve, thirteen, four—" her voice broke as a sob escaped her lips, "—teen."

"You sound as if you understand me now. You've got two more coming to you." I hit her once.

"Fif—" she sobbed, "—teen." Her body shook as she cried hopelessly.

I gave her the last one. "There. Your punishment has been served by your master. What do you say to your master?"

"Sixteen," she said with tears flowing, her voice cracked. "Thank you, Master."

Had it been Fiona on my lap, I might not have given her so many lashes. But I knew Hilda could take the harsh punishment since I'd trained her for years. I knew she enjoyed receiving it as much as I loved giving it.

I put the belt down beside me, then ran my hands over her red bottom. "If you didn't betray my trust, I wouldn't have had to do that."

"Yes, I understand. I was bad."

Pulling her cheeks apart, I leaned over, running my tongue along the crack of her ass. "For the next part of your punishment, I will fuck your asshole orally, and you may not orgasm as I do it. If you

51

do, it will mean twenty more lashings for you. One at a time, painstakingly slow. Do you understand me?"

"I do, Master."

I moved one hand under her to manipulate her clit while I tongue-fucked her asshole. And like the trained submissive that she was, she took it all and never came.

Hilda was something to be proud of, yet I couldn't tell a soul about her. She took all I had to give, and she made me a better man by doing it.

But I wasn't a better man to my wife, who lay crying on our bed at home. I wasn't a better man to my wife, who now carried my child. I wasn't a better man to her because this woman on my lap— this woman who was so ready to take the punishment that my wife should've gotten—ruled my heart and my cock.

Anger flooded me, and I picked Hilda up, then lay her out on the sofa. Looking down at her, I saw torture on her face. "You want to come, don't you?"

She nodded. "But I won't."

"You were right to take the punishment meant for her, you know that, don't you?"

She nodded. "I do."

"If you were not the temptress that you are, then I wouldn't be here, cheating on my pregnant wife. If you weren't the evil slut that you are, I wouldn't be here with you so many nights when I should be in bed with my wife. You're a filthy whore, that's what you are. And you've stolen my heart. I don't have it to give to the woman I'm married to. You've ruined our sex-life."

"I am sorry."

"You will be, you dirty whore."

Standing, I took the rest of my clothes off, then picked her up by the hair, and flung her to the floor. She landed on her back, and I pounced on her, shoving my fat cock into her tender pussy. A pussy so swollen with arousal that it made it hard for me to get all the way in. But I pushed and thrust until I was balls deep in the bitch.

She clawed my back as I fucked her with no mercy. "Please," she begged.

"Please what?" I bit her on the neck.

Her nails clawed me once more. "Please, don't."

"Don't what, you nasty bitch?" I bit her earlobe as I slammed into her again and again.

"Don't stop loving me, Master." She sobbed. "I can't live without you."

Slowing down, I looked at her, watching the tears running down the sides of her face. "As if I could, you seductress. As if you would allow that for even a second. My heart is yours, and you damn well know it."

"And mine is yours, and it always will be." She caressed my cheeks, pulling me in to kiss her.

Our tongues tangled as she arched her body to mine. I didn't know where I ended and she began—we were so much a part of one another.

As I took her for what was surely the millionth time, I wondered if my wife and I would ever share what my submissive and I did. A love so pure that it had an abundance of patience and the never-ending desire to glue us together as one entity.

Our bodies gave in to each other, and I collapsed on top of her, trying to catch my breath as she tried to catch hers. I would never share this type of intimacy with my wife. And for that, I was sad.

Fiona carried my child, and yet I felt more a part of Hilda than I had ever felt with Fiona.

And I couldn't imagine that changing.

LILA

July 1988 – Carthage, Texas

One day after my eighteenth birthday, I met Coy at the courthouse, where we bought our marriage license. The clerk behind the desk smiled as she said, "You have to wait three days before you can legally get married. This license is only good for ninety days, so you have to get married before time runs out."

"We're going to come back up here and let the Justice of the Peace marry us in three days," Coy informed her.

"Okay then. He'll know that the signed license has to be turned in within thirty days of the legal marriage." She beamed at us. "You two make a cute couple. I'm sure you'll be happy together. Congratulations!"

Coy handed me the paper. "You hold onto this. Keep it in your purse so we'll have it when we come back."

Even though I was the happiest I'd ever been, there was still a ton of nerves bubbling in my tummy as we walked to the doors of the courthouse. "Okay, I'll have it with me when we come back." I hated that we couldn't be seen together; we were taking a huge risk just by being in the courthouse together. "I'll leave first, and then you take off in fifteen minutes."

He nodded, pulled me to him, and kissed me. "Soon, all this sneaking around will be a thing of the past."

"I hope so. I really do." Carefully placing the marriage license into a zippered pouch inside my purse so no one would accidentally see it, I zipped up my purse, then walked out the door.

Looking around, I made sure that no one I knew was around before taking off. My house was half a mile away, and I had to walk all the way.

I couldn't have asked my father if I could borrow the car—he would've wanted to know why. So, I'd taken off on foot, telling my mother that I was walking over to one of my friend's houses to hang out with them.

As I walked along the sidewalk a few minutes later, I heard the familiar sound of Coy's truck as he drove past me. He gunned the engine playfully, making me smile.

Coy was the best-looking guy I'd ever dated—or even knew, for that matter. He had bigger muscles than any guy I'd gone to school with too. He said that was because of the rigorous exercise regimen they did at his boarding school, which focused a lot on sports.

But the thing that really set Coy Gentry apart from all the other boys I'd ever known was his sweetness. He was kind, gentle, and caring. He was also much more mature than any guy I'd met. I chalked it up to having to live away from home since he was a little kid. He'd had to grow up fast and learned not to depend on others for ordinary things like comfort and even love.

Coy had loads of love to give, and I thanked my lucky stars that I got to be one of its recipients. Life with him as my husband was going to be amazing. There wasn't a doubt in my mind.

I knew things had moved fast for us. And I knew that that alone would've been cause for concern for my family. But I also put the blame for our rushed marriage squarely on their shoulders.

If our families could've stayed out of our business and not let whatever feud they had to interfere with our relationship, then we would've had more time to date before rushing into marriage.

This was their fault, not ours.

My hope was that everyone would accept us once we were

married, and there was nothing they could do about it. But that was a long-shot, and both of us were aware of it.

Coy had been preparing for the worst. He'd pulled money out of the bank account his father had opened for him when he had turned sixteen. Being afraid that someone might find it if he stashed the cash in his house, he'd given it to me to hide. Again, my purse was serving as our hiding place.

He'd withdrawn the money in hundred-dollar bills, so the stack wasn't that thick. Still, there was so much of it in my wallet that it was getting hard to close.

I knew I would have to get an envelope to store whatever else he ended up taking out of the bank account. I hadn't even dared to count the cash we had so far.

When I got to the next crosswalk, I saw Coy parked in a used parking lot down the street and wondered what he was up to. Heading that way, I wanted to check things out. Not that I could walk up to him in public in the light of day.

Walking by slowly, I acted as if I wasn't looking his way, but I still caught some action out of the corner of my eye. But what I saw had me stopping and turning my head all the way to look at Coy, who was taking a set of car keys from the salesman.

Coy walked over to a tan Honda Accord, got inside, and started it up. I walked around the corner to hide myself from view as I watched him drive it around the block and back into the parking lot.

My heart raced as I saw him get out, nodding as he and the salesman spoke. Then, they went into the office, and I had a distinct impression that Coy was going to buy the car. And I also had the impression that he was going to give it to me.

My mother didn't even own her own car. No one I knew had their own car. There were family cars—everyone had one of those. But no one I knew had a car of their very own.

And I knew that if Coy gave me that car, I couldn't take it home. Maybe not even after we were married, for fear my father would have my brothers ruin it.

Dad could be mean. I knew that. I'd seen it.

It seemed like the men in my family and the men in Coy's had a few things in common. That was one reason why I found Coy to be so special—he didn't seem to have a mean bone in his entire body.

His mother had been my third-grade teacher, and from what I remembered, she was very nice. I figured he must take after her. But she wasn't standing up for her son when it came to his future, which I found not so nice.

I began walking once more, as Coy had been inside the salesman's office for quite some time. Not in any hurry to get back home, I walked at a slow pace, wondering why a woman as nice as Mrs. Gentry would be onboard with Operation Keep Lila and Coy Apart.

I'd heard about her car accident. And I knew she'd be in a wheelchair for quite some time. Two of the bones in her lower back were broken. I was sure that her injuries had something to do with why she wasn't defending her son and his right to choose who he dated.

A car came barreling down the street, horn honking and tires squealing as it came to a stop right next to me. "Lila!" Janine, my best friend, shouted from the passenger side of the car her boyfriend, Dave, was driving. "There you are! Your father is looking for you. One of your little brothers told him that he was looking in your purse and found lots of money. He's sure you've been seeing that Gentry guy that he told you to stay away from. He's pissed, too. And he's out driving around, looking for you."

Clutching my purse, I didn't know what to do. "Thanks, Janine. I've gotta go do something real quick. Don't tell anyone that you saw me. Please."

"I won't. Geeze, you should know that you can trust me—I'm your best friend, Lila." She rolled her eyes as if she couldn't believe how I'd been hiding things from her. "What kind of friend do you think I am?"

"A good one. And I'll tell you more later on. Right now, I've gotta get someplace." I took off running back the way I'd come. I had to get the money back to Coy, or my father would surely take it from me. And he would surely look through my purse, so I had to give Coy the marriage license to hold on to as well.

Coy was still inside when I got to the used car lot. So I got into his truck and squished myself into the floor so that no one would see me if they drove by. I wasn't sure if anyone in my family knew what kind of car Coy drove, so I was still freaking out that I might be found before I could give everything to Coy. They were the most important things in the world to us at that time—I couldn't let him down by letting my father get a hold of them.

When I heard Coy's voice, I finally felt okay. "I'll be back in three days to pick it up. Make sure it's all detailed for me."

"Will do, sir. It's been nice doing business with you," the salesman called out.

As soon as Coy opened the driver's side door, he saw me, and his blue eyes flew wide. "Hey." He got into the truck as if he wasn't worried about why I was hiding on the floor. "So, what's up?"

"One of my nosy brothers must've been snooping in my purse last night and saw the money you gave me. He told my father, and now my father is searching for me."

"And who told you this?" he started the truck and started driving away.

"One of my best friends saw me walking and told me." I took my wallet out of my purse and placed it on the seat. "Here, take this and hide it." I got the marriage license too and put it on the seat next to my wallet. "And this too. If he finds it, he'll rip it up and do only God knows what to me."

"This isn't good at all." He sped up as his dark brows furrowed. "I hate this."

"Me too." I didn't know what else to do, though. "What will I tell my father when he finds no money?"

"Tell him that it wasn't real money, just some play money that you got from the dime store to play poker with your friends. And get that friend of yours to verify the story too. Tell her to say that you guys have been playing for a couple of weeks, and that's why you had it."

He parked the truck. "I'm going to run into the dime store now and get you some of that fake money to make the story sound legit."

At that moment, I thought Coy was the smartest man on the planet. "I love you and your amazing brain."

"I love you too, and soon we'll be laughing about all of this." He left me with a grin, and I began to feel that everything was going to be fine. With Coy on my side, nothing could go wrong.

As I waited for him to come back, I tried to figure out how to become the best actress I could possibly become when I ran into my father.

A half-hour later, I had the play money in a wallet Coy had picked up at the dime store and was walking back home. That was when my father pulled up next to me, and my three brothers got out of the car, yanking my purse off my shoulder. "Hey, what the hell are you doing?" I shouted as if I had no idea.

Tony tossed the purse into the car to my father, who sat behind the steering wheel. "Check it, Dad. You'll see. Her wallet is full of money."

"What?" I laughed as I shook my head. "You went through my purse?"

"Yes, and don't even try to lie, Lila!" Tony shouted at me.

My father had already gotten into my purse and had the fake money in his hand. "What's this shit?"

"Play money, Dad," I said. "Me and some of my friends have been playing poker with fake money."

My father shoved the money back into my purse, then threw it out of the passenger window. "Get back in the car, you idiots."

"So, can I get an apology?" I asked, knowing damn well that none would be given.

They sped off as my father cussed like a sailor, and I had a smile on my face that would not quit.

That worked like a charm.

FIONA

November 14th, 1970 – Carthage, Texas – Local Hospital

Cradling my son in my arms, I finally knew what love felt like. "Coy Marcus Gentry."

"Coy *Collin* Gentry," my husband said as he sat down on the hospital bed next to me.

I wasn't sure I wanted my son to have the same name as his father, even if it was only a middle name. He already had the bad luck of having his last name. "Why don't you like Marcus?"

"Why do you like that name?" He picked up the paper and pen off the tray. "We've got to fill this out for the birth certificate. I'll write down our names as the parents while you think about what it means to me that my son carries my name."

"He is a Gentry, you know." And that was already one strike against the poor boy.

Living with Collin's parents had been an eye-opener for me. He was a carbon-copy of his father. And the worst part of that was that Collin didn't act like his father because he looked up to him; he did it because he was terrified of the man.

I'd never heard anyone speak to another human being the way Collin's father did to him when he was disappointed in something he'd done. And I didn't want Collin to treat our son that way.

As it was, we were already meeting his father's wishes by naming our son Coy, which was Collin's father's middle name. And now Collin wanted me to saddle the kid with two names that were associated with hard asses. I just wasn't sure I wanted to do that to my son.

"It would make my father happy, you know." And that was all he had to say to me.

I wasn't about to bring down the buckets of guilt his father would rain down on him if he were to disappoint him. "Fine. Coy Collin it is then."

He hurried to write it down on the paper before I changed my mind. "Good."

"The next boy gets named after *my* father." I had to stand up for myself, at least a little. "And I get to pick all the girl names too."

"Then I get to pick all the boy names, after the second one."

"It's a deal." I looked down at the tiny face of my son and smiled. "He's so adorable."

"He's small though." He put his huge hand on top of our son's little head, dwarfing it. "See. He's a runt."

My ire sped to the surface. "He's not a runt. Seven pounds and nine ounces is average. Were you thinking he'd come out full-grown?"

"No." He laughed as he backed away from me. "I just thought, seeing as he's *my son*, he'd come out bigger." He gestured to his large stature. "I'm six-three you know. And Mom said I weighed ten pounds when I was born."

"Well, your mother is a lot bigger than me. I'm glad he didn't weigh that much. I can't imagine having to give birth to a baby that size."

Shrugging, he said, "Yeah, it would've probably ripped up a frail woman like you anyway. I guess it's best that he came out small."

"He's not small. He's perfectly average." I saw nothing wrong with being average.

"Anyway, now that you've had him, you know there will be no going back to work for you, right?" He'd been on me to quit my teaching job at the elementary school since the day he found out I was pregnant. But I wasn't about to let down all the kids in my class by dumping them. They would've to spend the remainder of the year being taught by a substitute.

Thankfully, I'd trained a student teacher to take over for me for when I had the baby. She was nice, and the kids liked her. And if I wanted to stay home with the baby, she'd make a suitable replacement. But I wasn't sure that I wanted to do that yet.

"We'll see about that later on when he's a bit older. I don't want to make any big decisions right now. I just want to look at my adorable baby and fall in love with him." I couldn't stop looking at my perfect little angel.

I saw my husband rolling his eyes before he left with the paperwork to give them to the nurse. He was in a huge rush to turn them in. "I'll be right back. You want anything? A soda pop or something?"

"No, thank you." I was as content as I could be with my baby in my arms. "Momma loves you."

He wrapped his tiny hand around my pinky, holding it tightly. I felt it was his way of telling me that he loved me too. I'd never been so happy in my entire life.

I heard a knock on the doorframe and was startled to see the first doctor I'd gone to all those months ago when I thought I might have been pregnant. "Hi there. I saw your name on the door and thought I'd stop by to see how you two are doing?"

I could feel my cheeks stained pink with a blush. I was a bit embarrassed that I'd just stopped going to him cold turkey. But Collin had been so upset by what he'd done that I didn't want to push it. "Oh, Doctor Nelson, thanks for stopping by. We're both doing very well."

He came to the side of the bed to look at my son. "He's a nice-looking boy, Fiona. I was just in the hospital checking on a patient who delivered yesterday. When I saw your name on the chart out there, I had to stop by. I hope that's okay with you."

I had to offer him a reason why I stopped coming to him. "I'm sorry about switching doctors. I decided I wanted a female doctor instead. You must understand, I'm sure."

"Sure I do. A lot of first-time mothers opt for a female doctor. It's a hard time for them, and it helps them feel better about everything. I totally get it. But keep me in mind for your next baby. I'm sure now that you've been through everything, you're much more at ease with all the things that go on when you're pregnant."

"Yes, I am. I'll keep you in mind when we have our next one." It was lie; Collin would never agree with me ever going back to see him.

He looked over his shoulder, then back at me. "Did you and your husband work out that little problem you were having?"

"We did." We hadn't, but I wasn't about to tell him that. "Thanks for all your help."

"Not a problem." He patted me on the shoulder. "You know, back in the old days, women came to doctors all the time with what they called hysteria back then. The ladies were aggravated and snapping at their husbands and families, and no one could figure out why. The story goes that a doctor during that time began asking intimate questions, and he found that all of these ladies who were being treated for hysteria had one thing in common."

I felt my cheeks heating up as I blushed. "They didn't have orgasms."

"Yep. So, this doctor began to manually stimulate the clitoris of each one of his female patients who'd been diagnosed with hysteria. He ended up with so many patients seeking his unique treatment method that he ended up building a vibrating machine to make his job easier and not so hard on the fingers. Plus, it sped up the climax, that way, he could see more patients."

"And I bet he ended up selling his machines to his patients so they could tend to themselves at home."

"He did, and now the world is a much better place." He laughed, and then his eyes cut to one side as my husband's large frame filled the doorway. "And this must be Mr. Gentry." He walked towards him with his hand extended. "Hello, I'm Doctor Nelson."

As Collin shook the man's hand, his eyes moved to me. "Is that so?"

"He saw my name on the chart and stopped by to see how the baby and I are doing." My heart sped up as I knew Collin had put two and two together.

"So, you were my wife's first doctor then," Collin said. "The one who told her that she was going to be a mother for the first time."

I prayed my husband would stay in control of his jealousy and his temper. "Honey, did you get me that soda I asked for?" I knew I'd turned down his offer, but I had to do something to separate the two of them.

"You said you didn't want one." He looked at me with a furrowed brow.

"You must've misheard me, dear. I would really like one. I'm so thirsty, and I'm tired of drinking water."

"I can grab you one if you'd like," the doctor offered. "It's no trouble at all."

"I'll get it." Collin stepped back, and the doctor was finally able to walk out the door. "See you, doc. And I'll be right back with the soda, Fiona."

"Bye now," the doctor said as he left us.

I let out a long sigh of relief as they both left. "What a fiasco that almost was, my son. What a fiasco indeed."

Later that night, after Collin had gone home to sleep, a woman wearing an apron with red stripes came to my room. She wheeled in a cart with magazines on top of it. "Candy striper. Would you like anything to read?" Her long dark hair was pulled back into a ponytail, and her caramel lips were curved into a smile.

The baby lay sleeping in his tiny bassinet, as the nurse hadn't come back for him yet after I'd finished feeding him. The young woman pushed the cart next to me, then went to stand over the bassinet.

"He's a cutie, isn't he?" I picked up a couple of magazines, opting for entertainment over education.

"Yes, he is." She ran her hand over my sleeping son's head. "He's precious."

"I agree. He's our first child. Are you married?" I flipped open the latest copy of Reader's Digest.

"No." She let out a long sigh as she gazed at my son. "And I don't have any babies of my own." She looked at me out of the corner of her eye. "You said he's your first child. Does that mean you plan on having more?"

"Oh, yes. My husband and I want as many children as the good Lord sees fit to give us." As I moved to resituate myself, the discomfort of recently having a baby was brought back to my attention. "But I think I'll give it a year or so before I try to get pregnant again. Not an easy thing, childbirth. I think I'll need time to forget the pain before I purposely put another bun in my oven."

"And your husband agrees with that?" She turned to face me, placing her hands on the cart.

"This is *my* body. I make the decisions about when I get pregnant." I held up the three magazines I'd picked out. "Thanks for these. I'm sure to be entertained now."

The sound of voices coming from the hallway made her jerk her head to look at the door. "I should get going. There are more mothers who need something to read."

I looked at her apron and saw no nametag. All the other candy stripers I'd seen around the hospital had nametags. "I think you lost your nametag, miss."

A frown turned her mouth into a horseshoe. "Oh, yeah. Well, I'd better backtrack to see where it came off. Congratulations on the baby. He looks like a fine boy."

"Thank you."

"You know, you look to be around my age. My husband and I are the same age. Are you from Carthage?"

She nodded. "Born and raised."

"You most likely went to school with my husband, Collin Gentry." I watched as she ducked her head, eyes on the floor.

"Yes, we did go to school together. He and his father employed some of my brothers from time to time. I even did a short stint as a maid out at the ranch." She pushed the cart towards the door, hesitating for a moment before leaving.

I took the chance to say, "Tell me your name, and I'll tell my husband that I met you. He'll get a kick out of that, I'm sure."

"Oh, sorry, gotta go." And with that, she left.

I could hear the sound of the cart's squeaky wheels going fast down the long hallway. It sounded as if she was in a hurry, passing in front of all the other rooms instead of stopping as she'd said she was going to.

Something about her felt odd. I couldn't quite put my finger on it, but there was something about the young woman that bothered me.

But then again, she may have just been embarrassed for telling me she'd been a maid at the ranch I now lived at. The haves and have-nots of the small town didn't often speak to one another. Not that I was like that. I'd talk to and befriend anyone.

Collin and his mother and father weren't like me, though. They only associated themselves with the people they deemed to be on their level in society, which I found snobbish. The young woman must've been ashamed she'd told me about her past as a maid.

Poor girl.

COLLIN

On the day my son turned six weeks, I made my last visit to Hilda. Only, she had no idea this would be the last time we would see each other.

Pulling into the drive, I found her coming to the door, opening it to welcome me inside. "Long time no see, stranger."

It had been a few months since I'd come to her. Becoming a father had hit me hard, even before my son was born. I had tremendous responsibilities now. And I could no longer tempt fate by messing around with Hilda.

The time had come to let her go.

The majority of my heart now lay in the palm of my infant son's tiny hands. But there was still a little piece that belonged only to Hilda. So, what I had to tell her was going to hurt me badly.

Stepping inside the home—the last time I'd ever do that—I took a look around. She had always kept it very neat and tidy, not a speck of dust to be found. "I'm glad you've taken good care of your home, even in my absence."

"I did not know whether you might show up or not." She closed the door, then walked towards the kitchen. "Would you care for a glass of iced tea? I'm not used to seeing you in the light of day. I'm not sure how to act."

Her unique scent filled my nostrils, and I inhaled it deep into my lungs, desperate to keep a part of her with me forever. "I don't want anything to drink. This isn't going to be the most pleasant visit, Hilda."

Walking back into the living room, she took a seat, a grim expression on her face. "You found out what I did, didn't you?"

I had no idea what she was talking about, but I acted as if I did. If she'd done something that might get me into trouble, I needed to know. "I want *you* to admit out loud what you did."

"It's true. I went to the hospital after your son was born. I saw him—and I saw her." She clasped her hands in her lap as if to prepare herself for my wrath.

She went to see Coy and Fiona?

"Tell me what you said." I kept my chin up high, acting as if I already knew everything—which I certainly did not.

"I didn't tell her my name. But I did tell her that I worked for a short time as a maid at the ranch, and I told her that I went to school with you. But that's all I said." Her eyes held the floor as she waited for me to dole out her punishment.

But there wouldn't be one. "It sounds as if no harm was done." Fiona hadn't said a word to me about their interaction, so I knew there wasn't anything to worry about. "Thank you for being honest with me."

Wide eyes met mine—she looked utterly confused. "I thought that's why you weren't coming to see me. I mean, not for the months before his birth, but afterward. I thought you were so angry with me that you kept yourself away for my own protection."

"No, that's not why I stayed away." I continued to keep my distance from her, pacing on the other side of the living room. I was as far away as I could get from her without leaving the room.

"So why did you?" She couldn't pull her eyes off of me. Eyes that were full of worry and concern. "You're making me nervous, Collin."

I faced her, squaring my shoulders as I prepared myself. "Becoming a father has changed me in ways I hadn't expected. Well, that's not entirely true. I had the feeling that I would begin thinking of my life differently than I had before. There's more I can lose now."

"No one has found out about us in all these years, and *now* you're getting worried?" She stood up but kept her distance from me. "Why now? And what do you think anyone would if we were found out? Take your son away? Not likely."

"My father can still throw me out, Hilda. And he can let my wife and son stay on at the ranch, without me. Believe me, I've thought this through. I don't want to lose you. But I really have no choice. It's my *son* I'm talking about here. My *blood*."

"You can't do this to me. You took everything away from me— and my only consolation was having you. And not even all the time or all to myself either."

"We did talk about the fact that I would have to marry someone else one day and that I would be expected to have a family too. I *am* expected to provide more heirs for the ranch, and you know that." I couldn't believe how she'd conveniently scrubbed that off from her memory bank.

"You talk like you're some sort of royal or something. You're just ranchers, Collin. Who the hell cares who ends up with that damn ranch after you and your father are dead?" She threw her hands into the air. "I can't believe you would do this to me over that godforsaken piece of land."

"This is about my son, not the ranch." I hadn't expected her to act this way. I had expected lots of crying and pleading. But arguing with me wasn't something I'd thought Hilda would ever do. For as long as I'd known her, she'd worshipped me.

As intoxicating as that had always been, I had to end what we had. But I couldn't let her think she was on her own, and I wasn't exactly abandoning her, leaving her to figure out how to make money after I'd taken care of her for the last few years. "Hilda, I've already bought you a home in Shreveport, Louisiana."

She plopped down on the couch. I hadn't ever seen her look this way. She had an agitated air about her, and for once, it seemed like pleasing me was the furthest thing on her mind. "I need you to tell me what the hell you're doing. I'm desperately trying to understand why you would buy me a home in Shreveport when all of my family is here in Carthage. Am I to live in solitude? And for what? So you can have your family and forget I ever existed?" She made it sound so selfish.

My son needed me to do this. "Do you think this isn't hurting me? Killing me? Because it is. I—I" I'd never said the words out loud to her. But she needed to know how I felt. "I love you, Hilda Stevens. But I also love my son. And I hate to say this to you, but I love him more than I love myself. I have to do right by him."

"You should see things the right way. I've done your bidding for my own reasons. Reasons you could never understand, and I will never explain to you. But you need to know that I know you have never loved me. Nor have ever I loved you. We've *needed* each other. We've *used* each other. And that is all." She nodded. "What I don't understand is why I have to leave town and move to another state." Her hands covered her face as she began crying softly. "I don't want to lose you. I don't want to lose us. I can't do the things we do together with anyone else."

My heart ached, and my arms itched to hold her in them. But that would only make what I had to do harder. "Hilda, I've bought you a decent home. And I've already gone up there and opened a bank account. The checks will be mailed to you at your new place. The account is in your name only. But I'll make weekly deposits in the same amount I do for you now."

"So this is it then." She pulled her hands away from her face, which was red and tearstained. "You'll take care of me until you die, and *I* will die alone."

I didn't want to think about death. "I don't know what the future holds, and you don't either. Let's not think that far down the road."

"You and your *wife*," she said the word as if it had thorns that cut her tongue as she spoke, "will have many children, according to her. And your children will keep you away from me. *Always!*"

What could I possibly say? She wasn't wrong. Not that I could tell her that. "Look, we don't know what the future holds. My father won't live forever."

"And after he dies, there will be your mother to keep happy. After she dies, you will have to keep your wife happy. It will *never* end. You and I will never be. Not ever! You're a coward, Collin Gentry. A coward and a liar."

I was stunned by her anger. "Hilda, please try to understand. I'm going to take care of you, no matter what." I'd never seen these expressions on her face before, and it made more uneasiness creep up inside of me.

"I don't care about a house or money if it means we will never be together. Death may be better than not having you anymore." Her chest rose and fell noticeably as she took several deep breaths.

"Watch what you say to me." I wasn't about to allow her to bully me with threats of suicide. "You *will* go to the home I bought for you. This one has already been sold. You'll be moving out today. I hired movers to pack your things and take them to the new place. You're to get into your car and follow them." I reached into my pocket and took out the set of house keys, then tossed them onto the coffee table. "Those are the keys to your new place. It's much nicer than this one. So what do you say?"

"You expect me to thank you?" Her body shook as if she was in shock. "You expect me to simply do whatever you say?"

"I do." I'd made things so easy for her ever since I'd come back from college. "I've given you a home of your own and that new car that's parked in the garage. I've given you thousands and thousands of dollars, and I pay all of your bills. I expect you to do as I say."

"And if I don't, then you'll cut me off?" She stood, then turned her back to me as if she could no longer stand to look at me.

"Yes." I would have no choice but to cut her off if she refused my very generous offer. "Don't make me do that. Just take the new house and the money. And we'll see what the future holds."

"I know what it will hold." She turned to me, tears freely cascading down her reddened cheeks. "You will live a happy life with your kids and your wife, and I will live a lonely existence with no one."

"You have my permission—" I had to stop and swallow as a knot formed in my throat. The idea of Hilda being with another man made me sick. But I had to stop being so goddamned selfish. "I'm sorry. As you can see, this isn't easy for me, Hilda. You have my permission to find another man."

"How *heroic* of you, Collin," sarcasm dripped off her tongue with words she did not truly mean. "May you live the life you deserve and have the family you deserve. You no longer need to keep me in your mind since I'm nothing but a taboo to you and your family."

Her words hurt, but hearing them gave way for some relief—and a little hope. Hope that I might finally cast off this dark obsession I had with her. That I could resist my dark desires—so long as she was far away from me.

FIONA

1976 – Dallas, Texas – All-Boys Boarding School

It seemed like a punishment to me. Since being blessed with Coy's birth, we hadn't had another child. And Collin put the blame squarely on my shoulders. Now he was sending our only child—six-year-old Coy—away to boarding school. Even if he wouldn't admit it, I knew he was doing it to punish me for what he thought were my failings.

Coy sat in the backseat of our car, his eyes wide as he looked out the window at the tall buildings in downtown Dallas. "This isn't like home, Daddy."

"It's still a good place, son. You'll really love it here. And you'll have lots of boys your own age to play with. You don't have anyone to play with at home," Collin looked at me, "since you don't have any brothers or sisters."

"He made friends in kindergarten last year when he went," I pointed out. "And he'd be in class with most of them this year too. This isn't necessary, Collin."

"I want my son to get a good education, and Carthage public schools just won't cut it." That was one of the many great reasons—or so he said—why our son had to leave home. And he had his father's backing him up, so it seemed that things were set in stone. "I grew up as an only child, Fiona. It was a lonely existence, and I don't want that for Coy."

"You seem to forget that I'm an only child too, Collin. I had lots of friends and was perfectly happy. Coy is a lot like me. He makes friends easily."

Collin didn't make friends easily, so he had none. But Coy wasn't his father. He was much more like me. Unfortunately, my husband wouldn't see that in our son.

"What did I tell you about talking about this in front of him?" he growled at me.

"Daddy, I don't want to leave home to go to school. I can play with my friends at my old school. I'll miss you all so much. Please don't make me go," Coy pleaded.

Collin glared at me as if this was all my fault. "See what you've done. Fix it, Fiona. Fix it right now."

I knew my husband wasn't going to bend on this. Trying my best not to roll my eyes, I turned in my seat to look at Coy. "You know, maybe Daddy's right. Maybe this *will* be a good thing for you. It will be like having lots of brothers. That'll be nice. Don't you think so?"

He shook his head as his lower lip drooped. "No."

Collin had said we'd pick up Coy for the holidays, but looking at my sweet boy's sad face, I made an executive decision at the last minute. "I tell you what, Coy. We will pick you up every Friday once school is out, and you can stay with us, at home, until Sunday evening. We'll have to bring you back Sunday night, but at least you'll see us every single week. That's three days out of seven that you'll be with us."

"We never agreed to that," Collin grumbled. "I'm not even sure that's something I can do."

"I can go and bring him back if you're too busy. I do drive, you know. I have my own car." I'd gone back to work, teaching at the elementary school last year when Coy started kindergarten. And I would be working that school year too. I wouldn't even have to ask him for money to go get our son. "It's not a problem for me. I want to see him each week."

"I want that too, Daddy. Please, let her," Coy whimpered.

I wasn't about to let Collin make the decision. I'd already made it. "I *will* come to get you on Fridays, son. You'll be with us Friday nights, all day and night on Saturdays, and all day on Sundays too. And then there are all the holidays you'll get to come home for. It won't be so bad, you'll see."

Collin didn't like it when I made decisions. He didn't like the fact that I decided to go back to work. He didn't like when I had any independence at all. But I did it anyway. Collin had to learn that he wasn't in charge of me. And he needed to learn that he wasn't in complete charge of our son either.

I saw his knuckles turning white as he clutched the steering wheel, trying not to blow up at me in front of our son. "Fine, Fiona. Have it your way."

Smiling at Coy, I was happy when he smiled back at me. "Thanks, Momma. I feel better now."

It wasn't everything I wanted—what I wanted most was Coy at home with us. But at least I would have him there more than I had thought I would.

When we arrived at the boarding school, I felt myself falling apart. Knowing that I couldn't do that in front of Coy, I sucked it up as we got out of the car in the parking lot of the huge building.

"This place is enormous. So much bigger than the pictures on the pamphlet." I took Coy's little hand in mine. "But it's really nice looking. Isn't it, son?"

"It's really big, Momma. What if I get lost?"

Collin came up on Coy's other side. "You won't get lost. There will be lots of other boys around, and there're teachers here too. There's nothing to worry about."

Coy looked up at his father. "Why didn't you go to a school like this, Daddy?"

"I wish I had gone to a school like this, Coy. But my parents didn't know there were such things as this when I was a kid. I think you're incredibly lucky to have a father who found this place for you." Collin shot a look at me that told me he had no intention of being the bad guy. "I'm doing this for you because I love you, son. And I want what's best for you."

He could spout that all he wanted. I knew better than that, though he'd never admit it. No matter how many times I'd asked him if he was angry with me for not being able to have more children, he would always tell me that it wasn't an issue.

Collin said the right things. He did tell me that he didn't think it was my fault. But he didn't say that it might be him who was to blame either.

The lack of children was a subject he didn't like talking about. To him, it was what it was, and there was nothing anyone could do about it. But from time to time, I would catch him looking at me with pure disgust, and I knew why that was—even if he wouldn't admit it.

Collin's mother and father only had one child as well. It wasn't planned that way; it had just happened that way. I had the feeling that a low sperm count was to blame in both my husband and his father.

I was also an only child, but my parents had had more of a say in that. My mother had high blood pressure, and when she'd been pregnant with me, it had nearly killed her. So, right after birth, the doctor gave her a tubal ligation to prevent any more pregnancies.

Much like his father, Collin didn't like to take the blame for anything. If a woman could be blamed, then she was. I'd watched Collin's father blame his wife for things that she'd never done, time and time again.

Collin tried to do that with me, but I wouldn't accept the blame the way his mother did. I wasn't as weak-willed as his mother. It was obvious that Collin hadn't thought I would be so strong-willed when he'd asked me to marry him. He'd often mumble underneath his breath that he'd married me too soon—that he hadn't gotten a chance to get to know the real me.

But when I'd ask him what he said, he'd say, "Nothing." And that would be it.

I knew what I'd heard, though. And I knew sending our son away was only done to hurt me.

But I wouldn't let him. As hard as he might try, Collin Gentry would never break me.

COLLIN

May 1988 – Carthage, Texas

Standing in the middle of the dance floor at the American Legion in Carthage, I privately congratulated myself. I'd truly outdone myself. Putting together a high school graduation party for Coy all by myself had been quite the undertaking.

Fiona hadn't been able to help since she'd been injured in a car wreck a few weeks before the big event. Now she was in a wheelchair. She'd broken both her legs and had fractures in her two lower vertebrae. The wreck had taken its toll on her body, which I'd always thought had been on the frailer side anyway. The doctors had said that she would make a full recovery, but it could take a year or longer before that occurred.

Without Fiona to help me, I'd had to do it all—decorations, refreshments, guest list. I'd invited the entire senior class from the local high school too. That way, Coy could reconnect with the kids he'd gone to kindergarten with.

Now that he'd be living back at the ranch, working for me until it was time for him to head off to college in the fall, I wanted him to think of Carthage as his home.

Coy hadn't hung out with any of his old friends when he came home to visit. His mother monopolized his time too much for him to be able to spend it with anyone outside our little family circle. But that would end now. I'd make her back off of him and let him become the man he now was at eighteen years old.

It wouldn't be hard to do either, since she wasn't in the best of health. Her strong will had taken a hard hit with her injuries. Not only was she unable to take physical care of herself, but she also wasn't able to work and wouldn't be able to until next year. And that was only if everything healed as it should.

I'd hired a full-time nurse to tend to Fiona. Not that it made her happy. She hated being so dependent on others. Her mood wasn't often happy anymore.

The party would begin shortly, and when the doors opened, I turned to see who was coming in. It was my parents, followed by my wife and son. Coy pushed his mother's wheelchair, both wearing big smiles as they looked at what I'd done.

I opened my arms to gesture at the decorations. "So, did Dad do good by you, son?"

"I'll say." He looked all over the place. "Dad, this is amazing."

Fiona couldn't wipe the smile off her face. "Collin, I can't believe you did this all by yourself."

"I am a capable man." Walking to the table filled with drinks, I filled a small cup with fruit punch and took it to my wife. "Try this out."

"Is it spiked?" she asked with knowing eyes. "Because I've just taken some pain meds so I could come out here. If I mix alcohol with them, I might end up dead."

My father patted her on the shoulder. "Now, now, Fiona, he wouldn't put alcohol in something meant for a bunch of underage kids, you know."

She still looked at me to make sure of that. I laughed. "Fiona, seriously, do you think I want to tend to a bunch of drunk teenagers?"

With a nod, she took a sip. "You would never want to deal with that."

Coy went to look around at every single thing in the hall, his blue eyes full of excitement. He had my dark hair, my tall height, and my muscular build, but he had his mother's blue eyes. I was sure that if he'd gone to a high school with girls instead of the all-boys boarding school we'd sent him to, he would've had to beat the girls off with a stick.

The stage was set with instruments for the band that would be starting soon. "You got a live band?" he asked.

"I did." I couldn't have wiped the smile off my face if I'd wanted to.

"Wow, Dad!" He jumped up and clicked the heels of his cowboy boots. "Yee-haw! A real band!"

Not much later, the band came in, and people started showing up. Since I hadn't done much in the community, I wasn't sure about the kind of turnout we'd get for the party. But the live band and free food and drinks had them coming in droves.

Before we knew it, the dance floor was crowded, and everyone was laughing and having an excellent time. Coy had no trouble making friends, either. Many of the kids who he'd gone to kindergarten with recognized him immediately.

I sat at the family table with my wife and parents as we watched Coy have the time of his life. I leaned over to my wife. "He's doing great, isn't he?"

"He is," she agreed. "I guess going off to boarding school was good for him after all."

I couldn't believe she was finally agreeing with me on that. "And going off to college will have him coming back home with even more enthusiasm for life." Our son had such a love for life; it defied my imagination.

His heart was huge, too. He loved his grandparents, me, and his mother with all his heart. I was sure that he didn't know how to love any other way. And I hoped that the girl he ended up falling in love with would give him back what he had to give to her.

Coy was everything I could never be. And I had his mother to thank for that. God knows he didn't get his affinity for goodness and love from me or my side of the family.

I knew our reputation in town was that of a bunch of hardasses. Neither my father nor I put up with anything. If we ordered two-thousand bales of hay, there better be that many in the hay barn

79

when they were through delivering it. We'd count each bale, and if it came up short, there was hell to pay.

A Gentry wouldn't be cheated on.

Tonight though, things were different. The Gentry family had put on a party for the whole town, and they'd come out to enjoy it. I knew why, too.

My wife had gained a good reputation as a teacher in town. She'd taught most of the graduating class at some time or another. She'd been a third-grade teacher, and she'd also taught fifth grade for the last few years, before her accident. She'd been teaching before Coy was even born, so she was all smiles as some of her old students waved at her.

It was because of her that we were able to have a successful party. Fiona was our key to acceptance in the town because no one cared for me or my father. Not that either of us cared. But everyone liked Fiona.

As the evening progressed, I saw Coy dancing with the same girl for at least ten songs. They swayed slowly, holding each other while talking.

The girl had dark eyes and silky dark hair. She was a real beauty, with caramel-colored skin and more curves than most of the girls her age. I could see why my son seemed to have an interest in her.

Since I had no idea of the names of anyone there, I asked my wife, "Who is he dancing with?"

"That's Lila Stevens." She smiled. "She's a nice girl. I taught her in third grade. She's really turned into such a beauty."

My heart froze as I heard her last name. "Do you remember her parents' names?"

"I know her mother's name is Beth, but I can't remember her father's name..." she tapped her chin as she tried to remember.

I recalled something that Hilda had mentioned when I had told her about Fiona being pregnant. "Arthur?"

"Yes, that's it. Arthur and Beth Stevens." She looked around as if looking for them. "I don't see them here, though."

That's because Arthur would never come to a party I'm throwing.

Arthur was Hilda's brother. He was one year younger than her.

She'd told me that it was such a coincidence that he and I were both going to become fathers in the same year.

The girl my son was dancing with, the same one he was making calf eyes at, was Hilda's niece. And that was not good.

My father sat on Fiona's other side, and he'd overheard everything we'd said. He looked at me with one cocked brow as if telling me that I knew what I had to do.

I sat there, though, not wanting to move, not wanting to tell my son what I knew I had to.

In all the years that the Stevens family had lived in Carthage, they'd never pulled themselves out of the gutter. They were all just as poor as they'd always been. Most of them didn't even have high school diplomas, and none of them had college degrees.

A part of me thought that Coy could have a little summer fling with the girl, then he'd go off to college and find a real woman to marry and bring home.

Another part of me thought that he might fall in love with the girl and want to take her with him to college. I'd wanted to do that with Hilda. I'd wanted to pay her way through college. I'd wanted to bring her up to our level, so my father would finally accept her.

But I didn't handle the money at that time, so it was impossible to do what I wanted. And my father had made sure that I understood I was to leave Hilda behind, to keep her hidden right where she was.

The night before I'd left for college, my father had come into my bedroom. I'd had no idea that he knew about me and Hilda. I'd thought I'd successfully kept it a secret from everyone.

But my father had found out somehow, and he'd woken me up with a smack of a leather belt on my bare back. "Get up!"

"Ow!" I'd jumped out of bed, wearing nothing but underwear. "What's that for?"

"You thought I'd never catch on. You thought you could get away with it." Another strike of the belt had my cheek burning like fire after he struck me in the face.

"Dad, I've got my first day of classes tomorrow. Please!"

He'd hit me in the stomach next. "I will beat the flesh off of your bones, boy. You knew you were doing wrong when you did it—

fucking that piece of trash, that whore, from that good for nothing family. I know you knew better than that. That's why you've been hiding it from me for so long. So, tell me what I have to hear, or I won't stop beating your ass before you're laying on the floor."

He would've done it too. He'd done it before. "I'll stop seeing her. I swear to you that I'll stop."

I'd gotten ten more lashes before he stopped, after I'd begged and begged for him to please quit beating me. I wasn't far from passing out when he left the room, leaving me with one last threat. "If you ever see her again, I will disown you, and you will be out on the streets without a damn thing."

He wasn't the kind of man who made idle threats—I knew that I had to go off to college and leave Hilda behind. I was able to do that for four years. It was only when I came back home and married Fiona, only after I found her to be such a prude, that I was left with no other choice but to go back to Hilda.

My father hadn't ever figured me out. Although he'd never caught on to the affair I'd had with Hilda, he now knew my son was attracted to someone from her family. And that was not good.

The first chance I got to talk to Coy alone, I took it. He was walking to the bathroom when I caught up to him and pulled him through a side door. "Hey, son, you look like you're having a good time."

"Dad, I really am," he gushed. "Thank you so much for doing this for me. It's really amazing. Everyone keeps talking about how great this is and how cool it is of you for putting it all together." He smiled. "For once, it seems like the town people like you, Dad."

"Yeah, I'm not used to this." And now I knew it wouldn't last. "Son, I know you don't know this, but our family isn't one to rub elbows with those people in town who don't try to make something of themselves."

His eyes flashed with anger, just like his mother's sometimes did. "What's that supposed to mean?"

"The girl you've been dancing with—"

He cut me off. "She's great. I really like her, and she seems to like me too. I've already asked her if she'd go out with me tomorrow night. She said yes. I'm going to take her to Dallas to show her my old school, and then I will take her out to eat at that restaurant that's shaped like a sphere and rotates."

"You can't do that."

"I can." He merely shook his head, thinking he could make his own decisions.

"No, you can't."

He set his jaw, and I knew he wasn't going to be easy to sway. "Why not?"

"She doesn't come from a good family. She won't be accepted by your family. Do you see what I'm getting at here?"

"Mom will accept whoever I bring home." He puffed out his chest. "And you will too."

"No, I won't." I—above all people—knew how unfair I was being. But my father was still alive, and I didn't want him going into my son's bedroom one night and beating the shit out of him. "Just find another girl, son. That's all I'm saying. Find one who's going to college, the way you are. That's all I ask."

"How do you know that Lila isn't going to college?" He was so much like his mother. And that worried me.

"I don't." But I didn't know of even one member of that family who had gone to college. "Did you ask her about that?"

"I did. I told her how I was going to be going to Lubbock to go to Texas Tech, just like you and Mom have."

"And what did she say?" I thought if I could go back and tell my father that this girl was going to go to school in the fall might make it okay for Coy to see her.

"Well, she said that her parents don't have money to send her. But if they did, then she would go."

"See, she comes from a bad family. If she had a good family, they would have made it a priority to save money so their kids could go to college. I'm sorry. You have to find yourself another girl, son."

Cocking his head, he looked at me as if I were crazy. "Dad, I'm not going to find another girl. I'm going out with Lila, and that's that. Come out of the Stone Age, and join the rest of the world." And then he walked away from me.

Just like his fucking mother!

FIONA

The night of our son's high school graduation party had been going extremely well. Until Collin pulled Coy outside to talk to him. I found Coy coming back with a scowl on his face, and soon after, Collin came in looking the same way.

I had no idea what could've set the two of them off. When my husband came back and sat next to me, I asked, "What's going on?"

"Your son is too damn much like you, that's what's going on." He pulled off his cowboy hat and ran his hands over his hair as if he had a headache.

"I still don't understand."

He pointed at the dance floor, where our son was dancing again with Lila Stevens. "See. He's doing that just to spite me."

I was completely lost. "How's that?"

"I told him to move on to another girl. But he can't take an order to save his fucking life." He huffed and closed his eyes as if he couldn't stand watching his son having a nice time with someone.

"If you ask me, the boy was spared the belt, and it shows," Collin's father said.

"Why do you care who Coy is spending time with, Collin?" I tried to ignore his father's remarks; the old man spoke like some ancient caveman most of the time.

"You wouldn't understand, Fiona. But the fact is that I told him he needs to find another girl to dance with, and he's clearly not doing it." His ears had turned as red as beets. I knew that meant he was angry.

But I still couldn't understand why. "Just let him dance with whomever he wants." Collin's controlling nature could get the best of him at times. And I hoped he wouldn't ruin our son's party.

"You'll never understand things in this town, Fiona. That girl is from the wrong side of town. The name Gentry means something here. I fully expect my son to protect the name the same way my grandfather and my father did. The way I did."

"I can't see how he's smudging the family name by dancing with that girl." This was just too much.

"I didn't get to do it, and neither will he," Collin said with such anger in his voice that it actually frightened me.

His words just confused me even more. "Was there some girl from here that you weren't allowed to see, Collin?"

"Never mind," he growled before getting up and leaving.

His parents followed a half-hour later, and I was left sitting alone at the table, wondering what the hell was happening. When Coy saw me sitting alone, he came to me. "Where has everyone gone?"

"Home, I suppose." I'd ridden with Coy but had assumed Collin would take me home. "I hate to put a damper on your evening, Coy, but it seems I'll need you to give me a ride home."

"Of course, Mom. No problem at all." He sighed and shoved his hands into his pockets. "Man, Dad's a real snob. I never knew how much until tonight."

"What did he say to you?" *I might finally get some answers.*

"He told me that I can't see Lila. He said she comes from a bad family."

"Oh, I see. And you must've told him that you will see her if you want—or something of that nature." My son was like me in many ways. I was proud of him for that.

"Yep." He rocked on his heels. "Mom, I just can't let him dictate my life. And I really can't let him tell me who I can and cannot date. Sorry, I just can't do that."

"I know you can't." I was the same way. "Well, I'll talk to him.

85

Not that I have any control over him, but sometimes I can make him understand that he's not in control of everyone else."

"I would appreciate it if you did that for me. I don't want to argue with him. But I'm not about to stop seeing someone I like just because of their family or how much money they might or might not have. I honestly have no idea why Dad is so pissed off."

Collin's father's words about Coy being spared beatings came to mind. "I'm sure it has something to do with your grandfather, Coy. I'll do what I can to put a stop to this nonsense. But how about that ride home now? I'm exhausted and in need of more pain killers."

Coy took me home and got me into the house. "Mom, I'm gonna go back into town to get Lila. We're gonna hang out for a bit longer. It's only a little after midnight. I'll be home in a few hours."

"You be careful, son." I knew he hadn't dated anyone before, and that worried me. "You don't know anything about this girl, so guard your heart until you get to know her better. She's the first girl you've gone out with, you know."

"I know. That's why I want to talk with her some more. I'm not trying to rush anything. But I like her, Mom. I like her a lot."

"Don't mistake physical attraction for something more. You should be intellectually attracted to a girl too." I trusted Coy. He was a good boy. "Good night. Have fun. I'll see you tomorrow."

"Good night, Mom. I love you."

"I love you too."

I wheeled myself to the downstairs bedroom, which I'd moved into after my accident. Having to have my nurse help me dress and undress and move from the wheelchair to the bed made it so that I had to have a separate bedroom from Collin. Waking him up wasn't an option.

The nurse's bedroom was right next to mine; she heard me as the floorboards creaked under the weight of my chair. "There you are. I bet you're in need of your pain medication."

"You are so right, Lucy. And I'd love to get out of this chair and into my cozy bed."

The next morning, I was woken up by my husband, who wore an angry expression. "When did he finally come home?"

"Coy?" I pulled myself up to a sitting position, which made my back spasm as the brace around me slipped. "Ow!"

Collin hurried to help me, slipping the brace back into place and pulling the strings to tighten it back up. "You have to be careful."

"Well, you woke me up, and I'm out of sorts, Collin." I panted as my lower back throbbed. "Hand me the pain killers, please."

Moving quickly, he got me a pill and handed me the glass of water I always kept on the nightstand. "Here, take this."

It took me a few minutes before I could start thinking straight, and when I finally could, I asked, "What's your problem, Collin?"

He stood there with his arms crossed over his chest. "Our son needs to do as I tell him. Did he leave after he brought you home?"

"Yes, he did. He went back into town to spend some time with Lila. And you need to mind your own business." I wasn't about to side with my husband on something this stupid.

"I'm saving him from himself. You wouldn't understand. He listens to you. I need your help with this."

He was a fool if he thought for a second that I'd help him. "Collin, you know that I don't feel as if myself, you, or your parents are above anyone else. Coy is not above that girl. There is no above. We are all just people. And we can date and even fall in love with anyone we damn well please, regardless of their color, bank account, or family background. So, what did the Stevens family ever do to the Gentry family that made them persona non grata?"

He closed his eyes as his face went a shade of red that I hadn't seen before. "Look, I had to follow my father's rules growing up, and so does everyone who lives in this house or on this ranch. If Coy wants to continue living here, he will have to listen to what I say. And he can't date anyone from that family or any family that my father deems beneath us."

"No." I wasn't going to be a part of this idiocy. "I won't back you or your father on this. It's against my moral code, Collin. And it sounds like it's against our son's as well. He's eighteen—a man now. And I'm proud of him for sticking up for what he believes in."

"You leave me no choice then. If you aren't with me, then you are against me. If you don't back me up on this or accept whatever I choose to do to Coy, then you can get out of this house."

"I'm at your mercy right now, and you know that. I can't work for maybe a whole year. How will I pay rent? How will I get around? How will I pay my nurse if you send me away?" My father had already passed away from a heart attack, and my mother's high blood pressure had gotten so severe that she had to live in a nursing home. I had no one to go to if he sent me away.

"Don't make me send you away then. I'm not saying that you have to make Coy do as I say because I know that might well be impossible. He is so much like you, after all." He didn't make it sound like a compliment. "But I do expect you to back whatever I say and whatever threats I make or go through with. I'm not doing it to hurt our son. I'm doing it to save him from himself."

"You were interested in someone from that family a long time ago, and your father didn't allow you to pursue it. I can see it in your eyes. Did he beat you over it?" I'd seen enough of the ugly side of the Gentry's to think otherwise.

"He did. You're right. And I learned to obey what he fucking said, too. Do you want that to happen to our son?"

"I wouldn't allow it, and I expect you not to allow it either." I hated being so incapacitated at a moment when I truly needed my strength.

"He won't do it when anyone is around. And we both know that Coy won't fight back. Plus, my father can disown me if I can't make my son protect the family name. He's told me before that if I don't do as he demands, he will leave this ranch to the state before giving it to me."

I knew Collin's father was a hard-ass—that he could even be cruel at times. But I had no idea he could be so downright evil and spiteful. It made me sick to think that I'd lived in the same home as a man who was capable of such atrocities.

"Collin, we should move out of this house. We should leave the ranch anyway. We can't allow that man to control us or our son. You have a degree and loads of experience. You can get a job as a ranch manager in no time. It's not nearly as much money as you have, but it's an honest living, and then no one can tell you how to live your life or how to treat your son."

"I can't do that. And believe me, you wouldn't want me if I left

88

this ranch. Tell me what I need to hear from you, Fiona, or I'll pack your things and send you away this very day. I swear to you that I will do it."

My heart skipped a beat. I loved my son more than anything, but in this condition, what choice did I have?

I could only hope that one day, Coy would understand.

COY

July 1988 – Carthage, Texas

Driving home, I decided that I had to give my parents one more shot. I'd never been in an argument with either of them, and it occurred to me that I didn't know how to argue my point with them. But I had taken a debate class, so I knew how to argue.

As I walked into the house, I tried to make a list of pros that I could think of about me and Lila. There were a lot of them. And the only cons pertained to my family and hers.

My mother sat in her wheelchair alone in the living room, reading a book. She looked up at me with a smile as I came into the room. "There you are. You've been so busy this summer. Where've you been today?"

For a moment, I wanted to tell her the truth. But even if she didn't like the idea of me being with Lila, she would hate knowing that we'd gotten a marriage license and planned to get married in three days. Without her there.

So, I lied, "Just messing around with some of the guys I was in kindergarten with. You know, the ones I reconnected with at the party you guys so generously threw."

"That's nice." She put her book on the table next to her, giving me her full attention. "We're having chicken fried steak for dinner this evening. Your favorite."

"Good." I was hungry. I just hoped I would still be hungry after our conversation. "So, while Dad's not in the house, I want to talk to you about something."

Her jaw tightened right away, and she clasped her hands in her lap. "About what?"

I took a seat so that we were on the same level. "Mom, it's about Lila Stevens. I don't understand why we can't see each other."

She looked over her shoulder as if trying to make sure no one would hear us, then looked back at me. "Son, I know this isn't right. I'm not the kind of person who thinks anyone is any better than someone else. But I'm not your only parent. And your grandparents own this house and the ranch. Your father hasn't inherited it yet. And, frankly, I'm not one hundred percent sure he'd allow you to see Lila, even if he were in charge right now."

"But why?" I couldn't understand why my father had to take a stand on this.

"Your father was raised differently," she said. "His parents instilled their values in him, and they soaked in thoroughly. This ranch is everything to him and your grandfather. And they will do anything they deem necessary to make sure the next generations uphold their strict values. And these values make it so that any children of theirs have to hold themselves to the same standards as they do."

"Mom, come on." I knew she didn't think the way they did. "Can't you talk some sense into them?"

A weak smile curved her pale lips. "I have tried. But your father won't hear another word about that from me. He's made it clear that if I'm not with him, then I'm against him."

"Mom, you know that you can have your own opinion. And you know that your opinion matters." I didn't like seeing my mother like this. "Why are you backing him on this? You're a strong woman."

"But I am not independent—especially not right now. I rely on your father for everything. I am so sorry that my injuries are interfering with what you need right now. I truly am. But there is absolutely nothing that I can do about it." A tear ran down her cheek, and she quickly wiped it away. "Just do as he says, Coy. Don't make waves. There are more fish in the sea, I promise you that. And college is going to start in the fall, and you'll meet many young women from all over the place there. Women who are as energetic and educated as you. Women who you might be more compatible with."

"Mom, Lila and I are extremely compatible."

"I'm sure that you think that, Coy." She shook her head. "Lila is a small-town girl who probably hasn't ever been further away than Dallas. She's not going anywhere."

"So?" I had no idea why that would even matter. "I'm coming back here to this ranch after college, so I'm not going anywhere either. I'll eventually take over this ranch and live out the remainder of my life right here. What makes me any different from her?"

"You've gone to a better school than she has, for one. And you'll get a college degree that will make you even more well-rounded. When you come back for your first visit after being in college for a semester, you'll see that you've outgrown the likes of a small-town girl."

"I don't even believe that for a second." Sighing, I didn't know how to make her believe that I was in love with Lila. "Mom, we've been seeing each other in secret."

"I'm going to pretend that I did not hear that. And I don't want you to repeat it. I need you to stop seeing her. This is for your own good. You must trust me on this. Forget about her, let the future show you what it has in store for you. I met your father in college. I'd had a couple of boyfriends before him, but it was different when I met him. It could happen for you just like that too."

"Mom, I've found the one for me. I don't need to date anyone else to know that."

Shaking her head, she hissed, "Stop saying things like that. It makes it sound as if you've been spending time with her. Your father will see right through you. And you can't let him do that."

I had a strong feeling that she didn't believe anything she was saying—that there was another source behind all of this. "I think I'll go talk to Grampa."

All color drained from her face, and her mouth fell open. "No.

92

Promise me that you won't do that. It would be unbelievably bad for you if you did that."

"The worst thing that anyone can do to me is take away my inheritance."

"You are wrong. You have no idea how wrong you are." She wrung her hands in her lap; it was obvious that I'd upset her. "Drop this, now. End things, now. I am pleading with you, Coy."

"Coy Collin," I said with disgust. "Named after the two most stubborn men I've ever met. Why do they refuse to understand that the heart wants what the heart wants? I can't have whoever *I* choose. I must take whoever *they* approve of." I looked at my mother, who was the epitome of a prim and proper wife. "Look at yourself. A college-educated woman who knows her place. Seems Dad picked you because you fit the role, Mom. Tell me how many times the word *love* has been said between you and my father."

"Coy, please stop," she whimpered, which was unlike her. "I didn't raise you to be cruel like this. You might be a man now, but you're still young. There's still a lot you don't know about how the world works—about how marriages work."

"I might be young, but I know what I want. I know I want a marriage with *love* at its heart. Not similar educations. Not playing a role. *Love*, Mom. *Love* is what makes the world go 'round. *Love* will see you through everything. Not being on the same financial tier. Not being on the same level." I had never felt more disgusted with my mother in my entire life. "You didn't stand up for me when I didn't want to be taken and left at boarding school when I was six, and you won't do it now either."

"I can't." She ran her hands over her injured legs. "I'm in no condition to fight a battle with your father. And to be perfectly honest, I don't think it would be worth it, in the end. She is the first girl you've ever kissed, and I think that's why you've formed this bond so quickly." She ran her hand over her face. "Life is too big to marry only for love. Life hits you hard at times, and you need a partner you can trust. If you listen to nothing else I tell you, at least listen to that. And you need to heed the advice of those who love you and have your best interests at heart. Which your father and I do. Son, I feel as if I made the decision to marry your father too

93

soon. And I don't want to see you do something similar to what I did. Just wait before marrying this girl, please."

The sounds of my father's boots against the wooden floor echoed in the living room. Mom's eyes begged me not to say a word to him about what we'd talked about.

But I couldn't do what she wanted. "Dad, I'd like to have a rational conversation with you." I got up and went to pour him a glass of whisky, hoping it would help.

His lips curved into a small grin as he took a seat with a solid thump and took the glass from me. "Rational? As if I am anything but that." He took a sip, looking at me over the rim.

"Coy," Mom said. "Could you go see how long it'll be until dinner is ready? And let them know that your father is done with work."

She was just trying to get rid of me. "Mom, let me talk to my father."

"Yes, Fiona. Let him talk to me." Dad said as he held the drink with his two hands, and his jaw squared.

"I would like your permission to date Lila Stevens." I thought I should start there, just to see how bad his reaction would be.

"We've gone over this already, and I won't revisit the topic." He took another drink before asking my mother, "What's for dinner, anyway?"

"Chicken fried steak, mashed potatoes, cream gravy, and green beans." She smiled. "Coy's favorite and yours. You two have a lot in common. Don't you think so?"

"We have too much in common, that's the problem. Only I was brought up with a firm hand while our son was spared the rod." Putting down the glass, his haggard expression made him look like a man who'd made many mistakes in his life. "Spare the rod and spoil the child, as they say. And it seems that we've spoiled him."

"I am anything but spoiled. I grew up without my parents." I walked away, not wanting to say things that would hurt them, even if they didn't care that the things they said hurt me immensely. "You are all from a time that has to come to an end. You believe that money can separate the good from the bad—but you are wrong. You are wrong about so many things. And I hate that I'm just

94

beginning to figure that out. I am from a family that I never really knew. And you did that to me, Dad. You sent me away so that I never got to chance to get to know any of you. Not really."

"Stay away from that girl, Coy," my father said. "Or you will hate the outcome."

"Maybe *you* will hate the outcome far worse than I will. Maybe *you* will find that losing your son—your only child—wasn't worth your fucking pride. This is a ranch—and one I barely even grew up on. A fucking ranch. Some goddamn dirt that cattle shit on all day long. It's not Camelot. It's not a kingdom. You are not royalty either. And I will do as I damn well please before I sacrifice my life for a piece of dirt that I hardly give two shits about!"

Leaving the room, I could feel the hot glare my father gave me. And I could hear my mother weeping.

But I didn't care.

LILA

Even though I had only seen Coy for a short time that night, I still fell asleep with a smile on my lips. I couldn't help but smile when I thought about our future together.

In only three days, we'd become man and wife. Coy had explained to me that I would need to pack as much as I could while being as discreet as possible.

After the marriage ceremony was to be performed by the local Justice of the Peace, Coy would take me to the used car lot to pick up the car that he'd bought me. And then we'd travel to Lubbock and move into the house his father had already bought him.

He was sure that his father would cut him off—at least for a while—but we'd stay at the house as long as we could. In the meantime, Coy would get a job to make ends meet. I was sure that I could find some way to make money to contribute to our household too.

Although terrified about everything, I was extremely excited to start a new life with the man I loved. I knew my family would cut me off for a while too. Not that there was much to cut me off from, other than communication. With time, they would come around. At least, I hoped.

My happy slumber was abruptly interrupted—I found myself

completely confused when I woke up with something pulling at me. My arms and legs were bound, and something was shoved into my mouth to keep me from making any noises that would alert the household to what was happening to me.

Dark shadows moved around me. One of these shadows snapped what sounded and resembled a paper bag. I then momentarily saw my oldest brother's face before the bag was put over my head.

With my hands tied at the wrists and my ankles bound together, I was helpless as one of them threw me over their shoulder and carried me out of my bedroom.

I felt the cool night air on my bare legs and arms, my slip of a nightgown offering no protection from the elements. I heard the sound of our car starting up, and then I was laid down on a hard surface. A whooshing sound was all I could hear before the slam of the trunk told me that I was being taken away from my home in the dead of night.

Tears started pouring down my face as I realized what this meant for my happy dreams. I knew something had to have happened to alert my father about the plans Coy and I had made. As worried as I was for myself, my heart held even more worry for Coy.

God, I hope they didn't do anything to him.

Even though I had no idea where they were taking me, I knew that my father and brothers were responsible—they were the ones who had done this to me. That knowledge alone made me feel slightly better as I knew that at least they wouldn't kill me.

Once I got to wherever they were taking me, I would figure out how to get back to Carthage and back to Coy. If I had to go directly to the police to make sure Coy was okay, then that's what I would do.

My father had no idea what he'd sparked inside of me. I was going to fight like a bear to return to the man I loved. If someone got hurt in the process, then too damn bad for them.

The car ride went on forever before we finally stopped. The trunk was opened, and I was picked up and tossed over someone's shoulder.

97

I heard what sounded like an old screen door opening with a loud squeak. "Bring her inside," I heard a woman say. "Back here. I've prepared a room for her."

Whoever this was, she'd been expecting me. I knew that meant this whole thing had been planned. And it had to have been planned recently since Coy and I had only gotten our marriage license the day before.

Someone had told on us. But I had no idea who even knew about our relationship. More worry for Coy built up inside of me and what might be happening to him at that moment.

I was dropped on what felt like a small bed, then something was wrapped around my waist, and I heard the click of a lock. "You've set this up very well, sister," I heard my father say, suspicion in his voice. "Who knew you had so much experience with restraints?"

"Never mind about that. You all leave. I'll deal with her now," the woman said.

"Are you sure that you can keep her here like this? For as long as it takes?" my father asked.

I had no idea what he was talking about. What was going to take so long? I wiggled and twisted on the bed, trying to free myself. Her voice came from somewhere right beside my head, "Don't do that, or I'll tighten the chains, Lila."

"Hilda," my father said, and I finally knew where I was. I was with my Aunt Hilda. "Make sure to take care of her—feed her well, and give her water too. I want my daughter back in a healthy state once this is over and done with."

"I won't kill her if that's what you're asking."

As soon as I heard the sound of their receding footsteps, leaving me alone, I let out a sigh of relief. At least I knew I was going to be okay. And as long as I had some strength left in me, I had a chance of escaping.

Knowing exactly where I was helped as well. My aunt had moved to Shreveport when I was just a baby. She hadn't come to Carthage ever since, but we'd gone to her house for several holidays during the past years. I remembered that it took about an hour to get there.

I'm only an hour away from home.

For the first time ever, I felt thankful that I'd never had a car. I was used to walking; I could walk several miles in a day without even getting tired. If I could make it to the highway, I was certain that I would be able to get a ride back to Carthage.

All I've got to do is free myself.

"Let's get that bag off your head," Hilda said as she came back into the room.

When she pulled the bag off my head, I blinked as the bare light bulb above the bed shined in my eyes. She pulled the gag out of my mouth and tossed it to the floor. "Thank you." I thought that if I was civil with her, she might see it fit to let me out of the chains sooner rather than later. "Aunt Hilda, why did they do this to me?"

"You've fallen for the wrong guy, honey. That's why you're here." She took a large pair of scissors and cut the zip ties that held my wrists and ankles together. "The chain around your waist will allow you to move around enough to get to that wastebasket over there. That will be your bathroom."

I looked at the small trashcan. "You want me to use the bathroom in that thing?" I couldn't keep the disgust and repulsion from my voice. "Why can't I use the bathroom?"

"Because the chain won't reach that far." She went to the door, then turned to look at me. "Take my advice, Lila. Put the Gentry boy out of your mind. He'll only cause you pain, sorrow, and loneliness. And you won't like that kind of life—believe me. I'll be back in a bit with some breakfast."

I wasn't hungry at all. All I wanted was to learn more about what had led me here. "Aunt Hilda, how do you know anything about the Gentry's? Did you know Coy's father?"

"No." She walked away, leaving me to my own thoughts.

I knew she had to have had something to do with someone in that family, and it must not have gone well. In fact, it must have gone horribly. There was no other reason for this insanity.

That meant she must have known Coy's father or grandfather because there wasn't anyone else. And the idea of her having an affair with the grandfather was pretty sickening.

As I lay there, trying to figure out what secret had led to all this, I started thinking about what I knew of Hilda. She had lived her whole life in Carthage, and then she had moved away all of a sudden.

I'd heard my mother and father talking about it on different occasions. They had both wondered why she had moved away when there was nothing for her in Shreveport.

Closing my eyes, I didn't really care what their damn secrets were. All I cared about was finding out if Coy was okay. "Aunt Hilda," I called out.

She came back to the door, leaning against the frame. "Yes."

"Is Coy okay? I have to know if he's okay."

She laughed as if that was the silliest question she'd ever heard. "He's a Gentry. Of course he's okay. *You've* been removed so that he can't get to you, but nothing has happened to him. I suppose his heart will ache when he finds that you've moved away without a word, but the boy is going to college soon anyway. He'll meet someone else, and he won't even spare you a thought. And that's when you can go back to your home with your father and mother. But not until then."

"So, I'm to be chained to this bed until that happens?" I'd never felt afraid of anyone in my family before, but everything that had happened in the last couple 0f hours was so far beyond normal that I didn't know how to feel anymore. I started to question how safe I was here—I was no longer certain that Aunt Hilda wouldn't harm me. This wasn't protection, this was punishment. It was more than punishment.

"I guess that depends on you, dear." She smiled as if she felt no empathy at all. "Whether or not you see the truth. This is a lesson on falling in love with a Gentry. Only pain comes with that. Once you've learned this lesson—however long it takes—then you, too, will have no desire to have him in your life anymore. And he'll have moved on long before."

Her words terrified me. Not because I believed them—Coy was a good man, he would never hurt me if he could help it—but because of the look in her eyes as she said them out loud. They were filled with nothing but bleakness. Whatever had happened to Aunt Hilda in the past, I knew it had made her believe in every word she was saying.

"I don't know which one of the Gentry's hurt you, Aunt Hilda, but I can assure you that Coy isn't like any of them. He's a good man. He's a caring man. He's not like his father or his grandfather." Suddenly, it occurred to me that she must be in contact with someone if she knew about Coy's plans for college. "Who are you talking to in the Gentry house?"

"That's none of your concern. You should be thinking about what you will do when you're taken back home. You'll want to get a job. You'll want to be able to take care of yourself."

That might have been the first bit of good advice she'd given me, and it made me wonder. "And where do you work, Aunt Hilda?"

"I don't." She turned and began walking away. "So, you won't be alone here in the house, if you were thinking you could escape. I'll be right here at all times. Even my groceries will be brought to me to make sure you don't have a moment all by yourself."

"So, someone is paying you to keep me here." I knew my family had no money for that. But the Gentry's had more than enough.

COY

As usual, I went to the park in town where Lila and I would meet each morning at six—so we could watch the sunrise together. Only she wasn't there. I went back just after dark, too, for our usual second meeting of the day. Again, she wasn't there. I waited for her until midnight, but she still never showed up.

The next day was the same. That's when I really started to worry. The day after was supposed to be our wedding day. I knew I had to do something to find out where she was and what the hell was going on.

Has she changed her mind about marrying me?

If the marriage was something she'd grown concerned about, we didn't have to go through with it. I loved her and wanted to marry her, but I didn't want to force her or make her feel pressured into doing something she didn't want.

I needed to talk to her to let her know my thoughts. I needed to see her, touch her, kiss her. It had only been a couple of days, but I missed her more than I knew I could miss anyone.

Since I knew where she lived, on the morning we were supposed to get married, I parked on the street from her family's small house. Waiting for someone to emerge from the house, I finally saw two young teens walking out, heading towards the opposite direction of my truck.

Following them at a distance, I drove slowly so they wouldn't notice me. One of the boys split from the other, went up to a house, and headed inside as the other kept walking.

Taking my chance, I pulled up next to the boy and rolled my window down. "Hi. You're Lila's little brother, right?"

"Yeah." He looked at my truck. "You're the guy she doesn't want to see anymore, aren't you?"

I shook my head. "Is your sister home?"

"My sister moved away a couple of nights ago. Dad told us that she wanted to get away from this town." A frown told me he missed his sister. "Cause of some guy."

"She didn't tell you goodbye?"

"No. Dad said that she woke him up, and she was crying. She said she wanted to leave because she couldn't face this guy she's been seeing, but she didn't want to see him anymore. So Dad took her to live with our aunt. He told us that when her heart is better, she'll be back. But that might take a long time."

There was no way in hell I would believe that story. But this kid seemed to believe all of it. "You miss her, don't you?"

"Yeah. Lila's a great sister. She always hangs out with me and my brother, even when nobody else gives us the time of day. And she cooks for us, too. She makes the best grilled cheese sandwiches in the world." He wiped his eyes with the palms of his hands. "I didn't think she was sad. I'd never seen her happier. But I'm just a kid, so what do I know about things like that anyway?"

I bet he knew a lot more than he realized.

I had to get the address of where she'd gone. But I highly doubted the boy knew it. "I'd love to write her. We were just friends." I didn't want him thinking I was the guy she'd run away from. "But I'd like to keep in touch with her. You know, let her know that she's missed around here."

"Oh." He looked at the ground, scuffing his bare feet across it to kick up dust.

He wasn't catching on at all. "So, do you think that you can find out the address for me? I could meet you at the park at the end of the street just before dark tonight so that you can give it to me. I've got a few bucks I can give you if you do that for me."

His dark eyes lit up. "You'll pay me to get you the address?"

"Sure." I needed him to keep it a secret, though. "I'll give you a whole twenty bucks if you can get it without letting anyone know what you're doing." I reached into my pocket and pulled out a ten, then held it out to him. "Here, take this as a sign of good faith. And I'll give you that twenty when you come to the park with the address. Make sure to write it down, so you don't forget any of it."

The way he stared at the money in his hand told me he wasn't used to seeing it there. "Wow!"

"I know, right? Wait until you're holding twice that amount in your hand. Do we have a deal? And what's your name, by the way."

"Paul." He looked at me. "And your name is?"

"John," I lied. "I'll see you at the park just before dark. If we have a deal."

"We've got a deal! I'll be there. I do know this much, she's staying with my father's sister—Aunt Hilda. She lives in Shreveport, Louisiana."

Only about an hour away!

"Cool. Well, see if you can get me that address so I can send her a letter. I'll make sure to tell her how you helped me out, Paul. Anything you'd like me to tell her from you?"

"Tell her that I love her and that I miss her and her grilled cheese sandwiches. And I hope her heart gets better very quickly so she can come back home."

"I'll do that. See you later, Paul." I drove away, feeling slightly better about things.

One thing I was pretty sure of was that someone had told her father about us. And I was sure he'd taken Lila to his sister's against her will.

As I drove back home, I had to wonder if my father or even my mother had had anything to do with Lila's father finding out about us. I'd just had that talk with my parents the night before Lila stopped showing up—the night her little brother said she'd asked her father to take her away.

Could my parents really be this heartless?

Once I got home, I walked into the house and went straight up to my bedroom, not wanting to talk to anyone. Ditching my boots at the door, I walked inside and fell face down on my bed.

Nothing made sense to me. I felt as if I didn't know my own family. Sure, I'd grown up in boarding school, but I did spend summers with them, and all the holidays too. For the first year, I'd even been picked up to come home for the weekends. But in all that time—or that little time—I had missed out on learning who my family really was.

My mother and father had always been strong figures to me. But now I could see that my father ran roughshod over my mother. My mother's strong façade was just that—fake.

Then there was my father. He said the right words to me, telling me he did everything for my own good. But those words were spoken merely to pay me lip service.

When it came down to it, everything he did was for his own best interest and no one else's. Who I dated should have never been any of their concern. And now it seemed that my own family might go so far as to take away the person who meant the most to me in my life.

What was worse was that they might have pushed Lila away from all the people she knew and loved. She had friends and family in Carthage. I just knew that somehow, someone in my own family must've made sure her father got her out of town, away from me.

Whatever had happened to forge a line of steel between our families didn't have a damn thing to do with either of us. We shouldn't have been put in the middle of their stupid feud. We should've been left alone.

Rolling over, I saw the clock on my nightstand.

Noon. We should've already been married by this time today.

Getting up, I went to my dresser. I'd made a fake bottom in the middle drawer to hide the things I couldn't let my parents find. The thousands of dollars in cash, the marriage license, and the wedding rings I'd bought two days earlier.

I'd been so excited to show them to Lila. But I'd never gotten the chance.

This was unjust, unfair, and unacceptable. I had to put a stop to this. I couldn't let my family continue acting this way.

And more than anything, I needed to make sure that Lila was okay.

I heard the sound of a telephone ringing in the distance and knew it was coming from my parent's bedroom down the hall. At the time, with my mother's injuries and her being in a wheelchair, my father was the only one using that room.

When I heard the ringing stop, I got up and crept along the wall, being careful not to make a sound. Placing my ear against the door, I could hear my father talking. "This isn't an open invitation to keep in contact with me."

Who would he say something like that to?

"He's here. Yes, I'm sure. I saw his truck in the driveway. How would he ever find your place?"

The hair on the back of my neck stood up. I was sure that he was talking to whoever had Lila. And Paul had said she was with her Aunt Hilda.

"So what if she said that? He has no idea who you are or where you are. Plus, I'm going to suggest that he and I take a trip to Lubbock to check out his new house. I think that'll help take his mind off of her."

I knew it!

"What do you mean, you have a gun?" my father asked with concern. "If he somehow finds her, you better not harm a hair on his head. Do you hear me? Do you?"

I did not like the sound of that. Not only because it put me in danger, but it meant that this person who was keeping Lila from me —Hilda—wasn't afraid to use violence. And that bothered me to no end. If I weren't there, who would protect Lila?

"Just don't open the door if he somehow finds you. Don't let him in. Act as if no one is home, for God's sake. Do I have to give you explicit instructions on every little thing? Damn."

Even though I was hearing the words come out of my father's mouth, it was still unbelievably hard to imagine that he could do such a horrible thing—not only to his only child but to Lila, too.

He made someone leave their home just to keep them away from me.

I had no idea what I should do. I loved Lila with my whole heart and soul. I would do anything for her. I would even lay down my life for her.

She didn't deserve to be treated this way. She didn't deserve to be taken from her own home, and away from the town she grew up in. She didn't deserve any of this.

I'd already felt terrible that my family wouldn't accept her. And now they'd gone and turned her entire life upside down.

I felt as if I was some sort of poison to her. All I wanted to do was love her. But the people I came from had not only forbidden it, but they had done whatever they could to put it to a stop.

My father surely had no heart. Any parent who did something this heinous to their child was pure evil.

All Lila and I wanted was to love each other the same way everyone else got to. We weren't asking for much—and yet, look at what had happened.

For the first time, I wondered if maybe Lila was better off if I stayed out of her life.

LILA

Wearing a white cotton dress, I walked down an empty aisle to meet Coy, who stood at the front of the room. He wore a suit and a tie and looked more handsome than I'd ever seen him.

My heart raced as I walked up to him and took his hand into mine. "Coy Gentry, I take you to be my lawfully wedded husband."

"And I take you, Lila Stevens, to be my lawfully wedded wife."

We kissed, and the next thing I knew, we were in bed, rolling around naked and laughing as we made love. Sunlight shone through the window as birds chirped and sang outside.

Life would be better now that we were joined as one. Things would change. Coy and I would live life on our own terms.

"I love you, Lila Gentry." Coy looked down at me as he moved his body over mine.

He pressed himself into me, making me sigh. "I love you too, my handsome husband."

Moving like waves on the ocean, we made love, holding each other, laughing, sighing, and even crying over the beauty of it all. We were husband and wife—and no one could come between us anymore. No one could separate what God had joined together.

"Wake up," I heard someone calling.

Startled, I woke up with my eyes swimming in tears. Wiping

them away, disappointment resonated within me as I realized it had only been a dream.

Coy and I were supposed to get married that very day. But I was still chained up, unable to get to the courthouse where we'd agreed to meet at eight in the morning.

Hilda put the plate of food on the bedside table. "Here."

"What time is it?" I asked as I sat up.

"Does it really matter?" She walked towards the small television she'd brought in for me. Turning it on, she stood there in front of it for a moment. "Days go by. Time goes by. And nothing—absolutely nothing—changes." She turned to face me. "That's life when you love a Gentry man."

"When are you going to tell me what went on between you and Mr. Gentry?" I still wasn't sure which one of them she'd been with, but I was certain that she'd been with one of them.

"Eat your eggs before they get cold." She walked out of the room, then came back with a bucket of water, a washcloth, and some clean clothes for me to put on. "After you eat, wash yourself and then put these on. You reek."

"It *has* been three days." I wouldn't be ashamed of stinking when I'd been kept away from the bathroom and clean clothes.

She went to the trash can that served as my toilet. She picked it up and held it away from her as she left the room. Again, I felt no shame in having used the only thing she gave me—it was her shame, not mine.

I smiled as a thought crossed my mind—what if I could make the room stink so badly that she would have to set me free? Even if only to make me clean it myself. And then I would hit her in the head with whatever I could find and run away.

I looked at the panties she'd given me. They were huge and an ugly tan color. And the other piece of clothing was just an old, threadbare nightgown in a greyish color.

I supposed she thought I wouldn't dare run outside in such a sad outfit. But she was wrong. If I had no clothes on, I was still going to make a run for it as soon as I got the chance. I'd use tree branches to cover my body if I had to.

When she came back in with the cleaned trashcan with a new

liner inside, she placed it right back where she'd picked it up from. "You still haven't finished eating yet?"

"No." I saw no reason to hurry. I'd been civil, and that had gotten me nowhere, but I still tried. "I don't think you're getting paid enough to deal with this. Do you?"

She laughed. "I have to agree with you. But I'm not in charge."

"Then who is?"

"Someone." She left me alone again.

I took my time eating. Then I pulled off the clothes I'd been wearing the night I was abducted from my own bed. Tossing them into the trashcan, I saw no reason to keep them. They were soiled and ripped from the rough treatment I'd had to undergo.

Washing my body with the cold water, I tried not to cry. I had to be strong. I couldn't let myself get run down or worn out. The idea here was to break my spirit and my love for Coy. It wasn't going to work, though.

I knew he'd wait for me. I knew he wouldn't find someone else to love, not with things unresolved between us. No matter what he'd been told, I knew his heart belonged to me, and mine belonged to him. I had to believe he was telling himself the same thing.

His parents didn't understand him. He was a passionate, independent man who stood up for what he believed in. He was the way he was because of what they had done to him when he was a little kid. Sending him away at only six years to live with strangers—it had turned him into a different sort of young man.

He'd never really felt loved, he'd told me once. And now that he had felt my love, he wouldn't let it go. I prayed he knew that I wasn't about to let it go either.

They could only keep us apart for so long. My friends would be stopping by the house to ask for me. Janine would keep bothering my family until they told her where I was. Or she might even go to her parents to seek help to find me.

I also had high hopes that Coy wouldn't believe whatever garbage he was told about my disappearance. I hoped he would know that my father had taken me somewhere and that he'd maybe even go to the cops.

Someone had to do something. Someone had to miss me

and want to know where I was. I had good friends. I knew that they could get together and demand to know my whereabouts.

But will they?

All of my friends knew that my father could be a real asshole. And he had control over my older brothers, making them real assholes too. So, there was a chance that they wouldn't want to deal with them, and they might not try that hard to get information about me.

My mind infuriated me. I would be thinking positively for one minute, and then it would flip on me and take me down a desolate road—a road with no help along it.

Getting dressed with a chain around one's waist was a real pain in the ass, and when I caught Hilda snickering at me as she walked back into the room, I clenched my jaw. "You know, a real shower would be nice."

"I bet it would. Just think how much better it's going to feel when you haven't had one in months." She looked around the room. "Where are your dirty clothes?"

"I threw them away." I shimmied the gown down my body after shoving it through the chain, which only gave about a half-inch gap around my body.

She went and retrieved them from the trash. "I'll wash them. You'll wear them again."

I wasn't about to waste my breath arguing with her. It didn't matter what the hell I wore anyway. "Why are you doing this to me, Hilda?"

She stopped and looked at me. "Why should you get something when I couldn't have it?" And then she left.

I sat down on the bed, wondering what, exactly, that meant.

Did she want to marry Coy's dad or grandfather?

Since no one had told me why I'd been taken away, I had no idea what they exactly knew about me and Coy. Maybe no one knew about the marriage we'd been planning. Maybe they just found out that we'd been seeing each other in secret.

So, did she mean that she had wanted a secret relationship with one of the Gentry men and hadn't gotten it?

As I fell back onto the bed, I rested my hand on my forehead. My brain hurt from all the thinking I'd been doing.

I knew this much. It did not matter what Hilda or any of the Gentry's had done in the past. What mattered was me and Coy. What mattered was my life. And that meant I had to figure out how I was going to get out of the damn chain and out of the damn house.

Feeling frustrated, I said to myself out loud, "Coy will figure out where I am, and he will come for me."

Eventually, I did figure out what time it was. When the daytime soap opera that my mother watched came on the little television, I knew it was noon.

And not long after the show started, I heard Hilda talking on the phone to someone. "Hey, it's me." There was a pause before she added, "Is he there with you right now? Are you sure? I don't know. I mean, she said something about him coming to get her. It's got me worried."

She's got to be talking to someone in Coy's family.

"I've got a gun. I'll use it if I have to," she said, building up fear inside of me. I sat up, trying to hear each and every word she spoke.

Would she really shoot Coy if he came for me? Would she shoot me if I tried to leave?

I never would have thought it of anyone in my family, but she had me chained up to a bed, using a trash can as a toilet. I could no longer predict what she would or wouldn't do.

"I hear you. But what am I to do if he shows up here?"

Does she really have any reason to believe that Coy might be able to find me?

"I'm sorry that I called you. I'll deal with things on my own—as usual." I heard her slamming down the phone, cursing under her breath. "Damn that selfish man. Damn him to hell for all he's done and put me through. When will this torture end?"

Now I knew for certain that there was something between my aunt and one of Coy's relatives. My gut was telling me it was his father who Hilda had a past with.

If Coy's father was against our relationship, then it made sense that his father before him must've felt the same way if he'd been seeing my aunt. She was from the poor side of town, too, just like me.

The two of them must've been forbidden from being together. But had they really stayed away from each other, or had they had a secret relationship the same way Coy and I had?

And why do I keep caring about that?

That didn't amount to a hill of beans. Who cared about their past?

Knowing the truth wouldn't help me get out of the situation I was in. Coy and I weren't going to follow the archaic rules of the Gentry family. We were going to get married and live our own lives —far away from Carthage, if our marriage wasn't accepted by our families.

We had love. We had tons of it. And when you have the kind of love, you don't need anything or anyone else. You could live on that alone.

Somehow, I had to get free. Coy and I had to show our families that they couldn't stop love. Not a love as true and faithful as ours.

I closed my eyes and pictured Coy's face as I repeated silently, *I am in Shreveport with my Aunt Hilda. Come find me. Go through your father's things to find the address if you have to. I have no doubt that he has it.*

The phone call I'd overheard also confirmed my suspicions that Coy's father was paying my aunt to keep me away. I bet he'd paid for a lot of things—things that his wife didn't know a damn about.

Keep fucking with me, and I might well end your marriage, Mr. Gentry!

COY

Anger coursed through my veins as I stood outside my father's door. I made a quick knock before opening it and barging in. "And to whom are you telling my whereabouts?"

He stood by the desk in his bedroom, looking at me with wide eyes—eyes that held a fair amount of fear in them. "I wasn't telling anyone anything about you, Coy."

I had a sharp memory, so he wasn't going to get away with that. "I heard you say these exact words: *'He's here. Yes, I'm sure. I saw his truck in the driveway. How would he ever find your place?'*"

"*He* could be anybody, Coy. What makes you think I was talking about you?" His mouth was working hard to convince me that I was wrong. But it was his dark eyes, wide open, that told me I was right on point.

"Okay, then tell me who *she* is. I heard everything you just said on that call. About me not knowing who the person on the phone was, about your idea of a little trip to Lubbock to take my mind off of *her*. Who else has a new house in Lubbock besides me? And who else needs his attention taken off a girl? Don't try to lie to me, Dad. I've found you out."

"You're not being reasonable. You're acting like a frenzied animal, son. You need to calm down, and I'll explain the conversation you eavesdropped on—a conversation meant to be private."

"Oh, I'm sure you wanted that conversation to remain private, Dad. Especially the part about a gun."

My father turned away from me so I could no longer witness the shocked and rather pitiful expression on his face. "You didn't hear that right, son. I never said anything about a gun. I don't know why you think you can remember so much of what was said, but you didn't get it right. Sorry that you've misunderstood everything, but I was talking about one of the ranch hands who's been having some family troubles. I'm not at liberty to talk about his private affairs with you either, or I would fill you in on the whole sordid story."

"Dad, I was in every one of the school plays while I was in boarding school, not that you came to any of them. I've got a great memory for words, so I know I recall everything perfectly and exactly as you meant it."

He walked away from me, ignoring what I'd said, and grabbed his car keys off the dresser. "I've got tons to do today, Coy, otherwise, I'd love to stay here and play this little game of nonsense with you."

"Tell me what the name Hilda means to you, Dad." I inhaled, preparing myself for his reaction.

He laughed as if that was some sort of joke. "I went to school with Hilda Stevens, if that's who you're talking about. She's that girl's aunt. Don't know why you're asking me about her, though."

"I have reason to believe that you know a lot more about that woman than you're letting on." I crossed my arms over my chest and stood in the doorway so he couldn't leave. "I'd like to know more about her."

"Why? Because she's the girl's aunt?" he asked as he took a seat on the bed, crossing his arms over his chest to mimic my posture.

"Sure, let's say that's the reason why." He knew that I had some suspicions now, and I could tell it made him uneasy. I watched as his eyes started darting around the room instead of staying on mine.

"Well, she was shy and quiet in school. I never heard her say much of anything. She moved out of town a while back. Not that I know why. I just heard it through the grapevine. I don't know much about most people around this town—Hilda Stevens included.

"Stevens?" I asked, finding that a little odd. Paul had told me that Hilda was his father's sister, but he hadn't told me she still went by her maiden name. "She's your age and still has her maiden name?"

"As far as I know, she never married. So what?" he asked as if it wasn't a big deal.

"So what? Why didn't she ever get married? She never had a boyfriend?" My suspicions about my father's past involvement with the Stevens were coming to fruition.

"I don't know, son. I wasn't close to the girl. I got married fresh out of college, if you will recall. I didn't care about what anyone else in this town was doing. I've got to get going." He got off the bed and walked toward me. "You can come and give me a hand if you want. There's a cow in labor in the barn, and the vet might need all the help he can get."

The last thing I wanted to do was help my father or grandfather on the ranch. Not when it was the very thing that made them think they were better than other people. "No thanks."

I walked back to my bedroom. Knowing he would be busy in the barn, I decided I would take that time to pack some things and get ready for whatever was coming. I didn't exactly know what that would be, but I had to do something.

I was supposed to meet up with Lila's little brother a little before dark, and I'd have the address then. I could get on my way to Lila, and once I had her, I wouldn't be bringing her back anywhere near here. I wasn't about to take her any place where she wouldn't be safe —not until I had changed her last name to mine.

I'd snuck out one day with the keys to the house in Lubbock that my father kept in the desk drawer in his bedroom. I'd had a couple of copies made for me and Lila, and had hidden them in the drawer with our other things.

It was time to take my stash out so as to have it with me at all times. I wasn't sure how things were going to play out, so I wanted to be ready for whatever was coming.

One thing I knew for sure was that I wouldn't be backing down to anyone when I returned home with Lila. And neither would she.

If Lila was still up for marrying me, I wouldn't bring her back to Carthage until we were legally married. If my parents refused to accept our marriage, then that would be their loss.

In the late evening, after I'd managed to get everything to my truck, I walked through the living room to see if my mother was there.

She looked up at me as I came into the room. "You look nice. Where are you off to tonight?"

"Some guys are having a party. There's going to be drinking too. I'm gonna crash at one of my friend's houses so that I don't have to drive. Gotta be responsible."

Nodding, she asked, "What's the friend's name? I did teach most of the people in your age group, you know."

I hadn't thought of that. "Oh, his name is Paul. He's not from here. I think that's why we get along so well. He's sort of an outsider —like me."

"I hope you don't really feel like an outsider here, Coy. You belong in this town, just like everybody else. You're going to be a huge part of the community someday when you take over this ranch. You know, it's a big employer." She looked around quickly as if to see if anyone would overhear her next words. "You can do things differently than your father and grandfather once you take over."

I looked around the big living room. I'd never thought of this place as my home. I'd grown up and spent the majority of my time at the boarding school. In my mind, I hadn't ever had a real home or a real family. I'd certainly never thought of this place as mine.

I also knew next to nothing about ranching. All I could do was ride a horse and listen to my father order the ranch hands around. I supposed he thought he was teaching me to do what he did. But since he never explained himself—ever— in reality, I wasn't being taught a damn thing.

Nevertheless, her words struck me. I could do things differently than my father. She didn't know it, but that was exactly what I was doing. I wasn't about to let history repeat itself—not that I exactly knew what that history was.

"Yeah, I know. Maybe I'll learn more in college. I just don't have the experience Dad has with the ranch. I'm not sure I'm cut out to run it."

"You'll learn. Once you get done with college, you'll come home, and you'll learn how to run the place. It's your legacy, Coy. You were born to take over this ranch."

I didn't want it. I didn't want to have anything to do with it. Now that I was pretty sure my father had interfered with my relationship with Lila as much as he had, I didn't want anything to do with him or my grandparents.

Mom was the one person I wasn't sure I wanted to cut out of my life. But I wasn't even completely sure about her.

"Yeah, we'll see what college does for me."

"You don't want to stay for dinner and eat before you go to this party? We're having steak and baked potatoes tonight." She smiled at me, and it made my heart hurt.

Both of my parents kept trying to act like all the arguments and the accusations I'd made during the last few days hadn't happened at all. I didn't want to feel this way. I wanted things to be the way they had always been. I wanted back the family that I'd thought I had. I wanted that to be real. And it seemed that they wanted that too.

So much dishonesty. So many secrets. But the manipulation, the bullying, and the horrible deeds were too much to take. I didn't even want to eat a meal with my family at that time.

It was all I could do to pretend that nothing was wrong. But I knew I had to do that if I didn't want them to stop me—or try to, anyway—from leaving the house.

No matter what my father had said, he knew that I was right about what I had overheard. And that meant he'd be thinking that I might go renegade on him.

It had never been my intention to ruin my parents' marriage. But if they wanted to ruin my relationship with the woman I loved, then a turn about was fair play.

If I found Lila with her Aunt Hilda, and I got Hilda to confess about having a relationship with my father, either prior to his marriage to my mother or afterward, then I was going to use that information to my advantage.

"There's gonna be food there, Mom. See you tomorrow. I'll most likely sleep in, so don't expect me to be here early or anything. You probably won't see me before afternoon." I went over and kissed her on the cheek, feeling as if I might just cry.

I loved my mother. Out of everyone in that house, she had a good heart. It was just that my father knew how to control her. How to use that good heart and hold it over her head.

"I love you, Coy." She hugged me tightly. "So much."

"Me too, Mom." I hugged her back, then pulled away and turned around so that she wouldn't see my tear-glossed eyes.

Damn, I hate that it's come to this.

LILA

Listening to my aunt mutter to herself for an hour after the phone call, I got the distinct impression that things between her and Coy's father had been much more serious than I'd assumed.

Initially, I thought they might have had an ill-fated young fling. Now, I was starting to suspect there might have been an affair. Or maybe the two of them had been secret lovers before he got married, and then he went off to college and came back with a wife. But she mumbled some things that made it seem as if they'd had a very long and extremely intimate relationship. One that had ended before she was ready for it to be over.

I heard a pot slam down on the stove, and then she muttered, "I gave him everything I had." Something else crashed, and I thought she must've thrown it. "Children. All for him!"

I sat there, mesmerized by what she was saying. *She gave up children for him? How?*

"How can he still hurt me this way?" she mumbled as something else crashed to the floor. "Why do I allow it?"

On and on she went. And I sat there, listening to every word.

Then she came into my room with dinner. "I burnt the meatloaf. The potatoes are lumpy. The tomato gravy has too much salt." She put down the plate on the bedside table, then turned to leave.

"Aunt Hilda, would you like to bring your plate in here and eat with me?" I wanted to know more. I wanted her to feel comfortable with me so she would confide in me.

It was purely manipulative, and I knew that. But I needed some ammunition if I was going to be able to get out of this prison.

"I'm not going to be good company. And I don't know why you would want to eat with me in the first place. I am your jailer, after all." She left me before I could think of anything to say.

But she came back with a glass of water, so I got another chance to gain her trust. "You know that I could hear how angry you were with whoever you were talking to earlier. I do have ears. And I do have compassion for a woman who has been hurt. Why don't you come sit with me, and tell me why you're so upset?"

She leaned against the doorframe, her head cocked to one side, and her hands clasped in front of her. "Lila, my only dear niece, you would never, not even in a million years, understand why I am such a bitter old woman."

"Try me." I took a bite of the meatloaf. It was burnt, but I acted as if I liked it anyway. "Hey, this isn't bad at all. I like it."

"I was a shy girl when I was younger." She left the room after that, and I wondered what had happened. But then she returned with a glass of red wine. She leaned back against the doorframe as she took a sip. "When I look back on it now, I realize that I was an easy target."

"Who targeted you?" I took a bite of the lumpy potatoes. "These are good too."

"You're only saying that because your mother is a horrible cook." She sighed. "Your mother was able to get a good man. But not me."

"Well, my father isn't that good." He was mean and strict. Plus, he'd kidnapped his own daughter, so he had an evil streak as well.

"I mean that he did the right thing by your mother—even though she couldn't cook worth a damn. And let's face it, she's got the brain of a turnip."

My mother wasn't completely stupid. But I wanted to pull Hilda in, so I agreed. "Yes, she's so ignorant."

"Yet, as ignorant as she is, she got a husband. She got to have children with this man. She's someone's wife. Even if she doesn't deserve it." She took another drink, then held the glass with both hands. "I can cook like a chef. I can clean better than the finest maid. And I can please a man better than any woman I know."

My cheeks heated with her words. I had the idea that my aunt had been quite a woman—despite what years of what I now saw as bitterness had done to her, she was still an attractive woman. I could only imagine what she must've looked like when she was young and full of hope. And yet, no man had ever taken the time to get to know her.

"You know, maybe it's your quiet demeanor that's kept you single all this time. One of my mother's older sisters lost her husband last year to cancer. She's going to church on the lookout for men she might be attracted to."

"Church isn't a place I would find the right kind of man. Anyway, my heart no longer belongs to me. I don't have it to give to any other man."

"And why can't you be with the man who has your heart?" I was sure that was because he was already married.

"It doesn't matter. It never has." She downed the glass, finishing it off, then leaving me once more.

I took another bite as I waited to see if she'd come back. Although she'd said that she could cook like a chef and clean a house like the finest maid, I found the food bad, and the cleanliness of my room and what I could see outside it to be wanting.

She's delusional—and depressed.

Who wouldn't be if they were in her place?

I heard the sound of her sweeping up the things she'd probably thrown on the floor. Then I heard her gathering them into a dustpan before throwing them into the trash.

She went from one thing to another, cleaning up the house. And then she came into my room. "You're done with your food, right?"

I'd eaten every bite, even though it wasn't that good. "Yes, Aunt Hilda. Thank you."

She smiled at me. "You're going to make a fine woman someday, Lila. You don't let things hold you back."

SHE CARRIED MY EMPTY PLATE OUT OF THE ROOM, AND WHEN SHE came back, she had brought a broom with her and began sweeping. "I've got to get this place clean. I've been letting things go, and that's not like me at all."

"Are you depressed?" I asked as I watched her move with grace while doing such a mundane chore.

"Yes," she said so quickly that it made no sense. Not many people were willing to share something like that—at least not so quickly.

"Is it because you're in this place all alone?"

She nodded. "Yes."

"Then why don't you move back to Carthage, where your family is? You would have plenty of company if you moved back there."

She didn't say a word as she finished sweeping and then left the room again, only to return with a dustpan. She bent over to collect the dirt she'd gathered in a pile. "If I could, I would." With that, she left again.

I sat there wondering why in the hell she couldn't move back if she wanted to. As soon as she returned again with a mop bucket in one hand and a mop in the other, I asked, "Is it because you don't have enough money or a job?"

"No." She plunged the mop into the bucket, then began from the far end of the small room, mopping with such precision and grace that stupefied me.

"You love sweeping and mopping, don't you?" I asked as I watched her almost dance with the mop.

"I do." She laughed. "I used to love doing housework. I loved to make it fun and exciting." She shrugged her shoulders. "And pleasurable."

I'd never heard of anyone calling housework pleasurable. "Do you mind telling me how you make yourself see chores as pleasurable?"

She stopped mopping and leaned against the handle. "Well, you're chained up, aren't you?"

"I am." I had no idea what she was getting at.

"And if you were let out of those chains after the three days, you would find pleasure in being able to move around, wouldn't you?"

"I suppose I would." I still had no idea what she was driving at.

"So, if you were set free and told to clean the house, then you would find some freedom in being able to move around. And that alone would give you pleasure. Such a simple thing can give one so much pleasure." She closed her eyes, and a smile curved her lips. "And if you had the right kind of man, he would treat you to something nice after a job well done."

"Something nice?" I wasn't following her at all. My father didn't give my mother anything for cleaning the house. He'd never even made a comment about it—he just expected her to do it.

"You know, a trinket of some kind. And that would be followed by a nice long bath together, where he'd wash your body and hair. And then you would do the same for him. You would take care of each other—in all ways."

"A trinket for cleaning a house? I'd rather get a gift because a man loved and respected me, not because I performed some duty well for him." Her idea seemed a little transactional—a little old-fashioned. Not only that, but a bit demeaning as well. I liked the idea of being equals. "And you said something about being chained up and then set free? That sounds pretty bad to me, especially if you're only being let free to clean the house." This was maybe one of the weirdest conversations I'd ever had.

"It's not bad at all." She began mopping again. "When a man really takes care of you, it's the best feeling in the world. You don't have to make any decisions because he makes them for you. And he takes care of everything for you too. There are absolutely no worries."

Except being chained up, apparently.

I had no idea what my aunt was into. But her moving away from her family was finally making sense to me. And the connection between her and the Gentry's was becoming even more worrisome.

Mrs. Gentry was a good woman. If her husband was some sort of abuser, she didn't deserve it.

I thought about seeing her in the wheelchair at Coy's party. I had to wonder if there really was an accident or if her husband had been the one to put her in those leg casts.

Is Mr. Gentry into hurting women for his own pleasure?

Though I was young, I wasn't naïve. I had older brothers, and gossip about people's lives—even the most intimate parts—was rampant in our neighborhood.

I had to find out more. "So, this being chained up, and then set free to do housework and take a bath together...does it also involve something a little more—let's say—taboo?"

"Spanking can come into play if the sub has earned it. Or she might just want it. Subs can find themselves needing discipline for things that happened a long time ago, things that they might've gotten away with."

Drunk Aunt Hilda was much more informative than sober Aunt Hilda. I tried to keep my blush under control. I'd heard my brothers whisper that word before—sub—when Mrs. Richards down the street had been caught having an affair. I needed to hear her admit more, though. "You should tell me all about this stuff. I had no idea this was a thing."

"It's been a thing for years. Centuries even." Her eyes turned glassy as she looked up. "I miss being a sub to my master. I miss it more than I miss anything else."

Holy shit! What has my aunt been into—and with whom?

COY

I sat in my truck, waiting for Paul to show up at the park near his house. Twilight came and went, leaving me in the darkness. But still, I waited, hoping like hell that he'd come through for me.

He may have had trouble getting the address. Or he might've had trouble getting out of the house for some reason. And now that it was dark, he might've been unable to leave the house.

I had no idea what kept him away. But I knew I had to stay right where I had told him I would be, or I might miss my chance to find Lila.

An hour after the sun had set, I saw a shadow moving up the road. I watched as it got closer and closer, seemingly coming towards my truck.

My heart pounded hard in my chest as I started feeling hopeful that I would soon be able to find Lila. Only three days had passed, but to me, they felt like years.

"John?"

Breathing a sigh of relief, I answered, "Yeah, it's me, Paul. Did you get me the address?"

He came up to the side of the truck. "Yeah. My mom keeps everyone's addresses and phone numbers in a book by the phone in the kitchen. It was easy to get the address. I don't want you to pay me anything else since it wasn't hard to get."

I handed him a twenty-dollar bill anyway. "A deal is a deal, Paul." As I gave him the money, he gave me the slip of paper that held my world on it. 'Thanks, man."

He shuffled back and forth a little as if he was nervous. "You promise not to tell that guy she was seeing about this, right?"

"I promise." The way he acted made me a little uneasy. "Did your father tell you something more about her leaving? Is that why you're late? Were you thinking about not giving me the address?"

"Sort of," he confessed. "I heard my mom and dad talking this afternoon. Mom was asking about Lila. She's feeling bad that Lila hadn't come to her to talk to her about her boy problems."

Because she didn't have any.

"Oh, so she didn't say anything to your mom about why she wanted to leave town?" I found that odd. Mostly because after her father had forbidden her to see me, she'd told me that he was an ass. It made no sense that he was the one she had gone to if she needed help getting out of town.

"Not a word. So, Mom's been asking Dad every day if he's heard from Lila. Each day he says that he has and that Lila just wants to be left alone." He shrugged. "Girls, I can't figure them out."

If Lila had truly wanted to get away from me, I knew she would want to talk to her mother about things, not to her father. She definitely wouldn't be calling to give him updates—she would be calling her mother. "So, why hasn't your mother just given Lila a call herself?"

"She has called our Aunt Hilda, who Lila's staying with. Aunt Hilda has told her every time that Lila is resting and she doesn't want to wake her, but that she's doing fine. She even said that Lila's told her that she might want to remain with her and get a job up there in Shreveport."

That does sound a little bit more legit than anything her father has said. "Why do you think she really left, Paul?"

"I overheard my father yelling at her at the beginning of summer.

He told her that she couldn't see this guy named Gentry—that's his last name, I think. And she was mad at our dad for telling her that." He laughed as he shook his head. "But she must've been seeing this guy anyway—even without our father's consent. Dad said that she told him that she couldn't keep seeing that guy because if she did, he was going to be disowned by his family, and he would lose everything. She said that she couldn't be the one responsible for him losing his inheritance, which is tons of money and a huge ranch. I think that's why she left—not because he was a bad guy or anything."

Crap. That makes sense.

But what about the call I heard at home? Could my dad have been telling me the truth? My trust in my family had been shaken the past few months, but maybe I was hearing things that weren't real.

"Do you think she'll stay up there and get a job?" I was on the fence about going to get her now that I heard all this.

With a shrug, he said, "Who knows? I just know that I'm gonna miss her if she stays up there. Anyway, I've gotta go. I'm supposed to be outside feeding the dog. Someone might notice that I haven't come back into the house yet."

"Thanks, Paul."

"Yeah, thanks for the money, John." He ran off into the night, and I had an inkling that I would most probably never see the kid again.

Looking at the address, I continued second-guessing myself, wondering what I should do. Maybe Lila had left because she wanted to. Maybe I should just go ahead and move to Lubbock so that she returns back home. I could write her a letter, telling her that I knew she'd left so I wouldn't lose everything. I could write that I left Carthage and that she could come back home to her family and friends.

It's not like I had anyone except her in the small town anyway. And now that she was gone, there was no reason for me to stay. It wasn't like I would want to hang around my parents since it was because of them and their goddamn lunacy that Lila had left.

With both of our fathers forbidding us to see each other, I could completely understand why Lila had run away from me. She didn't want to leave her life, her family, and her friends behind just to be with me. And she wasn't wrong to want that either.

As I sat there, thinking about all the things she and I had done and said to each other, I began to see a pattern. I'd been blind to the fact that I was a lot more like my father than I had realized.

From the first time I saw Lila, I'd wanted her. I'd gotten her in record time, too. I'd wanted to be with her as much as I possibly could. And I'd gotten that too.

The only thing I hadn't gotten was my father's blessing.

And maybe that was where things turned so dramatic. Maybe that was why we moved so fast with each other. Maybe the fact that our fathers had told us that the other person was off-limits had awoken the inner rebel in both of us.

Almost every moment we'd had was stolen. Every kiss we shared, forbidden. And when we'd made love, we'd broken all the rules.

After meeting that first night at my graduation party, we'd sped through the bases. First kiss was on night number one. Night number two, we rounded second base with extremely heavy petting. Morning number three, we made out in my truck just before the first specks of dawn, landing squarely on third base.

That same night, we slid into home plate when we made love in the back pasture of the ranch under the glow of a full moon and a blanket of stars. That was the first of many times we'd used that pasture and the night to hide us so that we could get as intimate as two people could possibly get.

We'd moved way too fast for a couple of virgins.

Better said, I moved way too fast.

Lila couldn't stop telling me how handsome I was and how she'd never touched muscles as big as mine. She would say how she wasn't anywhere near my league and that this had to be a dream.

I took advantage of her lust for me.

The one thing we knew for sure when we'd made those fast moves was that we weren't supposed to be together in the first place. And that there would be plenty to lose if we were ever discovered. Yet, we did it all anyway. And we continued doing it for another month.

Then I came up with the idea of getting married and moving away. I couldn't recall actually asking her to marry me, though. I did remember saying that I was going to make her my wife. But I never asked her to marry me.

I'm a goddamn fool!

Of course she'd gotten scared and ran away. Of course she felt bad about me being disowned and disinherited. Of course she'd asked to get out of town so that she didn't have to tell me to my face.

The only thing that didn't make sense was that she'd asked her father for help.

But at that point, I'd already manipulated her—even though I hadn't meant to—into having sex for the first time with a guy she'd only known for three days. And I continued rushing her when we got our marriage license and told her we'd get married in three days.

By that time, she was probably desperate enough to get away from me that she'd ask just about anyone for help. I was Mr. Three Days, after all. *Stupid! Stupid! Stupid!*

When you really love someone, you don't hurry things along. At least, I guessed that's what you didn't do. I'd never been in love, so I had no idea how things were supposed to go. Maybe she had realized that.

Normal couples dated for a while, several months even before they moved on to having a sexual relationship. And then they dated —sometimes even for years—before the man asked his girl to marry him.

Not me, though. I went right for it. Sex—boom! Marriage— boom, boom!

I am such a moron.

Now I wished that I did have a party full of guys my age to hang out with and drown my sorrows. I needed some good male advice about women and the timeframe that went along with a good relationship.

But I hadn't even tried to get to know any of the guys at my party. Instead, I had focused all my attention on Lila. Like a freaking predator.

Lila was right to run off.

Her father had said that she didn't want to be the reason I lost everything. But that might've been the nicest way she knew how to say that she didn't want to see me anymore.

I knew that if she'd come to me and told me what she'd apparently told her father, I would've said that I didn't care if I lost everything. All that mattered was that I still had her.

After one month, I had the nerve to say something that fucking stupid.

Yet, even as I told myself how stupid that sounded, I couldn't help but feeling the same. I was only heartbroken that Lila didn't seem to feel that way as well. But if she had gone to so much trouble to ensure that I didn't throw away my future for us, then she must still care about me. Even if only a little bit.

Of course she did, she was that kind of girl. The kind who cared about everyone.

And she still deserved the world—even if she didn't want it with me. She deserved to live at home, close to her friends and family. And she needed to know that I would leave her alone to live her life.

I owe her that much.

Reaching into the backseat, I grabbed my book bag. I'd write her a letter and get to the post office so it could go out first thing in the morning.

I wanted her to know that I would leave so that she could come back home and that I was as sorry as a person could be for what I'd done to her. And I wouldn't use the word love, not even once.

My hand shook as I held the pen at the top of the page, not knowing what the hell to say first.

Tossing the things into the passenger seat, I shouted, "Fuck it! I'll tell her in person."

LILA

My eyes flew open as I heard a familiar sound outside.

Coy's truck?

I had no idea how long I'd been sleeping or what time it was. It was dark in the room, which meant that it was still dark outside. The engine shut off, and then I heard a soft knock at the door.

Hilda had continued drinking wine, even after our long talk. I assumed she was passed out and couldn't hear the knocking on her front door. "Hilda," I shouted. "You have company."

More soft knocking came, but there were no other sounds. The knocking grew louder and more insistent. Then I heard Coy's voice. "Hilda, I know Lila is in there. Let me in. I just want to talk to her!"

Something crashed, and then I heard Hilda stumbling around. "No, no, no. This can't be happening."

"Coy!" I shouted.

Hilda was there in an instant, shoving a sock into my mouth, then wrapping a cord around my wrists to make sure that I couldn't get the sock out of my mouth. "Be quiet, or I'll shoot your little boyfriend."

I went still right away, not wanting anything bad to happen to Coy. He'd said that he knew I was in the house. I knew he wouldn't leave without seeing me for himself. I became very patient as I waited for things to play out.

The pounding never stopped. It seemed Coy wasn't about to give up. "Come on, Hilda. You've got to let me inside. I *have* to see her. I'll leave as soon as I tell her what I came here to say. I swear."

She looked at me with wide eyes. "You'd better be quiet."

I nodded and watched as she closed the door. I heard a sound as she slid something in front of it. She must've been making it look as if the door didn't exist.

Coy had to be smarter than Hilda if he was going to find me. But I knew he was smart. He could do it; I believed in him. So I stayed quiet. In my mind, though, I shouted to him that I was there.

The wooden floor creaked under Hilda's feet as she went from her bedroom to the front door. But I heard the sound of her cocking a shotgun, and my heart stopped. "You need to leave," she shouted. "I've got a shotgun—it's cocked and loaded. Unless you're bulletproof, I suggest you get back into your car and drive back to where you've come from."

"I can't go back until I've told her a couple things. Please, Hilda, let me in so I can set things straight with her. I'm begging you."

"I can't let you in," she told him.

"I won't tell a soul that you did it. And I'll give you any amount of money you want if you just let me in."

She was quiet for a long time. From the part of the house and the things in it that I could see, everything seemed to have been there for a very long time. The curtains, the blankets, and the sheets in the room I was in were so old that they were nearly see-through. It was obvious that she didn't have a lot of money.

I began moving my arms back and forth, trying to loosen up the cord she'd wrapped around my wrists. If I could get the damn sock out of my mouth, I could scream to alert Coy of my presence. And if he couldn't get inside to see me, he would call the cops.

Coy, please get help if you can't get inside this house!

"I can't do that. You need to leave." I could tell by the creaking floorboards that she'd slowly began moving closer to the door. If she got close enough, she could shoot him right through the door.

My heart sped up as panic spread through me like wildfire. Coy

133

hadn't ever had to deal with something like this. I had no idea how much he even knew about guns and wooden doors and how easily the bullets could penetrate them. He might not even realize how vulnerable he was, standing on the other side, unaware of everything.

Aunt Hilda had not tied my feet. So I got out of the bed and kicked over the nightstand, making an enormous sound that brought Hilda running back to me.

A scraping sound told me she was moving whatever she'd put in front of the door, then it flew open, and she slapped me so hard that I stumbled back onto the bed.

Moving like lightning, she yanked the cord off the back of the little television and jumped onto the bed to sit on my legs. Holding them as still as she could as I kicked for all I was worth, she lashed the cord around my ankles, securely tying them up.

I'd never seen anything like it. And then I realized that I had. She'd used the same technique a cowboy used when he was tying up a calf's legs after roping it.

Hilda had some impressive skills, much to my dismay. I looked at her with wide eyes. Eyes that begged her to stop this insanity and to let Coy inside so that he could help me.

But she wouldn't look into my eyes as she left me again, closing the door and pushing something in front of it once more. She had no idea how much Coy and I loved each other—that was her biggest mistake.

Coy would never leave this place without seeing me. I knew that for a fact. Hilda would've been better off answering the door and telling him that I wasn't there. But she'd chosen the wrong approach.

He knew I was there without a doubt now. Hilda's mistakes were paying off for me—big time. Coy knew I was inside this house. She'd made sure of that.

"What's going on in there?" Coy shouted. "You sound as if you're running all over the place. You don't need to be afraid. I'm not about to hurt you or anyone."

Hilda's voice sounded far away now; she must've been right at

134

the front door. "*She's* running, Coy. She's trying to hide from you. She's afraid of you."

"Don't say that," he pleaded. "I'm sorry for what I've put her through. I want to apologize to her. I didn't realize I was rushing her —I didn't know that she might've felt I was manipulating her. It must be in my goddamn DNA. I don't know. But I have to apologize to her for scaring her—for making her feel that she had to run away."

I had no idea what he was talking about. *We* had gone that fast —not just him. I was part of everything we had done. I had wanted everything as much as him.

Why does he think he's manipulated me?

"She can hear you, so you have apologized. But she doesn't want to see you. I'm sorry. I'm her aunt. I have to do as she wishes," Hilda said. "And she doesn't want to see you, Coy. She's afraid of you."

My entire body froze with her lies. I wasn't afraid of Coy. I had never been afraid of him. I had no idea why he would think that, but he was wrong.

I loved Coy more than I'd loved anyone in my entire life. I was ready to leave my hometown for him. I was ready to leave my family for him. And I was ready to walk away from my friends for him too.

He can't believe her lies!

"I understand," came his weak response. He sounded as if he'd been stabbed directly in the heart.

And I felt the same way. *Please, God, don't let him leave me here.*

"Now go away, and don't come back," Hilda said.

"Hilda?" he asked with a voice full of tears.

"What?"

"Please let me in. I won't do anything to her or you. I've never been violent in my life, not even for one day. I'll give you every cent I have just to be able to see her."

With my eyes closed, I kept praying that my aunt would let Coy in. If he just got inside, then he would find me. I knew he would.

"If I let you in, you will have to understand that I can't let her go with you."

"Yeah, I know," he said.

"Okay. Give me a moment to get her ready. And be prepared to find her in a state that won't allow you to take her away. Okay?"

"Okay."

I couldn't believe it. She was going to let him in.

But she didn't come to set me free. She didn't move the barricade from in front of the door. She didn't do anything for such a long time that I wasn't even sure whether she was still awake.

Finally, Coy got impatient. "Hilda, what's going on in there?"

She walked in place, making it sound as if she was walking to the door from somewhere else. "Okay. I've got her ready. You do have money for me, right?"

"Yes, I have it in my hand. I'll give it to you as soon as you open the door."

"I have the shotgun. I'll use it on you if I have to."

"Yes, I know you will," he said with reverence.

I heard the locks clicking open as Hilda began unlocking the door. The squeak of the rusted hinges followed, and I couldn't believe that Coy was finally here to save me.

"You look look just like him," I heard her gasp. "Your father. Except for those eyes of yours."

"Apparently, I'm more like him than I knew. That's why I have to see Lila. I have to apologize for what I've done."

"You hurt her, didn't you?" she asked.

"I didn't mean to. But I must've hurt her for making her run away from everything—from me, her home, her town, her family and friends. I just want her to know that I'll accept the fact that she no longer wants to be with me, and then I'll leave Carthage so that she can get back to her life."

"That's incredibly sweet of you," Hilda said.

I started yelling behind my gag. I wanted to know why he thought all these things when none of them were true—but I knew he couldn't hear me.

"Who told you that she was here?" she asked.

"I'm not telling anyone that information. It doesn't matter anyway. I'm not going to try to change her mind. I just want to let her know that I'm incredibly sorry for what I've done."

"Don't be disturbed by what you see when I take you to her. I did this for her own good. And yours as well."

The sound of something being slid away from the door made my heart skip a beat. And then the door opened, and the light over the bed was turned on, nearly blinding me.

Coy gasped, and I blinked until I could see him. He had his hand over his mouth as he looked at me. I saw my aunt standing behind him with the gun aimed at his head.

With a sudden movement, he ducked and turned around fast, taking the shotgun away from her. She stumbled backward, as he'd slightly pushed her to get the gun. "No!"

Coy pointed the gun at her. "Unchain her right now, or I *will* kill you."

COY

I could not believe what I was seeing. Lila, with a chain around her body, hands and feet bound, and something shoved into her mouth. My stomach turned on itself as bile rushed up my throat.

How could she do this to her own flesh and blood?

Moving like the wind, I bent and bobbed as I turned to face Hilda, shoving her back. At the same time, I grabbed the barrel of the shotgun, jerking it out of her hands.

Cowering in front of me, she held up her hands. I wanted to shoot her for what she'd done to the woman I loved. But murder—even if justified—would put me in jail.

I have to stay free for Lila.

"Unchain her right now," I said sternly, "or I will *kill* you."

"Don't shoot me. I'll set her free. Just don't shoot me." Hilda moved like a serpent to get to the other side of the room. "The key to the padlock is in this drawer." She looked at me with worried eyes. "I've got to open it to get it out."

Lila's eyes stayed on me as I nodded. "If you pull anything other than the key out of there, I'm going to squeeze the trigger."

"Got it." She slowly opened the door, then pulled out the key.

Red filled my vision. I'd never been so angry in my entire life. The things this woman had done to Lila were horrifying. Lila had been gone three nights. I couldn't believe Lila had had to endure this torture for that long.

I wasn't about to let Hilda get a hold of anything sharp—and it would take something sharp to cut the electric cords that tied Lila's hands and feet. Glancing around the room, I saw a large pair of scissors on the floor in a corner.

After Hilda had unlocked the padlock that to the chain around Lila's waist, I said, "Put that chain around your waist now and use that padlock to close it. Then toss the key over here, to my feet."

Nodding, she did exactly as I'd said. Only then did I put the gun down near the door, out of Hilda's reach. I quickly moved to get the scissors, but before doing anything else, I took the thing out of Lila's mouth. "Coy, I'm so glad to see you!"

"I'm getting you out of here." I cut the cord binding her feet first. I looked at Hilda, who stood by the bed with her head hanging low— I needed to let her know that I wasn't going to let her get away with this. "I want you to tell me who asked you to do this to her."

"No one asked me to do this," Hilda lied.

"I know that's a lie!" My hand shook as I pointed the scissors at her. "Lila's father brought her to you. I already know that much. Now, tell me who orchestrated this entire thing. And tell me who told you to chain her up."

Hilda still wouldn't lift her head up to look at me. "Her father brought her to me. I was to chain her up only for one night. After that, I was supposed to let her out of the chains. But not until after I had talked some sense into her about staying away from you. I hadn't gotten that far yet. That's why she was still bound when you showed up."

"Tell me what role my father played in all of this." I was going to get to the bottom of this and make all of them pay dearly for what they'd done to Lila.

She finally lifted her head to look into my eyes. "Your father?"

I snipped the cord between Lila's wrists, setting her free. She immediately jumped into my arms and hugged me like she'd never let me go. "Coy! Thank God for you! I love you so much!"

"I love you too, baby." I used the blanket underneath her to cover her up as the rags she was wearing were barely covering her body. Turning my attention to Hilda, I said, "Yes, my father. Tell me how he was involved in all of this."

"I haven't spoken to your father since our high school days. This was all done by Lila's father. He wanted her to stay away from you. He'd forbidden her from seeing you, but she continued doing it anyway. So, he brought her to me. He wanted me to help make her accept the facts. Gentry men and Stevens women don't get to be together."

"Well, they do now." I didn't believe her for one second that she hadn't spoken to my father in years—I knew she was the person he'd spoken to on the phone. But my main concern was getting Lila the hell out of there. "I'm not sure what Lila and I are going to do about you and her father. She and I will make that decision together. You will never know whether the law is coming for you. Let that uneasiness rest solidly on your shoulders, Hilda Stevens. Kidnapping, false imprisonment, and torture can get you life in prison. Think long and hard about that."

I picked up the key to the padlock. Looking around, I wanted to be sure to place it somewhere she could get to and set herself free. But I wanted her to have to work for it.

There wasn't much in the room. But there was a dresser. I walked over to it, then lifted it up to examine how heavy it was. And it was very heavy. So, I leaned over and pushed the key underneath to make it extremely hard for her to reach.

"There you go. I've given you more than you ever gave Lila. And let me leave you with this. I hope you, and all who worked with you to do this to the woman I love, rot in hell for eternity. And may your life on Earth until your death be full of sorrow and hopelessness, because I am sure that's what Lila has been feeling since you people ripped her away from me."

A soft hand took mine, and I turned to find Lila shaking her head. "No, don't wish bad things on anyone. I'm okay, and you're okay, and that's what really matters."

She'd been the one who had gotten hurt, and yet here she was, telling me to leave the people who'd hurt her alone. "You're an angel. Do you know that?"

"Come on, babe. Let's just get out of here. I'm more than ready to move past this." She held my hand tightly, pulling me away to leave with her.

As we walked to the front door, I saw the cash I'd given Hilda lying on the coffee table. "I'm not about to let her keep this. Do you have anything else here that we need to get?" I picked up the several hundred dollars and put it into my pocket.

"No," she said as she pulled me to leave. "They took me out of my bed, tied me up, gagged me, and put a bag over my head before tossing me into the trunk of the car. I came with nothing more than the nightgown I'd had on."

I could not believe her own father had done that to her. There was absolutely nothing I could say to make things any better. But I would try to make her life happy until the day she died—if she'd allow me.

At one in the morning, Lila and I drove away from her aunt's house, heading toward Interstate 20. That would take us all the way to Dallas. I didn't want to take her anywhere near Carthage. Not yet.

"What were you talking about back there when you said that you'd manipulated me, Coy?" She pulled the ratty blanket around her shoulders a bit tighter, her eyes locked on mine.

"Well, I thought that you'd left town to get away from me. So, I thought about why you would've done that."

"Yeah, but I didn't leave you."

"I know that now."

"So why do you think you manipulated me?"

"I think that I pushed you without meaning to. I think I moved too fast. What do you think about the pace we've been moving at?"

She looked away from me, staring out the window as she fell quiet, presumably thinking about what I'd asked. When she looked back at me, she had a twinkle in her eyes. "Coy, I love you. I don't have a single regret about anything we've done in the short amount of time we've been together. We have moved fast, but we've continued moving forward with our relationship this whole time. I'm happy about us and our plans for the future. But if you're having doubts and want to wait, I'll understand."

"You don't want to wait to get married?" I thought I should rephrase that. "Wait a minute. I never asked you if you wanted to marry me in the first place. I just sort of told you that I wanted to marry you, didn't I? So, Lila, do you want to marry me?"

"I do." She smiled. "Do you want to marry me?"

"I do." I reached over and took her hand in mine, pulling her across the seat to sit right next to me. "How come you're sitting way over there when you can snuggle up against me?"

"I don't smell that good right now." She laughed as I tugged her. "Really, Coy. I stink. I haven't had a shower in three days."

Like I cared. "Get over here, girl." I pulled her to me, then draped my arm around her. "I don't care what you smell like. I just want to be able to hold you." It felt good to have her beside me again. "I'm gonna get us a hotel room in Dallas. After a shower and nap, we'll get up and go find a judge or Justice of the Peace to marry us. I brought our marriage license."

She sighed, and it sounded sad. "Coy, I'll need my driver's license to get married."

"You gave me your wallet. Don't you remember doing that?"

Perking up right away, she nodded. "Oh, yeah! This is great. We've got everything we need then."

"Are you sure that you're alright with making such a huge decision right now?" She'd been through hell. "I don't want you to look back on this and have regrets."

"Coy, the truth is that I'll feel much safer with you as my husband." She placed her hand on my thigh, moving it back and forth. "With all that's happened to me, I feel as if I don't have a family anymore. You and I can be a family. We can make our own family."

"You want to start a family too?" I hadn't even thought about kids.

"If you do." She smiled coyly. "Why not start having kids right away? We've done everything else quickly. Why not get our family going too?"

"I don't know. I've got four years of college to get through. Plus, I'm pretty sure that I'll have to work for at least a little while. Dad will surely cut me off once I tell him that you and I are married. We should hold off trying to start our family until we know what our future holds."

"You're right. I guess we can take at least that one thing slow. Kids will come. I know that. But for now, I will be completely satisfied with being your wife."

I kissed her on the cheek. "I'm going to be more than satisfied by being your husband, Lila soon-to-be-Gentry."

"Wow," she whispered. "Lila Gentry. I bet your family never thought that a Gentry would marry a girl from the wrong side of town. Not even in a million years."

"We're gonna make some big changes in that little town we were born in. Just wait and see, Lila Gentry."

I meant that, too. Once I took over the ranch, things would be so different. And the Gentry name would be something my kids could be proud of—without their pride poisoning them into thinking that they were better than everyone else.

LILA

The next day, I sat in the truck next to my husband, wearing the white cotton dress he'd bought me. He wore a dark blue button-down shirt with black jeans and looked every bit as handsome as he had in the dream I'd had about marrying him.

With my left hand in his right one, I kept looking at the gold band he'd put on my finger only a few hours earlier. "I still can't believe we're married. This feels like a dream."

"It's not a dream. It's one hundred percent real." He pulled my hand up and kissed the ring. "You *are* my wife."

I laughed as that sounded crazy good to hear. "And you *are* my husband."

"I am that." He was driving out to the ranch to tell his family about our marriage. His plan was to tell them what had happened to me, hoping the insanity of my ordeal would help them change their minds about us.

It had never been my intention to get in the way of Coy and his inheritance or between him and his family. But he assured me that I wasn't in the way of anything. He said that if anyone was in the way of his happiness, it was his family, not me.

So, I sat there next to him with butterflies swarming inside my stomach. "I wonder if they'll accept us."

"You know, I'm still not sure about trusting my family just yet. I'm sure I heard my father talking to Hilda on the phone."

"We can't worry about that." I didn't want him to be angry at anyone over what had happened to me.

"Lila, I have to worry about that. If my family acts as if they accept this, then it might be a ploy to make us feel comfortable so you can be kidnapped again. And this time, they might take you even further away and make it harder—or even impossible—for me to find you."

"And you would call the police if that happened." I didn't think anyone would try to do such a thing to me again. They'd tried their best to stop us from being together, but now that we were married, nothing could separate us.

"I've just got this uneasy feeling. So, here's what we're going to do. We're going to tell my family about the marriage, and then we're going to tell them that we're moving right away to the house in Lubbock. I don't want us to spend even one night at the ranch."

"So, the plan is to let them know what we've done. Then, you'll get some of your things and pack them in the truck. After we'll go to my house where we'll tell my family, and I'll grab as many of my things as I can, and we'll be on our way to Lubbock?" It sounded like a lot of work and a lot of traveling. But how could I argue when he might be right not to trust any of them?

When we pulled into Carthage, he headed to the used car lot. "We'll pick up the car I bought for you before we do anything else. You can follow me out to the ranch. We'll leave the car at the gate just in case my father pulls some really shitty stuff with me."

"Like what?" I didn't know his father or what he was capable of. After talking to my aunt, I did have some vague ideas that he was into some rough stuff. But they were only ideas, not facts, so I kept them to myself.

"Hell, I don't know, Lila. I just don't want to risk losing everything we have. So we'll move everything that we have in the truck to the trunk of the car. And I mean everything. I'll even empty my pockets before we go and talk to them. I don't trust anyone but you at the moment."

"I hate things are this way." This was no way to start our lives together. I had to leave some hope in my heart that our families would see that we can't be stopped. There would be no reason to keep trying to keep us apart when we'd already gotten married.

After getting to the car, I got to work filling the trunk with Coy's bags, and then he took out his wallet and placed it there too. "That's it. That's everything we have, Lila. If everything goes to shit, we've got four-thousand dollars to our name."

I pointed out that we had more than that. "We've got the keys to the house in Lubbock as well, Coy. We will have a roof over our heads once we get there. And we'll also be stopping by my house to pick up some things." Suddenly, I realized that I didn't know much about the house in Lubbock. "Is the house furnished? Are there pots and pans, dishes, curtains, a television? You know, the stuff people use every day?"

"It's completely furnished with everything we'll need. All we really need to pack are our clothes and anything else that's personal. Everything else is there, waiting for us. There's even a washer and dryer from what my father told me."

"Cool." At least we would have the basics—that is, if Coy's father did take everything else away from him.

After closing the trunk, Coy and I stood there, looking at each other with rather grim expressions. He took me into his arms, holding me as he kissed the top of my head. "Change of plans. Let's go get your things before we go out to the ranch."

"Are you sure?" I had no idea how things would go with my family.

"Yeah. Leave the car here, and let's go in my truck. We'll come back and put your things in the car, and then we'll head out to my place."

Although I felt uneasy, I got into the truck with him, and we went to my house. The car was gone, and that gave me some relief. "Looks like Dad might not be here. Come on, let's hurry." I'd packed most of my things in several bags in the closet before I'd gone to bed the night they took me away. It wouldn't take long for me to grab my things. Plus, I didn't have much in the first place.

Mom sat at the table as we walked through the door. Her eyes moved to Coy. "Hello." Then, she looked at me. "Lila! You're back home! I missed you so much." She got up, and I ran to hug her.

"Momma! It's so good to see you." I didn't want to let her go, but I knew we had to hurry before my father and brothers returned home.

Paul and Roman came running into the kitchen. "Lila!"

I let my mother go so that I could hug them both. "Boys!"

When I let them go, I saw Paul looking at Coy as he asked, "John? What's going on?"

"My name isn't John. I'm sorry that I lied to you, Paul. I'm Coy Gentry."

My mother sucked in her breath. "No!"

"Momma, it's okay. Coy rescued me. Dad took me to Aunt Hilda's."

"Yes, I know." She looked at me, confused. "But he did it because you asked him to. I called your aunt each day you were gone, and she told me that you were resting." My mother sat down hard in the chair. "What's going on?"

"Mom, I don't have much time. We need to leave before Dad and the boys get back. We don't want to make a scene, and I'm sure they'll cause one." I held out my hand to show her my ring. "Momma, we're married. I'm Lila Gentry now." I looked at my younger brothers. "Boys, can you grab the bags I have in the bottom of my closet and take them out to the truck? Coy and I are moving to Lubbock. He's got a house there. Once things settle down, I'll call you."

My brothers took off to get my things, and I followed to make sure we got everything. Coy came too, his hand in mine. "This is uncomfortable."

"Yeah, I know." I'd never felt so uncomfortable in my own home. But then again, I'd never been kidnapped by my own father either. "Let's get the hell out of here." I picked up the small suitcase with my makeup and hair products, then followed my brothers out to the truck.

"Don't wait too long to call us, Lila," Paul said. "I love you, sis."

"I love you both too. Be good for Momma." I felt a knot form in my throat and tried not to cry.

Getting into the truck, I gulped hard and grabbed my husband's hand as we left my family behind me. I felt as if it would be the last time I would be seeing them.

We drove in silence towards the car. Then, I got out of the truck and into it, following Coy to the ranch. Parking the car outside the entrance of the ranch, Coy and I began moving the things I'd gotten from my house into the car. The trunk and the backseat were now full of our things.

"There's not much room left," I said as I looked at everything.

"I don't have much left at home. I've already packed most of my things. What's left can fit in my truck. Dad gave me the truck for graduation. I don't really think he'll try to take it away from me. I mean, he might cut off my bank account for a while, but I don't expect him to do much more than that."

"But you never know," I said. "My father and aunt went to insane lengths to try and stop us from being together. And I'm still pretty sure your father was involved in some way or another. We have no idea what he'll do next."

Nodding, a frown formed on Coy's face as he took my hand and led me to his truck. "Let's go see what kind of welcome we receive from my family, shall we?"

Biting my lip the whole way up the long, winding driveway, I felt like I might throw up. And as we parked the truck outside the side entrance, I felt like I might even pass out.

I clung to Coy as I walked beside him. "Coy, I'm so afraid."

"Don't be. We have each other, and that's all we will ever need. Everything else is just icing on the cake, baby."

Smiling, I didn't know how he was always able to make me feel better, but he had. "You're right."

We hadn't gotten to the door yet when his father stepped out. "What in the hell do you think you're doing, Coy Gentry?"

"I have something to tell you, Dad." Coy didn't bat an eye as he stood tall and faced his father. "Lila and I are married now. There's nothing anyone can do about it. And you should know that her own father kidnapped her, and she was chained up at her Aunt Hilda's house in Shreveport. For three days, this young woman was held captive by her own family. And I am here to ask you if you had anything to do with that."

I wasn't even aware that he was going to ask his father that. I'd thought we were going to give them the news of our marriage and see how they took it.

The sound of his mother's voice came from behind Coy's father, "He most certainly did not have anything to do with that, Coy. How dare you accuse your father of anything so heinous!"

Coy's eyes narrowed as he looked at his father. "I expect you to accept this marriage and to accept Lila as my wife and as part of this family. It will be our children who inherit this ranch someday."

"You think that you can shove this down my throat?" he asked with a grin. "You think that you can have what's mine to give?"

"I would like your blessing on my marriage," Coy said.

"No. You can't have that." Coy's father took a deep breath, his chest rising and falling, before he said, "You have a choice to make, son. You can get the marriage annulled and remain an eligible heir to Whisper Ranch. Or you can stay married and become a penniless son-of-a-bitch."

"Collin!" Mrs. Gentry gasped. "Don't do this."

"I won't have him doing this to our good name, Fiona. This is the way it has to be."

"Coy, please agree to the annulment. Don't give up everything for a girl you barely know," his mother begged.

I'd never seen the sheer determination that took over Coy's expression. "How long do you think you can go without seeing me?"

"Forever," his father said with no hesitation at all. "I will never be bullied by anyone. You will do as I say, or you can go to hell for all I care. So, is it an annulment?"

"I'm never leaving my wife. I love her, and I will never stop loving her. If you can't accept that, then you can go to hell." Coy's hand gripped mine so tightly that it hurt.

"Give me the keys to your truck," his father said. "You can leave this ranch with the clothes on your back, but nothing more than that. I'll have the bank account closed in minutes, and you can kiss the house in Lubbock goodbye as well as your college education. I won't be paying for any of it. I can sell that house back to the realtor in a matter of minutes."

Coy let go of my hand and walked toward his father. "Mom, can you get me a pen and some paper before I leave this Godforsaken place forever?"

"Coy, please listen to reason," she begged.

"Please, just do as I asked, Mom."

I had no idea what he was about to do as I stood there and waited, chewing my fingernails. Staring at the ground, I'd never been so nervous in my life.

Coy was giving up everything for me. He'd have nothing if we remained married. I wasn't sure I could take that kind of pressure.

When I looked back up, I saw Coy with the pen and paper. He placed the paper against the house's wall and then scribbled something on it. "Lila, can you come here please?"

I walked on shaky legs to his side, and then I saw what he'd written on the paper. He was giving up everything. He'd written that he and I never want anything from his family. The note stated it all in plain words. He signed it and then handed me the pen to do the same. Which I did.

I handed him the pen and stepped back. "Are you sure about this?"

"I've never been so sure of anything in my life." He put the paper on the step and then placed the pen on top of it. "There you go. You've successfully lost your son. Congratulations to you both."

Coy draped his arm around my shoulders as we walked away from his family, his inheritance, his ranch, and his life as he'd known it.

Kissing the side of my head as we walked down the long driveway, he said with such sincerity that it made me cry, "I've never felt freer. Thank you for giving me this, baby. Thank you for loving me and marrying me. It won't be the life I had hoped it would be, but it will be full of love and devotion."

And he was right. We'd found our happily ever after.

And I wouldn't have changed a single thing.

EPILOGUE

COLLIN

October 1990 – Carthage, Texas – Whisper Ranch

Things were never the same after Coy left us. Fiona never laughed again after that awful day. I never saw another smile curve her lips, which had become thin from the perpetual firm line she kept them in.

She never blamed me for his leaving. She never blamed me for anything. Maybe that's because she rarely spoke more than a word or two at a time since he'd left.

Even though her legs and back had healed, Fiona never moved out of the bedroom on the ground floor. And I never entered that room.

The maid had found her that morning. Lying in bed, hands clasped over her heart, Fiona wasn't breathing. The maid shouted for me to come, and I hurried to the bedroom.

My wife didn't move when I called out her name; her eyes remained shut. When I touched her cheek, I found it cold. "Call for help."

Plenty of help came. Only no one can bring the dead back to life. The coroner said that he would have to do an autopsy to confirm the cause of death, but he was fairly certain that her heart had given out. And I agreed with him.

Fiona's heart had shattered into a billion pieces the day we lost our only child. It was a miracle that she lasted the two years that she had.

My father died three days after Fiona's passing. And while we were burying him, my mother suffered a fatal stroke at the graveside service.

I found myself utterly alone for the first time in my life. And for a short time, I walked the halls of the ranch house in a numb state, waiting for death to come and find me.

My loneliness grew and grew until I realized that there was someone to blame for all that I'd lost. So, I sent for her. I had her brought to the ranch where I'd built a room just for her.

I hadn't laid eyes on her in many years. And the first time I saw her again, she kneeled in the room I'd made for her in my home. Her head tucked into her chest, dark eyes on the floor in front of her. "You failed at the one task I gave you, slave."

"And for that I am truly sorry, Master."

"You certainly will be." I picked up the black whip I'd brought in from the horse barn. "I've lost everyone because of you."

"I am truly sorry, Master," her words came out strong. But by the time I would be finished finished with her, she would barely be able to muster a whisper.

"My heart wasn't enough for you, was it?" I pulled back my arm, letting the whip's end dangle behind me. "You had to make sure I lost more than that. So you let my son take the girl. You let him ruin his life and mine."

Crack!

With the one lash, I'd split the naked caramel-colored back down the middle. "One."

The blood that peppered the thin line made me think about death. "My wife is gone because her heart could no longer take living without her son in her life." I pulled the whip back to ready myself to give her another lash. "For some reason, my father died, and then my mother died too. Within a week, I went from being a part of a family to being alone."

I let the whip fly and added another red stripe to her back. "Two."

"Now that I am all alone, you will serve to fill my time. I will use you any way I want. And I will punish you without mercy for what you've done to me." I gave her another red stripe on her bare back.

"Three." She sniffled as the blood ran down her back, pooling on the floor underneath her.

She'd had enough. But her pain—like mine—wouldn't end until we met our ends.

The pain began with us, and it would end with us. Only with my passing would Whisper Ranch become what it was meant to become.

Although my son would never see the ranch again, the heirs he gave me would someday call the place their own. They alone would fulfill the legacy their father had turned away from. They alone would have the opportunity to turn the ranch into something neither my father nor I ever could.

The future rests in the hands of those who have not yet been born. May God help them avoid the curse of being a man who carries the last name Gentry.

LILA

Present Day - Dallas, Texas

"I'm glad you saw my post on Facebook, Robert. It's been forever since I've been able to speak to you." I'd only recently gotten on social media to reconnect with family members I'd left behind in Carthage.

After leaving, Coy and I had made our way to Dallas, and that's where me made our home. We'd had three sons in that little house. But they'd left their father and me after Collin Gentry died. They had inherited Whisper Ranch and everything that went with it.

"Lila, it's so good to hear your voice. I can't recall the last time we spoke," my cousin said. "As soon as I read your post, talking about how your sons inherited their grandfather's ranch in Carthage and came into billions, I thought about my five nephews who lost their parents when they were kids."

"I heard about your brother and sister-in-law, Robert. Dying in a house fire is a tragic way to go. I can't imagine how those boys dealt with all that loss." My heart hurt for those kids, who had grown into men since losing their parents.

"Despite their bad luck, the boys have grown into good men. They all work hard, too. And they're as smart as can be. When I saw that your sons want to invest some of the money they've inherited to help their relatives make something out of themselves, I knew my nephews would be grateful for their help."

"What are they doing for work now?" I hoped things would work out for all of them.

"They're all in the hospitality industry, and one of them is a chef. They've talked about opening their own hotel or resort or something. But they don't have the credit to get the loans they would need to get things rolling. Maybe you could set up a meeting between them and your sons."

"I tell you what, why don't you talk to your nephews to find out if they have any worthwhile ideas, and then I'll relay that information to my sons?" I knew there would be many long-lost relatives who would want money from my boys. I was ready to weed out the good from the bad.

"Sure, I'll get back to you soon, Lila. And it was great hearing from you—even if you're not in love with the boys' ideas."

"I'm glad to hear you say that. I'd love it if we could all be close again. Now that my father has passed away, I finally feel like I can be around my family again. I look forward to hearing from you, Robert. God bless."

Coy came up behind me, wrapping his strong arms around me and kissing my cheek. "Sounds like you're already getting some nibbles. I'm glad our sons will start meeting some of their family members. And I'm happy they're going to help some of them get started with their own businesses. We raised great kids—even if we didn't have lots of money."

"The Nash brothers from Houston might be the first ones our sons help out." Turning in his arms, I wrapped my hands around him, then kissed him softly. "I'm proud of us, Coy. Damn proud."

***The End of the Beginning* –**

2. MAKE HER MINE

Billionaire Boss Romance
(Irresistible Brothers Book One)

BLURB

Telling my boss my BIGGEST secret was just one of many mistakes...
> **#1 I revealed that I was still a...you know what.**
> **#2 I also confessed I'd never experience the big O.**
> **#3 I don't even have to spell it out do I?**

Look, I NEVER expected him to make it his mission to help a girl out,
> But I can't say I haven't fantasized about it.
> Even when I want to slap his arrogant face,
> I wouldn't mind tearing his suit off in the process.

As much as I want to let him take me in every way imaginable,
> My mission to find the big O,
> Quickly turns into Oh shit!

Falling for him wasn't part of the plan...or the agreement.
> **Will I always just be another conquest for my billionaire boss?**
> **Or can I fall out of his bed and into his heart?**

TYRELL

Carthage, Texas – Panola County
January 1st

The limousine moved slowly, almost stoically, through the newly fallen snow that covered the road. My younger brothers and I were on our way to a new life. A life we'd never even imagined.

On Christmas day I got a phone call from an Allen Samuels, an attorney in Carthage. My family came from Carthage—that much I knew. What I didn't know were the reasons we'd never met our grandparents.

Later that day, Mr. Samuels sat in front of us in the limo looking through a folder he'd brought with him when he picked us up at the airport. A private plane had brought us to Carthage from Dallas. Being that Dallas wasn't that far from Carthage, we all wondered why the extravagant lift was necessary.

"The whole of the estate that includes Whisper Ranch, a thirty-thousand square-foot mansion, and all the vehicles, including the Cessna Citation II you came in on, belongs to you three gentlemen now." The attorney looked over his shoulder, then tapped on the dark glass that separated us from the driver. The window rolled down with a quiet swish. "Davenport, we need to make a stop at Mr. Gentry's bank, please."

"Sure thing, sir." The driver rolled the window back up, giving us privacy once more.

Mr. Samuels looked at me, probably because I was the oldest. "Tyrell, what have you been told about your paternal grandparents?"

"Not much." That was no lie. My parents rarely spoke about either set of their parents. "My mother's famous quote was that if one couldn't say anything nice about a person, they shouldn't say anything at all. We'd assumed our grandparents weren't very good people."

Jasper took over, "Yeah, we stopped questioning Mom and Dad when we were very young. Just asking them who our grandparents were put them in a foul mood."

"I see." He looked out the window as we pulled into the parking lot of the Bank of Carthage. "Here we are. You will become the Ranch's accountholders. We can transfer the remainder of your grandfather's funds into accounts each of you will open here." His eyes scanned us all. "If that's okay with you. Certainly, you can open accounts elsewhere if you'd like to. Your grandparents used this bank exclusively for years. I can assure you that the president appreciates Whisper Ranch's business and does everything to keep their customers happy."

Looking at my brothers who flanked me on either side of me, I shrugged. "This bank seems as good as any. What do you guys think?"

Cash, the youngest at twenty-two, ran his hand through his thick, dark hair that hung to his shoulders in waves. "Sounds fine to me. It'll be my first bank account anyway."

Jasper, only a couple of years younger than me at twenty-five, shrugged. "Sounds fine with me, too. All I've got in my bank is about twenty bucks. Hell, I might not even have that. I bought a bottle of Jack before getting on the plane that might've overdrawn my account, actually."

"This bank will do for us, Mr. Samuels." We started getting out of the car since the driver had opened the door for us. "Thanks. Your name is Davenport, right?"

The older man nodded. "Yep. I can also drive the various

tractors and trucks at the ranch. You need a ride, call me, and I'll get you there."

I thought it kind of funny that the man was clearly a farmer and not a chauffeur at all. And to be called Davenport seemed on the comical side. "If you don't mind me asking, what's your first name?"

"Buddy." He smiled at me. "Your grandfather liked to put on airs."

"We're not like that. Mind if we call you Buddy instead?"

He shook his head. "Not at all. It would be nice, in fact."

Jasper clapped the man on the back. "Nice to meet you, Buddy. I'm Jasper, this is Tyrell, and the feller there is Cash, the youngest of the Gentry family."

None of us were kids anymore, and Cash always took offense at how Jasper teased him. "Jasper, you're the littlest out of all of us, you jerk."

Flexing his left bicep while threading his fingers through his dark hair, Jasper replied, "By a smidgeon of an inch, Cash. You're shorter."

"Also, by a smidgeon of an inch." Cash walked ahead of us. "This bank is pretty fancy."

"It's the best one in town," Allen said as he hurried to get in front of Cash to open the door. "Here we go. Mr. Johnson is the bank president; he'll handle this for us."

"The *president* will handle all of this?" That was unorthodox. "How much money are we talking about?"

Cocking his head to one side, Allen looked confused. "Are you telling me that even with the jet, the mansion, and the ranch, you still don't understand how much capital your grandfather was worth?"

"Not a clue," Jasper said as he stepped into the bank's lobby. "Whoa. Posh."

As I stepped in behind him, my eyes went to the chandelier in the center of the ceiling. "I haven't seen many banks with a thing like that hanging above peoples' heads before."

"This bank deals with a lot of exclusive businesses here in Carthage." He led us to the back of a large open area as all eyes inside soon fixed on us. "They can afford certain luxuries other banks cannot."

A lady sat at a desk inside the first office we came to. "Hello, gentlemen. You must be the Gentrys."

I reached out to shake her hand. "Tyrell."

Jasper nodded. "Jasper."

She smiled at Cash. "Then you must be Cash."

"Yes." He shook her hand and gave his most charming smile. "And you are?"

"Sandra, the executive assistant." She let go of his hand to lead us to her boss's office. "And if you gentlemen will follow me? Mr. Johnson will get things started." As she opened the door, her eyes scanned me. "Judging by the blue jeans and t-shirts, you all will be greatly surprised by what you're about to inherit."

I figured we'd be lucky to get a million bucks and a hefty amount of debt from the Ranch. From what Dad told us before we left Dallas, our grandfather had been making more enemies than friends when Dad and Mom left town. Dad also said not to get our hopes up for what we were about to inherit, which might be more problems than profit.

The man sitting behind the large desk smiled and got up as we came into his large office filled with furniture that looked as luxurious as it was stunning. Mounts of various game animals adorned the walls. "Bryce Johnson, at your service, gentlemen. Please take seats anywhere you'd like. May I offer a cigar? They're Cuban. Or a drink perhaps? A thirty-year-old Scotch would be perfect for this occasion."

My brothers and I sat down on a sofa that felt a lot more like a cloud than a piece of furniture, and then I got right down to it.

"Okay, Bryce. We're quite certain this ranch is swimming in debt right? And we're not even close to being ranchers. Our father's advice was to find a buyer for it and move on."

Cash looked at me with narrowed eyes. "I'd *love* a Scotch, Tyrell. Let the man handle this meeting, will ya?"

"Scotch for everyone then," the bank president told his assistant who hurried off to fetch them. Turning his attention back to us, he asked, "So, Allen hasn't informed you?"

"I have. Not the exact numbers, but I've told them about everything they now own." He sighed and looked a bit put out. "They don't seem to get it, Bryce."

Sandra came back with a tray of crystal glasses half-full of a dark liquid. "Here you go, gentlemen. Enjoy." She held the tray out for us to grab a drink, and we each took one.

"A hell of a lot of hoopla, don't ya think?" I asked as I pulled the glass to my lips.

"You're all worth it," Sandra said before putting the tray down on a nearby table then taking a seat on a chair that looked spoke of affluence.

Bryce picked up some documents from his desk, then handed one to each of us. "I'll let the numbers speak for themselves."

When I looked at the page, there were more numbers in a row than I'd ever seen before. "Not sure how to say this number," I admitted. "And not sure I understand what it even means. Our father told us there has to be debt the ranch has built up."

Laughing, Bryce shook his head. "Whisper Ranch is one of the most profitable businesses this bank deals with. What each of you are looking at is your allotted third of the money Collin Gentry had in his personal accounts." He handed one paper directly to me. "This is what's in the ranch account."

Again, more numbers in a row than I'd ever seen before. "If I'm seeing this right, the ranch is worth millions."

Bryce shook his head. "You're not seeing it right. Look again."

"Oh, thousands." I squinted trying to make sense of the numbers.

Cash sounded out of breath as he said, "Tyrell, the ranch is worth *billions*, and we've each inherited fifteen *billion* dollars."

That didn't sound right. "Dad said there'd be more money to pay than receive."

"Your father was wrong," Bryce informed me. "Your grandfather went from raising cattle alone, to raising racehorses. You might've heard of some of his famous horses. *The General's Son? Old Faithful? Coy's Burden?*"

"We've never followed horse racing, sir," Jasper let him know. "I guess those horses are on the estate?"

"They are. And they all are prize-winning stallions," Bryce acknowledged. "Your grandfather began selling their semen and making a good penny from it. Those sales, along with the cattle, and the racehorses have made him a pretty penny. Pennies that now belong to the three of you."

It hurt me to think our grandfather left his only child out of his will. "Our father isn't mentioned?"

Allen looked at me with compassion. "Look, it may be difficult to understand, but let me show you in writing why that is." He pulled a paper out of the files and handed it to me. "Your father signed a statement that he wanted nothing from Collin or Fiona Gentry from that date forward. He wasn't forced to sign it. Coy did it to prove a point to his parents when they refused to acknowledge his marriage to Lila Stevens."

What is he talking about? "Wait. What?"

Bryce took over, "Your grandparents wanted to make the Gentry name something akin to royalty around here. But your father fell in love with a female from the wrong side of the tracks. A woman whose family lived on welfare. A girl who'd once worked as a maid at the ranch house."

My brothers were just as confused as I was. "Why would they never tell us about that?"

Allen had the answer, "Most likely because they didn't want you to know what they walked away from. They chose love over money *and* over their families. Your mother's family was just as against their marriage as the Gentrys were."

"Wow," that was all I could muster up. "Seems our parents hid a hell of a lot from us."

"There's one more thing you need to know about the will, gentlemen," the attorney said. "It stipulates that neither your mother nor father is ever allowed on the property. And your grandfather's money can never benefit your parents in any way. If you so much as hand your parents five dollars, the entire estate will revert to the state of Texas."

"Harsh," Cash muttered.

"Yeah," Bryce agreed.

"Your grandfather was considered to be a harsh man. So harsh that most people think your grandmother died at the age of forty-five, only two years after your father left the ranch, because of his hard ways."

What the hell?

ELLA

"Ella, get your hind end in here, girl!" Mom shouted for me.

Hurrying to see what she wanted, I knew today wasn't the day to screw things up. Sliding into the foyer that I'd just cleaned every nook and cranny of, she was eyeing a spot up very high on the ceiling. "What's wrong, Mom?"

"Girl, I know you can see that up there on the chandelier." Her blue eyes met mine, a tad of aggravation in them. "They're coming today. For the first time ever, those boys are going to see the domicile their father declined in order to be with their mother. This place has to shine, sparkle, dazzle. You know what I'm saying, right? You do get it, don't you?"

"Sure, some brats are coming to live in their rich, old grandfather's mansion. And we're their servants." I rolled my eyes so hard it actually hurt.

"I've told you about them, Ella." Mom put her arm around my shoulders. "They aren't moneyed. Well, now they are, but they weren't before inheriting Mr. Gentry's riches and this ranch. Look at it this way; they don't have to keep us if we can't make this place look as great as it can. Got me?"

"Sure, to keep this *great* job, and I'm being sarcastic just in case you can't read my tone, Mom, I'll get up on that loathsome sky-high ladder and dust that damn crystal monster overhead." I hated dusting the lighting in the house. There were so many chandeliers it made my job miserable.

"This is a great job, young lady," Mom chastised me. "Not many maids earn what you do."

"A whopping fifteen dollars an hour, Mom?" I didn't believe her. As the house manager, she oversaw the hiring and firing of the house staff. She employed my older sister, Darleen, for a few years until she went to college to become a vet. If the wages were so great, then why'd my sister quit?

"Most maids make minimum wage," she told me. "You're making over twice that amount. You should be thankful."

Looking up at the shiny crystal that hung from the ceiling, I thought the wage wasn't nearly enough for all the hazardous duty that came with keeping the place pristine. "Thankful, huh? For what? For *having* to climb up on a ladder, then carefully wipe down each and every little crystal teardrop up there?"

"Yep," she said matter of factly. "And hop to it, child. The new proprietors will be here in about an hour. This room, in particular, needs to shine. It's the first one they see."

With a huff, I strolled to the back to get the indoor ladder out of the shed. I grumbled and growled as I carried the heavy thing inside, all the way into the lobby to set it up. "I don't get it. Who cares if it has a little dust on it? These guys aren't used to seeing things like this anyway. They won't even give it a second look. They'll be so overwhelmed by this place that they won't look too hard at anything."

After getting one half of it cleaned up, I climbed down the ladder to move it over to reach the other half. The front door opened as I was halfway up, and I nearly lost my balance supposing it must be the new owners. "Shit!"

"Classy, Ella," my brother Kyle commented as he came in. He looked up at me with a grin. "You missed a spot." He pointed at the half I was about to clean.

"You missed the bus." What did that mean? It came out just the same. Often, I just said what came to my mind, whether it made any sense or not.

"Whatever that means." He passed the ladder, stopped and took a step back, putting his hands on either side of it. "What if I gave this a little shake? What would you do, baby sister?"

"Kick your ass." I held on tightly because he'd shake it and laugh as I screamed for mercy.

"Kick *my* ass?" He gave it one shake. "You sure about that?"

Shrieking, I glared at him. "Stop! If you make me fall, Mom will kill you for getting this floor all bloody. And God forbid my head bust open and my brains get all over this floor, Kyle Finley!"

"Yeah, the new owners might slip on your gore and fire us all." He laughed, then walked out of the room.

Kyle worked with our father who has been the foreman on the ranch since before any of us were even born. He and Mr. Gentry were as close to being friends as that old bastard ever got to be with anyone else. Perhaps 'cause Dad understood the cranky old man.

The door opened again, and I chastised myself for not having the job done yet. Luckily it was Dad who walked inside.

"You better hurry the hell up, Ella. They should be here any second now. The only reason I came inside was to greet them when they arrive. And I can see up your skirt. You need to wear bigger knickers, young lady."

Using one hand to dust and the other to hold my skirt closer, I muttered, "I don't want to wear bigger panties. I want to stop wearing this stupid maid's uniform and wear jeans, a t-shirt, and some freaking tennis shoes. These dumb maid shoes look horrible. And I'd love it if my job never entailed getting up on a ladder in the first place so people could see up my damn skirt."

"Try your best to curtail your sass, Ella." Dad gestured for me to get down. "Come on, that's good enough. I know your momma thinks every little thing needs to shine to impress these men, but they won't give a lick about a little dust. And their first impression shouldn't be one where your undies are showing."

I nearly had it done anyway. "Dad, I'm almost finished. Momma will send me back up here to finish the job. And you dang well know she'll do it, too."

"Well, just scurry then." He left the lobby, shaking his head as he mumbled, "That girl is going to be the next to go. I just know it."

167

Like I cared if the new guys fired me. I could get another job. Most likely one with better pay. Of course, I hadn't gone to college after graduating from high school. That shouldn't be important in getting a great paying job.

My parents had been asking me since my twenty-first birthday a month ago about what I'd like to do for a profession. When I told them it would be fun to be a stand-up comedian, they laughed at me. That proved I could be successful as a comic since I'd made them laugh without even trying.

However, I hadn't really meant that. I didn't know what I wanted to be. So, for now, a maid was it. One day that would change—I just knew it would.

"And this is the ceremonial entrance to your new home, gentlemen," came a voice from behind me.

Looking back, I saw that lawyer Mr. Gentry had around the place a lot during the last year when he was sick. He was bringing the new owners through the back entrance, and they caught me with my guard down.

"Oh, shit!" Scrambling down the ladder, I skipped a rung and began a fall that was sure to leave me looking like an idiot as my body splayed out on the granite floor.

Only I didn't hit the floor. Instead, a pair of strong arms caught me. "Got ya."

Opening my eyes, which I had squeezed shut while falling, I saw his eyes first. Blue like the sky, they twinkled as he looked down at me.

"Put me down! I didn't ask for your help." *Damn, he's hot! Too hot!* His dark hair made those blue eyes really stand out. And talk about muscles! Whoa!

I looked at the three new owners and found them all pretty damn devastating. But the one who caught me really shook me up. And I don't get shook up. Not ever.

"Sorry if I offended you by saving your neck." He placed my feet on the floor.

Straightening out my shirt and skirt, I then ran my hand through my pony to make sure it was on point. "You didn't *save* me."

The man's eyes scanned me. "I, at the very least, saved you from an embarrassing fall. Some people would say thank you."

"I have cat-like reflexes. You'd have seen them in action had you kept your meaty paws to yourself." Going to take the ladder down, I found the man stepping in front of me, taking it down himself. "I…"

"No, I've got this." Tucking the ladder under his arm, an arm with a massive bicep bulging under the long-sleeve brown tee he wore, he kept his eyes on me. "I'm Tyrell. And you are?"

"The maid." I reached out to take the ladder from him. "If my mom, who's also the house manager, catches you taking that out she'll kill me. I don't need that today. Not with you guys here."

The lawyer seemed taken aback as he said, "Who the hell are you?"

Mom and Dad walked into the room, both with ashen faces as my father said, "That's Ella, our youngest." He looked at me with a grim expression. "Get that ladder and work elsewhere, Ella."

The man who caught me shook his head. "She's much too small to be carrying this around. I'll put it up. Come on, Ella. Show me where this thing goes. And by the way, these are my brothers, Jasper and Cash. "

"Duh." I led the way out of the room, ignoring my parents' dropped jaws. "Come on. I'll show you. What did you say your name is again? I missed it." He kind of made me all wiggly inside, including inside my brain.

"Tyrell," he said with a southern drawl. "Tyrell Gentry. And you are Ella?"

"Finley. My parents have run this place forever. I think my dad was your grandfather's only friend." Opening the door to the back, I pointed to the shed. "It goes in there. Thanks, Tyrell Gentry."

"For catching you?" His eyes sparkled again.

Damn, he's too hot for his own good. "Sure. Even though I didn't *need* your help."

"Next time I'll let you fall." He kicked the door shut behind him as he walked out. And I watched him him walk away through the window next to the door, my mouth watering as well as other parts of my anatomy.

TYRELL

Cash, Jasper, and I decided to tour the rest of the house on our own, preferring to scout out our new digs alone. "You wasted no time, did ya, Tyrell?" Jasper asked as he opened a door with a movie theater behind it. "Would you look at this?"

"Doing what?" I leaned in to see what else was in our private movie theater. "Wow, I wonder if we get Netflix."

Cash laughed as he slapped his thigh. "Seems we've died and gone to Heaven."

"Real cool, Cash," Jasper said with a frown. "Our grandparents did die and go to Heaven, or we wouldn't have this. And I meant how you fondled that cute, petite housekeeper in the foyer, Tyrell."

"You mean caught and saved her life, not fondled." I followed my youngest brother, ignoring my pain in the ass middle brother.

Cash walked down the corridor to the next door. "If Mom and Dad hadn't given up their fight, we would've grown up with this."

"To be fair, we have no idea how hard that fight was," I said as I looked into the room Cash had just opened. "Nothing but theater supplies in here. Popcorn, pickles, hot dog buns, we've got it all. We could make a living just selling tickets to movies and snacks here."

Jasper chuckled as he walked down to the door across the

hallway. "We could add that one to all the other ways our grandfather already made money from this place. Hey, a sauna!"

We all hurried to see it and found he'd made the entire room into a steam room. I couldn't believe it. "We may never have to leave home, guys."

Cash shook his head. "Unless one of these doors has some single women behind it, then we certainly have to leave, at least every now and then."

"We just barely got here, Cash," Jasper reminded him. "We should settle in and get to know the locals before looking for chicks. Otherwise, we may end up with the loosest women in Carthage, of which I believe are aplenty."

Cash laughed as he walked away to see what we'd find next. "What's wrong with loose women, Jasper? I'm not picky. If they want to give it, I'll take it."

"*And* their diseases?" Jasper asked as he raised one dark brow. "I think not, little man."

Cash grabbed his crotch. "I've got your little man, Jasper."

"That you do." Jasper chuckled as I opened the next door we came to. And we all went silent.

Red walls, black carpet, and chains hung on one wall. Something like a bed, but it had no mattress, was at the end of the rectangular shaped room.

"You know what this is, don't you?" Jasper asked.

"This is going to be locked up, then boarded up." I pulled the door closed only to have Cash open it again.

"Don't be so quick to make hasty decisions, Tyrell." He walked into the room. "Gramps was a freak. Who would've ever guessed?"

"You boys finding everything alright?" a woman's voice came from behind us.

We turned to find an older version of the young maid standing there. "You must be Ella's sister," I said.

"Correct. I'm Darleen." She was about a foot taller than tiny Ella, but just as pretty with long dark hair and eyes as cobalt as the ocean. "Ella's *older* sister. And you must be Tyrell, Jasper, and Jasper, the new owners of Whisper Ranch."

I introduced us all. "I'm Tyrell, this is Jasper, and that's Cash. Do you work here?"

"Nope." She grinned. "So, you can't fire me. I do live here though. So, I guess you could evict me. I'm going to college. I'm specializing in cattle and horses. Hopefully, I'll be able to charge you for my services. Much the same way your grandfather did. But that's our little secret, 'kay?"

Cash started coughing, Jasper's jaw dropped, and I asked, "Do you mean that you and he," I pointed to the room, "in this room, here?"

She nodded. "Yep. And I'm still available if any of you have that particular calling. Your grandfather paid for my college education. But I could use a new car."

Our grandfather had been one hell of an old man! "I'm afraid none of us are into that sort of thing, ma'am. Sorry."

Unexpectedly, she burst into gales of laughter so hard that tears filled her eyes and dripped down her cheeks. "You guys are too easy to fool. Really? Would you *really* think I'd do something like that? Oh, hell. That was fun."

"So, you didn't go at it with our gramps?" Cash asked.

"No," she assured us. "Not in a zillion years. Not even if he'd left this place to me. But he did provide work for someone for this room. She left when he got sick last year. Hilda was his mistress for about twenty years. He took her on after your grandmother died, is what my mother told me."

"But he never married her?" Jasper asked.

Shaking her head, she looked into the room. "Nope, just some sadomasochism when he felt like it. He did pay her well for it. She got a very nice home and quite a bit of funding for her trouble. He wouldn't have married her anyway. He never took her out in public. She wasn't in his class."

"Like our mother," I said looking at the floor, wondering what it must've been like back then. "To think that Mom was looked down upon makes me kind of hate this man we never met."

Darleen smiled and lightly punched me in the arm. "Look at it this way, no matter how hard he tried, he didn't succeed. Your parents got to keep their love, and you guys get to keep everything your grandfather ever made."

"Yeah." I supposed there was some justice in that. "But our parents can't ever reap the benefits."

With a grin, she said, "Betchya a billion bucks, they don't want a thing that man had."

Cash nodded. "That's what Mom told me before we left Dallas. She said take it, enjoy it, and make the most out of it. She wanted nothing to do with Whisper Ranch nor anything our grandfather had ever touched."

"Can't say I blame her." Darleen walked to the next door, and we followed her. "Let me show you Hilda's bedroom."

Pushing open the door, they saw a stark room containing only a twin bed with nothing on it. There was not a single thing else, not even a curtain covering the one window. I looked at the pitiful space and felt sick at my stomach. "Why'd he want to keep her like this?"

Darleen slowly shook her head. "He made everyone around him wretched. It was like he got off on it." Her eyes met mine. "I don't mean to talk badly about him, but he was an ass, you guys. The name of Gentry isn't one many people care for around here. Hopefully, you guys can change that."

"You and your sister are like night and day," I said closing the door. "How's that?"

Her narrow shoulders shrugged. "Mom had her when she was in her thirties. Maybe she was made out of a rotten egg."

While my brothers laughed, I frowned. "Or maybe she was a casualty of a mean older sister?"

"Nah, that can't be it," Darleen said with a grin. "*I'm* an angel."

She probably wasn't quite the angel. "I'm sure your sister can be an angel when she wants to."

"I'm sure you're wrong." Darleen laughed, then turned to leave us. "I'll let you guys check out the rest of the quarters on your own. I just heard your voices down the hall and wanted to introduce myself. I'm sure we'll get along just fine."

"Me, too," I said, then added, "Even with Ella."

Her laughter echoed all the way down the long foyer as she left us. Then Jasper's shoulder hit mine. "Methinks you're thinking about that petite maid too much, big brother."

"No, I'm not." I walked to the next door. "Hey look, it's a massive shower."

Cash wrinkled his nose as we all walked inside. "Perhaps we should board up this entire area."

"The other two rooms, I agree with, but why this?" I asked as I held my arms out in gesture to the biggest shower I'd ever seen.

"Grandfather apparently was in here after they… you know." Cash made a gagging face. "Yuck."

I had to agree. "Yeah, yuck."

Jasper looked at us and nodded. "We've got some changes to make around here and around town, too, if we want to be amiable." We walked out of the giant shower room and back into the hall.

"Oh, shit," came a soft curse uttered by a feminine voice.

We all turned to see Ella running back down the hallway away from us. "Hey, wait up," I called out.

But she kept on running as if she'd seen a ghost. "You going to chase after her, Tyrell?" Jasper asked.

"What for?" I turned to walk in the other direction.

Cash bumped his shoulder to mine. "'Cause she seems to have a crush on you."

"You're wrong." I headed for the next door, but Jasper stepped in front of me. "What?"

"She's acting that way 'cause you got her stimulated. Aren't you going to get her settled down?" Jasper's dark brow raised. "That might be fun."

"I like my women a bit more refined. And not quite so mouthy." I pushed open the next door to find a room covered in sketches. A chair by the window had a table next to it, and a pad of paper and colored pencils sat on top of it. "You don't suppose this is why Ella was up here? You don't suppose this is *her* stuff?" I ran my fingers over a picture of a cardinal that hung on the wall. The red feathers looked almost real. "She's gifted."

"You don't know this is hers, Tyrell." Cash pointed at the initials on the bottom of the paper that were written so tiny I could barely make them out. "What does this mean?"

"I think it's the signature, or rather, the initials of whoever drew this." Squinting, I tried to make them out. "I do believe it's an E and an F. As in Ella Finley."

"Or you'd like to believe that, anyway," Jasper said. "I see two Es."

Cash picked up the case of colored pencils as he looked out the window. "Oh yeah, this is hers alright. I can tell."

He held the case he'd picked up to his forehead as if using his mind to see who it belonged to.

"So, you're doing your old fake psychic thing, Cash." I took the thing away from him to find Ella written on the case in black Sharpie.

Who are you, Ella Finley?

ELLA

I had plans of going to my secret room to draw when I saw the new landlords coming out of the enormous shower on the second floor. They had their clothes on, thankfully. I felt Tyrell's blue eyes burning into my back as I fled, his deep voice calling out to me kindled something in my body.

Returning to my family's section of the mansion, I headed to my bedroom to lay down and chill after finishing work for the day. Passing through the living room, my older sister, Darleen, was smiling at me. "I heard you met the guys, Ella."

"What?" I stopped, putting my hand on my hip. "What did they tell you, Darleen? I want to hear every single word."

"*They* didn't say much." She lay back on the couch, her dark hair splaying out on the armrest as she grinned like the Cheshire Cat from Alice in Wonderland. "Tyrell is the one who talked about you. Get this; he thinks you could be an angel. *You.*"

My heart sped up, my body heated. "He said what?" my voice came out a bit on the high side.

Darleen sat up quickly, one long finger pointing at me. "You *like* him."

"Hell, no." I switched my weight to the other foot and moved my hand to the other hip. "Why'd he say I could be an angel, Darleen?"

"I said I was one." She lay back down. "They're all studs, huh?"

I nodded, only because I couldn't help it. "But so what, who cares? Tyrell is old. He's thirty if he's a day."

"He's twenty-seven," she alerted. "Jasper is twenty-five, and Cash is twenty-two. I've done my research. Cash is more your speed, I think. Leave Tyrell to me since he's just a year older than me. It makes the most sense, don't you think?"

"Um, no." Something was happening to me that had never happened before. I was getting mad for no reason. "You better ask Mom and Dad if you can go out with any of them before you get into trouble. They may not want us to mix business with pleasure."

"What would you know about pleasure, baby sis?" Darleen sat up again, laughing. "Ella, you never even held hands with a boy, much less locked lips with one. What do you know about pleasure?"

"Shut up." I walked away to the kitchen to get a drink and opened the fridge, my eyes landing on Dad's beer. I was keyed up and had no idea how to take it down a few notches, so I took one of Dad's beers and popped the top, taking a long sip, then choking on the bitter taste. "Yuck."

Darleen looked around the corner to see me with the can in my hand. "You better finish that."

I walked over to the sink and poured out the remainder. "I'll leave a buck for him under the magnet on the fridge. This stuff is so gross. I don't see how you guys drink it."

Darleen went to grab an apple off the counter. "That's 'cause you're a kid still, Ella. One day you'll understand why people drink alcohol and have sex."

"Darleen, you're quite possibly the worst big sister in the history of big sisters." Watching her eat the apple, I had to know more about what Tyrell had said about me. "Was there anything else he said?"

"He said you and I were like night and day." She took another big bite as she nodded. "Me being the day. Like… I'm nicer than you."

My foot began to tap, my arms crossed over my chest. "So, what?"

"*You* asked, Ella." She walked over to the fridge and got a bottle of water. "Seriously, don't make a fool out of yourself over those guys. They're way out of your league. Maybe, before they were loaded, you could've stood a chance, but now that they've got money—well, there's no way now."

An even more intense heat filled me as I glared at my sister. "Oh, but *you* have a chance?"

Laughing, she walked out of the kitchen and reclaimed her seat on the couch. "Probably, but I don't crap where I eat, if you know what I mean."

I grimaced. "That's just disgusting, Darleen. You're saying that you wouldn't go out with any of them because you live under their roof?"

"Correct." She laid the apple core on the coffee table, then lay on the couch again. "I'm going to take a nap. School wore me out today. We did a canine autopsy; it was mind-numbing."

The door opened, and Mom looked at me as she wiped the sweat off her forehead. "There you are. I've been calling your cell for thirty minutes, Ella Finley. Tasha called in sick, and Chef Todd needs you in the kitchen to serve dinner."

I checked the cell in the pocket of my apron and found it on silent. "To them?" I shrieked. "Mom, no! Please!"

"Yes, you *have* to do it. It's their first meal here, and I want it to be grand." She pulled a napkin out of the pocket of her apron and wiped more sweat off her brow. "I'm helping Todd with the cooking; you need to serve. In my closet, there's a server's uniform. Put that on and get your butt to the kitchen, ASAP. The appetizer is ready, and I've told the men to get seated in the dining room."

Darleen sat up, and for a second, I thought she would volunteer for the job. "Mom, why do you have a server's uniform in your closet?"

"Never mind, nosy." Mom gave me a quick shake of her finger. "Ella, you hurry now. If I have to come find you, it'll be your hide, young lady."

"You'd spank me?" I couldn't believe it. "Are you serious?"

"Our jobs are on the line, girl. I'm serious. Now scurry!" Mom left, leaving the door open, footsteps thumping as she ran down the hall back to the kitchen.

Looking at Darleen, I began to beg, "Darleen, please do it. I'll give you anything you want. You really liked the necklace I got from Grandma this Christmas; you can have it if you do this."

"Um," she pursed her lips contemplating my offer, and then her eyes set on mine. "No way in hell. I need a snooze. And you better hurry up."

I hated the fact she no longer needed to keep a job at the estate. "What a selfish piece of work you are, Darleen." I ran to Mom and Dad's bedroom and found the outfit, a short black skirt and white button-down shirt. And then I saw the high heels that went with it. Mr. Gentry always made everyone wear what he called *proper attire* for their jobs.

Carrying the stuff to my room, I found a pair of black pantyhose in my top drawer but pulled a rip in them right off the bat. Black stockings were part of the get-up. I went back to Mom's room to see if she had another pair, and when I opened her top drawer, I found not pantyhose, but stockings—fishnet ones. But they were black, so I had no choice.

After getting changed, I looked at my reflection in the mirror and blushed. "I thought the maid attire was bad enough."

Walking through the living room, Darleen's eyes were closed, but she must've opened them because I heard her snickering. "Oh, hell."

I lifted one hand, showing her my middle finger. "Thanks, big sis."

"Be careful not to bend over too low, Ella. Your ass will be on display for sure if you do." Her laughter followed me down the hallway as I went to the kitchen.

Todd nodded toward three bowls of salad. "There, Ella. Take the salads out. And see if they want something to drink. Be courteous." He rolled his eyes as he pounded a piece of chicken to make it thinner. "What am I saying? And to whom? *Try* to be nice, Ella. *Please*. Our *jobs* depend on it."

"Fine," I snapped and picked up a tray and put the bowls on it.

"Ella, you need to get the silverware," Mom added. "Come on, honey, think."

"No one set the table?" I huffed while collecting the utensils. "I've got to do *everything* around here today?"

Neither of them said a word as I carried the tray out. Going into the outsized dining area with a massive central table, I saw they were sitting at the far end. Tyrell was at the head of the table and his brothers were on either side of him.

The way Tyrell grinned made me shaky. "You're working the dinner shift, too, I see."

Placing the bowls and silverware in front of them, I nodded, "Yeah, the girl who normally does this called in. Stupid Tasha."

"Looks good," Cash commented as he dug right into his salad.

"Um." I stood there, trying to remember what Todd told me to do. "Oh, yeah. You guys want something to drink?"

Jasper nodded. "A Jack and Coke would be great."

Cash looked at me as he asked, "What do you have?"

Shifting my weight, I didn't have an answer for that. "Tell me what you want, and I'm sure we can fix you up."

I felt a hand on my arm, and turning, I found Tyrell's meaty hand there; bolts of lightning shot through me, and I jumped back. The damn heels had me stumbling backward, then those hands were on me again.

"Whoa, Ella." He held me for a second. "Saved you again."

"The wall would've stopped my fall. I'm not used to wearing heels." I moved out of his grasp, heading toward the kitchen to get away from the man who made me act crazy.

"I'll have sweet iced tea," Tyrell called out.

Cash added, "Me, too, I guess."

In the kitchen, I tried to settle down. "Todd, I need a Jack and Coke and two sweet iced teas." I ran my hands over the front of my skirt nervously. "God, I hate doing this. I hate wearing this."

Suddenly a deep voice came from right behind me. "So why are you wearing it then?"

I turned to see Tyrell had snuck in. "How'd...? Why...? What are you doing in here?"

"Cash changed his mind. He wants a Jack and Coke, too. And I want to know why you're wearing something that makes you feel uncomfortable, Ella." He looked at Mom as my tongue had gone limp inside my mouth. "From now on, let the staff wear whatever they feel the most comfortable in. This isn't a five-star hotel. We don't care what anyone wears."

"Okay, Tyrell," Mom said with a nod. "I'll get that memo out after dinner."

"Thanks." He turned to leave.

As I watched him walk away, I felt weird. "Thanks."

He stopped and turned to look at me with a funny smile. "For?"

"For catching me." I ran my hand down the short skirt. "And for noticing how uncomfortable I feel in this outfit."

With a nod, he walked out, and I couldn't take my eyes off the door until Mom yelled at me, "Ella, get out of your stupor and take the drinks out! Damn, girl!"

TYRELL

With so much to consider, my brothers and I hopped in one of the ranch's trucks and drove to Dallas to talk to our parents. Having spent the night, none of us knew exactly what the right thing to do was. Plus, I wanted to know more about the situation. Like why Dad's father was such an inflexible man?

I drove, Jasper sat in the passenger seat, and Cash sat in the middle of the backseat that morning. "If we sell the ranch, you might never catch Ella when she falls again," Jasper chuckled. "Who knows? Without you around, she might finally meet her end with how clumsy she is."

Cash leaned forward. "I don't think she's clumsy. She's intimidated by Big Brother here. And how is it, Tyrell, that you always jump to catch the filly anyway? One of us could've done it just as easily."

"I didn't see either of you jumping to do that." I put on the blinker to get on the ramp to the highway. "And believe it or not, I don't want to keep the ranch just to catch Ella from time to time."

"Time to time?" Jasper asked with a goofy grin. "Yesterday you caught her twice. I almost wonder if she fell on purpose to get you to scoop her up in your strong arms, Romeo."

"Cool it." We had better things to discuss besides the young housekeeper. "Now, tell me how we're going to do right by that ranch."

Cash seemed optimistic, "We can learn, can't we? Now that we've got loads of cash, we can learn things."

"A Cowboy college?" Jasper joked. "I don't think they have one of those. Not even in Texas."

"Yeah, but we have Zeke Finley," I reminded them. "He's been around that ranch forever. He'd teach us everything we need."

Cash's eyes narrowed. "You know what? Why do we have to learn a damn thing? We've got money to pay everyone to do everything for us."

Living a life of doing nothing seemed like a bad way to live to me. "Cash, the idle rich seem to get into a lot of trouble. I think it best if we all work at the ranch. *If* we keep it."

As we came into the outer suburbs of Dallas, we passed the historical Mesquite Rodeo Arena. "Hey, how about we get into the bucking bulls game?" Cash suggested.

Indeed, we could use the ranch to not only make money but to learn some things while we were at it. "If that's something you'd like to do, then go after it. Once we settle on staying or selling."

Jasper's eyes glazed over as he said, "You know what we could do?"

"What?" I asked as I took the exit to Mom's and Dad's house.

"They can coach us how to cowboy up! The guys working at the rodeo arena could teach us the basics at least. That way, when we go back to the ranch, we wouldn't be such greenhorns about everything."

"Sounds good. Get on that," I advised, taking a right on the street we grew up on. "*If* we choose to keep the place."

"*We've* got ideas, Tyrell," Cash said. "What are your ideas?"

"At the present, I'm looking for a real estate broker to talk to." I didn't want to run the property into the ground because of our lack of knowledge. More people than just us count on it to make a living.

Parking in front of the modest two-bedroom home we'd grown up in, I couldn't help but sigh. Cash and Jasper did, too. Jasper looked at me with a frown. "I don't know about keeping them out of our newfound wealth, Tyrell."

"Me, neither." I got out of the truck, and we all headed inside.

Mom never had a job. Dad wanted her to stay home with the kids instead. Dad did not go to college. With no education and no work experience other than some labor work, he had a tough time finding employment when they moved to Dallas. Eventually, he landed a job with a construction company. But it didn't pay well. Not that our father ever complained.

Mom threw the front door open and held out her arms. "You're back! My boys are back home!"

"We've only been gone one night, Mom," Cash laughed. "How could you miss us already?"

Her dark eyes glistened with what might be tears. "I was worried that you would see what we had left behind us and suppose we were insane and write us completely off."

Why did they leave? "Mom, can you and Dad please tell us the truth about everything? We need to know."

Nodding, she hugged us then let us go so we could get inside. "Coy," she called out. "The boys are back. They want to talk."

My father came out of the bedroom. His robe untied, wearing night clothes, he looked tired and a bit sick. "What do you want to talk about?"

As Jasper and Cash took seats on the couch, I put my hand on our father's shoulder. "Are you doing okay, Dad? It's noon, and you're still in pajamas? Are you sick?"

Mom patted me on the back. "Go take a seat, Tyrell. Your dad just tied one on last night is all."

We've never seen Father with a hangover. "Why'd you do that, Dad?"

He sat in his threadbare chair, hollowed out where only his butt ever parked. "I thought we might lose you to the life we left behind. We know how alluring wealth can be. No one would blame you if you did take it and leave us. You see, I know about my father's Last Will and Testament. His attorney sent an e-mail to us. We got it yesterday, not long after you took off."

"Just 'cause we can't give you anything doesn't mean we'll walk away from you guys," Cash said. "You're our family. Money won't get in the way of that."

184

"We'll give it to the state then," I said because of how they were taking things. "We never had anything before, and we don't need it now."

Mom shook her head taking her seat next to Dad's. "No. Don't do that. Keep the ranch and create something good. Too much bad has already occurred. Change things. Your father and I never wanted anything from our parents. And we don't need anything from you, either. Well, that's not true. We need your love. We need you, our children. But we don't want anything other than that."

I wanted to know more. "Mom, what happened? You don't talk to your family, either. Now this grandfather of ours, well, we've heard enough to understand why you guys didn't want to deal with him. Your family, though? We don't know about them, either."

Mom looked at my father, and then ran her hand along his shoulder to rest it there. "My family told me to know my place in this world and accept it. I worked as a maid at the ranch for a month before your father and I discovered a mutual attraction that both our families thought taboo."

"That's stupid." It was so archaic.

Dad nodded. "Yeah, it was. I loved your mother the first moment I saw her. I didn't care where she lived or who her family was. I had to have her and make her my wife. My father wasn't about to allow that to happen. He used everything in his arsenal to stop our nuptials. He even bribed the town's justice of the peace, getting him to refuse to marry us."

Jasper nodded as if he comprehended. "So, you cut out Mom's family, too, because they tried to hold her back?"

Mom's hand ran down Dad's arm, and they clasped hands. "They took money from Collin Gentry to get me out of Texas. One night, I was woken up, and my own father had me tied up and gagged. He and my two brothers carried me out of our home and threw me into the trunk of the car. They drove for hours. Finally, we stopped, and they let me out, took off the ropes, and told me I'd be living with my Aunt Hilda in Shreveport, Louisiana. I was not to come back to Texas."

"But you must've come back," I alleged.

"Nope, I went to find her." Dad's thumb ran over the back of

Mom's hand. "I paid her youngest brother to tell me where she was. She was a wreck. Her aunt kept her locked up so she wouldn't run away. I paid her aunt to let me see her with my promise that I wouldn't take her away with me. But I did, and we returned to Carthage where I told my father he couldn't impede our marriage."

Mom smiled as she looked adoringly at my father. "We stopped in Dallas to get married before going back home."

"When I showed my father our marriage license, he told me I no longer had a home. Everything he'd given to me, he wanted it all back. Your mom and I were on our own." Dad looked at Mom with starry eyes. "I wrote out a statement saying I didn't want a thing from him—and never would."

Jasper nodded. "Yeah, we saw that. But this doesn't feel right without you guys getting something, too."

Dad nodded. "We got you! And neither of us needs anything other than the love we share. To be honest, I've lived the life of a rich man. This one is better. Take what you've been given. Why should the state get what's rightfully yours? Plus, some people count on that ranch for their homes and livelihoods."

"There are quite a few." I looked at Mom and saw the love in her eyes when she looked at her husband. I wanted to find a love like that. "I presume we *should* keep the ranch and do our best by it and those who depend on it."

My brothers nodded and, just like that, our judgment had been made.

ELLA

Everyone seemed to be on edge with the exit of the Gentry brothers. I had no idea why. So, what if they left? "Momma, why's everyone on pins and needles today?" I ran the dust cloth over the banister to shine it up.

She'd been on her way upstairs but stopped when I asked. Turning to me with concern in her eyes.

"Honey, don't you understand? If these men don't take on the ranch, then it'll go to the state. The state won't keep it the way it is. We'll all lose our jobs. And in our case, our home. The only home we've had since before you kids were born."

"Why is that?" The state wouldn't shut the ranch down.

"How many state-run ranches have you heard of, Ella?" She rolled her eyes at me. "If the state keeps it as a working ranch, they'll probably fill the place with prisoners who'll do the work, and the state will reap the benefits."

"Oh." I hadn't thought of that. "So, we need the guys to stay then, right?"

"Yes." She nodded, then put her hand on my shoulder. "And you need to be a lot nicer. The way you talk to Tyrell … Mind your mouth, young lady."

"I doubt Tyrell would give up this ranch on account of my mouth." The idea was nuts.

Mom stared at me blankly. "Ella, you could get fired, and he could tell us he no longer wants you on his property."

"Why would he do that?" I shook my head in disbelief.

"Maybe because you'd be getting on his nerves." With a huff, Mom ascended the stairs. "Please, Ella, just keep your mouth shut whenever they are around."

"Yeah, whatever." I doubted that Tyrell gave a damn about anything I said, no matter what Momma thought.

After shining up the banister, I took a break, sitting on the front terrace, loving how the snow looked as it covered the ground. The sound of a truck coming up the long drive had me standing up to see who it might be. I didn't expect it to be the brothers yet. They'd only been gone for a few hours.

The shiny red hood of the truck they'd taken off in came into view, and I muttered, "Shit," then took off inside of the house to hide.

With work still needing to be done, I decided to start cleaning the bathrooms upstairs in whatever bedrooms they slept in. They'll probably stay downstairs for a while, talking to Mom and Dad about their plans.

Where had the guys slept? I searched for all the rooms with messed-up beds. When I failed to find not one bed unmade, not one room disheveled, I decided to look a bit harder.

There were six bedrooms in the residential wing upstairs. Six more downstairs, but Mom said she saw them going up when they left the dining area. But even close inspections of each attached bathroom didn't provide a clue as to where they slept. Mom must've been wrong, so I headed down the stairs—and there was Tyrell.

He held up one hand. "Better not topple down these stairs, Ella."

Maybe it was my deer in the headlights expression? Shaking off the initial reaction, I spoke hastily, "Since you allowed me to drop the old-fashioned dress code your grandfather enforced, I've got on tennis shoes. Falling is highly unlikely. Too bad, huh?"

"For me?" he asked as we met halfway on the landing.

"Yeah, for you." I didn't look at him but noticed his eyes roaming over my body, taking in the jeans and t-shirt. "Since I won't be falling anymore, you won't have to fulfill your hero fantasy—or whatever has you thinking I'm a damsel who needs rescuing."

"*Excuse me.*" He moved up the stairs.

Where are their rooms? "Hey, where did you guys sleep last night?"

Tyrell turned around with a wide grin. "Why? You want to lie on my bed and sniff my pillows?"

"You're seriously going to make me gag." But the idea wasn't all that bad. The man smelled splendid. "I'm the housekeeper. It's my job to clean your rooms every day. In particular, the bathrooms. They can get malodorous."

"We clean up after ourselves," he informed me. "And we do a good job of it. Our dad made sure we helped Mom with the chores. It took us a while to find where to take the towels this morning, but we managed."

"That's my job." I put my hands on my hips. "You want me to lose my job, Tyrell Gentry?"

His look made me blush all over. "You're mine, Ella."

"Huh?"

"My maid. I'm your boss." He laughed, then turned around again. "The only person who can take your job away from you is me. Come on, I'll show you the bedrooms we picked."

My legs, though shaky, took me up the stairs behind him. "May I ask what you have decided to do about the ranch?"

"We're keeping it." He stopped at the top of the stairs to let me catch up. "Looks like you're going to be stuck with me, Ella."

I walked ahead of him. "Who says I'll be a maid here forever?"

"Not me." He moved to pass me. "Mine's this one here." He opened the third door on the left. "I like the blue hues." He pointed across the hallway. "Jasper's is there, and Cash took the first one off the right." He led me into his room, and I looked around.

"Um, if you put your dirty clothes and towels and stuff in the bathroom hamper, I'll launder them each day. It's been our practice to wash the sheets once a week, on Mondays. If that's okay with you, I'll keep on doing that." Mom told me to behave myself, and I tried to conjure my inner maid to do just that.

"I rather do my own clothes." He went to open the closet. "We've been doing our own laundry since we were fifteen. I prefer to wash my own boxers." His eyes went wide as he looked at the massive closet space. "Whoa. This is nearly as big as the bedroom."

"Yeah, there are some huge closets in these suites." He didn't have enough clothes to make a dent in the space. "You should go shopping. You know, fill this bitch up."

"Not much of a shopper." He closed the door, then turned to look speculatively at me. "Care to make a buck helping me do that, Ella?"

"Helping you do what?" I ran my dust cloth over the already-clean dresser.

"Shopping." He came to me, took the cloth out of my hand, then tucked it into the pocket of my apron. A frisson of sensation sparked in me from his touch. "I have no clue where the stores are. I'll pay you, of course."

"Nope." I shook my head. "Since you already cleaned your own rooms this morning, that will be just another part of my job. I can help all of you. When do you want to go?"

Biting his lower lip, he seemed to be mulling it over. "Sometime tomorrow. It's too late to go today."

"The morning might be good." We can get the shopping out of the way first thing. "Get with your brothers and let me know." I turned to leave, but then felt his hand on my shoulder. Why my damn knees had to go weak confused me.

"So tonight then, can you show me around town?" Tyrell turned me back around to face him. "You know, show me the nightlife?"

The man clearly wanted to use me for more than just helping him to find places to buy clothes and get his party on. "I'm not interested." The guy would be one of those love 'em and leave 'em kind of men. And I had to live with this one.

"In?" he asked as if he didn't know.

"In you." I took a step back to make more space between us.

"Didn't think you were." He seemed cool about it, but the way he slid one hand through his dark hair told me I'd kind of blown him out of the water with my remark.

"Cool. I know about guys like you, Tyrell Gentry." I walked backward toward the door. "You like to screw anything you can."

"Wrong." He walked toward me. "You don't know me, Ella. Not at all."

"You think you're so cute, don't ya?" I wasn't looking for an answer; he thought he was God's gift to women!

"What do you think about yourself?" He kept coming my way.

I stopped and held up one hand. "What do you think you're doing?"

"I'm going down to grab my bag out of the truck." He went past me, walking out the door. "Since you suppose I've got a high opinion of myself, how about you? Where did you get that idea? I wanted to pay you to show me where to shop and hang out. You're kind of conceited, don't ya think?"

He had other intentions, I was sure of it. "You rich guys are all the same, Tyrell Gentry. Don't act like you're not. I'm not one to put myself in situations and get more attention than I want. Find yourself another person to show you around town."

He stopped in his tracks, and then turned to face me. His right eye twitched. "Ella Finley, I've never had more than a few bucks in my pocket until yesterday. I'm not who you say I am. But *you're* exactly who I think you are."

My hand went to my hip as I lashed out, "And just what do you think I am?"

"A very young girl." With that, he turned back around and went down the stairs as I stood there with my jaw dropped.

"Am not," I whispered. "Big jerk. Thinks I don't know what he's up to. He wants to get in my pants. He can say what he wants, but I know he does."

"You talking to yourself, Ella?" a man's voice came from behind me.

Spinning around, I saw Cash and Jasper standing there. "Where did you guys come from?"

"Our rooms. We brought our bags up," Jasper told me. "Looks like you didn't hear us when you and Tyrell were in his room."

Their smiles made my heart freeze as I thought about what they overheard. "Yeah, I didn't hear you. I'll tell you what I told him then. If you'll put your dirty laundry in the hamper…"

Jasper held up his hand. "We do our own laundry, thank you. Just leave our rooms and restrooms off your list of chores, 'kay?"

"But…"

Cash put his arm around my shoulders, and Jasper came up on the other side of me as they took me down the stairs. Cash reminded me, "We haven't always been rich, Ella. We haven't ever been catered to or picked up after. And we're not about to start acting like spoiled rich men now."

Just as we got to the bottom step, Tyrell came into the foyer. The look on his face when he saw his brother with his arm around me was priceless. His mouth gaped and he froze in place.

Cash moved his arm as I said, "I've got it. Leave your bedrooms suites alone. Does that go for you, too, Tyrell?"

He stood there, looking oddly at his youngest brother. "You can vacuum my bedroom every day. How's that?"

"Your wish is my command." I rolled my eyes, walking away from the three of them. As soon as I got out of their view, I fell against the wall as my legs went wobbly.

That look on Tyrell's face told me more than I wanted to know. *He likes me!*

TYRELL

The intense jealousy that came over me when I saw Cash's arm around Ella made no sense. Neither did the words that came out of my mouth as soon as I knew Ella was no longer in the lobby, "What the fuck, Cash?"

He looked like he had no idea what I mean. "What's up?"

"Your arms." I gestured to his two ape-like appendages. "All over her."

"What?" Cash laughed, and so did Jasper. "You look peculiar, Tyrell. Are you envious?"

"Fuck no," I busted. "We need to show our employees the same respect we'd show someone who worked in an office for us. Avoiding sexual harassment lawsuits is wise."

"Sure." Cash didn't seem to care about that. "She knew I meant nothing sexual by that. You, on the other hand, seem to think so. Wonder why that is?"

Jasper elbowed him in the ribs. "'Cause he's sweet on her."

"Will you both just shut up?" I picked up my bag that had fallen out of my hand when they came down the stairs, looking like they just had a threesome.

Taking the stairs two at a time, I went to my room to put my things away. We decided to stay, so I wanted to make the place feel more like home.

Locking the door behind me, I started pulling things out of my bag. When I put them away, I found the amount of clothes to be pitiful. Why not shop online?

Who needs Ella Finley to help anyway?

Just thinking of the girl made me hot. The shower looked inviting as I passed the bathroom. Stripping, I figured why not enjoy a hot shower?

There were jets everywhere, and when I turned them on, they made a loud sound that muted everything else. My mind slipped away as the jets pummeled my body from all sides.

Why'd Ella have to think so badly about me? I'd had one girlfriend all through high school. She left for college in Austin, and we lost touch.

Sure, a few women after her, but nothing serious. That didn't make me a man-whore.

The right woman just hadn't come along yet was all. And not because I was some wolf who pursued a woman until he got what he wanted, then left. I wasn't that guy.

But what kind of guy was I?

I want *the maid*, for God's sakes. Not that it was awful that she was a maid, but she was *my* maid. And she lives in *my* home. That's what made it appalling.

But even as I pictured her sweet face, my cock went hard. I ran my soapy hand over it. "You really shouldn't get so excited. She should be off limits. She *works* for me. What if we didn't work out? I'd see her all the time! I couldn't fire her just because we didn't want to see each other anymore."

And now I'm talking to myself!

Closing my eyes, I leaned back and let the water work its magic. But my mind was doing some magic of its own. Ella steps into the shower and drops her clothes. "Can I come in?"

"Sure, come on in, baby. The water's fine." I pulled her into my arms. "Glad you came to your senses."

"Me, too," she cooed. "Tyrell, did you know that I've wanted to do this since you first caught me in those strong arms?"

"Tell me, baby. You can do anything you want." I kissed her red lips.

Barely breathing, she batted her long, thick, dark lashes. "I want to wrap my legs around your waist and have you fill me with that long, thick dick of yours, Tyrell Gentry."

Her ass in my hands, I lifted her up, and she put her legs around me as I sunk deep into her hot core. "Oh, yeah. You fit me like a glove, baby."

"Oh, Tyrell, you're so big." She put her head on my shoulder as her body stretched to accommodate my girth.

"You'll get used to the size, baby. You certainly will." I moved back and forth, using her tight cunt to stroke my hard cock. "I'm going to show you what it feels like to belong to me. You'll feel things you've never felt before."

"Tyrell?" she raised her head to look at me. "Are you going to give me an orgasm?"

"Over and over again." I kissed her as I pinned her to the wall, the jets pounding our bodies as I pounded her with a passionate ferocity. "Your cunt is so tight."

"Your cock is so big," she moaned.

"Your *tits* are so big." I leaned down to take one into my mouth.

Her nails raked over my back as she arched up to allow me to suck her tit. "Oh, Tyrell, you make me feel like a woman. Sorry I was so childish. I promise never to behave that way again."

"See that you don't." I moved to bite her neck, leaving my marks up and down her creamy flesh as she whimpered and begged for more. "You're all woman, Ella. *My* woman."

"Oh, oh, oh," she cried out as I gave her more than she'd ever expected. "Tyrell!"

Her cunt clenched all around my cock, but I wasn't about to give in. "You like that, baby?" I slammed my cock into her pulsing walls even harder. "You like it when I fuck you raw?"

"Yes!" she gasped. "Fuck me, Tyrell. Fuck me hard. Oh, God!"

Her body gave into mine, letting me take her any way I wanted to. "Your body was made for me. Your cunt hugs my cock like a glove."

"Your cock is so hard and huge I was made to ride it." She ran her tongue up the side of my neck. "Fuck me all night long, Tyrell Gentry. Show me who owns me."

"*I* own you." I slammed into her hard and heavy, over and over until my body could take no more. "*You* are *mine*." I took her face in my hands as I came inside of her. "You are mine, you hear me?"

She nodded. "I don't want anyone else."

I kissed her body as she went into another orgasm, milking my cock for all it would give her. Out of breath, we held onto each other until both of our bodies no longer pulsed or throbbed.

When my eyes opened, I looked in the foggy mirror, only seeing the shape of my body. "Not her, Tyrell. Anyone but her."

Sagging against the wall, I watched the powerful shower jets wash my cum down the drain. I couldn't recall such a vivid sexual fantasy ever. Not even in my teen years when I discovered what my hand could do.

Ella was young, feisty, prickly, and mean. She thought I was out for one thing and one thing only. And damn if that girl wasn't right.

I wanted her. I wanted her tight, tiny body. I wanted to feel that rosebud mouth move over my hard cock. I wanted to watch her pretty head bobbing at my waist. Her legs wrapped around me, my cock buried in her sweet pussy...

"Argh!" I turned off the water, then got out of the shower.

I need to find a bar. Some booze to chill me out and get my mind off of Miss Spitfire. Wrapping a towel around my waist, I went out to see if my brothers had come back up.

A quick knock on Jasper's door, "Who is it?"

I opened the door, and he looked at my state. "Let's go out. Get ready."

"I'm in." Jasper got off his bed and went to prepare himself.

Next door in Cash's room, I found him flipping through the channels on the giant television. "What's up?"

"Get ready. Let's go out." I shut the door, then heard women talking downstairs.

For some reason, I stood there, looking down, waiting for them to come into view. When I saw Ella and her sister walking side by side, I clenched my jaw as my cock jerked.

Although I hadn't made a sound, Ella's head turned, and she

looked up at me. Putting her hand over her mouth, her eyes were aimed directly at my dick.

When I looked down, I saw what she was looking at. "Shit." My cock had gone hard.

Walking back to my bedroom, I couldn't remember a time I'd been so humiliated. I needed copious amounts of alcohol to get that girl off my mind. I *had* to get her off my mind; I couldn't have her. It would be wrong.

What's worse, she knew it all along. I lied to myself, but she didn't. And now I had to forget her.

Booze and women would be the only priorities I'd have for tonight. Hopefully, Cash was right and the women of Carthage, Texas, would be easy to coax into some sexual activity.

I must've needed to get laid pretty badly if a fantasy about screwing the sassy housekeeper had me going. And to get a hard-on just seeing her, too? I was out of it!

Maybe it was all this change? Or all the wealth? Perhaps a combination of the two? What had gotten into me? But I had to get into some other woman, or I'd sure as heck dip my dick in Ella's hot pussy.

She'd be in my bed before she knew what happened. She might not have known that, but I did. And I couldn't let that happen, no matter what I had to do to stop it.

ELLA

Sunday brunches were my favorite. Christmas was the only other time Chef Todd prepared more food than his famous Sunday brunches. To top it, Sunday was my day off.

Feeling happy for no other reason than the free time and the tons of splendid cooking, I skipped to the dining room—dubbed the Brunch Room. The smell of smoky bacon, cinnamon, and coffee was in the air. My mouth watered as I made my way down the long corridor.

"Wow, what a spread," I heard Jasper remark.

I stopped, not wanting to see Tyrell after seeing him wearing nothing but a towel the day before. A towel that had tented over his boner. It was quite intriguing—but mostly repulsive.

I was glad Darleen hadn't been paying attention and she missed it. Well, most of it. She did see him running away though, and we both cracked up.

"Do you think Tyrell will come down to eat?" Cash inquired.

Jasper answered, "I don't know. He got pretty lit last night at The Watering Hole. And he was dancing with anyone who'd let him. He's probably worn out. We might not see him much today."

I fisted my hands at my sides. The Watering Hole was a bar in town. It was a pretty rough place—bikers went there on occasion.

The women were promiscuous. And Tyrell had been dancing with them. Who knows what else he'd done?

Suddenly, I wasn't hungry. I was livid; I turned around and hurried back up staircase. What am I doing? Why am I doing it? At his bedroom door, I paused and pounded on it.

About the fourth round of consistent knocks, I heard his gravelly voice, "What the fuck?"

Then it hit me. I had temporarily gone out of my mind. I ran down the stairs as fast as lightning. In record time, I made it to the Brunch Room and stopped to catch my breath before going inside to join the others.

Walking in like I hadn't just run the length of the entire mansion, I said, "Good morning. How was your night?"

Jasper turned away from the buffet with a plate piled so high it defied gravity. "Morning, Ella. We had quite the time last night. We found this bar called The Watering Hole and had a few drinks, danced with some nice ladies, and then came home. And what did you do?"

Picking up a plate, I looked at the vast array of foods. "I stayed home. Watched some Netflix. Sounds like you guys had fun though."

"Tyrell mentioned he invited you to come along, but you turned him down," Cash commented as he took a seat with a plate stacked equally as high as his brother's.

I waved a fork to gesture at their plates. "You guys know you can come back for more, right? No need to pile those plates so high."

They looked at the amount of food they had, and both laughed, then Jasper acknowledged, "We don't have a refined bone in our bodies."

Mom came in, carrying a carafe of fresh-squuezed orange juice. "Good morning, everyone." She looked at the two men who sat at the big table. "Where's Tyrell?"

I took a seat a few chairs down from Cash and looked at them for their reply as if I had no clue to why Tyrell wasn't there. Cash shook his head. "He probably will not be coming down, Miss Finley. He imbibed a bit too much."

"Oh, that's a shame," Mom said as she put the juice down, then made herself a plate.

Dad and Kyle came in; both had dirt on their jeans already. "Morning," Dad stated, sounding gruffer than usual.

Jasper caught on right away. "Are you having troubles this morning?"

Kyle nodded. "One of the cows had a stillborn calf—a male. Two more are in labor now. It'll be a stretched day, I'm afraid."

Jasper looked at Cash. "Hey, maybe we can help them out?"

"Sure." Cash looked at my father. "Mr. Finley, would it be alright if we came along with you guys after breakfast?"

"That would be great!" Dad smiled, which was unusual. "The more hands, the easier it'll be."

"Cool," Cash said as he dug into his meal. "We'll see childbirth."

Mom laughed. "It's not exactly the same as when a woman has a baby, but it's fascinating just the same."

With much to go tend to, the men ate quickly, then headed out to spend the day in the cattle barn, helping the cows along with their labor. Mom and I ate much slower than they had, preferring to enjoy the food, instead of gulping it down like mountain lions.

My sister's voice drifted down the hallway, "You look like hell, Tyrell."

"I feel like hell, Darleen," came Tyrell's voice. "Something woke me up out of a dead sleep. With this headache, I couldn't get back to sleep. Maybe if I eat something, then take a handful of aspirin I might live."

Darleen wasn't lying about Tyrell's appearance. When they walked in, he had dark circles under his eyes, his hair wasn't neatly combed, parted to the left as usual, and he had dark stubble over his chin and jaw line.

I was staring at his face when his bloodshot eyes met mine. "Top of the morning, Ella." He looked at my mother who sat across from me, "Mrs. Finley," then went directly for the coffee.

I got up to get some of the tiny sausages. Standing next to him as he poured the coffee, I asked, "Why did you drink so much?"

He shrugged those massive shoulders. "I don't know."

"Your brothers went with my dad and brother to lend a hand in delivering calves. If you want, we can go down there on the golf cart after you eat." I picked up another dish. "Here, let me make you a plate. You look like you're about to fall down. Go sit, and I'll bring it to you."

"*You're* being nice to me?" He looked at me with drooping eyes. "I must really look horrible."

"Believe me, you do." It wasn't a joke. "Go sit down."

Taking his coffee, he shuffled to the table and took a seat. My sister stepped up beside me, making her plate as she whispered, "Look at you being all nurturing, Ella."

"Hush." I grabbed a dish and put two poached eggs on a scoop of hash browns, a thick slice of Canadian bacon, a cheddar cheese scone, and then carried it to him. "Here you go. Eat as much as you can. I bet it'll help. And there's some chicken tortilla soup. I'll fix a bowl of that for you, too. What kind of juice do you like? There's plenty to choose from."

"Water," he said as he picked up his fork that I lay next to the plate. His eyes came up to mine. "Thank you, Ella. This is kind of you."

My mom stared coldly at me, but I ignored it. "You're welcome, Tyrell."

After getting his water and filling a piping hot bowl of soup topped with fresh cilantro, I took a seat across from him.

"This soup looks like it has everything but the kitchen sink in it," Tyrell said, eyeing the broth.

Mom clued him in on what was in it, "Todd makes the chicken soup with rice first. Then he cuts up fresh jalapenos, onion, and garlic, and adds them along with chopped tomatoes, salt, and pepper. The cheese from Oaxaca in Mexico goes on the bottom. Fill the bowl with soup and add some avocado and cilantro on top."

Tyrell took a bite. "This is great. But you left out the tortilla chips that are in here, Mrs. Finley."

I spoke up, "I crushed them in the bowl before I poured the soup in."

His blue eyes settled on mine. "Well, it's all delicious. Thank you. I feel better already."

I couldn't help but smile. "You're welcome."

Mom got up, taking her plate with her. "I have some shopping to do in town today. Darleen, would you care to join me?"

"Yeah," Darleen said. "I've got some things to do as well."

Mom put her plate in the tray for the dirty dishes as she looked at me. "Ella, your father thinks it's a good idea for the men to get familiar with the ranch. Could you take Tyrell on a tour of the horse facilities once he feels up to it?"

"Oh, I'm up to it," Tyrell said quickly. "This miracle soup has done the trick. I'll just shower," he ran his hand over the dark stubble on his face, "shave, then put on some jeans and boots and meet you, Ella."

"'Kay." I couldn't believe how excited I was over something so simple. "I'll be in the garage. The golf cart is probably charged up."

Half an hour later, on our way to the horse barn, the cold wind hitting us in the face made our cheeks red. A scarf was wrapped around my neck as I drove the two-seater cart. Tyrell looked at me, then reached over and pulled it up to cover my nose. "That'll help keep the cold wind off your face."

I smiled under the scarf. "It helps. Thanks."

Stopping in front of the barn doors, we jumped off and headed inside. I pulled the scarf off my nose as Tyrell looked at the many stalls. "Are these all full?"

"No. We've got some empty ones." I walked over to the first one and pointed to the gold plaque on the wooden door. "This is Coy's Burden. Dad said he's named after your father."

"Why did my grandfather name him that?" Tyrell reached in to run his hand over the black stallion's nose. "Hey there, boy. How're you doing?"

"No one knows the reasons behind anything that man did." I walked to the next stall where Fiona's Secret stood, waiting for some attention. "He didn't believe in the need to explain things or respond to anyone."

Tyrell turned to face me. "Did you know about my grandfather's mistress?"

"Hilda?" Everyone who worked here knew about her. "I felt

sorry for her. It was like she felt guilty or something. Like she deserved to be treated like that."

"Why was that?" he asked then his eyes went wide. "Ella, do you know Hilda's last name?"

"Stevens, why?" I asked him.

"That's why!" He leaned back on one of the stalls. "She's my mother's aunt. She used to live in Shreveport."

"Yeah, she did." I never did understaand everything about that woman. "Mom told us she just showed up one day. It was before Fiona died. Your grandmother was beyond pissed and told her to get out of the house and to never set foot on the property again. Fiona yelled that she'd set her up in a nice house in Shreveport if Hilda had promised she'd never come back to Carthage."

"So, my grandmother made my mother's aunt leave town." Tyrell looked puzzled. "My mother was taken to her aunt's. My grandfather had paid off her family to run her out of town. It's making more sense, but not entirely. When did Hilda start coming back around?"

"Mom said it wasn't long after Fiona passed away." That was odd, too. "Your grandfather brought Hilda here. He kept her at the mansion for a while, then took her back to the house he bought her in town when he got tired of having her here. Not that she got to do anything other than stay in her rooms when she was here."

"This is all so confusing." Tyrell looked at me. "Could you could take me to meet Hilda?"

"Why?" Apart from being his great aunt, why would he need to meet her?

"I've got questions." He bit his lower lip. "Lots of questions, Ella."

TYRELL

Climbing into one of the estate's trucks, Ella and I set out to meet Hilda. I hadn't been so excited about anything in a long time. Part of it was getting some information on my family. The other part was spending time with Ella. And she wasn't being snippy with me, either. She was actually being nice for a change.

"So, who'd you meet at the bar, Tyrell?" she asked as we made our way into town.

I turned off the county road to head to the main street. "It would be a lie to say I remember anyone's name. I don't know why I drank so much." I did know why; I was trying to get Ella off my mind! And I did for a while. But then I came home and dreamt about her.

"That's not a very nice place to hang out," she said, then pointed up ahead. "Take a left there."

"It's a little rough, I'll give ya that." I looked over at her, liking the way she had her dark hair up in a loose bun. She looked adorable. "I can see why you think that way. It's certainly not a place for you."

She looked at me with narrowed eyes. "You think I'm some little girl, sure, you've told me. That's not why I don't like that bar. It's because only trampy women go there."

"Darleen said she'd gone there more than a handful of times." It's a valid point that not all the women who went to The Watering Hole were tramps.

"Do you know my sister's reputation, Tyrell?" Ella shook her head. "It's not good. Last year alone, she had three different boyfriends!"

"She's single now," I said.

"How do you know?" Ella's sapphire eyes had a fire in them.

She seemed to be jealous? Even though I shouldn't have been trying to make her that way, my mouth kept on chatting, "She told me."

Ella crossed her arms over her chest. All it did was accentuate her cleavage that peeked out from underneath her pink sweater. "Why'd she do that?"

"Cash asked her." I smiled, knowing that got me out of the hot spot. "He's nosy like that."

"Oh." Her arms came down to her sides and her eyes widened. "Why hasn't he asked me if I'm single?"

He knew I had a thing for her is why. Even though I protested that I didn't, my brothers knew better. "Who knows? Who cares?"

"Oh, this is it right here." She pointed at a large pink house with a pink Cadillac parked in the driveway. "This is where Hilda lives. That's her car. Your grandfather gave her that, too."

Parking the truck, I felt a little nervous. "How am I supposed to do this?"

Ella opened the door. "Come on. Don't fret. I'll be with you. I'll start the conversation."

As we got out, I wondered why in the hell she was so helpful out of the blue, but I didn't dare ask. Following her on the sidewalk, I stayed behind as she rang the doorbell. Moments later, a woman who slightly resembled my mom opened the door with a frown.

"Ella, what are you doing here?"

Ella took a step back and reached for my hand. Taking it, she pulled me forward. "Hilda, this is your great-nephew, Tyrell Gentry. He wanted to meet you."

We both just stood there, staring at each other. I saw my mother in her, and she probably saw the same in me. "I'd like to ask you some questions, if I may?"

She nodded, then stepped back. "Come in."

The living room, filled with expensive furnishings, looked like it was a showplace instead of a habitat. "Nice place."

Hilda nodded. "Thank you. When Collin was here, he wanted things to be nice." She took a seat on the sofa, crossing her long legs. "I suppose you've heard about our relationship."

Nodding, I took a seat next to Ella on the loveseat across from Hilda. "Yeah. My grandfather drove my mother out of town. And the marriage of my parents happened anyway. What happened between you and my grandparents sending you to Shreveport in the first place is beyond me."

"It won't hurt to let you in on things." Hilda closed her eyes as if she was going back in time. "We met in high school, Collin and I. It started way back then. Everything we did was shrouded in secrecy. Our families never knew a thing about us. We graduated from high school, and he went to college. He lived in an apartment in Lubbock, and he got me one as well."

"Still, he kept you a secret then?" I inquired.

She nodded. "Yes. Even when there was no one to hide from."

"That had to be upsetting," Ella sympathized.

"It was. But I'd take whatever Collin would give me. Any time he had for me, I was available." Hilda took a deep breath. "While in college, he met Fiona. He took her home to meet his family. I remained in Lubbock alone. When he got back, we argued about what he'd done, and he announced we could never become more. He'd asked her to marry him in front of his family and she accepted."

Ella put her hand over her mouth. "Oh, Lord."

"Yes," Hilda said softly. "That's when I lost it. I went to Fiona and told her everything about us. That didn't work out as I had expected it to. She told me to leave him alone. He was now *her* fiancé and soon to be *her* husband, and our fling was over."

"But it didn't end, did it?" I asked.

"Not at all." Hilda smiled. "Your grandfather loved me. He came to me that very night and cried on his hands and knees. He begged me not to end things with him. He said he'd still have time for me, too."

"So, you kept on seeing him," Ella said. "Even though you knew you'd always have to stay concealed."

Hilda nodded. "I knew my place in life. I was from a poor family, not in the same league as Collin Gentry's wife. Fiona truly belonged there. She came from a prestigious family in Dallas. She was refined and elegant. And she gave him a son just under a year after they were married."

"You and he never had children?" I requested.

Her face told me the answer wasn't a good one. "Your grandfather took me to a doctor in Dallas when I was eighteen. We had a pregnancy scare the year before, and he didn't want that to take place again. I had my tubes tied."

"He ruined you," Ella gasped.

Hilda nodded. "Yes, he did. You see, Fiona wore his wedding ring, and I wore his collar. I was his mistress, nothing more nor less. One day Fiona found out. After sixteen years of devotion to that man, his wife ended it. At least for a while."

My grandmother sent Hilda away. "She paid for you to move to Shreveport and got you a house there. How did you pay your bills? Did you get a job?"

"I never had a job in my life," she told me. "Your grandmother paid the bills. She sent me a check each week to cover my expenses and took care of me. Collin couldn't find me. He'd have killed us both if I hadn't stayed hidden."

"Wow," Ella exclaimed, then looked at me. "This is so harsh. You come from terrible grandparents, Tyrell. Are your mom and dad anything like them?"

"Not at all." I bumped her shoulder with mine. "Don't be anxious about us being like that."

"So, you two are seeing each other?" Hilda asked.

"No," we both said promptly.

I smiled at Ella. "She dislikes me."

Ella didn't say a word; her eyes were glued to the carpet. Hilda chuckled. "When your grandmother died, my family told me. I still stayed where I was. Collin paid my family to spill the beans, and he came and got me, brought me back to this house, and took me out to the ranch from time to time as well."

"Yeah, we heard about that." How did she get by now that he was gone? "Did he leave you anything?"

"I'm on the estate's payroll." She tapped her temple. "The ranch pays me for consulting. I make a pretty penny."

Ella frowned. "But you don't really do a thing."

"No, I don't." Hilda sat there, looking at me. "Now that you know that, you'll have those payments stopped, Tyrell. Your mother must've told you what I did. You must hate me."

Shaking my head, I had no intentions of cutting her out. "You can keep getting the money. My grandfather screwed you over enough as it is. Thanks for being honest with me, Hilda."

"How is your mother?" she asked. "Is she happy?"

"My mom and dad are very happy." I never had a clue what they walked away from, but they made the right decision. "We'll get out of your hair now."

Hilda got up, walking us to the door, she said, "It's nice to know that she's happy. I've felt accountable for a very long time. Responsible for keeping her locked up. And then letting her go with your father when he came for her. They thought they made the escape behind my back. They hadn't. I watched them leave; I just didn't do anything to stop them. I felt guilty over both of them. Had I kept her hidden away better, your father wouldn't have lost everything."

"My father didn't lose a thing. He found love." I knew now that love was worth more than all the money in the world. "Stop feeling guilty. None of what happened was ever your fault, Hilda."

She nodded, but just saying that wouldn't ease her guilt. She had carried it for a long time. But at least I knew things better than before.

As we got into the truck, Ella looked at the floorboard. "Times were really shitty back then. Your grandfather didn't marry the woman he really loved because of her being from a poor family. Your dad wasn't supposed to marry your mom because she was from a poor family and a maid at the ranch to boot."

She should know I had no problems like that. "Being a maid

doesn't mean you're less than anyone else. And it definitely doesn't mean you're not marriage material, Ella."

She looked at me with wide eyes. "Do you really think that, Tyrell?"

"I do." I took my fist and lightly cuffed her chin. "I bet you have to beat the boys off with a stick."

She shook her head. "Not so far, I haven't."

I took off to go back to the property. "So how many boyfriends do you have?"

"You don't want to know." She looked out the window.

"Come on, tell me." I pulled onto the main street to find barely a car on the road. "Damn, this town is empty on Sundays."

Ella looked at me. "How many girlfriends have you had, Tyrell?"

"A few. Nothing serious, though." I took a left to get to the county road. "So how many boyfriends, Ella?"

"Tyrell, I've had no boyfriends. I haven't even held hands with anyone before. Not like for real holding hands, you know." She bit her lower lip; she was out of her element talking to me this way.

"Then, you've never been kissed either, huh?" My cock swelled in my jeans as she shook her head. "You're a virgin?" She nodded, and my heart stopped a beat.

ELLA

Being alone all day with Tyrell had me feeling different. I'd thought about him a lot once we parted ways for the night after dinner.

We filled everyone in on Hilda. It felt good to be a part of Tyrell's endeavors. And when dinner was over, he walked out of the dining room with me. His shoulder touched mine. "Ella, we're trying to figure out what to do on this ranch. Any ideas?"

He was asking for my opinion! "To be honest, Tyrell, I don't know what you're good at."

He laughed, and the sound made my insides melt. "I'm good at most things I try. And I can learn, too. I saw you messing with a rope in the barn earlier today. Can you teach me how to do that?"

"Maybe." I stopped as we'd come to the place where I go one way, and he another. "I'm off tomorrow, too, if you want to learn then. It's not too difficult."

He looked over his shoulder, then back at me. "Cool. Teach me what you know, and I'll teach you what I know."

The way my body went white-hot made me uncomfortable. He didn't mean what I thought. Did it mean he'd teach me about sex? That idea wouldn't go away as I laid in my bed that night.

Tossing and turning, I felt so ill at ease. Everything ached. Even as I rubbed my arms, my legs, my boobs, nothing made the pain go away. What was worse was the ache inside of me.

I'd never experimented with masturbation. Frankly, it seemed kind of nasty to touch myself. But without will, I found my hands moving on their own to ease that throbbing ache Tyrell had caused in me.

Closing my eyes, I just let it all go and did whatever came naturally. Tyrell's blue eyes hovered over me as he eased his naked body over mine. "You're so beautiful, Ella."

I ran my hands over his stubbled cheeks. "You are, too, Tyrell."

Moving slowly, he inched forward until our lips met, and he pushed his tongue into my mouth. Fireworks went off inside my head as he kissed me deeply, yet so softly.

His hands moved over my tits, then down to my waist. I sucked in my breath as his fingers moved over my clit, then through my hot wet folds. His finger pressed against my virgin pussy, then he pushed it in.

I cried out with desire, "Yes!"

He pushed it in and pulled it out with slow movements. I spread my legs so he could push his finger into me even deeper. His thumb grazed my clit until it was swollen and hard.

"I'm going to make you come, Ella." He leaned over me, his finger still pumping, then his warm lips pressed against my clit. Kissing it, he groaned, then licked it over and over until I was arching my back and screaming, "Tyrell! Yes! God, yes!"

The way my insides felt... My legs shook, my breathing was gasping and erratic, and my heart pounded like I'd run a mile as fast as I could.

Getting off my bed, I was dripping with sweat, and I went to take a shower. My legs were shaky as I made my way to the bathroom; even my vision was blurry. "Oh, shit. What have I done?"

Starting the shower, I got it nice and hot, then slipped under the cascade, letting it relax me. My body had reacted bizarrely! What would happen if the real Tyrell had done that?

"I probably would've died and gone to heaven." I put my face under the stream of water as it fell out of the showerhead.

I've never done anything like this, and another thought came into my head. *What if I'm not a virgin anymore?*

Had I messed up my hymen in the process of fingering myself? Concerned, I got out of the shower, put on a clean nighty, then went to see if my sister was still awake.

Softly knocking on her door, I heard her inside, "Who is it?"

"Darleen, it's me. Can I see you for a second?" My hands knotted thinking of what I'd say.

"Yeah, come in," she called out.

Upon entering her room, I felt some heat as embarrassment filled me. "Darleen, I might have messed up."

"You?" she asked with a giggle. "Doubtful. Nothing is so bad, sis."

"How many ways are there to lose your virginity?" I blurted.

"You and Tyrell were alone a lot today," she said, then crossed her arms over her chest. "Did he do something to you?"

"No." I shook my head ferociously. "He's not like that. It's me. I did something."

"To him?" she asked. "He didn't get you to suck his dick, did he?"

"God, no!" Everything she was coming up with was worse! "I did something to myself."

She ran her hand over her face. "While he watched?"

"No!" *Wow, she's got some gnarly imagination!* "Darleen, I stuck my finger inside my pussy. Have I de-virgined myself?"

She was close to being speechless. "Okay, you did this while you were alone? Tyrell was nowhere around?"

"Yes. He wasn't around. I just did it." I wasn't about to tell her that he was there in my imagination. "I've never masturbated before, that's why I'm asking you."

Her eyes narrowed. "If you've never done it before, why now?"

I didn't want her to know that Tyrell was the reason. "Look, have I screwed up my virginity? It's a simple question."

"Did you bleed?" Darleen ran her hand just above the covers over her genital area. "You know, here?"

"No." I hadn't seen blood when I'd taken a shower, and there was none on my bed, either. "Does that mean my hymen is still intact?"

"Yes. Plus, your finger isn't long enough to break it. If that were the case, the first time you used a tampon would've done that." She smiled at me. "I'm glad you came to me, Ella. Looks like you're maturing."

"Uh-huh." I turned to leave. "Thanks, Darleen." Then I wanted to clarify something and turned around to find her pulling something out of a drawer. "Don't you tell a soul about this, agreed?"

"Of course." She held out a long white box. "Come here. I bought this last week but haven't used it. You can have it. It's way better than using your finger, trust me."

Walking back to see what it was, I flipped the box open to discover a long, projectile object. "What's this?"

"Are you serious, Ella?" she asked with an astonished expression.

"Yeah." I pulled the wiggly thing out of the box. Shaking it, I asked. "What do you do with this?"

She reached out and took it away, then pushed a small button at the base. It began to hum. Then she pressed the tip of it against my cheek. "Feel that?"

"It vibrates." I took it from her, looking it over.

"It's a vibrator." Darleen confided. "You know what I'm talking about, right?"

I tried to close my hand around it, yet it was too big. "Use it to massage your body! My body has been aching. This could help. I guess."

Putting it against my arm, I looked at my sister who said, "It goes between your legs, Ella."

I pulled my nighty up to put it between my legs. "Like this?"

"Ella! For God's sakes!" Darleen grabbed the vibrator and turned it off. "It's a dildo—a fake dick. It goes in your vagina. God, are you really that naïve?"

I couldn't believe she'd given me that! Aghast, I said, "That would certainly take my virginity away, Darleen! I should've never come to you about this." I turned to leave, dismayed.

"Ella, it's not the same thing. Come here, you fool. Take this!

Experiment with it," she suggested as I walked hastily toward the door.

"No way. I'm not spoiling myself with that. Yuck!" Shuddering, I opened the door. "You're so gross, Darleen!"

"Wait," she interrupted. "Ella, look at me!"

With my hand on my hip: "What?"

"Start thinking about birth control. If you're experimenting now, you may find yourself wanting to actually have sex," she said. "And that's perfectly natural. But be on some type of contraception. I'll make an appointment for you tomorrow at my clinic. Be careful with things like this!"

"Won't a doctor have to examine me?" I didn't want that.

"If you get pregnant, more than one doctor will have to treat you," she said. "Think about it. I'll make an appointment first thing in the morning. Get your ass up nice and early, and I'll take you."

"I don't know." I started feeling sick about the arrangement. "I think I'll decline. For now,, Darleen."

"Look, you think you've got time, but you don't," she warned me. "I've seen how you look at him, Ella. You've never looked at anyone the way you look at him."

"Who?" I had no idea who she was talking about!

"Tyrell, chickey-poo!" she exclaimed. "He looks at you that way, too. Better to be safe than sorry. I'm making that appointment, so be ready. You're getting on birth control tomorrow. I'm not taking no for an answer."

"Fine." I left her room, my feet feeling heavy, and stumbling to my room. "Being a grown-up kind of sucks."

TYRELL

I spent the night before fantasizing about Ella again. She had gotten under my skin even more after spending time with her the day before. I'd begun to think that trying to forget about her was pretty damn useless. And she'll teach me how to work the rope the next day, so I had high hopes we'd end up spending the whole day together again.

As I got to the breakfast nook, my brothers and Mrs. Finely were there, but no one else. "Good morning." I went to get a cup of coffee and tried to smother my disappointment at not seeing Ella.

Jasper lifted his cup of coffee in a greeting. "Good morning, Tyrell. Cash and I are going with Mr. Finley after breakfast to the feed store. Care to join us?"

"As fun as that sounds, I better pass." I took the coffee and went to sit at the table.

Mrs. Finley frowned at me, her hand on her hip. That was something her youngest daughter did a lot, too. "Boy, aren't you going to eat something?"

I'd thought to see if Ella showed up before making a plate. "Um, not yet."

With a sigh, she pulled the lids down on the silver chafing

platters. "Don't wait too long. Eggs don't set well for more than an hour in these things."

Cash picked up a piece of bacon and waved it at me. "You better get some of the bacon before I eat it all up! Bacon is never this good! How come you don't want to go to the feed store with us this morning?"

Come up with something! Or they'll bother me until I came with them or told them the truth. "The horses are appealing to me. I'd like to make them my special interest."

"That's a good idea, Tyrell," Mrs. Finley said with a nod. "You *should* find things that interest you here."

Fidgeting in my seat, what's keeping Ella so long? Even her sister... Or had they already come? "Where are the girls this morning, Mrs. Finley?"

"Oh, they went into town this morning. They left together, which is a bit unusual." She walked toward the door, then looked back at me. "You eat now, Tyrell. If you're waiting for anyone, you'll be waiting for nothing."

I got up and made myself a plate, then took a seat as my brothers stared at me. Jasper asked, "You were waiting for Ella?"

"Not really." I took a bite of the eggs.

Cash didn't seem to believe me. "Then why'd you make a plate only after you found out she'd already gone?"

"No reason." They were getting into my business too much! "When are you guys leaving to the feed store?"

"After we're done eating." Jasper arched one eyebrow. "Why, do you want to go now that you know Ella isn't around?"

"Nope." I had no idea when she'd be coming back and didn't want to be gone when she did. She might get the wrong idea about me and think I didn't want to spend time with her if I wasn't here waiting for her.

How out of character is that? I never waited around for anyone! But I couldn't make myself go with my brothers.

"So, what are you going to do at the horse stable all alone?" Jasper teased.

"Check it all out. Get to know the horses." That's what I'll do. I had an idea of how today would go, and it wasn't going that way at all.

My brothers got up and put their empty plates in the dish bin, then walked out, shaking their heads as they left me alone. They probably thought I was stupid for sitting around, waiting for Ella to return. Somehow, I didn't care what they thought. I *wanted* to wait for her.

So, I waited. In the library, I discovered some books on racehorses. Three hours went by as I found out all sorts of cool things about the horses. When I checked my cell for the time, I just about lost it. "Where the heck is she!?"

The library was close to the garage, and I knew I'd hear the car pull up when they returned. And as I stood there, looking out the window, I thought about how dumb it was to hang out, doing nothing but waiting.

But I kept on waiting anyway.

Grabbing my coat from my bedroom, I went down to the garage for a gold cart to head on down to the horse stable. At least Ella wouldn't think I'd sat around in the house waiting. The last thing I needed was for her to think she had the upper hand.

Another hour later, as I roamed around the barn examining things, the dogs barked. Someone had come up the drive, so I got back on the cart and hightailed it up to the house. Sure enough, Ella and Darleen were pulling into the garage.

Slowing down, so it didn't look like I was hurrying, I pulled into the space designated for the golf cart and plugged it back to charge the battery up. "Oh, hey there, ladies."

Darleen looked at me as Ella hurried into the house. "Oh, hi, Tyrell. Whatchya been doing?"

"Checking out the horses. I've taken an interest in them." I tried not to hurry into the house to find out why Ella hadn't even said hello to me. So, my walk was purposely slow and ambling. "Guess lunch is about ready now. Thought I'd come up and see about that."

"It's almost noon; I'm sure it's nearly done," Darleen remarked as she went inside in front of me. "At least I hope so. Ella and I left before eating this morning. I'm famished."

Why they had left so early? How to ask without sounding like I cared? "Yeah, I noticed you weren't there for breakfast."

Walking beside her through the empty kitchen that still smelled of food, I pushed the door open to the lunch area where Todd and Mrs. Finley were setting it up. "Oh good, you're home, Darleen. Where's Ella?" their mother asked.

"Probably in her bedroom. She didn't feel that great." Darleen put her purse down on a chair, then went to make a drink.

I wanted to ask about Ella but thought better of it. Instead, I got a glass of iced tea and examined the food. "Burgers. They look great, Todd."

"Sweet potato fries, too. I used an air fryer," he announced as he pulled the silver top off to show them. "Guilt-free and so flavorful. You have to try some."

"Don't mind if I do." As I started making my plate, my brothers came in with Kyle and Mr. Finley. "Hi, guys. Did ya have fun at the feed store?"

"We got some baby chicks," Cash beamed a smile a mile wide. "I've always wanted a few. A man with chicks! Ha ha!"

"I had no idea." I put some lettuce on my burger, then found an assortment of cheeses and had to taste a sample of each one before deciding to go with one called Havarti. "Who knew there were so many types of cheeses! And you never serve American cheese, Todd. Why's that?"

"Because it's artificial," he told me. "Why do we, as Americans, allow our good name to be used on that crap?"

Jasper agreed, "Right. It tastes like plastic with yellow number 5."

As I took a seat, I felt bad Ella wasn't here. "Maybe someone should bring Ella a meal."

Darleen shook her head. "She's in a terrible mood. Just leave her alone. She'll come out when she's ready."

"Maybe she's in a bad mood because she hasn't eaten?" I offered.

Mrs. Finley looked at me. "Maybe so. I'll go check on her." She left the room, and it made me feel better.

I'd never thought so much about anyone in my life. Why was Ella always at the forefront of my mind? But she was there.

Managing light chit chat with everyone, I got through lunch, then headed to the sitting room where Ella liked to hang out. There was a big picture window she liked to sit by to watch the meadow.

She wasn't there, so I went to the other room upstairs where she likes to hang out and draw, but she wasn't there, either. With no other options, I went to the Finley's quarters.

I'd never been so nervous, and it made me feel insanely stupid. My fist hung in the air, millimeters from the door. Taking a deep breath, I knocked. No answer came. So, I knocked again—still nothing.

Looking around, I saw nor heard anyone around and checked to see if the door was unlocked. It was open. The place looked like an ordinary apartment. I stepped into the living room; it had a kitchen to the left and a hallway in the back.

She must be down there in her room. Which one was hers? I could knock on each door as I found it. As I went back there, all the doors were open, except one. It had to be Ella's.

The closer I got to that closed door, the harder my heart beat in my chest. Holding my breath, I knocked on her door. "Ella?" Nothing. Knocking harder. "Ella, are you in there?"

"Tyrell?" she asked.

"Yeah, it's me. Can I come in? We were supposed to go down to the horse barn, remember?" I shifted my weight feeling like a loser standing there on the other side of the door.

Typically, in other situations such as this one, I'd go on into the room of a girl I was interested in. But something about Ella had me feeling nervous.

"No, you can't come in," she shouted. "What makes you think you can even come into our quarters? I came in here for privacy. Get out! Now!"

"I was just concerned, Ella. Damn." She overreacted, and it pissed me off. "You don't have to be so rude. I won't give a crap about you, okay? How's that?"

"I don't care. Go away." I heard the lock click, and I knew she locked the door so that I wouldn't barge in.

As if I'd ever do that. "Fine. I'll go away. God, you're such a brat, Ella Finley."

Leaving the Finley's quarters, I went right up to my bedroom to pace and berate myself for even trying. "She ain't worth my time. She's so adolescent. She's so mean!"

And I'd never felt so screwed because no matter how mad she made me, I couldn't stop thinking about her.

ELLA

After hours of kicking myself for being such a baby, someone was trying to come into my bedroom. "Hey, why'd you lock your door, Ella?" my sister called out from the other side.

Lying on my bed, I thought that I should get up and let her in. I needed to talk to somebody; it might as well be her. Padding across the room in my bare feet, I unlocked, then opened the door. "Come in. I'm ready to talk."

"It's about time!" She came in, closing the door behind her. "What happened at the clinic that took so long and put you in such a foul mood?"

Sitting on the edge of my bed, I took a deep breath, then let it out. "First, they wanted me to pee in a cup."

"Totally normal, Ella." Darleen sat down on the chair in front of my vanity. "That wasn't bad at all, huh?"

Shaking my head, "It wasn't bad, but I couldn't make myself pee in that cup—not a drop would come out. I was in there for thirty minutes when the nurse came and asked me if I needed something to drink to help me go."

"Okay, so you got some water, and then you went a short time later?" she gathered.

"No, I did not." Crossing my legs Indian-style, I went on. "It took an hour. Then I was able to fill that cup and then some. I peed all over my hand, and that made me feel sick."

"It happens," Darleen said with a nod. "That's why there is soap and water in the bathroom, Ella. Then you got to the exam?"

Shaking my head, I explained what happened. "I acted like I hadn't peed. I stayed in that bathroom for as long as I could until the nurse knocked and made me come out."

"Dear Lord, Ella." Her cheeks went a shade of pink. "Girl, I have to go back there and face those people! They know we're sisters! You should've held it together better than that!"

"If it makes you embarrassed to be related to me, then this next bit is going to kill you." I had definitely humiliated her. "See, I went into the exam room, got naked, put on the paper robe and got up on the table where I waited for a whole five minutes."

"Ella, don't tell me…"

I told her anyway, "I got off that table, dressed myself, and then left."

"I asked you how it went, and you said fine." The astonishment shone in her eyes. "Ella, how could you lie to me like that?"

"It had gone fine." That wasn't a lie. "I hadn't been poked or prodded. No one saw me naked. And I hadn't gone through with the exam. It was fine. But then as I walked out of there, the regret set in. That's why I got quiet and didn't want to talk."

"I thought you were just shaken was all. I had no clue you hadn't gotten the exam and the birth control pills." With a huff, Darleen got up. "You better stay away from that man if you're not mature enough to take care of things like this. Until you're able to do the mature thing, Ella, you shouldn't be doing what adults do." And then she left me alone.

Falling backward, I put the pillow over my face and tried not to cry. Did Tyrell even like me that way? That was why I didn't go through with it. Why go through it for no reason at all?

I had to do something to grow up at least a little. But what?

Drawing always helped me, and I left my room to sneak upstairs to my colored pencils and paper. There, I became Ella, the famous artist, destined to travel the globe to various art shows where my work would be displayed for all to see and purchase.

With most of my artwork, I let my mind take my hand on the journey. And this time it had me sketching Tyrell's ruggedly attractive face and his almond-shaped eyes—the blue had to be just right. The dark brows, thick eyelashes, and the length of his nose had to be just right, too.

The sound of an engine rumbled from outside, and I looked out the window to see the four-wheel-drive truck the brothers loved to drive going down the ranch driveway. It was almost dark outside, and the taillights took a left at the end of the drive, heading into town.

Instinctively, I knew Tyrell was in the truck.

I closed the sketchpad and put it in the bottom drawer of the desk before looking for someone to tell me where he'd gone. But I had to ask in a way that didn't hint to the fact that I had a massive crush on the man.

Dad was the first one, and I greeted him sweetly, "Hi, Daddy. Where's everybody at?"

"Out," he said as he plopped down on one of the big chairs in the media room. "I'm going to watch some television. You want to join me? Oh, wait. You're mother said you haven't eaten all day. Get yourself something, then come here and we can watch some old westerns."

"Sure." I really didn't want to. "Kyle went out, too?"

"No, just the Gentrys." He flipped through the channels, searching for the perfect western. He'll tended to only get through about five minutes before falling asleep. That's what always happened when my dad sat still for a few minutes. "The Watering Hole called their names is what Jasper told me before they left."

"All of them went?" I felt my blood getting hot thinking about Tyrell going back to that place!

"Yep." He ended his search on a John Wayne flick. "Now get yourself something to eat. You can't go to bed on an empty stomach."

I left the room, stomping not to the kitchen but to my bedroom. Throwing myself on the bed face first, I cried. I could've spent the day with Tyrell again, but I got so mad at not going through the exam to get on birth control, that I'd missed out. There he was, going to get drunk and end up dancing with random women of ill repute. He might even have sex with one of them.

Somewhere inside of me, I knew we would've spent the day together if I'd just been nice to him. He might not have left with his brothers and stayed right here with me. We might've gone to the theater room to watch a movie together. We might've even held hands—or even—made out.

I had to ruin everything by being a big infant. Why couldn't I act my age? Why did I have to be so juvenile?

I could blame my family for treating me like a baby my whole life. And so that's what I did. I stormed out of my room and saw my mother and sister sitting on the couch. "Why'd you do it?"

Mom looked taken aback. "Why'd I do what?"

"Not just you, Mom. All of you." I threw my hands up in the air. "I'm adolescent. I've never acted my age. And it's all you guys' fault. Daddy never let me help him the way Kyle and Darleen do. Mom, you only gave me work because I'm your kid, and you felt like I couldn't get a job elsewhere."

"Not true," Mom said defiantly. "Ella, you have the job because you know what I expect out of a maid. You have an eye for spotting what needs to be cleaned. Most of the time."

"I've got an eye, Mom, because I look at things and draw them. You didn't know that?" I asked her accusingly.

Darleen got up and took me by the shoulders. "Midol, Ella. Go to the medicine cabinet and get a handful. You're obviously PMSing."

"Am not!" I shook her hands off me. "I'm having a mental breakdown, and you aren't helping me." I stormed back to my room, slamming the door behind me.

Turning around, I saw my reflection in the mirror above my vanity. My hair was in two braids, I wore no makeup, and my eyes were red from crying.

I had enough! No matter how much I'd been babied in my life, no one had held me back. I couldn't blame a soul except myself.

I've always been a loner. I pushed people away for various reasons. But I didn't want to do that anymore. I wanted to be like everyone else.

Average.

Slowly, I looked at my closed closet door and walked to it. Opening it, I found my best cowboy boots, my newest pair of blue jeans, and the most enticing shirt I had. Sure, it wasn't too sexy, but it had buttons that can be undone at the top.

I showered, washed and dried my hair, then styled it, making it curl around my face. Pulling on the tight jeans, I put on the maroon chenille button-down sweater, tying it at my waist, and leaving the top four buttons undone so my cleavage showed. I found the silver hoop earrings Darleen gave me for my eighteenth birthday and added them to my accoutrements. Then I put on a necklace, the silver cross with diamonds, to hang between my breasts.

I felt almost ready to go out. But then a quick look at my fingernails, which hadn't been painted in forever, had me grabbing the burgundy nail polish my sister kept in the bathroom. With them painted shiny cherry, I was now ready to go.

I left a note on my bed saying *I've gone to The Watering Hole*. That way if anything terrible happened, at least they'd know where I had gone. Just because I was growing up a bit, I wasn't about to stop being responsible.

It was nine-thirty; I made it out of the house without anyone seeing me as everyone had gone to sleep already. I went to the garage. The keys to all the cars and trucks hung in a lockbox on the wall.

Scanning the many automobiles, I took the keys to the yellow Corvette. If I was going for it, go all the way! If Tyrell didn't notice me, someone would for certain.

TYRELL

With the third Tequila shooter down, I sat back in the chair and let out a holler that made me feel lighter. Dark, dank, and smelling of booze, the place matched my soul at the time.

"You want me to get another round, Tyrell?" Cash asked as he eyed the attractive barmaid.

"Are you trying to get me drunk?" I laughed, picking up my mug of beer. "I have this for now, you know?"

"Yeah, but having another shooter in front of you, in case you start on another tangent about Ella and how she's such a pain in the ass, might be helpful." He got up, walking to the bar without me even saying anything to him.

I looked at Jasper. "Cash has been here almost every night."

He jerked his head in the direction of the bar. "Looks like he's got the hots for that bartender, Bobbi Jo. Her mom works at the feed store, and Cash bent her ear but good, asking about her daughter. That's the genuine motive behind us going to the feed store today. Bobbi Jo told Cash her mom works there. What she hadn't told him, and her momma did, was her dad is the sheriff here."

I looked at the blonde, petite, pretty female, and then the door opened, and a woman who looked exactly like her walked in.

"Whoa, would ya look at that?"

Jasper whistled. "Cash told me she had a twin sister. But from what he said, Betty Sue had nothing on Bobbi Jo. They look identical to me."

"Me, too." I smiled at him. "Go say hello. Introduce yourself."

"Why don't *you* do that?" he asked, then took a sip of his beer. "Oh, yeah. I forgot. You're all starry-eyed over Ella."

Kicking him under the table, I saw the door open again, and this time Jasper's eyes bulged out of his head. "What?" I asked.

Jasper's eyes were glued onto the leggy redhead. "Doesn't she look a lot like Tiffany McKee from back home, Tyrell?"

"The girl you dated in high school?" That was a long time ago.

"Yep." He couldn't pull his eyes off her. "It's been seven years since I've seen her, but I could swear that's her."

The woman scanned the room, then her eyes landed on Jasper, and a smile broke out over her red lips. She came right up to our table. "Jasper Gentry, it's been a while, hasn't it?"

Jasper got up and took her into his arms. "It sure has, Tiff." They moved off to another table, leaving me alone with my beer.

Shortly afterward, a blonde sat down in the chair Jasper left empty. With my brothers entertained, I figured I might as well enjoy —or try to, anyway—the young woman's company.

"Hi, I'm Felicity."

"Tyrell." She had nothing to drink, so I waved the waitress over. "Can you fix the lady up, please?"

Felicity smiled. "Thanks. I'll have a gin and juice."

"Another beer for me." I put the half-empty mug down to give my attention to the lass who had enough guts to sit at my table. "So, Felicity, what do you?"

"Work for the local newspaper, the Carthage Chronicle. And you are Tyrell Gentry." She took her cell out and pushed it toward me. "If I could get your number, that would be great."

"I'm not sure I like talking to you yet. How about we chat for a while first?" I picked up the beer and took another sip.

Dragging her cell back across the table, she frowned. "Okay. It's just that your story is worth telling. And I'd like to be the one to tell it."

"I'm not interested in becoming Carthage's newest celebrity,

Felicity. But thanks anyway." I took another drink of the beer as I watched Cash flirting with the barmaid. Her sister looked on with interest, too. Being that I was sitting with the town reporter, I asked, "What do you know about the twins up there?"

"Ah, the Baker twins," she said with a smile. "They're as different as night and day. The one behind the bar is actually very good. Her sister though, well, she's far from it. Your brother better watch out for her. Betty Sue has been known to impersonate her sister on more than one occasion. It's gotten her into trouble at times."

She was good. "How do you know that's my brother?"

"Are you kidding?" The waitress brought our drinks and placed them in front of us. "Thank you, Sarah."

"You know everyone, don't you?" I asked.

She nodded. "Born and raised here. And you were born and raised in Dallas. Your father left town with Lila Stevens, whom he'd eloped with before coming back to tell his father to screw off."

"What do you know about Ella Finley?" Since the town gossip was sitting with me, I might as well find out everything about Ella.

"Ella Finley works as a maid at Whisper Ranch. She recently turned twenty-one. She's never been spotted with any man—or woman—so one can't assume she's a lesbian. She is quiet and keeps to herself." Felicity leaned forward to whisper the next part. "She's never had a friend in her life, Tyrell. Ella's tough to get along with."

"I know." I finished my beer, then went to work on the new one. "Something about her intrigues me."

Shrugging, she got up. "I'm meeting someone. I better get to my own table, so he doesn't get pissed. If you want to let me in on your story, you can find me at the publishing company most workdays. Just stop by."

"Don't hold your breath. It was nice meeting you, Felicity." I nodded as she left. Jasper came back, taking his seat again. "Did you two reconnect?"

"Kind of, not nearly enough." Jasper looked over his shoulder as Tiffany went out the door. "I noticed Felicity came to talk to you. She's prying for our story. Cash and I both told her it's not quite the story she thinks. Plus, we don't want to be front page news in our new town."

"Me, neither." I watched the door open again, and some hot brunette came walking in, swaying her hips. "Who's that?"

Jasper turned to see who I was talking about and did a double take. "Naw. It can't be."

"She almost looks like…" I squinted to try to see better.

"Ella," Jasper said in a hushed whisper. "It's Ella, Tyrell."

"No way." Getting up, I made my way to where she'd taken a seat at the bar but stopped when I saw Cash talking to her. When he looked back at me, but she kept looking ahead, it was in his eyes. It was Ella!"

"What in the hell?" I went back to sit down with Jasper. "What is she doing?"

Jasper moved his chair around so he could observe. "This ought to be interesting. Ella Finley at a local dive."

The barmaid put a shot glass in front of her and filled it with whiskey. "She isn't going to drink that. It'll come right back out of her mouth."

Cash looked back at us as Ella picked the glass up and took it all at once. He looked as stunned as I when she put the empty glass down on the bar, then nodded. The glass was filled again, and I shook my head at Cash who merely shrugged as Ella downed that one, too.

"She's old enough to drink, Tyrell," Jasper alleged as he put his beer mug to his lips.

"But she's not a drinker, Jasper. She's making rookie mistakes right there." My eyes went to the door as some guy walked in, and his eyes went right to Ella. He walked over and took the empty barstool next to her.

He uttered something to her, and she seemed to be talking back. Then he held up two fingers, and the barmaid put two beers in front of them both. He extended his arm, which Ella accepted, then they took their drinks and went to sit at a small table, sitting so close their legs touched.

Jasper looked at me with a grin. "Would you look at that?"

I could barely see through the fury that filled my vision. "What the hell does she think she's doing?"

"It looks like she's trying to act ordinary for a change." Jasper took another drink as he turned his chair around. "Boring."

Watching Ella was anything but boring! I was infuriated! She'd been so mean to me, and here she was talking it up with some strange dude! And she was all dolled up, too. She even knew how to put on makeup and curl her hair!

"She's got work tomorrow; maybe I should go over and remind her?" I picked up my beer and started to get up when Ella stood and went back to the bar alone. "Or, I'll sit back and see if she's going to do the right thing on her own." I watched her take the seat she'd left, and she ordered another shot. "That's way too much for her."

Jasper laughed. "Relax, Tyrell. We're right here. We won't let her drive home drunk. Maybe she took a cab?"

Taking advantage of her back to me, I got up to go out to see if she drove one of the cars to the bar. Peeking out the window, the yellow Corvette was parked right up front. When I went back to sit down with Jasper, I let him in on the scoop, "Seems she took the Corvette."

Jasper's expression was one of astonishment. "She drove it here?"

"That's what it looks like." When Ella went rogue, she pulled out all the stops.

After downing the third shot, she held up her finger, and I saw the guy she left at the table stand up and come behind her. His hands on her shoulders had me just about to get up, then he leaned down, his lips touched the side of her face, and she quickly turned around. Then he put his arms around her, and she put her hands against his chest.

It's hard to say what happened after that. A chair hit the floor as I rushed across the room. The guy went flying, and Ella was thrown over my shoulder.

Her tiny fists hit my back as I carried her out to the Corvette. Tossing her into the passenger side, I took her purse to get the key fob.

"Tyrell!" she screamed, then leaned out to puke as I backed away.

I let her get it all out before helping her lie back in the passenger seat, then buckled her seatbelt and drove us home. Her head lolled back and forth as she'd passed out.

Even passed out drunk, she was still gorgeous. What am I going to do about her?

ELLA

Quiet snoring sounds met my ears as I woke up. My mouth felt as if cotton balls had been shoved into it. My head felt like someone hammered on it, and my eyes burned when I opened them.

Quickly I closed them back up. What did I do last night? Nothing was coming back to me, so it might be just a cold.

Running my hands down my body, I found my shirt and jeans were still on. What's going on? I sat up, opened my eyes even though they stung like crazy, and that's when I saw a large lump on the floor of a bedroom that wasn't mine.

"Shit." I reached up to my hair to find it a tangled mess. "Where am I?"

The room was still dark. Why am I anywhere other than my own bedroom? A pounding headache made it difficult to process. But then a scent drifted through the air that seemed familiar. *Tyrell?*

Looking closer in the dark room, I saw nightstands on each side of a large bed. The blanket was azure, soft, and the same kind as Tyrell had on his bed. Looking to the left, I saw a darker spot in the room where the bathroom door was left open. I was in Tyrell's bedroom!

But why?

Moving my hands over the sweater I wore, I felt the chenille fabric and had the slightest recollection of putting it on. I tied it at the waist, but it hung loose and untucked. When I moved my hand up the row of buttons, all were buttoned up—all the way to the top.

I left the top few undone… So unlike me! Then it hit me all at once. I went to that bar I was sure Tyrell would be at and had some shots— something new for me.

Oh, God! I took the Corvette, too!

How did I get home in an apparent drunken state? After never messing up even once, I'd gone and jumped off the deep end and would soon find that I'd drowned!

Climbing out of the bed as quietly as possible, I tiptoed to the door to make my escape before Tyrell woke up. Will I get a lecture? Or worse? Had I done something with the guy that I was completely unaware of?

But he was sleeping on the floor. And my clothes were still on. All that was missing were my boots that I couldn't find. I would have to get them later. For now, I had to get back to my bedroom before my parents woke up!

Moving like a ghost, I left the room, closing the door gently behind me and then hurrying downstairs. I had no idea where my purse was; my cell was in it, so that was lost, too. For all I knew, my boots were lost as well.

"I am never drinking again!"

When I got to the door to our quarters, I heard my father and brother talking on the other side of it. Instead of going in to explain myself, I hid in the room across the hall. It took them forever to leave.

I forgot that they begin their day at four each morning. Mom would be getting up in an hour, and I am expected to begin the housework by nine. I so didn't feel like working! I needed sleep and lots of it.

After Dad and Kyle got far enough away, I slipped out of my hiding spot and went into our quarters, then to my room where I closed and locked the door behind me.

Stripping out of the tight blue jeans and chenille sweater, I got rid of my bra and panties, too, then climbed into bed. After a few hours of sleep, hopefully, I'd feel better.

It took no time to fall back to sleep. When I woke up, it was to the sound of pounding on the door. "Ella? What the hell's going on?" Mom hollered.

"Huh?" I sat up, bleary-eyed and felt a sharp pain going through my head. "Ow."

"Ella?" she called out again. "What's wrong? It's ten o'clock! Didn't you hear the alarm go off on your cell?"

Moving slowly out of bed, I felt nauseous. "Mom, I'm not feeling well. I'll be there in a bit." I headed to the bathroom. "I've caught a bug or something. I might need to throw up."

I heard the door handle wiggling. "Let me in, Ella."

With not a stitch on, I looked around the room then saw a t-shirt tossed on the floor. Intending to pick it up and put it on, I leaned for it and got so dizzy that I fell over. "Ow."

"Ella, what's going on?" she asked. "Let me in!"

When I got up, I caught a glimpse of myself in the mirror over my dresser and saw makeup smeared all over my face. "Shit!"

"Ella?"

"Mom, I'm going to take a shower, then I'll get to work, okay?" She can't see me looking like that! She'd be made of questions if she saw the state I was in.

"Well, okay. Come find me once you get cleaned up and ready. I'll be in my office doing payroll." I heard her walk away and then slunk to the bathroom, still feeling hideous.

The hot water washed away all the makeup caked on my face; I cleaned my hair, and that made me feel a bit more alive. But I had Tyrell to face, and that wasn't good at all.

I put on sweatpants and a t-shirt to do the cleaning. I wasn't up to doing much, but I had to try to do what I could. Before getting down to work though, I should find my purse.

Figuring I left it in the Corvette, I snuck out to the garage and saw it parked right where it belonged. The keys were in the lockbox on the wall, so I took them to unlock the car. But once inside, it wasn't there.

That meant Tyrell had most likely taken it into his bedroom. Why had he done that? It was eleven o'clock. He should be awake and most likely out of his room by now.

Heading up there to track down my things, I knocked nonchalantly on his door. "Tyrell? Are you in there?"

Not hearing anything, I opened the door and went inside. The blanket he'd been laying under still lay on the floor; the bed was still a mess. Now that it was drenched in sunlight, I saw my boots on the floor by the dresser, and my purse was on top of it.

Grabbing my things, I turned to leave the room when the door opened. "Hey, you."

My eyes closed as awkwardness made my entire body flush. "Hey."

"You look better considering your state..." I didn't turn around, but his voice was moving toward me.

"I still feel like hell." Finally, I turned around to find him wearing only a towel around his waist. "Oh, God!" I closed my eyes. "Sorry! I just wanted to see if my things were here. I didn't think you were even here! I'll leave you alone so you can get dressed."

"Really?" He chuckled as if I was being silly. "After what you did last night? You still feel uncomfortable with me?"

What was he talking about? I opened my eyes to look at him. "What happened last night?"

"What do you recall?" He walked over to his closet, then stepped inside and closed the door.

The thought of him dropping the towel and buck-naked looking for something to put on...

"Not a lot. I remember driving to the bar, getting out and going inside. Cash was there. I had a drink, and then, well, then I don't know what else."

"So you *were* drunk after that first shot then. I suspected as much. You had a few more shots and a beer, too."

He didn't seem upset about the Corvette, but I had to know what he thought about me driving it home while I was drunk. "So, you're not pissed about me taking the car?"

"I'm not thrilled," he said then came out of the dressing room with jeans and a button-down shirt on, his feet were still bare, and they looked fine. Not many people had nice-looking feet, but Tyrell did. "But you had no problem letting me drive it back here. You had no problems at all, Ella."

Staggering back to the bed, I sat on it as my mind raced with what else I let him do. "You don't mean we…"

He walked right up to me, put his hands on my shoulders as he looked me in the eyes and said, "Ella, you don't remember a thing we did last night?"

I shook my head slowly. "Not a thing."

"Do you recall talking to a guy at the bar?" he asked with a frown.

I shook my head again. "Did I talk to some guy last night?"

"You sure did." He stood over me, towering and somewhat imposing. "And that guy put his hands on you. He was going for a kiss. In the state you were in, it seemed like you might just let him do it."

"I didn't, did I?" I felt sick thinking about my first kiss with some random dude that I can't even remember.

"No. I wouldn't let you do something like that." He smiled. "You're lucky I was there."

I wouldn't have been there if he hadn't been there, but he didn't need to know that. "Thank you for preventing that, Tyrell." I couldn't remember how he stopped it, but I was appreciative. "And what did we do after getting back here?"

His smile went devious. "You don't remember a thing, Ella?"

"Tyrell, please don't tease me. I am appalled. If we… um… uh… did anything, please tell me." I braced myself for the worst. I was attracted to the man. In an inebriated state with my inhibitions all gone, I was sure at least a kiss happened at some time or another.

"I should be truthful about everything that went on last night." He took a seat next to me on the bed and put his hand on my thigh, sending chills all through me.

Oh, God, what have I done?

TYRELL

Ella and I hadn't done a thing, other than me carrying her up to my room as she passed out. She should be more careful about getting into such a state! "What if you'd gone home with that guy at the bar, Ella?"

She looked at the floor. "I wouldn't have done that."

"If I hadn't been there, you might've gotten yourself into terrible trouble." What would've happened if I hadn't been there? "You were out of it, Ella. So inebriated that you didn't wake up when I carried you up here to my bedroom. What if someone else had done that? What do you think would've happened then?"

Her entire body shuddered. "I don't know."

"You wouldn't have known a thing. You couldn't stop anything from happening." I wanted to be sure she never did anything so reckless again. "I took your boots off, I untied your shirt, then buttoned it all the way up, and you had no clue. That could've gone the another way, you know. Someone else might've taken your clothes off, and you would've been at their mercy. Let me tell you, most drunk men have little, if any, compassion."

"So, we didn't do anything?" She couldn't even look at me.

I pulled her face to where she had no choice but to look at me.

"Ella, do you honestly think I would ever take advantage of you, or anyone else, for that matter?"

She shook her head. "And *I* didn't try anything either?"

"You passed out after you threw up." I brushed her hair back off her face.

"I threw up?" She really didn't recall a thing!

"You did, in the parking lot. You barfed it all. Then you promptly passed out and stayed that way." I felt she had learned her lesson. "You worried me, Ella. Promise me you'll never drink so foolishly again."

Nodding, she whispered, "I promise. When I woke up feeling worse than ever, I swore I'd never drink again."

"You can drink, Ella, just do it responsibly. You were downing shots like a frat boy." I laughed, recalling the way she'd taken the shots. "And they knocked you on your ass almost immediately. Now, would you like to tell me why you went to a place you told me wasn't the best choice?"

Her eyes glazed over as she looked away. "I just felt like going out..."

"You came home yesterday in a dreadful mood," I reminded her. "That's not really what a person in a bad mood does. What's the real reason?"

"That's it." She got up. "I've got to work. It'll take me until midnight to catch up."

"I could help you!" I got up, then went to get my sneakers.

"The boss helping do the chores is frowned upon." She went to the door.

"I'm serious, Ella. I want to help you. You must have one bad hangover." I sprinted to catch up to her. "I'll clean the toilets. That alone might trigger a barfing session for you."

Her hand went to her hip as she pursed her lips. "My mother will want to know why you're helping me."

"Only if she catches me." I smiled, then led the way out of my room. "We don't have to let her in on our arrangement, do we? Does she know where you went last night? Or that you took the 'Vette?"

"No one does." The way her face fell made me feel bad.

"My brothers and I know. And none of us are mad about it. So, it's not a big deal. Next time, ask one of us for permission before you take one of the vehicles, please."

She hadn't been thinking clearly when she took the car in the first place. Something told me she had a horrible day. "I don't have you guys' numbers, though." Smirking, she went on, "Not that I would've called. Things hadn't gone the way I planned yesterday. It made me angry. Mostly at myself. Then I heard you guys went to the bar, and it only made me madder."

Walking at her side, I liked the fact she was being so open with me. "And why would *our* going to the bar make you mad, Ella?"

Her cheeks went pink. "It just pointed out to me that I stay home all the time when I could be going out. That's all I meant. It wasn't about you guys. I've been hanging on to my childhood for too long. Not taking the steps most people my age have taken. I can't seem to do things, and when I do, I do them off beam."

"You need guidance." I opened the linen closet and found the cart she used, then rolled it out. "I can help you."

She shook her head. "Um, no, you can't."

"Sure, I can." Pushing the cart, I led her to the upstairs media room. "This room and bathroom need to be cleaned. With my help, you only have to clean the rooms we utilized in the last couple of days. We'll be done in no time. What makes you think I can't help you?"

"You're a guy. You don't know what it's like to be a woman." She opened the door to push the cart through.

"I know what it means to be a grown-up." Taking the cleaner, I went to the bathroom. "You dust and vacuum, and I'll clean up the bathroom while you do that."

"The mansion has a central vacuum system, you know that, right?" she asked.

I stopped and turned to look at her. "What's that?"

Handing me a broom and the mop off the cart, she walked in front of me to the bathroom. Pointing at one of the baseboards, she said, "Do you see these small openings around the floor's edge?"

"Yeah. Funny how I've never noticed them before." I stooped down to take a better look. "What are they?"

"Miniature vacuums. Well, not exactly; there's a button in the kitchen, and when it's turned on, the dirt that's swept up against the openings is sucked in. Push the dirt to these holes when you sweep. And you can't mop until I go down and push that button." She left me to my work, and I got to it.

After a half-hour of intensive cleaning—I didn't want her to think I'd half-assed the job—I went out to find her finishing up the dusting. "Done. Well, until you go down and press that button."

Smiling, she took the cell she'd taken out of her purse and put into her back pocket. "I usually don't do that. Tasha, the chef's assistant does."

Waiting, I watched her make the call. Why didn't she say that in the first place? Ella was a complex individual. Helping with her labor, along with what I'd done for her the night before, would hopefully get her to see me as an ally. More than anything else, I wanted to be Ella's first real friend.

That she was known for not having friends made me feel bad. Not that she'd want me to feel that way, but I couldn't help it. She had her sister, but they didn't seem to be that close. Everyone needs someone to confide in, and Ella didn't seem to have anyone.

Ending the call, she tossed me another spray bottle. "You can mop now. Just spritz the floor with this, then mop it. After that, we can clean the next room."

Later, after cleaning everything, I bumped my shoulder against hers as I put the cart back into the closet. "How about I take you out for a greasy burger and some fries?"

She put her hand on her stomach. "That might make me puke for sure. I still don't feel well."

"You'd be amazed how much it'll help." I closed the door, then took her by the hand. "You gave me chicken soup when I had a hangover; let me show you what my usual remedy is."

"I don't know." She hesitated as she looked at our clasped hands. "What would people think if you and I went to eat together?"

"What do we care?" I asked with a grin. "Ella, I'm not humiliated to be seen with you. Are you?"

"No." She laughed. "Tyrell, you and your brothers are the talk of the town right now. Who knows what people will think if you and I are spotted together?"

"Oh, like when my mom and dad were going out?" I asked, pulling her along with me.

"Yeah, like that. She was the maid here, too, remember? And that stirred up all kinds of hullabaloo." She tried to pull her hand out of mine.

I held on, not willing to let it go. "You're coming with me, Ella. I don't give a rat's ass what anyone thinks." Thinking it best, so she didn't start to feel uncomfortable, I added, "It's just a late lunch. No one thinks a couple of people grabbing a late lunch is a date of any kind."

"Is that how that works?" She eased up and started coming along.

"Yes, that's how it works. If you and I were all dressed up and went to some fancy restaurant, then that's considered a date." Pushing the door to the garage open, I asked, "Can you pick up the keys to the 'Vette?"

She grabbed them and held them out. "Here you go."

"Nope. You're driving." I wanted her to feel older than she'd allow herself to feel.

"No way." She jiggled the keys. "Come on, take them. You drive."

"No." I let go of her hand and got into the passenger side. "You're driving, Ella. Consider this part of your training as an adult. I said I would help you."

Smiling, she got into the driver's seat. "It was fun driving this car last night."

"I thought so, too, when I drove it back home." Putting on my seatbelt, I prepared myself to not freak out if she made mistakes. "How long have you had your license?"

"Since last year. It took me a while before I decided to get it." Looking at me, she wrinkled her nose. "I take more time to do things."

"There's nothing wrong with that. But don't be frightened of doing things you've never done before." By that, I meant *all kinds of*

241

things. Getting Ella to try new things filled my mind with possibilities.

There were so many things she hadn't done, and I wanted as many of those firsts as possible.

ELLA

Was it was the effects of the hangover? I wasn't being my usual
myself as Tyrell and I ate at Dairy King. "This is helping. You were
right about greasy foods, Tyrell. Who would've ever thought to eat
something like this on an upset stomach?"

"Not sure who came up with the idea, but fatty foods have an
incredible effect on stomach acid." He took a big bite of his burger
and some oil actually dribbled out the bottom.

"Yuck!" I said, then took another bite of mine. "It looks yucky,
but it's so yummy!"

He nodded knowingly, then wrapped his lips around the straw
sticking out of the bottle of Dr. Pepper. Sucking down half of the
cold drink, he ended with, "Ah. Nothing like a nice cold D.P., is
there?"

"It's my favorite, too." Taking a drink, I realized I've never gone
out with anyone other than members of my family. "Seems we have
similar tastes."

"Indeed." His eyes moved to watch the person who just entered.

When I turned to look over my shoulder, I saw the tall redhead
walking in, and I immediately felt heat run through me. It was envy.
"She's pretty." I tried not to glare when I looked back at him.

"She's Jasper's old high school girlfriend." He smiled. "What's that in your eyes, Ella?"

Blinking, what he was talking about? "Is there something in my eyes?"

He laughed. "They actually sparkle when you get irate. Did you know that? It's uncanny how your eyes convey that sentiment. You must've thought I was checking Tiffany out."

My heart raced. Am I that transparent? "No. Not at all. Why would I care if you check out some girl?"

"Yeah, sure." He laughed as I blushed. "And why would I knock some guy to the ground when he tried to kiss you?"

Taken aback, I sat there looking at him. "You did what?"

"When I saw that guy put his hands on you last night, I kind of lost my marbles." The way he smiled all crooked made me jittery inside. "Everything after that point was a blur. He went down, I threw you over my shoulder like Tarzan, and out to the car we went."

Gulping, I asked, "Why'd you do all that, Tyrell?"

He took another bite of his burger and shrugged his broad shoulders. I had to look away as a flush heated my body up. I knew why he'd acted that way, and he knew why as well.

Sitting there, realizing he could've violated me while I was passed out, yet, he didn't. He appreciated me. That had to be it. Tyrell just respected me. It wasn't that he *liked* me. Not like that.

Not having made any friends had me processing things differently. Tyrell was five years older. He was all man, and no way in hell he'd be interested in a fool like myself. He was being nice to me because he liked me as a friend. Stop thinking it is anything other than that, or I'll become a bigger schmuck than I've demonstrated already.

Suddenly, the redhead was unexpectedly standing beside our table. "Hi, Tyrell. I didn't get a chance to say hello last night. Jasper filled me in on what you guys are doing in Carthage."

"And why are you here, Tiffany?" Tyrell asked.

"My parents bought this fine establishment." Her green eyes came to mine. "Hi, I'm Tiffany McKee."

I didn't know what to say at first, then I opened my mouth and declared, "I'm Ella Finley, their maid."

"She's more than that." Tyrell reached across the table and put his hand over mine. "She's our good friend, too."

"Is that right?" she asked crossing her arms over her ample chest. "It's nice to meet you, Ella. We'll probably see each other now and then since Jasper's in town now."

Tyrell slid his hand off mine as he asked, "You two will try things out again?"

"Oh, no. No, no, no," she protested a bit too much. "I have a kid now. You know, responsibilities and such. I can't bring Jasper into my chaos. But we're good friends."

"Bring your kid out to the estate," Tyrell offered. "What child doesn't like horses, dogs, and tons of room to run?"

"My kid." Tiffany looked over her shoulder as another customer walked in. "I have to get to work. Mom and Dad took off already. It was nice to see you, Tyrell, and to meet you, Ella."

We both watched her as she hurried away. "Why doesn't she want to bring her kid out to the property?"

Tyrell looked at me with a knowing expression. "Probably cause the kid's hyperactive. Her little brother, Bo, was like that. It might be the case here as well."

To be sure she didn't overhear me, I whispered, "Looks like Jasper dodged a bullet then, huh?"

Tyrell's laugh was so deep and sexy, it made my insides ache in a way only he could. "He may have. They were so in love back then. He probably won't give up on her since he knows she's here. He's willful that way."

"Like Cash?" I asked. "He's gone to that bar every night. But last night, seeing him with that bartender told me why."

His eyes narrowed, his lip twitched. "You've been noticing when Cash goes out?"

Cash left about the same time I was in my drawing room. The car lights beamed on the ceiling up there. But Tyrell shouldn't know the lame way I spend my free time. "I've noticed him leaving, yes."

"Why's that?" His eyes flickered. That's interesting!

"I'm just near a window when he goes is all." Deep in his eyes it looked as if he was exhibiting a bit of jealousy. "I don't like him like that, Tyrell."

245

He jerked his head to one side. "I never claimed you did."

"Okay." Things had gone in a weird direction, so we should halt it. "Do you think ice cream would be okay to eat?"

"Yeah, I do." He got up and took our empty food baskets then went to the counter.

I got up and tossed my empty cup in the trash, then went to stand next to him. "I like strawberry ice cream."

"Noted." He sighed, then looked down at me. "Would you like to take a walk while we eat our cones?"

A stroll? Now?

"Okay." Maybe he just wanted to walk off the junk food? The man kept himself in tip-top shape. Long walks after scarfing down fast food had to be something he's always done.

Tiffany came to take his order. "Would you guys want something else?"

"A couple of cones would be great. One vanilla and one strawberry." He looked at me. "One scoop?"

Nodding my answer, I quietly stood at his side. This was probably how a date ensues. And a great one!

Although many would think it lame, to me, simple things were better than fancy ones. Burgers, fries, and then ice cream sounded better than dining on lobster at some expensive restaurant.

Tiffany handed us the cones. "Enjoy the walk and the ice cream. It's on the house."

"Thanks, Tiff," Tyrell said, then gave his a lick.

"Yeah, thank you," I said as I gave mine a lick, too. "Yummy. It tastes homemade."

"That's because it is." She smiled and waved as we turned to leave. "Bye now. Come back again, ya hear?"

"We will," Tyrell let her know. "This is the best ice cream I've ever tasted."

"They don't call us Dairy King for nothing," she shouted as we walked out the door.

A small park was only a short walk away. Kids played on the playground, laughing and screaming. Birds chirped, and the sound of cars driving slowly around the streets made the place seem charming. I never thought of my hometown as charming before. Not until I walked around it with Tyrell Gentry.

Through the park we strolled, then down to Main Street where we looked in the windows of the various shops. "Antiques," Tyrell said. "I've never gotten why people want to buy old things."

"Me, neither. My granny has what she calls her collectibles. They look worn out, yellowing… She's told me I stand to inherit a good amount of those breakables. I've never told her how little interest her aged stuff gives me."

"Well, I'm not talking about family heirlooms—just stuff that other people held onto for longer than they should have." He finished off his ice cream and tossed the napkin in a nearby trashcan. "Keep whatever your grandmother has given you, Ella. Take it from someone who's never known a single grandparent; you'll want something to remember her by."

"You have the manor to remember your grandparents by," I remarked, then took the last bite of my cone.

"Since I never met them, the luxury of remembering them is spent." He stopped and looked inside the next store window. "Clowns. Who would have a store that only sells clowns?"

"A sadist?" Shivering, I looked at the painted faces in the window. An old woman moved around behind them, scaring the crap out of me. I jerked and screamed, then Tyrell took my hand, and off we ran.

We didn't stop until we made it to the end of the block and down an alley. When we at last stopped running, he didn't let my hand go. Instead, he held it as we caught our breaths.

The alley was dark and empty; it seemed we were absolutely alone. He ran his free hand through my hair. "Have I told you how pretty you are?"

My heart felt as if it was in my throat as I shook my head. Gulping, I tried hard not to tremble; he shouldn't know what was happening to me.

"I like it when we get along like this." His hand squeezed mine. "I like it when you talk to me. I feel like your ally, Ella. Do you feel like we're friends, too?"

Friends?

TYRELL

What happened to Ella's good mood? Something warped it. "Can you take me home now?"

"Ella, I asked if you think we can be friends," I said holding tightly to her hand. "And now you want me to take you home?"

She nodded. "Please."

Maybe her stomach was acting up? Pulling her along with me, we walked back to the Dairy King parking lot. She yanked her hand out of mine. Okay…

When we got to the car, she tossed the key fob up in air at me as she walked past me. "You drive."

Not about to argue, I got in the driver's seat and we drove home in silence. Even the radio was so low the lyrics of any of the songs that came on were inaudible. Finally, I pulled into the garage, and she got out without saying a word.

I sat there for a few minutes, going over the exact words I said and if they offended her somehow. After reviewing them all in my mind, there was nothing that should've upset her.

It must be her stomach.

Getting out of the car, I went back inside and hoped she'd feel better and come to the media room we hung out in. But she never came, and I eventually got tired of waiting.

As a result, I went to her family's quarters. That is what a friend would do after all. A quick knock and Mrs. Finley said, "Come in."

Opening the door, I went inside. "Hi, Mrs. Finley. Is Ella here?"

"She's in her room." She directed her head at the hallway behind her. "Third door on the left."

"Thanks." I headed back to knock on her door. "Ella, it's Tyrell. Can I come in?"

"Ugh," she huffed. "Why?"

"I just want to see how you're feeling is all." I bit my lip trying not to yell at her about being rude.

"It's not locked," she told me.

Opening the door, she was laying on her stomach on her twin-sized bed. "Are you feeling better now?"

"I'm fine." She kept her eyes on her phone screen. "I'm playing a game."

"Would you like to watch a movie with me?" I felt a little odd asking her as she obviously wanted to be left alone.

"Not in the mood." She swiped the screen. "Damn, lost again."

Taking the phone out of her hands, I got on my knees in front of her. "Good. Let's do something. Don't sit here all alone..."

"I *like* to be alone." She took her phone back out of my hand.

What to say? It was apparent why she hadn't had any close friends. Why am I spending so much time trying to be one to her? "So, you don't want to be friends with me?"

Her eyes fixed on the screen once more, she said, "Friends are great until you want to spend time on your own and they won't let you."

Pinching the bridge of my nose, I wanted to say so much more but knew it would only cause a fight. "At least can you say something nice about today?"

She finally looked at me. "Oh, yeah. Thanks for taking care of me last night. That was nice of you. And thanks for helping me clean today and taking me for the burger, etcetera. Anything else? Did I miss anything else?" Sarcasm laced her last few words.

"You know what? That shit isn't necessary, Ella." Being patient is not in the cards for me. "Why do I even try?"

"Me, neither." She pulled herself up to sit Indian style, the phone in her hands, still playing the darn game.

"You're not only immature, you're a fucking jackass to boot! Has anyone ever told you that before?" I turned to leave her room.

"No, Tyrell," she snapped. "No one has ever told me that. I have no friends."

There it was. She didn't have friends! Even though I had many clues as to why, it still upset me that she was alone most of the time. So, I turned around, giving her another chance. "Ella, I want to be your friend. I really do. Can you stop acting this way? It seems you're afraid things won't work out and our time together will end. It won't. I promise you."

Tossing the phone to the end of the bed, she looked down. "When I was five, I went to the first day of kindergarten. Lacy was sitting in the chair across from mine. We were desk mates. She and I were friends. We said we'd always be friends. Guess what, we weren't always friends. Do you want to know why?"

Nodding, I truly did. "Please."

Lifting her head, she looked me square in the eyes. "She kicked the bucket."

Shock ran through me. "No."

Nodding, tears in her eyes, she went on, "She didn't show up for school one day. That turned into a week. The teacher told us that my first friend passed away. Our parents were called to take us from school as we all were upset. On the way home, my mom had the car radio blaring and a news report came on. That's when I heard the real story. My friend, Lacy Peters was drowned by her very own mother in the bathtub at her home. If that doesn't make you see why I don't believe in humanity, then I don't know how else to make you understand why I don't want to have friends."

"I had no idea, Ella. That's terrible." Slowly I moved toward her, opening my arms for her. "Come here. Let me hold you."

This time, there were no tears in her eyes, only a glare that confirmed she didn't want to be held. "No. I don't want to rely on anyone for comfort. I got through that by myself. I can get through anything by myself."

What to do or say? "Ella?"

"Can you leave now?" she asked in a hushed whisper.

Nodding, I did as she'd asked. Going to the living room, I softly asked her mother, "Did Ella really have a friend in kindergarten who was killed by her mother?" She might be messing with my head.

"Oh, Lord, yes," Mrs. Finley confirmed. "It was awful. She told you about that?"

Nodding, I shuddered. "She did. Just now."

"Wow," she whispered. "Ella hasn't discussed that with anyone in ages. We took her to see a therapist when it happened. Ella was inconsolable, and we *had* to do something. She wanted to put that friendship out of her mind. Anytime anyone asked how she was doing, she'd snap that she just wanted to forget it all. So, we eventually learned not to bring it up at all. Why did she bring it up to you?"

"I was trying to be her friend, I suppose." I shoved my hands into my pockets. "She has no close friends. It made me feel awful."

Her mother nodded. "She's a loner, Tyrell. Always has been."

I knew better than that. She wanted friends at one time. She just believed that pain came along with having friends, and apparently, she wanted no part of that.

"I'll get out of your way, Mrs. Finley. Have a nice evening." I walked to the door.

"Tyrell, it's nice you to want to be her friend. I'm afraid she'll end up making you dislike her though. She pushes people away. Even us at times." With her sigh punctuating that last statement, I left her.

How lonely an existence did Ella have? She must've felt miserable most of the time. I made my way t0 the room she drew in. Looking at the drawings on the wall, I saw the detail in them.

Going to the desk, I pulled open the top drawer and found a sketch pad inside. Opening it, I found picture after picture of the same little girl. The girl was probably Lacy. She hadn't ever forgotten her. For not wanting to think about her, it seemed she thought about her more than anyone knew.

I put the pad back exactly as I found it and left the room. Maybe it wasn't right to snoop? Maybe I shouldn't hurt over her. But, it wasn't as if I could help my feelings...

Because of what scarred her when she was just a little girl, Ella didn't want to grow up—not entirely. Maybe she wanted to stay a little girl because Lacy remained one? For whatever reasons, I couldn't give up on her now. Not now that I knew what the problem was! Maybe trying to be Ella's friend wasn't the right thing?

In her mind, she had one—just one. She didn't want another. After all, Lacy didn't have the privilege of having another friend, so why should Ella?

When I got to my bedroom, I desperately wanted to talk to someone about my discovery. But I knew Ella wouldn't want me to tell a soul about what she told me. I should hold onto that information and deal with it on my own, the same way she had for all those years.

I thought about Ella before the ghastly murder: a sweet little girl, full of mirth and joy. She had loved with all her heart and had no shred of the current attitude.

Just because someone has cracks in their heart doesn't mean they can't be mended. Ella didn't need another friend; Ella needed to feel loved. She needed to feel special to someone.

Could I make her feel that way? Loved and special? Would she let it happen? Should I?

I'd never even tried to make anyone feel cherished before. No one mattered that much to me. Ella is as important to me, but I couldn't pinpoint exactly why. Her delight meant something. I wanted to see her happy and stay that way for a long time.

Would it be a waste of energy to try? Would it end up hurting me?

It's not manly to not do something just because one might get hurt. No, I'm not the type of guy who turns away from something just because there is some pain.

I could show Ella there's more out there than just grief. Even if it slayed me, I'd show her.

ELLA

I couldn't sleep that night. What I said to Tyrell stayed on my mind. I hadn't spoken about Lacy in years. She never left my mind for long, but I didn't talk about her. It upset me too much.

After her loss, for years I had nightmares about her and the way she passed. It tore me apart that her own mother held her under the water until she stopped fighting for her life. I couldn't imagine the panic and fright Lacy had gone through.

Worse, I found myself not trusting my own family as much as I had before. Somewhere inside me, I thought *no one* could be fully trusted—not when a mother could kill her own child so brutally.

It sometimes helped to go up to draw pictures of my old friend. So, I got out of bed, wrapped a robe around me, and went upstairs to see if that would help.

I had a notebook with my portraits of Lacy in the desk. Taking it out, I ran my hand over the cover before opening it up to find Lacy's big brown eyes staring at me. "Hi there, Lacy. It's nice to see you again. I hope you've been doing well."

Taking the sketchbook with me, I went to sit by the window; the full moon lit up the night sky, and I used only its light to draw that night. Flipping through the pages, I looked at each picture that I had penciled of my best friend who still plagued my dreams at times. "Why'd she do it? Why would anyone do that to anyone, much less their own daughter?"

There were no answers to my questions. I asked my therapist time and time again why this had to happen, and she had no clue. Some things we're not meant to understand, but the age-old answer didn't cut it for me.

So, I didn't comprehend most things after that. I didn't identify with the other children in my class and how they could go on and play as if nothing had ever happened. Or how they all bonded and made long-lasting friendships when at any minute it could be torn away.

Didn't they have a sense of self-preservation? Didn't they worry about feeling the terrible pain that came with losing a friend? Or am I the only one who felt that way?

Growing up, I learned it was pretty much just me, indeed. Others gave their lives to chance. Not me, though. Being alone was much safer than pretending friends are for a lifetime. I didn't need anyone anyway.

But I had had a blast with Tyrell today. And he helped me get my work done when I felt so out of it. He also saved me from making a mistake of enormous proportions the night before.

Tyrell is a good man. Why waste time on me? Well, I definitely put him off sufficiently.

If I ever fell for that man, it would surely devastate me if anything happened to him.

Taking the pencil out of the holder , I laid the tip on a blank page as my mind only conjured his face instead of Lacy's.

For a long time, I just sat there with the pencil poised to draw, but I couldn't make a single mark. Finally, I put the pad down and got up to get a different one.

Going to the bottom drawer, I took out the other pad where I'd drawn a picture of Tyrell. Looking at his handsome face, I sighed, then filled in more of his features to finish out the picture.

"What is it about you, Tyrell Gentry? Why do you make my heart beat so hard? Why do you care about me?" I drew one of his ears, then the hair that grew over it. Dark and thick, shiny and silky,

I continued until I had his whole head done. "Why are you so darn gorgeous?"

Putting the sketch pad down, I looked outside at the moon. A set of headlights turned up the drive, and a truck pulled up. Cash didn't park it in the garage this time. He stopped in front of the house, and when he got out, he went around and opened the passenger door. A feminine silhouette stepped out, and the two walked inside. It was probably the bartender he'd been after.

The thought of people having sex in the manor made my heart pound for mysterious reasons. And his bedroom was just down the hall from where I was! Tyrell's room was steps away, too!

What would Tyrell do if I slipped into his room? Into his bed? Would he tell me to get the heck out? Or would he pull me into his arms, kiss me, and tell me he was glad I visited?

I'll never know; I'm not the type of person who'd do such a thing. Then it dawned on me that it wasn't because of morals. I secluded myself because of fear.

I've been lying to myself for years convinced that I had higher standards than others. That was why I kept to myself and never even held hands with a guy. But it was all a lie. I'd done it out of fear, and not even a bit out of principle.

After Cash and the woman giggled up the hallway, after the sound of his bedroom door closing, I left the drawing room to return to my own bedroom for the evening.

Padding down the hall in my bare feet, I stopped at Tyrell's door. He was inside, sleeping, maybe even dreaming? I put my ear to the door to listen, hoping to hear him breathing.

"Yeah, baby," came his deep voice. "Yes, I do love you. Come on now, stop making me chase you."

Jerking my head back, I couldn't believe what I'd heard! Tyrell must've been on the phone with some girl who he said he loved!

Bolting away, I ran until I reached my bedroom, then closed and locked the door. My heart felt as if it was breaking into a million pieces. I buried my face in the pillow and screamed with anger, "Why did you make me think you liked me? Why did you want to be my friend if you love someone else, Tyrell Gentry?"

I barely slept a wink that night. The next day I moved at a snail's pace, and noticed Tyrell wasn't around. He even missed breakfast. Not that I had eaten either; I just passed by the Brunch Room to see if he was in there. The other two brothers didn't make it to breakfast, either—a little odd since they all made it all the other mornings.

As noon came around, the Gentrys were still gone. I finished cleaning the upstairs and was about to begin working on the downstairs area when the doorbell rang. Going to answer it, a man was standing there with a large bouquet of red roses in his hand. "Hello," I greeted him. "Can I help you?"

"I'm looking for Ella Finley," his words surprised me.

"That's me." I shook my head. "But those can't be for me."

"These are for you, and there's a note, too." He handed me the flowers and the note. "Have a fantastic day, Miss Finley."

"Thanks." Who would've sent me flowers for no reason whatsoever? It wasn't my birthday or anything like that. Not that my family ever sent me flowers on that occasion anyhow!

I went to the kitchen to find a vase. Placing them on the bar, I got a funny look from Todd when he came out of the pantry. "Flowers?"

Nodding as I opened the envelope, I clued him in. "They're for me. Who would send me flowers?" As I pulled out the miniature card, I gasped. "No!"

My sister walked through the rear entrance, her eyes as big as saucers. "Whoa, who got those beauties?"

Todd bursted, "Ella. But she's yet to tell us who they're from."

"So?" Darleen asked, "Who sent them?"

I picked up the roses, then promptly shoved them into the trash can. "Some jackass." I tossed the note in, too, and turned to walk away.

Leaving the kitchen, I stormed to my bedroom, trying not to cry. Why did Tyrell send me flowers when he was telling some other girl that he loved her? It was infuriating!

Plopping on the bed, I once again buried my face in my pillow to scream obscenities until I fell asleep. Hours later, my sister pounded on the door. "Ella, wake up! You've been sleeping all day."

My head hurt when I picked it up from the pillow. "Huh?" The room had been lit by sunlight, yet now it was dark. "What time is it?"

"Eight," Darleen called out. "Come on, you need to eat something."

Climbing out of bed, I ran my hands through my hair as I went to open my door. "I must've dozed off."

"For six hours?" she asked. "That's not dozing, that's full-on passed out. What's up?"

Shrugging, I went past her to go get a drink from the kitchen. And that's when I saw the flowers again. They were put into a vase and sitting on our kitchen table. "Who brought these here?"

"I did," Darleen declared. "They're dazzling, and you shouldn't have thrown them away."

"I *don't* want them." I went to get a bottle of water, trying to ignore the powerful scent of the roses. "They reek." They didn't stink at all; they smelled wonderful, but I didn't want them.

Darleen picked up the note that came with them off the table. "Tyrell sent these. He left his number and asked you to call him once you got them. I think he'd like to ask you out on a date."

My brother Kyle walked in through the front door. "Who's asking who out on a date?"

Darleen smiled. "Tyrell is asking Ella out. At least I think he wants to." She handed him the note, then gestured to the flowers. "That came with these."

Kyle's face turned ruby red. "That son of a bitch! Who does he think he is?" Turning on his heel, he headed toward the door.

Why is he so mad? "What are you doing, Kyle?"

"I'm going to go kick his ass and set him straight." He flung open the door, then stormed out.

Darleen and I looked at each other surprised then ran after him. "No," she shouted. "Kyle, don't do anything stupid!"

I caught up to him and grabbed him by the arm. "Kyle, he'll fire you!"

"So what?" He jerked his arm out of my hand. "Let me deal with this."

Darleen grabbed me as Kyle flew out of the house. "It's no use. Let him go. At least Tyrell won't bother you anymore. That is what

257

you want, right? I mean you did toss those flowers in the trash. You must not want anything to do with the guy."

Panting after getting heated up by Kyle's reaction, I nodded. "Yeah, I guess."

We returned to our quarters, and she put her arm around my shoulders. "Why don't you want anything to do with him, Ella?"

"The same reason I don't want anything to do with anyone." I stepped away from her to go inside. I didn't want to admit I was afraid, or for anyone else to know what I knew now.

Tyrell would hate me soon. My brother would see to that. Maybe it was all for the best. He could stop pretending to like me. He could focus on that girl he was talking to the night before and leave me out of his sights.

That's just fine with me. But why does my heart ache so much if it's perfectly fine?

TYRELL

Hours had passed since I got the text that the flowers had been hand-delivered to Ella. I've been at the Dairy King, hoping she'd call. My number was on the note, and the delivery man assured me he handed it to her. I asked her to give me a call. But she hasn't called.

So, I went to The Watering Hole for a few drinks to give her more time to respond. This was Ella, after all. She needed more time for just about everything.

I ordered my third beer after Jasper ditched me when Tiffany came in. "Later, braddah. I hope Ella shows up."

Waving at Tiffany, I turned to my cell to distract me while I waited. Was it all in vain? My mind has been focused on Ella, even when I slept. I was tired of fighting it and her. I just wanted to be with her already.

The flowers were meant to show her I cared. They were not about showing everyone else—they should already know I was crazy about Ella! I might've been just plumb crazy, but I couldn't stop thinking about her. That must mean something.

Knowing how innocent she was, I knew we wouldn't be getting to the good stuff as quickly as I had with anyone before her. But we'd get there. I knew we would.

My fantasies of her had been off the charts. The night before, I used the word *Love* with her. I'd never used that word with any other woman before, not even in my dreams!

Not sure that I actually loved her just yet, but I cared about her . She needed more than just *some guy*. Ella needed a man who could value her. A man with thick skin who could soften her shitty attitude. A man who could douse those flames with soft kisses and unveil what's been hidden under her rough exterior.

Ella just needed to give me a chance to uncover some of that sweetness she'd pushed far down inside of her tortured soul. I couldn't right what had happened with her very first friend; no one could. Ella needed to come to terms with that fact of life.

She needed to know that men and women were meant to make love and complement each other. One was no better than the other; both had roles to play, but it took two to tango.

Ella needed to feel a man's caress, to know what it felt like to be touched by loving hands, not lusting hands. No, Ella was too special and too psychologically frail. She'd need a commitment before I took her virginity. I wouldn't expect her to accept anything less.

Ella was a rare find, and I'd treat her as such. If she'd let me begin showing her, I could be the man she needed and deserved. We could be each other's everything. But she has to stop being so afraid.

When she told me about Lacy, it was apparent that fear kept her virginity in place. I could be gentle with her body and her mind.

Lifting the frosted beer mug to my lips, the door opened, and Kyle Finley walked in. Usually, the man looked cheerful. Not now. No, Kyle wore a grim look, his lips were formed one tight line, and his color was on the red side.

I sat there, watching him as he scanned the room. Whomever it was, I would've hated to be in their shoes. Kyle looked like he could spit glass at that moment.

When his eyes met mine, I smiled, hoping to lessen his anger—for whatever it was over—but then he came at me, his fists balled at his sides and flames shooting out of the top of his head.

Well, maybe not actual flames, but he sure was hot-headed. And why was he coming at me? "Hey, Kyle, buddy. What's up?"

"Get your ass up, Tyrell," he snarled. "I'm about to kick your ass."

"*My* ass?" I couldn't believe my ears.

His eyes looked like the eyes of a rattlesnake. "Yeah, *your* ass."

"Why mine?" I got up just to be on the safe side.

"You've got some nerve coming into our home and thinking you can play slap and tickle with my baby sister." He put his fists up in front of him. "Get ready to get your butt whooped."

"*Slap and tickle?*" What is he was talking about? "I've never touched your sister, Kyle. Why are you so angry? I've never done anything untoward to your sister."

His fist came through the air right at my nose, and I quickly dodged out of the way, feeling the air rush by my face. "Liar!"

People, including my two brothers, began to gather around us, and a few began to chant, "Fight, fight, fight…"

"There ain't gonna be no fight," I said calmly. "Kyle, I can see you're furious."

Another blow came at me; again I dodged it just in the nick of time.

"I'm pissed as hell, Tyrell! You must have touched my baby sister to have sent her all those flowers. Don't lie to me! What do you want with her anyway? Another notch on your bedpost? Well, forget it! She's not about to fall for your charming bullshit."

"I don't want that at all." I ducked just in time to miss another punch. "Kyle, chill, dude. We can talk about this like rational men."

Jasper came up behind me, and I turned to look at him for only a second when Kyle's fist connected with my jaw.

"Oh, shit!" Cash caught me as I stumbled toward him. "Bro, you shouldn't have turned your head."

Squaring up, fists at the ready, I wasn't about to let Kyle *actually* kick my ass. "Sucker punch, huh? Let's see how you like it." I had more fighting experience than Kyle could've ever imagined. I landed one controlled punch right on his jaw. "There, we're even. Let's chill."

"Fuck you!" He swung again, and thanks to Cash pushing me forward a bit, it hit me square on the chin.

"Cash, Goddammit!" I took only a second to check my chin to

be sure there was no open wound. "Oh, you are so lucky you didn't split my chin open, Kyle." Thrusting my fist out so fast he never saw it coming, I connected with his chin. "We're even again. Stop this now. I don't want to hurt you, man."

My hit had knocked him back a few steps, and when he regained his footing, he let out a roar, then came at me like a linebacker. "You're pulp!"

An alarm went off as I got ready to take Kyle on, then water splashed on us both from above as a woman's voice came over a bullhorn, "This stops now!"

The cold water seemed to pull Kyle out of his angry state as he looked up. "What the hell?"

The bartender pushed and shoved people out of her way as she came between Kyle and I. "I've got each of you two shots of whiskey and some ice-cold beers to chase them with. They're all yours if you'll take seats at the bar and talk this out like real men do."

Cash moved in behind her. "Come on, guys. Don't give the lady a hard time." He kissed her on top of her blonde head. "Good thinking, Bobbi Jo."

"Yeah, it just came to me to set off the fire alarm." She eyed Kyle, knowing he started everything. "Come on, big fella. Let's talk this out now."

He followed her, and I walked behind them with Jasper at my side, who whispered, "What the hell is this about?"

"I don't know. Let's find out and settle it."

After Bobbi Jo turned the sprinkler system off, we took seats at the bar, leaving an empty one between us. I held up the first shot glass. "To peace and harmony."

Kyle nodded. "To peace and harmony."

We downed the shots, then I asked, "Okay, please tell me what's going on."

"You sent Ella flowers. The note said to call you," he continued as he rubbed his jaw. "She is difficult to get along with, so I immediately thought you took advantage of her and gave her flowers as a thank you gift."

"You are mistaken." I picked up the next shot glass, and he did the same. "To understanding each other and talking like adults."

Kyle smiled. "To being adults."

We downed the shots, then I told him of my intentions. "Kyle, I've got it bad for Ella. All I can think about is her. I even dream about her. But never—not in a million years—would I ask her to do anything she isn't ready for. And I won't hurt her or use her or abuse her in any way, shape, or form; it's a promise. I truly care for her more than I've ever cared about anyone."

His brow furrowed. "Why?"

I kind of thought he might ask that.

ELLA

Waking up at one in the morning, I heard Kyle as he careened down the hallway, hitting the walls on either side. Jumping out of bed, I ran to the door, throwing it open. "What happened?"

He stopped and turned slowly to face me. His drooping eyes assured me that he was hammered. He put one finger to his lips. "Shh. Don't wake up Dad. He'll holler if he finds out how late I'm getting in."

"Okay," I whispered. "But what happened with Tyrell?"

"Don't you worry one bit about him, baby sister. I've got it all taken care of. He's not going to hurt you." He turned away from me and lurched down the hall until he got to his room.

What did he mean? It didn't make a lot of sense! Slipping back into bed, I thought about Kyle's face. It looked puffy in places.

Did they get into a fistfight?

Kyle couldn't have gone so far as to assault Tyrell, his boss...? Maybe he didn't have a job anymore? Maybe Tyrell told him we were all fired? He would've had every right do that.

Pulling the blanket over my head, I chastised myself, "This is all your fault, Ella Finley. What's wrong with you? Why can't you be ordinary? Any other girl would be blissful getting flowers from Tyrell

Gentry. Not you, though. No, you get mad, and then your brother beats the man up."

We are so screwed! I have to fix it! Dad has worked here nearly his whole life. We'd grown up on the estate. I didn't want to leave the only home we'd ever known.

All of us will have to leave because I am a scared little girl. The whole world frightened me! It was an unsafe place, and no one could be trusted.

Man, I'm really screwed up!

And now my mental hang-ups would affect my entire family. How mad will they be when they wake up to find we had neither jobs nor home?

Maybe I could do something to fix it before they all woke up? So, I did what I had to do and put on a robe over my pajamas and then went to see if Tyrell made it home yet.

I'd just have to explain that my brother wanted to protect me. I'd say that we love our jobs and have always called Whisper Ranch our home and to please forgive my idiot-Neanderthal brother for beating him up.

As I got to his door, I wondered how badly Kyle beat him. I hope his cute face is okay. I knocked on the door. "Tyrell?"

I heard some fumbling, then the door opened, and there he stood, smelling of alcohol, smiling like a fool, with a slight swelling on his chin. "Hey, you." He leaned on the door, looking like he might fall over if the door wasn't there to steady him. "I missed you today. Did you get the flowers I sent ya?"

"Yes, I did. Are you okay?" His hair was disheveled, and he had starry eyes. "Did my brother hurt you?"

"Naw." He shook his head. His southern drawl had really taken off, "He's a good guy—a great big brother, Ella. He just cares about ya, is all." His hand moved and the next thing I knew it was on my cheek. "You're so pretty. Have I told you that before? Wait. Yes, I have." The way his thumb stroked my cheek made moisture pool between my legs. "Did you like the roses?"

He still acted as if he liked me. And I was done keeping what my thoughts to myself. "Tyrell, you're drunk. And you might not even recall this conversation in the morning." I wanted to clear that up before saying anything else. "Did you fire Kyle tonight when he hit you?"

He shook his head as his hand dropped off my face. "No. There's no reason to fire a great guy like him. We traded a couple punches is all. Nothing serious. We're fine. Don't worry about us, Ella."

While glad we still had our jobs, I wanted to know about the other woman in Tyrell's life. The one he'd never told me about. "Did you leave someone behind in Dallas when you came out here to Carthage?"

His lips curled, his eyes drooped. "Ella, I'd ask you to come in, but I respect you. Did you know that? If you didn't, then now you do. I respect you a lot. And I care about you. Like, I can't stop thinking 'bout ya. Like, not ever. When I sleep, I dream about ya all the time. But I respect you." He put his finger on the tip of my nose. "And I know you're afraid, but I'm going to prove you don't have to be afraid of me."

He hadn't answered my question, and now I had even more. "So, who'd you leave behind in Dallas, Tyrell?"

"Did you know that I've never had a girlfriend with dark hair before? Not ever." He held up one finger. "All blondes. All of them. You've got the most beautiful hair I've ever seen."

This felt like a conversation with a three-year-old. "So, what's the blonde's name who you left behind, Tyrell?" I might be able to trick the answer out of him.

He let out a long sigh, then his bleary eyes settled on mine. "And you've got the prettiest blue eyes. Your lips are like red rose petals. That's why I picked red roses to send you. They reminded me of your lips, so soft and smooth. I'd like to kiss those lips." He held up his finger, moving it back and forth. "But I won't do that until you're ready. When do you think that'll be, Ella?"

I put my fingers to my lips and felt moisture springing up in my lower area. "Tyrell, you're being silly." I felt a blush heat my cheeks. "You're drunk."

"I am drunk." He hiccupped. "But sometimes, even without the alcohol, I feel drunk when I'm around you. Is that weird? Cause it's never happened with anyone else before. I'm high on you, Ella Finley."

"You're something alright." I better let him get to bed. "You know what? It would be better to have this conversation tomorrow. It's late, and you're not quite yourself. It was wrong for me to bring anything up. I was only worried Kyle might've hurt you."

"Nah," he said then waved his hand through the air as if trying to swat a fly. "I'm not hurt. And you won't be, either. Did I tell you that I dream about you?"

"Yes, you did." We're not getting anywhere with this. "Well, good night then. Sweet dreams."

"Oh, I will." He put his hand to his mouth, then kissed it before holding his palm out to me. "Tomorrow, my lady. For tonight you will sleep with me in my dreams. The way you have for many nights. But one day I hope we can be together in real life."

That was it. He'd gone on too much. "Tyrell, I heard you last night."

His eyes went all shiny. "Last night was the best dream ever. I said, 'I love you' in that dream."

"Wait." Stunned, I wondered if I heard him wrong? "You did what?"

"In my dream last night, I told you I loved you and to stop making me chase you." He hiccupped again. "You *should* stop making me chase you, Ella. It's making me nuts."

Alcohol? Truth serum? Or worse, a liquid that brings lies to life?

"You didn't get a phone call from someone last night?" Why do I bother asking a drunk man anything at all?

"Nope. Why do you ask?" he stumbled backward, taking the door with him. "Whoa. Where ya going' Ella?"

"It's you who's going, Tyrell." I stepped closer to stabilize him before he fell on his ass. "Here, put your arm around my shoulders, and we'll get you to bed. You really need to get some sleep."

"Aw." He put his arm around me. "You do care about me, don't you?"

"I can't just stand here and watch you fall down." I let him lean on me as we stumbled to his bed. "You still have all your clothes on.

If you sit down, I'll take off your boots. The rest is up to you. You were nice enough to help me out when I drank too much."

"You're sweet. I knew you could be." He plopped down with a thud.

I lifted up his right leg to get the cowboy boot off. "I suppose I can be sweet, when the stars align just right." The boot was off and then I went to pull the other. "This one's a bit tight, Tyrell." I turned my back to him, then straddled his leg to get a better grip. I've taken off my daddy's boots hundreds of times the same way. "Now give my butt a push with your other foot, and I'll have this boot off in a…" I went flying across the room as he'd pushed me a little too hard. "Tyrell!"

Somehow, I caught myself before plowing into the wall. When I turned around, he was laying flat on the bed with his legs dangling off the side. His loud snores told me he'd passed out.

Walking back over to him, I heaved his heavy legs up onto the bed, then covered him with a blanket as best I could. As he lay there, mouth slightly open, eyes closed, chest rising and falling with each snore he made, something in my heart stirred.

He wasn't talking to anyone. He loves me—in his dreams at least.

Reaching out, I ran my fingertips along his swollen jaw, then over the chin where a bruise was beginning to appear.

He cared about me. I cared about him. Maybe it was time to do some growing up and put the fear behind me? Maybe I could stop hiding behind that fear and actually start living life? A life that possibly could include him?

Easing my fingers over his lips, I traced them, wondering how it would feel if those lips pressed against mine. Taking my hand away, I turned to leave the room, chiding myself. *What, now you're something akin to a necrophiliac? Do what you need to become what he deserves.*

Looking at him as I closed the door, I turned off the overhead light, then kissed my fingertips and blew across the room to him. "Sweet dreams, Tyrell."

Now to get some kind of a plan.

TYRELL

Rolling over, I saw her lying there, her dark hair splayed over the blue pillowcase. Right next to me, Ella slept. Moving my hand up her arm, I gently ran it along her soft skin, finding it all bare. Her naked breasts rose and fell with each breath she took.

Ella Finley is in my bed!

Moving my hands over my body, I was naked as well. Whatever happened while I slept was about to happen again while I was awake! Kissing her neck, I caressed her body to wake her up. "Ella, baby?"

She stirred, moaning, "Tyrell, go back to sleep, babe."

"What happened?" I whispered in her ear, then nibbled on it, making her moan.

"You know what happened." She turned to her side, her blue eyes open. "You told me that you love me."

Pulling her close to me, our bodies flush, I smiled. "Oh, yeah. Now I remember." My lips took hers with a gentle kiss. "I do love you."

"And I love you, Tyrell Gentry." Her hands moved up to wrap around my neck, then she tugged me to get on top of her. "Come on back up here and show me what it feels like to be loved by you."

My cock sprang to life as I scooted on top of her. "You want more, huh?"

"I can't seem to get enough of you." Her eyes sparkled as I eased into her. "What you do to me doesn't seem real."

I felt as close to Heaven as I'd ever been while buried deep inside of her. "This is all very real, baby. To hear you say that you love me takes my heart to new heights." I moved up and down, holding my body a bit above to keep my weight off her.

She ran her hands under my arms, then pulled me down. "Get closer to me. I want to feel your body on mine." Her lips caught mine with a hungry kiss. Her sweet breath mingled with mine as our tongues fought for control, mine winning out in the end.

Bending her knees, I sank into her deeper. "You feel amazing!"

She moaned, arching her body up to mine. "You do, too! I shouldn't have held off so long. This is better than I ever thought possible!"

"Sex?" I asked as I nibbled her neck.

"Not just sex, Tyrell. Making love with you. I can't imagine this being any better with anyone else." Her nails ran down my back as she wiggled. "Oh, that feels good right there."

I made slight move. "That?"

She nodded and groaned. "Yes, there."

"I don't want you this way with anyone else, Ella Finley. You hear me?" I gave her another special move that had her whimpering with pleasure.

Her words came out in a soft grumble, "Oh, I hear you, Tyrell. And the same goes for you. Do you hear *me*?" She squeezed her legs tightly around my body. "You are mine."

"I hear ya, girl." Kissing her again, I held her down while making slow, torturous strokes that left her body quivering, needing more. Not too fast! I wanted this to last!

Having her in bed was a bolt from the blue. The girl was chock full of surprises.

It would've been nice to recall what happened, but at least she's where I'd wanted her for some time. I wasn't about to let this end.

"Oh, baby, faster, harder, please," she begged as I kissed her neck, driving her into a frenzy of lustful passion. "Tyrell, oh, my God!"

Shaking, her body was on fire and about to blow sky high. "You hold on, baby. Let me take you on a wild ride you'll never forget."

Her legs held me tightly as she kept me inside of her. "Just give it to me, babe. I need it."

"Wait," I whispered. "Wait until I tell you to."

Her nails bit into my flesh, then her teeth did, too, as she moaned with agonizing desire. "I'll try."

Reaching back, I grabbed one of her ankles and pried her leg off me, pulling it up until her knee was by her ear. Going in even deeper had her whimpering, and I loved the sound. "You want me to go faster?"

"Please," she begged. "Faster. Harder."

I wanted to feel her hot juices all over my hard cock, so I gave her what she wanted. Moving fast, all I could hear was the sound of our heavy breathing and the slapping of flesh.

Harder and harder I rode her until she screamed, "Yes! Tyrell! Yes!"

Her body clenched around mine as she orgasmed and thrashed violently. I couldn't hold back; I came, too, with an inhuman groan, "Ella! God, what have you done to me?"

I didn't know it could feel this way. How could love make it feel so incredible? I never wanted this to end!

Softly, I kissed her neck as we caught our breaths. Her body still shook underneath mine. Our hearts beat so hard; hers was banging against my chest. "Shh," I hushed her as she whined. "Everything's going to be alright. I love you, Ella. This will never end. Not ever."

Her hands moved to catch my shoulders, pushing me up so she could look at me. "What does that mean, Tyrell?"

"I'll make sure this never ends. I'll treat you like a queen and make sure your every need is met. There will be no reason in hell to end what we've found. Not ever." I kissed her quivering lips softly. "I love you, baby."

When our mouths parted, I found her staring at me with shining eyes. "Does this mean you don't want me to go back to my own bedroom? Like forever?"

I nodded. "I want you right here, where I can hug and kiss you anytime I want."

She smiled slightly. "And I can hug and kiss *you* anytime I want to as well? I like that idea." Pulling me back to her for another kiss, she held me tightly in her petite arms. "Loving you is better than strawberry ice cream, Tyrell Gentry."

I had to laugh. "Girl, loving you is better than the greasiest blue cheese burger in the world."

I felt lost and found at the same time. It was the oddest, but best sensation! I would've waited as long as that girl wanted me to. I was glad she didn't delay any longer. Nowhere but forward to go now.

Stroking my hair, she whispered, "I must've fell in love with you the first day you came here."

Smiling, I smoothed a few stray hairs off her darling face. "I know you did."

Laughing, she punched me in the arm. "You did, too. When you caught me the first time, you had googly eyes for me."

"Maybe I did." The moment I caught her, she felt different in my arms—a *great* different.

"You did," she said with a nod. "And I had them for you, too, only I conceal stuff like that much better than you."

"To be honest, I thought you hated me." I kissed the tip of her cute nose. "But that was just a front. My beloved Ella, you've hidden behind fear for long enough. It's time to discover life isn't daunting."

"With you by my side, I can do anything." Her foot ran up the back of my leg, sending chills all through me. "Want to have another go at it?"

"Insatiable, aren't you?" I moved a tad, trying to get it the way she liked.

"Um, hm," she moaned as I moved slow and steady. "When will I get out of this bed with you? Do you think Momma will look for me when she realizes I'm not in my room?"

"She might." I kissed along her collarbone. "We might want to get you back before that happens, huh?"

"I'm not some child." She pulled my face to look into my eyes. "You've made me a woman now, Tyrell. *Your* woman. My momma will have to get used to the fact that I'll be here a lot more than in my own room."

I wanted her there all the time. "You'll always be here. I ain't about to let you sleep in your tiny bed alone. Not when you feel so good in my arms."

The smile that filled her made my heart skip a beat. "So, do you think my family will be on board with this arrangement?"

"We'll convince them, don't you think?" I kissed my way along her chest. "I'm not about to love you and leave you, the way you thought. I'm in it for the long haul."

"You talk like you want to marry me." She pulled my face up once more.

"And if I do?" We're talking about this rather soon, but now that we are, why not clue her in on my true intentions?

"When you make the real proposal, I'd like a ring in your hand." Her lips pressed against my cheek. "Just so you know."

"Got it, ring in hand, on one knee, and the biggest smile you will ever see." Rolling over with her, she was on top of me now. "Your turn to ride me, cowgirl."

"Giddyup!" I bucked, and she shouted. "I've got me a live one here!"

"That you do, baby." Holding her by the waist, I moved her up and down, watching those double Cs bounce with every movement. "What a sight!"

Putting her hands on my shoulders, she jiggled her tits near my face. "Here ya go, cowboy." Taking one hard as rock nipple into my mouth, I sucked it, making her squeal. "Tyrell! Oh, Tyrell!"

Some knocking sound came from the door. My eyes flew open, my hand on my hard cock. 'Tyrell? You up?" Jasper asked from the other side of the door.

No one else in my bed but me... My jeans were still on, just unzipped. Even my shirt was on. "What the...?!"

Another round of knocks. "Tyrell? What the hell, man? It's noon already. Are you alive in there?"

Not nearly as alive I thought. Damn!

ELLA

"Darleen, come here," I whispered as she passed my bedroom door.

Pausing, she looked into my room. "What? And why are you whispering?"

Wiggling my finger, I encouraged her to come inside, "Come here." It was still early in the morning; we hadn't even got ready for work yet. Mom was in the living room, reading a book. She'd listen to us talking and shouldn't hear what I was about to say.

Darleen came in, closing the door behind her, understanding the need for privacy. "What's the hush-hush all about, Ella?"

"Tyrell said he loved me last night." I bit my lower lip trying not to burst out with some happy song.

"He did not!" she said with wide eyes. "You mean in your dreams or something? You went to bed way before they got back from the bar. Or did you go to his room afterwards? Oh, Ella, don't tell me you did! Have you given up your virginity to a drunk?"

"Relax," I said with a scowl. "What you might think of me is pretty appalling. I would never do something like that. I went up there after seeing Kyle when he got back. His face was swollen. I was worried he hurt Tyrell and went to check on him."

She sat on the edge of the bed frowning. "Not smart at all.

Going to a grown man's bedroom late at night isn't something an innocent girl should be doing. Did you go into his room?"

"Not at first." I stopped as she ran her hand over her face.

Her blue eyes rolled. "Ella, before you go on, please tell me you did nothing. Not so much as a kiss. Please?"

"Not a thing! But listen! "I needed her to shut the heck up! "He really likes me. He wants to start seeing me. And he said he had a dream the other night, and in that dream, he said he loved me. He was so smashed he passed out not long after saying that. I pulled off his boots and tucked him in, leaving him alone. I did the appropriate thing. The same way he did when I got drunk and passed out in his bed the other night."

The expression on her face reminded me I hadn't told a soul about that. "You did what? When? How? And why?"

"After not going through with the exam at the clinic, you all had gone to bed that night…" I really put my foot in my mouth this time. "I saw the black truck leaving. Dad was downstairs falling asleep in front of the television. He told me the brothers had gone to The Watering Hole."

"*You* went *there?*" Her eyes were as big as saucers. "You got drunk at that bar?" She paused. "What car did you take?"

I'd get a lecture if she knew, so no mention of the corvette. "Look, that's old news, Darleen. Honestly, nothing awful happened that night. That's because Tyrell was there and rescued me from making a dreadful mistake in the nick of time. He took me home and put me in his room."

Getting up, she began to pace. "He put you in the bed, and you slept together in it? That's *so* not okay, Ella."

"He didn't do that." She saw the worst in everyone! "He put me in his bed, taking off only my boots and buttoning up the sweater I purposely left unbuttoned enough to show off my boobs. Tyrell slept on the floor, also with his clothes on. He was a gentleman. And the next morning he helped me with my duties. We went out for lunch after that and had the best time. Then he freaked me out and ruined things by asking me to be his friend."

"What an ass," she said with a marked amount of sarcasm. "So that's why he sent you those flowers? He wanted to improve things since you acted like a jackass, huh?"

"Yes." I didn't like to think of myself as a jackass, but she was correct. "But after talking to him last night, it's been a mistake hiding from things—him especially."

"So, do you want me to make you another appointment at the clinic?" she asked. "Because condoms are great, but not as effective as birth control. So, I do not recommend relying on them alone when your special time comes. And it will come. Sooner than you think. Tyrell is all man; he'll sweep you off your feet with the first kiss. And you'll lose all the will to stop him from going further. You'll become putty in his hands."

"Will not." I got up and rolled my eyes. "That's just stupid. Anyway, he said he respected me and wouldn't even kiss me until I was ready."

"That's decent of him. But when you give the go-ahead on that kiss, you need to be ready for what follows." She came up behind me as I looked at my reflection in the mirror over my dresser.

"I do." Turning to face her, I let her in on my design. "I didn't want to see the doctor because I thought that one day I'll pass her on the street and will want to crawl in a hole in shame."

"It's honestly not that awkward. She's seen lots of female anatomy in this town. Why would you stand out more than anyone else?" she asked with a grin.

"Okay, it's just me. I'll be trying to dodge her, and who knows, I might run in front of a moving vehicle just to avoid her." I did have another idea though. And the fact she kept butting in was slowing me down. "Our cousin, Sherry lives in Dallas. I could go there and spend a week or so to visit a clinic where no one knows me. How long does it take for birth control to kick in?"

"It depends on which one you get." She tapped her chin with one long finger as she contemplated.

"I'm only getting on the pill. The other options are not for me. I can handle a pill every day like my Flintstone chewable. The other pill can be popped at the same time." Great idea!

"That one takes thirty days to kick in," she announced. "And like I said before, don't use condoms alone, too risky. And you certainly don't want to get pregnant right off the bat."

"So, I need to stay away for a month then," I mused. "I'll have to ask Mom for time off. And I'll have to make sure Sherry is fine with me staying with her that long."

"What are you going to tell Mom?" Darleen asked.

"That's why I asked you to come in here. Help me make up a good reason." I tapped my foot and crossed my arms over my chest. "You're great at filling in the blanks."

Darleen went into the zone she'd go to when faced with a problem. "What's in Dallas you could possibly need to do?"

Something sparked in my brain. "Hey, what if I said Sherry will be out of town and needs me to dog sit for her?"

Darleen's head tilted to one side. "What if Mom calls Sherry's mother, and asks about that? They're sisters…"

Nodding, she was right. That's why I asked for her help after all. "True."

Folding her hands in front of her as she paced back and forth, she finally stopped. "Sherry might actually need your help. I talked to her a few months ago. She said she was starting up a daycare business. I bet she could use your help, in a volunteer role. We could get that worked out for you. And I'll let her in on what the real deal is. She's cool. She'll go with it."

"How soon could you get that going?" I wanted to get moving on it as soon as possible.

"I'll grab my cell and give her a call. I'll be back in a little while." She walked to the door, her hand on the knob. "Are you going to tell Tyrell?"

Shaking my head, I wasn't about to have a conversation with him about that. "No way. Are you nuts? How awkward would that be?"

Clucking her tongue, she shook her head. "In my opinion, Ella, you're still too adolescent for this."

"I agree. But I've got to mature somehow. Getting away for a month, being with our cool cousin, finally getting the exam most women had at least a few of, should put me on the road to maturity. I plan on being a different person when I return." Visions of me walking back into the mansion, maybe at dinner time, Tyrell checking me out as I'd be wearing something awe-inspiring outfit that I picked up in Dallas. A new hairstyle, total makeover. His jaw would drop. He'd be lost for words.

"Um, that's a pretty tall order." She opened the door. "You really should go talk to him. See how he acts in the light of day and sober. I doubt he'll be as lovestruck as he was last night."

"You're wrong. He's crazy about me." I had faith in the guy. He'd wait for me. He understood things about me before I had. Tyrell would know instinctively that I'd gone to gather myself and become a real woman for him.

I started packing, knowing Darleen would get it all finalized. Then I got online and looked up the bus schedule. I'd never driven in a big city before, so I couldn't ask to take the family car to Dallas for a month. Bus first, then I could take Ubers to get around while there.

This was going to be it: the first step in becoming set for a mature relationship. Tyrell would be stunned and he'd know without a doubt I was ready for him.

A chill ran through me thinking about what that really means. Me and him, kissing, hugging, holding hands, and even doing the deed. Over and over again, at that. It was thrilling me more than anything!

Darleen came back a while later as I waited to purchase the bus ticket. "You can go as soon as you want. She's even going to ask her mom who could help her out for a time. Sherry is so cool; she'll make it seem it was her mom who'd come up with the idea of you coming to help."

Not even an hour later, my mother found me cleaning and asked, "Ella, could you go to Dallas to help your cousin with the daycare she's opened up? She's desperate."

Acting as if I had no idea if I could go or not. "What about my work here?"

"Tasha's aunt can take over while you're gone. She's always looking to make some extra money." Mom took the broom out of my hand. "I'd let you take our car, but I doubt you'll like driving in

Dallas. Everyone drives as fast as they possibly can. But I can take you in, and then you can catch up with her."

"How long are we talking about, Mom?"

"Most likely, a month. She's distressed, Ella. Don't let her down," Mom pleaded.

"Since you put it that way, how could I say no?" I took the broom from her. "I'll put these away, get packed and ready to go. But you don't have to drive me. I can take a bus. It's not a problem." I actually wanted to do it on my own for once.

Mom looked concerned. "Oh, I don't know."

Putting my hand on her shoulder, I looked into her eyes. "I'll be fine, mom. I'll even pay for my own ticket. Sherry needs help. She's a great cousin and I'll have fun in Dallas, too."

"You probably will. Sherry will make sure of it." Mom's smile warmed my heart even if we were pulling the wool over her eyes.

TYRELL

After chugging down two bottles of water, I thought I might make it after all. "I really tied one on last night." My brothers sat in my suite as I tried to recall exactly what happened once I got home. "I made it to the bedroom, pulled my wallet and cell out of my jeans. But after that, it goes blank."

Cash pointed at my boots placed neatly by the dresser. "You took your boots off. But they're put away much too neatly."

That's a valid point. I stared at the boots for a long time but had no recollection of how they got there. "Apparently I got them off somehow, then passed out, totally dressed. I even managed to pull a blanket over me."

The vivid dream of making love to Ella was still in the forefront of my mind. "You guys won't believe the lucid dream I had. I thought Ella was in my bed."

Jasper put his hand over his mouth as he gasped, "What if she was, Tyrell?"

"Nah, she'd never do a thing like that. She has no idea how I feel about her anyway. She never responded to the flowers... Maybe she doesn't like me the same way I like her?"

Cash seemed taken aback. "Are you serious? Tyrell Gentry

thinks a woman isn't as into him as he is into her? What's the world coming to?" He laughed as if he thought it was hilarious.

"She's different, Cash. She's had some rough stuff in her life. You'd never understand her." I smiled thinking about her. "She's not transparent by any means. You never know what's going to come out of her mouth. It's interesting just to be with her. It's never clear if you're going to be smiling or frowning or wanting to yell at her."

"Sounds rather tragic, Tyrell," Jasper opined. "I like knowing if you're going to have a great time with a girl or not. If the answer is no, I'd be the guy who thinks of something else to do, anything other than spending time in her company. But that's just me."

"I'm the youngest and closest to Ella's age, but she's extremely adolescent, Tyrell." Cash got up and went to look in the minifridge. "All you got in here is bottles of water?"

I nodded. "Yeah, why?"

"I figured it would be full of beer." He got out a couple of bottles, tossing one to Jasper.

With no recollection of the night before, it's best I slow down on the drinking. "I'll leave the bar alone for a while. You see, Ella is a exceptional young lady. Everything I do with her will be her first time. I'd like to remember those firsts."

Jasper nodded. "Oh, I see now. She's a virgin."

Cash laughed. "Duh."

With a shrug, Jasper went on, "I hadn't realized that. I suppose you two have been observing her more."

What's wrong with that? "You're sweet on Bobbi Jo, right?"

"Very sweet," he said with a grin.

"So why have you noticed this much about Ella?"

"You're my big brother. She's a year younger than me." Where is he going with this? "If a woman your age was after me or vice versa, you'd size her up, wouldn't you? You know, watch out for me?"

"Perhaps." I still didn't like that he had so much interest in her. "Have you noticed how she puts her hands on her hips a lot? The way her nose crinkles when she believes something's not good?"

"Um, no," he informed me. "None of that. Just that she's less mature than other girls her age. That alone told me she was a virgin. Girls who've already been around the block a time or two don't act the way she does."

He was right. "Yeah. Seems I'm insecure about her. I've never been apprehensive about anyone in my entire life, but I keep asking myself if petite Ella Finley really likes me or not?"

Jasper shrugged. "The other night at the bar should've demonstrated enough, Tyrell."

"You'd think so. But after that night, we had lunch together and she went quiet on me when I asked her to be my friend. Then I sent her flowers and still nothing." She had to let me know if we were on the same page.

Cash came over to tap me on the back. "At least now you have Kyle's approval to see his sister, so the family won't be in your way. Now to just find out what Ella thinks about you."

"You know what?" I got up and headed to the shower. "I'll clean myself up and do just that. She has to let me know one way or the other. I'm tired of pussyfooting around. Virgin or not, some things are considered plain rude."

My brothers left, and I got myself cleaned up, then went to find Ella. She works today, so I began my search downstairs. "Ella? Where are you at?"

I should've had her cell number, but instead I had to hunt her down.

After walking about and calling her name for some time, I decided to check the kitchen. Or her mother's office? Someone in there should know of her whereabouts. Her mom was walking out of her office as I rounded the corner.

"Oh, Tyrell. My, don't you look dashing this afternoon. But I suppose sleeping until noon would have you getting plenty of beauty sleep."

Long and hard sleep makes me look dashing? "Thanks. And I won't be doing much sleeping in anymore. At least not because of overindulging in the booze." Ella's mother needed to know I wasn't a drunk. "Do you happen to know where I can find Ella, Mrs. Finley? I'd like to talk to her about something."

"She went to Dallas." What?!

"For how long?" I asked. "And why?"

"To help her cousin with a daycare she's opened." She looked up as if thinking how long she'll be gone. "My sister told me Sherry would need Ella's help for a month or so."

"A month?" My heart stopped. "Why so damn long?"

The way her mother looked at me with disapproval told me she didn't like my cussing. But she didn't have to say a word. I got it.

"I suppose she needs Ella so *dang* long because of the number of kids versus the amount of workers, Tyrell." She walked toward the kitchen. "I need to do the inventory for the kitchen. If you need anything, just let me know. Tasha's aunt will take over Ella's job in the morning."

Standing there, my mind rushing with all kinds of questions, "How'd she go to Dallas? When did she leave?" Might I be able to catch her? She hadn't even said goodbye!

Stopping her retreat, she turned to look at me. "She left about an hour ago on the bus."

"I would've let her take the private jet." I shoved my hands into my pockets. "Had she told me, I would've accompanied her on the trip to make sure she made it there safe and sound."

"Her cousin will pick her up at the bus station in Dallas." Mrs. Finley turned to walk away again. "Sherry will take good care of Ella. Don't worry one bit."

"At least she can come home on the weekends if she wants." I couldn't stand the thought of not seeing her for an entire month. "The jet is still at her disposal. I'd like to tell her that myself. Can I have her cell number?"

Stopping again, she turned around and wiggled her finger at me. "Come here, Tyrell." She pulled her cell out of her pocket.

I hurried to her. "It's just that she's so innocent. If anything happened to her…"

She chimed in, "It would devastate you." She showed me the number, and I typed it into my contacts. "The flowers you sent her… They're gorgeous. Sorry she didn't accept them. She's not one to be doted on, I can tell you that much."

"I won't dote then. Thanks for the advice." I walked away to make the call to her in private.

Shaking her head, she muttered something about me ending up with a broken heart.

What lay ahead of me now? I'd already begun preparing myself for a hard road ahead, but like anything worth having, it took some work and patience.

ELLA

Sitting on the bus, I played a game on my cell to distract me. Then a call came in from a number I didn't know. Refusing the call, I swiped the screen, then got back to playing my game of shooting balls at bricks.

A text came in after that, and I saw it pop up, then disappear too quickly for me to see more than a name. "Tyrell?"

He didn't even have my number, so why would he be texting me? I checked and saw it was him indeed; my mother gave him my number, and he asked me to call him back.

My heart pounded with the thought of talking to him. What could I say? But I called the number back anyway.

He answered immediately, "Ella, you left without saying goodbye."

"Did that upset you?" It appears so!

"No." He got quiet. "Okay, some. You could have taken our jet to Dallas if you would've told me. I would've ridden with you, made sure you got to where you're going safely. But you took off without telling me a thing."

He would've let me go on the jet? It kind of made me mad that I hadn't told him goodbye. "Looks like I made a mistake, huh?"

"It looks like it," he said. "But you don't have to worry, Ella. I can come get you and bring you home for the weekends if you want. It only takes about twenty minutes to get to Dallas."

He wants me to come home on the weekends? "Um, why do you want me to come back home, Tyrell?"

"Obviously, I will miss you, Ella." He laughed lightly. "Did you not understand what I meant when you got the flowers?"

"Tyrell, I know what you meant. We talked, you know," I reminded him. "I know exactly what you want. And I'll become the woman you need me to be."

"You're that now." He hesitated. "What do you mean, we talked?"

Of course he wouldn't remember our little conversation the night before! He played with my head; why not play with his a bit? "I came to your room last night to check on you, remember?"

"Um, sure." He didn't sound sure.

"And you told me how you'd wait for me. Did you mean that?" I asked playing with a lock of my hair, loving that I had the upper hand this time around.

"What else did I tell you?" he asked with a sigh. "And how long did you stay in the room with me? What did we do exactly?"

He had no clue! "You said you had the best dream ever, and that you said you loved me in that dream. And that I should stop making you chase me. By the way, that's far from the truth, Tyrell."

"Then why'd you leave? Your cousin could find someone else. You didn't *have* to go. You *wanted* to go," he sounded upset.

My presence, or absence, really mattered to him! "I have some growing up to do before committing to you in any way. That'll take a month or so. Can you wait for me?"

"Can I come get you for the weekends?" he asked.

"No, you cannot. I need a solid month, Tyrell." Darleen was right; if he kissed me, I'd be putty in the guy's hands.

"Away from me?" He didn't sound happy.

"Yes, away from you." I didn't want to get into the *whys* of the situation, especially not on a public bus

"I don't understand," he supposed. "Why stay away for a month for us to be together, Ella? I need an explanation."

"You won't get one. This is personal, Tyrell." I bit my lower lip as I was getting increasingly uncomfortable. "You don't need to know why."

"That's what people in relationships do, Ella. They let each other know where they're going, why they're going, and why the other can't go with them," he explained.

"We aren't in a relationship, are we?"

"I want to have one with you. Admittedly I don't recall last night's exchange. Can we have one now? One that I *will* remember?" He paused to give me a chance to say something.

"I can't have a relationship with you at this time, because I'm not ready yet."

"And the magic time is a month?" he asked. "Why is that?"

"I've got my reasons." I couldn't believe people in relationships had to know so much about each other. "You probably wouldn't understand even if I told you."

"So that's it then? You're humiliated by something?" he deduced. "You don't have to be embarrassed with me, Ella. Not about a thing."

Sure I don't.

"Look, Tyrell, if you want to be with me, I have some oats to sow..." All adults said things like; they sowed their oats or something like that. What did it meant exactly? Taking care of their adult things, supposedly. And I had to prepare myself for sex in a conscientious way. I did everything the responsible way. That made the most sense.

"Oh no," he opined. "You have no wild oats to sow, Ella. Whatever you sow, you'll sow with *me*."

A smile pulled my lips up. "That's so sweet. But you don't know what my wild oats are, Tyrell."

"Wild oats entail on hooking up with random strangers and getting liquored up—among other things," he informed me.

"Oh." That's what that phrase meant? "You can be sure that's not what mine are."

"Tell me then." He refused to give up.

And that melted my heart. "I can't." I didn't care what he said; I wasn't going to talk to him about it, birth control-wise.

"You can," he said with authority. "And you will, Ella Finley. Hey, what's your middle name anyway?"

If it would get him off the real subject, I'd tell him anything else, "Jean. And what's yours?"

"Montgomery," he said. "So, Ella Jean Finley, what are these oats you have to sow?"

I pretended not to hear his inquiry. "Tyrell Montgomery Gentry. That is a mouthful, isn't it? I mean it has like..." I counted on my fingers. "Bran-don Mont-gom-ery Gen-try. Seven syllables. Wow, that's a mouthful. Mine only has four. Our names are kind of like us. Yours is long and distinctive and mine is short and simple."

"I'm not distinctive," he opposed. "And you are anything but simple."

"You are, too," I said thinking about his place in life after the inheritance. "You're a Gentry. You own Whisper Ranch. Those two things alone make you distinctive. Why have you set your sights on me when you could have any woman you want?" Not like I wanted him to find someone else...

"Is that what you want, Ella?" he asked. "Do you want me to forget about you and find someone else?"

I sat there silent and feeling a little sick. "If you want to, then get to it so we can stop this."

"What the hell are you doing?" he asked again.

"I can't tell you," I reiterated. "But if you feel like seeing someone else, then tell me."

"Girl, you're making me crazy! I don't want anyone else; I want you. And I want you to be around, so we can see each other. If not every day, at least on the weekends," he was exasperated. "I didn't say to find someone else; I asked if you wanted me to do that. But I'm taking that question back. You took it all wrong. But you've never talked to me this much before. Can we at least talk on the phone while you're away?"

This guy didn't have to beg girls to talk to him or stay around. It must be weird for him to do that. "We can talk." *One can't get pregnant by talking on the phone.*

He let out a sigh. "At last, we can agree on something. Alright then. Since we're talking, tell me everything we said to each other last night."

I thought about my touching his lips after he passed out. I won't admit that. "You were clearly under the influence. And my brother was angry when he left to find you."

"Why was he so mad anyway?" he asked.

Shrugging, I didn't really understand that. "To be honest, I'm not sure."

"He did say, after we exchanged a few punches, that he thought the flowers were because we had done something physical. Which we had not." He waited a beat. "Is that the case, Ella? We didn't kiss, did we?"

Would I have been able to stop things from going further? It was unlikely he would've stopped himself, either. "We didn't kiss. Tyrell. Neither of us should be drinking when we kiss for the first time. That'll be a unique kiss, and we should remember every single moment."

"That's another thing we agree on, Ella. You have my word, no alcohol when we have our first kiss," his words gave me chills.

We will have a first kiss. Now I know that for certain!

TYRELL

The days went by with Ella and I talking every day for hours at a time. She hasn't told me exactly what she was doing to mature in Dallas, so maybe her sister could clue me in on things?

After Sunday brunch, I followed Darleen as she left the dining room; she was rubbing her stomach and aiming to her quarters, most likely to nap off the meal. "Hey, wait up, Darleen."

She stopped, then turned to see me coming up to her. "What's up, Tyrell?"

"I thought we could talk a little bit."

"About?" She started walking again.

"Ella, and what she's doing in Dallas." I talk to her every day, and she's never at the daycare. "She's not helping her cousin—not at the daycare anyway."

She stopped again to look me in the eyes. "You've been talking to her?"

"We talk every day," I acknowledged. "I've been pretty transparent about my interest in her, Darleen."

"Sure, but what I can't understand is *why*." She shook her head. "If you're supposing Ella is playing a game, making you pursue her, you're wrong. This isn't a diversion. This is the real Ella. She's immature, Tyrell. And frankly, she's not ready for an adult relationship. Are you?"

"She's old enough, Darleen. She just hasn't let anyone in before. She's letting me in. She told me about the friend who was murdered by her mother." A chill moved through me. *How could a mother do that to her own child?*

"It would be wrong to tell you the true reason she went to Dallas." She pushed her hair back off her face, showing an odd expression. "So, I won't tell you why exactly. But can I ask you this? Have you guys talked about sex?"

"No." Why did she ask? "I'm not that way. Not with her, at least." With other girls for certain, but Ella was poles apart. "She's a virgin; she *has* told me that."

"In every way, Tyrell. She's never kissed a boy or even held hands." She took off again toward her room. "I need to take a nap today. School has been grueling this week."

"She's told me about her lack of experience." I wasn't as out of the loop as Darleen thought. "We haven't talked about what to expect when the time comes. That's better left as a revelation."

"You think so, huh?" She stopped when we made it to the door of their quarters. "And along with that revelation would come the one about birth control, right?"

I had condoms! "Darleen, rest assured I've got that covered."

"So, you talked about protection then?" She put her hand on her hip the same way Ella and her mom did.

"No." No need to talk about that with Ella. She probably wouldn't let me. "She's inhibited about stuff like that."

"Yes, and that's exactly why she's not ready for what you have in mind." She opened the door, then looked at me smirking. "Do us all a favor and give her time, Tyrell. Consider what you're really doing here. Ella isn't playing games; she's truly an innocent girl with much to learn about life. And she's also a shrew most of the time."

"She can change." She's been nothing but nice when we talked on the phone. "And I can smooth out her rough edges."

"Don't think I'm being crass, please," she said with a stoic look on her face. "Is your interest in her about her being a virgin?"

"No," I said quickly.

"You said that pretty damn fast, Tyrell." Darleen stepped inside. "Ask yourself if that's the God's honest truth. Taking a girl's virginity should not be taken lightly, you know."

"I wouldn't know." I never had a virgin before.

"Oh, I see." She winked at me. "Interesting, don't you think? You've come across a virgin, and you got a hard on for her. It's not the first time a man's been in your position, is it? Promise to think about her more than you're thinking about yourself. She has a lot going on inside of her. If you hurt her, it'll break her in ways other women can't be broken."

"Of course." I understood that completely. "I'll think about what you've said. Thanks for talking to me so honestly. I really do appreciate it, Darleen."

Going up to my room, I couldn't get her words out of my head. What if it really was just a hard on for the pretty virgin? What if I was interested, not in Ella's mind, but her body and her virginity?

Sitting on the bed and thinking about things, I picked up my cell to check something out. I called Ella every time we talked. Except for that one time when I sent her a text, asking her to call me.

Maybe she wasn't that interested in me? If I hadn't made the first move, would Ella have ever thought about me?

What is the right thing to do? I'll put the ball in Ella's court. If she really wants to be with me, she'll call and keep things going. If she didn't, here was her chance to let me know.

Ella wouldn't know how to break up with a guy! She's never done it! She never had to even brush a guy off before. Have I been taking advantage all this time? Perhaps I was taking advantage of a woman who lacked too much in life experience to know what was happening?

Not once had I thought of myself as a predator. But the fact was that I never had sex with a virgin. Did that make me into a creep?

Would my male instinct to seek out a female who'd never been touched make me into something akin to an animal? At this point, all I knew was of my hots for Ella. But did she have it just as bad for me?

It wouldn't be fair if she didn't. Why pressure her into giving her virginity to me if she wasn't as into me as I was into her? That wouldn't be appropriate.

"When did you become so damn moral?" I asked myself.

I couldn't recall any girlfriend's family I got to know so well. Maybe that's it? If I talked in depth to their older siblings, I might've seen things differently.

A knock on the door. Jasper. "Hey, Tyrell, I'm going to ride around the ranch with Kyle and Mr. Finely on horseback. You should come, too."

Getting up, I decided to go. Why wait around for Ella to call? Why not give her some space? "Coming."

Meeting him in the hall, Cash was stepping out of his suite, Bobbi Jo at his side. "Hey, we're going, too," he called.

Jasper bumped my shoulder with his and muttered to me, "He's grown a bit attached to her it seems. She's been staying here most nights."

"Why wasn't she at brunch?" I asked.

"She probably feels somewhat awkward." He gestured to our surroundings. "It's quite ostentatious here, don't you think?"

Even so, we should make Cash's girl feel more at home. I looked over my shoulder as they came up behind us. "Glad to have you joining us today, Bobbi Jo. Chef Todd is barbequing our supper tonight. You have to try his ribs. They melt in your mouth."

She smiled. "Looking forward to it!"

Cash put his arm around her, beaming. "His potato salad is awesome, too. I'm glad you'll join us for a meal, Bobbi Jo."

Jasper looked sideways at me with smirk. "Us, too, Bobbi Jo."

Saddling up in the barn, we took off with Kyle and Mr. Finley leading the way. Jasper and I were the last to leave. I thought to ask him for his advice. "Jasper, I need your honest opinion on something."

"You've got it," he said as he swayed in the saddle.

Making sure everyone else was out of earshot, I asked, "Do you think I'm only interested in Ella because she's a virgin? That's what her sister thinks. And her brother didn't really understand what I saw in her. Am I deceiving myself?"

"I don't know," he said as he looked up at the blue sky. "Men will always be interested in having firsts from women. And sex isn't about love. Not to a man, it's not."

He was right. I didn't need to love to have sex. But Ella should have that before we got intimate. And a real commitment before taking her to my bed wasn't off limits. But now... I might be lying to myself about my feelings for her.

"If people are meant to be together, do you think spending time apart, not even talking, would prove if it is real or not?" It seems time would let us know if what he had was real.

"Maybe." He smiled. "I loved Tiffany back in high school. She was the girl who took my cherry after all. Now I'm not sure. When I first saw her again, I thought so. But some things were broached that make me wonder if I could really love her. She isn't the person I thought she was. Maybe Ella isn't who you think she is either. Women can keep secrets, Tyrell. Secrets about many things."

Jasper sounded like he had other things on his mind, so I didn't bother asking him for more guidance. I knew what to do. Although should Ella be privy to it or not?

If she really cared, she'd call. If she called, then I'll let her in on my experiment.

ELLA

Midnight rolled around, and Tyrell still hadn't called. I turned off the lamp beside the bed and closed my eyes. We talked every day for hours. Why did he suddenly didn't call?

Even though I planned lights out at midnight if he hadn't called, I was fighting it. I'd gone through the awkward gynecological exam. And what was worse, a male doctor performed it. But I didn't leave; I didn't freak out; I didn't cry either. I just stared at the ceiling and thought about Tyrell. I thought about how life would be different very soon. This was only a part of it.

Not being able to sleep, I got out of bed and went to get a drink of water. That and a cracker or two might help me sleep. As I stepped in the living room, Sherry came out of her bedroom. "You can't sleep, Ella?"

Shaking my head, I admitted why, "He hasn't called all day."

"Hmm." She went with me to the kitchen. "That's weird, huh?" Pulling open the fridge, she got out the milk. "I'll make some hot cocoa with honey. Care for some?"

"I'd love a mug, thanks." She must've been having trouble getting to sleep too. "What's keeping you up?"

"Tomorrow is a big day." She filled a small saucepan with milk then nodding in a gesture to one of the cupboards. "Can you grab the chocolate out of there?"

I got out the chocolate cubes and put them next to the stove. "Here you go. What's so big about tomorrow?"

"The state is making its fourth visit to the daycare. Everything's in order as it should be, but I get fretful anyway." She stirred the milk, adding the chocolate slowly. "Talking to you would help me focus less on my small problem, which isn't even a problem, just my dang insecurities that crop up every so often. So, tell me what has you worried about your guy, Ella?"

I took a seat on a barstool at the kitchen island. "Everything." I chuckled because it was the truth. "I've never been so interested in anyone. How to act? What I am supposed to be doing? And since he hasn't called, has he found someone else? I've gone through so much for him, and if he's moved on... It's going to really screw with my head and my heart."

"I'll be upfront with you, Ella." She poured the finished drink into two mugs, grabbed a jug of honey, and then came to sit with me at the island bar. "Here ya go. Careful, it's hot. Add the honey when it cools off a tad" She blew across the surface of her mug, making wisps of steam stir in the air. "You had a traumatic event when you first started school. That would scar anyone. It's no secret your family has babied you. It's to be expected. Aunt Ruth and Uncle Zeke weren't expecting to be parents again in their thirties."

"It was a 'happy accident' is what mom says." I smiled, then added some honey to my drink. "I'm okay with that." Stir, stir...

"Yeah, I know you are." She looked at me with wise eyes, even though she was only ten years older than me. "I learned a lot about your family the summer I stayed with you guys and worked at the ranch. I saw how your family interacts. They all hid things from you, keeping you as innocent as possible. I suppose because of what you'd gone through. But also, I think it was because of how special you became to all of them."

"Funny, I don't feel special at all." I didn't think my family members thought more of me than anyone else.

Sherry smiled dumping more honey in the mug before taking

another sip. "Ella, they shelter you from everything. And even from growing up. You freaked out over a standard pap smear!"

She was right. "Kyle confronted Tyrell about the flowers. And Darleen said I wasn't ready to be in a relationship if I couldn't talk to Tyrell about birth control."

"Here's the thing, Ella." She bumped her shoulder to mine. "Most people don't talk a lot about that in the first place. And Darleen came to me when she was sixteen and asked me to take her to get on birth control. It even helps regulate menstruation."

I felt my lips pull down into a frown. "That sneak."

"Darleen and Kyle had relationships, but they never bring anyone around.," she mentioned. "They kept you from seeing ordinary, adult issues. Don't be mad at any of them; they're doing it out of love. But pay mind to when they're actively keeping you a little kid."

Nodding, I wondered if one of them said something to Tyrell to stop him from calling me. "Would it be wrong for me to call him, Sherry?"

"No," she said with a smile. "He might be waiting for you to make a move, Ella. He could be just as insecure as you are. I mean, he's living at the estate, and your family has access to his ear, right?"

"Boy, do they." All of them probably said something to him. It was Sunday after all. Everyone had brunch on Sundays. "Do you think I'm making a mistake, Sherry?"

"Staying away from him for a month because Darleen told you?" She nodded. "Yeah, why? What did the doctor say at the appointment?"

"He said it'll take a month to get in my system and to use condoms until then. And if I'm unsure of my sexual partner's sexual health, to use one anyway, even while on the pill." Darleen was right. "See, my sister was pretty adamant about not relying on condoms."

"That's because she got pregnant when she was seventeen. She was on the pill, but she skipped a whole week before she realized how risky that was. She said they always used condoms, too." Sherry looked at me with narrowed eyes. "Do not tell anyone in your family this secret, promise?"

"Not even Darleen?" This new information was perplexing.

"Yes, you can talk to her." She took another sip of cocoa. "She really should have told you about that so you'd have a clue of what could happen if you're not cautious."

"What happened to the baby?"

"She lost it." Shaking her head, she looked sad. "When she figured out she missed those pills, she took a whole week's worth at one time. This was about two months after the fact. She came to Dallas and told me she skipped her period both months, so we got a pregnancy test, and it came out positive."

"So, she lost it because she started taking the pills again?" That was one of the saddest things I'd ever heard!

Shrugging, she said, "I don't know. There's no way to tell. She went home and was going to tell the father. But on the ride back, she began bleeding and returned here. We went to the emergency room where she lost the baby. Since then, she's been a stern believer in not using only a condom. Plus, she started using another form of birth control; no pill involved."

"So, as long as I take the pills correctly, and within these first thirty days we use a condom, then I could have sex without much risk?" Darleen might have been a little too overzealous...

"If you feel you're ready, Ella. Don't force yourself. And you should be in love." Sherry sighed. "If I could do it over again, I'd wait for love. You and this guy might find that if you're honest."

"Do you really think so?" Since he hasn't called, who knows?

"Look, he's already done more for you than any guy has for me," she smiled. "He's beaten up a guy for trying to kiss you. He's taken your drunken butt home, put you in his bed, left you alone, and even helped you do your job the next day! He's called you every day since you've been here. And the jet is at your disposal? That's something, girl, let me tell you."

"And here I am, too anxious to call him." I felt so stupid and childish. "You're right about my family. Now that you've brought it up, I recall tons of times they've stopped me from doing things. Including going to summer camp when I was fifteen. This one girl invited me, and I sort of wanted to, but was on the fence about it.

298

Then Darleen and Kyle said how awful it is and how they make you do things I'd hate, so I dropped it."

"They'd do that." She got up and put her empty mug in the sink. "So, after the state inspections, I usually go to Chili's to get a margarita and some of their guacamole dip. You should join me, Ella."

That sounded like a grownup thing to do! "Yeah, I will. That sounds great. I'll do some shopping in the morning."

"If you want some company for that, one of the girls who works at the daycare is about your age. She's got tomorrow off, and she's got great taste in fashion. Her aunt owns one of the best hair salons in Dallas. She could get you in." Sherry headed off to bed as I washed and put our mugs away.

"Leave me her number, and I'll give her a call." Not having any friends was not entirely my doing... There were times I'd talk about some girl at school and either my sister or brother were quick to point out problems in their families.

Maybe they just wanted me to stay home and be safe? Whatever their reasons, their fears would not hold me back any longer.

Seemed I've been hiding behind my fears and all of theirs as well.

TYRELL

One in the morning came around when I picked up my cell off the nightstand to check for the zillionth time if the ringer was on and if it was charged up. "Damn. That girl is not going to call."

Maybe I'd been wrong to put the ball in her court without telling her? My finger hovered over the screen thinking about calling her even though it was late, and Ella had probably already gone to sleep.

That pissed me off! If she'd gone to sleep without talking to me, then she obviously didn't care. And since when was it me who cared the most in a relationship?

Putting the cell down, I turned over on my side and pulled the blanket up to cover myself. Things had to change. I couldn't let some girl pull my chain. What Ella's sister said about the way she acted was not a game, but it still wasn't acceptable.

It took two people to have a relationship. Not one guy who does it all and a girl who sits still and waits. Maybe she was too juvenile for me?

The cell rang, and it was Ella's ringtone. My heart sped up as I turned to get the phone. "Ella?"

"Hi," came her soft voice. "You still awake?"

"Yeah." I sat up, feeling on the overjoyed side. "You?"

"Yeah." She took a deep breath as if getting ready to say something important.

Fear rushed through me. "Ella, I missed you today."

"If that's true, then why didn't you call me?" she asked, sounding upset.

"I thought putting the ball in your court would be a good idea. Seems I was wrong." It was time for me to be as honest with her as I'd ever been with any other girl. I've been taking it easy since she was so immature. "Look, it takes two, Ella. I can't be the only one to try to make things work. You've got to do your part, too. That means you can pick up the phone and call me sometimes."

"Were you worried I wouldn't call?" she sounded bewildered.

What to say? I was never on this side of a relationship before. But honesty seemed like the best thing to me. "Kind of."

"Can I ask you a question?" She waited.

After all the conversations we had, it was funny she'd even ask. "Ella, ask me anything. And you can *tell* me anything. What will it take before you understand I'm *all* into you?"

"I'm sorry, Tyrell." She sighed before going on, "Does the reason you didn't call today have something to do with a member of my family?"

I didn't want to rat Darleen out, especially since I went to her. But I had to be honest. "Kind of."

Another long sigh came then she said, "Tyrell, we should probably leave my family out of our business from now on. They mean well, but they see me as a kid, and they can't help themselves for trying to keep me as innocent as they've always known me to be."

"You're right about that." I wanted to see Ella so bad it hurt. "My parents are celebrating their anniversary this Saturday. My brothers and I will be in Dallas Saturday morning. It's a big deal with my family. Since we inherited this year, and nothing can to be handed to them, Cash —with Bobbi Jo's help—has planned a festivity at the Hyatt-Regency. I want you to come with me."

"Oh, I don't know," she said with a ton of hesitation in her voice. "You know how socially awkward I am. And meeting your parents, too? Tyrell, that's a lot in one evening to ask of me."

"Not really." She'd be okay. "I'll be with you at all times. I'll never leave your side, scout's honor! Go with me, Ella. I want Mom and Dad to meet you."

"I'll think about it. Tomorrow I'm getting some new clothes and hopefully getting my hair done." She went quiet; she must be contemplating my request. "After that, I'll let you know. Will you ask someone else if I don't?"

Chuckling, the answer was easy, "Ella, I don't want to take anyone else. If you don't feel up to it, I'll go alone. Jasper isn't taking anyone, only Cash is."

"Sherry told me something today," Ella said. "See, I don't have anyone to compare you to."

And if I have my way, you never will. "That's not a bad thing, Ella."

"It kind of is," she said. "Because the things you've done for me... The fact you beat that guy up who tried to kiss me is pretty heroic. And then you took me home and put me in your bed alone. That's a rarity, too, from what Sherry said. You do a lot that other guys don't. And I've taken that for granted. I'm sorry for doing that, Tyrell. You're a special kind of man, and I'm lucky you think so much of me."

"You're a special kind of lady, Ella, and I feel lucky." A smile filled my face as I thought we were getting a lot closer to being the couple I could see us being. "To have you at my side for any event would be an honor."

"You really want me to go to that anniversary party, don't you?" she asked.

Not to put undue pressure on her... but I wanted her to do all sorts of things with me! Best to pick and choose my battles appropriately. "Ella, it's just a party. What I really want is just to spend more time with you. And I'd like to do it sooner than a month from now."

"It's only three more weeks now," she said. "Maybe less."

"Ella, please tell me why you're staying with your cousin in Dallas." I need to know. From what Darleen said, there was more to it than helping Sherry out—something Ella wasn't doing anyway. "You said you're going shopping and to get your hair done. That's not helping out at the daycare. You didn't go there to do that, so what is it? Come clean with me."

"It's confidential," she said. "No, I'm not here to help Sherry. I came to get her help. And I've got it. She's helping me with responsibilities, Tyrell. Can you take that answer for now?"

If it meant that much to her, sure. "I guess so. I just wish you trusted me more. For instance, what's your favorite pastime?"

"What does that mean?" she asked.

"What do you like to do when you have time to waste?" She liked to draw, and I'd like her to tell me more about it. She was talented, and I wanted to tell her that and discuss her taking classes and maybe doing it professionally one day. But she had to let me in on that before I could make her dreams come true. If that was her dream. What are her dreams? She wouldn't talk about herself that much.

"I play games on my phone when I'm bored." For a moment I thought she might divulge a bit more information. "It's not like I've got loads of time to waste."

With a sigh, I let that go. "Okay. There's a lot of other stuff to talk about. Like what's your favorite color?"

"Crimson," she whispered. "Like the red bird. We've got loads of them out at the ranch. Each one has its own personality. Some are more skittish than others. Some are more daring, but each is his own bird."

"Wow." Ella was insightful and loved nature. She had a thing for cardinals as she had many drawings of them in her hideaway. "Would you say that's your favorite bird?"

"I love their colors, but my favorite bird is the Mountain Jay or Steller's Jay." She sounded engrossed as she went on, "We'd gone up to a small park outside of Denver, Colorado. We were there on vacation. One of a handful we've taken in my life. I saw this sapphire-colored bird with a black head. Its body type reminded me of a cardinal. While I love the red more than the cobalt, the way that bird behaves! It's like an old bird who's lived in the rugged mountains forever."

"We should take a trip there," I said. "Whenever you want to go, just let me know, and we'll jet off to Colorado. You know what's super cool about dating a billionaire, Ella?"

"Lots of things, I bet." She laughed.

"Yeah, I would imagine so. But the cool thing is that I can take you anywhere in this world you might ever want to go. I can take you to see whatever you want to see." I found a way to get her brain working on what she could do with a boyfriend who had more money than he could spend. "When I get to Dallas, even if you won't come to my parents' party, we could go do anything you want. There's a great art museum we could check out."

"You like art?" she asked.

A little, but I knew that Ella was a covert artist who needed to come out of the closet. "Sure, who doesn't? I don't know much about it, but I can discern appealing things. So, what do you say, will you join me this coming weekend?"

As quiet as a mouse, Ella said nothing for the longest time. I sat there, patiently, then she said, "That might be nice."

It almost sounded like she agreed to go out with me. "I'll take that as a *yes* and make the plans. We can do it on Sunday. Think about coming to the party with me, too. But we'll for sure go to the art museum on Sunday, no matter what." I wasn't letting her back out. "And we'll do brunch before we go. You love brunch and plenty of restaurants serve magnificent ones in Dallas. Ones that can rival Todd's Sunday brunches."

"Is this our first date, Tyrell?" she asked, warily.

I wasn't going to let her think it was anything else but that. "Yes, that will be our first date. Unless of course, you go with me to the party. Then that will be our first date. And I am extremely pleased that you've accepted."

It might've taken me some time to finally go out on a real date with Ella, but I was about to show her things not many men could.

ELLA

Pulling one item after another out of the wardrobe, I just couldn't find something to wear to the museum the next day. It wasn't just that Tyrell was in town. I'd been too insecure to go to the anniversary party with him. "No, that's not any good either, Sherry. I've got nothing to wear. I'm not going."

She took out the new red dress I purchased. "This would be perfect for the party."

"I'm not going to that. I told you that already. Tyrell's not troubled with my answer, why are you?" I tossed a pair of heels on the bed. "Those hurt my feet. Why did I buy them in the first place?"

"Because they're a staple of every girl's wardrobe, Ella. And I'm not taking no for your answer because you obviously want to see Tyrell and go to this party. You're just being shy and insecure. Stop giving in to those feelings, Ella." She pulled out the azure dress Meagan made me buy. The girl who worked at the daycare proved to be a control freak, but a talented fashionista.

"No," I held my hands up. "That one is way too…what' s the word?"

"Stunning?" Sherry said looking at the shiny minidress. "Glamorous? Awe-inspiring?"

"Slutty," I said.

Sherry shook her head. "No, this is not one bit slutty. This is a classic design, Ella. And with those tall stilettos, you'll look like a runway model. I'll go plug in the curling iron and the curling wand. Let's do your hair and makeup, and I'll even join you, so you're not alone when you walk in."

"But Sherry," I whined. "I don't want to meet his parents."

"Life is tough." She took me by the shoulders, pushing me toward the bathroom. "Shower, do not shampoo. You did that yesterday. Hair styles stay better that way. You have ten minutes to shower and shave, then throw on a robe and come to my room so I can fix you up."

"If you're coming with me, when will you have time to get ready?" How could she do us both in enough time?

"Don't worry about me; I'm a seasoned veteran." She pushed me the rest of the way into the bathroom. "Oh, and don't give Tyrell a heads up that you're coming. Surprising him is a lot better."

"I don't know about this." I felt nauseated. "I might be coming down with a bug or something." I burped and looked at Sherry with wide eyes. "See."

"It's called nerves. Shower." She closed the door, and I obeyed her.

Since I've never crashed a party before, my anxiety was crippling. Amazing how severely it could affect a person! "Lord, if I'm this sick about going to a party, what's going to happen when we actually kiss? Oh, Lord! Or have sex?"

Sherry called out, "I can hear you, Ella. More showering, less worrying."

Small apartments were the worst. Back home, the walls were so much thicker! So, the remainder of her shower was in silence.

Once finished, I felt no better as I went to Sherry's bedroom to be powdered, plumped, brushed, and curled. "I don't want false eyelashes," as I eyed them on the vanity top.

"Those aren't for you anyway. You've got lovely long eyelashes, unlike the rest of the family. Lucky." She pulled a lock of hair up to run a straightener over it.

Some parts she straightened, others she put into hot rollers, and still others were curled. What is the end game? It's not making a heck of a lot of sense to me! "What if they're gone by the time we get there?"

Sherry laughed. "I doubt they reserved a place like the Hyatt to go home early. Don't worry, I'm nearly done here, and you can put your dress and heels on while I get dressed, then we'll go."

"Tyrell should know I'm coming..." I looked at my nails that were done at the salon a few days earlier. "What if he hates the way I look?"

"Umm," she hummed as she reviewed me in the mirror. "He will *not* hate it. You look gorgeous. I'm not just saying that. The haircut, the nails and matching pedicure, everything is coming together in an amazing way. Don't agonize Ella, that guy will love what he sees when he lays his eyes on you tonight. And he won't be the only man who will not be able to keep his eyes off you."

"Oh, I don't want anyone else to be looking at me, Sherry." I felt so weird as it was! I didn't quite recognize the woman who looked back at me in the mirror.

"Too bad. You're going to stun them all." She took pins with zirconias and put them in my hair until it looked magnificent.

Sitting there, looking at my hair and makeup, I found myself speechless. "Wow. Is that really me?"

Sherry nodded. "It is." She pulled me up. "Now go put that dress on and let's get the heck out of here."

Fortunately, she took a few minutes to get ready, which gave me time to walk in the heels. Circling the living room, each time I passed the mirror by the front door , I caught my reflection and didn't recognize myself. "Man, he's going to freak out."

"He sure is," Sherry announced. "Time to go."

My heart pounded so hard she probably heard it. "I can't."

Taking my hand, she tugged me along. "You can and will. You're dazzling. And you're about to see what happens to men when they see women as beautiful as you."

Sherry wasn't looking too shabby herself. "You look elegant yourself, Sherry." She pinned her blonde hair up in a messy bun and wore a black dress and heels that made her look sophisticated.

"It wouldn't be so bad if I met a handsome bachelor at this

party. Hopefully, there will be a few of them!" We got into her car, then we proceeded to the anniversary.

Taking deep breaths to calm myself down, I looked good, so that helped. But I still was me on the inside, and that was disconcerting. "Do you think it would be okay if I stayed quiet tonight?"

"I don't see what it would hurt." She smiled as we pulled up in front of the hotel. "Here we are. Just be yourself. He likes you already. You don't have to win him over. This isn't for him, Ella, this is for you: a woman everyone notices. It's powerful. You need to know how it feels. And it builds up your security, your femininity, too, which carries over to how comfortable you are with your sexuality."

"So doing this will help me mature?" I asked as the valet opened my door.

"Welcome to…" He stopped talking; his mouth hung open as his eyes nearly popped out of his head. "Hi."

"Hi." I held out my hand to get help stepping out of the vehicle with a tight dress on. "Could you lend a hand?"

"Oh, sure." He took my hand, pulling me up. "And welcome to the Hyatt-Regency. I hope you enjoy your stay with us." He didn't let my hand go once I'd gotten out of the car. "How long is that going to be?"

"I'm only here for a party." I smiled. He was enamored with me without even knowing me!

"I hope to see you when you leave then. You have a nice time." He finally let my hand go as my cousin came up on the other side of me and gave him the keys. "Bye." He waved as he gazed at me with adoring eyes.

We got inside and both laughed. "He acted so silly!"

Sherry nodded. "You look fantabulous, Ella."

Approaching the information desk, all eyes were on us. "We're here for the Gentry party," I declared.

One of the men nearly ran from behind the desk. "I'll show you to that party." He came up on my side. "Please follow me."

Our heels clicked over the Italian tiles as we proceeded and Sherry asked, "How many people are attending this party?"

"About fifty," he said, then stopped in front a set of closed double doors with music coming from behind them. "May I say you two ladies will be the belles of the ball tonight? None who've come so far even come close."

Smiling, I felt my cheeks heating. I'd never imagined anyone being so impressed with my appearance. "Thank you, sir."

He opened the door. "No, thank you for coming. Both of you will have a wonderful time tonight."

My tummy was rolling, my head spun, and my mouth had gone dry as a bone... "I need a drink. Nothing with alcohol." Tyrell and I might share our first kiss, and it shouldn't be spoiled.

"Hello," some guy said who fell in beside me. "You want a drink?"

"No, thank you," I let him know. "I'm here to meet someone."

He winked at me with dark eyes. "Well, blow *him* off and meet *me* instead. Has anyone ever told you how beautiful you are?"

"As a matter of fact, yes." Tyrell had told me a number of times. "Thank you for the compliment though."

Someone grabbed him, and Sherry and I walked toward the bar. The place was dimly lit with a disco ball spinning around; it made it difficult to see anyone, and the music was quite loud as well.

As I waited at the bar while Sherry ordered us something to drink, I saw a tall figure on the dance floor. "Tyrell?"

TYRELL

Cash had invited tons of our old friends to the party. It looked like *we* were having a party. He and Bobbi Jo had done a great job of planning the whole thing.

As I stood at the bar, a familiar face walked in. Along with her came a young girl. As soon as she spotted me, she came right to me. "Tyrell Gentry. Aren't you a sight for sore eyes?"

"Hi, Beth. It's been a long time." I hugged my old high school girlfriend, then looked down at the child. "And this pretty young lady is?"

"This is Samantha." Beth looked at me with slightly sad eyes. "Me and her daddy are on the outs right now. Your best friend, Marco, isn't being such a nice guy to me lately. But I didn't want to miss the party just because he's being an ass."

"So, he's not coming?" I hoped to see him.

"He might." She leaned in to whisper. "To be honest, he was jealous that I wanted to come when we got the invitation. With all this new wealth for you guys, he might be afraid I'll ditch him and come back to you."

That wouldn't even be an option, but no reason to say something that rude. "I've got a girlfriend. Call Marco and tell him to come up here. It's been forever since we got together."

"I told him that." Beth smiled. "You've got a girlfriend, huh? You better watch out, Tyrell. Women, will be coming out of the woodwork for you now that you've got money."

"She's not like that." Ella should have come to the party, but I knew better than to push it too much. She'd accepted the date for the next day, and that's good enough. "I wish she was here so you could meet her. She's apprehensive about meeting my parents."

"Is she from Carthage?" Beth asked.

"She's actually part of the staff at the estate. Funny how Mom and Dad fell in love at Whisper Ranch, just the way we have." We hadn't said the words yet, but I loved Ella.

Her little girl grabbed my hand, tugging it. "I'm Samantha. I'm six years old. Daddy said you are his friend from a long time ago."

I leaned down to talk to the little girl. "It's nice to meet you, Samantha. I'm Tyrell. Marco and me were great buddies in high school."

"I like to dance. Mommy said we can dance at this party." She grinned at me. "Can you dance with me since Daddy didn't come?"

No harm in that. "Sure, Samantha."

She tugged me with her and didn't let go of her mother's hand either. Beth looked at me apologetically. "You don't have to do this, you know."

"No, it's okay." I just hoped Marco wouldn't show up and think I was after his wife. We never fought over Beth. He started seeing her a few years after we broke up, no need to start now.

The little girl never let go of our hands as we all danced to an ABBA song. Everyone had smiles on their faces. Mom and Dad sat the song out and enjoyed watcing their guests dancing and having a good time.

The looks on their faces made my heart sing. I couldn't remember when they were so content. Brilliant of Cash to do this for their anniversary.

As I danced and scanned the room, someone was hurrying away from the bar and heading to the exit. Someone with dark hair, a blue dress that hugged every curve, and high heels. Heels that had her swaying a bit as she hauled ass, a blonde right behind her, trying to catch up.

When the blonde grabbed the other woman's arm, she spun around and then I saw her face. "Ella?" Stooping down to Samantha, "Honey, this was fun, but I have to go. Sorry."

Letting go of her hand, I hurried to the woman who looked like Ella, only a much glamorized one. She and the blonde were arguing, and she jerked her arm out of the other woman's grip.

That's when the heels got a life of their own, and she began stumbling backward. I got to her just in time, catching her in my arms. "Got ya."

Her eyes shone as she looked up at me. "Let me go."

"You look amazing, Ella." I said smiling as I righted her on her feet.

She glared at me, then took off again. "You have some nerve!"

Why is she so mad? But I wasn't about to let her go! Grabbing her by the waist, I hauled her away to a remote corner where we could talk. "You are going nowhere, young woman."

Ella seemed to be breathing fire as her eyes met mine. "I *saw* you. You said you wouldn't bring anyone else if I didn't go. *You* lied to me."

"Oh, that?" I looked out to see Samantha and Beth still dancing. "I didn't bring anyone. The little girl asked me to dance, and she dragged her mom along! Nothing to get mad about, Ella."

"You expect me to believe that, Tyrell?" She took a few steps back. "I'm not about to let you make a fool out of me."

The blonde approached with a scowl on her face. "Ella, you need to quit. I've asked around. He came here alone. He's not with her. So, chill."

Ella looked at the other woman. "Are you one hundred percent sure, Sherry?"

"Oh, you're Sherry," I reached out to shake her hand. "Tyrell Gentry. It's a pleasure to meet you. You convinced Ella to come, thank you very much."

"Sorry for how things have started." Sherry looked at Ella. "Maybe giving the man a head's up would've been a better idea."

"It's okay," I let Sherry know. "I'm getting used to Ella seeing the most tragic scenario instead of the reality of a situation. You know what? I love her anyway."

Ella's jaw dropped. "You what?"

Laughing, I repeated, "I love you, Ella Jean Finley. Now come and dance with me before I introduce you to my parents. You'll be the first lass I can tell them I love. Now, you don't want to spoil that, right?"

Sherry smiled as she waved at her cousin. "You go out there, Ella. You've got one heck of a good guy here. Don't blow it."

I held Ella close to my side as we headed for the dance floor. "Sorry, Tyrell. Not sure why I overreacted. I just saw you dancing with a woman and went bonkers with jealousy."

"Kind of how I got harebrained when that moron tried to kiss you," I reminded her. "Yeah, I get it." Pulling her into my arms, wrapping them around her the way I wanted to, I whispered in her ear as we swayed to the music. "I love you, Ella. Do you have anything you'd like to tell me?"

Pulling her head back to look at me, her eyes sparkled. "I love you, too, Tyrell Gentry. I wouldn't have done all this if I didn't."

"You looked nice before." I stepped back to look her over, then twirled her around before pulling her back to me. "You look hot as hell now. Both of your looks are pretty smoking. Now, tell me what it is that you really love doing, Ella?"

"What are you talking about?" She really had no clue!

"You're an artist. Certainly, it's wrong for me to be snooping, but it is my home after all. I found your hideaway and your art."

She buried her face in my shoulder. "I'm not that good."

"You're amazing!" I sent her out for another spin, then pulled her back into my arms. "And you should become the best artist you can be."

"I had fantasies about having my own art show." She smiled, taking my breath away. "Do you sincerely think I'm good? Not a soul has seen my drawings."

"My brothers have. You are *incredible*. And I'll be proud standing by your side at your very first art show." I twirled us both around the dance floor as she held on tightly. "You also are a natural dancer, baby. Who knew?"

"Umm, I've danced a lot. Alone, but a lot." She giggled as I swept her across the dance floor. "It's better to dance with you though."

"I should hope so." The music took us away, and we danced until we couldn't take another breath. I stood there on the edge of the dance floor holding her. Everyone else kept on dancing. No one seemed to be aware of us falling in love.

Ella bit her lower lip, stained red with shiny lip gloss. "You wanted to know why I came to Dallas, Tyrell? I'm ready to be a mature woman with you. The kind of woman you ought to have. And I want to be the woman I deserve to be."

"I like the sound of that." And she was ready to explain why she went to Dallas. But mostly, when is she was coming back? "Whatever the motive was, can it be over now? I want you home, Ella. The ranch isn't the same without you. I miss you more than you can ever understand."

Nodding, she gulped, then said, "I'll return when you guys all leave. See, I've been following some advice, but it isn't helping me much. I came here to get on birth control pills. And they won't be effective for another couple of weeks."

"And you wanted to stay away from me because you thought I'd pressure you into having sex with me?" That wasn't going to happen.

"I thought so, yes. Not that you'd force me, though," she added. "I think once you kiss me..."

With a chuckle, I let her know how things would be after we kissed, "You will want me that way, Ella. But guess what?"

"What?" she was curios.

"I won't take your virginity until you have my last name. I'm doing it the old-fashioned way. I am not hurrying a darn thing with you, girl." Pulling her close, I let her know one more thing. "I haven't had a drop of alcohol today, have you?"

She shook her head as a smile curved her plump lips. Lips as red as rose petals and looking as soft as them, too. "Not a drop of alcohol today."

"Would you mind if we share our very first kiss now?" My eyes glued to her lips, my mouth watered to taste her.

"I wouldn't mind at all." She eased in closer to me. "I can't think of a better time."

The music was slow and romantic, and the atmosphere gave a hint of what was yet to come as our lips touched. Stars filled my head as her lips parted and our tongues played together. The stars gave way to fireworks as our kiss went on and on—and then on some more.

When we parted, I gazed into her cobalt eyes. "Damn it, girl. I am head over heels in love with you."

"Let's keep it that way." She pulled me to her again. "'Cause I'm head over heels in love with you, too, Tyrell Gentry. Kiss me again because I've never felt something like this in my life."

And neither have I.

ELLA

One year later...

From what I'd been told, I was supposed to be a bundle of nerves on my wedding day, but I'd never been so calm. I walked with Daddy's arm linked with mine and the most handsome man in the world looking at me by the altar, waiting for me.

Tyrell told me once he'd wait for me for as long as it took, and he hadn't lied. The guy stayed true to his word, even when I whined about getting to the good stuff already; he kept his pledge.

Tyrell Gentry was marrying his naughty little virgin, as he dubbed me not long after we began seeing each other. Six months after our first official date—the one to the art museum—he proposed and gave me a giant rock of an engagement ring. We set a wedding date for six months after that.

My fiancé wore dark blue Wranglers, black cowboy boots, and a starched to the hilt white button-down shirt tucked neatly into the waist of his jeans and a snakeskin vest. A black belt topped the jeans that hugged his lower half, defining his muscular legs and butt. I was getting a prime, Grade A chunk of man, and I treasured that.

We chose a white wedding dress for me. The soft silk felt like clouds against my skin. I wore flats so I wouldn't fall over again. That's the last thing I wanted; it had already happened too much already.

Each step I took had me closer to my future, a future I was ready for. With Tyrell's help, I'd grown up by leaps and bounds. I signed up for an art school in Dallas. Tyrell took me to the class twice a week on the jet.

And once he took me to Paris, just for a dinner and a movie. Tyrell had broadened my horizons by millions of miles. I didn't think it possible to love anyone more than I loved him. And now we'll be married, and he could take me to *our* bed and transform me to a complete woman.

"I'll take her from here," Tyrell's deep voice told my Daddy. "Hey, beautiful. How you doing this fine day?"

"I'm just fine. You look nice." I handed my bouquet to my cousin Sherry, who was my bridesmaid. "Here you go, Sherry. Thanks for everything."

She took the bundle of red roses. "You are welcome."

Tyrell took both my hands in his as we gazed into each other's eyes through my sheer veil. "Ready to become my wife?"

"I've been ready." I gave him a wink.

Turning to face the preacher, Tyrell and I said the vows that bound us together until death do us part. Then he kissed me for a moment before sweeping me off feet and retreating down the aisle. "You're about to have more pleasure than you've ever had in your life, Mrs. Gentry."

"Are we going to do it in the limo?" I asked him, as I was down with that.

He laughed. "Hell, no."

Rats.

Slipping into the backseat of the limousine, our driver, Michael, took off toward the reception hall as Tyrell sat me on his lap. His hands moved over the top of my dress, then he unbuttoned the tiny pearl buttons until the camisole underneath shown. "You've got layers and layers on, don't ya?"

I nodded. "It's a jumble of clothes, Tyrell. But we're stopping by the house to change. You need to help me get out of all this stuff." I had hopes he'd be keyed up, seeing me nearly naked, and take me then and there.

"You're being naughty again," he warned me. Then his lips pressed against mine. He had this way of stopping my wicked behavior with his magical kisses. Only this time, we were married and could do so much more. So, his kiss only brought out more naughty in me.

Moving my hands down his back, I eased them around until I could feel the lump in his jeans. Wrenching my mouth from his, I made him an offer he wouldn't refuse, "How about you let me kiss you some other place, Mr. Gentry?" Before he could answer, I let him in on something, "I've watched some videos to learn how."

With a nod, he gave me the go-ahead, and I slid off his lap. Undoing his jeans, I freed his hard dick and marveled at the sight before looking back up at him. His eyes glistened. "I love you, baby."

Grinning at him, I whispered, "I love you, too, Tyrell." Then I licked my lips and took his male appendage in my hands and kissed the tip of his massive organ.

The skin was softer than I imagined. The taste was much better, too. Easing my mouth over him, I took him all in, and the way he groaned sent chills through me. He liked it! It was my first time, and he's already pleased!

And soon he'd please me! Over and over again, he'd pleasure me until I was a drained muddle of a woman. And I couldn't wait!

TYRELL

AFTER WATCHING ELLA DO SOMETHING I'D ONLY DREAMT ABOUT, I couldn't wait much longer. When the limo pulled up to the chalet and I climbed out, I gathered her in my arms and took her inside. Michael hadn't gotten out in time to open the door, and he stood there with his mouth ajar, watching me hurry inside.

"I'll be out here waiting to take you to the reception, sir."

"'Kay," I called out as I stared into Ella's eyes. "He's going to have to wait a bit."

She giggled. "Yay!"

I took the stairs two at a time to what was now *our* suite. Kicking the door closed behind us, I put her feet on the ground, then began the arduous task of removing the wedding dress .

Finally, she stood in front of me with nothing on but a smile. "Your turn, Tyrell."

Kicking off my boots, I undressed in record time, then picked her up and carried her to *our* bed. "Oh, girl, you have no idea what's about to happen to you."

Her cheeks went red; her arms flew open. "Show me."

I wasn't about to just hop on and take a ride. "You just lay back and relax and let me do what I do best." Pushing her legs apart, I pulled her to the side of the bed until her legs hung off, then got on my knees.

When my lips touched hers, she moaned, "That feels amazing, Tyrell."

"Girl, I haven't even started!" She was in for a surprise, that was for sure.

Running my tongue through her warm folds, I kissed and licked until she was screaming with an orgasm, "Tyrell! Oh, God!"

Only then did I stop and move my body up hers, kissing every inch of her along the way. Pulling her legs up to bend her knees, I put my cock at the cusp of her virginity, then thrust it in nice and quick. "You okay?"

She moaned and moved her foot up the back of my leg. "Oh, yeah, babe, I am more than okay, I'm on fire for you."

Moving with ease, I found she wasn't fragile in the least. "Damn, Ella, just like dancing, you're a natural at this."

She arched her body up to mine. "I've sat on the shelf longer than most. Can we do this for the rest of our lives?"

The way her tits squished between us, the way her hipbones pressed into my stomach, the way her body moved with mine, it was better than any fantasy I had about her. Moving faster, making harder thrusts, I loved the sound of her breathing as the air was pushed out of her lungs with every plunge I made.

We became nothing more than two bodies tangled into one. No one knew where one ended, and the other began. Her clit convulsed around my cock, and I gave it all to her, every last drop.

We lay there, breathing hard, sweating profusely, and out of our minds with love. Ella stopped taking the birth control pills shortly after telling me the reason of the trip to Dallas. I wanted us to have babies after we got married. I wanted us to have all the babies possible. She said up to three babies, so we agreed to what she preferred.

I didn't want to get off her or to part our bodies. "This was meant to be, Mrs. Ella Jean Gentry."

Her fingertips ran over my shoulders. "You're right, my dear spouse." She laughed. "I have a husband! And not just any ol' guy! The best looking, most considerate, gentlest husband ever. And the sex is off the charts, too. Throw in all that money you got and this estate, and I've hit the lottery, haven't I?"

"It's me who's hit the lottery, baby." I kissed the tip of her cute, pudgy nose. "I've got the prettiest wife who's talented and sure to be a successful artist in no time. She's honest, sweet when all the stars align just right, and even when she's naughty, my kiss brings her back around. Plus, I love her more than ever I knew possible."

"Me, too, Tyrell." Her eyes glazed over as she got sentimental. "I love you more than I can even comprehend. And I can't wait to make a family with you."

"Me neither, baby." I kissed her sweet lips once again. "What do you say to skipping our reception and staying here for the rest of the night?"

"I say that I think we've found it, Tyrell." She hugged me tightly.

"Found what exactly, baby?" I asked because with Ella you never really knew.

"Our happily ever after, of course!"

Yeah, she was right, we had found that. And I had a feeling it would go on and on and on.

The End

3. MAKE HER MINE EXTENDED EPILOGUE

TYRELL

Two Years Later...

"What do you mean, you're losing her?" I ran my hand over my face in aggravation as the veterinarian only shook her head. "We can't lose her. She's my wife's horse. She loves this mare. Can't you give her a C-section or something?"

"It's too late. The foal is lifeless, Mr. Gentry." Doctor Fontaine stood, pulling her gloves off. "Miss Rose had this dead fetus inside of her for too long. If you called a few days sooner, things might be different. She's developed an infection. This animal is in agony, Mr. Gentry. It's best to put her down. If your wife would like to say her goodbyes, then now's the time."

"She can't take that." I paced back and forth as the sounds of Miss Rose's labored breathing filled my ears and tore my heart. "Just do it. I'll deal with my wife after the fact."

Ella made me promise her mare would be okay—that she'd make it through this pregnancy without a hitch. In error I stand. And now there was only me to blame.

I forced the issue. Coy's Burden—the stallion named for my father—was about to be put out to pasture. As his age demanded, we took him off the eligible sperm list. When Ella bought the mare, I thought it prime time to see if old Coy could father his own. And he got it done. But then Miss Rose had complications during the pregnancy, and now we not only lost a foal, we were losing the mother, too.

Ella will be distraught.

The barn door opened. When Darleen walked in, tension was in the air as she eyed the veterinarian. "Did you pull the stillborn yet, Margaret?"

"No need, Darleen, she's too far gone. There's no need to torture this poor animal any longer." Pulling a syringe out of her bag, Doctor Fontaine prepared to put Miss Rose down.

Darleen's indigo eyes shot to mine. "We don't have to do this, Tyrell. Ella loves this horse."

"She shouldn't suffer anymore, Darleen." What else to do? I couldn't put this burden on Ella. "I'll deal with Ella once this is done."

"Dismiss her," Darleen said with a firm tone.

"Who, Doctor Fontaine?" No way!

Nodding, Darleen went on, "Margaret, do not administer that yet."

"Darleen, learn to let some things go, I've told you this before." The vet ignored Darleen, kneeling in front of the horse.

"Do it, Tyrell," Darleen growled. "Dismiss her now. I can deal with this."

"You're not licensed yet, Darleen," She had to be reminded that she wasn't a full-fledged veterinarian yet.

"I've got everything I need to take care of Miss Rose, so let me do it." She stepped closer to me. "Please, Tyrell. Let me take care of her!"

I didn't know what else to do, so with a nod, I decided, "Okay, Doc, step down. I'm letting Darleen take over from here."

"This will be a mistake, Mr. Gentry." She disagreed, but she got up and put the needle away. "When you decide this horse has suffered enough, just call me."

Darleen shot her a look that could kill. "We won't need your help, Margaret. Worst-case scenario, Tyrell will shoot her."

I'll do what?

The vet nodded, then left the barn as Darleen turned her attention to me. "Get Dad and Kyle. They'll pull the foal, and I'll administer the antibiotics. This horse can be saved, Tyrell. I know she can. Ella won't have to go through this loss. Not right now, she won't. We can do this together. Now get moving! We've got no time to waste!"

Hurrying to find her father and brother, I went out and jumped into my truck, hauling ass to the cattle barn where the men usually were. My cell rang as I drove across the ranch. Seeing Ella's name on the screen made me feel sick to my stomach because I need to sugarcoat the situation. "Hey, baby."

"How is she?" the very first thing to come out of her mouth. "I've been getting concerned. This is labor has been going on too long."

"I'm getting your dad and Kyle to help pull the colt out. It didn't make it, baby."

"So, there's no baby?" she sounded upset. "Miss Rose is like me? She can't have a living baby either?"

In two years of marriage, Ella had two pregnancies that went to the second trimester, but no further than that. "No one says you can't bring a baby to term, Ella."

"No, the doctors won't say it, but the fact is I can't." She got really quiet, and my heart hurt for her. "I can't even have a baby horse, it seems. Sometimes, I feel like this estate is cursed. Like happiness isn't meant to last here."

"We're happy," I reminded her.

"Yeah, sure," she sounded hopeless. "So, is Miss Rose going to be okay?"

What to say? She's already disheartened; it's in her voice. "We're doing our very best."

With a heavy sigh, she ended the call, "Don't make anymore promises, Tyrell. Please, just stop making me pledges you can't keep."

The silence made my heart heavy. She was right. I made guarantees I had no right making. Promises that we'd have a healthy baby each time she got pregnant. And even assurance her mare would have a healthy foal and things would be fine.

Maybe Ella was onto something? Perhaps the property was indeed under some curse? Things went wrong a hell of a lot around this place. Maybe keeping the mansion hadn't been such a great idea after all.

❦

ELLA

I moved down the hall to where we set up a nursery only a few months after getting married—we'd gotten pregnant right off the bat—I went to sit and think about existence. While I couldn't complain even one little bit about my life with Tyrell, the one complaint was not being able to have a child.

I've done everything right. Eat healthy, exercise, take my vitamins the way to the doctor ordered. *So why couldn't the babies develop to term?*

Death became a recurring thing after we married. I got a puppy not long after losing the first baby. It took a walk with us, barked at one of the bulls, and got stomped on; it was killed instantly.

Tyrell thought a pet fish might be better, so he got us a goldfish. On the third day we got up in the morning, and it was floating upside down in its bowl.

I even took an interest in one of the many feral kittens living in the cattle barn. No one knew I adored that tiny kitten. One day it went missing; I never saw it again and had no clue what happened to it. Is it me or the ranch that was cursed? Either way, there certainly was a curse.

Opening the door to the nursery, I went inside and sat in the big, white rocking chair. Slowly, I rocked back and forth looking at the crib. We chose a white one, so it would work for either a boy or a girl.

The first baby we lost, a boy we named Jonah, was buried on the property in the family cemetery. We put his minuscule casket as far away from Tyrell's grandparents as possible.

His sister, who we lost next, lay in a casket right next to his. We named her, Mary. I never was a religious person, but when we lost our son, I began reading the Bible for comfort. That's when I decided to name our little boy after someone in the Bible. I did the same with our little girl. It made me feel the tiniest bit better that they'd get to Heaven, and everyone would know their name.

There were times I thought about Lacy being up there with our two babies, playing with them, keeping them happy until the day I would be with them. It was only pretend; no one knew of this—not even Tyrell.

He'd been so good to me when we lost our children. He never blamed me or looked at me differently. But he was disenchanted. *I* disappointed him.

Sitting there, rocking and rocking, I thought about my horse that lay in wretchedness out in the barn. She had a dead baby inside of her the same way I had. And I wondered if she felt as sad thinking about what she lost.

Gulping back tears, I took the cell out of my pocket and called Tyrell. "Hi, babe. Tyrell, bury the foal just outside the fence where our babies are. It should be close to them. Maybe it'll find its way to Heaven to be with Jonah and Mary. Do you know if it's male or female yet?"

"We got it out. It's a male," he told me. "He looks like his dad."

A name came to me, and I blurted it out, "Moses. His tombstone will have that name written on it."

"Moses, it is, Ella. Don't worry about a thing," he said. "And Darleen said she's not leaving Miss Rose's side until she sees an improvement."

"Darlene is there? Tell her I'm coming down to sit with her, too. I should be there with Miss Rose. I know what she's feeling after all." I got up and wiped the tears with my hand. "I'm not the only one who's suffered a loss."

"I'll come up and get you, baby." He ended the call before I could protest.

Maybe he needed to be with me? Maybe witnessing another dead baby being pulled from its mother had him feeling the same pain I did? We needed each other. Not one of us was stronger than the other where the loss of our babies was concerned; we found comfort in each other. At least we had that. We had our love to see us through. And now our little angels had a pony up there with them. I supposed my puppy, kitten, and even the goldfish was up there, too.

I was tired of loved ones getting sent up to them. I wanted to keep at least some people and animals down here with Tyrell and me. But who's in charge of things like that? Somehow I have come to terms some things were just out of my control and Tyrell's, too.

Leaving the nursery, I went down to meet my husband. It had been some time since we had sex. Six months had passed since we lost Mary. Six months had passed since we found the will to make love.

TYRELL

Driving up to the house to get Ella, I thought about everything we lost. Our son and daughter, buried in the family burial ground, seemed a poor start to the family I hoped to create with my wife.

The doctors told us both fetuses had heart defects and that's why we lost them. They checked Ella and I and nothing was out of the ordinary. It made no sense why our babies had these defects!

Not one to think about something as irrational as curses, is something truly plaguing us? After all, there was no reason why our babies perished.

When I pulled up to the garage, Ella was standing outside, waiting for me. The way she wrung her hands told me she's not having an easy time. She looked at me as she climbed into the truck. "Tyrell, something came to me while I was waiting."

"About?" I backed up to return to the stable.

"Your grandfather's mistress." Her brow furrowed, she looked confused and upset. "Tyrell, do you remember how his mistress, Hilda, said your grandfather got her tubes tied so she couldn't have babies?"

It has been years since we talked to that woman or said anything about her. "I do recollect. Why?"

"What if she cursed all of you?" she asked with wide eyes. "What if we can't have babies because she did something to make sure the Gentry bloodline would end with him?"

That was nonsense! But I couldn't tell her that. "I don't know a thing about stuff like that."

"We should go see her," she said. "Like right now."

If it would help my wife, I'd do anything. It had been over six months since we made love. After the miscarriage of our daughter, Ella had lost all desire for sex. And I understood completely. So, I didn't push her. "Okay, we'll go now if that's what you want to do."

Turning in the opposite direction of the barn, we went to town to find Hilda. Fifteen minutes later, we pulled up to the curb in front of her house, the same Cadillac in the drive.

Ella sighed, then got out of the truck, and I followed after her as she bolted to the front door. "We have to choose our words carefully, Ella."

With a swift knock and three rings to the doorbell, Ella seemed to be on a mission. How much control does she have at this moment? When the door opened, a skeletal woman stood there. I barely recognized her!

"Ella?"

"Hilda?" my wife asked. "Um, I'm sorry. You look exhausted. Are we bothering you?"

The woman looked more than tired. She looked to be as close to death as I'd ever seen anyone!

When she opened her dry, cracked lips, she said, "Come on. I'll tell you about it."

Going inside, the house wasn't the showroom it was before; everything was a mess. Dirty dishes piled everywhere; laundry lay on every available surface. The stench was awful, and I had to fight the urge to gag.

"Hilda, what's wrong?" I asked.

Pushing some dirty clothes off a spot on the sofa, she pointed at the chair. "Just throw that stuff on the floor."

Ella shook her head. "We don't need to sit down. Hilda, are you sick?"

"I'm pretty sure of that," she said, then coughed, covering her mouth with her thin hand.

I waited for her to stop coughing before asking, "Have you been to the doctor?" As far as I knew, Hilda still got the paychecks my grandfather had set up before his death.

She shook her head. "I'm not going to a doctor."

Ella looked at me troubled. "I don't like this, Tyrell."

I didn't, either. But what can we do about it? "Hilda, we can take you to the emergency room. You really should be seen by someone right away."

My offer met with a shake of her head. "I won't go. Now, tell me what has you two coming to see me after all this time?"

With a sigh, Ella knew when she'd been beaten. "This might sound crazy to you, Hilda, but Tyrell and I had two miscarriages in the last two years. I thought perhaps the Gentry men have been cursed? Conceivably, you might have something to do with it."

That sounded insane! "Hilda, I'm sorry we bothered you. We'll leave."

"No," she said in a hushed voice. "She's right."

"Say what?!"

Hilda looked at me with dark eyes, circled by even darker skin. The woman was beyond ill. "There is a curse on all the Gentry men. Just before your grandfather died, he asked me for help."

Ella leaned against me, clutching my arm, "Did you put a curse on Tyrell and his brothers, Hilda?

"When I was banished to Louisiana, I met a woman there. She was a voodoo priestess," she admitted. "Out of resentment, I asked for her help. Not a year later, Collin's wife was dead. The death occurred so quickly and Fiona wasn't old, so there was an autopsy. She died of a heart defect they never found in her before. But the doctors chalked it up to the fact she hadn't sought much healthcare after the birth of Arnold."

All we knew was my paternal grandmother died of something that sounded similar to what our babies had. And that worried me.

ELLA

"Hilda, what did you do?" I looked into the woman's darker than death's eyes. "We need to know."

"I didn't do a thing, Collin did." Hilda took as deep a breath as she could to gather strength. "Where Fiona was concerned, I did ask for that. But the curse on the son of Collin and the sons he bore has nothing to do with me."

It didn't seem possible, "Did Collin get some witch to curse his sons and grandsons? Is that what you're telling me?"

Hilda's nod answered my question as she went into another fit of coughing. Left speechless, I looked at Tyrell with tear-filled eyes. He moved his hand around my shoulder, pulling me closer to him. "We should leave, Ella."

I asked Hilda once more if she'd let us take her to get medical help. Once she stopped coughing, I pleaded, "Hilda, please let us take you to the emergency room. This is no way to live."

"Oh, this isn't living, Ella," Hilda said smirking. "This is dying. We all have to do it someday. It's just my time now."

"Don't you want to be somewhere you can get pain medications, Hilda?" How could someone not want relief?

Shaking her head, she explained, "This is karma for having the priestess put a curse on Fiona and taking her life. Getting relief isn't a thing I deserve."

Tyrell couldn't hold back, "Hilda, what my grandmother died from didn't have a thing to do with curses. She had a heart condition. We've had two miscarriages and both fetuses had heart abnormalities. Curses aren't real. And at least one of my brothers has a child, so that whole idea makes no sense."

"When did he have it?" she asked.

"Six years ago," Tyrell told her.

"That was before your grandfather did the hex." Hilda shook her head. "He made it only hours before he died. Sorry about this. If I hadn't sought that priestess, none of this would've happened."

Tyrell thought she was crazy, and a fair amount of my mind

328

thought that way, too. But there was that nagging doubt that some magic charm plagued us, and we wanted to get rid of it. "If one can make a curse, one can break a curse, right?" I looked at Tyrell who shook his head. "Come on, Tyrell."

"No." He tugged me to come along with him. "We'll get out of your hair, Hilda. Thank you for the information. It will be quite helpful."

"I hope so." She lifted a hand to wave goodbye. "And when I get there, I will try to make things right for you again. Culpability is a dreadful thing to live with. Once I can change things, I will. Believe in what I say. The curse will lift after my death."

Tyrell nodded, and I smiled at her as we walked through the door and I called back, "Thank you, Hilda. I hope you can break this hex Mr. Gentry put on his relatives. We have two babies in graves already, I don't want to put even one more in that cemetery before I die myself."

I didn't get to say anything else as Tyrell pulled me out of the house and took me to the truck. "Baby, don't believe that crap."

"Why not?" I got into the truck. Why is he thinking everything has to be so black and white? "You don't know everything, Tyrell Gentry."

"I know what I *don't* believe in." He closed the door, then went around to the driver's seat. "And I don't believe in witches or curses. But I do believe in genetics and if my grandmother had a heart condition, then our kids could've gotten it."

My cell rang. It was Darleen. Swiping the screen, I asked, "Do you have good news?"

"Miss Rose is recovering."

I clutched my heart. "Yes! Thank, God."

"Come and see her when you can. I think she misses you, Ella. She keeps nibbling my cheek, but she's looking around for you," Darleen told me.

Darleen wasn't right about who she was looking for. "I know that feeling. She's looking for the foal. She doesn't understand what happened to it. She can still smell him there." It broke my heart the poor horse had to endure that feeling of loss. "I will see her when we get back."

Tyrell took a turn that led us to the doctor's office, instead of the estate. "I want to stop by and see our doctor. She needs to know. Maybe she can get a copy of my grandmother's autopsy report and match it with that of the fetuses?"

"It's worth a shot." I still hung onto the curse thing, but he was right for seeking other answers. "We'll see what happens after Hilda passes away. That sounds morbid, but after what she said, this idea things will change was insistent."

"Our doctor can make the changes we need. We may have our babies another way, but we will have our family, Ella. I promise." He reached over and took my hand in his, then kissed it. "And I know you told me to stop making promises I can't keep, but I'm making you this promise: we *will* have healthy babies someday, Ella Gentry."

TYRELL

Her body underneath mine felt like Heaven. Our ragged breaths filled the room. Undulating, moaning, and diving so deeply into each other, neither of us had an inkling of the passion that would come that night.

Dragging her nails across my skin, Ella growled, "I want you more than I've ever wanted you. I want you to fill me with your hot seed. I want to have your baby, Tyrell Gentry."

We only just found out about what might have caused the miscarriages. "I want you to have my baby. I want that more than I've ever wanted anything." Thrusting into her hard and fast, I gave everything I had and she did the same for me.

"I love you, Tyrell Gentry," she moaned as her foot ran up the back of my leg.

Catching her leg behind the knee, I pulled it up, slipping deeper into her. "I love you. Ella Gentry."

Our eyes met, our bodies moved as one, and I saw our future. Blue flames filled her eyes as she screamed with her release. I followed quickly with my own, her body milking mine for every last drop of the life giving liquid I produced.

Panting, I fell on top of her, completely spent. Pushing my hand through her hair, I tried not to think about us having another baby. To have my heart broken again wasn't a thing I wanted. But I couldn't help it.

I wanted another chance to be a father and make her a mother. That's all I wanted.

Her fingers trailed lightly over my back. "After six months, this feels like the right thing to do. Like they say, if you fall off the horse, you've got to get back in the saddle and try again. We can't stop trying, Tyrell."

Kissing the top of her head, I agreed, "No, we can't stop trying. We may not have a healthy baby this way, but we will definitely find a way."

Pulling my face to hers, she kissed my lips before saying, "We'll be just fine. My instinct tells me as much."

We fell asleep in each other's arms that night.

Waking the next morning, we went down to breakfast and saw Ella's mom looking a bit off. "Morning, Mom," Ella greeted her. "You look kind of out of it. Is everything alright?"

Looking up from her plate of untouched food, she blinked a few times. "I just got a call from the police. The officer said someone left a note with the house number on it. It said to call the number and let the people know the curse has been lifted."

My heart raced. We haven't told anyone about our visit the day before with Hilda. "Is Hilda dead?"

Nodding, she looked like she'd seen a ghost. "Yes, she died around midnight last night is what the officer said. But how'd you know it was her I was talking about?"

"Just a wild guess," I said as Ella smiled at me.

"Everything will be alright now, Tyrell," she whispered.

Her mother looked at her with confusion. "What in the world are you talking about?"

"Nothing." I didn't want anyone—not even her own mother—to know about Ella's silly belief in the hex and how Hilda's death might lift it.

No one needed to think my wife was crazy.

ELLA

"Come on, baby," Tyrell coached me. "One more push and she'll be out."

"I can't," I whined. "I'm tired, Tyrell."

"Well, that don't matter cause you have to do this." He took my hand, holding it in a loose grip. "Now when you get that next contraction, push like you haven't pushed before."

With a loud grunt, I bore down, and the doctor said, "She's almost out, Ella. Great job. Only one more push."

"God, why's this so much work?" I complained. "No more, Tyrell. Promise me that I won't have to do this again."

"I promise." Kissing me on my sweaty forehead, I hoped he recalled making the compromise we had when we first got married.

One more push and little Karina's high pitched cry filled the air. We all breathed sighs of relief as the nurse whisked her away to clean her and check her vitals.

"Okay, Ella, come on now," Tyrell coached me some more. "Let's do this again."

Two minutes went by without a thing happening, then I moaned, "Here he comes."

The doctor at the ready, said, "I'm ready for Layne's arrival. Push him out, Momma."

One hard grunt and I heard our son's cries. "Way to go, baby." Tyrell kissed me on the cheek, then smiled.

"I can't do that again. I'm drained, Tyrell." I wiped the back of my hand over my sweat-soaked brow.

"One more time," he assured me.

It wasn't like I had a choice. With another hard contraction, I barely had to push as little Melvin came out and took his first breath, then cried along with his siblings. "There's our three, Tyrell. Just like I promised you."

"You did it, little Momma." My husband looked at me with shinning eyes. "Did we just get lucky with these triplets? Thank God for their good health and for yours, too."

"Don't forget to thank Hilda," I told him. "If she hadn't passed away to lift the curse, we might not have been so lucky."

His laugh told me he still didn't believe it. That didn't matter. We finally had our three children and that was all that mattered.

Our happily ever after could keep going on and on...

The End

4. COLLIN'S CURSE

A Make Her Mine Extra

Even though we were young, passion cared not about our ages...

I was all of sixteen years old when I first laid eyes on her.

She'd just moved to our small town.

Her family – so different from mine.

Times not in our favor.

Even though everything seemed to be against us, we found love anyway.

I taught her how to be what I wanted.

She taught me that love would never be enough – not when your last name is Gentry...

COLLIN

She walked into my math class, head bent, eyes on the floor, her dark hair shiny and satin-smooth. "This is Hilda Stevens," Mr. Reinhold told the class. "She's a new student whose family has moved into Carthage from Mission, in the valley."

No one said a word as the girl took a seat at the back of the class. With my desk only two rows over, I could see her from the corner of my eye. Her small chest heaved with the nerves I knew coursed through her.

She did not speak one word throughout that class, then the bell rang, and we all left the math room to go to lunch. I followed behind her, interested in where she'd go to eat. She headed straight to the benches and picnic tables, then took a seat on one of the benches. Opening her book bag, she took out a cylinder of aluminum foil and pulled it open, revealing a flour tortilla filled with something I couldn't make out.

The girl's large, dark eyes made my cock stir. Her slender, almost willowy figure proved easy on my eyes. Something about her did it for me.

I took a seat on one of the picnic tables nearest to her. Johnny Franklin came up to take a seat too. "What's up, Collin?"

"Not much." I didn't care much for Johnny. I didn't care much for anyone. But the girl who sat all alone had my attention, nearly all of it.

Johnny's blue eyes went to the girl I had mine on. "Hey, who's that? She's new, huh?"

"She was in my math class," I told him as I shoved my hand through my hair. "The teacher said she came here from the valley."

"Oh, yeah?" Johnny asked, then got up and went to take a seat right next to the girl who'd been introduced as Hilda Stevens. "Hi. I'm Johnny. And you are?"

Slowly, she turned her head to look at him. Her lips quivered as she answered, "I'm Hilda."

"So, you're new," he said as I listened intently to every word they said. "You a junior too?"

She nodded. "Yes, I am." Wrapping the foil back around the filled tortilla, she put it back in her bag, seemingly embarrassed to be eating it for some reason.

"What's that thing?" he asked her as he watched her put it away.

"A burrito. My mother makes them for our lunches." The girl looked at the ground again.

"So, whereabouts do you live in Carthage?" Johnny asked as he got up, standing in front of her.

"I, um, my family lives on Sabine Street." Pulling her arms around her as if hugging herself, she seemed to be bracing for something.

"Southside, huh?" Johnny looked at me, then winked. I had no idea what he'd done that for, but I soon found out. "So, Hilda, what do you say about giving me your address?"

Her dark eyes met his, her expression confused. "Why?"

"It's pretty common for girls from that side of town to put out to guys – sometimes for money." He smiled at her. "So, how much?"

My heart sped up, my fists balled, and I almost said something. Almost.

The girl got up and walked away, maintaining her dignity, even as Johnny erupted into laughter. He came back to sit on top of the table near me, and I said quietly, "She's from a poor family then."

"Yeah, I'll say." Johnny laughed again. "Too bad. She's kind of okay in the looks department. But you know what they say about the

336

girls from the southside, you can play – just don't tell anyone you're playing over there."

I knew the rules. I knew them very well. And I followed them, lest my father beat the devil out of me. One did not go against the rules my father laid out, nor that of civil society for that matter.

A Gentry was born to follow the rules. One never prospers if one deviates from what society expects out of them. As the owner of one of the largest ranches in Panola County, my father helped set the standards the citizens of our town lived by. Bucking the system meant bucking him. And my father definitely wasn't one to be bucked. You could ask any person who'd ever seen him break a spirited horse about that.

Father spared nothing when breaking his horses. The whip, his constant companion, always seemed to be ready to knock the resistance out of anything and anyone.

As the bell rang and the next class started, I saw the girl walking to my same class. This time, I took the seat right behind her. Never uttering one word to her, I breathed in her scent. Fresh linen, a hint of lemon, and utterly female took my breath away.

Why she had to be from the wrong side of town, I didn't know. No one had ever stolen my attention as much as that girl. Not that I'd ever be able to do anything about that, though.

My father would skin me alive if I did so much as talk to the girl. After class, I followed her to the next one and the one after that. It seemed like we'd been put on the same schedule. I found that interesting.

Maybe we had a destiny that no one could stop – not even my controlling father.

HILDA

I never wanted to leave Mission. My friends were there. Most of my family lived there too. But my father took us to a town where we would never fit in. As the oldest of seven children, it was my responsibility to help the others get used to our new town and home.

Blanca, my one year younger sister, came up beside me after school. "How was your first day, Hilda?"

"I don't know." I walked slowly, holding my books in front of my chest. My breasts had begun to swell, and I hated that.

"You don't know?" she asked with a wrinkled brow. "How do you not know how today went?"

Joe, our brother who was a year younger than Blanca, ran up to us. "We've got to get to the junior high to make sure the others are okay. I got picked on during gym class. Who knows how their first day went."

Picking up the pace, the three of us tried to hurry without looking like we needed to rush to find out if our two siblings in the junior high school were doing fine. As boys, it seemed my brothers would get the physical abuse. As girls, I knew we'd get the mental torture. I couldn't stop thinking about what that boy had said to me at lunch.

"Ricky," I called out when I saw my brother just under Joe. "Where's Alfonso?" He was a year younger than Ricky. Our parents had their children back to back; not more than a year separated us.

Ricky turned to look back, then we all saw Alfonso coming out of the building. One black eye and a swollen lower lip told us how his day had gone. "Oh, poor Alfonso." I went to him, taking his books out of his hands.

"It's okay," he said. "I'll be alright. Let's get to the elementary to get to Juan and Rosa."

Thankfully, the two of them were all smiles when we got to them. It seemed the younger kids hadn't learned how to be so mean yet. Down the street, we all walked past the stores, the nice homes, all the way to where the people with very little money lived.

Gulping, I looked around myself in a way I hadn't before. In the doorways, I saw the young women that that boy had talked about at lunch. It seemed he hadn't been lying about things on the south side of our new town. "We don't need to be outside after dark," I let my younger siblings know. "You boys, especially." I nudged Blanca's shoulder. "Nor us, sister."

Blanca followed my eyes, seeing the women, barely dressed at all, leaning on the doorframes of their small, shack-like homes. "Oh, I see what you're saying, Hilda."

The sound of a car coming up behind us had us moving to one side of the street. Slowly, it went by, the driver barely looking at me, but he did look. I recognized him from my classes. He'd been in every one of them. I didn't know his name; he seemed to be just about as quiet as me.

I watched as he stopped at a house two houses down from ours. Honking the horn had a man running out of the house like his tail was on fire. "Coming, Collin!"

He jumped into the back of the truck instead of inside of it. The truck moved down the street, honking again, and another man ran out to join him in the back.

Before we could get inside our house, the truck came back and stopped next to us. "Any of you boys need to make a little money?" the driver, who I now knew was named Collin, called out.

Joe and Ricky stopped, seemingly interested in what the boy had to offer. Alfonso ducked into the house as everyone else. Only I stayed, waiting to hear what he wanted from my brothers.

My brothers approached the car as Joe said, "We could use some money. What do you need done?"

"My father owns Whisper Ranch outside of town," Collin told them. "Most afternoons, he lets me pick up some people to do work around the ranch. You know, shovel shit, hose down horses, grunt work. It comes with a meal that's served at seven when the workday ends. Plus, you get paid in cash, then I drive you back home."

Ricky's brow cocked. "How much cash?"

Collin smiled, revealing perfectly straight, pearly white teeth. "Three bucks for each hand. So, you guys in or what? Cause I've got others that I can put to work. I just thought – with you all being new to town – you might need the break."

Joe looked over his shoulder at me. "Tell Dad what we're doing, Hilda." He handed his books to Ricky, who brought them to me.

I stood there with their things and mine in my arms. "When will you get your homework done?"

Joe looked at me with a smile after he'd jumped into the back of the truck. "I'll give you a nickel if you do mine for me."

Ricky jumped into the back too. "Hey, me too, Hilda. Even Blanca could do it if she wants to make some money."

Nodding, I turned to go inside when I heard the boy say my name, "Hilda?"

Turning back around, I asked, "Yes?"

"Tell your father that I'll have your brothers home by eight." And then he just took off. My brothers waved at me as they drove out of sight.

Going into the house, I had no idea how our father would take the news. One never knew with him. If he didn't find any alcohol to drink, he might not take it well. But if he'd find some, then he might be overjoyed. One just never knew what to expect.

Mother was busy making tortillas for supper. "How was school, Hilda?"

"It was school, Mother. I suppose I'll get used to it. Joe and

Ricky have found an after-school job." I looked down the hall when I heard my father coughing. "How's Father's mood this afternoon?"

She shook her head, then turned away. I caught the bruise on her cheek, and I knew right away that not only was he not going to take the news well, but he might take it out on me for not stopping my younger brothers as well.

COLLIN

Lying in the hayloft, the stars peeking in at me through the cracks in the roof of the old barn, I held my cock in my hand and thought of Hilda. Her long, luscious, dark hair hung down her back. Her dark eyes loomed in front of my face. "Collin, I am here for you. Do to me as you want."

Taking her chin in my hand, I pulled her lips to mine, taking them with a long, soft kiss. "Will you be mine, Hilda?"

Nodding, she wrapped her arms around me, then I pushed my hard cock into her soft, warm pussy. She whimpered, "Yes, I will be yours, Collin."

Thrusting into her with hard strokes, I loved the way she gasped for air with each move I made. Pushing her to her limits, I pushed more before letting her come all over my cock that jerked and spilled into her sweet cunt.

"Collin?" I heard my father call out. "Boy, where the hell are you?"

Shoving my spent dick back into my jeans. I crawled over the loft floor to hurry to my father. "I'm up here, Father."

As I climbed down the ladder, I felt his hand on my shoulder. "Why the hell did you leave your bedroom, boy?"

"I wanted to look at the stars," I told him, trying to sound firm and not nearly as scared as I really was. When you showed my father fear, he let you know exactly why you needed to fear him.

"That's a pile of horseshit." Throwing me back, he went up the ladder. "Who's up here?"

"No one is up there, I swear it." Getting up off the dirt floor, I walked toward the barn door to leave. "I just wanted to lay up there and look at the stars, is all."

Not wanting to give him a chance to catch up to me and cuff my ears or thump my head, I went inside the house and straight to my bedroom. Given time, my father usually cooled off.

Hilda's brothers had worked for us for a few months. Each day I got to see her in our classes and when I picked them up after school. We hadn't said more than a few words to one another in all that time.

Things had begun to get to me. I wanted to talk to her. I wanted to do a hell of a lot more than that to her. But I knew neither of us could let a soul know if we did what I wanted.

Bright and early on the next morning, I got up and drove the truck to school. During the night, I'd come up with an idea. There was going to be an assembly at school that day. The football team was going to state, and there would be a loud celebration. One so loud that it would be nearly impossible to hear a couple of love-starved teenagers going at it under the bleachers.

I just had to get Hilda to agree to meet me underneath them after the festivities started.

In the first period, I took the seat behind her. Writing her a note but leaving my name off of it, I asked her if she'd like to get to know me better. Slipping the note into her bag, I had to wait to see if she'd find it.

In the next class, I took the seat behind her again. When she turned sideways with the note in her hand, she smiled at me. I nodded, then she did too.

Somehow, she'd understood that it was me who'd written the note, and so I wrote her another one, telling her to meet me under the bleachers that day. Then, I slipped it into her bag.

In the next class, I couldn't sit behind her as Lisa Jenkins beat me to that place. I had to take one clear across the room. But her eyes found mine after I saw her take that note from her bag. She nodded again, filling my cock with hot blood as I knew that our time had come.

Soon, Hilda's hot cunt would be surrounding my aching cock, and I'd bury myself in her so deep that it wouldn't be possible to tell where I ended and she began.

HILDA

The sounds of the playing band filled the auditorium we'd all been brought into for an assembly. I didn't care about the football team going to state that year. All I cared about was the fact that Collin Gentry wanted us to get to know each other better. Not that we really knew each other at all, but I was ready to see what he meant by what he'd written to me that day.

With the music loud and the students and faculty cheering like crazy, I made my discreet exit to find my way underneath the bleachers as Collin had instructed me. In the dimness, trails of light, tendrils of dust flowing through them, I saw a shadow. "Collin?"

"Hush," came his southern voice.

Standing perfectly still, I didn't know what I was supposed to do. "K."

He came to me, his hands took mine, then he pulled me back until the darkness covered us as thick as a wool blanket would've. My back against the wall, his body pressed against mine so hard, I could feel every bit of him. And the hard lump between his legs made my legs shake.

His hand moved behind my neck, holding me as his lips pressed against mine with a hard kiss. The way his tongue pushed at my lips until they parted startled me. When he slipped his tongue into my mouth, I nearly gagged, it seemed like such a gross thing to do.

But then I began to like it as he kissed me, ran his hands over my body, my breasts, my stomach, and then in between my legs. I caught him by the wrist, trying to pull his hand away from a place I'd never been touched before. "No," I hissed after wrenching my mouth away from his.

He didn't even take one step back, his dick pulsed against me. "No?" Moving his hips, he made a grinding motion against me. "You sure about that?"

I ached for him. But I wasn't that kind of girl. "Yes."

Moving his hand back to where I'd pulled it away from, he pressed the back of my hand against my now very warm sex. I couldn't believe what he was doing. "Stop."

"I'm not doing anything," he whispered in my ear, "you are."

Moving my hand hard and fast, he had my body on fire, and all I knew was that I wanted to feel his hands on me instead of my own. So, I pulled my hand away. "Okay, you do it."

"Good, girl. You do what I want, and you won't be sorry. I promise you that." His fingers pulled the top of my pants down until he could reach inside to run his fingers over my bare flesh.

Quivering with fear and desire, I didn't know what to do. But I didn't want it to stop. "Collin, what do you want from me?" I had to know what he meant. I wanted to know if he wanted me to be his girlfriend. If he wanted us to hold hands while walking down the hallways, carry my books for me, eat lunch with me each day — that's what I yearned to know.

Pressing his palm against my sex, he let me know what he wanted, "I want this."

I'd never given that to anyone. And I knew I should've told him that. But he kissed me again, even harder this time. His mouth on mine, his hand in my pants, touching, stroking, then one finger pushed inside of me.

I nearly dropped to my knees when his finger pumped inside of me. He rammed it in hard and fast. My fingers curled into his shoulders as he shoved his finger in deeper and deeper until I thought I might cry from the pain.

348

When he pulled it out, I inhaled a breath of relief. But what he did next stopped me from breathing entirely. He stepped back for only a second. His pants hit the floor, then he pushed mine down too, put his foot on the crotch of my pants, and picked me up, so I had nothing on below the waist.

Pushing me back against the wall, he issued his first of what would become many orders, "Legs around my waist."

I moved them quickly, why I didn't know, but I did as he'd told me to. Not one word came out of my mouth as he slammed his hard cock into my virgin hole.

A scream began to rise in my throat as pain filled me. The burning and the ripping were intense. But I knew that no one could know what we were doing underneath the bleachers. Burying my face in his shoulder, I let the tears flow, but the sounds remained inside.

He made soft grunts, low groans and pressed his lips against my neck as he kept up a fast, hard, steady rhythm. Finally, the pain ebbed away, followed by a numbness that filled my entire body, and I had to admit that it filled my mind as well.

On and on he went as I held on for dear life. I had no idea what this meant for us. No idea if when we walked out from under those bleachers, we'd go hand-in-hand or what we'd do. But I knew one thing. I knew I felt a connection with him that I'd never felt with anyone.

His teeth grazed along my neck as he kept up his furious pace, then growled in my ear, "You know not to talk, right?"

I didn't know what he meant. "I guess."

"No one can know." He pulled back, and even in the darkness, I could see his face. Boyishly handsome, Collin was the epitome of what I called Texas royalty. Ranchers, bankers, and actors held those prestigious positions - in my head anyway.

I wasn't sure if he meant that no one could know about the sex or about us. And I wasn't about to ask. "K."

It's not like I cared anyway. I didn't need anyone to know that he and I had this connection. I didn't need him to walk around holding my hand. I didn't need anyone to know anything about us.

What we had wasn't meant for others to know about. Judge.

I knew people would judge him if he dated a poor girl like me. How could I fault him for not wanting to deal with that?

His mouth took mine again as he went at me harder, more feverish. I had no idea what was going on since I'd never done that before. But when his body shook, followed by wet heat filling me and thick strands of a substance that I didn't know what was running down the insides of my legs, I knew only one thing. The boy was mine.

And I knew I was right when his body went soft against mine, his voice so soft, "Thank you, Hilda Stevens."

A smile pulled my lips up. "Thank you, Collin Gentry."

He couldn't look at me as he said what he had to say next. Instead, he kept his face buried in my neck. "You're my first."

"And you're mine too," I let him know.

When he pulled his head back to look at me, I saw an odd expression on his face. "I'm what?"

"You're my first too, Collin."

"Shit." He let me go, pulled up his pants, then left me there. Alone.

COLLIN

How could she have been a virgin? I kept asking myself that over and over as I drove home.

Once I'd left her, I took off. I didn't know what else to do. I didn't want to see her or anyone. I'd never thought of that girl as a virgin. In my mind, she was as sexually advanced as any of the girls on the wrong side of town. Only this girl was prettier than the rest of them. Plus, she smelled better.

I'd taken her innocence, though. And that didn't sit well with me. Once I got home, my mother noticed me running to the bathroom. I had to shower, get our combined scent off of my body. "Where are you going in such a rush?"

"I need a shower. I got really sweaty in gym class today. I reek." I got into the shower without even waiting for the water to heat up. Lathering up, I scrubbed until every bit of that smell was gone.

Later, I lay in my bed, staring up at the ceiling. I wanted more with Hilda — more than I could ever have. Why did things have to be so complicated? Why couldn't two people — no matter how different their places in society were — just be together if they wanted to?

Even if Hilda Stevens had been living on the right side of town, her cultural combination wouldn't have changed a thing for us. Her white father – known to be a raging alcoholic who'd inherited his home in Carthage from his grandparents – had no job, no skills, and no way in hell would my father ever allow me to have a thing to do with his daughter. Her mother — rumor had it – was born in Mexico.

There wasn't a chance in hell for us, and I'd gone and taken her virginity. Deep inside, I knew blowing that girl off after doing a thing like that would be wrong in so many ways.

But how could I do the right thing by her when no one would allow it?

I sat in silence at the dinner table that night. My father kept looking at me. "So, the boys took off for the big game in Dallas then – huh?"

Nodding, I shoved a forkful of greens into my mouth so I didn't have to say anything.

Mom looked at me with a perplexed expression. "If they're going to play in Dallas, Collin, why haven't you left to go watch that game?"

Then it hit me. Most of our small town would be gone to Dallas for that game.

I can see Hilda tonight!

Gulping down the food, I found some hope and said, "Oh, I'm going. Right after dinner, I'll leave. It'll be late when I get back."

My father pulled out his wallet, then slipped me some cash. "Here ya go. Stay in a hotel in Dallas and just come back in the morning."

I couldn't believe it. I had enough money to rent a room somewhere. I wouldn't go to Dallas, but I could go one town over, and I could pick up Hilda and take her with me. "Thanks, Father. I'll do that. It's safer than driving that late in the night anyway."

Scarfing down the rest of my food, I hurried to pack a small bag, then went out to my truck. The task of getting Hilda to come with me, without anyone knowing, wasn't an easy one.

Driving to her street, I went slowly in front of her house. Her brother Joe ran out. "Hey, boss. You need some help today?"

"Nah." I didn't need his help. But then I had an idea. "Mother needs someone to help her in the house. Can you ask one of your sisters if they'd like to make a couple bucks? And it's an overnight job. Mother's cleaning out the attic and said it's going to be an all-nighter. I can bring whoever wants the job back in the morning."

"I'll ask Hilda and Blanca if one of them wants to take the job. But let me run it by our father first." He turned to go back inside as I waited, fingers crossed that Hilda would figure out what I was doing.

If her sister came out, I had no idea what I'd do.

Five minutes later, Hilda came out of the door with a small bag in her hands. She slipped into the truck, then I took off. Her lips were pressed so tightly together that they formed one thin line.

I knew she had a million questions, so I let her in on things. "First, I didn't know you were a virgin. Second, I wouldn't have done things the way I did. And third, I'm gonna make up for it tonight. We're going to a hotel in Beckville for the night."

Slowly, she turned her head to look at me. "What does this mean, Collin?"

"It means we're kind of seeing each other," I let her know. "You know we can't be seen out in public, right?"

Her dark eyes drooped. "Yes, I know. I'm not good enough for someone of your class."

"Just by society's rules, Hilda. Not by mine." Moving my arm to lie over the back of the seat, I patted my hand to draw her attention. "Come on over here and sit next to me. We're out of town already."

Sliding over, she smiled as I put my arm around her shoulders, then kissed her cheek. "Collin?"

"Yeah?"

"How long can we keep doing this?" She looked at me with hope in her eyes.

I had no intentions of letting her go. "As long as we keep this a secret from everyone, we can do this for a very long time, Hilda."

With a sigh, she relaxed and leaned her head on my shoulder. "I like the sound of that."

I thought I'd found us the happiest ending she and I could ever have. And I hoped she thought so too.

The End

5. HIS REVENGE

Secret Baby Romance
(Irresistible Brothers Book Two)

BLURB

I don't believe in seconds chances,
   Especially when they come in the form of Tiffany.
   The only woman I've ever loved.
   The only woman to shatter my heart and skip town
like I never mattered.

She hasn't been the only woman in my bed,
   But she's the only woman that I could never forget.
   The day she left, I swore I'd do everything to forget her,
   But hell if the feelings don't come rushing back the minute I
see her.

What the hell is she doing back in this town?
   She's still as beautiful as the day she left—but something's
different.
   The little girl she brought back home with her,
   Looks exactly like me.

I'll be damned if she thinks she's going to show up here,
   With zero explanation and secret so big it could blow up my
entire life.

I'm going to make sure she knows the pain she caused me,
One slow, toe-curling orgasm at a time.

Revenge can be sweet,
And I plan to make sure she knows exactly what she missed out on.
I just have to keep my heart from falling for her all over again.

JASPER

Carthage, Texas—Panola County
January 1st

In the matter of one week, our lives changed drastically. My older brother, Tyrell, sat between me and my younger brother, Cash. A limo had picked us up at the small airport in Carthage, Texas. We'd come in on a private jet—I'd never felt so cool in my life.

We'd never met our grandfather who'd passed away a little before Christmas last year. We'd never met any of our extended family though, so it wasn't that strange—for our family anyway.

We'd grown up in a suburb of Dallas, Texas, called Seagoville. The town we drove through wasn't a thing like what we'd come from. The population sign at the Panola county line said there were only a little over six thousand people who called the place home. It wasn't the smallest town in the world, but it sure was close.

Our grandfather's attorney, Allen Samuels, sat across from us. Taking a piece of paper out of a folder he had on the seat next to him, he finally started telling us why the hell we were summonsed to Carthage in the first place.

"The whole of the estate—that includes Whisper Ranch, the thirty-thousand square foot home that's on the ranch, and, of course, all of the vehicles, including the Cessna Citation II you came in on—belong to you three men now." He tapped lightly on the window that separated us from the driver and the chauffeur rolled it down. "Davenport, we need to make a stop at Mr. Gentry's bank, please."

"Sure thing," the driver said, then the window up slowly rolled back up.

The lawyer gave my older brother his attention. "Tyrell, what have you been told about your paternal grandparents?"

"Not much," Tyrell said. "My mother's famous quote when any of us asked about our grandparents was that if one couldn't say anything nice about a person, they shouldn't say anything at all. We'd assumed our grandparents weren't very good people."

I added my two cents. "Yeah, Mom and Dad didn't even like to be asked about them. So, we stopped asking early on. Just asking them who our grandparents were put them in terrible moods."

"I see." The man's brown eyes seemed a little on the sad side to me. "Here we are." Looking around, I noticed we'd pulled into the parking lot of a bank. "I'm going to have you all added to the ranch's bank accounts. And then we'll transfer the remainder of your grandfather's money into personal accounts for each of you— if that's okay with you. You certainly can open accounts elsewhere if you'd like to. Your grandparents used this bank exclusively for years. I can assure you that the president appreciates Whisper Ranch's business and does everything they can to keep their customers happy."

Since neither Cash nor I spoke up, Tyrell looked at us, then shrugged. "This bank seems as good as any. What do you guys think?"

Cash pushed his hand through his thick dark hair. "Sounds fine to me. It'll be my first bank account anyway."

I just shrugged. It wasn't like I had anything better to do. "Sounds okay to me, too. All I've got in my bank is about twenty bucks. Hell, I might not even have that. I bought a bottle of Jack before getting on the plane; that might've overdrawn my account." I'd never been real good at keeping track of my monetary gains.

None of us were that experienced with money as we were pretty young. Tyrell was twenty-seven, I'd just turned twenty-five, and Cash was only twenty-two. And none of us ever had great jobs either. Money and The Gentrys didn't exactly go hand in hand.

Tyrell let the man know what we wanted to do. "This bank will do for us just fine, Allen." We got out of the car, and I saw the driver standing there. Tyrell greeted him. "Thanks. He said your name is Davenport, right?"

The old guy nodded. "Yep. I also drive various tractors and trucks at the ranch. If you need a ride, you call me, and I'll get you there."

Tyrell being who he was, didn't much cotton to formalities. "If you don't mind me asking, what's your first name?"

"Buddy," the man told him. "Your grandfather liked to put on airs."

"We're not like that at all." Tyrell shook his head. "Mind if we call you Buddy instead?"

"Not at all." The old man smiled. "It would be nice, actually."

I figured we ought to introduce ourselves to the man who'd occasionally be driving us around. "Nice to meet you, Buddy. I'm Jasper, this is Tyrell, and the little feller there is Cash, the baby brother of the Gentry family."

I loved teasing my baby brother; it pissed him off.

"Jasper, you're the littlest out of all of us, you jerk."

I flexed my bicep and shoved my hand through my hair in the sexiest of fashions. "By a smidgeon of an inch, Cash. You're shorter."

"Also, by a smidgeon of an inch." Cash wasn't waiting around for us; he walked up to the door of the bank. "This bank is pretty fancy."

"It's the best one in this little town." The lawyer got in front of Cash to open the door. "Here we go. Mr. Johnson is the bank president; he'll be handling this for us."

"The *president* will handle all of this?" Tyrell asked like he thought that was kind of weird. "How much money are we talking about, Allen?"

The lawyer gave my brother a look that said he couldn't believe he'd asked such a dumb question. "Are you telling me that even with the jet, the mansion, and the ranch, that you still don't understand how much money your grandfather was worth?"

"Not a clue." I finally made it into the bank lobby and looked around the big space kitted out with all sort of leather seating and cowhide rugs on the marble floor. "Whoa. Posh."

Tyrell looked up at the giant chandelier. "I haven't seen many banks with a thing like that hanging above peoples' heads before."

"This bank deals with a lot of exclusive businesses here in Carthage."

Everyone inside had turned to look as us as the lawyer escorted us to the very back of the building.

"They can afford certain luxuries that other banks cannot."

We went through a door and a woman jumped up from behind her desk. "Hello, gentlemen. You must be the Gentrys!"

Tyrell reached out and shook her hand. "Tyrell."

I gave her a nod. "Jasper."

Her face lit up when she looked at Cash. "Then you must be Cash."

He shook her hand. "Yep." With a smile, Cash asked, "And you are?"

"Sandra, the bank president's personal assistant." She turned to lead us through the door behind her. "And if you gentlemen will please follow me, I'll let Mr. Johnson get things started." As she opened the door, she looked Tyrell up and down and smiled. "Judging by your blue jeans and T-shirts, I'm going to guess that you all will be greatly surprised by what you're about to inherit."

Our dad had shared some things when we got the call about inheriting the ranch he'd grown up on. He'd said not to get our hopes up, that we'd get much more than a headache from the massive debt he was sure our grandfather had gotten himself into.

Mr. Johnson rose from his desk as we entered his large office. Gesturing to the many seating options, he said, "Bryce Johnson, at your service, gentlemen. Please, take seats anywhere you'd like. Can I offer you cigars? They're Cuban. Or a drink, perhaps? I've got a thirty-year-old scotch that would be perfect for this occasion."

The three of us sat down on the nearest couch as Tyrell got right to the point. "Okay, Bryce. We're pretty sure this ranch is swimming in debt. And we're not even close to being ranchers. Our father's advice was to find a buyer for it and move on."

Cash gave Tyrell a look that could kill. "I'd *love* a scotch, Tyrell. Let the man handle this meeting, will ya?"

"Scotch for everyone then," Mr. Johnson said, and his secretary hurried away. "So, Allen hasn't filled you all in on things?"

"I have. Not the exact numbers, but I've told them about everything they now own." The lawyer made a long sigh. "They don't seem to get it, Bryce."

In no time at all, the woman returned with our drinks. "Here you go, gentlemen. Enjoy." We each grabbed one, and just by the smell alone, I knew I held something expensive in my hand.

"A hell of a lot of hoopla, don't ya think?" I asked before taking a sip.

"You're all worth it," the woman said as she took a seat.

Mr. Johnson handed us all papers as he explained, "I'll let the numbers speak for themselves."

After reviewing the sheet, Tyrell said, "Not sure how to say this number and not sure I understand what it even means. Our father told us there has to be built-up debt."

The numbers didn't make sense to me either.

Mr. Johnson just laughed out loud. "Whisper Ranch is one of the most profitable businesses this bank deals with. What you are each looking at is your third of the money that Collin Gentry had in his personal accounts." He handed another paper to Tyrell. "And this is what's in the ranch account."

I'd never seen a more confused expression on my older brother's face. "If I'm seeing this right, the ranch is worth millions."

"You're not seeing it right," Mr. Johnson said. "Look again."

"Oh, thousands." Tyrell just wasn't getting it.

Cash did get it though. "Tyrell, the ranch is worth *billions*, and we've each inherited fifteen *billion* dollars."

Still unable to believe it, Tyrell said, "Dad said there'd be more money to pay out than we'd get."

Mr. Johnson just shook his head, grinning, as he said, "Your father was wrong. Your grandfather went on from raising cattle alone to raising racehorses, too. You might've heard of some of his famous horses. The General's Son? Old Faithful? Coy's Burden?"

I still felt more confused than ever. "We've never followed horse racing, sir. I guess those are horses on the ranch?"

"They are." Mr. Johnson nodded. "And they all are prize-winning stallions. Your grandfather began selling their semen, and he made a killing from it. Those sales, along with the cattle and the racehorses, have made him a pretty penny. Pennies that now belong to you three."

"Our father isn't mentioned at all in the will?" Tyrell asked.

The lawyer had compassion in his eyes as he looked at Tyrell. "Look, I know it's difficult to understand, but let me show you in writing why that is." He pulled another paper out of a folder and handed it over. "See, your father signed this paper, stating that he wanted nothing from Collin or Fiona Gentry from that date forward. He wasn't forced to sign it. Coy did it to prove a point to his parents when they refused to acknowledge his marriage to Lila Stevens."

Tyrell seemed incapable of understanding any of this. "Wait. What?"

The bank president, Johnson, tried to help out. "Your grandparents wanted to make the Gentry name something akin to royalty around here. But your father fell in love with a girl from the wrong side of the tracks. A girl whose family lived on welfare. A girl who'd once worked as a maid at the ranch house."

Tyrell looked at me and Cash, both of us just as confused as he was. "Why did they never tell us about that?"

The lawyer spoke up. "Most likely because they didn't want you three to know what they'd walked away from. They chose love over money *and* their families. Your mother's family was just as against their marriage as the Gentrys were."

"Wow," Tyrell said. "Seems our parents hid a hell of a lot from us."

"There's one more thing you need to know about the will, gentlemen," the lawyer said. "It stipulates that neither your mother nor father are ever allowed on the property. And your grandfather's money can never benefit them in any way. If you do so much as hand your parents five dollars, the entire estate—that includes the money—will revert to the state of Texas."

"Harsh," Cash mumbled.

"Yeah," Mr. Johnson agreed. "Your grandfather was considered to be a harsh man. So harsh that most people think your grandmother died at the age of forty-five, only two years after your father left the ranch, because of his hard ways."

Who do we come from?

TIFFANY

We'd had a particularly hard day at the Dairy King, the little café my parents bought seven years back. We'd moved out of the Dallas suburb of Seagoville when they bought the place in Carthage. The café came along with a small two-bedroom house that sat behind it. Mom and Dad, along with my younger brother and sister, had moved into it, and I got a small apartment not too far from them for my daughter and me to live in.

With Jasmine at my parents', I decided to hit the local bar, The Watering Hole, for a little drink before going home myself. Dad had put corndogs on sale for a quarter at the Dairy King, and the whole town had to have what seemed like five apiece. I'd spent the entire day on the fryer. My legs ached, my back hurt, and my brain was just about as deep fried as all those corndogs I'd dunked.

Heading into the dimly lit bar, I looked the room over to see who all I knew there. I could hardly believe my eyes when they landed on a tall, dark-haired man with the brightest blue eyes I'd ever seen.

I couldn't help the smile that spread over my face. Like a moth to a flame, I was drawn to the man—much the same way I'd been back in our high school days. "Jasper Gentry. It's been a while, hasn't it?"

Jasper had grown into quite a man over the years we'd been apart. He stood and wrapped his strong arms around me; he smelled like leather and sunshine, and I felt like I'd come back home with him holding me like that. "It sure has, Tiff." He let me go but left one arm draped over my shoulder as he steered me to sit at another table. I noticed that he'd been sitting with his older brother, Tyrell, and I should've said hello to him, but I couldn't quite pull my attention away from Jasper for even a second.

The broad shoulders and wavy dark hair that I knew was so thick and lustrous and soft to the touch, that it all came together, reminding me of the days when he and I were like one. "I just can't believe I'm seeing you here in Carthage, Jasper."

I took the seat he'd pulled out for me, my eyes glued to him as he sat down in the other chair, then pulled it closer to me, the sound of the wooden legs scraping against the hardwood floor.

"I can't believe I'm seeing you here, either, Tiffany McKee. It's been a very long time since I've laid eyes on you. How long have you been here?"

"Since high school graduation." I'd left town without telling him a thing. I'd thought it best to do that at the time. "My parents bought this little café here in Carthage, and we all made the move with them."

"So, Bo and Carolina are here, too?" he asked.

I shook my head. "Carolina got married last year. She moved to Abilene. And Bo joined the Marines. He's on his second tour."

Jasper's eyes went wide. "Wow, it's hard to believe that hyper little brother of yours went and joined the military. And the Marines of all things. Just, wow. And you're doing what now, Tiffany?"

"Working at the café. It's called Dairy King." I wasn't sure if I would tell him about my daughter or not. So, I didn't say a thing about her.

"You living with your folks then?" he asked as he reached over and played a little with a lock of my hair, making me tingle just a little inside.

"No, I've got my own place." I knew what he'd ask next.

"So, you wanna show it to me?"

I laughed. "No." His bearded face was so familiar to me, yet so unlike how he used to look. "I see you finally got enough hair on your face to make a real beard instead of that peach fuzz you used to have."

His fingers grazed my cheek. "Yeah, I'm all grown up now, Tiff. And so are you. Come on. Let me come over."

It wasn't like I could actually allow him to come over anyway. "Look, I've got a little girl to think about. I don't want to ever have men coming and going around her. That's why you can't come over."

I saw his chest stop moving as he held his breath, then slowly released it. "You and her daddy have anything going on?"

"No, we do not." I hadn't had a thing to do with Jasmine's daddy since leaving Dallas. "He's not in her life—never has been."

"I'd say that was a real shame, but then I'd be lying." With a sly and sexy smile, Jasper leaned in real close—so close I thought he might kiss me. "I'm glad to hear you have no ties getting in my way of getting you back where you belong, girl."

I couldn't ever get back together with Jasper Gentry. "I don't want you to take this the wrong way, but I can't start seeing you. I can't start seeing anyone. Since I had my daughter, I've kept to myself. It's best that way."

"Even mommas need love, Tiffany." His lips barely brushed my cheek. I felt the whisper of his warm breath on my skin.

The flood of desire that rushed through me took my breath away. "Oh, Jasper, you are still bad, aren't you?"

He leaned back, giving me space. "I wouldn't say that. I still have it bad for you, Tiff, that's all. Always have. When your whole family disappeared without a trace, I did more than worry about you. And to be honest, I was kind of hurt that you hadn't told me a thing about you leaving. I mean, why not tell me, the guy you were seeing, why you had to move and where the hell you were moving to?"

I had my reasons—good ones. "We were kids, Jasper. I'll have you know that most young couples don't last. It was time to move on. How would you have gotten to Carthage to come see me anyway? You had no car, no money, no way of getting to me. So, why tell you where I'd be? I felt it best to sever all connections. I stopped talking to my friends from Seagoville, too. I just wanted a brand-new start."

I wanted to be where no one could look at me with sad eyes and wonder what had happened to little Tiffany McKee—she'd had so much potential until she met that boy and got herself into trouble.

At least in Carthage, no one knew me. I would've experienced those looks and more had I stayed in my hometown. But I couldn't explain that to Jasper.

"Yeah, I know you stopped talking to them." His blue eyes moved slowly over my body. "I asked around about you. I asked them all. No one knew a damn thing. Not even your younger brother's and sister's friends. Why did they dump their friends, too, Tiff?"

They did it for me.

"We all wanted a fresh start." I knew that sounded insane, but I had nothing else to say.

His eyes cut away from me as if he were a little upset or mad about my answers. "I had no idea life was that damn bad for you guys back then."

It hadn't been bad at all. My father had managed a popular restaurant in Dallas and made great money doing it. We'd had plenty of money, a nice home, nice cars—the works. My brother, sister, and I made good grades and were popular in school. Our abrupt departure didn't make any sense.

"It wasn't that bad." I boldly reached over and ran my hand over his shoulder, feeling the muscles he had grown in our time apart. "It was more like we came to this town to start a business and wanted to give it our all. I enrolled in an online college and got my bachelor's degree in food science, so I could bring more to the table at the café. We dove into the business headfirst."

"But you'd always talked about going to Texas Tech," he reminded me. "And not for food science, either. You wanted to get a degree in agriculture so you could work with animals one day. So, your parents buying some little café changed everything you'd ever wanted? Them buying a café made you not want me anymore, either? I could've come with you, Tiff. I didn't have a damn thing else to do."

I couldn't tell him that I chose online courses, because I didn't want any of my schoolmates to see my big belly.

"I wouldn't have asked you to follow me around, Jasper." And I couldn't have counted on him to be able to do what was best. The fact was, Jasper Gentry was on the immature side when we'd graduated. His only goal after graduation was to get a job flipping burgers, so he could get free meals. "What did you end up doing anyway?"

"I got a job at the Piggly Wiggly stocking groceries at night." A smirk pulled his lips up. "But I don't do anything at the moment."

I knew he'd turn out to be a loser.

"So, your older brother moved here, and you came along for the ride," I said, knowing that was what had happened. Jasper wasn't one to have big dreams.

I couldn't fault him. His father made very little money and didn't seem to care at all about trying to get a better paying job. He had poor role models; I'd never blamed Jasper entirely.

"Nope." Jasper looked me right in the eyes. "I'm not riding anyone's coattails, Tiff. My brothers and I have recently inherited our grandfather's ranch. Whisper Ranch is now ours, and so is all the money that comes with it."

Whisper Ranch is theirs?

"I knew the man who owned it was a Gentry, but how in the hell was he your grandfather when you all lived the way you did?" I knew it came out sounding rude, but I was at a loss.

"My mother and father have been keeping secrets. My grandfather didn't approve of their relationship, and my father chose love over money." His hand trailed over my shoulder. "We Gentrys are passionate men. I thought you needed to be reminded of that fact."

I didn't need to be reminded of anything—I'd never forgotten how passionate this guy could be. And that was back when he was just a teenager. By now, he just had to be out of this world in bed. "Jasper, no one ever said you lacked passion—just money."

"Well, I've got more than I can ever spend now, honey." Once again, his eyes moved over my body. "But you don't care about that, do you?"

Not about that.

JASPER

Pulling her cell out of her back pocket, Tiffany frowned as she looked at the screen. "I've gotta go. My daughter wants Mommy to give her a bath and put her to bed." Looking over her shoulder, she huffed. "I'd wanted to get at least one beer before I had to go on mommy duty. Oh, well." She turned back to look at me softly. "It really was nice seeing you again, Jasper. Since you live here now, I'm sure we'll see each other from time to time, especially if you come down to the Dairy King. I'm always there when it's open."

Getting up, I pulled out her chair and helped her up. "It was really nice seeing you, too, Tiff. I wish I could see a hell of a lot more of you, but I get it. You don't want me around your kid. I can't be too pissed about that. Since you won't even let the kid's father be around, how can I be mad?"

Looking a little nervous, she nodded. "Yeah, how can you be mad?" She turned to leave, but I stopped her by grabbing her hand.

Pulling her back to me, I hugged her nice and tight to remind her of what she was walking away from. "I've missed you, girl. And don't you ever think I stopped."

I felt her body sag in my arms, and for a second, I thought she'd change her mind about us. "I've missed you, too, Jasper. Not a day goes by that I'm not reminded of you."

Letting her go, I had the idea that—given time—she'd want me back in her life. "See ya around, hot stuff."

The smile on her face made my cock twitch.

"Hot stuff? I haven't been called that in forever."

"About seven years, if I'm not mistaken." I smacked her ass as she walked away, making her look over her shoulder to give me another huge smile. "Be good, honey."

"*You* be good." She headed to the door, then left me standing there like a fool.

I went back to the table I'd left Tyrell sitting at alone. Only he hadn't been alone long, because Felicity, a nosy reporter from the local paper that we met earlier, had joined him. But now she was vacating the seat I'd left open when Tiffany came in.

Giving her a nod, I looked at my brother as he asked, "Did you two reconnect?"

"Kind of. But not nearly enough. She left." I looked over my shoulder as Tiffany went out the door. "So, I noticed Felicity came by to talk to you. She's got a hard-on for our story. Cash and I have both told her it's not quite the story she thinks it is. Plus, we don't want to be front page news in our new town."

"Me, neither." Tyrell's eyes went to the door. "Who's that?"

I turned to look at who he was seeing and did a double take. "Naw. It can't be." It looked an awful lot like the little maid from our new home whom Tyrell had caught on more than one occasion already. But she wasn't the type to be hanging out in a bar. Ella wasn't the type to be anywhere but at the mansion.

"She almost looks like…" Tyrell squinted as he peered at her.

"Ella," I whispered. I'd never been more sure of who I was looking at. It was the little maid who'd never worn any makeup or had her hair out of a ponytail. But there she was, all dolled up. And I had good reason to believe she'd done that for my older brother—to catch his attention. Little did she know, she already had it. "Yep, it's Ella, Tyrell."

"No way." Tyrell stood, walked halfway across the room and then abruptly returned to take his seat again. "What in the hell? I have no idea what she's doing."

I pulled my chair around, so I could see her, too. "Well, this ought to be interesting. Little Ella Finley, drinking at a bar."

The barmaid, Bobbi Jo, the girl Cash was interested in, put a shot glass in front of Ella, then filled it with whiskey. Tyrell said, "She ain't gonna drink that. It's gonna come right back out of her mouth."

Cash looked back at us as Ella picked the glass up and took it all at once. He looked stunned when she put the empty glass down on the bar, then nodded. The glass was filled again, and Tyrell shook his head at Cash who merely shrugged as Ella downed another shot.

"She's old enough to drink, Tyrell," I reminded my brother before I took a sip of the beer I'd left on the table before Tiff had shown up.

"But she's not a drinker, Jasper. She's making rookie mistakes right there." Tyrell looked at the door as some guy walked in, and the man's eyes went right to Ella. He walked over and sat in the empty barstool close to her.

Seemed Ella knew the guy, as he ordered them both drinks and extended his arm, which Ella took. They took their drinks and went to sit at a small table together. I couldn't help but grin; it was pretty damn obvious that the girl my older brother was interested in was out with someone else. "Would you look at that?"

Tyrell's words came out in a growl. "I'd love to know what the hell she thinks she's doing."

"It looks like she's trying to act normal for a change." I took another drink, then turned my chair back around. Watching Ella on a date wasn't as captivating to me as it was to Tyrell. "Boring."

Tyrell couldn't let it go. "She's got work tomorrow; maybe I should go over and remind her about that." He picked up his beer and started to rise. I watched him as he stopped himself again. I noticed that Ella had gotten up, too, and was returning to the bar by herself. "Or, I'll sit back and see if she's going to do the right thing all on her own." But he didn't sit back down. He stood there, watching Ella as she ordered another shot. "That's way too much for her."

I had to laugh, because my big bro was losing his mind. "Relax,

Tyrell. We're right here. We won't let her drive home drunk. Maybe she took a cab."

Tyrell peeked out the window, then came back and took his seat. "Seems she took the Corvette."

Now, that surprised me. "She drove it here?"

"That's what it looks like." He took a long drink of the beer in his hand as he looked confused as all get out.

I had my own things to think about, and I decided to ignore him. But Tyrell made that impossible as he suddenly jumped up, knocked the chair over, then flew into a rage toward the bar.

I got up and watched as my brother grabbed the guy who'd left his table and now stood at the bar, holding Ella in his arms. Holding the front of his shirt with one hand, Tyrell clocked him with the other, sending the dude flying backwards. Next, Ella was flung over his shoulder like a rag doll, and the two exited the bar. Her fists pummeled Tyrell's back as he carried her out.

Sitting back down, I chuckled and drank the last of my beer, then walked over to the bar to sit next to Cash who was looking a little stunned.

"What are you guys doing?" I asked him, then held up a finger to Bobbi Jo. "Uno más, por favor."

Cash let out a loud laugh. "Um … did you catch what just happened here, Jasper?"

"Yeah, Tyrell went all ape on that poor guy who had the bad luck of hitting on Ella." I took the beer that Bobbi Jo put in front of me. "Thanks, pumpkin. And put that poor guy's drinks on my tab, will ya? Tell him Tyrell Gentry is paying for them, though. I don't want him to have hard feelings for my deranged brother. Can you do that for me, baby?"

Cash gave me the stink eye. "Watch it."

Chuckling, I winked at Bobbi Jo. "Seems he's sweet on you, girl."

She blushed. "You think?"

Cash's face went red. "Jasper, I swear to God."

"Nope, don't do that." Patting my brother on his back, I tried to settle him back down. "I want to ask your girl here some questions about Tiffany McKee."

Bobbi Jo's twin sister, Betty Sue, took an interest in our conversation and came down the bar to sit next to me. "I'm drinking scotch and soda, Jasper."

"Cool for you, Betty Sue." I nodded at her sister behind the bar. "I'm talking to your sister right now, so if you don't mind ..."

"I kind of do mind," Betty Sue said. "Hit me with another drink, and I'll take your mind off that boring redhead you asked about. I can tell ya right now, that girl hasn't seen even one man since they moved here seven years ago. I wouldn't get my hopes up that she'll give to you what she ain't given to no one else in all that time."

The girl had no idea what the hell she was talking about. We hadn't been in town but a week and already I knew better than to trust a thing Betty Sue had to say. Tiffany did have a kid after all. She had to have seen someone since she left Dallas and me behind.

"If I buy you another drink, will you do me a favor and stop talking, Betty Sue?" I asked her.

Once she nodded, I gave the go-ahead to Bobbi Jo to give her sister a drink on me. "This is gonna be your last one though, Betty Sue," Bobbi Jo informed her sister. "This makes your third within the same hour. You're hitting it too hard."

"Yeah, well, I've got troubles I need to drink away." Betty Sue ran her hand over my shoulder. "I was hoping you'd help me forget about them, Jasper."

Normally, I didn't have a problem with loose women. But now that I knew Tiffany was around, I didn't want a thing to do with anyone but her. "Sorry, girl. I'm not in the mood to fix your troubles. Have the drink, and that's all."

Taking her new drink, she walked away, mumbling, "Damn, he's hot, too. Rich and hot—a killer combo—and he's only looking at that stuck-up redhead. What a crying shame."

Cash ignored Betty Sue as he asked, "Why's Tiffany McKee here in Carthage anyway?"

Bobbi Jo answered, "Her family owns the Dairy King. It's got the best junk food in town. And on Sundays, Tiffany has her own menu. It's nothing like the fast food they serve the rest of the week.

It's all healthy, locally sourced fresh food. You've got to make a reservation; it's that exclusive."

"So, this is where they came to when they left Seagoville," Cash mused. "I've always wondered about that family. You and she were tight, Jasper. Are you going to try to get her back?"

"I am." I took a drink of my beer as I contemplated how I would go about doing that. "Tell me what you know about Tiff, Bobbi Jo."

The frown she put on her face didn't do much to convince me that she'd be a wealth of information on the woman I thought of as my first love and only heartbreak.

"You know, Jasper, that girl stays to herself. She's friendly and all that, but she's just not into having relationships outside of her family."

"What do you know about her kid?" I had to get some kind of information out of her.

"I don't know anything except that she has a daughter."

Bobbi Jo was useless. So, I turned to look for Felicity, the local reporter. But she'd slipped out with her date.

"Damn. Who else would know anything about my girl?" I shook my head as a hopeless feeling came over me. "If I can't get her back, it's gonna drive me nuts. Just seeing her again filled my heart up in a way no one ever has. She has to let me back in."

She just has to.

TIFFANY

As I washed my daughter's long, dark hair—hair so much like her father's—it staggered my mind. Jasmine had never asked even once why she had blue eyes and dark hair when no one else in our family did. I had red hair and green eyes, as did Mom and Bo. Dad and Carolina were both blondes with brown eyes. Jasmine stuck out like a sore thumb in our family. If Jasper ever saw her, he'd know in a heartbeat what I'd kept hidden for seven years.

"Momma, where'd you go after work tonight?" Jasmine asked as I rinsed her hair out. She looked at me with her father's blue eyes.

I hadn't lied to Jasper when I told him I was reminded of him every day. Our little girl had kept that man fresh in my mind since her birth. *Should I let her know I'd seen her father?*

Shaking off the stupid thought, I said, "I went to get a cool drink after work, honey. I had a tough day."

"Oh, what kind did you get?" she asked, then picked up the little rubber duck out of the basket of bath toys.

"I didn't end up getting one at all." Meeting Jasper again had stopped that from happening. "I met an old friend and we talked. Then your Gam-Gam called me and told me you wanted a bath, and only I would do."

"Yeah, I need you to wash my hair 'cause only you know how

376

long to leave the conditioner in so my hair's not frizzy. Gam-Gam just doesn't have the patience you do, Momma." Jasmine pointed at the water faucet. "Warm it up, please."

I turned on the hot water to give it a bit more heat. "How much longer do you think you're going to want to soak in here?"

"Probably for a little while," she said as she laid back in the sea of bubbles. "I fell off the swing on the playground at school today. My butt hurts."

"Aw, my poor baby." I ran my hand through her hair, pushing the conditioner all through it. "Let this soak in too then."

"Who'd you meet, Momma?" she asked as she kicked her feet gently to make the bubbles move around.

I froze, unable to think of what to say. But then finally I thawed out. "A boy I used to know when I went to high school back in Dallas."

She sat up, eyes wide. "A boy? Are you going to date him? Is he cute? Is he funny? I bet he's funny. I bet he's really cute, too. So, are ya?"

"No, I'm not going to date him." I chewed on my lower lip as my stomach twisted and a flush of heat crept over me.

I did want to see Jasper again. But I had Jasmine to think about now. I couldn't let my lust for him lead me. I had to use my brain.

"Is that 'cause he's ugly, Momma?" she asked.

"No, he's not ugly at all." I turned the hot water off. "That should be hot enough."

"Is he not that funny?" she asked.

"He's okay." Jasper wasn't exactly a comedian. Jasmine loved funny stuff; she loved to laugh.

"If he's not ugly and at least kind of funny, then why don't you want to date him, Momma?" she asked with an innocent smile. "I won't be mad. I want you to have a boyfriend."

Since she'd started school, she'd seen that other kids had two parents and had been hinting that it would be nice if she did, too. And now her father was right here in the same town. But I still didn't know if it was the right thing to do to tell him yet—or ever.

Now that I knew he had money, I worried he might think I was just trying to pin a kid on him, so I could have some of that money, too. It might start a horrible drama, and he might be pretty mad that I'd hidden the whole thing from him.

"What if I don't want a boyfriend, Jasmine?" I asked her, then pulled her around so I could rinse the conditioner out of her hair.

Her frown told me she wasn't going to give up easily. "Why wouldn't you want one?"

"Maybe one day, when you're a lot older, I'll get one," I offered. "For now, it's the me-and-you show, kiddo."

She laid her head back, so I could rinse her hair. The smattering of freckles that ran over the bridge of her nose was just about the only thing she'd gotten from me. "Momma, you know you're very pretty, right?"

I supposed she thought I considered myself unattractive since, I didn't want a boyfriend. "I know I'm pretty, Jasmine. I know I'm smart and a real catch, too. But I'm not in the market right now. I want this time to be about us, you and me and no one else."

"Mom, that's silly." She sat up as I'd finished rinsing her hair out. "I'm going to have a boyfriend one day, then what will *you* do?"

Pulling the plug, I grabbed a towel and helped her out of the tub. "You're not getting a boyfriend anytime soon, young lady. How about we talk about something else?"

"Like what?" She pulled the towel around her tightly. "It's cold, Momma. Turn the heater up."

"Once you get your hair dry, you'll be warm and toasty." I began pulling out the blow dryer. "Go put your jammies on while I get ready to dry your hair."

"Okay." She took off running, laughing as she went.

Is leaving Jasper out of her life fair?

I got so much joy from even the smallest things Jasmine did: the sound of her laughter, the sight of her smiling face, the hugs and kisses she gave me so freely. How fair was it of me to keep her away from her father?

Before he'd come to town, I'd never contemplated it much at all. I'd figured he was working some nowhere job, doing the same things he'd always done back home. But he wasn't there anymore. He was here now. He had lots and lots of money and one hell of a nice ranch.

Jasmine would miss out on so much if I kept them apart. And I would miss out, too.

After drying her hair, I snuggled my daughter into her bed with her Disney princess blanket. "You sleep tight now, Jasmine. I love you. Have sweet dreams."

"You, too, Momma. I love you." She kissed my cheek as she put her arms around my neck.

I kissed her back, then left the room. Heading to the kitchen to make myself a cup of hot tea, I pulled out my cell to call Mom and give her the news. "Did you get her to bed, Tiffany?"

"I did." Pouring some water into my teakettle, I put it on the stove. "I saw an old friend today, Mom." My parents never had any animosity toward Jasper, so I knew she wouldn't be mad. But I did wonder what I was supposed to do now.

"Oh, you did?" she asked. "Who was it?"

"Jasper Gentry." I waited for that sink in as I went to get a bag of Earl Grey.

"You don't mean …"

"Yes. Him." The whistle of the kettle let me know the water was ready, and I poured it over the translucent tea bag, turning the clear water to a deep brown. "He lives here in Carthage now. At Whisper Ranch, of all places."

"Did he get a job there?" she asked, then sucked in her breath. "The old man who owns that ranch died right before Christmas. His name was Collin Gentry. You don't suppose …"

"I do suppose." I sipped the hot tea. "Jasper and his brothers now own that ranch. Jasmine's father is a billionaire." As I said the words, it began to sink in for me, too.

Jasper is a billionaire.

"Well, what did he say to you, Tiffany?" she asked, sounding a bit frantic. "And what did you tell him?"

Taking the tea, I went to the living room to sit down. "I told him I had a daughter. I didn't tell him how old she was. He'd shown interest in getting back together. I shut him down about that though."

"Good." She was quiet for a moment before adding, "What are we going to do about this, Tiffany? This town is too small. He's

379

bound to see her one day. He'll notice the resemblance, her age, and he'll be so mad that we hid this from him all this time."

"Maybe coming clean right away is the best thing to do." I held the teacup in my hand, relishing the warmth of it and wondering what telling Jasper would do for him and me.

"I don't think so, Tiffany." Mom had always had an aversion to telling Jasper anything about Jasmine. "He's got loads of money now. He can take her away if he wants to."

"I don't think ..."

She didn't let me finish. "You don't know for sure. There's a lot to feel out about the man before you go telling him anything. Worst-case scenario, we sell the café and move again. We can't lose our girl."

I wasn't sure that would even work again. "Mom, he's got the funds to get an investigator to track us down now. We have to remember he has abundant resources—things he never had before."

"There are lots of things we need to think about. And we need to do all that thinking before we make any decisions, Tiffany." Her tone was adamant; she wasn't going to let me be reckless with Jasmine. "How terrible would it be if he ripped Jasmine away from the only people she's ever known and took her to a place she's never been, with people who are strangers to her?"

It sounded terrible, and I knew deep in my heart that it could happen in the worst possible circumstances. But I trusted Jasper a bit more than that. But then again, he might not trust me anymore once he knew I'd hidden something this important from him for this long.

"I'll play it safe, Mom. I promise you; I'll watch what I say to him." I was pretty sure I'd see Jasper sooner rather than later.

"Get some rest, sweetie. I'll see you in the morning after you drop Jasmine off at school." She took a deep breath as if calming herself. "I hope he doesn't have any reason to go to her school."

"Even if he did, I highly doubt he'd be able to tell she's his when mixed up with all the other kids. Plus, he wouldn't ever grab a kid and take off with her, Mom. He's not a maniac."

"Yeah, well, people can do crazy things when they feel angry or done wrong. I'll see you tomorrow."

Putting my phone away, I sat there staring a hole into the floor. I hadn't ever planned on this day coming. That might've been a bit naïve of me, but I truly had never planned on seeing Jasper again or having to tell him what I'd done.

I needed to come up with a plan now, though. What would be the best way to tell a man that you had his baby without him knowing and never planned on letting him know about her? And what kind of a reaction could I expect him to have?

An apocalyptic one, I suppose.

JASPER

Seeing Tiffany again after all these years made me horny as hell for her. I'd barely made it home, before I had to climb into bed, my cock hard for her. That girl had made me hard from the very first day I laid eyes on her. The memory of that day came easily.

Wearing a cute little cheerleader uniform, her auburn hair in pigtails, she'd sparkled on the football field. I'd been in the same grade as Tiffany McKee since school began, but I'd never noticed her until our junior year of high school. That year she became a cheerleader and seemed to have blossomed into a hot, young thing overnight.

I barely saw the game that day as my eyes couldn't move off of her. Long legs kicked as pom poms shook, and that girl was taking my mind to places no one ever had. I knew I had to get to her before some other guy did.

Going down to the refreshment stand as soon as I saw her heading that way, I managed to bump into her. "Hey there, Tiffany. Good game, huh?"

Her hand on her hip, she sighed. "I hear the sarcasm. We're down by twenty points. What a disaster. But still, we have to keep on cheering as if there's a chance in the world that our boys will make a comeback."

I'd had no idea what the score was or that we were losing. "Yeah, it sucks. But you sure do look cute out there, shaking your new pompoms. I didn't know you were on the cheerleader squad. When did this happen?"

"Rachel fell and broke her leg last week," she told me. "I've been an alternate since our freshmen year. This is the first time I've gotten to actually cheer with the other girls." She ran her hand over her uniform. "This has been in my closet for a little over two years, and it's the first time I've been able to wear it in public."

"It makes your legs look like they're a mile long." I ran my eyes up and down her body.

Her cheeks went red. "Oh, I must look like a giraffe."

"No." I hadn't meant it as anything but a compliment. "I mean, you look hot, Tiffany."

The shade of red went even deeper as her eyes flitted away. "Oh, Jasper, you're being silly."

"No, I mean it." I took her hand. "Come on, let me buy you a Coke." I had all of two bucks to spend, but I'd be damned if any other boy was going to buy her something to drink.

"Well, thanks, Jasper. How nice of you." She came along with me, not even trying to pull her hand out of mine. "I'll have a Dr. Pepper. But just a small one."

"Cool." That meant I could get one, too. I held up two fingers to the kid behind the counter. "Give me two cans of DPs." I laid the two bucks on the counter, then took the drinks he gave me. I handed one to her. "Here ya go."

Popping the tops meant we had to let go of each other's hands. But as soon as the sodas were open, I took her hand again and liked the smile I saw on her red lips. "You know, I don't think you and I have ever said this much to each other."

"Yeah, I'm a guy of few words." I took a sip of the drink, trying to look as cool as possible. "What do you plan on doing after the game?"

"Well, we're all planning on going to Pizza Palace to eat. You should totally come, too, Jasper." Her invitation was appreciated, but I had no more money.

Before I turned her down though, I thought about asking her to do something else. Something free. "After the game is over, the playground is a cool place to hang out. No one's around since everyone leaves. I like to chill, lay on the merry-go-round, and check out the stars. But hanging at the noisy pizza place sounds good, too."

Looking up at the night sky with the lights of the stadium too bright to see even one star, Tiff said, "I like your idea better, Jasper. If it's cool with you, I'd rather hang out with you after the game."

Nothing could've been cooler. "Yeah, no prob." We walked, hand in hand, back to the front of the bleachers. "I'll just be sitting here, watching you cheer your little heart out for the Dragons, even though they can't win now." That little blue-and-white cheerleader uniform of hers did things for me that made me wonder if it was magical.

"Don't watch me too hard, or I'm sure to mess up, Jasper." She handed me the half-empty can. "And can you hold this for me? We're not allowed to have anything on the field."

"Sure, I'll hold it for you, hot stuff." I liked the way she blushed and grinned.

Then she went and did something that surprised me. Tiffany McKee leaned in and kissed my cheek. "Thanks, Jasper. This next cheer is just for you."

So, I sat back and watched her cheer and cheer, and her smile did things to my heart that were irreversible. Later, after everyone else had left, Tiffany and I went to the playground.

"Here, get on this swing and I'll give you a ride." I held it steady for her, and she took the seat. Giving it a little push, I stopped it when she got back to me.

She looked up. "Why'd you stop me?"

I didn't say a word, just made my move, leaning down to kiss her soft lips. Everything stopped: time, my breathing, my thinking. It all just stopped as we kissed.

She wasn't my first kiss, but she was the best. The way she tasted turned me ravenous for more. I pulled her off the swing and pushed her up against the wall; our hands moved all over each other, and before I knew it, we were panting, pawing, and losing ourselves to the moment.

We didn't go all the way that night, only because Tiffany McKee was a respectable girl. But after three months of talking on the phone every night and holding hands as we walked around the school, I'd saved enough money from picking up cans around town to take her out to dinner.

She had a car that she'd let me drive for our first real date, and I took her to The Red Lobster. They were having a lobster fest, and I'd found out that night that my girl had a thing for lobster—a thing that turned her into an animal.

Once we got back in that car, she scooted over to me and took my hand, putting it right on the crotch of her jeans. "Can we?" Her green eyes shimmered in the lights of The Red Lobster parking lot as she looked at me. "I've got fifty bucks. We can rent a room. My parents think I'm staying the night with a friend."

"I don't have any protection," was all I could think to say. I'd had no idea she'd be ready to do this. We hadn't talked about it at all.

Pinning her lower lip between her teeth, she nodded, then said, "Well, you can pull out, can't you? You know, when the time comes to—you know—you can just pull out and spill it on my stomach."

"Hell, hot stuff, you've been thinking a lot about this." I had, too, but not so much about the birth control part of it. "Let's go, baby."

As I lay there in my bed now, I recalled the first time she let me have her completely. Her hair splayed over the white pillowcase, her eyes shining in the dim light the bathroom gave off. The sound of the television was in the background—some spooky movie was on, and the music was eerie. "You scared?" I'd asked her.

Her head shook, and I could hardly believe her. I was scared shitless. "No, I trust you, Jasper. I've never trusted anyone like I trust you."

"Is this your first time?" I had to know if I was the only one coming to this as a newbie.

"It is." She ran her hand over her naked tit. "And I think it must be yours, too, Jasper Gentry."

I hadn't planned on admitting that but thought I should now that she had. "Yeah, this is my first time, too. But I've got lots of experience watching how it's done in the movies. I think I can get the job done."

"Well, climb on and let's see what this sex thing is all about." She spread her legs, and I just about had a heart attack.

"Damn it, hot stuff; you're gonna kill me." I climbed up, moving in between her legs as she smiled at me.

"Before we do this, I want to tell you something that I ain't never told anyone before." She licked her lips. "Jasper, I love you."

My heart pounded in my chest harder than it ever had. "Oh. My. God. I can't believe it. You love me. And we're about to make love. And I think I love you, too, Tiff. I really do. I think about you all the time. I can't wait to see your pretty face every day. I race to school just to see you. I do, Tiff. I love you, too."

And then we kissed. Long, slow, soft, and it meant something. When I pushed my hard cock into her soft recesses, I knew we were really going to be something. She and I would last and last, and nothing would ever break us up.

Her body, so tight around me, felt insane. Each stroke I made only felt that much better. Every single atom of my body lit up, and it was only for her.

The way she made these soft little moans did things to me that nothing ever had. The way her breath ran over the skin of my shoulder as she held on to me as I moved inside of her, made every bit of my flesh hot.

Kissing her neck, I felt her insides tighten around me even more. She liked that, so I kept it up as I moved back and forth. Her legs wrapped around me as she arched up. "Jasper, I think something is happening."

I kept moving, nipping and sucking her neck and wanting to know what it would feel like when she climaxed while I was buried inside of her. "Give it to me, hot stuff."

Her legs began to shake as she made a shrill noise. "Jasper! Oh God! Jasper! Ahhh!"

I cried out, too, as her pussy clenched around my cock so hard that it almost hurt. *Almost.* It was the oddest pain-slash-pleasure I'd ever experienced. I'd jacked off before, plenty of times, but this was very different.

Bucking wildly, Tiffany was going crazy, making loud cries, then soft whimpers, and all the while scratching my back and shoulders. And that felt insane-great, too.

With all the commotion going on, I felt my cock jerk inside of her, then had to pin her shoulders to the bed. "I've gotta come."

"Yes!" Her eyes were wild. "Do it, Jasper. I wanna feel it inside of me."

Shaking my head no, I held her down with one hand, then pulled my engorged cock out of her with the other and finally came all over her stomach and breasts. "Oh, shit! Damn! Fuck me!"

Panting, we looked at each other, both of us smiling like crazy, then she whispered, "Wanna take a shower, then do that again?"

"I sure as hell do."

Lying on my bed now at Whisper Ranch, my now-spent cock in my hand, I couldn't do anything but wish like hell that Tiffany would give me another chance. And this time I could be so much more for her than I ever could've back then.

If she just gives me a chance, I can win her heart again. I know I can.

TIFFANY

Slicing tomatoes, I felt a chill, then looked up to see Jasper at the door to the Dairy King. He pulled it open, ringing the bell. I should've known he'd put the pressure on right away.

It took him no time at all to find me as he scanned the kitchen area. With a wink, he came to the counter where Felicia asked, "What can I get for you today, sir?"

"How about a heaping helping of that redhead in the back there?" His smile was as wide as the Rio Grande as he looked at me.

Poor Felicia looked back at me over her shoulder with a frown, not knowing what to do or say. So, I came to her rescue. "This is Jasper Gentry, Felicia. He's an old friend of mine and thinks he's funny."

"Friend, huh?" He held out his arms for a hug as I came from behind the counter.

I couldn't help myself and slipped right into his strong arms. "We *are* just friends, Jasper."

Swaying back and forth, he whispered, "You know how long I'll let that last, don't ya?"

His words had me remembering the first time he showed me any attention. That boy took my hand at a football game and never let go of it unless he absolutely had to. I wondered if he'd changed much from how he was back then. I got the feeling that he hadn't. And that terrified me. "Let's go back and take a seat, Jasper. You want something to eat or drink?"

"Nope. I just came here to see you, hot stuff." He let me out of his arms but took my hand, pulling me to the farthest booth in the back corner.

I slid in on one side, then he slid in right next to me. "You know, there's room on the other side, Jasper."

"I like it right here." Leaning in close, he sniffed my hair. "You still like to use jasmine-scented shampoo. I like that. Every single time I've caught a whiff of that scent, it's reminded me of you."

My love of the fragrance was part of how my daughter got her name. The other part was because Jasmine seemed like the female version of Jasper to me. I had no idea if anyone else considered that to be true, but I did. The two things I'd loved combined to make the name for my daughter, who I loved more than anything in the entire world.

I loved her so much that I would keep my libido in check where her father was concerned. Albeit it was not easy to do when he was all up on me the way he was. "And every time I smell freshly cut grass, I think of you." He'd taken a job cutting lawns one summer, so he could take me on dates. That boy smelled like fresh-cut grass all summer long.

"I took those jobs for you—you know that, right?" He played with a tendril of my hair that had escaped the bun I'd had it in. "I've never seen anyone else whose hair was as pretty hair as yours, Tiff. I've missed running my fingers through your silky hair. I've missed kissing those pouty rosebud lips of yours, too. Have you missed anything about me?"

Everything.

But I couldn't say that, or he'd get the idea that I wanted to give us another chance. "Sure, I have. But I've got a kid to keep me busy. Her and this job fill up my time. So, you can see where it wouldn't be fair to you if I led you on, right?"

"I think you could find time for me. I don't mind sharing you, Tiffany." He slipped his arm around me, pulling me close. "Back then, I know I was greedy with you. Maybe you think I'm still that way, but I'm not. If you let me show you, then you'd see that I can share now."

"How about you give me more time, Jasper?" I needed lots more time to make the decisions I knew I would have to make eventually anyway.

"How about you give me a kiss, and we'll see how much more time you think you're going to need …" A sexy grin curved his lips. "I happen to know that you liked what we had just as much as I did."

Yeah, too much.

It had been me who'd begged him to come inside of me the last three or four times we'd had sex. Don't ask me why, 'cause I plain don't know myself. My body took my brain over. I had wanted to feel it, to know what it would do to me. And I found out—the hard way. It would get me pregnant.

"We both know what happens when we kiss, Jasper Gentry." At least I could be truthful with him about that. "I get all hot and bothered and crazy as hell. You're like a drug to me, and you know it."

"Oh, come on now." His finger traced my lips. "I ain't like no drug to you. For one thing, you quit me way too easy for me to be like that to you. You obviously weren't addicted to me, or you wouldn't have run away without telling me why."

If he only knew.

"I'd like to be honest with you about that, Jasper." I could tell him some of what I'd gone through without telling him everything. "I cried like a baby for a solid month when we moved. For the first week, I couldn't even get out of bed."

"I would've loved to have gotten to lie in bed and cry," he told me with a smirk. "I had to get up every day and go to work."

Grinning, I said, "I thought you said you'd worked at night stocking groceries."

"You know what I mean." His fingers trailed over my collarbone, sending chills all through me. "My problem was that I kept thinking you were gonna show up one day and tell me what had happened. Or maybe you'd call to let me know where you were. I had hope, whereas you clearly had none."

I had a good reason to have no hope of ever getting back together with him. But I couldn't tell him that I was pregnant back then and had to try to make the best decision for my baby.

"To make a fresh start, I thought it best not to hold onto the past. I didn't know it would hurt so bad to let it all go, but it did. I got through it, though." I felt a certain amount of pride in the fact that I had gotten on with my life.

"And this fresh start, Tiff …" He reached back to pull the band out of my hair to release it from the bun. I shivered. "It sounds as if you didn't let anyone into your life except your family. And that's just not like you at all." His hand moved through my hair, making me wish he'd stop before I gave in.

The thing was, he was right. I'd always had friends. I'd always been outgoing. And now I had no one and went nowhere. "Well, I got to thinking that I was living life all wrong."

"All wrong, huh?" His glistening eyes told me he didn't believe me. "What's wrong about anything you did? You had a boyfriend who adored you. Except for the sex, which I don't think was wrong since we loved each other, you didn't do a thing wrong. You didn't drink, smoke, do any kind of drug at all. Hell, girl, you wouldn't even speed when you drove your car. So please explain to me how you were living your life all wrong."

Needing to hold back the fact that I'd gotten myself pregnant didn't make explaining myself easy at all. "Those last few months before graduation, I was like a sex fiend with you."

"You'll never hear me complain about those last few months. You made them the most awesome months we had in our two-year relationship." He moved his hand to run it back and forth on top of my thigh, dangerously close to my hot center.

The way moisture pooled inside of me had me gulping. "Yeah, well, that's not how a nice girl acts, Jasper. I'm not blaming *you* or anything. I'm just saying that I lost myself back then. I needed time alone to become who I needed to become. No friends. No boyfriend. No one but my family could help me become the person I needed to evolve into."

"And why the rush to evolve anyway?" His hand stopped

moving. It rested on my leg, and I felt my pussy pulsing, wanting his touch.

I had to become a mother is why. "I scared myself with you, Jasper. I terrified myself at what I'd become."

"You didn't become anything bad, Tiff. There's nothing wrong with wanting to be with the man you love." He moved his hand only a smidgeon nearer to my now hot-as-hell pussy.

"I was only eighteen, Jasper. I don't expect you to understand. Now that I have a daughter of my own, I don't want her getting intimate with anyone until she's at least twenty-one." I meant that, too. She'd floored me when she'd said she was going to get a boyfriend one day. If I had it my way, she'd stay away from boys until I was dead and buried.

"Good luck with that, Tiffany." Bringing his hand up, he caught me by the chin. "But that explains nothing, since you didn't have her yet when you decided you were being such a bad girl. And you weren't bad at all. You were fantastic—giving, accepting, willing to try just about anything. And you did it, because you knew you could trust me and could trust that I loved you. I'd thought that I could trust you when you said those words to me, too. It hurt real bad when I figured out that you didn't mean them. I wondered if you *ever* meant them."

I couldn't let him think that. "Jasper, I did love you. I loved you with everything I had. Don't ever think I didn't. I just got in over my head is all. I had to get out of the water to get my head back into reality. The time for living a fantasy was over; I had things to get to. And I got to them all on my own. Well, that's not true. If I hadn't had the support of my family, I don't know what I would've done."

Looking skeptical, he said, "You talk like someone who had to get off drugs or something. I have a feeling you're not telling me everything. Was there another guy or something? Is that the case? 'Cause I've got to be honest, the more you say, the more I don't understand."

"There wasn't another guy, Jasper. You were the only one. God knows you gave me more than I ever needed." My body heated up even more as I thought about how well he handled my body back then.

"Well, you were with someone else at some time or another," he pointed out. "So, you decided to go back to having sex, letting little 'hot stuff' back out to play."

Biting my lip, I didn't know what to say to him about that. There had never been anyone else in seven years.

Thankfully, the door opened then. "Oh, hell. The lunch crowd is here. I've got to get to work, Jasper. We can talk more later."

Saved by the bell.

JASPER

With Tiffany being too busy to talk to me anymore, I left the café, not one bit closer to getting her to start seeing me again. And I had more questions than ever about what had gone on in her life during the seven years we'd been apart. The girl was full of secrets, and I had to get to the bottom of at least one of them.

Who is her daughter's father, and why has he been shut out of the kid's life?

Since Tiffany didn't want to give me any straight answers, I went to the know-it-all reporter who had been hounding both me and my brothers for our story since we arrived in town. Perhaps she'd give me the scoop on the McKees if she thought I'd give her our story in exchange—which I wouldn't, but I wouldn't let her know that until after she told me something about Tiffany.

Walking down the sidewalk, I made my way to the publishing company where Felicity worked during the day. And as I walked, it bothered me more and more that Tiffany didn't want me to be around her kid.

I wasn't a bad guy. I'd never been around little kids much, but I didn't have an aversion to them. And Tiff knew I didn't have a mean or hateful bone in my body. *So why keep me and that little girl apart?*

If that was really all that was stopping us from getting back together, then I had to fix it. And I could. I could buy the kid a pony or something. I could make her like me; I knew I could. Tiff was just being stubborn about it.

I came up to the glass door with "Carthage Publishing Company" on it. Pushing it open, I could smell the ink they used to print the local newspapers. "Felicity? You in here?" The place seemed empty.

After hearing some shuffling sounds, I saw an old man with ink-stained fingers coming into the lobby. "Hey there. What can I do you for?"

"I'm looking for Felicity. Is she around?" I looked behind him to see if anyone else was back there.

"She's out to lunch." He jerked his thumb over his shoulder. "It's Friday—printing day here—and I've got my hands full. If you'll come help me with my work, I'll let ya bend my ear till she gets back."

"Sure, why not?" I followed the old guy, who'd probably worked there since he was a kid riding a bike and tossing newspapers on lawns. "I suppose you've been here a while."

He pointed at a bulky stack of papers as he nodded. "Can you bring those over here for me?" Pausing, he looked at me. "Oh, I'm Peter. And you are?"

"Jasper." I picked up the stack of papers with ease. "Gentry."

"Whoa! The Whisper Ranch Gentrys?" he asked as he pointed at where I needed to put the papers down.

"Yep, that's me." Laying them down, I found I already had black ink smudges on my hands. "What else ya got for me, Peter?"

"See them boxes over there?" he asked. "They've needed to be moved for a year now. We ain't got no one strong enough to move them though. Wanna give it a try? They need to be moved to the back room."

"I'll do it." As I went to get a box, I thought I'd see what he knew about the McKees. "So, the family who owns the Dairy King —what's their story?"

"Jason and Darla McKee came here about seven years ago," he said as he fed more paper into the printing machine. "Their oldest is Tiffany. The middle kid is a boy named Bo. That kid was a real mess. Always getting himself into trouble. Then he up and joined the Marines. And the last kid was a girl named Carolina. She got married last year. We had a lovely spread in the paper about that wedding."

"What do you know about Tiffany?" I asked as I picked up another box. then took it to the small room at the back.

"I know she's a pretty great chef. You've got to make reservations if you want to get a taste of her Sunday menu." He smacked his lips. "Some real great cooking, she does. And she's got a little girl, too. Now the only thing about her is that I can't ever recall seeing Tiffany while she was pregnant. I don't know if she hid out or what, but I never did see her with a big belly."

"How old is the kid?" I asked as I got the last of the boxes.

He only shook his head. "Don't know. I haven't ever seen her. They didn't ever put her birth announcement in the paper, or I'd know when she was born. I got one of those crazy memories. I can't recall what I did ten minutes ago, but if it was ever in the newspaper, it's in my brain for life."

"Did you ever see Tiffany with the father of this little girl?"

"Nope." He shook his head. "I've seen that girl around town, at the grocery store, the Watering Hole, and of course, at the Dairy King. She's always alone. And come to think of it, I've never seen her daughter with her. For the longest time, no one knew she had a kid at all. A couple of years ago, word started to spread that she had a little girl."

"So, she might only be like two or something then?" I asked as I scratched my head. If that kid was that young, then I saw no real reason to keep me from meeting her. It wouldn't be jarring to a kid that young to meet a new person. "Do you know her name?"

He stopped, tapped his finger to the side of his head, then his eyes went wide. "Yes, I do know her name. It's Jasmine. And I know that she has the last name of McKee. No father has ever been mentioned."

Everything I'd found out only served to make more questions pop up in my head. "I thank you for the information, Peter."

"I thank you for moving that heavy stuff. See ya around, Jasper

Gentry. It was nice to meet you. Sorry about your grandfather being such an ass."

I had to laugh. "Yeah, me too. Did you know him personally?"

Nodding, he said, "We went to school together. That seems like a million years ago. He was quiet and kept to himself." He ran his hand under his nose to scratch an itch and left a black trail over his top lip, giving himself a little Hitler mustache.

"Ya got a little something there, Peter," I let him know.

"I suppose it wasn't entirely Collin's fault he became the ass he did." He ran his hand over the spot again, only making it worse. "I can't count the times that boy showed up at school with marks on him where his father had beaten him. Once, in our senior year of high school, he missed school for a week. When he came back, his arm was in a cast, and he looked like he'd been run over by a herd of cattle. But the whispers were that his old man had done that to him. And over a girl, too. Your grandpa had the poor judgment to secretly date a girl from the wrong side of town. His papa put a stop to it—for a while at least."

"Wow," I said as I thought about how harsh my father's family had been. "I'm glad my dad wasn't a thing like his father or his grandfather. He's never laid a hand on us."

"Well, that's 'cause your daddy got plenty of the same treatment his daddy had gotten," Peter said. "Be thankful your daddy got out of this town. If he'd stayed—well, then I guess you boys wouldn't have ever been born."

"I guess you're right." I headed out and found Felicity walking up the sidewalk with a taco in her hand. "Hey, I came to talk to you."

"Great," she said, smiling broadly. "I've been hoping one of you boys would give me what I'm after."

"Well, you're sure to be disappointed then. I just wanted to ask you some questions. Peter answered them for me." And yet I wondered if she might know a little more than he did. "Tiffany McKee's daughter—how old is she?"

"Oh, that I do not know. I've never seen her. Tiffany doesn't take her out." She shook her head. "I don't know why that is.

Maybe it has something to do with the absent father. No one knows who he is. She's never told a soul even so much as his name."

"Maybe you should ask her," I said. "Knowing everything about everyone is your forte, is it not?"

"Well, that's her personal business, Jasper. I'm not one to get into things like that," she said. "Especially where a child is concerned. I mean, you never know if she escaped an abusive relationship, and that's why he's never been seen. Or maybe she had some celebrity's baby, and she's afraid if he ever found out, he'd take the kid away. I mean, when you're talking about a kid, knowing the whole story doesn't justify messing their life up."

"Yeah, I guess you're right." It seemed no one could tell me what the hell Tiffany's real deal was.

But the woman herself could. I deserved to know. She'd left me without a word. She'd known she was moving and didn't think I needed to know.

We were in love. Or so I'd thought. We spent every available moment together. It made no sense that she didn't think I should know her family was going to move. And I was tired of being put off about it.

"You don't happen to know where Tiffany lives, do you?" I asked Felicity. "She and I were together in high school. We just met again yesterday, and she had to get going. She forgot to tell me her address. She won't be mad at you for giving it to me. I won't even tell her who I found out from. It can be our little secret, Felicity."

"You're going to have to give me something first, Jasper."

I'd had a feeling she'd make that stipulation. "I tell you what. My brothers and I will let you give us a set of questions that we'll answer for you. No more than ten questions, so make them count."

The fire in her eyes told me I'd just bought myself an address. "You got it. I'll have those questions ready for you on Monday. Stop by and pick them up then. I want them answered before Friday so I can write up a story for the following week."

My brothers might want to kick my ass for what I've done. But it'll be worth it in the end.

TIFFANY

Taking off early from work, I picked up Jasmine from school, then
we went home to spend a peaceful evening together, just watching
Netflix and eating pizza. "So, what do you want to do this weekend,
Jasmine?"

Picking the pepperoni off her slice of pizza, she shrugged.
"Dunno. What do you want to do?"

"Not sure." I watched her carefully pull each round bit of meat
off the pizza. "Jas, you always say you want pepperoni pizza, but
then you take the meat off. Why not just order a cheese pizza if
that's what you really want?"

"Momma, you see where the pepperonis were?" She pointed at
an orange spot.

"Yeah."

"Well, those spots taste gooder than the plain old cheese. I don't
like the way the pepperonis feel in my mouth, but I like the taste."

"I see now." I liked the way my six-year-old could communicate
so well. I chalked it up to how much time she'd spent with grownups
since her birth.

No one but my immediate family had ever watched her. Until
she started kindergarten a couple of years back, she hadn't even
been around other kids. It showed in her vocabulary, too.

I couldn't help but smile as I watched her eat her pizza very neatly, wiping her mouth after each bite to make sure there wasn't anything on her face. "Is it gonna rain or snow this weekend, Momma?"

"Not that I know of. Would you like to do something outside?" I asked. "Maybe go to Dallas tomorrow to the zoo?"

"We did that last year around this time, and the animals barely came out," she reminded me. "How about something inside? Tammy from my class said that her family went all the way down to the coast and saw lots of fish in a giant aquarium."

"The coast?" I asked. "That's kind of too far for a day trip. I've got my Sunday reservations at the café to think about."

"I know." She looked at me with hopeful eyes. "But can we do it this summer when it's hot outside? Tammy said they also went to the beach. It sounds so cool, Momma. And she got these really cool sunglasses, too. She wears them all the time. She looks like a movie star when she puts them on. I want some, too. Hers have little mermaids on them. I want some just like that."

"Well, we can certainly make plans to take a vacation down there this summer." I liked the fact that we'd struck a deal. "As for this weekend, I think I can find us something to do indoors. Maybe check out what's playing at the IMAX theater in Dallas. We'll see how we feel tomorrow."

She nodded as she put the last bite into her mouth, then got up with her paper plate and threw it in the trash. "Sounds good, Momma. Are you ready to find a movie for us on TV?"

I'd finished, too, and got up to toss my empty plate. "Yeah, I'm thinking something funny."

"Of course," she said as she put her little hands on her hips. "I love funny stuff."

The sound of a loud vehicle pulling up in my driveway had me going to the window that overlooked the front of the house, and I saw a big four-wheel-drive black truck parking behind my car. My heart stopped, and I froze completely when I saw who got out. "Jasper."

Turning to find Jasmine sitting on the couch, I ran to her. "Hey, let's walk off that pizza." I grabbed her hand, taking her toward the backdoor.

"Aw, Momma, I don't wanna go for a walk," she moaned.

We heard him knock on the door just as we went out the back. "Come on. Let's hurry."

Jasmine looked back as I closed the door. "Momma, someone's at the door. Aren't you going to answer it?"

"No." I had no idea what to tell her. "I wasn't expecting anyone. I'm sure it's some salesman, and I don't want to deal with that right now."

The knocks turned into pounding as Jasper got impatient and shouted, "Damnit, Tiffany. I know you're in there. Your car's here. Now let me in."

"How does that salesman know your name, Momma?" Jasmine asked.

"That's one of their tricks to get you to buy what they're selling, baby girl. Let's hurry up and get to the park." I tugged her along and found she was just slowing us down, so picked her up and carried her as I nearly ran to the street behind ours, then zig-zagged through the streets to get to the park.

In the park, there were a few picnic tables under a grove of trees that made it impossible to see from the street. If Jasper drove around to look for me, he wouldn't see us there. Jasmine pointed at the slide. "Hey, can I slide?"

"Sure can." I put her down and watched her climb up the stairs. When I heard the sound of a big truck, I turned to see if it was Jasper. It was. *He's driving around looking for me.* "Shit."

"Momma!" Jasmine cried out. "You said a naughty word. Shame on you."

"Yes, shame on me. I—um." I had to think of a plausible excuse for cursing in front of her. "...stepped on a pinecone and it freaked me out."

"Oh, okay then." She slid down the slide. "Wheeee..."

The kid loved slides more than anything. But I couldn't smile the way I normally would when my daughter was having such a great time doing something so simple. Not with Jasper actively looking for me.

I had to do something. At this rate, he'd catch me with Jasmine sooner rather than later. We needed to leave town, and we needed to do it right away. But what in the world would I tell Jasmine?

There would be a lot to do. I would have to cancel the Sunday reservations that had already been made for my special meals at the café. Plus, I would have to call to cancel the delivery the farmers made to the café with their fresh produce on Saturday. I had lots to do and little time to do it.

Jasmine slid another four times, and Jasper came by the park two more times. I figured he'd look elsewhere, and I would have a small window to get packed and get the hell out of town.

"Jas, come on. We should get going. I just had an awesome idea. We can leave right away and go to Dallas. We'll spend a couple of nights in a fancy hotel and go do all kinds of fun things this weekend."

"Oh, yeah, Momma!" She sprang off the end of the slide, running to me. "Can we go to a fancy spa and get our nails done like we did that one time?"

"We sure can." I picked her up and hurried back to the house. In the distance, I could still hear Jasper's truck, and it made me move even faster. "We can even stay at the Lorenzo Hotel. You loved that one. Remember, it's all lit up, and you loved looking out the big window at the Dallas skyline?"

"Oh, yeah!" Jasmine was getting excited. "I loved that one. Oh, I can't wait, Momma. Let's hurry."

As we came in the backdoor, I put her down. "Go grab your bag out of your closet, and I'll be in to help you pack. And get your toothbrush out of the bathroom, too." She took off, and I went to the front door to see if Jasper had left me a note. He'd left a sticky note on the door—his phone number, name, and in all caps, "CALL ME!"

Taking the sticky note off the door, I put it in my pocket, then a chill rushed through me. "You know what, Jas? Momma's gonna buy us everything we'll need." I ran to my room, grabbed my purse and my daughter, then left the apartment. I knew something was very wrong with Jasper, and I wasn't ready to deal with that.

Maybe someone had told him something they shouldn't have. I

had no idea. He hadn't been acting like that when he saw me at the Dairy King earlier, so I wasn't sure what had happened. All I was sure about was that I wasn't ready to come clean with the man and that he'd talked to someone to get my address.

Buckling my daughter into her booster seat, I found my hands shaking. "Momma, what's wrong? Look, you're shaking." She put her hand on mine.

"I'm just really excited." I kissed her on the forehead. "This is so spontaneous, right? So not like us."

"Yeah, we've never done this before." She put her hands on my face. "Momma, just calm down. We're going to have lots of fun, but you don't need to get so excited that you shake."

Taking a deep breath, I knew I had to chill the hell out. "You're right, baby girl. Momma's gonna chill."

I got into the driver's side and backed out of the driveway nice and slow. Then I took the most direct route to get onto the interstate and get the hell out of Carthage before Jasper saw me driving around. I knew he'd go to great lengths to stop me if he saw me.

"I'm gonna get pink on my nails," Jasmine said as she looked at her hands. "My toes, too. What color are you gonna get?"

I tried to settle my mind and get into the groove like she was. "What do you think about coral?"

"That's kind of like pink and orange, right?" she asked.

"Yeah, kind of like that." I looked at her through the rearview mirror as I went up the ramp to get on the interstate. Just being that far out of town made me a lot more relaxed than I had been.

"Well, I think it sounds very nice." She looked out the window as darkness fell and car lights started to come on. "Is it going to be very late when we get to the hotel?"

"Well, we've got to stop somewhere to get what we need. That'll take an hour or more." I thought about how hairbrained my idea to flee was. "Yeah, it's gonna be kind of late. But we can sleep in. I've got calls to make, so can you be very quiet for me while I make them?"

"I *can* be very quiet, Momma." Her eyes were glued to the passing cars. "I like watching the lights anyway."

I'd never had a friendship like the one I had with my daughter.

Although she'd never been planned, she was meant to be mine, and I knew that. "Thanks, sweetie."

A knot formed in my throat as I drove down the road. I'd had all this special time with Jasmine, and Jasper hadn't ever had a moment with our daughter. When I felt a pain in my heart for Jasper, I thought it must be because I'd done him wrong in more ways than one.

I'd never meant to see the man again. But I guessed we should've moved farther away than we had. But then again, maybe he was meant to find us. Maybe he was being led to find the little girl he'd never known he had.

But he sure seemed mad when he was yelling out for me. I could feel the anger coming off him when I read the note he'd left. He was really mad, and that meant someone had told him something about Jasmine.

But who in town knows anything about our daughter, other than my parents?

JASPER

I drove by Tiffany's apartment one more time, only to find her car gone. I had to give her the benefit of the doubt. Maybe she hadn't been home when I'd come by. Maybe she'd taken her kid out to play or something.

Going by slowly, I saw the note I'd left was gone. So, she had my number and still she hadn't called. And that kinda pissed me off.

A simple phone call wasn't that much to ask of someone who once loved you. Just a little old phone call, and I wouldn't be mad. Only Tiffany wasn't going to give me even something that simple.

It kept gnawing at me that she was hiding something big from me. And her kid kept coming up in my head, too. Not knowing how old the girl was bothered me immensely. If I knew that, then I'd be able to move on.

For now, I had nothing else to do, so I headed home to have dinner with my brothers. I had to let them know what I'd traded to get Tiffany's address; now was as good a time as any.

When I went into the formal dining room, I saw Cash and Tyrell had beaten me to the table. They sat there, drinking iced tea while waiting on the appetizer to be served. "Hey there, gentlemen."

Tasha, the cook's helper, came in. "I thought I heard you come in, Jasper. What can I get you to drink?"

"I need a beer. A big one." I took a seat as she left the room.

Tyrell eyed me. "You look kind of agitated. What's up?"

"Tiffany is what's up." Tasha came back in with my beer, putting it on the table in front of me. "Thanks, Tash."

"You're welcome." She walked away. "Enchilada soups are almost up, guys."

Cash smiled. "Yum."

Tyrell still eyed me. "What's up with Tiffany? I saw her at the Dairy King the other day. She seems fine to me."

"Yeah, well, I've got the notion she's hiding something from me." I took a long drink of the cold beer. "And I've got to tell you boys something."

With a huff, Tyrell asked, "What is it?"

"Well, I talked to Felicity today." I waited a beat as both my brothers shook their heads.

Cash pinched the bridge of his nose as he asked, "Did you make a deal with her, Jasper?"

"Kind of." I took another drink to help me rustle up some courage. "I told her she can give us a list of ten questions that we'll answer for her, and she can make a story out of that."

The way Tyrell's nostrils flared told me he was as pissed as I'd thought he'd be. "You did what?"

"I had to know where Tiff lived, and Felicity wasn't going to tell me the address until I gave her something. It's not that much, guys. Ten lousy questions is all. And I'll be happy to answer them if you guys don't want to be bothered. I *had* to do it. I had to know where I could find Tiffany. You understand, right?"

When all I got were shaking heads, I knew I'd jumped the gun. "Okay, I'm going crazy. All right? I know this. And I wish I could stop myself, but I can't. I went to her house and banged on the door yelling that I knew she was home because her car was there. I'm sure her neighbors think I'm insane."

Cash cleared his throat. "Jasper, you've got to face the fact that she might not want to see you again. There are more fish in the sea, bro."

"If that's true, then why do I see the sparkle in her eyes when she looks at me?" I wanted to know that. I had to know that.

Tyrell said, "You're her first love, Jasper. I think it's natural for her to look at you that way. But it doesn't mean that she's *still* in love with you. Do you honestly believe that you're still in love with *her*? I mean, you don't know the woman she's become at all. How can you say you're in love with her if you don't really know her? And how can you expect her to just jump back into your arms when she doesn't know who you are anymore?"

Even though what he'd said was completely logical, it didn't make me stop thinking the way I had all day. "I think she's hiding something big from me. Her story has too many holes in it. And she won't tell me how old her kid is either—or who the father is. Now that's big. Don't you agree?"

Tasha came in with three steaming bowls. "Here's the first course, gentlemen."

"It looks great, Tasha," Cash said as he smacked his lips. "Tell Chef Todd I said that. He loves when he gets compliments on his food."

"I'll let him know." She left us alone again.

While Cash dug in, I took my time, not feeling all that hungry.

Tyrell noticed the way I ate slowly. "Jasper, you don't think that kid is yours, do you?"

I looked up at him thoughtfully. "How can I know for sure?" I hadn't been one of those guys who told other people about every little detail of his sex life, but I knew how reckless Tiffany and I had been the last few times we'd had sex. "If I knew how old she was, then I would have a better idea if the kid is mine or not."

Cash asked in between bites, "Weren't you and Tiffany real close, Jasper? Don't you think she would've told you that she was pregnant if she'd known that before she moved away? Or wait! Maybe she only found out after she moved and didn't know how you two would make it work while living so far apart."

"Even if that's true, why not tell me now?" If I was that kid's father, then I should've been told a hell of a lot earlier. But I could forgive that. What I couldn't forgive was being here now and *still* not being told. "If I only knew how old this kid was, then I could stop with all this thinking shit. I could get onto making Tiff mine again, without all this pent-up anger getting in the way."

Tyrell shook his head. "I can understand that. It's not like you're some poor man working as a night stocker at Piggly Wiggly anymore. You've got lots to offer now. And it would be a crime to keep any kid of yours away from you when you've got so much to give now. I'd be mad, too, if I knew someone was actively keeping my child away from me."

At least I had his support. Cash just kept eating. "And what do you think, Cash?"

"I think this soup is freaking awesome," he said, then took another spoonful.

"Not about the damn soup," I said. "About this situation."

Gulping down the last of his soup, he wiped his mouth with a napkin. "Look, Jasper, you don't know anything for sure yet. So, I wouldn't go getting my panties in a wad right now."

"I left her my phone number, and she hasn't called yet. I think that's a red flag." I took another drink of my beer and knew I'd be drunk by ten that night if Tiffany didn't call me soon.

Cash shook his head. "She's got a kid, Jasper. I'm sure she's doing things with her and won't have time to call you until after she puts her to bed. Be patient, bro. If Tiffany still likes you, she'll call. And if she doesn't, then my advice is to leave her alone."

That wasn't like me at all. "I go after what I want, Cash. You know that." Sitting back, I thought about the little girl's name. "Her name's Jasmine. Don't you think that means something? I mean, it's close to sounding like my name, you know what I'm saying?"

Tyrell looked up at the ceiling with an exasperated expression. "Jasper, that doesn't mean a damn thing. Maybe she liked the name. Maybe it was her grandma's name. You don't have any idea why she named her little girl that. Do yourself a favor and let this go. For now, anyway. Give Tiffany some time to do what's right—*if* the kid is yours. I bet she ain't your kid, if you want to know what I think."

"It sounds like she might only be about two." I knew that much. "Maybe I'm making myself crazy for no reason at all. I hope that's it. Because it's making me hate Tiffany to think she's kept a kid away from me for this long, and that she's had the chance to tell me about her, yet still doesn't."

"You're beginning to hate Tiffany?" Cash asked. "That's not good at all."

"I know." I drank the rest of the beer just as Tasha came back in with the main course. "Can you hit me again, Tash?" I put the empty mug on the table.

"Of course." She placed a plate of beef enchiladas, rice, and beans in front of me. "You seem out of sorts, Jasper. Is everything okay?" She moved around the table, serving my brothers.

"Not really." I cut into the cheesy sauce-covered enchiladas. "But I'll take care of it."

One way or another, I would take care of it. I would make Tiffany tell me all about that kid. She owed it to me after leaving me without a word.

Cash asked, "You wanna come to the bar with me after dinner, Jasper?" He cut his eyes to Tyrell. "I'm sure big bro here is gonna spend the evening cuddling with Ella."

"You're right," Tyrell said. "She got a late start to work today since we stayed up late last night, watching movies. She's going to be done with work anytime now, and we plan to do a little stargazing tonight."

I still didn't understand why my brother's fiancé still worked as our maid. "When are you going to let her quit that job, Tyrell?"

"She can stop any time she wants to," he said. "She's a lot like her momma. She takes a lot of pride in how this place looks. To be honest, I think she'd like to take over her mother's job of being the house manager someday."

I could see that happening. "And her brother, Kyle, wants to take over as the ranch foreman when his dad is ready to retire. Which he should've done a decade ago, but I bet he won't give that job up until he's dead."

We all laughed, knowing the crusty old man would probably do just that.

If I had a kid who could be enjoying this new life I had but couldn't because of a mother who wanted to keep her all to herself, then I had no idea what lengths I would go to. I'd grown up poor. I knew that wasn't the case for Tiffany and her daughter. She had money, a lot more than my parents had when we were growing up. But the fact was, I had a hell of a lot more money now and an awesome home on the ranch. Any kid would love to grow up here.

"What good is this mansion and ranch if you can't share it with your family?" I asked.

Cash looked confused. "You mean you want Mom and Dad to come live with us here? You know they can't and don't even want to."

"Not them, you idiot." I threw a linen napkin at him. "Stay on the subject, would you? I mean, if that little girl is mine, she belongs here, on this ranch, living in this gorgeous mansion. She deserves to have all I didn't. That's all I want, really. I just want her to have the best."

"But she might not be yours, Jasper," Tyrell reminded me. "Go have some drinks with Cash at the bar and see if you can't get out of your own head for the rest of the night. You're making yourself crazy."

He's right. I am *making myself crazy.*

TIFFANY

After making calls to make sure my absence on Sunday wouldn't disappoint anyone, I thought about calling my mother to let her know where I was going. But then I wondered if she or Dad might've been the ones to tell Jasper things about Jasmine they shouldn't have.

If that's even what has Jasper acting so out of character.

Putting my hand in my pocket, I pulled out the little yellow note with Jasper's number on it. I laid it on the passenger seat, then looked in the rearview mirror to see that Jasmine had nodded off.

After stopping at a Walmart to get the things we'd need for the weekend, we'd gotten back on the road, heading to Dallas. It hadn't taken long for Jasmine to pass out.

I knew I couldn't make the call to Jasper, even if she was asleep. She might wake up and hear our conversation. I would have to make it on my handsfree device since I was driving. It was already almost ten. By the time we got to the hotel, it would be nearly midnight. I didn't think I should call him that late.

I didn't know if I should call him at all.

If he knew what I'd hidden for so long, he might be outraged. I'd never had to deal with Jasper being mad at me before. We'd never had so much as one argument in the two years we'd been together.

That was one of the big reasons I didn't tell Jasper about me being pregnant. I'd known for a month before we moved that I was. I'd known for three months before the move that we were moving.

Maybe that's why I had gotten so reckless with sex with him. When I looked back on it, I thought maybe it was because my brain hadn't fully formed yet. Why else would I have asked him to come inside of me?

When my parents had told us all that they'd found a little café in Carthage and that we'd be moving right after I graduated from high school, I wanted to run and tell Jasper all about it. I wanted to stay with him but knew I couldn't.

Jasper had no means of providing for us, and his family surely didn't. Even so, I'd thought about getting a job in Dallas and asking Jasper if he wanted to move in with me so we could try to make it work.

For some reason, I never talked to him about it. I kept going back and forth on things. Then I missed a period, took the pregnancy test, and found out I had a baby to think about now.

Living with Jasper was out. He and I couldn't make enough money to support a child. And I would have to work, leaving our baby only God knew where. It would've been such a disaster. And our poor baby girl would've been the one to suffer.

No matter how things had turned out, I knew I'd done right by our daughter. She was a wonderful little girl, and I knew that was all thanks to what I'd given up.

Living with my parents for the first couple of years of her life made it easy for me to take care of her while I went to college online. Then once she was two, I went to work in the café while one of my family members took care of Jasmine. We'd kept her secluded to make sure no one could ever take her from us.

Deep down, my parents and I knew the Gentrys didn't have the money to search for us. I assumed Jasper hated me for leaving him without saying a word of goodbye. Even still, I'd had this sick feeling that one day someone would show up and take Jasmine from me.

And now I wondered if my parents had betrayed me by telling

Jasper things they'd never planned on telling him. I knew my mother could be weak, and she got nervous easily. It might not have been on purpose that she'd told him anything that would hurt Jasmine and me. But she might've blurted out something, not meaning to.

At the time, I thought it best that my parents didn't know where I was. Who knew if they'd tell Jasper, and he'd come find me. The man could be relentless; I knew that much about him.

I also knew that running away wasn't going to be the answer. I had a good amount of money saved up. I could stay gone for a year at least, without even working. But that wouldn't solve a thing. I knew Jasper would be able to hire someone to find me if I did that.

Time is what I needed—time to come to terms with knowing that what I'd always wanted wasn't going to happen. I'd take the weekend to figure out how to tell Jasper the truth about our daughter. I'd figure it all out.

"Momma, are we there yet?" came Jasmine's tired voice.

"You woke up," I said as I glanced back at her. "We're about an hour out. All that shopping took us longer than I thought it would. Soon you'll be looking at the lights of the Dallas skyline as we lay in a comfy bed. Won't that be nice?"

"Yes." She leaned her head back. "I was having a dream. There was this man's voice calling me. He kept saying my name over and over. It was dark, and it seemed like I was in the woods or something like that. We couldn't find each other." She sniffled. "It made me feel sad."

"I'm sorry it made you feel sad." It made me think about Jasper looking for her. "We can get milk and cookies when we get to the hotel. Remember how they make them at night?"

"Oh, yeah." She smiled. "They're so good. I can't wait. How far now, Momma?"

"A little less than an hour." I turned the radio onto the channel with kids' songs on it. "Wanna sing along with the radio?"

She shook her head. "Not right now. I still feel kind of sad about that dream. Maybe it's 'cause I miss Uncle Bo. Do you think he's okay?"

That brought up even more concerns. "I'm sure he's fine." How could I be sure of that when my little brother was doing a tour of—I didn't even know where. But there was so much danger out there in the world; I couldn't kid myself into thinking he was in any safe situation.

"I hope so," Jasmine whispered. "I *have* to see him again. I love Uncle Bo so much."

"Me, too." I thought about the day he'd left and how much we'd all cried. "I don't want you to worry about Uncle Bo. We'll see him again."

She nodded. "Yeah, I think we will, too. I just miss him."

We all did. When a family member left like that, it was hard to take. Carolina was gone, but we all knew she was safe. With Bo, no one knew what was happening to him at any given moment. It made it hard to think about him sometimes. And my imagination had proven to be my enemy more than a few times.

I had to admit that about Jasper, too. I'd imagined him being so mad at me for not telling him about Jasmine, that he'd take her away from me just to make me hurt the way I'd hurt him.

As I looked at my little girl in the backseat, I wondered how I would ever take it if he actually did that. Then I had to shake the thought out of my head. I couldn't deal with that. Not at all.

"Hey, if you look real hard, you can start to see the city lights, Jasmine. We're about a half hour away now." I pointed out the window at the horizon that glowed ahead of us. "Not too much longer, and we'll be nibbling on cookies and looking out the window at all the pretty lights. It'll almost be like Christmas."

Clapping, Jasmine squealed with delight. "I can't wait!"

Even though her cheery attitude usually made me smile as my heart filled with joy, I didn't feel it at all. All I could think about was how Jasper was missing this with her. And how it was all my fault.

I glanced at the note on the passenger seat again and knew I could make this pain go away with one phone call. But then my eyes went to my daughter, and I knew it wasn't the right time yet.

Jasmine needed time to get used to the fact she would have a father now. When she found out about his ranch and the mansion, she'd be well out of her wheelhouse.

How would Jasmine react to suddenly becoming the wealthiest

little girl in Carthage? How would she handle all that attention? With Felicity's knack of finding stories in our little town, I had a feeling she'd push for ours. And I would come out like a villain in that story. I didn't want the whole town to know what I'd done.

There were just so many things that would make me look bad that I just wasn't ready to face. Jasmine had gone this long without a father, what would a few more weeks change? And Jasper had gone this long without knowing he had a child, so again—what would a few more weeks change?

"You know I love you more than anything in this world, Jasmine, right?"

She nodded. "And I love you more than anything else in this world, too, Momma. We're best friends."

A sharp pain hit me square in the heart. Would a best friend hide something like what I'd hidden? Would a best friend keep her away from great things, like having a dad who would love her?

I knew *no* true friend would do the things I had. The past, and the decisions I'd made, I could stand by with pride. I'd done the best I could for our baby back then. And I'd fight Jasper to the end over that.

What I couldn't fight him on was what I'd done since he'd come to town. That was all my wrongdoing. And I couldn't seem to stop doing it.

"Jasmine, we're going to have the best time ever this weekend." I would make her time as happy as I could. I had no idea what the future would hold for us, but at least we'd have this weekend.

"I think so, too, Momma." She smiled and pointed up ahead. "I see the round lights of that restaurant! Look! We're almost there!"

Happy to see the lights getting closer too, I smiled. For this weekend, I'd leave my worries behind and just enjoy the time I had with my daughter. Things would have to change, and God knew I hated change, but changes happened anyway.

I hadn't lied when I'd told Jasper how much I'd cried when we first got to Carthage. That transition was hell on me. And I was sure this one would be pretty bad, too.

JASPER

Opting out of spending the night at the bar, I'd stayed home, hoping that Tiffany would call. I didn't want her to think I was some kind of a barfly. She needed to know that I could be the kind of man a woman could bring her kid around—or baby—or whatever age her kid was.

The age thing bothered me like crazy, so I'd decided to go down to the Dairy King. I wasn't going to leave until I had at least one answer to the one question that wouldn't leave me alone: *How old is Tiffany's kid?*

On my way to town that Saturday morning, I drove by Tiffany's apartment to find her car still gone. Hoping she'd be at work, I headed that way. Today would be the day to end my insanity. I'd promised myself that much.

Not in my entire life had I ever been so consumed by anything. It was an unnatural thing for me, and I truly hated it. My dreams had even gotten into the mix. Last night, I dreamt I had been playing hide and seek with a little girl—a girl I called Jasmine.

I had this feeling that even if the girl wasn't mine, she needed me in her life. She needed a daddy, and I could be that to her. I'd seen a future with Tiffany starting all the way back in high school.

Sure, I hadn't mapped it out the way I should've before we

graduated. But then again, if Tiff had told me about her family's move, then I might've gotten the steam under me to make better plans. Maybe I'd have gotten a better job so she and I could get a place together.

If she'd only told me about things, I would've done everything I could've done back then to keep her with me. I'd never wanted to let her go in the first place.

Every girl after her dimmed in comparison. No one had ever filled her shoes—not mentally nor physically. One would think sex would have been just about the same with anyone, but it wasn't.

I didn't know if it was because Tiff had been my first, and I'd been hers, but no one had been as good as her. That girl had been free with me, and I had been the same way with her. I've never felt that level of a connection with anyone else since. And now I was pretty damn sure that I never would.

With Tiffany within my reach, I no longer even looked at other women. So, yeah, if her little girl needed a father, then I was ready to be that to her. Tiff and I could make a family no matter what the circumstances were.

All I needed was to talk to Tiffany, to make her understand that I was no longer the same kid she left all those years ago. I might not have decided yet what I wanted to do to fill my time work-wise, but I knew how I wanted to spend my free time. And work wasn't a thing I had to worry about since I'd inherited more than I could ever spend.

I'd never been able to spend much money on Tiffany when we were younger. The fanciest place I'd ever taken her to was Red Lobster. But now I could take her anywhere she wanted to go. I could take her, and her little girl too, to places they'd only dreamt of going.

If she gave me a chance, I knew I could show Tiff that I could be the man for both her and her daughter. As I pulled into the parking lot of the Dairy King, I noticed her little blue Sonata wasn't parked there. It hit me that she might be trying to hide from me.

But why?

There I was again, thinking she was hiding something very important from me. And there was the anger again that I couldn't seem to control. Slamming my fist on the steering wheel, I gritted my teeth. "Why does she have to be some damned closed off right now? What is she hiding?"

An ache began in my stomach as I thought the worst. I had two terrible scenarios in my mind. One, that I was the father, and she didn't ever want to tell me for some reason. Or two, she'd cheated on me and got pregnant before her move and never wanted me to know that.

If there was some guy who she'd met after her move and made a mistake with, then I highly doubted she'd be acting this way. The holes in her stories, the hiding her kid away from everyone, the worry about me being around her kid … none of that made sense. At least it made no sense if the father was anyone other than me or someone from our hometown who I would know.

Even then, why would she keep her kid hidden from the people in Carthage?

My gut twisted as I thought the worst once more.

The little girl could have something wrong with her appearance that Tiffany thought would make people ridicule her. Or maybe she had a mental issue. It wouldn't bother me if she did. I mean, I'd feel bad for the little girl, but it wouldn't mean that I'd turn tail and run.

That has to be it.

That had to be the reason she felt no one could be in the child's life. *Poor Tiff. Poor Jasmine.*

Since it was still early in the morning, the café had only two customers inside, one of which was Tiffany's mom. I got out of the truck, intending to get some much-needed answers.

The bell rang as I came inside, and when her mother looked at me, her jaw dropped.

"Hi, Mrs. McKee. It's been a long time." I walked up to the counter. "Do you have a minute to talk to me?"

Her green eyes darted back and forth as she shoved her hand through her red hair, the same shade as Tiffany's. "Oh, I'm here alone, Jasper. I don't know."

Which possibly would work in my favor. If she was in a rush to speed up our conversation, she'd spit answers out faster in hopes of getting me out of her hair. "I can help out. Put me to work, Mrs. McKee."

She seemed a little upset as she pointed to the rack with red aprons hanging on it. "Well, put one of those on and come back here. I've gotta get things cut up before our cook comes in, so I can run the counter."

Grabbing an apron, I put it on, then went to wash my hands. Moving in next to her at the prep table, I took a knife and began cutting up some onions. "How about I take these for you? Save you some tears."

"Thank you, Jasper." She ran the back of her hand over her forehead. "You always were a helpful boy."

I'd always tried my best to show Tiffany's parents that I was the right guy for their daughter. "So, where is Tiff this morning?"

"I honestly don't know." She looked at me, the truth showing in her eyes. "This is her day off, but to be honest, it's not like her to go anywhere without telling me. And I found out when I came in this morning that she canceled the vegetable delivery she gets every Saturday. She even called to cancel the reservations that had been made for her Sunday meals. Did she tell you about what a great cook she's become?"

"She hasn't, no." I picked up another onion and chopped it up quickly. "Others have, though. Tiff's been tight-lipped with me since we found out we're living in the same town again."

"Has she?" she asked, as if she didn't know.

"Especially where her daughter is concerned." I watched her mother's shoulders tense up. "I found out her name from someone yesterday. Jasmine is a pretty name. I know that's Tiff's favorite scent."

"She does love that smell," Mrs. McKee agreed.

"Did she tell you about how my brothers and I inherited our grandfather's ranch?" I asked just to be sure she knew I was rolling in the dough now.

Turning her head to look at me, she smiled. "She did tell me about that. I think that's awesome for you guys, Jasper. I know things weren't easy on your family, financially speaking."

Mom and Dad came into my head. "The will made sure we

can't share anything with our parents and that kind of sucks. I mean, they've told us that they wouldn't take anything even if we tried to give it to them anyway. There are so many hard feelings between them and our grandparents on both sides."

"That's a real shame. I don't know what I'd do if I couldn't see my granddaughter. And Carolina just told us a couple of days ago that she and her husband are two months pregnant." She sighed with the thought. "To live a life not knowing how your grandkids are doing sounds like hell to me. Even now, with not knowing where Tiffany and Jasmine are, I hate the feeling it gives me. Does that sound controlling?"

"It sounds like you care." I nudged her shoulder with mine. "Jasmine is lucky to have you as her grandmother. You were always such a caring mother. And your lasagna has never been topped."

"You always came over for dinner every time I made that." She laughed with the memory. "You and Tiffany were practically inseparable."

"Yeah, we were. It's funny how I'd gone to school with her for ten years before I really saw her." That little cheerleader uniform had really fit her well. "But when I finally did—wow. I mean, wow. She stole my heart."

"She loved you so much, too, Jasper," she said. "That girl cried for a month over you when we moved."

"She could've called," I reminded her. "She had our home phone number."

"Oh, I think she just thought it best to make a clean break." Her hand shook as she picked up another tomato.

"Yeah, I can see that." I didn't want her to get too nervous and cut her fingers off. "I've got all the onions done. You want me to do the tomatoes, and you can start forming the hamburger patties?"

"Sounds good to me." Mrs. McKee walked over to the bowl with the meat in it and went to work making patties.

"Tiff told me how she went to college online." I sliced up one tomato, then added, "She'd always talked about going to a regular college, like the one in Lubbock—Texas Tech. Why did she change her mind?"

"Oh, that." She shook her head and bit her lower lip as if she had to think about why that was. "Well, she just didn't want to go after all."

That seemed pretty thin to me, so I pushed it a bit. "A woman has the right to change her mind. I'm just glad she still went to college. Tiffany is one smart girl. It would've been a real waste if she hadn't furthered her education. But I guess having a baby gets in anyone's way when you want to go away to college."

"It sure does," she agreed. "Tiffany was so self-conscious about her body when she was pregnant; she didn't go out at all for the first couple of years we lived here."

And that told me Tiffany *had* been pregnant when they'd first moved to Carthage. "How old is Jasmine again?"

"Six. She's in the first grade now." Her green eyes met mine, then she frowned, knowing she'd just let the cat out of the bag.

"Is that so …" I felt eerily calm. "Is she as smart as her mother was at that age?"

Mrs. McKee nodded slowly. "She's every bit as smart."

So, no mental problems and, by the sound of it, no physical ones either.

Finishing off the tomatoes, I said, "Thanks for letting me help you, Mrs. McKee. Tell your husband hello for me. I'll let you get to it."

"Thank you for the help, Jasper. Grab yourself a pop on the way out," she called out as I walked to the door.

Waving, I just shook my head. I didn't want anything. Well, that wasn't true—I wanted my daughter.

TIFFANY

The weekend away gave me time to think. And think I did. A hell of a lot of it, as a matter of fact. And the conclusion I'd come to was that Jasper needed to be told about Jasmine. It was the right thing to do. But the courage to make the confession wasn't coming easily to me.

The whole day at work on Monday, I kept expecting to see Jasper walk into the Dairy King—especially after my mother told me about the visit he'd made on the weekend. She'd told him how old Jasmine was, too, so I knew he had to have a pretty good idea that she was his.

Mom said he hadn't acted mad in the least. Jasper hadn't even asked a thing about Jasmine possibly being his. I wasn't sure how to take that. Maybe he didn't want a kid; I had no idea. And I didn't want to force Jasmine on him if he wasn't into it. Being a father wasn't for everyone. When I added in the fact that he might've been mad at me for keeping the secret for so long, there was just no telling what was going through the man's head.

With the workday over, I felt a ton of anxiety. "Mom, do you think you can watch Jasmine for the night? I just need a night of free time to come to terms with things."

She looked at me with compassionate eyes. "I really thought

he'd come in today to see if you were here. Do you think you'll go out to the ranch to find him and tell him the truth? The sooner Jasper knows, the better."

I didn't think I could just roll up to the ranch. "For now, I'm going to go down to The Watering Hole for a drink—or fifteen—and try to calm myself down."

She laughed. "Well, you be careful, young lady. I'll take care of Jasmine for the night. You need some time to yourself to figure out how you're going to explain things to Jasper. I think he'll forgive you, honey."

I crossed my fingers behind my back. "I hope you're right, Mom. Thanks for taking care of Jas. Tell her I'll pick her up from school tomorrow."

"Will do." She pointed at my grease-splattered T-shirt. "You go home, shower, change your clothes, maybe do your hair. Make yourself presentable before you go searching out Jasper."

"I've got his number." I put my hand in my pocket to feel the small note in it. "I've just been too afraid to call him."

Nodding, I knew she had an idea of how I felt. "Maybe a drink will ease your anxiety, and you'll be able to be honest with the man. I think he might even be good for Jasmine. Don't you?"

"I hope so." I grabbed my jacket and left.

My heart had never pounded so hard. My brain had never hurt so much from thinking about all the things that might happen when I told Jasper I'd hidden his kid from him for so many years. And my body shook with the fear that he'd be extremely angry with me.

A couple of hours later—all cleaned up and looking the prettiest I could get myself—I went to the bar where I thought Jasper might come in later. If nothing else, I knew Cash would be there, as he'd taken an interest in the bartender, Bobbi Jo. If I came in alone, he might inform his brother.

The last remnants of sunset filled the horizon as I got out of my car. It was a bit on the early side—especially on a Monday night—to be heading into a bar. The half-packed parking lot told me that I wasn't the only one with troubles to drown.

Neon lights made the bar glow blue. Cash had his usual seat at the bar, talking to Bobbi Jo as she tended to the three other guys who sat at the bar. I looked around, then opted to take a table.

The waitress, Tammy, came to me right away with a grin on her face. "Hey there, Tiffany. Tough day at the Dairy King?"

"You saw that crowd at lunch." She'd been there. "It was brutal. Sometimes I feel like we're the only place in town that serves lunch. It gets so crazy."

"Speaking of how crazy it got today," she said as she pulled her hair back into a ponytail. "I forgot to leave a tip this afternoon, so your first drink is on me. What'll it be?"

"Oh, wow." I had to think about it for all of a second. "How about an ice-cold draft beer in a frosty mug?"

"You've got it." Her eyes went to the door as someone came in. "I'll be right back."

With the door to my back, I had no idea who'd come in and really hated the fact that I'd taken the seat at the small table for two that didn't face the door. Now I wouldn't have any idea if Jasper came in or not.

To rectify my problem, I got up and went to the jukebox to play a song. Playing "Burn Out" by Midland, I went back to my table, taking the seat that faced the door this time. And that was when I saw Jasper sitting next to Cash at the bar.

Maybe he didn't see me.

Tammy came back with my beer. "Here ya go, Tiffany. Did you play that song on the jukebox?"

"Yeah. I love Midland." I took a nice long drink of the cold beer to soothe my jagged nerves.

"They're playing in Austin this coming Saturday. What I'd do for tickets to that concert..." She ran her hands up and down her sides. "Those boys give me the chills just thinking about them."

"They *are* pretty hot." I thought about how cool it would be to go see them. Pulling out my cell, I checked online for tickets. "I wonder if they have any tickets left?" The idea sprang into my head to buy a couple of tickets and invite Jasper to come with me. We could make a weekend out of it. And maybe that would help him forgive me for keeping the secret of our daughter from him.

"Are you going to buy tickets, Tiffany?" Tammy asked as I swiped the screen.

"If there's any available." I looked up at her, seeing the envy in her eyes. "If they've got some available, you want me to get a couple for you? Maybe we could all ride together. If I can find a date."

"Yeah, put me down for two. I'll give you the cash." She squealed. "I'm so excited. I hope Bobbi Jo won't be a bitch and will let me off next weekend."

"Fingers crossed." I looked at the ticket site and smiled. "Oh, yeah, Tammy. It's a go. I'm getting four tickets right now."

Jumping up and down, she was on top of the world. "Now all I've gotta do is decide which lucky guy will accompany me." She scanned the bar. "Well, he ain't here yet. But I do have people who need drinks. I'll be back over here to check on you in a few minutes and to pay you for the tickets. I'm so freaking excited now!"

So was I. I had something to ask Jasper now. But before I could get to him, he got up and went to the men's room without seeing me.

Going back to my table alone, I sat and took another sip of my beer. I couldn't help the feeling that Jasper knew I was there and was just ignoring me.

I'd find out for sure when he came out of the restroom, as he'd surely see me sitting alone at the table for two. Taking a deep, cleansing breath, I tried to calm myself down. It wasn't like Jasper to ignore me.

Kicking myself mentally for taking so long to make the decision to tell Jasper about our daughter, I downed the rest of my beer. Thankfully, Tammy was quick to bring me another one. "Girl, tonight your drinks are on me. I'm so excited about going to Austin with you next weekend. Wanna know something kind of silly?"

"What?" I took another drink.

"I've always thought it would be cool to be friends with you. I mean, you never hang out with anyone." She smiled at me to lessen the blow.

I'd had shit to hide. But all that was about to change. "I'm turning over a new leaf. And I'm glad you're happy about our weekend getaway. It's been years since I had any girls to hang out with. I'm glad we decided to do this."

"I'm gonna keep the beers coming, new friend." Tammy left me, laughing as she did.

Just as she walked away, Jasper came out of the bathroom. His eyes on the floor, he never looked up even once. "Damn."

Taking my beer, I got up, gathered my courage, then went to sit on the barstool next to him without saying a word. He looked at me, then nodded. "Tiffany. How are you doing this evening?"

"Fine." I took another drink as nerves moved all through my body. "And you?"

"Can't complain." He held up a finger to Bobbi Jo who put a bottle of Budweiser in front of him. And with that, he turned his attention to the television at the top of the wall.

I looked at it, too, finding a soccer game playing. I knew Jasper could not care less about watching that game. He was actively ignoring me. And that pissed me off.

Getting up, I went back to the jukebox and played every Midland song I could find before going to sit back down at the little table for two. At least Tammy came around to give me new mugs of frosty beer, and we talked and laughed about how fun our trip was going to be.

As the night went on and on, I had no idea what the hell Jasper was up to, but I knew it wasn't going to be any good for me. He'd never ignored me before. He and I had never fought over anything, and I didn't want to start now.

So, I got up, gave Tammy a nod and a wave goodbye, then left the bar without saying another word to Jasper Gentry.

The hell with him anyway.

JASPER

Sitting at the bar, trying my best not to pay attention to what Tiffany was doing, I kept my eyes on the television screen. But that damn soccer game couldn't hold my attention.

Another song by the band Midland came on the jukebox, and Tiffany and the waitress, Tammy, whooped and hollered about it.

"Yeah! Austin, here we come!" Tammy shouted.

I'd had no idea what they were so excited about until I overheard Tammy asking Bobbi Jo for the next weekend off so she and Tiffany could go to Austin to see Midland. Tammy made sure to say that they'd be taking dates and would ride together to the event.

I knew Tiffany would ask me to go with her. She hadn't had any other guy in the time we'd been apart—why would she have one now?

What I didn't know was what my answer would be.

Something inside me had changed, knowing she'd hidden something so important from me. A sense of injustice came over me. Not only for myself, but for the little girl, too.

Jasmine had to grow up without a father, and I knew that could be hard on a kid. I might not have had much money before, but I would've tried a hell of a lot harder to make money if I'd known I had a baby coming. But Tiffany had robbed me of all that. And the fact was, I felt like a victim. It felt like shit.

That girl had no doubts at all that I'd loved her. Except for my lack of money, I saw no other reason why Tiffany would've kept me from our daughter. And that bothered the shit out of me.

Being poor didn't automatically mean you'd be a bad parent. Being poor didn't mean you weren't worthy enough to know if you were the father of a kid or not. Being poor shouldn't have meant someone else got to decide things for you—especially important things.

I had money now, and I had the upper hand over Tiffany. She'd stolen six years of my daughter's life from me. Now I had the power to steal however much time I wanted with my daughter away from Tiffany.

We'll see how she likes it.

Things that had always attracted me to Tiffany now bothered me. Her laughter, her voice, the way she smelled like Jasmine all the damn time. I found her revolting for what she'd done to our daughter and me.

As I sat there, trying to ignore the woman completely, something came to me—revenge was a dish best served cold.

I could get revenge on Tiffany for doing this horrible thing to me and our little girl. But to do it, I would first have to make Tiffany believe I would forgive her for what she'd done.

Putting on an act wasn't a thing I'd ever done. But then again, I'd never been so completely blindsided by another human being in my life. If anyone would've told me that my little Tiffany could do such a horrendous thing, I would've laughed in their face. *Not my Tiffany. She'd never have a baby behind my back, then lie to my face about it.*

But she had done just that. I'd asked her about the kid's father, and she made some shit up. She could've come clean. I wouldn't have been so damn angry if she'd come clean early on when she and I had met up again.

She knew I had money now. She knew I wasn't some loser. Yet, she still kept the secret.

How could she?

In my heart, I felt like I'd never really known the girl I'd fallen in love with when we were so young. That girl couldn't do such a horrible thing. It had to have all been a lie.

And now *I* would be the one who would lie. *I* would be the one to pretend I was in love—pretend I could forgive her. As stabbed in the back as I felt, Tiffany would feel obliterated when I was done with her.

With the power to take her world away, I would do it with ease after how she'd duped me. Jasmine and I never had the chance to bond the way they had. I would never know what it felt like to hold her as a newborn and fall in love with her tiny face. I never got to see her take her first steps, say her first words, or hear her first cry when she came into the world. Tiffany had taken those things away from me.

Life was about to change for all three of us. But in the end, only two of us would stay happy. Jasmine and I would win out in the end, and it would be Tiffany who sat on the sidelines, crying her eyes out.

But first, I had to play the part of a forgiving man. Though it wouldn't be easy to pretend that nothing wrong had been done to me, I would do it. I *had* to do it. I couldn't let Tiffany get away with this without any repercussions.

That would be a crime.

A crime against my daughter and me. She'd taken so much away from us both; it wouldn't be fair to let Tiffany off the hook. And how ironic that she'd been so close to having it all with me.

If she'd only told me the truth once we'd found each other again, everything would've been so different. But she didn't do the right thing. Again.

My jaw clenched when I saw Tiffany walk out the door. "I'll catch ya later, Cash."

"Going after Tiff?" he asked with a knowing grin.

"Yep. It's time I get my girl back where she belongs. No more messing around." I headed outside. I hadn't told a soul about what I'd found out. And I wouldn't tell anyone what my plan for revenge was either. This was best kept under wraps.

If Tiffany or her family got even the slightest whiff of what I was about to do, then they'd surely pack up and leave in the dead of night with my daughter. It could take years to track them down if they did that.

I wouldn't make the mistake of giving them the slightest hint of what I was going to do. They all had it coming to them. Not one of them had said a word to me about Jasmine being mine. They'd all hidden it from me.

Tiffany had to have known she was pregnant before she left. I damn well knew she'd known they were moving. She'd kept it all a big secret, shocking me back then when she'd disappeared, and shocking me now that I knew how much she'd hidden.

As I walked out to my truck, I saw her continuously missing the keyhole on her car door. The fact that she had a key fob in her hand told me she was too drunk to drive. Ambling up to her, I reached out for the keys. "Give 'em to me."

Her green eyes, bleary and somewhat watery, looked into mine. "Why?"

"Because you're drunk, and I've got a conscience is why." I took the keys. "I'm taking you home."

"And if I don't want to go home?" She put her hands on her hips, swaying with the chilly breeze.

"You're going to anyway." Taking her hand, I led her to my truck. "You get to pick: your apartment or my place."

"Huh?" she asked, sounding like she really didn't get it.

"I'm done chasing you, Tiffany McKee." I opened the passenger door of my truck, then lifted her up, putting her in the seat. "Buckle up, baby."

"Wait." She shook her head. "You wouldn't even talk to me in there, and now you're saying you're done chasing me. You *want* me?"

"Always have." I closed the door then went to the driver's side and got in. Her seatbelt still wasn't around her. Leaning over, I snapped her in. "It's the law, Tiff."

I thought about how the law worked, and how it was on my side now. She'd committed a crime against me. It wasn't smart to commit crimes against people who could afford the best lawyers in Texas.

"Jasper, I don't understand." Clumsily, she tried to put the key fob back inside her purse.

"You took off this weekend without telling a soul where you'd gone. You had us all pretty worried, Tiffany. I'm done with your games." Pulling out of the parking lot, I headed toward the ranch. "You must have a sitter for the night, or you wouldn't have tied one on the way you did. I'm taking you home with me. You got any problems with that?" I eyed her as she smiled, then looked down.

"No. I'm pretty happy about it, actually."

She wouldn't be that damn happy about it if she knew what I had planned. But I had to make her fall in love with me again — had to play the role of a gentleman. "I'm gonna fix you something to eat when we get there. I bet you haven't eaten all day."

"I haven't eaten a thing," she confessed. "I haven't eaten much at all since you got back, Jasper."

Yeah, lying to a man's face can really screw with your appetite.

"I guess knowing I was around again had you all shook up. Now that we can get past all this nonsense, your appetite will come back, you'll see. And I'm *making* you eat tonight."

"Oh, you are?" She took her seatbelt off then scooted over to me, clipping herself into the middle seat. "Can I sit next to you, Jasper?"

I put my arm around her, then kissed the side of her head. "Hell yes you can, baby."

Snuggling into my side, she whispered, "I bought tickets to a concert in Austin this coming Saturday night. Would you like to be my date?"

"I sure would. We can take the private jet." I gave her shoulders a squeeze. "Won't that be nice?"

"That would be awesome." She looked up at me with star-filled eyes. "Can Tammy and her date come with us, too?"

"I don't see why not." I found it odd that I could act the way I was, given how mad I was. "I'll get us hotel rooms, too. We'll have an awesome weekend. You can get a sitter, right?"

"Mom and Dad watch my daughter any time I ask." She laid her head on my shoulder.

A rush of red ran through me as she said *my daughter*. She knew damn well that girl was my daughter, too, and still, she said shit like that. "Well, good. We'll have us one hell of a great time, won't we?"

Her hand moved over my chest. "I know we will. Jasper, this feels right, doesn't it?"

"Right as rain, baby." I kissed the top of her head. "It's all going to be roses from here on out; I can promise you that. Hell, if you're real good, I'll even take you out to Red Lobster."

"You remembered," she said like I could ever forget one damn thing we'd ever done together.

"I remember everything about when you and I were together, Tiffany. *Everything*." And that included the unprotected sex she'd asked for.

Why she'd done that, knowing she had to move away, was a thing I couldn't understand. *If she never loved me, never meant to stay with me, then why did she purposely try to have my baby?*

TIFFANY

I rode in the truck with Jasper, snuggled up to his side, inhaling his unique scent—leather, musk, outdoors—and wondering what the hell had just happened.

He'd virtually ignored me at the bar but now, all of a sudden, he was done chasing. I didn't know we'd been playing cat and mouse, but I wasn't unhappy to have been caught by the man. I had come to terms with the fact that I needed to tell him about our daughter. Why not let my body have what it wanted, too?

We could get back to how we'd been in the old days. Back to being together, giving ourselves wholly to the other, without any fear or regret. I couldn't wait to get underneath that man again.

"You know what, Jasper?" I whispered as I kissed his neck.

"What, baby?" His voice was deep, smooth as whiskey, and sexier than it had been seven, long years ago.

"I think I can skip eating, and we can get straight to your bed." His earlobe tasted delicious. "I can fill up on you. What do you say to that?" The thought of having him all over me made me hungry for him and only him.

"You've had too much to drink, honey. You need some food in that little belly of yours." He took my hand, kissed it, then held it against his chest. "You just let me take care of you."

He could take care of me forever. As I sat at his side, holding onto him, it all came back to me how well this man had always taken care of me. "Okay, I'll let you take care of me, Jasper. It feels good, actually." I'd been the one taking care of Jasmine for what seemed like forever. Letting him take care of me sounded like a dream come true.

When we pulled through the enormous iron gate at Whisper Ranch, I gasped, as it was all lit up. Jasper just smiled. "You like?"

"I love." I thought about how big Jasmine's eyes would be when she saw where her daddy lived. "This is kind of crazy to me. It must be that way to you, too." He'd come from such a tiny home, nothing close to what he now, not only lived in, but owned.

"I'm getting used to it. I suppose it's in my DNA." He looked at me as we headed up the winding driveway. "I was born to be here. Not a day goes by that I don't feel a part of this ranch."

"You know what you should do, Jasper?" I asked as an idea sprang into my brain. "You should get some kind of a degree that would help you manage this ranch."

With a chuckle, he asked, "You gonna help me with my classes, Tiff?"

"I could if you needed me to." I'd always been pretty smart. "I'd love to help you, Jasper."

"I'd love that, too." He kissed my cheek as we pulled up in front of the mansion. "We're here."

"Dear Lord, this is amazing." There was too much house to take in all at once, especially because only the entrance was lit up. "So many logs. I've never seen so many in one place. I didn't know there were such things as log mansions."

"Yep, there are." He got out, then reached in to get me. "Come on, baby. Let's get you inside and filled up."

His hands on my waist as he pulled me out of the tall truck made my heart stop beating. I lingered there, looking into his blue eyes. "Jasper, can you kiss me?"

A slow smile pulled his lips up. "Not yet, Tiffany McKee. You're still drunk."

"Damn my low tolerance for alcohol," I said as he took my hand, pulling me along with him.

434

The foyer had a gorgeous split staircase. "This is home now, Tiffany. I want you to make yourself at home here, too."

Blinking at everything, I felt overwhelmed. "Wow, Jasper."

He took me through room after room—the lights going on as we entered, and off as we left—until we came to one hell of an enormous kitchen. "Here we are." He pulled a tall bar chair out for me and picked me up, sitting me on it at the island bar in the middle of the kitchen. "I'm thinking a peanut butter and jelly sandwich and a glass of milk."

"I'm thinking this is the fanciest and most cutting-edge kitchen I've ever been in." Looking around, I saw machines I'd never seen before. "You must have a professional cook, huh?"

"Chef Todd," he said as he pushed the wall. But then it opened, revealing the inside of a refrigerator. "And he's got assistants to help him. His Sunday brunches are famous in this house."

Mine were, too. "Seems I'll have competition for your presence at my famous Sunday brunches. I do them at the Dairy King. Now that I can see that dining at home is much better for you, I understand why you haven't eaten anything at our café."

"Tomorrow I'll have him cook us up a seafood feast like we used to get on our special occasions at Red Lobster." He winked at me as he took a loaf of bread out of a huge bread box. "You can be sure he out-cooks any chef at that chain of restaurants."

"I bet he does." I was growing more and more envious of that gourmet kitchen. "How strict is he about sharing this cooking space?"

"Don't know. I've never wanted to get in here to do much more than make a sandwich or a bowl of cereal now and then." He pushed another piece of the wall, and it opened into a pantry. "Would you like honey-roasted peanut butter or chunky original?" He stopped and shook his head. "Listen to me. You will love the honey-roasted kind; I'm gonna use that."

"And strawberry jam." I'd found my appetite. Seemed all it took was getting back into the groove with Jasper to do it.

"I remember." He whistled as he made the sandwich, poured the milk, then placed the plate and glass in front of me. "And here you are, my sweet Tiffany McKee." His lips pressed against my

435

cheek, and my heart raced. Then he moved back, giving me more space between us than I wanted.

"Thank you, my sweet man." I tried not to scarf it down, but the hunger that had suddenly built up inside of me wouldn't let me eat it the way a nice lady should.

Jasper cleaned up the mess he'd made and had barely put the peanut butter away before I was done. When he turned to find me at the sink with the empty plate and glass, he laughed. "Damn, girl! Were you starving yourself or what?"

I'd been so anxious about the lie and all the hiding that I *had* kind of starved myself. Nodding, I walked toward him, opening my arms. "Can I have a hug now?"

His chest swelled as he took in a breath but didn't let it out right away. "Sure, I think I can handle that."

It had been so long since his strong arms had really held me. Laying my head against his chest, I heard the familiar sound of his heart beating. "I've missed this more than I've ever let myself believe." Looking up at him, I saw a shimmer in his eyes. "Jasper Gentry, I've never stopped loving you. I swear that to you. Can we just pretend like seven years hasn't passed? Can we pick up right where we left off? Can we tell each other that we love each other again?"

"Is that what you really want, Tiffany?" He looked into my eyes as he stroked my hair off my face. "Do you want to pretend we were never apart? Do you want to pretend time hasn't come between us at all?"

With a nod, I ran my hands up and down his bulging arms. "I really do want that, Jasper. More than anything. I want to make it feel as if we haven't been apart." My hands rested on his biceps, and I yearned to feel his bare flesh, instead of the fabric of his shirt. "If you take me to your bed, I can try to turn back time."

Lifting me up, he carried me out of the kitchen, back through all the rooms we'd come through before, then up the left side of the split staircase. He never said a word as he took me up to his bedroom.

Once again, I found myself gasping as we entered his bedroom. Bigger than any bedroom I'd ever been in, the décor was ruggedly elegant—a thing I had no idea existed. "And this is where I've lain my head since moving to Carthage." He placed me on the bed, and I began to unbutton my shirt.

I stopped as he turned and walked away from me. "What are you doing?"

"Getting you one of my T-shirts to sleep in." He pulled one out of the top drawer then came back, handing it to me. "We're sleeping tonight. I'm not about to have sex with you for the first time in seven years when you have alcohol in your system." Then he walked away, leaving me with my mouth hanging open.

"Well, damn." I pulled my clothes off, then put on the T-shirt. He'd gone into the bathroom. "So not what I expected," I muttered. "So not like the boy I left behind. So not what I thought would go down tonight."

I climbed underneath the heavy blanket. Jasper's scent was all over the bed, and I snuggled down, breathing it in and loving the familiarity it brought to me. It felt like home to me already. I'd had no idea it would feel this way. And before I knew it, I'd fallen asleep.

The next morning, I woke when a sliver of light slipped through the thick curtains. The soft sounds of Jasper's light snores made me smile right away. He'd slept with me without trying to have sex with me.

I recalled being disappointed just before falling asleep, but now, waking up sober, I felt happy that we hadn't had our reunion marred by my overuse of alcohol.

Turning over to face him, I wrapped my arms around him, then kissed his cheek. The whiskers tickled my lips.

His eyes fluttered open, and he smiled back at me. "Hey, beautiful, it's nice to see you here. I wasn't sure I'd wake to find you still in my bed."

"I'm not going anywhere unless you make me go, Jasper." I kissed his lips softly. "I love you."

His hands moved around my body, pulling me close to him—so close I could feel the pulse of his cock as it came to life. "I want you right here with me, Tiffany. I want to hold you each night. I want to kiss you each morning. I want you. I want all of you."

His hands moved underneath my T-shirt, then he lifted it off me. Rolling over, he put me on my back as he gazed at my body. And all I could do was watch him as he took me all in.

I think everything is going to be okay.

JASPER

Her green eyes glistened in the dim light as I moved my body over hers. Her lips parted, and she looked at me with love in her eyes. *But how could she have love for me if she'd done me so wrong?*

The way her hands moved through my hair left me breathless. Her body arched up to mine as I held her. I couldn't do it. I couldn't just have sex with her. No matter what my plan had been, I couldn't do that to myself.

"I've gotta go to the bathroom first." Rolling off her, I got up and went to the bathroom. My cock was too hard to actually take a piss. It strained against the soft fabric of my pajama bottoms—the only thing I had on.

Dropping them, I set it free then looked at the thing that wanted Tiffany so desperately. "Look, I can't."

It pointed straight up as if trying to look at me and tell me that it could if I'd just let it do what it wanted. Trying to ignore it, I went to the sink and brushed my teeth.

Maybe it was because she hadn't told me yet about Jasmine being mine. Perhaps that was why I couldn't say the three little words she'd spoken to me.

A knock came to the door. "Jasper, can I come in?"

Looking at myself in the mirror, I found a grim expression staring back at me. "Yeah."

Stepping inside the bathroom, she left the door open behind her. "I have something to tell you before we do anything. I've been having trouble finding the way to tell you what I've done."

My head began to swim. I had to sit down for this. "Let's get back in bed." Walking past her, I grabbed her hand and brought her with me.

We sat up in bed, looking at each other as my heart pounded. Tiffany licked her lips then said in a whisper, "When I left, I was pregnant with your baby, Jasper. My daughter, Jasmine, is yours."

A rush of adrenaline ran through me. Before I knew it, I'd caught her up in my arms, kissing her face all over. "Tiff, I love you. I love you so damn much."

Emotion took over, and I pushed her to lie back, then pushed her legs apart and thrust my hard cock into her hot pussy.

She whimpered as I went into her. "Oh! God, it's been so long, Jasper."

Pumping into her, I could barely breathe. "Oh, baby, you feel just like I remember." I knew she'd never been with anyone else. She was as tight as our very first time together. "Shit, Tiff, you're tight as fuck."

Pulling her knees up, she helped me slip in deeper. "Jasper, you're even bigger now."

I slammed into her. I couldn't help it. I had to own her again. I had to make sure she never even thought about any other man. I had to show her that she belonged to me. "You're mine. Do you hear me, Tiffany? You. Are. Mine."

Her nails dug into my flesh as she gripped my shoulders tightly. "I'm yours, Jasper. Yours again. Yours forever."

"You're damn right you are." Moving harder and faster, I reminded her of what only I could do for her. "And you're not going to get away from me again."

Her eyes wide, she looked a little shocked. "I'm so sorry, Jasper. I really am." Tears fell down her cheeks, and I leaned in to kiss them away. Then our lips met, and explosions went off inside my head.

I felt it all over again: the overwhelming love for her, the devotion to her, the unending need for her. *Why did you ever leave me?*

Rolling over, I put her on top of me, pushing her up to ride me. I watched as she pulled her hair back, her hands running through the red strands. Her body undulated on top of mine. I took her tits in my palms then pulled her down so I could take one into my mouth.

Larger than they'd been before, I was reminded of the secret pregnancy. It infuriated me, and I rolled back over, pinning her to the bed as I growled, "You *should've* told me about her. You *should've* let me know."

Her body trembled as her eyes searched mine. "Jasper, I'm sorry."

On the verge of having a meltdown, I pulled myself back out of the anger and hostility I'd had for her. I had to make her think I was truly in love. I had a plan; berating her for what she'd done would only send her running away with my little girl again.

"I know you are." I kissed her to redirect my mind. Her touch, like velvet on my skin, took me all the way back to when things were simple. Us, in the backseat of her car, hands all over each other, lips on lips, tongues entwined. Remembering how we were back then, the words slipped off my tongue, "I love you, Tiffany."

A low moan came out of her sweet lips. "Jasper, it feels like I've died and gone to heaven, hearing those words come out of your mouth again."

It felt surreal to me, too. How I wished it could've been as real as it felt at that moment. But I knew when the high wore off, I'd be left with the anger her lying to me had invoked.

For now though, my body wasn't letting my head get in its way. It had longed for this woman for so many years; it wasn't about to let my brain screw things up. There were so many things to do with her now.

Pulling out of her, I heard her intake her breath sharply as I ordered, "Knees, now."

Flipping over, she got on her hands and knees, wiggling her ass at me. "I've missed this."

Getting on my knees behind her, I held her by the waist then pushed my hard cock into her soft, soaked pussy. "I guess you're still not on any kind of birth control."

She huffed as I thrust hard. "No, I'm not on any. You're gonna have to pull out like you used to do."

"You're gonna need to get on the pill, baby." I no longer liked to pull out. Plus, I knew our needs could make the whole pulling-out thing not a thing we could do.

The way she moaned made my body heat up. "Jasper, you're so demanding. I love it."

Glad to hear she was into me dominating this relationship, I gave it to her harder. "You're gonna like doing as I tell you, Tiffany." I already had a laundry list of things I'd have her doing—starting with bringing our daughter to live with me. And for the time being, Tiff could live with me, too.

I'd never been one to dominate much. But with a woman like Tiff, who thought it was okay to run off with a man's baby, I had to step up my game. I had to let her know that it wasn't okay to do that to a person.

There was a price to pay for what she'd done. No one gets off scot-free after keeping a child away from her father for six years. No one.

Not even little, lovely Tiffany McKee.

Laying her upper body flat on the mattress, she moaned. "Just come inside me this one time, Jasper. I need to feel it again."

The hell with that.

"You do, baby?" I murmured as I ran my hand over her ass, still pumping away.

"I do," she whimpered. "Please."

"I can't come inside of your pussy, Tiff." I pushed my finger into her ass. "But here I can. You want that?" I wasn't about to fill her up with another baby that I would have to watch like a hawk so that she didn't run off with it.

After I threw her to the curb after getting my daughter safely with me, legally, the last thing I would need would be a pregnant Tiffany. So, if she wanted to feel the heat of my come, she'd take it in the ass or her mouth, but nowhere else.

"It's been so long since we've done that. I don't know." She looked back at me over her shoulder as she raised her upper body off the mattress. "You'll go in slowly, right?"

"As slow as you want, baby." Smiling at her, I winked. "If you want it, it's that way or down your throat. It's all up to you."

"Not inside me, though?" Her eyes slopped down a little. "Because of our daughter?"

I couldn't let her think that even for a moment. "No. Because when we have another baby, I want it planned out."

"Oh." She smiled, happy it wasn't some kind of a punishment, which it wasn't—it was just me being smart. "In the ass this time."

"You got it." Pulling out of her, I used her natural lube, sticking two fingers into her soaked pussy, then easing them into her asshole.

The moan she made as she once again laid the upper half of her body on the mattress made my cock jerk to get back inside of her. After getting her nice and slippery, I eased my already slick cock into her ass as she made a sexy noise that made it impossible not to smile as I watched my thick dick disappear into her ass. "Jasper, Goddamnit that feels good. All I've had is a dildo to keep me sane. And not once did I stick it in my ass. I forgot how good this feels."

Her words had a scene springing up in my mind of her using a dildo to pleasure herself. "So, what would you think about when you fucked yourself with that thing, baby?"

"You. Always you. Not once did I think about anyone else." She moaned as I moved in and out slowly. "Harder now, Jasper. I can take it harder now."

Smacking her ass, I moved faster, thrusting harder until she was screaming my name. Only then did I stick my fingers into her convulsing pussy to feel it clench around my fingers. With her body going crazy, mine followed along, gushing come into her ass as I finger-fucked her orgasming pussy while she moaned and shrieked with pure ecstasy.

I could always make that girl lose herself. I could always make her nothing more than a satisfied puddle of her former self. It was because she trusted me—trusted me so completely.

Spent and panting, I pulled my cock out of her ass, then fell onto the bed beside her. "You good now, baby?"

She gasped. "I am more than good." Reaching out, she ran her hand over my cheek. "You look like you're more than good, too. That was righteous."

"I agree." I rolled onto my back, then pulled her to lie on my chest. Our hearts beat wildly against the other. "So, here's how it's going to be. You're moving in. You're bringing our daughter, of course."

"Of course," she echoed me.

"And we're gonna fuck like this all we want." I kissed the top of her head and felt her body tense up.

"Well, as much as we can." She lifted her head up to look at me. "With a kid around, it ain't always easy to get alone time. You'll see what I mean."

I knew that. And I hoped the kid would get in our way of having alone time a lot. That would make it a hell of a lot easier to toss Tiffany out of my life when the time came to do that.

And that time will come.

TIFFANY

The sex over, I knew the time had come to be honest with Jasper about everything. Sitting up in his bed, I pulled the blanket up to cover my bare chest. "I want to get everything out in the open. I want you to understand why I did what I did."

He sat up too, leaning back against the oak headboard. "I'd love to understand everything, Tiff. Please, enlighten me."

I wanted to put a good spin on things, even though I knew that would be nearly impossible. Honesty was the best policy, so I went with that, but with a fair amount of tact. "It started when my parents told us that we were moving after graduation."

"And about how long did you know you were moving before you actually left?" he asked with a tight jaw.

Running my fingers along his jaw, I knew he had the right to be mad. "Please remember that I was just a girl back then, Jasper. I hadn't matured yet. The choices I made, the decisions I made, they weren't done with a fully functioning brain."

He took my hand, kissed my palm, then held it loosely on top of his leg. "I know you were young and dumb. We both were. Go on. Tell me how long you knew about the move."

"Three months." I watched his eyes move to look up at the ceiling as his hand went tight around mine.

"You didn't say a word in all that time, Tiff?" Drawing his gaze away from the ceiling, he looked into my eyes. "You never said a thing about it. You even talked about going to Lubbock to see about going to Texas Tech. Was that a lie?"

"You know I'd planned to take a year off after graduating from high school." I felt a little like I was on trial and tried not to let that bother me. "So, the answer is yes. I really was going to take a trip to Lubbock that summer to visit the college. I was going to take you with me to check it out. But then—well, we're getting ahead of my story here, Jasper."

"Then please go on." He let go of my hand to shove his through his thick mop of dark hair.

Crossing my arms over my chest, I could feel the tension beginning to creep up inside me. "I think that knowing we were leaving right after graduation had me making stupid decisions. Like the few times I'd begged you to come inside of me, instead of pulling out. I think that somewhere inside my brain, I wanted to get pregnant with your baby. You know, to always have a part of you with me."

"If you would've just told me, Tiff, we could've made things work." He let out a loud sigh. "How long did you know you were pregnant before you left town?"

This was the hardest part. To know I'd held something back from him for so long would be hard for him to take. "Okay, now please don't forget that I was a kid and scared to death back then."

He nodded. "Okay."

Gulping, I closed my eyes because I didn't want to see the look in his eyes when I said the words. "I knew for a month before I left."

The silence was deafening. And when I opened my eyes, I saw he'd covered his face with his hand as he massaged his temples. "And why did you find it impossible to tell me about the pregnancy, Tiffany?"

"You had no money, Jasper." I knew he couldn't have done a thing to make things any better if he would've known. "And I was moving pretty far away, too. How in the world would we have made that work?"

Moving his hand away from his face, he looked at me, and I saw the glistening of unshed tears in his blue eyes. "We would've made it work. I can't believe you didn't trust or believe in me that much, Tiffany."

The funny thing was, I *did* trust and believe in him—just not the way he would've wanted. "Jasper, I believed that you would work a minimum-wage job because that's all you could've done back then. I also believed that you would try to fit me into your parents' house. I knew you would want me to stay with you, not move with my family. I couldn't do that. I grew up with my own bedroom—my own personal space and privacy. I couldn't move into a tiny, two-bedroom house with your two brothers and mom and dad. And to bring a baby into that place, too? Well, I trusted you to make me do that."

"So, me being from a poor family is why you didn't tell me anything about us having a baby?" he asked, looking upset with me.

I sat there a minute, trying to think of how to put it, so he didn't lose his shit. "Well, your family didn't have much money. Your older brother, who'd graduated a couple of years before you, still lived at home and worked at the car lot, detailing cars. You had no aspirations of your own, other than going to work at some fast-food joint so you could get free meals and all the soda you could drink. So, you tell me if my reason for keeping the pregnancy to myself was over you being poor or not."

He nodded. "Sounds like it was exactly that, Tiffany."

And he wasn't wrong. "Well, I didn't know what else to do, Jasper. I had a baby to think about. I loved you, but I had to do what was best for the baby I carried. And I knew you would make it very difficult to do what I needed to do—which was making the move with my family. I had to keep a stable home for our child."

He nodded. "And I wouldn't have been welcomed in that home, huh?"

"Jasper, my father would never have let you live me with under his roof." He should've known better than to even say that.

"Yet, my parents would've let you move in with us." He looked at me. "Think about that for a second, Tiff. We had little to nothing, yet we'd have all gladly shared everything with you. Your family had lots, yet no place for me so I could be there for my child."

"Well, when you put it like that, it sounds bad." I felt he'd taken control of my story and put a negative spin on it. "Look, this is about our daughter and what I thought best for her and only her. She was safe, well taken care of, and had all she needed and more. I got the help with her that I needed so I could take online college classes and get my degree."

He laughed. "A degree that's helped you get a job working at your family's café. Kudos, Tiffany. Glad I had to miss out on six years of my kid's life so you could make it so far in this world."

I bit my lower lip as that sank in. "I said I was sorry, Jasper. Doesn't that mean anything to you?"

"It helps." His fist moved through the air. "But damn it, girl, this feels terrible. Don't you get that? If my parents had had money back then, I would've known about our baby. Is that right?"

"How should I know?" I threw my hands up in the air. "All I can tell you is that under the circumstances we were both under at that time, I felt going with my parents and leaving you out of things was the best thing to do for our child."

Getting out of bed, he walked into the bathroom, slamming the door behind him. I had no idea what I was supposed to do. Sitting there in his giant bed, I ran my hand over his pillow and wondered if this was a thing he could get over.

I have to help him get over it.

I got out of bed, wrapped the sheet around me, then went to knock on the bathroom door. "Can I come in?"

I heard the sound of water running, but nothing else. When I went in, I saw Jasper in the shower. His beard half gone, he glared at me. "Were you ever going to tell me about her?"

Standing there, I tried to give him an honest answer. The words stuck in my throat but then I finally got the one word to come out. "No."

Nodding, he looked into the mirror in the shower and cut the rest of his beard off. "So, that's it then. You wouldn't have ever told me about my own flesh and blood. That girl is closer to me than you will ever be, and you have deliberately kept us apart. You remind me of my grandfather, Tiffany. It's all about what others see on the outside. Let's keep the picture pretty, the riff-raff out, so the world only sees perfection."

"I never meant it to be like that. I never thought about you as riff-raff. Don't go putting words in my mouth, Jasper." Heat began to fill me. "You had nothing. My parents had more than enough. And there was a future with them. They were about to open their own café—a place that I could take over one day. So, yes, I got a degree in something that would help me take that over when they were ready to retire. Sue me, Jasper Gentry, for having the forethought at eighteen years old to do what was best for our baby, instead of doing what I wanted."

His face clean of any hair, he looked at me. "And what had you wanted back then, Tiffany?"

"I wanted you, Jasper. You're all I've ever wanted." I felt tears stinging the backs of my eyes. "Before I got pregnant, I had planned on asking you to move with me to Lubbock when I got ready to go to college. But that all changed."

"Having the baby *with me* wasn't a thing you ever wanted?" he asked. "Is that what you're telling me? Because that's what I hear. I hear that you wanted me and only me. And then you got pregnant, and you wanted that baby to yourself, leaving me out. You wanted a piece of me, but no longer wanted me—the poor boy from the wrong side of town. You'd gotten what you were after, that piece of me that you could hold, love, and receive love from. And then you left me cold and lonely, not knowing why you left or where you'd gone."

My head fell; it felt heavy. He was right. I hadn't ever thought about it that way, but he was right. "I am so sorry. You have no idea how sorry I am, Jasper. I was a kid myself. I really had no business making those decisions back then. But I did make them, and I didn't think at the time that they were selfish at all. As a matter of fact, I thought them to be selfless. I thought that staying with you would be the selfish thing to do. I thought that saddling you with a kid, when I'd been the one to ask for the reckless sex, was the wrong thing to do."

"Seems you were wrong about a lot of things, Tiffany." He turned off the water, then took a towel from the rack and hung it around his hips. "But that's the past. We've got a future now, don't we? Because now I don't stock groceries at the Piggly Wiggly at night. I've got more money than I know what to do with. We have a lot to work out."

Turning around, I ran into his bedroom, hurrying to put my clothes back on. I pulled on a boot just before he came out of the bathroom. "Don't worry about giving me a ride home. I'll walk."

"It's ten miles to town, Tiffany." He tossed the towel away, standing there naked. "Just calm down. We had to talk about that."

We'd never argued, and I hated it. So, I did what I thought best. I ran out of that bedroom, down the stairs and out the front door then all the way to the end of the drive before calling my mother to come and get me.

This was the biggest mistake I've ever made.

JASPER

Pulling on my jeans, I berated myself for all I'd said. "You idiot! You were supposed to keep your mouth shut. Now she knows how mad you are and she's gonna run."

I'd tried to pull it back at the end, but it was too damn late for that. I wasn't quite the mastermind at vengeance that I thought I could be. But then again, I hadn't counted on her wanting to tell me everything. And I hadn't counted on not being able to control my anger when she did.

Shoving my feet into my boots, I grabbed my hat, then went to get into my truck to go find the girl who'd run off like the wind. Knowing she couldn't have gotten far in the five minutes it had taken me to get dressed, I never imagined I wouldn't be able to find her.

As I drove down the drive, I found no sign of her anywhere. Knowing she had to have gotten a ride from someone, I went to the bar where her car was still parked. She *had* to talk to me; I wasn't going to give her any other choice.

But when I drove up to the bar, I saw her car was already gone. My nerves started to kick in. "She's gonna run again."

Bobbi Jo's car was parked in front, so I pulled in to see if she'd seen who'd picked up Tiffany's car. When I walked through the door at eleven in the morning, I was met with a frown. "Jasper, we ain't allowed to open until noon," Bobbi Jo told me.

"Yeah, I'm not here to drink." I pointed at the door. "Did you happen to see who picked up Tiffany's car?"

"She did. Her mom brought her." Sweeping up the remnants of last night's dirt, she asked, "I noticed that you took her home to the ranch last night. I was there with Cash last night and heard you two talking in your room when I walked past it to leave this morning. Is everything okay?"

"No." I leaned back against the bar. "I found out something pretty upsetting, and when we talked about it this morning, she got mad at me for being mad and ran off."

"From way out there?" She looked stunned. "I guess she called her momma, and that woman must've flown over there to pick her up. You just missed them by a minute, Jasper." Taking a seat at the bar, she patted the chair next to hers. "Sit down and tell me all about it. Being a bartender, I've heard some things and know how to handle a lot of problems."

I sat down, knowing she'd never heard a thing like what I had to say. But I needed some feminine advice, so I started talking. "Back in high school, Tiff and I were together the last two years of it. Then she left, and I had no idea where they'd gone or why she and her family had left without ever saying a thing to anyone."

"Oh, they came here, right?" she asked with a knowing smile.

"They did," I said. "See, Tiff was pregnant with my baby—not that I knew a thing about it. She made all the decisions on her own and left to have the baby she'd never planned on telling me about. And she made those decisions based on the fact that my family was poor."

Her eyes went wide. "Harsh."

"Yes." I'd heard the same words said about my grandfather. "She finally came clean with me this morning. Although I didn't ask her to tell me the whole story, she did anyway, and I got mad about most of it."

"Naturally," Bobbi Jo said with a nod. "And she got mad when you did. I can see that. She must've thought that what she'd done was best for the baby and didn't like being second-guessed."

"Yeah." I tapped my fingers on the bar. "And now I don't know what to do. I'm afraid she'll run off with our daughter again."

"Well, you can't let her do that." Getting up, she went behind the bar and looked underneath it, then came back up with a card in her hand. "Here's a lawyer you can talk to about your rights as a father. You can't let your little girl go on not knowing you. Your family is great. It would be a shame to leave her out of it."

"I agree." I took the card. "I wanted to work things out on our own, but I'm not sure Tiff will do that now." The fact was, I was glad to have the lawyer's number, but I didn't want anyone to know that I had other ideas about how to get revenge on Tiffany and her family. The sweeping blow would have them all feeling the same way I did.

"Don't get me wrong: I really like Tiffany and her family. They seem like reasonable people to me, Jasper." Bobbi went to get the dustpan. "So, try your best to leave the law out of things, if possible. Put the little girl in first place. Make her the most important thing."

"Of course." And it was because of her, and all she'd lost out on, that I would do what I had to do to pay Tiffany and her family back for hurting both my daughter and me.

"Even if you and Tiffany can't work things out, don't make that hurt your kid." She stopped just as she got in front of me, then looked me in the eyes. "Always, and I mean always, think long and hard about anything you do now, Jasper. My parents used my sister and me as weapons when they split up for a year when we were eight. It was by far the worst year of your lives. I still blame that horrible year for how Betty Sue turned out. She never learned how to trust anyone after what our parents put us through."

"I won't use Jasmine against Tiffany." That wasn't what I wanted to do. I just wanted Tiffany to know how it felt not to have what was yours. "I just thought we'd be making plans for me to meet Jasmine today. It's disappointing. Tiff and I have never fought or argued over anything before. I think she doesn't know how to have an argument."

"That might be the case." Bobbi Jo leaned over to brush the dirt into the dustpan. "Here's an idea that just came to me. You two should go to parenting classes. Tiffany has no idea how to share her kid, and you have no idea how to be a parent, so why not get some help with that? There's this woman who comes in on occasion— she's a therapist. You can find her downtown; she's got an office on Main Street. Her name is Sylvia Patterson. You should totally go by there and get something set up. After that, go see Tiffany and tell her what your plan of action is. I think that'll prove to her that you're not out to hurt anyone."

But I *was* out to hurt them. "You're right. I'll go see if that therapist can help us figure out how to become a family. I had no idea it would be so hard to do. It doesn't seem like most people find it this hard to make things right for their kid."

"You'd be surprised, Jasper." Looking at her watch, she raised her eyebrows. "It's almost noon. You should get over to her office before she closes for lunch. And you should think about sending Tiffany some flowers or something to make up for the fight."

"Yeah, I should do that. We're going to have to talk about things." I got up and headed toward the door, then stopped and looked back at Bobbi Jo. "Do you think I can ever forgive her for keeping me out of our daughter's life just because my family was poor?"

Shrugging, she said, "I don't know, Jasper. It depends on what Tiffany thinks now about all that. Did she say she was sorry?"

"Many times." I had to give the girl that. She had said she was sorry, and I saw the honesty in her eyes when she'd said it. "But what she did was pretty damn horrible, both for our daughter and me."

"And it's in the past," she pointed out. "You all have a future now. A future where you and your daughter will get to be whatever it is you will become. My advice is to not let the past dictate your future."

I laughed. "You know what, Bobbi Jo? You're one smart cookie."

"Thank you, Jasper." She patted her hand on the bar. "I credit this bar for my education."

"I'm glad my brother found you, girl." With a wave, I left her to tend to her business, then got back into my truck to go find that therapist. Maybe she could fix all that was wrong with Tiff and me.

But then again, I didn't see how anyone could fix all the wrong that had been done by Tiffany and her family. *How can it be made right or fixed when precious time has been lost?*

I didn't see how things could move forward with Tiff and me. Not when she'd kept my kid away for no reason other than I'd had very little money. Now the shoe was on the other foot. Tiffany and her family looked like paupers compared to what I now had. But it didn't make me think I was any better than them.

I was a better person, that was for sure. I wouldn't have ever kept a kid away from someone based on their financial status. Hell, that girl didn't even give me a chance to change that about myself.

I was almost certain that I would've stepped up to the plate, gotten a higher-paying job, and found us a place to live on our own. I wouldn't have pulled Tiffany into a bedroom that I'd shared with my two brothers. I knew I would've made things work for us.

We'd been happy back then, never fought over anything, and never discussed much either. Maybe that was the problem with Tiff and me. We'd never learned how to disagree in a healthy way. We'd never done anything that either of us had ever had to apologize for.

Now Tiffany had done something she had to apologize for, and I supposed she just had no idea how to do that without getting upset —especially when I couldn't accept that apology so readily and move on as if nothing terrible had ever happened.

Well, it's time she learned how to accept the fact that every action has a reaction.

TIFFANY

"You didn't see him, Mom. I've never seen him so mad." I'd never seen Jasper mad at all. "He even cut off his beard. It makes me think he's devising a plan."

"A plan to do what?" Mom asked as she got out of the car, and we headed inside the café.

"A plan to take Jasmine away from me." I shuddered as a chill ran through me with the thought.

Mom grimaced. "Don't even talk like that, Tiffany. Can't you make him see that you made a mistake and that you're very sorry? Let him know that you won't keep Jasmine away from him. You can share her."

"It's just that I don't know why he shaved his beard off. Is he trying to look like a respectable man or something?" As we got into the café, the other workers were busy doing not only their jobs but those of mine and my mother's, too.

Since the lunch hour fast approached, I shut my mouth, shut off my brain, and got to work. I paid no attention to anything other than my work until my father came into the café with a grim look on his face.

He gave my mother a come-here-wiggle of his finger, and she

456

dropped what she'd been doing to follow him to the back office. As they walked away, I watched them and noticed how they never said a single word to each other. And then it crept into my head that I'd never heard my parents argue about anything in my entire life. Every time something came up where either of them took the opposite side, they left the room and when they came back, a decision had been made. How it had been made, I didn't know nor care. They'd taken care of things in their own way, and life went smoothly for us.

The only thing about that was that I'd never learned how to have a disagreement. There were times when Jasper and I were dating that I didn't particularly want to go where he wanted to go. Instead of speaking up about it, I went along with whatever he wanted without making a fuss.

Peeling a potato to make a batch of homemade waffle fries, I thought about why I didn't tell Jasper about the move we'd be making once I'd graduated. And I knew, instinctively, that I'd worried it would cause us to fight. And I didn't want to fight about it, mainly because I didn't know how to go about it.

As the oldest of three siblings, I'd taken on the role early on as the big sister. One didn't have spats with the big sister, at least that was what Mom would say to Bo and Carolina any time they tried to go against what I'd said.

When I saw my mother coming out of the office and back up front to work, I turned to the new girl. "Sierra, can you peel the rest of these for me?"

"Sure thing, Miss Tiffany." She took the paring knife I'd laid down and got right to work.

I went to help my mother clean off tables. "Hey, Mom, what was that about with Dad?"

"Oh, he didn't like the look of our electric bill at home. Says it's too high and I need to stop turning the heater up so high." She wiped off the table, her face pinched. "I get cold easily these days; that's why it's been higher lately. But I agreed with him that I could put on a sweater or two and try to keep warm that way." She looked at her hands with a frown. "The thing about that is, my hands get cold, too, and they ache. But I guess I can put on gloves. My feet get cold and hurt, too. But I suppose I can put boots and two pairs of socks on."

"What temperature does Dad want the thermostat kept on?" I asked as that sounded like a lot to do just to stay warm inside one's own home.

Her lips pressed into a thin line and the wrinkles in her forehead told me she felt aggravated. "Sixty."

"Sixty degrees?" That was way too cold for an indoor temperature—especially in winter. "He's crazy, Mom. You've got to get him to meet you in the middle. What have you been keeping it on to stay warm?"

She looked away as another group left a table that had to be bused. "He's right. I have it too high. I'll just do what he wants. I don't want to make a fuss about it."

Turning to go to the other table, she tried to walk away, but I reached out and grabbed her arm. "Mom, what temperature have you been keeping the thermostat on to keep warm?"

"Seventy." She pulled away from me and went to the other table.

Going to talk to Dad, I found it hard to believe that my mother would go to such extremes to avoid an argument. And it made me upset with myself that I would do the same if I didn't learn how to speak up without worrying about getting into a disagreement.

Pushing open his office door, I walked in and stood there as he sat at his desk looking at me. "Hi, honey. What's up?"

"Mom's cold is what's up, Dad." I closed the door, then took a seat on the chair on the other side of his desk. "Dad, sixty degrees is just too cold for anyone to have to live with. Mom said her hands and feet hurt when she gets cold. Did she tell you that?"

He shook his head. "No. We don't really talk to each other that way. In our marriage, I make the decisions, and she follows them. It's just easier that way. We've managed to avoid a lot of conflict in our long marriage. I'm proud of how we handle our affairs, Tiffany. It's not many couples who can say that they've never had an argument."

"But you have had different opinions, haven't you?" I asked as I crossed my arms over my chest, feeling a lot of aggravation that my father thought it just peachy that everything always went his way and my mother just shut up and caved.

"Well, everyone has different opinions, honey," he said with a smile. "Your mother and I made the decision before we ever got married to let me take control of things. See, we went to a preacher who gave us marriage counseling for a whole year before we got married. That has saved us so much heartache and pain throughout these years. His advice was just such a wonderful gift for us."

"Dad, did you hear me when I told you that when Mom's hands and feet are cold, they hurt?" Maybe he hadn't heard me say that.

He nodded. "Yes, I did. But she can put on more clothes to fix that, can't she? Do you know what our electric bill was this month, honey?"

"No." I found that to be not as important as my mother experiencing pain when she got cold.

"It was a little over a hundred dollars. Normally, it's below that. I don't want it to get out of hand." He pushed the bill over to me to look at. "See what I'm talking about?"

"Dad, growing up in your house, it was hot as Hades in the summer and cold as sin in the winter," I pointed out. "When I moved into my own place, I put the thermostat on a comfortable setting. Guess what?"

"You have an outrageous electric bill," he said as he nodded.

"If you call a hundred and fifteen dollars on average outrageous, which I don't, then I suppose you're right." I pushed the bill back to him. "Let Mom keep the temperature the way it is. It's not right to have to bundle up like you're outside in a blizzard over a few dollars, Dad."

Cocking his head to one side, he looked at me in a way he'd never done before. "Tiffany, what's up with you, honey? You've never questioned anything we've ever done before."

"You're right. I've gone with the flow, kept quiet, let you make the decisions for me." I didn't want to blame my father for what I'd done to Jasper, but he did have a part in it. "Dad, when I told Mom about being pregnant, she went to you. And it's only now that it's coming to my attention that she had no part in the decision not to tell Jasper about the baby. *You* made that decision. She went along with it, which now I see she's always done with every decision you've ever made. And I trusted you guys to know what was best for my baby."

"And we were right, too." He smiled at me as if he didn't see what I was saying. "Jasmine is a healthy, happy, well-adjusted little girl."

"Who doesn't know her father." I looked at him with as much love in my eyes as I possibly could. I didn't hate my father. He only did what he'd been taught by a man he'd trusted after all. "I shudder to think if I would've never known you, Dad. I love you so much. And I love Mom, too. Or I wouldn't be in here, fighting for her to get to keep warm in her own home. Because I've never fought for anything in my life."

"Because you're a good girl, Tiffany." He got up and came around to pat me on the back. "Just like your daughter. You both have learned that it's best not to argue over things when there's someone who can make the decisions that work the best for all of us."

I'd never thought that I would see my daughter's behavior as the best little kid I'd ever seen as a bad thing. "I love you, Dad. I don't agree with you, but I do love you. And I owe it to my daughter to teach her how to make her own decisions and to speak up when she feels she needs to. I should've spoken up back then. I should've told Jasper about the baby. I should've told him about our moving. And I'd made myself believe that it was because of his family's poor financial status that I'd made those decisions. But the truth is, I made those decisions because you and Mom had come up with them. I just followed along like the dutiful daughter I'd always been."

Dad seemed to be at a loss for words as I got up and left his office. When I went out, I found an enormous vase with what looked like three dozen pink roses in it, sitting on the edge of the counter. "Who's the lucky girl?"

Mom jerked her head at the flowers. "Read the card."

Taking it out of the tiny envelope, I read it out loud, "To Tiffany, the mother of my child. You should've gotten these from me

460

the day our daughter entered this world. I loved you then, and I still love you now. Here's to our family. Love, Jasper."

Tears clouded my vision, and I had to wipe my eyes with the back of my hand as everyone in the café clapped and cheered. Then I heard the sound of the bell ringing as someone came in.

I knew his hands the moment he touched me, pulling me into his arms. Jasper's lips pressed against the side of my head. "Tiffany, I'm sorry for the things I said. I love you, and I want us to make this work. I swear to you that I will do everything I can to be what you and Jasmine deserve. If you'll give me the chance."

The floodgates opened as everyone cheered, and I held onto Jasper for dear life. I'd never been so overwhelmed.

JASPER

It wasn't easy, holding Tiffany in my arms, hearing the sounds of people wishing us luck on making a family together. Not when I knew it was all an act to get her where I wanted her.

Her tears had soaked my shirt; I saw when she finally pulled her face off my chest and nodded. "I'd love to have you in our lives, Jasper."

To my surprise, her mother came up and put her arms around us both. "I'm so happy for you two and my granddaughter, too."

I saw her father coming our way, his hand extended. "I'm glad to see this happening too. You've come a long way, Jasper."

Yeah, how's that?

I'd come a long way only because a grandfather I'd never known had died. I shook his hand. "I'm trying."

Tiffany's red-rimmed eyes made my now-jaded heart thump with compassion for her as she whispered, "I'm sorry about everything, Jasper. We should talk."

For the tiniest moment, I felt like things might be okay. But then I looked at how her parents were looking at us—like they'd never been happier that we were together—and I found that anger inside of me again. "Can you leave now?"

Her mother quickly answered, "Yes, we can deal with this place without her."

With Tiffany under my arm, we left and got into my truck. Putting on her seatbelt, she looked at me when I got into the driver's seat. "You know what I've figured out?"

Pulling out of the parking lot, I asked, "What?"

"That I don't know how to have a disagreement." She pulled down the visor to open the mirror. "Oh God. I look terrible." She began wiping away the lines left on her cheeks from the tears.

"You and I had never disagreed before." That was true. "I've made us an appointment to meet with a therapist. She specializes in family situations. We're going to go see her this afternoon to help us do what's best for our daughter."

She nodded. "Okay."

Interested to know if she was really okay with that or just agreeing with me, so we didn't have another argument, I asked, "Tiffany, do you really agree with that, or do you have other ideas we should consider?"

With a heavy sigh, she admitted, "I don't know."

I'd never considered Tiffany McKee weak in any way. But as I looked at her slumped shoulders, her trembling lips, and the way her eyes would cloud with tears then clear back up, I knew she wasn't anywhere near as strong as I'd always thought she was.

"Well then, for now, we'll see the therapist," I said as I headed to her apartment. "We can wait for our two-o'clock appointment with her at your place." I thought I should try harder to include her in decisions. "If that's okay with you."

She nodded. "Yeah, it's fine with me." Her eyes moved to look out the window. "I'm realizing a lot about myself, and I'm not real proud of the things I've done—especially to you and Jasmine."

My heart leapt. My mind raced to a place where she and I could resolve our past and move on, become a happy family. But I couldn't let myself believe that yet. And I couldn't sell myself short either. I deserved some type of revenge after all.

Pulling up in front of her apartment, we got out and headed inside. A large picture on the living room wall drew my attention right away. I pointed at it. "That's her."

Tiffany nodded. "Yeah, that's Jasmine. It's her school portrait this year. She's getting so big."

And I've missed everything.

In a flash, my blood boiled. Taking a deep breath, I tried not to let Tiffany see my reaction. "She looks like me."

Coming up behind me, she wrapped her arms around my waist and looked at the picture with me. "She does. She's got my freckles across her nose, poor kid. Other than that, she looks just like you."

I couldn't help it; I'd always hated when she said anything negative about her adorable freckles. Pulling her around, I hugged her. "Your freckles make you stand out in a great way, baby. Don't knock the freckles. And I can see more of you in our daughter than just those. She's got your rosebud lips, too."

Tiffany gulped. "And she's got my sunny disposition, too. A thing I hope to change."

Laughing, I had no idea why anyone would want to change that in their child. "Looks like we're having our first parenting disagreement. Why on earth would you want to change that about her?"

I moved to take a seat on the sofa, pulling her onto my lap. She ran her hands over my now bare cheeks.

"Why'd you shave your beard, Jasper?"

"I was upset and just did it." I really didn't know why I'd done it. Maybe because I felt like I was going out of my mind. "This isn't easy for me to come to terms with. You should know that, Tiffany."

Nodding, she looked into my eyes. "I'd like to change Jasmine's sunny disposition, because it's not as mentally healthy as I've always thought it was. See, I don't want to blame my father completely for what I did to you, but the fact is, I've deferred to my father the same way my mother always has. It seems I've been taught to do that. I've taught Jasmine to do that, too."

"So, if he hadn't told you that leaving me out of the baby's life was what was best for her, then you might've told me about the pregnancy?" I had to know if this wasn't her fault.

Chewing her lower lip, she finally said, "Not entirely, but I did follow his guidance on all things. It's my fault for not using my own brain to make the choices that were mine alone to make." She looked at me then shook her head. "No, I don't mean that. The choices belonged to both of us, not just me."

At least she was coming to terms with that. What more could I ask for? "And how about now, Tiff? What do you think we should do now?" I'd told her what I wanted—for her and Jasmine to move in with me. But I hadn't heard what she thought best.

Leaning her head on my shoulder, she whispered, "I've kept you and Jasmine apart for such a long time. It wouldn't be right to do it any longer. If you still want us to move in, then we will. I can introduce her to you when she gets out of school and then you can take us out to the ranch. I think she'll be thrilled."

Tiffany's agreeable behavior had my anger subsiding. I wasn't sure how good of a thing that was. "Are you sure that's what you really want?"

Her body tensed, and she pulled her head up to look at me. "Are you sure that's what *you* want? I don't want you to feel forced to take us to your home, Jasper. That is one thing I never wanted—for you to feel forced into anything. If you don't want to meet her yet, then don't. That's up to you."

"No," I said quickly. "I want to meet her. I want her in my home. I want my brothers to meet her, too." It hit me that I hadn't told either of my brothers about my daughter. "You know what? I need to call them and tell them this news before I go bringing her home and shocking the devil out of them."

Tiff hopped off my lap then headed to the hallway. "I've gotta take a shower and change before we go see this therapist anyway. Make your calls, Jasper, and make yourself at home. There's stuff in the fridge if you're hungry or thirsty."

As she went to get herself cleaned up, I wandered around the small apartment, looking at the pictures on the wall of Jasmine through the years. My heart ached even more with each one I looked at.

Pulling out my cell, I called Tyrell. "Where the hell are you?" he said in greeting.

"I'm at Tiffany's place." I ran my finger over the baby face behind the glass—Jasmine's newborn picture of her in a clear bassinet in the nursery of the hospital she'd been born in. "I've got some news, Tyrell. You're an uncle."

"I'm a what?" He sounded winded by the news.

"You have a six-year-old niece named Jasmine. You'll meet her when I bring her and Tiffany home this evening." I looked at the next picture, finding Jasmine sticking her hand in a cake that had a number one candle on top of it.

Another thing missed I can never get back.

I heard the sound of boots clicking over the tiled floor of our home on the other end of the line, then Cash's voice came next. "Tyrell, you ain't never gonna believe this. Tiffany's kid is Jasper's. I just talked to Bobbi Jo, and she told me he came by the bar and told her that earlier today. Can you believe it? We're uncles."

Tyrell laughed. "Jasper beat you to the punch, little brother. He's on the phone right now."

Cash shouted, "Congratulations, Papa!"

Tyrell echoed, "Yeah, congratulations, Jasper. I can't wait to meet her. I can't wait for Mom and Dad to meet her. They're going to be tickled to death. You better call them right now and let them know that they're grandparents."

"Yeah, I'll do that. Thanks, you guys. It means a lot to have your support about this." I meant it, too. Without them, I might've already done something crazy.

At least I was making slow decisions about how I would make the McKees pay for what they'd done. If I didn't have my brothers to worry about contending with, I might've up and taken my daughter and ran off with her myself. At least this way, things would be all legal. I'd get custody of her the right way.

The next call I made was to my mother. "Hello?"

"Mom, it's Jasper. How are you doing today?" I found it kind of hard to tell her my big news.

"I'm fine. How are you, son?" she asked, and I could hear the smile she wore.

"Well, I am great, actually." I gathered my courage then blurted it out. "Mom, you're a grandmother."

"Am not," came her quick response.

"You are." I laughed. "Tiffany McKee had my baby after they

left town. I've got a six-year-old daughter named Jasmine. I'm bringing her and Tiffany to live with me on the ranch. I haven't even met my little girl yet, Mom. Is it weird that I'm nervous?"

"Um … are you joking with me, Jasper?" Mom asked.

"Nope. I'll be bringing her to meet you and Dad very soon." I hoped that Jasmine would want to meet them. "As soon as she's ready to meet you guys, I'll bring her. Me and Tiff are about to go to see a therapist to do things right by our daughter. Don't worry about us; we'll be what she needs us to be."

"I'm speechless, son." Mom got quiet again.

"Mom, it's going to be okay." I felt like she must have been freaking out. "Tiff's a great mother, and I'm sure she'll help me be the best father I can be."

Slender arms slid around me as Tiffany had come up behind me. "You will be the best father in the world, Jasper. I know you will."

How can you love and hate someone at the very same time?

TIFFANY

"Children are resilient," the therapist said to us as we sat on the sofa in her office, side by side. "I'm sure if you tell her slowly, she'll understand things. And give her time to let each word soak in. It'll be a bit confusing for her at first. But it is what's best for the child."

I agreed. "I think so, too."

Jasper held my hand and gave it a gentle squeeze. "Okay, so now we know how to tell her. Is school almost over?"

Nodding, I found him getting up and pulling me up with him. I looked at the therapist. "Should we pick her up together? Or should he wait at my place? I don't know what's best here."

She got up, walking us to the door. "In my opinion, it would be best to tell her at home where she feels safe."

"Then that's what we'll do," Jasper said. "We'll see you next week at the same time. Thanks, doc."

"Once again, I'm not a doctor, Mr. Gentry. I'm a licensed therapist," she said. "Good luck to you both and to your little girl, too. Having parents who love each other is a great thing for a kid to have."

I held onto his arm, looking up at him with so much adoration, it seemed impossible. "Thank you, Jasper. Thank you for trying so hard and doing your best to go about this the right way. I love you even more than I did before."

He stopped and looked at me, his blue eyes searching mine. "Why is that?"

"Why do I love you even more?" I had to ask.

He nodded. "Yeah."

"I guess because you're becoming the father I'd always wished you would." It was kind of hard to put into words. "You're taking steps that I consider to be very smart. I hadn't ever thought of going to see a therapist to make things right for Jasmine. You've got some natural fatherly instincts. It's not only admirable, it's sexy. Along with loving you more, I've never been more turned on."

His lips curved into a sexy grin. "My little hot stuff. You're a vixen." He lifted me up into the seat of his truck, then closed the door.

My body was on fire, and I had to cool it down. I didn't have time for a nooner. By the time we got back to the café where I'd left my car, I would have to go to the school to pick Jasmine up.

Jasper got into the truck then looked at me as he started it up. "I hope she likes me. Do you think she'll like me?" He ran his hand over his clean-shaven face. "Now I'm glad I shaved the beard. It might've scared her. I don't want to scare her. I want her to love me. I want to love her."

I'd never heard this man sound as nervous as he did now. Reaching out, I took his hand before he drove off. "She'll love you. What's not to love? Everything is going to be fine. You'll see."

Nodding, he took off and before I knew it, we were at the Dairy King. He held out his hand. "Give me your house key, and I'll go wait for y'all."

I dug in my purse to get it out. "You know, maybe you ought to stop by the store and grab yourself a beer. You're as nervous as a cat in a room full of rocking chairs."

"Nah, I'll be okay. I'll just take a lot of deep breaths and walk it out when I get to your place." He winked at me. "I want to remember every little thing about the first time I see her. I want it to set in my brain and never go away."

469

"That's sweet." I leaned over and kissed him as I put the house key in his palm. "I'll see you soon, babe."

"Yeah, I'll be there." He huffed, and I could tell he was freaking out in a way he'd never had before.

It pained me to leave him alone, but it had to be done. When I got to the school, I had some nerves of my own as my daughter got into the car.

"Hi, Momma. I drew this picture today. It's of our apartment. We had to draw our houses and our family standing in front of it."

She handed me the picture she'd drawn, with only her and I in front of our small apartment. "You know what would look great in this picture, Jasmine?"

"Yeah I do," she said with a smile as I belted her into her booster seat. "A puppy."

I laughed. After I closed the door, I pulled away from the curb. "I meant a daddy, Jasmine. Wouldn't a daddy look great in that picture?"

"Why would you say that?" I saw her drooping eyes as I looked at her through the rearview mirror. "You know I don't have a daddy."

"Everyone has a daddy, Jasmine. Even you." I felt pretty bad for not ever telling her about her father. "I've kept things to myself about your father, because I thought you were too young to talk about him. But you're six now. I think that's plenty old enough to talk about your father. Would you like to know his name?"

Her lower lip jutted out, and I thought she might be about to cry. But then she smiled. "Yeah, what's his name?"

"Jasper Gentry." I waited to let that sink in, the way the therapist had said to.

"Jasper Gentry." She twirled a lock of her dark hair. "Can that be my last name now? Cause every kid in my class has their dad's last name, and I would like to have mine, too."

"I think that can be arranged." I liked the positive reaction she'd given me. "What do you think about meeting him?"

Her eyes became huge. "Could I really meet him? Like, in real life? And when? And where? And can I hug him when I see him?

And can I kiss him on the cheek? And can he hold my hand? And can I sit on his lap? And—"

I had to stop her. "Yes, you can do all those things. He wants to meet you, too."

"What?" she shrieked as she put her hands on her now-red cheeks. "He does? He wants to meet me?"

I nodded as I turned down the street to our apartment. My cheeks ached from smiling so hard. "He *does* want to meet you. And he's at our apartment right now."

"No!" she screamed. "Mom, are you serious? Are you being serious right now? I can't believe it."

I pulled up in front of the house, right next to Jasper's tall, black truck, then got out to get her out. Picking her up, I pointed at the truck. "That's your daddy's truck, Jasmine. Your daddy has a ranch with cow, horses, and I think I heard some dogs barking around there, too, when I was there last night."

"That's where you went?" she asked with shock. "You went to see my daddy, and you didn't take me with you? Are you crazy, woman?"

Laughing, I carried her inside. "Yeah, a little. You ready to meet him?"

"Put me down. I don't want you to carry me inside like I'm a baby, Momma." I put her feet on the ground outside the front door. She ran her hands over her dress to smooth it out, then through her hair. "How do I look?"

"Adorable, as usual," I said.

"K," she said. "I'm ready. Open the door, please."

My hand shook as I took the knob in my hand. My heart pounded, and I broke out in a sweat, I was so nervous.

"Here we are, Daddy."

I pushed the door open and found Jasper standing there with wide eyes.

They both froze in place as they looked at each other. I felt like I would pass out as I looked back and forth between them, taking in their odd expressions. "Jasper Michael Gentry, this is your daughter, Jasmine Michelle."

Slowly, his arms opened wide. "It's nice to meet you, Jasmine. Would it be too much to ask you for a hug?"

She shook her head, then moved slowly toward him. "You've got my eyes."

He smiled. "You've got my hair."

I held back the sobs that filled my chest, my hand over my mouth to keep them in, as I watched the two people I loved most in this world fall into each other's arms.

The way Jasper's eyes closed when he wrapped his arms around his daughter for the first time told me how much he already loved his little girl. My heart ached for the time I'd stolen from them both. "This makes me so happy."

"This makes me so happy, too," Jasper agreed.

Jasmine's tear-filled voice added, "I'm so happy, too, but I'm crying and don't know why."

Jasper and I laughed as I wiped tears away. He had to wipe some away from his eyes, too. "Seems like we're all a bunch of crybabies." He sat down, putting Jasmine on his lap. She pulled her head back, and he wiped her eyes. "It's very nice to know you now, Jasmine. Things are about to change but only for the better. I would love it if you and your mommy would come live with me on my ranch."

I thought he'd said that a bit too early and took a seat as my legs grew shaky. Waiting for Jasmine's response, I bit one of my fingernails. I'd never been so nervous. It was like she held the whole future in her tiny hands.

"Do you have puppies on your ranch?" She sniffled as she looked at him.

He nodded. "And kittens, too. And you've got a couple of uncles there, too, who are dying to meet you."

"I've also got an Uncle Bo," she told him. "He's in the Marines. What are my other uncles' names?"

"You've got an Uncle Tyrell," Jasper told her. "He's my older brother. And you've got an Uncle Cash. He's my younger brother. And you've got our mother and father; they're your grandparents. I don't know what they want to be called because you're their first grandchild."

"I am?" Jasmine looked thrilled as she looked at me. "Just like with your family, Momma. And now I've got two sets of grandparents, just like everyone else does." Her eyes went back to Jasper. "And now I've got a daddy like everyone else does, too. Can I have your last name, Daddy?"

The way Jasper's Adam's apple bobbed in his throat told me he was just about to lose it. He nodded. "Nothing would make me happier, baby girl. You got it." He looked at me for a long time, tears shimmering in his eyes.

I couldn't tell what was behind those eyes. So many things seemed to pass through them—so many emotions—some I was sure he'd never had before. He pulled Jasmine in to hug her again, rocking from side to side with her.

"I can't wait to become Jasmine Gentry." She pulled back and looked at him with a questioning gaze. "I would love for me and Momma to go live with you at your ranch. Is it okay if I call you Daddy? I guess I should've asked you that first."

Pulling her back to his chest, he laughed. "Yes. Of course it's okay, Jasmine. I wouldn't have it any other way." Then he looked at me with much clearer eyes and mouthed, "Thank you for this."

That was when the sobs hit me. I had to run out of the room to break down.

JASPER

The pain in Tiffany's green eyes wasn't lost on me. My heart ached and my mind raced with what I could do to make it better for her. But something else hung strong inside of me. She'd brought this on herself.

Jasmine and I connected almost as if we'd never been apart. Her chatter in the backseat of my truck seemed familiar for reasons that I didn't know or care to understand. I just felt like she'd always been there. "Do you think you can teach me how to ride a horse, Daddy?"

"I sure can." I smiled at her through the rearview mirror. "Anything you want, you got it, Jazzy."

The smile that lit her face up had me smiling, too. "Jazzy? I like that nickname, Daddy."

Tiffany's hand on mine drew my attention. "Jasper, maybe we should just visit for the evening, then go back to our apartment afterward. I'm a little worried about how Jasmine will take sleeping in a strange place."

Already she was trying to pull away. But I didn't want Jasmine to feel upset. "If she wants to go back to your apartment, then we'll deal with that."

"Right now, all I want is to see this big house you were talking about," Jasmine said.

I turned into the gated entrance with the words WHISPER RANCH at the top of the metal gates. "Well, you're about to see it. We're here. Welcome to Whisper Ranch, Jazzy. Your new home. One day, this ranch will belong to you and whatever cousins and siblings come along."

"No way!" Jasmine gasped as we drove through the gates I'd opened with the remote. "Wow, look at that! The gates opened all on their own. Like the doors at the grocery store that know when someone is walking up to them."

I pointed to the little button by the rearview mirror. "I pushed this to open the gates."

"Cool." Jasmine's eyes were glued to the window as I drove down the long driveway. Cattle grazed alongside the left and horses did the same on the right. "Horses and cows?" She looked at me. "Wow."

"Yes, it's pretty impressive." I couldn't wipe the smile off my lips. I couldn't have ever offered as much if I hadn't inherited the place and the money my grandfather had left me.

That fact sat there, deep in my mind. If I'd been doing what I was doing before inheriting what I had, and Tiffany had come to me with this news, then how would Jasmine and I be taking things?

If I were taking her to my parent's tiny home, probably in a car I would've had to borrow from my father or a friend, would she still be wearing such a huge smile? If I'd had to leave her to work the night shift at the grocery store the same night I'd brought her home, would she still be so happy about me being her father?

Shaking my head, I tried to rid my mind of the troubling thoughts. Those things didn't matter anymore. I had things now, things I could give her to make her life more than what it was before I came along.

Pulling up to the front entrance, I found Jasmine looking at our home with wide eyes. She shook her head. "I can't believe it."

Tiffany squeezed my hand. "I hope this isn't too overwhelming for her, Jasper."

"She'll be fine." I knew she would be a hell of a lot happier here than any other place in the world. I would make sure of that.

Tiffany and I got out of the truck. She helped Jasmine out of her booster seat, then picked her up to get her out of the tall truck. "Daddy, I like your truck. It's cool and really high."

"There's a bunch of cars and trucks in the garage." I winked at Tiffany. "You can take your pick of what you feel is a more family-friendly automobile for us. I can already see that this truck is going to make getting in and out of it hard for our little girl."

Tiff nodded. "That would be nice." I could see how nervous she was as she looked at the huge mansion. "So, Jas, what do you think so far?"

Jasmine looked at me as her mother put her down. She came right to me, taking my hand. "I think I'm dreaming. I've got a daddy and a place to live that looks like some fancy hotel or something." Jasmine looked at her mother, holding out her other hand. "Momma, come hold my other hand. I want to hold both your hands. I'm a little nervous about meeting everyone."

"No reason to be nervous, Jazzy. Everyone is very nice here." I felt a tinge of something I'd never felt before—pride, maybe. As I looked at Tiffany and our daughter, we felt like a real family for the first time as we all walked toward the entrance of the house. "I think you both will see that this place can feel like home if you just make yourself at ease here."

Opening the door, I gave Jasmine a moment to take in the grandeur of the foyer. "Oh, wow!" She looked at the split staircase. "What's up those?"

I pointed to the set to the right. "These lead to the bedrooms. I'll take you up there, and you can pick one out. But first, I want to introduce you to everyone. It's dinner time, and they'll be in the dining room. One of five that we have."

"It's like the best hotel ever," Jasmine whispered.

Tiffany nodded. "It is. And you have to be very careful not to break anything."

I didn't want Jasmine to feel like she couldn't have fun. "I don't want you to worry about things like that, Jazzy. Just be yourself, have fun." I looked at Tiffany. "I want you to make this your home, Tiff. You can't do that if you're afraid you might break something."

She nodded. "You're right. This place just feels so—I don't know."

But I did know. "Expensive."

"Yeah," Tiff said as we went from one room to another.

Jasmine noticed how the lights came on automatically when we came into each room. "Is this house magic?"

I laughed as I shook my head. "It's just really modern and energy efficient. From what I've been told, my grandfather had renovations done about five years ago. He had everything updated."

"Where is he?" Jasmine asked. "Am I going to meet him, too?"

"No." I shook my head. "He's passed away. That's why my brothers and I have this ranch now. We never even met our grandfather. But that's a story for another time." I pushed open the dining room door. "Because now it's time to meet everyone."

Her tiny hand gripped mine tightly as she saw everyone seated at the large table. "I'm scared."

Tyrell got up, and the rest followed him. "Hey, there, Jasmine. I'm your Uncle Tyrell. Aren't you just about the prettiest little girl I've ever seen in my life?" He held out his arms. "You got a hug for me?"

Her small chest heaved as she let our hands go, then walked slowly up to Tyrell, looking up at him. "I guess so."

With a laugh, he picked her, hugging her. "Welcome to the family, Jasmine."

Before he could put her down, Cash came up beside them. "And I'm your Uncle Cash. Soon to be known as your favorite uncle, Jasmine. You got a hug for me?"

Jasmine smiled and nodded. "Okay."

He took her from Tyrell, giving her a hug. "I'm so glad that you're here. You're gonna love being a Gentry."

"I know," Jasmine gushed as she looked at the others in the room. "And who are you?"

Ella smiled and waved. "I'm Ella. I work here. And I'm dating your Uncle Tyrell."

Bobbi Jo had come to meet her, too. "And I'm your Uncle Cash's girlfriend; my name's Bobbi Jo."

Jasmine's blue eyes shined as she looked at my brothers, then me. "Hey, we all have the same eyes and hair." Her giggle made my heart melt. "I look like my family. Finally."

Tiffany sighed as she leaned into my side, slipping her arm around my back. "She's never looked like any of my family."

For a moment, some pretty scathing words bubbled up in my throat as I thought about how awful it must've felt for my daughter to feel like an oddball in her own family. But I managed to swallow them up. "Yeah, well, now she's got us." And she would never lose us.

Cash took Jasmine, placing her in a chair on one side of the one at the head of the table. "Jasper, why don't you sit at the head since you're the man of your family now?"

I pulled the chair out opposite of the one Jasmine was seated in. "Tiff, take a seat."

She sat down, then I took my seat at the head of the table. Tyrell smiled at me as he sat down next to Ella. "Fatherhood looks good on you, brother."

The way Tiffany ducked her head, then ran her hand over her cheek told me she'd shed a tear. I took her hand in mine, then pulled it up to kiss it. "And I've got this girl here to thank for that."

After dinner, I took Tiff and Jasmine on a tour of the house, then let her pick out a bedroom. As she pushed open the door across the hall from my bedroom, she put her hand on her hip as she walked inside. "And your room is over there, right?"

"Yep. Right across the hallway." I went to take a seat on the bed. "It's nice and comfy. And it's got a nice view of the front of the property, too, out those windows. We can have it done up in your favorite color, too." I got up, took her by the hand, then took her to the enormous walk-in closet. "And in here is where all of your clothes and shoes will go."

Her blue eyes were as big as saucers as she looked at all the empty space. "No way."

Tiffany leaned against the doorframe, watching us. "You don't have to fill her closet all at once, Jasper. No reason to spoil her."

But I had every reason to give my daughter lots of things. I picked Jasmine up, then kissed her cheek. "Would you become a spoiled brat if your daddy filled this closet with beautiful clothes for you, Jazzy?"

"I don't think I would." Jasmine looked at her mother. "I bet Daddy will fill a closet for you, too, Momma—if you're very nice to him."

I couldn't help the smile the curved my lips. "Yeah, Momma—if you're very nice to me."

Tiffany frowned at us both. "My goodness. I'm up against two of a kind now." She raised her hands in the air. "I give up. I can't take you both on and win. I can see that right off the bat."

Jasmine took my face between her small palms then kissed me on the tip of my nose. "Yay, we win, Daddy. If Momma will stay with me, I'd like to spend the night in my new bedroom tonight."

"Nothing would make me happier, Jazzy. Nothing at all." I looked into Tiffany's eyes as our daughter gave me a hug. *See what you would've taken away from us if I had let you?*

TIFFANY

One week in, with a baby monitor in Jasmine's bedroom, I was let off the hook. No more having to sleep with my daughter was a thing I'd been looking forward to.

Closing the door behind me, I left Jasmine sleeping soundly in her bed. Crossing the hall, I found Jasper pulling off his boots as he sat on the edge of the bed. "Just in time. I was about to head to the shower."

"Lucky me." I began stripping away my clothes as I went toward the bathroom. Sleeping with my daughter had taken me away from sex with my man. And it was time to get back into that sweet action. "I'm so ready to get you back where you belong."

Jasper's arms went around me just as I dropped the last article of clothing I had on. "Deep inside you?"

Nodding, I wrapped my legs around him as he picked me up. "It's been eight days since I got the birth control implant in my arm. I'm fired up and ready to rock, captain."

"So, we have no fear of getting pregnant then?" Jasper asked, sounding a bit skeptical.

"They told me that after seven days, I was cleared for takeoff. This is by far the most effective birth control on the market today."

Running my nails across his back, I kissed a line up his neck. "So, there is no fear of getting pregnant, babe."

The sound of him sighing turned me on even more as his body lost all the tension I'd felt in it. Jasper really had a thing about not getting me pregnant again. I hoped one day he'd get over that if we were ever to become permanent partners. Having more kids with him suddenly sounded like something I'd like to do in the not-too-distant future.

Sharing Jasper with anyone wasn't a thing I'd ever had to do. With Jasmine around, he paid most of his attention to her, which I couldn't blame him for. Our daughter was adorable after all. But her momma needed some of his attention, too.

Nibbling on his neck as he walked into the shower, the jets came on, pummeling our bodies from all sides. He shifted me, his hard cock burying itself inside of me. The moans we let out shook my body as he pinned me to the wall. His lips moved over my shoulder. "You're so tight; it defies my imagination."

"Well, you can look at it this way: you're the only one I've ever had, so I guess I've formed to fit you." Pulling my head back, I looked into his eyes. "Jasper, you seem happy. Are you?"

His lips pulled up only on one side. "Yeah, I'm happy. Having Jasmine around is uplifting somehow. Like whatever she does, it makes me smile. She was drawing pictures with Ella the other day, and she drew one of the three of us, standing in front of our house. When she showed it to me, a smile just took over, and it wouldn't leave my face."

"And how about having *me* around?" I knew he liked having Jasmine around, but he hadn't paid a hell of a lot of attention to me.

"Of course. I love having you around, Tiff. Always have." His lips met mine, taking me away to the place only he ever had.

Our bodies moved as one under the falling water. Our lips opened, tongues played, breaths exchanged. I felt like a part of him as he moved inside of me. It had always been this way, and I thought it always would.

Spiraling into passion, my nails raked over his back as he made hard thrusts. Each move he made took me that much closer to the ecstasy I knew he could give me. "I can't wait to feel your heat inside me." I nipped his earlobe.

"I'm going to fill you up good, baby." With a fistful of my hair, he yanked it back hard then sucked a spot on my neck as I begged for mercy.

He would give me no such thing, and I knew that. Every inch of me on fire, I fell into the flaming abyss with reckless abandon. My legs quivered as I fell apart, both inside and out. Nails dug into his broad shoulders as I moaned with the sweet release. "Yes, Jasper. Yes, babe. What you do to me should be criminal."

Releasing my hair, his words came out harsh. "Like what you did to me?"

Tension mounted even with my orgasmic release. "Jasper?" I looked into his blue eyes, seeing flames in them. "Honey?"

"When you stole—" He stopped, the anger in his eyes gone in a flash. "My heart." Pulling me to him, he took my mouth in a hard kiss as he drove into me even harder.

Even as we kissed, I had the feeling that Jasper wasn't being all that honest with me. Maybe he did have reasons to resent me. Maybe he was just trying his best to get past them, so we could have our family. All I knew was that he and I needed a lot more therapy if we were going to make our family work.

To take Jasmine and leave him would hurt all three of us. But I couldn't make a life with a man who hated me deep down. What kind of life would that be for Jasmine, to live with parents who hated each other?

No, I couldn't do that to my daughter. If Jasper refused to get help, then what we had would be over before it could even really begin. To me, that would be a tragedy. Not only for myself but for my daughter, too.

Jasper's body tensed. He pulled his mouth off mine, then bit my shoulder as he came hard and hot inside of me. "Shit! Damn! Fuck, that feels so damn good." When his cock stopped jerking, he pulled back to look at me, cupping the back of my neck in one hand. "Tiff, I fucking love you." Then he took my mouth with the tenderest kiss he'd ever given me.

Feeling as if I had whiplash, I didn't know what to expect out of

Jasper anymore. Sometimes he was beyond sweet; sometimes he didn't even seem to know I was around. And now the sex was getting odd, too.

When our lips parted, he rested his forehead against mine, and I asked, "Jasper, can you please talk to me and tell me what's wrong?"

"What makes you think anything is wrong?" He let me go, turned to pick up the shampoo bottle, then began washing his hair.

"You're not acting the way you normally do." I took the bottle he handed me and began washing my own hair.

"Well, I'm changing, Tiff." He leaned back to rinse the soap out of his hair. "I guess you went through some changes when you became a mother. You should understand what I'm talking about."

I rinsed my hair as I thought about what he'd said. Then it occurred to me that I'd had plenty of reasons to change. "You know, when I was pregnant and even after I had Jasmine, there were a lot of hormones gushing through my body. I pretty much blame those for the way I acted back then. But you—well, you're not being yourself hardly at all."

His hands ran over his body as he washed himself, thick suds moved in slow rivers down his muscular body. "Just because I'm not chasing after you like I've always done doesn't mean I'm not the man I normally am."

He was right. He wasn't chasing after me at all. "Do you think you've got me in the bag because of our daughter or what?" I didn't much care for him thinking that way about me.

The flames in his eyes came back but only for a moment. He blinked, then said, "Of course I don't think like that, Tiffany. Jasmine is taking most of my attention right now. I've missed so much time with her. And she's missed it with me, too. For now, since this is so new to Jasmine and me, I think it's perfectly natural for us to want to spend all the time we can together. This new love I've found in my heart for her is life-changing. You have to know what I'm talking about. You've experienced it, too. Now I am, but for the first time. And Jasmine is, too. She can't remember when you two, mother and daughter, fell in love. It's kind of mind-blowing to know that my daughter will remember us falling in love."

The wind left my lungs as I listened to him talk. He was right.

Jasmine would always remember how she and her daddy fell in love when she was six years old. My legs felt weak all of a sudden.

Grabbing a towel, I got out of the shower, then went to the vanity to comb out my hair. I began putting it in a braid so it wouldn't be frizzy when I got up in the morning.

What I felt seemed an awful lot like jealousy. Even though I knew it was stupid of me to be feeling that way, I couldn't seem to help it. "I think we've rushed into things, Jasper." I saw him stop rubbing the towel over his hair as he stepped out of the shower.

His eyes met mine through the mirror. "I think you don't like sharing Jasmine or me. I think you've got to keep us separate for such a long time that you don't know how to share us. Here's the thing, Tiffany: you've got to *learn* to share us. Moving back out won't fix anything. As a matter of fact, it'll only make things worse."

The anger that shot through me had me turning to face him. "And what do you mean by that?"

"I mean, Jasmine isn't going to stand by and just shut up if you try to take her from her home." He smiled at me to soften the blow. "She's very much at home here. She's got lots of family around all the time, too. She's a Gentry, through and through, even though you never told her about us. This morning, at breakfast, I saw her eating bacon the same way Cash does—pulling it into strips, making sure she didn't get any fat on the bites she took of it. And yesterday, she was tying her shoes, and I noticed that she makes the bunny ears the way Tyrell does. She's one of us, Tiffany. I can't see her letting you drag her away from us."

"She's a child, Jasper. She will do as her mother tells her to." I turned back around to finish the braid I'd started. "This isn't a popularity contest. This is real life. If I think it's best to back up some, then she will do as I say." I wasn't about to let him think for a second that I didn't have the upper hand where Jasmine was concerned.

The way he sauntered out of the bathroom, the towel wrapped around his waist, made me even angrier. "That reminds me: we've got an appointment tomorrow at my lawyer's office. He's got the papers ready for us to sign for the birth certificate. By tomorrow evening, Jasmine's last name will be Gentry. I think I'll make a huge deal out of that and throw her a party here at the ranch. Make sure you invite your parents. I'll have Todd make something special that Jasmine will love. And there'll be cake, too. Jazzy loves cake."

Then he left me there, standing with my mouth agape. Things were beginning to get a little too real.

I'm not going to be Jasmine's only parent anymore.

JASPER

Climbing into bed, I wondered if Tiffany would be joining me or not. The conversation we'd had after the shower felt more like an argument than anything else. She definitely tried to draw lines, and I'd drawn my own.

I'd never felt this way before. Jasmine was *my* daughter, too. Tiffany didn't have any more rights over her than I did. It was time she got that through her head. If we had to fight about it, then so be it. I would fight for my daughter if I had to.

Tiffany was in for a rude awakening, but she would be woken up to the reality that Jasmine belonged to me, too. And the ranch was her home now. I couldn't see my daughter ever wanting to leave it, me, or her uncles.

Jasmine had made quick bonds with all of us. It felt like she was a part of us right off the bat. Tiffany couldn't change that even if she tried to—which I sincerely hoped she wouldn't. That would only hurt and confuse Jasmine.

So, I knew that I had to try harder with Tiffany, too—for Jasmine's sake. I had to try to feel empathy for her mother. Putting myself in Tiff's shoes, I thought about how I would feel if I'd raised Jasmine from a baby, then someone came along and butted into our relationship.

But even as I tried to think about that, I got mad as I also thought about how Tiffany had hidden her from me in the first place. If she had never done that, then I would've been in my daughter's life from the very beginning.

Taking a deep breath to calm myself, I saw Tiffany coming out of the bathroom. Her little pink T-shirt and purple panties made her look hot. My heart sped up as she came toward me with a slight smile on her face. "Can we just forget what was said a minute ago?"

I held out my arms. "I think so. Come to bed, Momma."

I couldn't help it. The attraction I had for Tiffany couldn't be denied. *Now if she could just turn back time and fix what she's done to Jazzy and me, things might work out.*

Climbing over me, Tiffany laid by my side; her arm draped across my chest. "You know you have every right to hate what I did —hiding Jasmine from you for so long."

"And you weren't ever going to tell me about her," I added before I could stop myself.

"Yeah, that too." She snuggled in closer to me, throwing her leg over mine. "I can't get so mad at you for having normal emotions and feelings. It's not easy though, and I know I'll slip up now and then. If you could cut me some slack, I'll cut you some, too."

"I think I can do that." For Jasmine, I could try harder with her mother. "The one who matters the most here is Jasmine. You and I will just have to get over some things." I still wasn't sure how I was going to do that though.

"Yeah, we will have to get over some things," she agreed. "Like the fact that I won't be Jasmine's only parent anymore. That's going to be a tough one."

I had some pretty tough shit to handle, too. "Like the fact that I'll never know what it feels like to hold my little baby girl in my arms for the first time."

Tiffany's sigh let me know I shouldn't have said that out loud. "I really am sorry about that, Jasper." She leaned up on her elbow, propping her head on her hand. "You know, we could have another baby sometime in the future, and then you would get to have that experience."

All I could do was stare at her. I couldn't trust her enough to have another baby with her. But I knew that would start a huge fight. "Yeah, maybe."

With a huff, she asked, "What are we doing here, Jasper? I mean about you and me. What is the plan here? I would like to know before I get in too deep."

I hadn't thought she'd call me out so soon. "Well, Tiff, I don't know yet. We have to see how things go."

"Do you love me the way you say you do?"

I didn't have an exact answer for her. I did love her, but I had bouts of hating her, too. "Look, when I tell you that I love you, I really mean it."

"Here's the thing, Jasper." She licked her lips, nervously. "I love you. I don't have any reason to not love you. But you have reasons not to love me. All I want is the truth from you. Can you do that for me? Can you tell me what your true feelings for me are?"

She couldn't take what my true feelings were. "Tiff, I love you. I always have. Yes, I got mad that you left me without saying a word. Yes, I'm not happy that you hid my child from me and that you were never going to tell me about her." I had to stop talking as saying that out loud really hit me hard.

Tiffany ran her hand over my cheek. "It's okay to hate me for what I've done. I understand. But what I don't understand is why you want us here, living with you, if you hate me."

"I want *her* here, Tiffany." I looked her in the eyes. "I want you here, too. I want to get past this, I truly do. It's going to take time. Can you give me time?"

She nodded. "As long as you can be honest with me. So, do you hate me?"

As hard as I tried to tell her the truth, it wouldn't come out. "I don't hate you, Tiffany. But I do hate what you did to Jasmine and me."

She blinked slowly, looking as if she might cry. "I never thought about what I did as hurting Jasmine. It honestly never occurred to me that she was being hurt by not knowing you."

I had no idea how she could've honestly thought that. "You love your dad, right?"

She nodded. "Yes. But Jasmine never knew you. She didn't lose you; she just never knew about you."

"She knew other kids had dads, Tiffany." I found it hard to believe that she'd never talked to Jasmine about that. "Jasmine told me that she was so proud that she could go to school and tell her friends that she has a real daddy now. Can you imagine how much that hurt when she told me that? I mean, shit, the kid was the odd one out, all because she didn't have a dad."

"She's only been in school a couple of years," Tiff said. "I'm sure she's not scarred for life over it or anything like that."

"See, that right there is what I'm talking about." I had to point out this terrible flaw in her character. "Tiffany, Jasmine has feelings, too. When you refused to tell her a thing about me, she thought her father must be the worst man in the world. Did she ever tell you that?"

She shook her head. "No. But I didn't actively promote discussions about her father."

"Jasmine thought that she wasn't supposed to ask you or your mother and father about her daddy, because he was such a bad man that it would make you guys sad to talk about him." My heart ached for the little girl and what she'd gone through. Taking Tiffany by the chin as she'd dropped her head, I made her look at me. "It's time that you do some self-reflection. It's time that you own up to what you've done. Don't try to brush everything under the rug. Own it, Tiffany. Own what you did to our daughter. Me? Well, I'm a grown man. I can deal with the betrayal. Jazzy's just a little girl who doesn't understand why you did what you did to her."

"She's told you this?" Her words quivered.

"She has." I thought the fact that Jasmine told me the things she had meant she felt hurt by being kept away from me.

"I had no idea she felt that way." Tears streamed down her cheeks. "I thought she just didn't even think about her father. He'd never been a part of her life, so why would she think about a fictional character?"

"She's human. She saw other kids with both parents. And there she was, afraid of hurting your feelings by asking about her father."

I felt a bit on the bad side for making Tiffany cry. But she had to start taking responsibility for what she'd done.

I supposed I'd never gotten to know the real Tiffany back when we were young. The girl I thought I knew cared about other people. The Tiffany I knew could feel empathy for others. Maybe I'd only been seeing what I wanted to.

Maybe she was right. Maybe we were rushing into things. I didn't know the woman. I didn't know if I could stay in love with a woman incapable of thinking about others—especially her own kid.

"Maybe it comes from sitting back and letting my parents make all the decisions," she said in a whisper. "Maybe I've been taking the easy way out all this time. It's a lot easier to not think about things sometimes, Jasper. You cry a lot less when you don't think about other people."

No matter how much I didn't like what she was saying, it didn't make me feel any less sympathetic to her. Pulling her to lie her head on my chest, I ran my hand up and down her back to comfort her. "Tiff, I'm sure you can change your ways."

"You are?" She ran her hand over my shoulder. "I'm not. I don't like the way this feels, Jasper. I don't like it at all. I've felt a little guilty now and then about you. But I've never felt guilty about Jasmine. And now that it's sinking in, I have to admit that I really hate how it feels."

"I tell you what; I'll make us an appointment with the therapist tomorrow before we go to the lawyer's office. I think we both could use her help." I kissed the top of her head. "I'm just thankful that my grandfather left me so much money so I can get us all the help we need. And I think Jasmine should talk to someone, too. I'd hate for her to have a harder time with life because of all that's happened to her."

Gulping, I felt Tiffany's body begin to shake. "God, Jasper. What have I done to her?" Breaking down, sobbing terribly, I knew she was having a breakthrough.

She needed to cry. She needed to see what she'd done. If she didn't, then she would never understand what she'd put Jasmine and me through. I needed her to see it. If she thought we were okay, and what she'd done didn't hurt us, then how could we ever make a family?

Not that I was sure we could make one together anyway. The things I'd begun to see in Tiffany weren't things I liked. It was becoming clear that back when I was a teenager, I hadn't looked much deeper than her appearance and pleasant attitude. As a grown man with a developed brain, I could see past her beautiful exterior, and what I saw wasn't too appealing.

TIFFANY

My hand shook as I signed the paper that would make my daughter a Gentry. "Man, this isn't as easy as I'd thought it would be."

Jasper's eyes blazed as he looked at me. "Yeah, things are hard."

Allen Samuels smiled at me, trying his best to ease the tension that filled the room with Jasper's and my own emotions. "You know it's best for a child to grow up with both parents if at all possible, right, Tiffany?"

Nodding, I finished signing the paper. "I do know that."

Jasper took the pen I handed him and quickly signed the paper. "Do you have the other paper ready too, Allen?"

I had no idea what he was talking about but watched Allen nod, then pull another page out of the folder he'd taken the other one from. "Tiffany, this is just your standard custody agreement. Since you two aren't married, I asked Jasper if he wanted to have this legal document that would make sure neither of you could take off with your daughter and not give the other parent equal access to her."

"A custody agreement?" I didn't like this at all. "Jasper, why didn't you tell me about this?" I felt like bolting. I didn't want any legal paper telling me how much time I could spend with my kid.

"I didn't think it would be a big deal, Tiffany. I mean, it gives you just as much access to Jasmine as it gives me." He smiled to try to convince me to sign the paper. "Plus, if for any reason things don't work out with us, it protects you, too."

"How?" I couldn't see how getting to spend only half the time with my daughter could possibly be a thing I could live with.

"This paper means that I can't take her completely away from you either," Jasper explained. "See, how it protects you now?"

"All I see is that if I sign that, then I'm saying you can have my daughter half the time. Half!" I shook my head. "No way. No way in hell will I give up half of her, Jasper. You can't ask me to do that. I'm not asking you to do that. Why would you even think you could bring this up? You barely know her. And here you are, wanting to take her away from me."

"I'm not." Jasper looked at the attorney for some help. "Can you explain things better to her than I can?"

"Tiffany," Samuel began.

I held up my hand. "I'm not signing it." I'd raised my daughter alone for six years. "He has no idea how to be a real parent yet, Samuel. There's more to raising a child than just playing with them and giving them things. He hasn't had to deal with her when she's sick or upset or can't sleep because she's had a nightmare. How can either of you expect me to sign something that would mean she couldn't have me around if she needed me?"

Jasper shook his head as he gritted his teeth. "I'm not a moron, Tiffany. I *can* take care of her if I have to. And I'm not saying that I will ever have to do that all on my own. What I am saying is that I would like something concrete where my time with my daughter is concerned."

Slamming my fist on the desk, I glared at Jasper. "She barely knows you!"

"Bullshit!"

Samuel stood up behind his desk. "Stop it," came his calm voice. "No more shouting. This isn't about either of you; this is about your little girl. You both claim her as if she doesn't belong to you both. She isn't just your daughter, Tiffany, nor yours, Jasper. This custody agreement makes sure that this little girl doesn't lose either of you if you ever decide to part ways."

I wanted to know why Jasper thought we might break up. Eyeing him, I asked, "Does this mean that you *do* hate me, and you can't see us staying together?"

"No," came his quick reply. "This means that I don't know what the future holds for us, but I want to be sure that I get my half of the time with Jasmine if we decide we aren't in love anymore."

Samuel cleared his throat, taking our attention. "As a man who has been married for thirty years to the same woman—a woman who had four children for us—I can tell you that you will fall in and out of love if you two decide to stay together. Things will get hard—sometimes so hard that you think about parting ways. But then you will look at those kids of yours, and you will do whatever you have to do to make it work. And then you will fall back in love. Not that it's going to last forever this time either. Something will happen that will toss that hopelessly in love feeling into the garbage. But the thing about true love is that it's like this river that runs through you both. At times it's full, overflowing even, and at other times, it's barely trickling along as if there's been a drought."

His words hit me hard. "I do love you, Jasper. I always have."

Jasper reached out, taking my hand. "And I love you, Tiffany. Sign the paper or don't. Whatever you want to do is fine with me."

Nodding, I looked at the attorney who had a grim look on his face. "Tiffany, my advice to you is to sign this agreement now. If things go south, then this man has plenty of money, and he might seek full custody of Jasmine. That means you would get her every other weekend, instead of every other day."

Looking at Jasper, I couldn't make myself believe he would ever do that to me. "Would you honestly do that?"

When he only shrugged, I felt my heart stop. "I don't know what I would do if you tried to take her away from me, Tiffany. I honestly don't."

I could barely breathe. My head spun. "This is why I never wanted to tell you. I never wanted this to happen to her. She's *mine*, Jasper. She's always been mine. I carried her in my body. I made her. I took care of her all on my own. And now you expect me to just hand her over to you without a fight?"

"No." Jasper shook his head. "I just expect you to let me have her in my life just as much as you would have her in yours. It's a better offer than what you gave me. As it stands right now, if you decided to walk out of my house, you could take her with you. How do you think that would make me feel?"

"Pretty fucking bad, Jasper." I tried to convey my feelings to him as I looked into his eyes. "Let's not do this to each other or her. Let's not have this document looming over us. Let's try to make it work. We haven't even really tried yet. This is all just beginning. Let's not make this decision yet. Please."

Samuel took his seat again. Picking the paper up, he said, "If you change your mind about signing this, Tiffany, you can come to this office anytime you want, and my secretary will be happy to help you."

I looked at Jasper. "So, have you signed it already?"

"No." He got up to leave. "If you're not, I'm not. I already told Samuel that. I guess we're done here then. We've got a therapy session to get to, remember?"

I got up to go with him. "I remember. Bye, Samuel. Thanks for your help."

"That's what I get paid for." He walked us out. "You two try to make things work, will ya? For the kid, you know."

My chest felt heavy as we left. I knew it would be best for Jasmine if her father and I could make things work. But I didn't know if Jasper would ever get over what I'd done. And I wasn't about to try to live my life with a man who hated me.

We'd started using the Mercedes, instead of the four-wheel-drive truck. I got into the passenger side, then promptly put my face in my hands, as I had the overwhelming urge to cry. I'd never cried so much in my life. Well, at least since that time when I left Jasper behind and moved to Carthage anyway.

Jasper got in and noticed my state. "You know what we should do, Tiff?"

Trying to pull myself together, I raised my head to look at him. "What should we do, Jasper?"

"We should skip the therapist and go to the jewelry store and pick out wedding rings. You can get a big fat diamond engagement ring, too. How about that?" He started the car then took off.

I sat there with my head spinning. "Are you asking me to marry you?"

"It might be the best thing for our daughter." He turned toward the one jewelry store in town. "And it'll bind us together. Maybe we won't have these thoughts of not working out and splitting Jasmine between us if we're married. Think about it. It makes sense."

"I don't want to marry you, Jasper. And frankly, that's the least romantic proposal I've ever heard." I felt indignant that he thought he could ask me in such a way.

"Seeing as you've never had one before, I didn't think what I said would offend you." Pulling to the side of the street, he parked then gave me his full attention. "Tiffany, I'm tired of feeling this way. I'm tired of wondering if you're going to not come home after work one day. I'm tired of feeling worried that you'll take Jasmine away from me. I'm so tired, and I just want it to stop. I don't know what else to do."

"We're not exactly getting along very well right now." I had no idea why he'd even want to marry me with the anger he had for me. "I don't want you to ask me to marry you so you can feel secure about Jasmine."

Lately, everything the man did was about her. If he only wanted to marry me to keep our daughter in his life, that wasn't going to be enough for me. I wasn't a bad person. I deserved undying love to go along with a marriage proposal. What he'd done felt more like throwing me a bone to stick around.

"Then how about making me feel secure about her in another way?" Jasper looked over his shoulder, the attorney's office just behind us. "Sign the custody paper, Tiffany. That'll make me feel a hell of a lot more secure about Jasmine."

"It's all about her now, isn't it?" I asked as I felt a lump forming in my throat. "It's not about me. It's not about *our* love. It's just about her and your access to her. To hell with me. You could take me or leave me—as long as you don't lose Jasmine." The truth hurt so much; I couldn't take it anymore. "I'm getting out of this car, and I'm going to go stay with Mom and Dad."

"Don't," Jasper said in a whisper. "Don't leave me, Tiffany. We made a promise to each other that we would try. We have to try to make this work. It's what's best."

I nodded. "For Jasmine. Yeah, I know." I opened the door. "But what about what's best for *us*, Jasper? When did we lose *us*?" As I closed the door, I felt the brunt of an emotional explosion hit me and knew things would never be the same.

JASPER

I watched Tiffany walk away, her gait slow, nearly staggering. What was supposed to be a joyful day had turned on a dime. From the hard time she'd had signing the birth certificate paper, I could tell this was harder for her than possibly anything she'd ever done before.

My eyes stayed on Tiffany until she made it to the Dairy King, then walked around back to go to her parents' home behind it. I had to give her space. So far, everything I'd said only upset her more.

Heading to the therapist's office, I thought I needed professional help. My head a mess, I walked in and sat down without telling the receptionist a thing. She looked at me with a funny expression. "Are you here to see the therapist?"

"Yeah, Gentry's the name. There's supposed to be two of us, but I've gone and run her off it seems." My eyes went to the floor. "Seems I don't know how to keep a woman. Not that one anyway." And I had no idea what Tiffany walking away from me meant for Jasmine.

The side door opened, and our therapist waved me in. "Come on in, Jasper. Let's talk."

Dragging my feet, I went inside her office and sat on the sofa

498

alone as she took the chair across from it. "I don't know what's happening to my life, doc. I'm doing it all wrong. Nothing is falling into place the way I thought it would."

"Tell me what's going on."

I tried to think about where to begin with it all. The truth felt like the right place to start. "Okay, here's the deal. I wanted to hurt Tiffany as much as she's hurt our daughter and me these last six years."

"And how did you go about hurting her?" she asked.

It felt ugly saying it out loud, but I had to do it. "I planned on taking Jasmine away from her. I set it all up. I knew Tiffany wouldn't want to sign a joint-custody agreement; I betted on that. And that would leave the door open for me to file for sole custody. Then it would be *Tiffany* who would barely get to see Jasmine. Tiffany fell right into my trap, too. I could go file right now if I wanted. She got out of my car and walked away from me just a little while ago. For all I know, it's over between us. I could go right back to my lawyer's office and set things in motion."

"Yet, you came here instead." She tapped her pen on the pad of paper in her lap. "Why do you suppose you did that?"

Jasmine was who came to my mind first. But before I said her name, Tiffany's sad face came into my head. "I don't want to feel hate for Tiffany anymore, doc. I've got underlying love for her, but the hate seeps through at times. She sees it, too."

"Let me see if I've got this straight," she said. "You hate Tiffany for keeping your daughter a secret. Anyone could understand that. Now, you told me at the last session that she and your daughter have moved in with you. Were you able to bond with the girl?"

"Yeah, we get along like peas and carrots. My whole family loves Jasmine. She fits in so well with my brothers and me. I can't wait to take her to meet my parents. She's like a piece I never knew was missing until she came along. And the anger I had has only grown as Jasmine has told me about how she's thought her daddy was a bad man, and that's why her momma never wanted to talk about him. It kills me what Jasmine has gone through."

"I'm sure it does." I found her smile comforting as she agreed with me. "So, you and your daughter have been bonding. But what about you, your daughter, and Tiffany? How's the family bonding been going?"

We hadn't done anything all together. "I've been spending the majority of my time with Jasmine. Tiff either has hung back or left us alone. I guess she wanted to give us time to bond."

"Well, that's no good."

I didn't understand that at all. "And why not?"

"Well, as you should be able to see by now, as you said, Tiffany walked away from you. You've focused too much on one person in your family. One can't do that without icing out the other part of your family." She smiled sweetly. "Your family isn't just you and your daughter—it's all three of you. But your little plan of revenge seems to have made you focus far too much on Jasmine, leaving Tiffany out in the cold. If you hadn't had a plan like that, you might've given them both your attention and tried to make the family work, instead of trying to break it apart to hurt Tiffany."

"I hadn't thought about it like that." She was right. "I didn't see a downside to my plan. And to be honest, I didn't see Tiffany walking away from me on her own either."

"When one schemes, one is usually met with disappointment."

"I've never schemed before, so I had no idea." I just wanted the answer for how to make it all better. "Can you help me fix this?"

"I can't. No," she said. "*You* can fix this all on your own. And that's exactly what you should do."

"So, the sole custody thing is a bad idea then?" I asked her.

"Jasper, I will not tell you what to do. You've got to make your own decisions. If you feel that filing for sole custody is the right thing to do, then do it. If you feel that going to Tiffany and telling her that you've been going down the wrong path and you would like to go down the right path with her, then do that. If you want to put a wedge between Jasmine and her mother, if you feel that would be what's best for everyone, then do that."

I knew she didn't want me to do that. "I don't want Jasmine to lose what she has with her mother. They love each other." I had no idea what I'd been thinking. "I love Jasmine too much to try to take away someone that special to her." As I talked, my heart got lighter and lighter. "I guess I hate what Jazzy and I didn't get to do. But what I'm finding out is that our blood binds us in a way I never knew it could. It's almost like she's always been with me. Only when I start thinking too hard about not getting to hold her when she was a baby, you know, things like that, only then do I get mad."

"But you have firsts with your daughter now and you always will. Her first date, her high school graduation, her wedding, you becoming a grandfather for the first time. You will have all those firsts. So, you must ask yourself if you need to hold hate in your heart just because you missed out on some things?"

"It's more like I've felt like Tiffany needs to pay for what she's done to us."

"Pay, huh?" She sounded a bit put off by that.

But who wouldn't? "Yeah, I know, it sounds pretty childish, doesn't it?"

"If you think Tiffany hasn't paid the price for what she's done, I'm sure you're wrong. She made life harder on herself than it had to be. Being both mother and father isn't easy." Putting the pad of paper on the table next to her, she got up. "You've got a lot to think about and decisions to make. I hope you take the time to make wise ones."

"I've got a party this evening, too. We signed the birth certificate paper today; Jasmine is officially a Gentry." I thought about how that had to be hitting Tiffany. "You know, I'm sure part of Tiffany's meltdown had to do with that."

"Most likely." She walked to the door. "You've got lots to think about."

As I walked out past her, I nodded. "Thanks for not telling me what to do while telling me what I should do, doc."

"Thanks for coming to me instead of rushing to make decisions that could hurt people."

"Yeah, at least I was smart enough to do that." I left her office and headed for the jewelry store. I'd been doing things all wrong. A man wasn't supposed to blow his family to smithereens. A real man was the glue who bound them all together. I should've taken a page out of my father's book. Instead, it seemed like I had been thinking a hell of a lot like my dead grandfather—a man I'd never met.

Much like finding that Jasmine had so much in common with

my brothers and me, just by sharing our blood, I shared blood with that old bastard. I would have to keep a look out for falling into that kind of coldblooded behavior. I didn't want to be a thing like that man.

Yet, there I'd been, thinking just like him.

Revenge wasn't a thing my parents had ever taught any of us. Making people pay for what they'd done wasn't part of my growing up. Forgiveness, kindness, and understanding were all things they'd taught us. It scared me how easily I'd forgotten all that.

And now it scared me that Tiffany had been hurt too much to get over what I'd done to her. I *had* iced her out. Not completely though.

As I walked through the door of the jewelry store, I saw dollar signs in the man's eyes. "Mr. Jasper Gentry! Hello and welcome to my shop."

I hadn't seen the newspaper but was pretty sure the article had come out about us. "You saw my picture in the paper, did ya?"

"I did." He shook my hand. "I'm Ramon. And what can I do for you on this beautiful day?"

"Can I see rings you have for little girls?" I asked. "It's a special day for my six-year-old daughter, and I want to give her something to mark the occasion."

"Yes, yes." He took a key out of his pocket to open the case. "I've got some very precious ones right here. Does your little girl have slender fingers or chubby ones?"

"Slender." I leaned on the counter as he pulled out the tray of rings. "I like that blue one there."

"Ah," he said as he lifted it out of the tray. "My sapphire in a princess cut. The diamonds which surround it combine to a remarkable two karats. It's quite the treasure."

"You don't happen to have a matching necklace and earrings for that, do ya?" I thought about how adorable Jasmine would look all bejeweled.

"As a matter of fact, I do have some things that will match with this ring perfectly. Your little girl will be very surprised, I assure you." He took out his key to open another case. "What is this special occasion?"

"It's kind of like her birthday, I guess." I looked at the ring, knowing it would get me a hug and a kiss from my little girl. "Today her last name is changing to Gentry."

"Only today?" he asked as he placed a tray of necklaces on the glass countertop. "But you said she's six, right?"

"It's a long story. Her mother had the idea it was best to keep her from me." I waited for the anger to kick in like it always did when I thought about her doing that to me. But it didn't come. "I suppose that doesn't matter anymore. What's important is the future, and it's going to include my daughter now."

He laid out the necklace and earrings that matched the ring. "Do you like this set?"

"Yeah, I'll take it." It would make Jasmine happy and give her something to keep that would remind her of the day her last name changed to Gentry.

TIFFANY

"I thought I saw you coming back here." Mom came into the house, finding me gulping down a beer. "What in the world are you doing, Tiffany McKee? You've been crying, too. What's wrong?"

"He hates me, Mom!" I wailed, then pulled the bottle back up to my lips to pour more alcohol down my throat.

"Tiffany, it's only ten in the morning. What are you thinking?" She took the bottle away from me and poured the rest of the beer out as I broke into another round of sobs.

Going to the sofa, I fell face down on it. "He hates me. He can't get over what I've done. And I can't even blame him for it."

Mom's hand ran over my back. "Honey, what makes you think that Jasper hates you?"

"The way he acts. The way he has so little to do with me." I sat up, wiping the tears off my face. "He's all about Jasmine. That's all it's about now—her."

"I'm sure once everything gets settled, it won't be that way anymore." She patted my shoulder. "Don't you want them to get along well?"

"Of course I do." A hiccup came out of me. "I drank that beer too fast." I held my breath, then another one came. "Damn."

Mom got up and went to the kitchen. She came back with a spoonful of sugar. "Open up."

"Mom, that's an old wives' tale. Sugar doesn't get rid of hiccups." I had another one.

"Just open up. Let it melt on your tongue." She pushed the spoon into my mouth, and I had to take it.

After it melted, I said, "Tell me what to do, Mom. I don't know how to make things right between Jasper and me. And I want to make them right again. You have no idea how much I love him and how much this is killing me that I hurt him so bad that he hates me now. And I hate myself, too. I've also hurt Jasmine and didn't even realize it until last night."

"Don't you have anything else to say?" She crossed her arms over her chest, wiggling the spoon.

"Um … probably. I wasn't really done."

"About your hiccups," she pointed out. "They're gone. I told you the sugar would work."

"Oh, those." I waited to see if another one would pop out of me. "Seems they're gone. I doubt the sugar had anything to do with it."

Mom huffed, then put the spoon on the coffee table as she took a seat next to me on the couch. "Look, I know it's natural for you to feel guilty about Jasper and Jasmine. But what can you do about the past? It's over and done with. The most you can do is say you're sorry, mean it, then move on to the next chapter."

"And what if Jasper can't do that?" I had to know what I was supposed to do if he couldn't get over what I'd done.

"Then he's not the right man for you, honey." She made it sound so simple.

But it wasn't simple at all; it was complicated as hell. "Mom, there's Jasmine to think about!"

"If you and her father can't get along, then she should spend time with you both, but apart." Mom ran her hand through my hair. "You two could learn how to co-parent."

"I don't want to co-parent with Jasper. I want us to be a family." The tears came back. "But he doesn't trust me. I can see it in his eyes. I asked about having another baby, and he wasn't into it at all."

"Well, don't do that, Tiffany. My goodness. You two aren't even married. Why do you want to keep having this man's kids when he won't even marry you?" She looked beyond confused. "He's known about Jasmine for over a week. I thought for sure you two would be announcing your engagement by now. Instead, you're looking more like you're breaking up. Having a family isn't easy, honey. It takes lots of hard work, sacrifice, and trust in each other."

"And we don't have that. I mean, I've got it for him." I stopped to think about that for a moment. "Well, that's not true. I don't trust him right now. He tried to get me to sign joint-custody papers after we signed the paper for the birth certificate. Jasmine's last name is officially Gentry now." I felt my heart cramp and clutched my chest. "God, that's actually killing me. My daughter and I no longer share a last name."

"Joint custody?" Mom asked. "Why would he want you to sign a paper about that if you two are going to raise Jasmine together? You live with the man, for goodness sakes. That's just crazy."

"That's how little Jasper trusts me, Mom." My stomach ached as much as my heart did. "How long can I live like this? I feel like everything is being ripped out of me."

Mom wasn't one to fall into the abyss of depression. "Look, honey, all you've got to do is pull yourself together. Let Jasper see that you can handle yourself and that you're trustworthy. Let him know that you will never try to take Jasmine away from him. You've got to show him how much he means to you, too. You need to prove that you're in it for the long haul."

"How can I do it when he's always shutting me out?" I didn't know how I could do anything. "And how can I let him and Jasmine bond if I'm always around, making myself part of whatever they're doing?"

"This isn't just about Jasper and Jasmine bonding, honey. Being a family is about *all* of you bonding." Mom sighed as she leaned back and looked up at the ceiling. "Have your father and I taught you nothing?"

"You've taught me plenty." I had no idea what she was talking about. "Mom, just tell me what I'm supposed to do. I really don't know right now. Jasmine was all mine, and now she's his, too. And I see them having their relationship, and I just feel left out. Jasper is getting things I never got with her."

"Like what?"

"Like they're falling in love, Mom," I whined. "I can see it in their faces. I never got that with her. She was too little. Jasmine is going to have memories of when she and her daddy began to love each other. She won't recall a thing about when she first knew she loved me."

"Jealous?" she asked with a smirk. "I can't believe that, Tiffany. And you did get to see your daughter fall in love with you. I saw it. When she looked at you, she had love in her big, blue eyes. The girl adores you just as much as you do her. I don't like seeing you being jealous over your daughter loving her daddy and her daddy loving her."

"Yeah, me neither. Just another thing I feel guilty about." I looked at the fridge in the kitchen. "I really need another beer, Mom."

"No, you don't," she said. "What you need is to stop being childish. You're the mom, Tiffany. Do you know what that means in a family?"

"Not really. I thought I did, but now I don't." I'd grown clueless in the last week.

"A mother is the strength of the family. Most might think it's the man who has all the strength, but it's the mother," she said. "See, us moms manage all the relationships in our homes. We try to keep things peaceful between family members. That doesn't mean we get in the way of the other relationships because we know they're important, too. But the most important relationship in the family unit it that between the parents."

"And Jasper and I have a horrible one." We were doomed.

"For now, you do." Mom wasn't going to give up. "You've got this past to make up for. And I know you, Tiffany McKee. You can be very selfish with Jasmine. How many times did I have to get onto you when your brother and sister lived here, and you'd first brought Jasmine home?"

She'd had to get onto me lots of times about them. "Yes, I

remember. I was stingy with my baby. They were her aunt and uncle, and they needed to build their relationships with her, too."

"Because it's healthy, Tiffany. And it's healthy for her to have one with her father. Maybe it's been that green-eyed monster that has Jasper feeling insecure about losing Jasmine." Maybe she was on to something. "Maybe he sees that and thinks you might grab his daughter and run off because you can't stand seeing them having a healthy relationship."

"But you know what, Mom?" I asked as I thought about how I'd come around not long after Jasmine was born where my siblings were concerned. "I learned to love watching Jasmine interact with Bo and Carolina. It made my heart sing when I heard her tell them that she loved them and when they told her the same. I can do this, Mom. I can learn to love the connection Jasper and Jasmine have. I'm sure I can. If I could do that before, I can do it again."

"I do believe that you have it in you to be the strength in your family, Tiffany. Let Jasper do his part, you do your part, and let your family fall into place the way it uniquely will." She looked at her watch. "It's almost noon. We've been talking a long time. You look like you could use a nap and a long hot bath before you get on with your day. You've got lots to think about. I'll leave you to that."

I'd almost forgotten about Jasmine's party. "Mom, can you and Dad go out to the ranch for Jasmine's party this evening? Jasper's throwing her one for her new last name. I don't think I'll go, but Jasmine should have someone from my side there."

"I think you should come, too, Tiffany. You know, show Jasmine that you're happy for her." She got up, then looked at me with a smile on her face. "We'll be there. We're happy for her, too. She's got a daddy who loves her. And she's got one hell of a future in front of her. If I was her momma, I would be right there next to her, experiencing it all with her."

"And if Jasper doesn't want me anymore?" I asked.

"Well, I doubt that's the case. And it might take making some apologies and changes in your behavior as well. I think you can get him back. That boy does love you, no matter if he does hate the fact that he's missed out on six years of Jasmine's life. Be the strength, Tiffany. Find it in you to be not only the mother, but the partner of the father, too. Put your relationship with Jasper at the top, and everything else will fall into place."

I didn't think my parents had a healthy relationship and wasn't sure about my mother's advice. But I really didn't have anything else to compare it to. "I'll think about everything. I'm going to take that long hot bath you talked about and then maybe take a nap. I do feel a little better now. Thanks, Mom. I love you."

"I love you, too, honey. See you in a bit after the lunch rush thins out."

As she left me alone, I put my hand over my heart, feeling the beat of it. "I can be strong for my family. I know I can. Somehow, I've got to make Jasper forgive me for what I've done."

JASPER

"Where's Mom?" Jasmine asked as she got into her booster seat in the back of the Mercedes. The teacher made sure she was all strapped in before closing the car door.

That gave me a moment to come up with something. "Working."

"Oh." Rifling through her backpack, she pulled out a piece of red construction paper. "Look what I made today, Daddy."

Peering into the rearview mirror, I saw it as she held it up. "Jasmine Michelle Gentry. You used excellent handwriting."

"Is that my name now? Cause I told everyone that my last name changed today." Her brows furrowed as a worried expression took over her cute face. "You did do that today, right?"

"We did. You're my daughter legally now, and your last name is now Gentry," I said.

The smile that took over her entire face had me smiling, too. But then it went away as her eyes glazed over a little. "Daddy, what about Momma? Did she get a new last name, too? I want her to match with us."

"We would have to get married for that to happen." I looked back at her as I stopped at a stop sign. "So, the answer to that is, no. Your mom still has the last name of McKee."

"Oh." Her eyes went to the window, and she went silent as she watched the scenery pass by.

"To commemorate this great event in all our lives, Jazzy, I've had Chef Todd make a feast for the party we're throwing for you this evening. Won't that be fun?" I asked her to get her talking again. The girl was usually a chatterbox.

"It should be fun. Am I gonna get to meet your parents?" She started going through her backpack again. "I've got homework I should get finished with if there's gonna be a party."

"As a matter of fact, you *are* going to get to meet my mom and dad. Uncle Tyrell and Ella are coming back with them as we speak. They took the jet to Dallas to get them." I turned to go down Adams Street. "We're having the party at Rancho Grande, the Mexican restaurant. But Todd took over the kitchen, and they'll be closed for any other business. We've got the place all to ourselves." I pointed out the place to her. "See, it's closed, but Todd and his staff are inside busily working on everything."

Her eyes bright, she looked at the place she'd have her party in. "Can we go inside and see?"

"Let's let them fix it all up so you can be surprised. We'll come back at six this evening." I thought about how I'd changed the plans so my parents could come to the party. I pulled into the parking lot and stopped so I could text Tiffany. "I've gotta let your momma know that the party isn't at our ranch anymore." After tapping in a quick text, I put the cell phone back down, then pulled out of the parking lot to go home.

"Daddy, why did you have to change where the party is?"

"Well, my parents aren't allowed to go out to the ranch. And frankly, they wouldn't want to come to it even if they were allowed to. It's got too many bad memories for them," I explained as I drove home, noticing that Tiffany hadn't texted me back.

I knew she was upset with me, but not coming to her daughter's party wasn't a thing I thought she'd do. I hoped she was just busy with something. And part of me hoped she'd borrowed her parents' car and had already gone back home—but I wasn't going to hold my breath waiting for that to happen.

Tiffany had been more upset than I'd ever seen her when she

got out of the car. And she had every right to be. I had to give her time to calm down though before I could try to talk to her.

"What kind of bad memories do your mom and dad have of the ranch, Daddy?" Jasmine asked. "It's so pretty out there. How can anyone have bad memories of that place?"

"My dad and his dad didn't see eye to eye on some things." I turned into the gated entrance of the ranch. "But they're very excited about meeting you, Jasmine. They told me to tell you that you can pick out their grandparent names. So, you should get to thinking about what you'd like to call them."

"Hmm." She tapped her chin as she began to ponder things. "I know this girl in my class has her Nana pick her up from school. I think she said she calls them Nana and Papa."

"That sounds nice." I liked the fact that Jasmine got to pick their names out. It seemed like it might cement her even more into the Gentry side of her family.

"What are their names?" she asked.

"Coy and Lila." I pulled into the garage as Jasmine tapped her chin again.

"Well, I like their names." She unbuckled her seatbelt then hopped out of the car, joining me to walk inside. "Maybe Granny Lila and Grandpa Coy are good." She shook her head. "Nah, that sounded better in my head than when I said it."

"Maybe you'll know when you meet them," I offered. "For now, let's tackle that pesky homework of yours, then get you all fancied up for your party, Miss Gentry."

The giggle she made as I picked her up made my heart dance. "I'm Miss Gentry now!"

An hour later, two pages of math questions done, a bowl of cereal eaten, and Jasmine was raring to get herself all cleaned up. "When's Momma coming home? I need her help getting ready."

Ella overheard Jasmine and stuck her head into the dining room. "We're back. Your parents are at the hotel in town. I can help you out until your mom gets here, Jas."

Clapping, Jasmine jumped up and down, then took Ella's hand. "Yay! I want to smell like a million dollars. I've got some new bath bombs I can use. All I need is for you to start the water, so I don't burn myself."

"Thanks, Ella." I did appreciate her help. I had no idea what the rules were on bathing your kid, but I'd find that out.

I headed up to my room to shower and change. I had to look my absolute best after all. As I walked up the stairs, I pulled my cell out to find Tiffany still hadn't answered my text, but she *had* read it, so I left it at that. The ball was in her court now.

Now to see if this is fate or not.

An hour later, I was ready and went to check on Jasmine's progress. When I opened the door to her bedroom, the smell of jasmine filled my nostrils. "It smells like your mom in here."

A peel of laughter wafted out of the bathroom, then Jasmine stepped out of it, her dark hair curled in ringlets around her face. Ella had put her in a white dress that went to just below her knees; black flats finished the innocent look. "What do you think, Daddy?"

I held the bag from the jewelers in my hand. "I think you look adorable. But you're missing something."

"I am?" Jasmine turned to look at Ella. "What's missing?"

Ella shrugged. "Nothing. He's just joking around with you. I've gotta go get dressed myself now." She left the room, leaving Jasmine and me alone.

"I think I've got something that will tie that outfit all together. Wanna see?" I asked as I held out the bag.

"What's in that bag, Daddy?" She came to me, curiosity filling her blue eyes.

"Oh, just a little something to match your pretty eyes." I pulled out the ring box first. "Let me see your fingers, Jasmine."

She held out all ten of them, wiggling them as she smiled. "Oh, Daddy, did you get me a ring?"

Pulling the ring out of the box, I judged which finger it would fit then slipped it on the ring finger of her right hand. "It fits!"

Squealing with delight, she held her hand up, looking at the shiny trinket. "It's so pretty! I love it! And I'm gonna take good care of it, too."

"Please do. It's real, Jazzy. That's a real sapphire, and those are real diamonds all around it." I gave her some time to fully appreciate the gift before pulling out the small box with the earrings in it. "And these are to decorate your cute, little ears."

She gazed at the shiny earrings as I pulled the top off the box. "They match!"

"They do." I clipped them on for her. "When you get your ears pierced someday, I'll get you a pair of these for pierced ears."

"That's gonna be awhile. I'm scared of pain." She ran to look in the mirror over her dresser. "Oh, Daddy, they look so pretty!"

Coming up behind her, I pulled out the larger box with the necklace in it. "And this will top it all off." Putting it around her neck, I watched her finger the sapphire that hung from the gold chain.

"I can't believe this." Blinking, she turned and put her arms around me. "I love all of it, Daddy."

Picking her up, I hugged her, then kissed her cheek. "I love you, Jasmine Gentry. I just wanted you to have these things so you could always remember the day you became a Gentry."

"I won't ever forget." She kissed my cheek again. "I love you, too, Daddy."

Something told me that I would never get tired of hearing her say that to me. "Well, we'd better get going. You don't want to be late to your own party."

"Okay," she said as I put her down. "Wait."

"What is it?"

She looked a little confused. "Where's Momma?"

"I think she's going to meet us there, Jazzy." I hoped she would anyway.

"Can you call her to make sure? I don't want her to work and miss my party. I want both my parents there." She took my hand. "Come on. You can call her while we go to the car. I can't wait to meet my new grandparents."

Instead of calling Tiffany, I called her mother's cell. "Hi, did you get the memo about the change of where the party is?"

"We did," Darla answered.

"Okay, so we'll see you *all* there then, right?" I asked, trying to give her the hint that I was talking about Tiffany, too.

"Um, well … me and Jason for sure," she said, making me feel a bit deflated.

"Jasmine is so excited about having *both* of her parents there," I said.

"I hope she gets what she wants, Jasper. I really do. You two have a lot to work on."

She was right. Tiffany and I had to work on things—but I had no idea if she would even want that anymore. "Well, we'll see you there. Jasmine and I are leaving now."

"See you there." She ended the call as I opened Jasmine's car door. "Here you go, my little princess."

A grin pulled her lips up. "I like that, Daddy. And you're my sweet prince." She cocked her head as I buckled her in. "Or are you Momma's sweet prince?"

Good question.

TIFFANY

"Honey, we're leaving," Mom called out from the other side of the
locked bedroom door.

"Bye," I said, lying back down on the twin bed they had in the
guest room.

"Tiffany, you will come, won't you?" Mom asked.

"Bye, Mom." I didn't want to talk to anyone.

"Tiffany, Jasper called," she said. "He and Jasmine are looking
forward to seeing you there. This is a big day for both of them. You
don't want to ruin it, do you?"

I rubbed my temples, thinking about the things I'd done since
Jasper and I had moved in together. The long bath I'd taken hadn't
made me feel any better. Neither had the nap that I barely got two
winks of.

"Bye, Mom." I heard her walking away from the door.

Then another set of footsteps come to it. "Honey, this isn't like
you at all," my father said. "I know it's been you and Jasmine for six
years, but she needs her father, too. This is such a big day for them
both, Tiffany." And then he walked away.

I couldn't speak as I listened to him walking away. A knot was in
my stomach and my throat. I sat up, looked in the mirror that hung

on the wall across the room and hated what I saw staring back at me. "You're an ass, Tiffany McKee."

But the longer I stared into that mirror, the clearer things became.

Jasper had wanted me to sign that custody agreement for some other reason. He didn't push me that hard about signing it; he gave up too quickly. And he pretty much told me straight out that he *would* try to take full custody of Jasmine if things between us didn't work out. And so far, they weren't working out.

"That son of a bitch was playing you, Tiffany McKee. And you fell for it."

No wonder he didn't get out of the car to follow me. He wanted me to be the one to leave him. He wanted me to look like the bad guy, not only to our daughter, but to a judge as well.

"You clever bastard."

I had to hand it to the man; he knew me so well that it made it easy for him to get me to do what he wanted. He wanted me out of the picture—that was pretty damn clear now.

No wonder my idea of trying to make things work petered out of my head. Now I knew going back to him and admitting my wrongdoings would be a huge mistake.

I doubted he even wanted us to try to work on things. His text didn't say a thing about being sorry or wanting to talk to me. Just come to the party—witness the happiness he and Jasmine had over her finally becoming a Gentry. After that, I could get lost for all he cared.

Well, if he thinks I'm just going to sit back and let him take away my child, he's got another thing coming.

Getting off the bed, I went to put my hair in a bun and got dressed. As I looked in the bathroom mirror, I realized I had no makeup on, and I had none to use at my parents' house either. Nor anything other than the jeans and T-shirt I'd worn that morning.

"I can't go to the party looking like this."

I went to see if Mom and Dad's car was there, so I could go out to the ranch to get ready. But I found the driveway empty, as they'd taken the car.

"Shit."

Going back inside to sit down, I put my face in my hands, trying to figure out what I could do. I could walk the half mile to the restaurant they were having the party, but I couldn't walk in looking like this.

To top it all off, I'd left my purse in the car when I got out. All I took with me was my cell phone. I didn't even have lousy chapstick to put on.

Mom was three sizes larger than me, but I looked through her closet anyway. What I found only depressed me. She didn't have anything remotely nice that would fit me.

I went to see if I could find her makeup and found only a jar of wrinkle cream and a tube of brown mascara. I hadn't realized that my mother had become such a minimalist. Looking under the cabinet in her bathroom, I thought I might at least find a curling iron, but she didn't even have a blow dryer.

"How does she live?"

One block over, there was a beauty shop where Jasmine and I had gotten our hair cut a few times. I recalled seeing a woman getting a makeover there one time. I thought I could give that a shot. At least my hair and makeup would be on point. The only problem was, I had no money with me.

But I did have the café, and I could borrow some from the cash register.

Hurrying out the door, I went to the café to get the money, only to find it empty and locked up. "Damn it. They closed the Dairy King to go to that party."

I looked toward the beauty parlor and decided to ask if I could pay later. A gust of wind blew in just before I got to the door. I jerked the glass door open then stood there, the wind whipping all around me, red hair blowing in my face. "I need help."

"No shit," someone inside said. "Get in here, quick."

Pushing the hair out of my eyes, I pulled the door closed with my free hand. "I don't have any money on me. But I'll pay you first thing in the morning— twice what the cost is—if you can fix me up now and as quickly as possible. My little girl is having a party, and I need to be there."

One of the ladies turned her chair around. "Hop on and let me do my magic. You're Tiffany from the Dairy King, aren't you?"

I took the seat she offered. "I am. And I need to look gorgeous. I want to rub my daughter's father's nose in it when I let him know that I've figured him out. I want him to look at me and hate that he missed out on this."

"I'm Paula." She spun me around, put a cape on me, then started brushing out my hair. "What colors are you going to wear?"

"All I have is what I've got on."

She shook her head, then looked at the other girl in the small shop. "Gloria, you're her size. Go up to your apartment and get her something nice to wear. We can't send her off to this party in jeans and a T-shirt. Think fancy, girl. I'm gonna give her an updo that will make that man's mouth water."

The girl I now knew was Gloria jumped up, eager to help. "I've got the dress I wore on New Year's Eve. And I'll bring the jewelry I wore with it, too." She pulled my foot up. "A six?"

"I am." I smiled at her, happy for her help.

"Me, too! I'll be right back." She stopped just before opening the door. "There's no back on the dress. You okay going braless?"

I hadn't ever gone braless before, but there was a first time for everything. "I think I'll be okay with that. Thank you very much, Gloria. I will make it all worth your while when I come back tomorrow."

Cocking her head to one side, she put her hand on her hip. "No, Miss Tiffany, that's not necessary. Us girls have to stick together. I'm just doing this to help you."

"Well, that's very nice of you, Gloria." I smiled as I looked at Paula in the mirror.

She shook her head. "Not me. I'm working. I get paid for my work, Miss Tiffany."

Laughing, I said, "As you should."

A half hour later, I looked like a fashion model, complete with six-inch black heels, a tight-fitting black dress with just a small amount of sparkling sequins to catch the light, and some silver chains to set it off. Gloria reached into the front of her bra, pulling out a set of diamond studs. "They're not real, but they look like they are. Put them on, too."

After adding the earrings, I felt a hell of a lot better about my appearance. When I looked at the glass door, seeing the wind whipping around, I quickly deflated. "That wind is going to ruin me out there." I had to ask one more favor. "I don't have my car. Do one of you think you could give me a ride to Rancho Grande?"

Gloria looked at Paula as they both shook their heads. Paula said, "We don't have a car, Miss Tiffany."

I sat back down, putting my lower lip between my teeth. "Damn."

All this work and still I had problems keeping me from getting to that party. Looking up, I asked, "Collin Gentry, is this your doing?"

"You knew him?" Gloria asked.

"No." I sighed. "He's the grandfather of the man whose baby I had. He was a real piece of work from what I've heard. I'm afraid his grandson may be turning into him in a way. Jasper hasn't ever acted toward me the way he has since I told him about our daughter."

Paula picked up the newspaper, then turned a few pages. "This man here is your baby's daddy?" She pointed Jasper out of the three brothers in the picture. Then she pointed to the picture of another man. "This is Collin Gentry."

It felt odd to see him looking back at me from that page. "He's got Jasper's eyes. And my daughter has her father's eyes. Seems my child is much more Gentry than she is McKee." The idea made me feel sad. "All this time, I've felt like Jasmine didn't need her father. I've been thinking that she didn't even need to know the Gentrys at all. I had no idea the man who owned Whisper Ranch was her grandfather."

"So, you've lived right here in Carthage with that man's grandchild, and he never knew about her?" Gloria asked.

I nodded. "Yep. I didn't do it intentionally; I just didn't know he was related to the boy I'd left behind in Dallas when we moved here."

"Maybe he's mad," Paula said. "Maybe he's trying to get in the way of you and his grandson getting back together. I heard he was a tough man—hard to get along with."

"I've heard that, too." I watched as a beat-up old Chevy pulled in front of the shop. "Looks like you've got another customer."

The wind began letting up as the car door opened. The woman, tall and lean, walked into the shop. "Paula, can you cut my hair?" She ran her hand through her long dark tresses. "It's a mess."

"Sure, Lola. Come, take a seat." Paula turned the chair around for her to sit in. "Miss Tiffany, this is my good friend, Lola Stevens. Miss Tiffany is trying to get to a party, so she can show Mr. Jasper Gentry what he's missing out on. But she's having trouble getting there."

"Gentry?" Lola asked. "Of the Whisper Ranch Gentrys?"

I nodded. "Yeah, those guys."

"My older sister, Lila, ran off with Coy Gentry a long time ago. I was just a little kid when I saw her last."

"You don't say."

JASPER

Just as Jasmine and I walked into the restaurant, I saw my parents sitting at a table alone. "There they are, Jazzy. Your grandparents."

Mom and Dad got up, coming to us, smiles on their faces as Mom said, "Oh my goodness. You're so pretty, Jasmine. Can I have a hug?"

Jasmine's smile was off the charts as she threw her arms open. "Yes, you can!"

Mom picked her up, hugging her as she closed her eyes. "I'm so happy to finally meet you."

Dad watched them with glistening eyes. "She's a real beauty, son."

"I think so, too." I gave my dad a hug. "It's nice to see you guys. Thanks for coming."

"We wouldn't have missed this for the world, Jasper," Dad said, then tapped Jasmine on the shoulder. "You got a hug for your old grandpa, Jasmine?"

"Of course, I do." She let my father take her from my mother and hugged him. "I'm so glad you're here. I'm a Gentry, too, now."

Dad swayed back and forth with her. "And I'm so proud to call you my granddaughter, Jasmine Gentry."

Mom looked at the door behind us. "And where's Tiffany? We

haven't seen her in years. It's going to be nice having her back around."

Jasmine looked at me for that answer, too. "I think she's just running a little late."

The door opened and in came Tiffany's parents.

Jasmine shouted, "Come here, Gigi and Pop-pop! You've gotta meet my other grandparents." She looked at my dad, then put her hands on either side of his face. "Can I call you P-Paw?"

He nodded. "You're the first grandchild; you get to pick our names."

Jasmin smiled. "Good." She looked at Mom. "And can I call you Me-maw?"

"You sure can," Mom said with a smile.

My parents and Tiffany's parents caught up while Jasmine hung onto their every word, interested in how they all knew each other. I went to the kitchen to see how things were coming along. "Hey, Todd. You got it all put together back here?"

He pointed to the walk-in cooler. "The hamburgers are done, the hot dogs are about to be put on the grill, and the taco bar is set up and ready to roll out. The cake is ready and in the cooler over there. Care to take a peek?"

Going to the cooler, I saw it as soon as I opened the door. Three tiers high, the pink and white cake had Jasmine written on the top tier, Michelle on the second one, and Gentry on the third one. A diamond tiara topped the gorgeous cake. "Wow!"

Todd came up behind me. "Tyrell brought in the diamond tiara. Those are real diamonds up there."

"No way," I said. "He's turned out to be a great uncle."

Cash came in the back door to the kitchen. "Did I hear someone say something about a great uncle?"

"I said Tyrell is one." I pointed at the cake. "He gave Jazzy a diamond tiara. It's on her cake."

Cash was all smiles. "Come out here and see what a really, *really* great uncle gets his niece."

Todd and I went to the backdoor. "I hope it's not a car. She's only six, not sixteen." I pushed the door open and found a miniature horse standing there with a pink saddle, reins, and even pink-painted hooves, standing there looking at me.

Cash came out with a carrot. "Here ya go, Lucy. Have a little snack."

"She's more like a big dog than a horse," I pointed out.

"I know. Jasmine will love her," Cash said proudly.

Todd agreed. "We'll have to set her up in the backyard. I bet those two are going to be inseparable."

Cash nodded. "Already had a small barn put out there just a little while ago. The guy delivered it and used a small crane to set it up in the back so Lucy will be close enough that Jas can go see her anytime she wants."

"But can she really ride this little thing?" I asked.

"She can." Cash ran his hand over the horse's backside. "She's as gentle as a kitten. I'm gonna bring her out at the very end of the party."

"Jasmine will be shocked." I turned to head inside as Cash made sure the mini horse was securely tied to the post in back.

When I got back out to where the guests were, I scanned the room hoping to see Tiffany. But she still wasn't there. I'd hoped she would've ridden with her parents to the party. I caught her father as he went to get a drink. "Hey, Jason, is Tiffany coming?"

The way he looked at the floor made me think she wasn't going to. "Darla and I both talked to her. It wasn't a conversation as it was through a closed door. I don't think she's intentionally trying to ruin this for you two."

"So, she's not coming?" I asked, feeling kind of desperate.

"I don't think so." He sighed then went to grab a drink for him and his wife.

I leaned against the wall, knowing I had to do something to get Tiffany to come. I'd put the ball in her court, but she didn't seem to want to play. There was so much I had to tell her—so many things to ask her.

I knew I had to let her know how I felt and how sorry I was for everything I'd done. So, I texted her.

Tiffany, I haven't been myself since I found out about Jasmine being mine. Maybe some of that bad Gentry blood boiled up inside of me and came out. But the good part of it has taken over now. I'm man enough to admit when I'm wrong, and I'm admitting it to you. Girl, I love you, always have, always will. You don't have to worry about me; I'm never going to do a thing to tear this family apart. I'll work with you until I'm blue in the face before I walk away or let you walk away. So, this is it, Tiffany—I'm not letting you walk away from us. Jasmine and I are your family, and neither of us will ever let you go. So, get your fine ass over here and celebrate this day with us because we love you.

I hit send, then crossed my fingers she would read it and get over things so she could come to the party.

Everyone was there, and Todd wheeled out the taco bar. "Come and get yourself some tacos, everyone."

Jasmine clapped as she ran toward the festive-looking bar. "Yay! I love tacos!"

"I know you do," Todd said as he patted her on top of the head. "I've made all of your favorites, Miss Gentry. So, don't fill up on tacos alone, 'cause I've got more surprises coming."

"Thank you, Chef Todd." Jasmine beckoned him forward with a finger.

He leaned down. "Yes, Miss Gentry?"

She kissed his cheek. "You're a very good chef. Thank you for this."

"You're very welcome." Just as he turned to leave, the front door opened.

The sun was so low in the sky that it made it impossible to see who was coming in; only a couple of shadowy figures could be seen. One of them was slender and very tall. As the door closed behind them, I saw that one of them was Tiffany. And she was dressed to the nines.

The other woman looked around the room, then her eyes stopped on my mother. She went straight to her. "Lila?"

Mom nodded. "Yes."

"It's me, Lila. It's Lola—your baby sister!" She held out her arms.

Mom got up with her hands over her mouth. "Lola? You were so little the last time I saw you."

We all just stood there, feeling stunned. Then Tiffany was at my side. "A suit, Jasper?"

"Huh?" I pulled my attention away from my mother and her sister to look at Tiffany. "My God. Look at you. You look amazing."

"So do you." She ran her fingers along my collar. "You clean up nice, Jasper Gentry."

"So do you." I pulled her into my arms. "Forgive me and let's start over. Please."

"Only if you can forgive me, too. I've seen the light, Jasper. I know I've been jealous and have pulled away from you and Jasmine —all the while blaming you for leaving me out of things. I'm done with that. So, if you want to start over, I'm in."

Jasmine came up to us, looking at us holding each other. "Momma, you look stunning."

Tiffany caught the new jewelry all over Jasmine. "Seems you've been bejeweled, Jas."

"Yes, I have." Jasmine held up her hand to show her mother the ring. "This is to remind me of the day I became a Gentry. All the stones are real, Momma. They are all very 'spensive, and I must take good care of them all."

Tiffany smiled at me. "Nice, Daddy."

I let her go. "I wanted her to have something to commemorate this important day in our family. Take a look at the gems; they're really gorgeous."

Tiffany leaned over to look at the jewelry. "These are so pretty, Jas'. You're so lucky."

As her attention was taken with our daughter, I pulled what I'd bought for Tiffany out of my pocket. When she turned back around, she found me on one knee with a huge engagement ring in my hand.

Everyone stopped talking as they saw my pose. "Hi, Tiff."

Her hand flew to cover her gaping mouth. "Jasper?"

"Tiffany, I've loved you for many years. Some of them, we may have been apart, but my heart was always yours. You've given me more joy than anything else. And you've given me this beautiful little girl now, too. I don't care about any of the other stuff. All I care about now is the fact that Jasmine and I are Gentrys and you aren't. I'd like to fix that ASAP. I figure the best way to do that is to ask you to marry me, so we can get going on this family we started a while back. Jasmine needs some baby brothers and sisters after all. So, what do you say? Will you make me the happiest man alive and become my wife?"

Her entire body shook as she looked at me with tear-filled eyes. And for a moment, I wasn't sure what her answer would be. Then Jasmine tugged at her mother's dress. "So, will ya, Momma? Will you become a Gentry like Daddy and me?"

A slow nod made my heart start beating again. It had stopped when she said nothing at all. "I will marry you, Jasper."

I had to hold her shaking hand still to slip the ring onto her finger. "It fits." I got up, then pulled her into my arms. "Just like us —it just fits perfectly."

"I love you." Her arms slid around my neck, then her lips touched mine.

As we kissed, everyone clapped, and I knew she and I could build the kind of family we both could be proud of. Alone, we could do okay, but together, I knew, we could do great things.

I felt Jasmine tugging at my pant leg and pulled my mouth away to look down at her. "Can I have a hug from you guys, too?"

Laughing, I picked her up, and Tiffany and I kissed her cheeks as people took pictures and laughed. I saw Mom and her sister holding hands as they looked at us and knew that was the start of something good, too.

It wasn't happening overnight, but our family was healing, growing, bonding, and learning how to love and forgive—nothing could've ever made me happier.

TIFFANY

One year later ...

A month after our engagement, Jasper and I agreed that I should have the birth control implants removed so we could get going on our family that we wanted to grow. No one was more excited about that endeavor than Jasmine.

She'd even come with me to the doctor to get the little stick taken out of my arm. She said she had to be there every step of the way for her new baby brother or sister.

Of course, there was one crucial step she couldn't be there for, but for all the rest, she would be included. And Jasper was there as well. We were a three-pack, as he'd started calling us.

Even at our wedding, Jasmine walked with me down the aisle, leaving me at the end and telling us both good luck and that she loved us. Our little girl was the best.

So, when the year went by, and no baby news came, Jasmine got pretty disappointed. As I dropped her off at school that day, she saw one of her classmate's mothers walking down the sidewalk, her tummy round. "That's Stacy's mom. She's going to have a baby boy next month. Stacy's going to get to be in the room with her. She's having him at home. I thought you had to go to the hospital to have a baby."

"Some women would rather not go to the hospital," I said. "Now, you remember to take a long look at your spelling words before you take the test, Jas'. I know you can do better than you did last week. You've just got to try."

"I know." She waited for the teacher to come to get her out of the car, watching the pregnant woman waddling by. "If you ever do get pregnant, Momma, can we have the baby at home?"

"I don't know about that." I was pretty much a big wimp when it came to pain. "And I'm sure I will get pregnant someday, Jasmine. That birth control I had in my arm was strong. It's just taking a while to wear off." At least that was what I'd hoped.

After dropping her off, I went back to the ranch. I'd taken the day off work to help Jasper build a treehouse for Jasmine. We were close to getting it finished; I wanted to put the finishing touches on it as he put in the last nails and screws.

Climbing up the ladder on the tall oak tree, I tossed the curtains up to him. "Catch, Jasper."

He leaned out and caught them, then held out his hand to help me up. "Curtains, too? I think you're going overboard, Tiff."

"I think every home should have curtains." I climbed onto the board that served as the floor. "And I want to paint this floor pink before we're all said and done with this thing."

He pointed at the can of paint that sat in the far corner. "I picked that up this morning. We'll leave that for the very last thing." Smiling away, he pulled out his pocketknife to cut through some binding on a roll of something he'd brought. "I got her a cowhide rug too. Check this out."

A white-and-tan pattern covered the area he unfurled the rug on. "Nice. Is it one of ours?"

With a nod, he laid out on it, patting the place beside him. "Sure is. It's comfy, too."

I moved over join him, looking up at the tree limbs overhead that soon wouldn't be seen after he put the roof on. He'd gotten the walls up the day before, and the roof was today's most significant project.

Pulling me close, he kissed the side of my head. "She's gonna love this."

"I think you're right." I looked into his blue eyes as he gazed at me.

"We've got the walls up. No one can see us up here, Tiff."

I smiled, thinking he was up to something. "Oh, yeah?"

His fingers slipped into my blouse. "We could get naked and do naughty things up here if we had the urge to."

"We could." I moved my hand down his body until I felt the bulge in his jeans. "Seems someone has an urge."

He moved his hand in between my legs. "Someone seems pretty hot down there. I should totally help you out and pull those hot jeans off you—let you get some cool air flowing around."

We hurried to help rid the other of their clothes, then I found myself flat on my back, looking up at tree limbs and glimpses of blue sky as my husband moved his body over mine.

"I've never broken in a treehouse before." I kissed a line up his neck as he moved in a slow rhythm. "It's kind of nice, getting in touch with nature like this."

He hiked my leg up, slipping in deeper. "Yeah, I think I might need to build us a treehouse of our very own."

I liked the way he thought—and felt—as his muscular body moved over mine. His hot lips scorched my skin as he kissed my neck, then sucked the spot behind my ear, driving me insane. My nails dug into his back as he moved faster and I bucked, wanting more from him.

Sweat covered our bodies as the heat we'd made filled the area within the walls of the small structure. The occasional breeze coming in from the open roof was all the air we had. Our bodies slid over the other as the sweat slicked us up.

His pelvic bone rubbed my clit over and over until I was nothing but a mess of desire, clawing at his back, arching to meet each hard thrust he gave me. Then I spiraled into a frenzy of lust and passion that took me to the place only he'd ever taken me.

His cock jerked and filled me with his hot seed. He kept pumping and pumping until he had nothing left to give. "Damn, baby. You're on fire today. We do have to get ourselves our very own treehouse."

I laughed as I ran my hand through his dark hair. "We could call it our love nest."

"We sure could." His eyes glistened as he looked down at me. "You're so beautiful, Tiffany Gentry. Have I ever told you that before?"

"A time or two." I ran my foot up the back of his leg. "Have I told you how much I love you and how handsome you are?"

He rolled his eyes. "Just every day." Then he kissed me softly, slowly, deeply. If he'd never said any words of love to me, I would have known he loved me from this kiss alone.

When he pulled back, I felt tears stinging my eyes. "Wow. You never cease to amaze me."

"Ditto." He sighed heavily. "Well, I could literally do this all day with you, but we do have this treehouse to finish. Jasmine wants to have a slumber party up here tonight. And I'm gonna need a roof over us for that to happen."

Sitting up, I found my clothes in the pile that surrounded us. "I think she means she and some friends are going to have a slumber party out here. Not her and us."

"No way." He hopped up and put his jeans back on. "She means us, baby. We're the three-pack. We do everything together."

"If she's got friends to do this with, then we can have our own little camp out in our bedroom." Every once in a while, I liked to have a two-pack.

His dark brows raised. "We *could* do that."

I put my clothes on. "Good. Let's get this finished, then I'll make calls to Jasmine's friends' mothers to set things up for her slumber party tonight."

It took us the entire day to finish. But we got it done. And the look on our daughter's and her friends' faces when we took them all out back to the finished treehouse made all that hard work worth it.

"Daddy! Momma! It's so perfect!" Jasmine screamed as she climbed up the ladder, followed by her two best friends.

Jasper had his arm around me as we looked up at the girls and he said, "There's an intercom in there that goes to our bedroom. You can push that button and tell us if you need anything. As you see, we've set you girls up pretty good."

Their little heads poked out the windows as Jasmine said excitedly, "There's even a little television up here!"

Her friend Terri added, "And a mini fridge!"

"And you have three sleeping bags up here, too!" Her other friend, Leticia, called out.

"I think you girls will be just fine up there." I moved my hand down and patted Jasper's ass. "We'll be inside if you need us."

Jasper seemed a little unsure of leaving them out there all night. "Remember, you've got the intercom if you get scared, Jazzy."

"Yeah, I know," she shouted from inside of the treehouse. Then there was screaming. "Are you kidding me? Pudding pops, too? You guys are the best!"

Jasper and I turned to leave as he said, "We really are the best."

"I agree." As we headed inside, I found myself feeling pretty frisky and was sure our night would be even more fun than Jasmine's would be.

And boy was I right.

Two months later, I woke up out of a dead sleep and had to sprint to the bathroom as puke rose in my throat. When I was done, I turned to find Jasper looking at me. "You okay?"

I went to the sink to brush my teeth. "It just hit me. Maybe I ate something bad yesterday."

Jasper reached under the sink and pulled out my unopened box of tampons. "Funny how you haven't opened this box in two months."

Spitting the mouthwash out, I gasped. "You're right."

An hour later, we were dressed and in the car, going to buy a pregnancy test. It was on a Sunday, and Jasmine had slept in. She was barely waking up when her daddy and I got back.

Rubbing her sleepy eyes, she came out into the hall when she heard us going into our room. "Morning."

"Morning, Jasmine." I looked at Jasper, who nodded. "Wanna come in here with us? I might have good news." I held up the box with the test in it.

She looked at it with disbelief. "No way."

Jasper wasn't ready to believe it yet either. "Maybe. It's just a maybe at this point. But if you want to be in here when the results come in, it would be nice."

Taking the test, I went into the bathroom while they waited patiently in the bedroom for me. After peeing on the stick, I placed it on the edge of the tub, then closed my eyes and left the bathroom. "Two minutes, guys."

We all waited, looking at each other with blank stares until the timer on Jasper's phone went off. Then we all three walked toward the bathroom.

Jasmine put her hand up to stop us before we went in to see the results. "Wait. How will I know if you are pregnant?"

"If there's a plus sign, then I'm pregnant. A minus sign, then I'm not," I told her.

"Okay." She nodded. "Let's go."

All three of us leaned over to see the results, then Jasper whispered, "Looks like we're about to become a four-pack."

The End

6. HIS REVENGE EXTENDED EPILOGUE

JASPER

Five years later...

"Daddy, don't wait for me, keep going," Jasmine shouted as she tried to catch up to me. Her favorite cow was down with a calf coming. She'd started laboring in the south pasture and couldn't be moved up to the barn to have her baby. Jasmine was a wreck over it. She'd planned everything out, and nothing was going as she'd wanted it to.

When we'd gotten to the barn early that morning, we found out about the cow; my daughter had named, Josephine. We'd hopped on a couple of horses and headed out to find the cow. Jasmine, at twelve, wasn't as fast as I was on a horse. "There's really not a rush, Jazzy. These things take a long time to happen." I slowed down to let her catch up. I hadn't meant to leave her behind in the first place. She'd started out fast, then slowed down.

Just as she got up next to me, she rolled her blue eyes. "Dad, I want to be there for the birth. You know I want to be a veterinarian. This experience is priceless."

Now Jasmine wanted to be a vet, when her mom gave birth to

her baby brother, Collin, four years ago, she wanted to become a baby doctor – as she'd called it.

Yes, we made the decision to name our baby boy after my grandfather. I thought it would be a nice thing to do for the man since he'd left us the ranch and all his money.

My father wasn't sure it was such a great idea. He had the idea that our son might grow up to be an asshole like his namesake. I had no such worries. I truly believed that my grandfather was a product of his raising and nothing more than that. If he'd been raised to think of people as equals, then his life would've been completely different. That was my opinion anyway.

Jasmine pointed to a dark lumpy shadow in the field. "Over there, Dad. Let's go." She hurried off on her horse and now it was my horse who struggled to keep up the fast pace.

Like a pro, she pulled her horse up short as soon as she got to the cow, then slid off the saddle and went right to her knees next to Josephine. Hugging her thick neck, she whispered, "I'm here now, Josephine. It's all going to be okay." She pulled a wet cloth out of her backpack then laid it on top of the cow's head. "Here ya go, girl. This is going to help cool you down. Soon you'll have a little baby of your own."

I got off my horse, then went to stand next to her. "How's she doin', doc?"

Looking up at me, she wiggled her finger. "Come down here, Daddy. Cows get real nervous when you stand over them. And my cow needs to be calm."

Kneeling next to Jasmine, I tried to be what she needed me to. "Okay, doc. What should I do now?"

"Can you just pet her nice and slow while I go look at her – um, well, you know – to see how she's doing down there?" She looked at me as if she was entrusting me with the most important thing in the world.

"I'll do it, Jazzy. You can count on me to keep her calm. I did help your momma when she had Collin. I think I can remember how to do it." I ran my hand over the cow's head. "You okay there, Josephine?"

The cow grunted as if telling me that she could be better.

Jasmine went on her hands and knees to look at the situation at the south end of the bovine. "Well, I guess this is what it's supposed to look like."

"Yeah, it's kind of supernatural, isn't it?" I recalled seeing what had happened to my wife's hoo-hoo just before Collin's head crowned. It had nearly knocked me off my feet. There'd been that wonder if she'd ever be the same down there. But then I remembered that she'd had Jasmine and had returned to peak condition.

"What if the feet come out first, Dad?" Jasmine's question was valid. She'd seen that happen before to other cows.

"Then we get the chains, and some help and deliver the calf and pray that it's okay." There was little else one could do when that happened.

Jasmine ran her finger over her brow. "What if Mom's baby comes out that way?"

Tiffany was two months away from having our third child. Another girl and she was breech at the time. "Well, first of all, human babies don't come feet first very often. Butt first, is how they can come. But the doctor has ways of moving the baby around to come headfirst the way all babies are normally born."

"But what if she doesn't get moved, then what happens?" The cow made a deep grunt then Jasmine's eyes lit up as she pointed at it. "Hey, Josephine, I can see something. Keep pushing, girl. You're gonna have this baby out in no time."

Trying to get off the touchy subject of the baby, I asked, "Can you see the head?"

"I see something." She nodded. "And it's not a hoof, so that's pretty good, right?"

"I think so." I hoped nothing would go wrong. Jasmine had high hopes of training this calf. To do what, I didn't know. She'd just said she was going to train it.

"Whoa!" She moved back fast on her hands and knees. "Watery, nasty stuff just spilled out of her."

"It's almost here." I moved around to watch the birth too. "Are you ready, Jasmine?"

Nodding, she smiled. "I hope Josephine is ready too."

Not three minutes later a calf was on the ground, and I had to let Jasmine know she had a baby bull to train. "Well, it looks like you're going to have your work cut out for ya, girl. This is a bull."

A frown filled her face as she knew bulls weren't easy to get to do anything. "Oh man."

⬥

TIFFANY

"Collin, honey, please put on your pants," I coaxed our four-year-old son."

"No!" He took off like a flash of lightning, out of his bedroom then into the hallway – stark naked.

It wasn't like I could chase after him. My belly was huge, I carried the baby girl all out in front, unlike the way the other two had been carried, mostly in my back. At least I had, what my doctor promised, would be an easier labor with her, carrying her this way. *Back labor is the worst.*

We'd already dubbed her Penelope, Penny for short. Avid fans of Big Bang Theory, Jasper and I had come to a quick agreement on the name for our third born child.

Tyrell's voice filtered into the bedroom where I waddled toward the door at a snail's pace. "Boy, you better get your hind end into that room and let your momma get some clothes on you."

"I don't wanna," came Collin's reply. "I like being free."

The next thing I saw was Tyrell carrying Collin back into the bedroom. "Don't we all, but civilized people wear clothes. Sorry, Bubba."

As he put my son's feet on the floor, I moved as quick as I could to get some underwear on the rogue. "At least we got this much on him."

Collin tried to dash away, but Tyrell was much too fast for him. "Not so fast, Bubba. Let's get all your clothes on. Once you're dressed, I'll take you on the buggy to see your sister's new calf. It ought to be born by now."

"Okay," Collin said as he was now excited about something.

"I should've thought about that a long time ago." I rubbed my brow as Tyrell helped my son put the rest of his clothes on. "I'm just so tired lately."

"You look a little pale." Tyrell finished up with Collin then turned his attention to me. "You go lay down, and I'll deal with him this morning. You need lots of rest, Tiffany."

I'd been wiped out for two weeks. I wasn't sure exactly what the reason for it was, but I could barely keep my eyes open. "Thanks." I yawned as I headed across the hall to the bedroom I shared with my husband. "I'll take you up on that offer."

Tossing a pillow between my knees, I used another to hold up my protruding stomach. This pregnancy hadn't gone right since the get-go. I had still had periods for the first three months of the pregnancy. I'd had no idea that I was even pregnant until I went in for a check-up and found out that I was indeed with child.

The doctor said that happens sometimes. I'd never even heard of that happening, but she'd assured me that it was a fact. It was funny how the periods stopped coming once I knew I was pregnant.

My last visit had the baby in the breech position which worried me. Even though the doctor told me that the worst case scenario would be a C-section, I still wasn't at peace with it.

A sharp kick to my kidney had me wincing with pain. "Hey, not funny, Penny." She must've thought it was hilarious as she began to tap dance on my bladder next, sending pee out of me and soiling the bed. "Damn it, girl!"

Getting up, I went to take a shower, put on clean clothes, then I went across the hall to sleep in Jasmine's bed. I passed the new maid as I walked across. "You've got to clean the sheets, Clair." I pointed at my belly. "She kicked the piss out of me."

Trying her best not to break a smile, she nodded. "I'll get them cleaned and deodorize the mattress too."

"Thank you." I could've been humiliated, but that little scene had played out more than one time since I'd gotten huge just as the last trimester hit me. "There'll be some bonuses in your paychecks for dealing with me."

She shook her head. "No, Mrs. Gentry, that's not necessary. It is my job to clean for you and your family — even that little one who is still in your belly. I can't wait to meet Miss Penny."

"Me too." I really couldn't wait to have her out of my womb and into my arms. "I'm going to take a nap in Jasmine's room. You haven't cleaned in there yet, have you? I'd hate to mess up clean sheets."

"I'll leave her room to the last. I'll let you rest. You look so tired." She smiled at me to lessen the blow. "The baby is taking much away from you. You should ask Chef Todd to make you a steak for lunch. You look as if you need some protein and iron especially. Add in a spinach salad too."

"I will do that, Clair. Thanks for your concern." Having so many people around who were looking after us all was nice. I hadn't grown up that way, and it made me feel better that my children would get to know life in this way, with lots of help.

Going to lie down on my daughter's bed, I barely hit it when the urge to pee hit me. "Damn it."

Getting back up, I went to the bathroom for the fifth time that morning. How Penny had found any pee to kick out of me was a mystery. I supposed she'd found a reserve batch to pounce on.

As I sat down on the toilet, my head began to swim. I had to hold onto the wall and the cabinet to keep myself from falling off the thing. "I will not pass out this way. No one will find my ass in the air and my head on the tiled floor like some college girl after an all-nighter of drinking."

Then I tumbled over anyway.

Well, shit.

JASPER

It didn't take long for the calf to stand up on its own four wobbly legs. Tyrell laughed as it took its first steps. "Looks like you, Jasper, after a night at The Watering Hole."

Scowling at him, I pointed at my kids. "Too early, too many young ears, and so not cool, Tyrell."

Nodding, he grinned. "Okay, bro. I get it. You don't want the youngsters to know about your rough and rowdy past."

He'd brought Collin down to see the calf and told me that Tiffany had looked tired, so he told her to go take a nap. I felt I'd been a little too busy with things to pay enough attention to her lately. "Would you mind watching the kids while I go check on Tiff?"

He nodded. "Not a problem. Go see to her. She really has been looking worn out lately. Like even after a nap, she's still pale, and her voice is too quiet."

Getting on my horse, I had to stop before galloping off as Collin came to me, pulling at my boot. "Dad, I want to go too. I wanna ride the horse with you."

Tyrell came up, picking my son up and putting him on his shoulders. "How about I give you a ride over to Old Blue over there that your sister rode down here. I'll put you on him and give you a ride. Let Daddy go see to Mommy, k, Bubba?"

"Okay," Collin giggled as Tyrell jumped around like a bucking bronco. "Whoa, Uncle Tyrell!"

"Hang on, cowboy!" Tyrell hollered as he hopped over to the other horse.

Jasmine was all wrapped up in the new calf, bull or not; she was determined to bond with the thing. "And you're going to be a good boy, aren't you, Bully?"

"You might come up with a nicer name for him, Jazzy," I recommended. "Maybe something like Ferdinand or Sweet Pea."

She just shook her head. "No, he's gonna be called Bully, but he's gonna be nice. You'll see. I'm gonna feed him flowers every day."

Tyrell and I laughed as I took off to go see how Tiffany was doing. "I'll see y'all up at the house when you guys get done down here."

When I came into the barn, I saw Cash putting away some bags of horse feed. "Getting your cowboy workout, Cash?"

Hauling another fifty-pound bag out of the back of his truck, he nodded. "Hey, it works." He tossed the bag on top of the pile of them then flexed his bicep. "See."

Getting off the horse, I pulled the saddle off, flexing my own biceps. "And you think I don't know that?" But we had a gym in the mansion too. "It takes more than moving some hay and feed bags to keep fit. Thank God for that gym our old granddad had the foresight to put in before he kicked the bucket."

"Yeah, he was such a forward thinker." He laughed, and I joined him.

Our grandfather wasn't much into forward thinking. My bet was he'd had a designer come in when he had the renovations done to the wood cabin styled mansion.

"I'm gonna go see how Tiff's doing." I headed out after putting the saddle and bridle away then let the horse go to run out to the pasture. "She's been tired lately."

"She's looking pretty bad. Bobbi Jo even said something about that yesterday." Cash stopped pulling bags of feed out of the truck for a minute. "She said you should take her to the doctor because she's too pale."

"Tiff's a redhead," I reminded him. "Sure, she's got her hair dyed black for reasons I don't know. But she's naturally a redhead, and she's always been on the pale side."

"You know, you see her all the time," Cash pointed out. "Maybe that's why you aren't as alarmed by her appearance as everyone else is. When's the last time she saw the doctor?"

"A couple of weeks ago. And she's due to see her again in two weeks." I went to the barn door to leave. "I'm sure she'll be fine until that appointment. Until then, I'll get Todd to boost her nutrients. And I'll get her walking more. She's been sleeping too much lately is what I'm starting to think. She just needs to move more and get better food in her system." I was sure that was all she'd need to get back into her usual good health.

"The baby is still breech, right?" Cash asked before I left.

"Yeah." That had nothing to do with Tiffany's wellbeing. "Why do you ask that?"

"Maybe the baby's position isn't letting her eat enough. That's what happened to that one cow last year. Remember, she was pregnant but kept losing weight. When we palpated her, we found the calf was breech. Maybe that's what's happening to Tiffany."

"Maybe." I thought about it a second. "Well, if that's the case, then we'll need to get more nourishment into her by giving her fluids instead of solid food. Leave it to me; I'll get her back to where she needs to be."

"You'd better. Tiffany has two more kids that need her too, Jasper." He eyed me as if I didn't know that. "You can't raise them all on your own if anything should happen to your wife."

"Now, why would you even say a thing like that, Cash?" I left the barn, somewhat pissed at my baby brother. Sure, he was younger than me, but he wasn't any dumbass kid. His remark didn't sit well with me at all.

Once, I'd thought about taking Jasmine all on my own. But I'd dropped that foolish notion pretty damn quickly, and knew I couldn't do it all on my own anymore.

I had a lot of respect for Tiffany for doing it on her own for six years with our oldest child. As much respect as I had for her, I knew I wasn't up to the task she'd taken on when she was just a teenage girl.

Thankfully, I didn't have to worry about that at all.

TIFFANY

"Shit!" I'd fallen and ended up head over heels, bunched up between the toilet and the standup shower.

Cursing the small bathroom attached to Jasmine's room, I made a promise to renovate the smaller bathrooms. There was a lot of wasted space in the mansion; I was sure I could figure out a way to use some of it to make some of the small bathrooms larger. No one would know when an accident like mine might occur after all.

My belly got in my way as I tried to maneuver my body around so I could get up. If anyone found me that way, I would have to die. And that's when I heard Jasper's voice, "Tiff? Where are you? Clair said you were in here, in Jazzy's room."

"Jasper," I could barely say the words as my position had my lungs bunched up too. "I'm in the bathroom."

"Tiff?" he called out again. "Come out, come out, wherever you are."

"Help," I whimpered far too quietly.

I looked at the bathroom door and saw that I'd locked it. *Well, of course, I did, crap.*

The sound of the bedroom door closing made me almost cry. I was stuck, and it seemed like it was getting harder and harder to breathe. The baby started moving too, kicking, pushing, punching. I guessed she was having a hard time of it too.

I thought about Jasmine and Collin and how horrible it would be for them to say their mother had died from falling off the toilet and getting herself stuck in an upside down position with her hind end up in the air.

They would have to bury me in a closed casket because even in death, I'd wear a scarlet hue from embarrassment so bad, it would scar my cheeks. And what of little Penny in my tummy? What would happen to her?

Sounds in the bedroom perked me up as I heard Clair say, "She was in here, Mr. Gentry, I know for certain that she was. Did you check everywhere?"

"I did," he said.

"He didn't," I said in a hushed whisper as nothing more would come out.

My husband and I had been through this argument over and over in our marriage. He'd say he looked everywhere for whatever I'd sent him to find. But I would go into the room, find the thing exactly where I'd told him it would be. So, I knew that my husband never looked everywhere – not ever.

Hopefully, Clair would. Even though if anyone had to find me this way, I'd rather it be my husband over anyone else. But I couldn't look a gift horse in the mouth at that time. I was losing more and more air with each passing moment. I knew I'd pass out if someone didn't come to find me soon. After passing out, I was pretty sure the next thing would be to stop breathing. Penny nor I needed that to happen.

"I told her to go see Chef Todd," Clair said. "I bet she's in the kitchen. You didn't check with him, have you, Mr. Gentry?"

"No, I haven't," Jasper said. "I'll go check now."

"No!" I said as loud as I could. But I heard them closing the door behind them, making it even harder for someone to hear me.

It seemed like a long time had passed as I stayed there, stuck. It began to look hopeless to me. I thought about way back before Jasper, and I had gotten married. He'd had this idea of taking Jasmine away from me as revenge for what I'd done to him – keeping her a secret. He'd been sure he could raise her on his own back then.

Now I had to wonder if that could be true. *Can he raise Jasmine and Collin, and possibly Penny – if she makes it through this?*

I hated to think that way, but as the darkness began to descend around me, making me lose sight of any hope that I'd be found before it was too late, I had no choice.

Could Jasper be enough for our kids? Could he make sure they felt loved, secure, and happy all at the same time? He and I could pull that off together, but alone? Well, I had no idea if either of us could pull that off for three kids all on our own.

I needed him and knew that. And he needed me. We'd made a family together. We counted on each other for support with the kids. If the baby made it and I didn't, then Jasper would have long nights with her. He'd be waking up every two hours to feed her. And then where would that leave our other kids?

When Collin was born, it took us both to look after both kids, even though Jasmine was seven and very helpful most of the time. But then there was the rest of Jasper's family. Cash and Tyrell, as well as their significant others, had always been willing to lend a hand or even two when we needed it.

At least Jasper would have help. At least I didn't have to worry about him being completely alone.

The baby kicked me hard, and I grunted with the impact. I started thinking about Jasmine. We'd always had a connection that was deep. Maybe if I kept calling to her in my head, she'd hear it somehow and come find me.

Over and over again, I called her name out silently. I knew she was fascinated with the newborn calf, but maybe she'd pay attention to the niggling feeling that I needed help.

Crazier things had happened between us before. She and I were on the same wavelength more often than not.

Please listen to my voice, Jasmine!

JASPER

Slamming into the kitchen through the back entrance, Jasmine hauled ass passed me. "Dad, where's Mom?"

"That's a great question, Jazzy." I still had no clue where Tiffany was. "Clair said she went to your room to nap, but I didn't find her there."

Jasmine ran off, and Tyrell and Collin came in. "Jasmine just started freaking out about her mom. What's up?" Tyrell asked me.

Shrugging, I had no idea what was wrong with my daughter. "I've got no idea."

I picked up Collin and put him on my back. "Come on, boy, let's go chase after your sister."

"She's acting crazy, Dad." Collin held on tight as I headed to Jasmine's room again.

I'd barely topped the stairs when I saw Jasmine fly into her bedroom. "Mom? Mom? Are you in here?"

I came in behind her as she ran to the closet and through the door open. "I doubt she's in there," I said.

"We've got to look everywhere, Dad." She came out, shaking her head. "She's not in there." Pointing at the closed bathroom door, she asked. "Did you check the bathroom?"

"No." I didn't see why she'd use that little bathroom.

"Dad, how many times has Mom told you to check even the places that you don't think something might be?" Jasmine went to open the bathroom door as I put Collin down.

"A lot of times," I said. "But that's about things, not people. People can make sounds, Jazzy. They can answer when you call out for them. I did call out for your Mom a lot while I was in here and she didn't answer. I hate to keep looking in the same place when she has to be somewhere else."

544

Her hand on the doorknob, she looked back at me. "Dad, this door is locked."

"No way." I went over and tried to open it myself. Leaning in close, I shouted, "Tiff?"

Nothing.

Jasmine shook her head. "She can't answer for some reason. Dad we've gotta get that door open."

Collin looked like he was about to cry. "Where's Mommy?"

"Probably in here," I said to comfort him.

"Why isn't she answering?" he asked as he went backward to sit on the bed. "Something's wrong."

I couldn't think like that. I didn't know what I would do if something happened to my wife. "No, Collin. Nothing is wrong."

Jasmine ran out of the room, only to return with Tyrell who had a small tool bag. "Is she locked in there?" he asked.

"I'm not sure. But the door is locked." I unzipped the bag to retrieve a screwdriver to take the doorknob off.

"How are you not sure?" Tyrell asked.

Jasmine answered as I was busy taking out the screws. "She's not answering, Uncle Tyrell."

"That's not good," he said. "Maybe you kids should come with me. Let Daddy get in there first."

Jasmine shook her head while Collin ran to Tyrell and clung to his leg. I looked at him as I took out the last screw. "Okay, get him out of here. Jasmine stays."

With a nod, Tyrell left with Collin in tow. And I looked at our daughter. "Now remember, no matter what we find, we can deal with it together."

She nodded. "Open it, Dad."

When I pushed the door open, it stuck before I could get it all the way open. Then Jasmine stuck her head inside. "Mom! Mom, are you okay?"

When no one answered, I stopped breathing. "I've gotta call an ambulance."

Jasmine wiggled her way into the bathroom. "Dad, she's fallen. I don't think she's breathing."

I could only peek into the tiny bathroom and could see that Tiff had fallen off the toilet and lodged her body between it and the standup shower. Jasmine was too small to get her mother out of that precarious position.

After calling 911, I began to unscrew the hinges on the door then pulled it all the way off. "Jas, go get your blanket off your bed, honey. I'm gonna wrap Momma up in it."

She hurried to do as I'd said and I picked up my wife; her head lolled back as she was out cold. "Tiffany, baby, can you wake up for me?"

Jasmine came back, putting the bedspread over her mother. "I'll get a washcloth wet with cold water."

Jostling Tiffany as I carried her to Jasmine's bed, I felt my heart throbbing with each step. "Wake up, wake up, wake up."

Jasmine came to us with the cold cloth in her hand. She pressed it to Tiffany's forehead then kissed her on the cheek. "Momma, wake up. Please, wake up."

The slightest flutter of eyelashes had me breathing again. "Tiff?"

"Momma, please open your eyes," Jasmine pleaded.

Slowly, her green eyes opened. "Hi," she whispered. "You finally found me."

Nodding, I kissed her lips. "I swear to you and God above that from now on; I will search out every nook and cranny before I stop looking for anything, ever again."

The sound of sirens had Tiffany looking wide-eyed. "Oh, Lord. You called 911?"

"I had to."

Jasmine cut in, "You didn't look like you were breathing, Mom."

With an embarrassed expression, Tiff whispered to me. "Did you pull my panties up?"

I hadn't. "I was a little more worried about you, not your state of undress."

Jasmine laughed. "Come on, Mom, I'll help you. But you need to let them check you out just to be safe."

An hour later we were in the hospital. Seemed Tiffany had grown anemic and needed to be hospitalized for the duration of the pregnancy.

Two months later, Penny was born. She'd switched positions all be herself, and Tiffany had another natural childbirth, which she was ecstatic about.

"She's got my read hair and green eyes," Tiff said as she ran her hand over our baby girl's tiny head. "I'm gonna let mine go back to red. I only dyed it to match the rest of you. With Collin coming out looking like you too, I've been feeling left out. But now that Penny's here, I feel like a part of the family."

I'd had no idea my wife had felt that way. Kissing her sweet lips, I whispered, "You've always been the best part of the family, hot stuff."

Somehow, our happily ever after just kept going on, no matter what trials or tribulations came our way. And I was more than thankful for that.

The End

7. FIONA'S CATCH

A His Revenge Extra

Collin

Going to college at Texas Tech in Lubbock, Texas, was the best thing to ever happen for Hilda and me. With no one around who knew us, we could go out on occasion. Sure, it had to be really late and not many people could be around, but we could go out together, instead of staying in all the time.

I'd gotten her a small one-bedroom apartment in town. I lived in a frat house near campus. Alpha Phi Alpha was my home away from home. I didn't stay there much, though, as I preferred to spend my nights with Hilda.

She'd told her family that she worked at the college cafeteria as a cook. I wouldn't let her work, though. Her only job was taking care of me. And she did it so well too.

I'd left her that morning to come to my physics class. The start of a new school year had the campus chaotic, with new first-year students running around everywhere. I'd been there two years already; I knew where everything was and didn't ever have to rush.

Turning a corner in the main building, I ran smack dab into a dainty blonde who cursed with the impact, "Oh, darn. Sorry."

She moved to the right to get out of my way, but so did I. "Sorry."

We both dodged to the left. "Oh, my goodness!"

Reaching out, I took her by the shoulders to stop us both. "How about I go right, and you go left?"

She nodded. "Sounds like a plan to me." Then she bit her lower lip. "You don't happen to know where English 101 is, do you?"

"I can tell you this much; you're going in the opposite direction." I turned her around. "Come with me. I'll get you there."

"That would be a great relief if you did." She clutched her book bag as if it were a lifeline. "I'm so lost here. My parents dropped me off yesterday, and I've felt like crying ever since then."

"Oh, there's no reason to cry." I patted her on the back as we headed to our classes that happened to be right next to each other. "This campus isn't all that hard to get to know. I can show you around after class. I'm Collin, by the way."

"My name's Fiona," she looked at me with wide sky blue eyes, "Witherspoon."

"Of the Cape Cod Witherspoon's?" I had to ask as the family was famous for being presidents of many banks in the northern states.

"Well, my father isn't into banking. He's into textiles. But we are a part of that family, yes." She looked down as if shy all of a sudden. "And your last name is?"

"Gentry." I wasn't trying to impress the girl, but I thought she might be interested in knowing about our ranch. "My family owns Whisper Ranch in Carthage. Have you heard of it? We supply beef to most of the north."

"Are you kidding me?" she asked with a smile. "Your ranch's name is on almost every package of meat my family buys. What a strange fate, meeting you, Collin Gentry."

"Funny that we both know of each other without really knowing of each other." I laughed a bit as we arrived to our classrooms. "I'll be in that room there. If you wait for me when your class finishes, I'll show you around. That way, you won't get lost for the rest of the day."

"Or you could just walk me to my classes, Collin." She sighed. "I wouldn't be opposed to that at all. I feel so alone here."

It was the right thing to do for a girl in her position. "I think I can manage that, Fiona." We stopped at the door she needed to go through. "See you after class then."

All smiles, I couldn't help but notice how pretty she was. "Thanks, Collin. I really do appreciate your help."

"I'm sure you do." As she walked into the room, I watched her stance. Fiona stood up straight, her head high, her steps precise. She was the kind of woman a man of my stature would be expected to be with, even marry someday.

I walked away, thinking about that fact. I could never marry Hilda Stevens. Why not set my sights on a woman who would make a good wife for a man like myself?

Hilda didn't need to know what I did at college. Surely, she understood that one day I would be expected to marry a woman in my class. At least I hoped that she'd understand that.

I did keep Hilda in a nice place, and that wouldn't stop. I gave her money; I wouldn't stop doing that either. Nothing would be different, except that I would have another woman in my life. Surely, Hilda knew that would happen someday.

All throughout the class, I thought about Fiona. Her blonde hair, so shiny and soft-looking, made her look like an angel. Those sky blue eyes were so pretty too. Her small frame, so petite and shapely, was another plus. The young woman had it all in spades.

I'd be a fool to miss out on my chance to get to know the woman who didn't know anyone else yet. I held the advantage over every other man at Texas Tech. I'd be a damn fool to waste that chance.

So when class finished, I waited next to the door of her classroom until she came out. The smile on her face told me she was happy to see me standing there. "Oh, good. I was hoping you meant it when you said you'd walk me to my classes today."

"And take you to lunch too, if that's okay with you, Fiona." I thought I shouldn't let her get off on her own without me, or another man might swoop in and snatch up my little flower.

"Lunch too?" Her chest heaved as she took a deep breath. "I think I've found my first friend here in Texas."

Taking her hand, I looped it in my arm, then took her book bag. "I think you have too."

FIONA

His dark hair had curls upon curls. His eyes were as blue as the Atlantic Ocean. His hands were as large as platters. And his attention never left me.

Collin Gentry was all man. From his tall stature to his muscular build, I knew he had more strength than any man I'd ever known back on the East Coast.

We walked, hand in hand, down the pathway that led to the lecture hall. I had a biology class, and the professor had a speech to give us. "I'm not at all excited about this next class."

"I'm free. I can sit in on the lecture with you." He leaned in close, whispering in my ear, "If you want me to."

The way his warm breath tickled my ear made me giggle. "Oh, Collin, I'd love it if you came with me."

"Then I'll stay." He squeezed my hand, then let it go to drape his arm around my shoulders. "I like hanging out with you, Fiona. This last month has been a blast."

We'd done a lot in the last month. Our dates had consisted of roller skating, eating at expensive restaurants, and going to movies. Those were my favorites. We'd had our first kiss at the movies. His lips touching mine had sent shivers running through my entire body. No one's kiss had ever done that to me before.

The only thing I didn't care for was what had happened after that kiss. He'd asked me if I'd ever been kissed before. When I laughed and said, of course I had, he got distant, moody, and quiet for the remainder of the movie.

But when we walked out of the theater, he was fine again. I didn't want to ask him why he'd acted that way. I didn't want to spoil the rest of our evening.

"Here you go, Fiona." Collin held the door to the lecture hall open for me.

I went in before him. "Thank you, Collin."

Before I could find a seat, he took my hand, pulling me to sit in the back with him. "Let's stay back here."

In all honesty, I didn't get much of what my professor had to say. as Collin's hand on my thigh made it hard for me to concentrate. And after class, when we walked to lunch, he pulled me behind an ancient oak tree. His lips pressed against mine, then he pulled them away and asked, "Fiona, I need you to answer me honestly. Even if it's something you're ashamed of, please tell me God's honest truth. Okay?"

His finger moving along my jawline made me feel dazed. "Sure, Collin. I'll answer you honestly. What is it?"

"Fiona, I like you a lot. I'm falling for you hard. I know it's only been a month, but I've gotta know if you feel the same way I do?" He licked his lips as he stared into mine.

"Of course, I feel the same way, Collin. I wouldn't spend every available minute with you if I didn't like you a whole lot." I couldn't out the smile off of my face; I was so happy.

"Good." He kissed me again, then pulled his mouth away from mine as he looked into my eyes. "Now the real question. Have you ever been with a man before? You know what I'm asking, right?"

"In a Biblical sense?" I asked to make sure.

He nodded. "Yes."

My cheeks heated with embarrassment. "No, Collin. I have never been with a man that way before. I've dated in high school, nothing serious, though. But no more than that."

"You have kissed a man before." His lips formed a straight line. "How many men have you kissed, Fiona?"

Crossing my arms over my chest, I didn't like being asked such a question. It wasn't as if that should matter in the least. "How many women have *you* kissed, Collin."

He held up two fingers. "Now, you tell me your number."

"I've got one more than that. And that is including you. Is your number including me?"

He nodded. "I can't say I'm thrilled with your number."

"I can't say that it should matter, Collin. I'm not a child. I have been through adolescence. I dare you to find another woman who hasn't kissed a man before now." I knew I wasn't the primmest young woman in the world, but I wasn't promiscuous in the least.

"I don't want to find another woman, Fiona. I'm quite happy with you." He kissed me again, hard, wanting, pinning me to the tree.

My body went hot, and my hands moved up his muscular arms to hang around his neck. When our lips parted, both of us breathed heavy breaths. He leaned his forehead against mine. I felt as if we didn't have to say a single word about that kiss. It meant something. It meant we were moving forward.

"Do you have something else you'd like to ask me?" I whispered.

He reached into his pocket and pulled out something. Then he slipped it on my ring finger. "This is only a promise ring, Fiona. I want you to be my girl."

His girl!

"I accept." I pulled him back towards me, kissing him with a bit more passion than we'd ever had before.

When our kiss ended, he asked, "Will you come home with me to the ranch for the Thanksgiving holiday?"

"Only if you'll come home with me for the Christmas holiday." I couldn't wait to introduce my family to my cowboy.

"It's a deal." He wrapped one arm around me, leading me away. Pulling my hand up, he admired the heart-shaped ring he'd put on my finger, then kissed it. "My girl. Wow."

Yeah, wow!

COLLIN

"Because, I'd rather you stay here for Thanksgiving, Hilda." I didn't know how to tell her about how I was taking Fiona home with me the next day. "I'll only be gone for four days. I'll have to be back on Sunday for Monday's classes."

"And I have to sit here, alone?" Hilda asked with sad eyes. "Why can't I take a bus back to Carthage to spend the holiday with my family?"

Because I would have Fiona in our hometown and she couldn't see that. "Look, I'm going to leave you with lots of money. You can eat at that café you like so much. I saw a sign on the door that said it would be open on Thanksgiving. I'll be back before you know it."

Hilda sat on the sofa, looking at me with narrowed eyes. "Collin, are you being honest with me about everything?"

"Why would you even ask that?" I felt anger rising up in me.

"You haven't been staying the nights with me much since the new school year."

"My classes are a lot tougher this year. I expect the same next year too. And my frat brothers keep coming up with one idea after another that requires my presence in our frat house." I had to come up with something that sounded valid.

Looking away, Hilda sighed. "I feel a shift in our relationship."

Because there was one, but I wasn't about to end it. I sat down next to her, putting my arm around her shoulders. "Look, college isn't easy, baby. I'm sorry about that. But it's times like these that build relationships, make them stronger. Or it can break them entirely. Now, that's up to you. I'm in it for the long haul. Do you want out?"

"No." She took my face into her hands. "Collin, I love you. You know that. I don't want anyone else."

Gulping, I didn't know what to say. I did want someone else now. But I wanted Hilda too. The two women were so different. With Hilda, we had no preconceived notions about what we wanted. We wanted each other, and we wanted it all.

How can I stop having outstanding sex with Hilda?

The answer was that I couldn't.

"I don't like the way I've been feeling lately, Collin." Her hand moved up my arm. "It's almost like I'm losing you. I can feel it. I can't explain it, but in my head, you're moving on, leaving me behind."

I'd had no idea she could feel that. And it made me feel terrible. Kissing her, I held her tightly. Quite some time had gone by without us making love. Maybe she just needed that to feel better about us.

Moving closer, I pulled her onto my lap, running my hand between her legs. Heat met my hand as I pressed it against her mound. She moaned, then I stood up, carrying her to the bedroom.

Laying her on the bed, her dark hair splayed out on the pillow, I wished she could've been the one for me. I wished like crazy that she had come from a different background.

Not only was her father a drunk with no job, but he was also married to a woman he should've never married. It wasn't fair to their children to be what they were - mixed. Although it wasn't Hilda's fault, it didn't matter to society. She wasn't like me. And no one would ever allow us to be together.

Her father's family had shunned him for who he'd married. Mine would too if I did so much as publicly date Hilda. But what one does in private, as long as he keeps it private, is no one's concern. My fraternity brothers taught me that much.

You can have whoever you want, just keep it a secret. The

smartest thing to do was to keep the right kind of woman at your side in public. Most importantly, never let the two meet. That was the second cardinal rule.

Hilda spread her legs, enticing me to join her on the bed. Nibbling on her finger, she gave me that look that drove me wild. "Honey, you know you do it for me, right?"

With a nod, she wiggled her finger at me. "And you do it for me too. So come on and do it to me."

I couldn't imagine Fiona ever saying anything like that to me. She was a lady, through and through. And I needed her to be that for me. But Hilda could be my little, hidden love slave. No one would ever have to know.

Ditching my clothes, I climbed onto the bed, then moved my body over Hilda's. Slipping into her hot recesses, I felt like I was almost home. *Almost.*

Hilda could never be the woman who ran my home. She could never be the woman who had my children. She couldn't be the woman standing by my side in front of an altar where a preacher would join us in holy matrimony. That place was reserved for someone else.

What Hilda could be was my bed buddy, my partner in sex, and we did have love between us too, which made it much sweeter. All I had to do was keep them away from each other. A secret from each other.

It could be done. My frat brothers had shown me that. I could pull it all off. But Hilda had to do as I said at all times for me to make that happen.

Her soft words echoed in my head, "I will never stop loving you, Collin Gentry. I'm as much a part of you as you are a part of me. We're joined together in a way that no one can break apart."

"That's right, baby. No one can take away what we have." At least no one could if I played my cards right.

FIONA

"This is gorgeous, Collin." He drove up the long drive to the ranch house. Cattle were everywhere. "So many cows and bulls. I've never seen any up close before. This is amazing."

"Glad you like it." He pulled up in front of a large, whitewashed, wood-frame home. "Here's my family casa. It's the original house my father built when he bought this ranch. I was born in this very house."

"I was born at home too. Only my family home is a bit different than this." Brick and mortar made up our home. "I can't wait to meet your parents, Collin."

"They're eager to meet you too, Fiona." He got out and came around to open the passenger side door for me.

"A true gentleman," I said as he took my hand, helping me out.

"I aim to please." He held my hand as he led me to the front door.

His mother met us at the door. "Oh, my goodness. You are a living doll." She held her arms out to me, and I moved in for a hug, which I returned. "Fiona, it's so nice to meet you. Collin has told us all about you."

"All good things, I hope," I teased as she let me out of her hold.

A man loomed in the back of the living area, his hands in his pockets. I nodded as I saw his and Collin's resemblance. Collin took my hand, leading me towards his father. "Fiona, this is my father."

"Mr. Gentry, it's a pleasure to meet you." I extended my hand, which he caught, pulled to his lips, and kissed.

"The pleasure is all mine, Fiona. What a pretty little thing you are." He let my hand go as I blushed with the compliment.

"Thank you, sir." I leaned into Collin as he put his arm around me. "This ranch is beautiful. And this house is lovely too."

Collin's mother came up behind us. "Thank you. I made all the curtains myself." She pointed to the cow skins that adorned the wood floor. "And my husband and Collin made the rugs that are all over the house."

"How quaint." I knew my mother would die before allowing any part of a dead animal on her floors. But this wasn't Cape Cod; this was a Texas cattle ranch. I should've expected as much. And I knew I would have to give my parents the heads up about the things they would find in Collin's home – if things ever went so far that they should all need to meet.

Collin's mother took my attention, "Come with me, Fiona. I'll show you to your room so you can leave your things and freshen up. The ride from Lubbock to Carthage is a long one. I'm sure you'd like a little time to yourself. And Collin has some things his father would like to discuss with him."

I had no idea we'd be separated so soon. "Um, well, okay. Collin, come get me as soon as you're done."

With a kiss on my cheek, he said, "I won't take long, I promise. You just freshen up."

"Okay." As I followed his mother, my travel bag in my hand, I looked at the pictures on the walls. "Is that one Collin when he was a baby?"

Mrs. Gentry stopped and looked in the direction I pointed. "Yes, that's him when he was six months. Wasn't he a little cutie?"

"He was." His dark hair and blue eyes could be made out even in the black and white photo. "And Collin is your only child?"

"He is." She looked at me. "Didn't he tell you that?"

"Well, he didn't exactly say that. He's not a man of many words." I'd loved spending time with Collin, but the fact was that he spoke so little about himself that I really had no idea about his family. "Is your extended family large?"

"No." She started walking again. "Is yours?"

"No." I'd hoped to get in with a man with a large family. Coming from such a small one was a thing I felt needed changing. "I'm an only child. My father has two brothers who have nothing to do with us. They're the rich bankers, and my father is a lowly textile salesman. Not that he's lowly at all, but I suppose when compared with my super-rich uncles, he is."

"We don't care about such things around here." His mother opened the door to a small room with a twin bed inside. The green quilt on the bed was something she pointed at proudly. "I made that too."

"It's very pretty." I didn't much care for it but would never say a thing like that to her.

In my opinion, the whole place needed to be redecorated. The homey look wasn't a thing I desired. But it wasn't *my* home, so I tried to stop thinking about it.

"I'll leave you alone now. Collin will come for you soon." Mrs. Gentry started to close the door. "I'm making turnip greens, hog jowls, and cornbread for supper. If you'd like to learn how to cook any of those things, you're more than welcome to join me in the kitchen later on."

"Oh, thank you. I will." I had no idea what any of those were. "Are those things Collin likes to eat?"

She nodded. "He loves my cooking. If you and he are going to get married someday, then you should learn how to cook what he likes."

"Oh, he hasn't mentioned anything about marriage. I don't want to jump the gun." It wasn't ladylike to think a man was thinking about marriage if he hadn't said a word about it.

"He brought you home." Her hand went to her hip. "He's never brought anyone else home. I think it's safe to say that he's looking at you as a wife, Fiona."

He is?

COLLIN

I showed my father the engagement ring I'd bought Fiona as we stood in the barn. "I hope she says yes."

"Well, she came home with you, son. I think she knows where this is headed." He pointed up at the roof of the barn that needed replacing. "While you're home, I'd like you to go to town and get some of those boys you used to get to work out here. We need this fixed."

The guys I usually got were Hilda's brothers. "Um, well, okay." I knew I would need to hide Fiona from them, or they might tell their sister. Not that they knew anything about Hilda and me, but just gossiping might get me busted.

I would have to figure out how to handle Hilda when the time came for that. For now, I had something to take care of. "I'll go inside and tell Fiona that I need to run to town to get the workers, then I'll be right back." I wanted to pop the question before I went. "Care to come inside so I can ask her the big question?"

My father nodded, then we went inside. I found Fiona helping my mother in the kitchen. "Wow, you look great in an apron."

Fiona turned to face me, a bunch of greens in her hand. "Well, thank you. Your mother made this. It's pretty, isn't it?"

"Not as pretty as you." I took the greens out of her hand, then got down on one knee. "Fiona, I've never met another woman like you. I'm not smooth with my words the way some men are. So I'll just say what's on my mind. Will you marry me?" I pulled out the ring. "I got you a ring too.

She held out her left hand, wiggling her ring finger, the one that had my promise ring on it. Sliding that one off, I put the engagement ring on as Fiona whispered, "I will marry you, Collin Gentry."

I'd never felt more relieved in my life. Standing up, I grabbed her, lifting her feet off the floor, then kissed her right on the mouth. I didn't care that my parents were watching.

Later, I went to get the boys to work on the ranch. As I drove up to the house, I was shocked when Fiona ran out to meet me. Hilda's brothers stayed in the back of the truck as she waved at me. "Collin, my parents are going to come over for Thanksgiving. When I told them of our good news, they said they'd love to meet your family. They want us to get married in Cape Cod over the Christmas holidays. Isn't that great? They said they'll set up the whole wedding there. You and your family don't need to do a thing except show up."

"That's wonderful." I looked at the boys in the back of the truck and knew I had to make an introduction. "This is Miss Witherspoon, my fiancé."

The boys waved, then hopped out of the back of the truck to get to work. I couldn't help but feel like things were about to take a bad turn. I had no idea how right I was, though.

Getting back to Lubbock after the holiday and making a visit to Hilda had me knowing she'd talked to her family. Met with a slap to my face, I instinctively said, "I'm sorry."

"How could you, Collin?" Hilda walked away from the door to drop onto the couch. "I asked you for the truth, and you stood right here and lied to my face."

Walking inside, I closed the door behind me. "Look, nothing has to change with us." I sat down next to her, stroking her long, dark hair. "You must have known that I would have to get married someday."

566

She shook her head. "No, I didn't know that." Breaking down, she buried her face in my chest. "I love you, and you love me. What else matters?"

She knew there were lots of other things that mattered. "I am truly sorry for how life is, Hilda. All I can offer you is my secret love. If you no longer want it, then I understand."

Pulling her head up, the tears streaming down her face, she asked, "Do you still love me?"

I took her beautiful face in my hands. "Hilda, I love you. I always will. My marriage doesn't mean I'll love you any less."

"*She* will have your children."

I nodded. "She will."

"You wouldn't let me have them," she whimpered. "You took away the one we would've had together. You made me get that operation so I could never have children. And now *you* will have them; only you'll have them with *her*."

I nodded again. "She's going to be my wife, Hilda. That's expected. You – well, you will be my mistress. But, as always, we'll have to keep that a secret."

She got up, dropped to her knees in front of me, and sobbed, "Please, don't do this to me, Collin. I can't stand the thought of you with anyone else. Why can't it be the way it has always been? Why can't you and I just keep doing things the way we always have?"

She had to know that we couldn't keep living this way forever. "I'm a man, Hilda. A man with a family who expects me to keep our family going. That means getting married to a woman who is suitable for me."

"Something I'm not." She fell back on the floor. "I'm not suitable for you. I'm not suitable for any man."

"That's not true. I'm sure you're suitable for others like you." I felt terrible for her.

She blinked as she sucked in air. "Collin, I am not considered suitable for white men, nor Mexican men. I am a mixed breed, unsuitable for anyone. Even marrying another mixed breed is deemed taboo. What is to become of me?"

"I will always take care of you, Hilda." I meant that. "As long as

I'm alive, and even after I die, I will always take care of you. Never doubt that. Not ever."

Her eyes were glued to the floor. "Your wife won't like that."

"What my wife doesn't know won't hurt her."

I just have to keep the two apart, is all.

The End.

8. STEALING HIS HEART

An Accidental Pregnancy Romance
(Irresistible Brothers Book Three)

BLURB

The moment I saw that tempting spitfire I knew I was in trouble.

The way her petite little body called out to me,

All of my billions couldn't stop me from wanting her—needing her.

Life on my ranch was simple before she came along,

Calm, ordered, boring even.

The moment we met, everything changed.

We spent every waking, passionate moment together.

I was lost in her.

Consumed by her.

But she's got it in her head this is just a fun little distraction.

I want more—I need all of her.

My desire to own her has pushed us to the breaking point,

And I'm about to lose her...forever.

I'll fight like hell to not only prove to her I'm the man she needs,

But the man that will protect her and our unborn baby.

CASH

Carthage, Texas—Panola County
January 1st

As the snow fell, my heart pounded with each flake I witnessed falling to the ground along the side of the road. A grandfather I not only never had known but hadn't even heard of had left my brothers and me a ranch in a town a little over an hour away from where we'd lived. A suburb of Dallas was where we'd always called home; now I wasn't sure where we'd call home.

All I knew for sure was that Mom and Dad weren't on the attorney's list of the people who'd inherited Collin Gentry's things. Even though he was my father's father, the man had left everything he had to the three of us and no one else. Why? I didn't know.

Tyrell, the oldest of the three of us, was the one to get a phone call on Christmas day from the man who'd said he was Allen Samuels, our grandfather's lawyer. He'd set everything up and now we were in Carthage, Texas, about to see what he'd inherited. Our father thought it would be a real headache, but I had other ideas.

We'd ridden on a private plane from Dallas to Cartage's small municipal airport. From there, Allen came in a limo to pick us up. He sat in front of us, looking through a folder as we all sat quietly, waiting to hear what he had to say.

Finally, the lawyer put the folder down to look at us. "The whole of the estate, that includes Whisper Ranch, the thirty-thousand square foot home that's on the ranch, and of course all of the vehicles, including the Cessna Citation II you came in on, belongs to you three men now." Allen looked over his shoulder then tapped on the dark glass that separated us from the driver. I saw the window between the driver and us come down. "Davenport, we need to make a stop at Mr. Gentry's bank please."

With a nod, the driver said, "Sure thing."

Allen turned his attention to Tyrell. "Tyrell, what have you been told about your paternal grandparents?"

"Not much," my oldest brother said. "My mother's famous quote when any of us asked about our grandparents was that if one couldn't say anything nice about a person, they shouldn't say anything at all. We'd assumed our grandparents weren't very good people."

"Yeah, Mom and Dad didn't like even to be asked about any of them," my brother Jasper added. "So, we stopped asking when we were very young. Just asking them who our grandparents were put them in terrible moods."

The lawyer nodded. "I see." We pulled into the parking lot of the Bank of Carthage. "Here we are. I'm going to have you all put on the ranch's bank accounts. And we can transfer the remainder of your grandfather's money into accounts that you each will personally open with this bank. If that's okay with you. You certainly can open accounts elsewhere if you'd like to. Your grandparents used this bank exclusively for years. I can assure you that the president appreciates Whisper Ranch's business and does everything they can to keep their customers happy."

Tyrell shrugged as he looked at Jasper and me; we sat on either side of him. "This bank seems as good as any. What do you guys think?"

Thinking about what we should do, I ran my hand through my hair. "Sounds fine to me. It'll be my first bank account anyway." I'd always worked for cash and hadn't had any need for a bank account before. Now it seemed I would need one.

Jasper shrugged. "Sounds okay to me too. All I've got in my

bank is about twenty bucks. Hell, I might not even have that. I bought a bottle of Jack before getting on the plane—that might've overdrawn my account, and I might owe the bank something."

"This bank will do for us, Allen," Tyrell said as we started getting out of the car. "Thanks. He said your name is Davenport, right?"

The driver held the car door open for us. "Yep. I also drive various tractors and trucks at the ranch too. You need a ride, you call me and I'll get you there."

Tyrell didn't look like he was comfortable with something as he asked, "If you don't mind me asking, what's your first name?"

"Buddy," the driver said. "Your grandfather liked to put on airs."

"We're not like that at all. Mind if we call you Buddy instead?" Tyrell asked.

Buddy seemed happy about that. "Not at all. It would be nice, actually."

Jasper clapped the man on the back. "Nice to meet you, Buddy. I'm Jasper, this is Tyrell, and the little feller there is Cash, the baby brother of the Gentry family."

None of us were little fellers, and I always took offense at how Jasper teased me about that. "Jasper, you're the littlest out of all of us, you jerk."

Flexing his left bicep while threading his fingers through his dark hair, Jasper replied, "By a smidgeon of an inch, Cash. You're shorter."

"Also by a smidgeon of an inch." I walked ahead of them. "This bank is pretty fancy."

"It's the best one in this little town," Allen said he stepped in front of me, opening the door. "Here we go. Mr. Johnson is the bank president. He'll be handling this for us."

"The *president* will handle all of this?" Tyrell asked, sounding surprised. It had me thinking that bank presidents didn't often handle things of this nature. "How much money are we talking about, Allen?"

The lawyer cocked his head to one side, looking a little confused. "Are you telling me that even with the jet, the mansion, and the ranch, you still don't understand how much money your grandfather was worth?"

"Not a clue," Jasper said as he came inside and looked around. "Whoa. Posh."

Tyrell came in and looked up at the chandelier in the middle of the ceiling. "I haven't seen many banks with a thing like that hanging above peoples' heads before."

Everyone in the bank looked at us as the lawyer led us to the back of the large, open area. "This bank deals with a lot of exclusive businesses here in Carthage. They can afford certain luxuries that other banks cannot."

"Hello, gentlemen," a young woman said as we came into a small office. "You must be the Gentrys."

My oldest brother introduced himself as he shook her hand. "Tyrell."

Jasper nodded. "Jasper."

A smile went clear across her face—and a pretty decent face it was, too. "Then you must be Cash."

"Yep." I shook her hand as I smiled back at her. "And you are?"

"Sandra, the bank president's personal assistant." She let go of my hand, still smiling away. "And if you gentlemen will follow me, I'll let Mr. Johnson get things started." Her attention turned to Tyrell. "By the blue jeans and T-shirts, I assume you'll will be greatly surprised by what you're about to inherit."

Dad had told us that we'd most likely inherit only enough money to pay off our grandfather's debts. I didn't have hope for much more than that. But the way the lawyer and secretary acted told me our parents might not have been right about things after all.

As Sandra ushered us in, the bank president got up, greeting us warmly. "Bryce Johnson at your service, gentlemen. Please take seats anywhere you'd like. Can I offer you a cigar? They're Cuban. Or a drink perhaps? I've got a thirty-year-old scotch that would be perfect for this occasion."

As we sat down, Tyrell answered for all of us. "Okay, Bryce. We're pretty sure this ranch is swimming in debt. And we're not even close to being ranchers. Our father's advice was to find a buyer for it and move on."

I didn't see why my oldest brother needed to rush through anything. Narrowing my eyes at him, I let him know what I wanted. "I'd *love* a scotch, Tyrell. Let the man handle this meeting, will ya?"

"Scotch for everyone then," the bank president told Sandra, who left to get the drinks. "So, Allen hasn't filled you all in on things?"

"I have," the lawyer said. "Not the exact numbers, but I've told them about everything they now own. They don't seem to get it, Bryce."

Sandra came back with our drinks. "Here you go, gentlemen. Enjoy." Offering us each a crystal glass of expensive scotch, she gave me another smile. I was used to the attention. Most women did pay special attention to me. I credited my shoulder-length dark waves for most of the attention; my blue eyes didn't hurt either.

"A hell of a lot of hoopla, don't ya think?" Tyrell asked just before taking a drink.

Sandra winked at me. "You're all worth it." She put the tray down on a nearby table then took a seat on a chair nearest to me.

The bank president gave us each a piece of paper with some numbers on them. "I'll let the numbers speak for themselves."

"Not sure how to say this number," Tyrell said, sounding confused. "And not sure I understand what it even means. Our father told us there has to be debt that the ranch has built up."

The banker laughed as if that was the craziest thing he'd ever heard. "Whisper Ranch is one of the most profitable businesses this bank deals with. What you each are looking at is your third of the money Collin Gentry had in his personal accounts." He handed a paper to Tyrell. "This is what's in the ranch account."

Still wearing a confused expression, Tyrell said, "If I'm seeing this right, the ranch is worth millions."

"You're not seeing it right," the banker said. "Look again."

My oldest brother didn't seem to get it. "Oh, thousands."

Unlike Tyrell, I did understand the numbers on all the pages we'd been handed. "Tyrell, the ranch is worth *billions*, and we've each inherited fifteen *billion* dollars."

Still, my brother wasn't convinced as he said, "Dad said there'd be more money to pay out than we'd get."

The bank president set Tyrell straight. "Your father was wrong. Your grandfather went from only raising cattle to raising racehorses. You might've heard of some of his famous horses. The General's Son? Old Faithful? Coy's Burden?"

"We've never followed horse racing, sir," Jasper said. "I guess those are horses on the ranch?"

"They are," the banker said. "And they all are prize-winning stallions. Your grandfather began selling their semen and making a killing from it. Those sales, the cattle, and the racehorses have made him a pretty penny. Pennies that now belong to you three."

"Our father isn't mentioned at all in the will?" Tyrell asked.

The attorney took that question, which I wanted an answer to as well. "Look, I know it's difficult to understand but let me show you in writing why that is." He handed Tyrell another piece of paper. "See, your father signed this paper, stating that he wanted nothing from Collin or Fiona Gentry from that date forward. He wasn't forced to sign it. Coy did it to prove a point to his parents when they refused to acknowledge his marriage to Lila Stevens."

Tyrell looked as confused as I felt. "Wait. What?"

"See, your grandparents wanted to make the Gentry name something akin to royalty around here," the banker told us. "But your father fell in love with a girl from the wrong side of the tracks. A girl whose family lived on welfare. A girl who'd once worked as a maid at the ranch house."

We all looked confused as Tyrell asked, "Why would they never tell us about that?"

"Most likely because they didn't want you three to know what they'd walked away from," the lawyer said. "They chose love over money *and* their families. Your mother's family was just as against their marriage as the Gentrys were."

"Wow, seems our parents hid a hell of a lot from us." Tyrell looked at Jasper and me as we all felt shell-shocked by the news.

The lawyer wasn't done talking yet as he went on. "There's one more thing you need to know about the will, gentlemen. It stipulates that neither your mother nor father are ever allowed on the property. And your grandfather's money can never benefit them in any way. If you do so much as hand your parents five dollars, the entire estate, that includes the money, will revert to the state of Texas."

I thought that to be a bit much. "Harsh."

"Yeah," the bank president agreed. "Your grandfather was considered to be a harsh man. So harsh, most people think your grandmother died at the age of forty-five, only two years after your father left the ranch, because of his hard ways."

Who the hell am I related to?

BOBBI JO

"Yeah, pull two cases of Crown out of the back and some Jack
Daniels too." I walked around the bar to take stock of the beer in
the cooler. "And five cases of Michelob Ultra. That's our best seller."
Joey was new to the bar, and I knew I'd have to hold his hand for a
while. "Once you've got those things up here and put away, you can
go out to the parking lot and make sure it's clean. You know, no
cigarette butts, no trash, nothing but a sparkling clean area for our
patrons to park in."

His dark eyes met mine as he smiled crookedly. "And what is it
that *you* do, Bobbi Jo?"

"Really newbie?" I put my hand on my hip. "You've been here
all of five minutes and already you're sassing me?"

"Sorry," he said as he turned tail and went to the stockroom in
the back of the bar. "I'll get that done. Am I gonna get to make
some drinks tonight?"

"Hell yes." I planned to sit back and watch the new bartender
do all the work. "I'll be supervising tonight."

The smile he wore told me Joey was okay with working all night.
And I was glad he was. It had been several years of me working by
myself mostly. Finally, the owners of The Watering Hole had taken
my advice—or better said—pleas for help.

While Joey did the hard part, I tidied up a bit then played a few hands of poker on my cell. Friday afternoons were usually hectic for me, but not this one. I was chilled out completely when the first guests walked through the front door. "Evening, folks."

The man and woman weren't locals and looked around the empty establishment. "Um, are we early?" the man asked as he put his arm around the lady at his side.

"You are." I took the chance to help them out, leading them to a nice table for two near the bar. "I've got a table with your name on it over here. I'm Bobbi Jo, your hostess for this evening."

The couple took the seats, both smiling and seeming a lot more relaxed as the man said, "For a moment there, I thought we'd stumbled into one of those private bars where only members are allowed."

"Not here at The Watering Hole. We welcome everyone." I pointed at the chalkboard behind the bar. "Those are our signature cocktails. Of course, we serve every beer known to man. And if you're a teetotaler, we have sweet tea, a variety of cokes, and even coffee."

"How about something to snack on?" the woman asked.

I offered our most ordered snack. "How about some saltine crackers with summer sausage and cheddar cheese on them?"

"Sounds great," the man said. "We'll have a couple of beers— whatever you've got on tap will be fine—and that cracker thingy too. She's starving."

"Coming up." I went behind the bar to make the tray of snacks before filling icy mugs with the beer. Joey came out with a couple of cases of beer to refill the backup fridge. "I've got this table, but we're about to get busy. Around here, if people drive by and there's even one vehicle in the parking lot, they tend to stop."

Putting the bottles in the fridge, Joey responded, "Ready, boss."

"Good. I like being called boss." Putting the things on a tray, I carried them to the table just as more people came inside. "Looks like you guys are the party starters this Friday. I'll check on you in a bit. And if you don't feel like getting up, just raise a hand and I'll make sure a couple more beers get to you."

"Thanks," the lady said as she dug into the snacks. "I'm famished."

Famished wasn't a word often said in our little east Texas town. "Cool. Enjoy." People from out of town were always easy to spot.

The regular customers came in. Every one of them looked at the new guy behind the bar then at me. I just waved and smiled as they took their usual seats. Giving a quick glance at Joey, I cut my eyes to the tables where he'd need to get to in a hurry.

Taking my cue, he hauled ass to our best customers, and I knew then I really could sit back and watch him work. After putting some good music on the jukebox, I took out my cell and went to take a seat behind the bar. Tonight, I would oversee the cash register to make sure Joey knew how to use it and make change.

My feet propped on a barstool, I sat on another one, playing a game as more and more people came in. Joey was moving like lightning around the bar and I loved it. He went to the register to ring up a table, and I took the time to let him know how good he was doing. "Hey, you might just work out, kid."

"Thanks," he said, then took off again.

Sighing with relief that my hard days of working alone were over, I saw the door open again. This time three hunky guys came in. All tall. All ridiculously hot. All built like brick shit houses.

Joey hauled ass to the bar as the three men came toward it. "Uh, let me get them, Joey."

With a grin, he nodded. "Got ya, boss."

I gave the newcomers my full attention. "Hi. Welcome to The Watering Hole. You guys aren't from here, or I'd know what to pour you."

They took seats at the bar. Two of them looked around the crowded room while one looked only at me. His teeth, straight and white, glistened under the blue neon lights of the bar. "We like beer and plenty of it," he said.

By their magnificent physiques, I knew their brand of choice. "Three Ultras then." I grabbed frosted mugs from the freezer then filled them with the cold beer we kept on tap. Putting the drinks on the bar in front of them, I gave them a bit of southern hospitality. "On the house. It's not often we get newcomers in here."

One of them looked right into my eyes. His blue eyes matched those of the other two men. "Get ready to see us around. We're going to be living here now. We're the Gentry brothers. I'm Tyrell, this guy here next to me is Jasper, and that little guy on the end is our baby brother Cash."

The guy on the end was anything but little. "Nice to meet you, boys. I'm Bobbi Jo. And I'm very nosy. So don't be offended when I ask you lots of personal shit, 'kay?"

The guy on the end, Cash, nodded as he took a drink of his beer. "Keep my mug filled, and you can ask me anything you want, beautiful."

Filling a bowl with fresh peanuts, I put it in front of the men as I looked into the baby blue eyes of Cash, trying not to salivate over his dark waves of thick hair that hung to his broad shoulders. "Okay, for starters, how about you tell me what made you move to our little town of Carthage?"

The one who'd been introduced as Jasper answered my question. "We've inherited the Whisper Ranch."

"Gentry is what you said your last name is?" I mused. "So, you're related to old man Gentry—the rancher who rarely left home. Wow, I didn't know that man had any family."

Cash grinned at me. "Yeah, we've been told he was a hard ass. Not that we knew him or even of him. Our father didn't want anything to do with his father."

Tyrell asked, "Do you know how many people or who attended Collin Gentry's funeral?"

I had no idea at all. "I'm not into the whole obituary scene. I know a lot of town gossip though. You don't want me to tell you what kind of things I've heard about Collin Gentry though; I promise you that."

Tyrell looked at the pool tables then back at Jasper. "Care to let me beat you at pool?"

"I'll let you try." He got up, and the two of them left, leaving handsome Cash behind.

"So, you guys are living at the ranch then?" I asked as I picked up a glass and a white bar towel to clean it. It was a habit that I had.

Nodding, he took another drink. "That house is huge. I'd never seen a log cabin mansion before, and now I'm gonna live in one."

I'd never seen nor heard of the house on Whisper Ranch. "I bet it's awesome."

"You'd bet right." The way he smiled made my heart skip a beat —and my heart didn't do shit like that. "So what do you do, besides tending bar here at The Watering Hole?"

"Sleep mostly," I said with a laugh. "This is my job, my leisure activity, and most of the time, my social scene as well."

"You don't get out much is what you're saying?" He chuckled, making his chest move, taking my attention.

Mesmerized by the man, I answered, "If you ever want to find me, your safest bet is looking right here."

"Cool." He took another drink. "It's always nice to know where I can find a pretty girl to talk to. Care to hit me again, beautiful?"

Going to get him another frosted mug, I bit my lower lip as I caught him giving my ass the once-over through the mirror behind the bar. Maybe he thought I was as hot as I thought he was.

As I filled the mug, I had to let him know he wasn't the first customer to come onto me. "You know, I've heard just about every pickup line there is. And 'beautiful' is a thing I'm called at least ten times each night. I would think a man of your total hotness would have better lines than what you've come up with so far."

"That sounds like a challenge." He took the mug from me, his fingers grazing the back of my hand as he did so. "So, how about if I don't try to pick you up at all then?"

The way my blood ran hot told me I wouldn't hate it if he tried to pick me up, but I wasn't that kind of girl who wore her heart on her sleeve. "That would be best, Cash. I'm not the dating type anyway. You'd be wasting your time."

"Yeah, I can tell." His lips curved into a sly smile. "You'd be wasting your time too, as I don't like to date either."

My bets were that he didn't have to date. Women probably just fell at his feet, and he took them any way he wanted to.

"Cool. Glad to see we're on the same page, stud."

CASH

The petite blonde behind the bar had a glow about her that took my attention completely. Not many women could do that for me. I wasn't that easy to attract, but she was doing it without even trying to. "Yeah, dating is a joke." I sipped my second beer.

"I agree." She ran a white towel over the already clean bar. "Why go out to eat with someone to see if you've got something in common? I mean, we all have to eat, right? Why see if you have that in common?"

"Well, there are different tastes in food," I argued. "Once, I hooked up with this chick, and we went back to her place. She had a fridge full of nothing but cans of tuna fish. I thought she must've had a cat that I hadn't seen yet."

"Oh, hell," Bobbi Jo said with a wince. "Bet she didn't."

I nodded. "Yeah, she didn't have a cat. What she did have was a strict diet of canned tuna. Needless to say, I didn't stick around that night to see what that kind of diet had done for her."

"I bet it had done a number of things for her." She held her nose. "Including giving her that fresh out of the can scent in her nether regions."

"Yeah, that's what I assumed too." I ate a peanut that she'd put out fresh for us. "I didn't want to find out firsthand."

"Smart." Moving to the register, she picked up a pen and a piece of paper. "Tonight, you and your brothers are on the house. That's how we welcome new residents of Carthage around here. And, of course, we hope you'll come back to visit us often enough to make up for the treat."

"Of course." I already had a good idea that I would love frequenting the fine establishment. "We're from Dallas. I can't say this is the nicest or worst bar I've ever been in, but I can say that the bartender is quite charming."

She looked behind her at the guy taking a bottle of Crown off the shelf. "You talking about Joey?"

The guy looked at me, wiggling his dark brows. "Hey there, mister."

"Hi there, Joey. Name's Cash Gentry." I gave him a nod.

He stopped as he looked at me. "Gentry?"

"Yep." I took another peanut.

"Like the Whisper Ranch Gentry?" he asked.

"Yep." I had the feeling we could expect a lot of that. "You've heard of the ranch?"

"My uncle has the ranch on the west side of that one. The Castle Ranch," Joey let me know. "His name is Richard. He's a good guy. He's about the same age as your grandfather was. He told me they'd gone to school together."

"Cool." Maybe I'd drop in and say hello sometime. It might be nice to know more about my grandfather.

"The Seven Pesos ranch is on the other side if Whisper Ranch," Bobbi Jo said. "George and Lori Sandoval own it. Well, Lori now. George passed away last year. He was your grandfather's age too. George went last year; your grandfather went this year." She looked at Joey. "Hope your uncle keeps himself in better shape than those two did."

Joey shook his head as he walked away to take care of other customers. "Me too. My cousins will make lousy ranch owners. They're snotty pricks who go to college in Lubbock."

Bobbi Jo looked back at me. "You look like you're college age. You going to school anywhere?"

"No." I wasn't ever planning on going to college. "My parents didn't have enough money for any of us to go to college. And none of us made good enough grades to get scholarships. But now, I don't see why we'd need to go get some degree. We're rolling in the dough."

"Yeah, I can see that." She gestured to my old shirt and blue jeans. "You look like a billion bucks."

Running my hand over my T-shirt, I said, "We just got the money today, honey. There hasn't been time to shop. But the next time you see me, I'll be looking like I'm worth my weight in gold."

Winking, she teased me, "Isn't horse semen a different color than gold, Cash?"

"So you know Whisper Ranch has made its money in the horse semen market." I had to hand it to the girl; she did know the town well.

"Racehorse semen," she corrected me. "More than one buyer has come to have drinks here, I'm proud to say."

"I figure all my brothers and I have to do is sit back and let the bucks keep rolling in." I hadn't had time to think about it much, but why bother with finding something to do if you had money coming in hand over fist already?

The slightest frown on her pretty face made me wonder what she thought about that.

"I hope you don't become *that* kind of man, Cash."

"What kind is that?" I had a feeling I knew but wanted to hear it come from her.

"A trust-fund brat." She ran the cloth over the bar again and then I could tell that she would soon become bored with me if I were nothing more than that.

"So, what would you have me do?" I had no idea why I'd asked her that.

"Something," she said. "Anything. Just don't sit back and drink your days and nights way while chasing loose women. Be something. Do something. Don't let this money go to waste. You know what I'm saying?"

"It sounds like you think I should—dare I say it?—work?" I'd barely gotten stinking rich and already the first woman I'd met after getting that way wanted me to work. "See, that's why I don't date or have serious relationships."

She seemed puzzled. "Because a woman would expect more out of you? Shallow man. I didn't see that coming."

"You're not typical, Bobbi Jo." I took a long drink of the beer as I watched her out of the corner of my eye.

"I try not to be." She pulled her jacket off, revealing tight and toned arms. "See, I'm a lot more like you than you think, Cash. I don't like relationships either. I think they stifle people." She flexed one bicep. "I like to work out when I'm not working. I've got my own gym in the garage at home. Men don't like women who are stronger or tougher than they are."

"You are absolutely right." I winked at her. "How about a refill, doll?"

With a heavy sigh, she got me a refill then slid it to me. "See, the thing is, I don't care if men don't like me."

"Because you like girls?" I teased her. I didn't see her as that type.

"You're a riot." She snapped the bar towel at me, catching me on the wrist. "I enjoy the company of men—just not for extended periods of time."

"So, you're a confirmed bachelorette then?" I asked as I'd considered myself a confirmed bachelor since puberty.

"Confirmed?" She tapped her chin. "I guess you could say that. I've got no intention of finding Mr. Right and making babies, taking care of a house, and driving a minivan. But having a little fun isn't a thing I'm against."

"Me neither." I held up my mug. "To you, Bobbi Jo, a woman who knows what she wants and isn't afraid of what anyone thinks about that." I had to respect that about the girl.

A blush covered her cheeks for only a moment as she ran her hand through her blond ponytail. "I guess I am coming off kind of strong. I'm not a man-hater by any means. "

"Nor am I a woman-hater." But I wasn't looking for anything serious. "I'm glad you and I have put ourselves out there. I don't like to guess what a woman wants. I bet you don't like to guess what a man wants either."

"What's to guess?" she asked. "Men want simple things. A woman who will dote on him, cook for him, care for him, give him what he wants, when he wants it. I'm just not into giving anyone what they want when they want it."

"Hey, how about another round over here, Bobbi Jo?" a guy called out.

Nodding, she went to grab some more beers for the table. "Maybe it's my job of having to give people what they want when they want it that makes me the way I am."

"Who knows for sure?" I took another drink as I watched her. The way her tight little ass moved when she hurried to give the beers to the table of men took my attention. It was a great ass after all. And her tits were pretty perky and plump too. She had that cute little hourglass figure that most women only dream of having.

When she came back behind the bar, I heard her stomach growl. "Oh, crap. I've gotta call in something for dinner. If I don't eat three times a day, I get extremely moody. How about you, Cash?"

"How about me what?" I had no idea what she meant.

"Have you eaten dinner yet?" I thought she was sweet for asking.

"I did. We have a home chef. He's the best. He made chicken fried steaks, mashed potatoes, and green beans. It was the bomb. Better than I've ever had before." Even recalling the meal had my mouth watering.

"Damn. That sounds good." She pulled her cell out of the pocket of her blue jeans. "Maybe you bring me your leftovers from time to time, and I'll treat you to free drinks. For now, though, it's the Dairy King to the rescue."

"I'll make that deal with you." It didn't matter that I had more money than I'd ever imagined. If anyone wanted to trade food for alcohol, I was in. "Any requests? I think I can get him to cook whatever I want."

"I bet you can, seeing as you and your brothers are his new bosses." She texted her order to the place she'd spoken about. "For the record, I love steaks. All kinds of steaks. And I like them rare."

"Me too." I liked that about her. "People who overcook their steaks piss me off. I'm like, a cow died for you, bitch. Don't ruin what it gave you."

Her laughter sounded musical, and I couldn't help the smile that took over my face. "I've literally said that before. My cousin Gina and I went to this steakhouse once, and she ordered her steak well done. I was like, why would you ruin your steak? That cow died for us."

"Seems we think alike." I hadn't ever had a girl who was just my friend. I'd never liked any girl that much. But Bobbi Jo wasn't like any girl I'd ever known. Most of them were so worried about attracting me that they watched every word that came out of their mouths.

"I highly doubt that." She jerked her head at some girls who came in the door. "I bet you and I are thinking totally different things about those girls there."

Looking at them, and seeing them look back at me, I nodded politely. "I see four young women who work together at what I'd bet is a bank." The fact was, I'd seen them at the bank we'd been at earlier when our lives were forever changed.

"Did the nametags clue you in?" Bobbi Jo asked, then laughed. "Too easy, Cash. Way too easy."

Yeah, just like being with you is.

BOBBI JO

The Gentry brothers had stayed until closing time at the bar the night before, and I'd had plenty of time to get to know at least one of them. Cash sat at the bar the whole night talking to me. He was entertaining, to say the least. And I knew I was the envy of all the girls in the bar, as the other ladies' eyes kept moving to look at the man who seemed to only notice me.

Sitting up in bed, I stretched as the noon hour had me waking up. Betty Sue sat at the vanity, painting on her face for the day. "You finally up, lazy bones?"

I nodded. "I wouldn't call myself lazy. I didn't get to sleep until nearly four in the morning. I've only slept the normal eight hours." She had the curling iron on, so I knew she was heading out later. "And where are you off to today?"

"Lance is taking me to Dallas. We're spending the night in a hotel." She blew a kiss at her reflection in the mirror. I thought it funny how much she adored herself. She and I were identical twins; we looked exactly alike. I didn't think of myself as God's gift to humanity, but Betty Sue sure did.

"Lance?" That was the first I'd heard of this guy.

"Lance Strongbow." She raised her perfectly arched brows. "He's Native American—Apache, I think."

"Really?" I had my doubts about that. My sister was so easily duped it wasn't even funny. "What color is his hair?" I had to ask that because once she fell for this guy who said he was Chinese. The only problem with that was he had blonde hair, blue eyes, a height of six-one, and the build of a Viking.

Guys lied to my sister about their native origins because she started off conversations with a tagline about hating Americans. I don't know if she thought it hip to hate herself and the people of her country or what, but she almost always started conversations with new people with that stupid line.

"Black," she said with a matter-of-fact expression on her painted face. "Long, shiny, black hair that hangs to his waist. This guy is the real deal. His grandfather's name is Trotting Horse. Now that's a real Native American name if you ask me."

I'd never heard a name like that, so who was I to argue with her about it? "So, you're going to Dallas with this guy? How well do you know him? You've never talked about him before." My sister had no sense of self-preservation; one had to ask her what the hell she thought she was doing most of the time. "And does Dad know about your little overnight date?"

"How old are we, Bobbi Jo?" She looked at me through the mirror.

"Twenty-two." In my opinion, that was old enough for some but not her. "But we live under Dad's roof, and you know his rules."

"What Dad doesn't know won't hurt him." She turned around to face me, then stuck her tongue out. "You won't tell on me."

She knew I wouldn't tell on her. But that was only because at least I would know where she was if she didn't show back up after one of her dates with strangers. "I won't tell. But I want you to send me a text of where you are once you get to where you're going. Plus, I'd like to know where he plans on taking you before you even leave town. I want to be sure he takes you where he says he will. And—"

She held up a hand to stop me. "Okay, okay, I know the drill, mother hen. I don't think there's anything to worry about. And, if you must know, I like the sense of danger that surrounds these men I don't know. Not knowing where they're taking me is part of the rush."

Rubbing my temples, I really thought that one day my twin would actually kill me. Not physically kill me, but mentally kill me. "Betty Sue, you shouldn't think that way."

"You wouldn't understand since you're a prude who never gets laid. Although you could if you wanted to." She ran her hand in a circle around her face. "We do look alike, and I have no problem at all getting men to notice me and want me."

"I don't either. Only I am a bit pickier than you are," I said. "As a matter of fact, I had a gorgeous man sitting at the bar talking to me all night last night."

"But did you hit the sheets with him?" she asked, eyes wide.

"No." I wasn't like my sister. I had to have more of a connection with someone before I got into bed with them.

"What are you waiting for?" she asked with a grin. "Does a man have to propose marriage before you give him any?"

I wasn't even thinking about marriage. "Betty Sue, since you're always talking about yourself, you may not know this about me, but I'm not into making commitments. I hate to date. I hate to be part of a couple. And I hate having to think of someone else's feelings all the time."

Getting up, she went to the closet to pick out her outfit for the day. "I don't think of anyone's feelings, Bobbi Jo. I have my fun then get out. You don't have to become a couple to have sex and do some fun shit together."

"How sweet," I said as I rolled my eyes. "Aren't you just a living doll, Betty Sue?" I had no idea what guys saw in her. Shallow to the core, the girl was a walking, talking nightmare. "Love them and leave them" was her motto, although she never disclosed that information about herself until the date was over.

"So, enough about me," she said as she came out of the closet with a short dress. "Who is this guy you met last night? Is he from here?"

I pointed at the tiny article of clothing. "You know it's January, right? And there's snow on the ground too. That dress is more suited for summer, not the dead of winter."

"He'll keep me warm." She slipped it on over her bra and

panties. "So, this guy is …?" She waved at me to get me to say more.

"His name is Cash Gentry." I wasn't sure how much info I wanted to give her. "He and his brothers are new in town. They've just moved here from Dallas." I thought that was the basics and she didn't need to know more than that.

"How old is he?" She looked through the jewelry box for something to add to her little dress.

"About my age, I think." I sighed as I pictured him in my head and my mouth just said things all on its own. "His six-two, blue eyes, dark wavy hair that hangs to his broad shoulders, and he's quite possibly the hottest man I've ever laid my actual eyes on."

"Intriguing," Betty Sue said. "And you said he has brothers. Yes, I can see myself in one or more of their arms now. Are they all as hot as this guy?"

I nodded. "They are. I doubt they'll be single long. Even the one who talked to me all night had the eyes of every woman in the bar —even the ones who were with their own men."

"Sounds like you might have a man for once, Bobbi Jo. If he's so eligible, you had better latch onto him and don't let go. And I'm not just talking about the other females in town; I'm talking about me too."

Something came over me as my sister looked at herself in the full-length mirror. "You need to stay away from him, Betty Sue."

Turning to face me, she smiled. "Why is that? Do you plan on taking him off the market?"

"No." I never planned on taking anyone off the market, especially since I didn't care to be taken off it myself. "It's just that he's nice. And I think he trusts people—maybe too much. You'd chew him up and spit him out. I don't want to see that happen to him."

"Then don't watch." She placed her hands on her hips then shimmied around the room. "So, how does my ass look in this dress?"

"Well, the lower part is peeking out at me if that answers your question." I laid back down and looked at the ceiling. I didn't see the white-popcorn ceiling at all; I saw his face. Cash's strong chin, cheekbones, and chiseled lips filled my mind. His deep voice, throaty laugh, and flirtatious words echoed in my head.

A knock came to the bedroom door. "You girls up?" Dad asked.

I sat up as Betty Sue darted to the closet to get a coat to cover up her daring outfit. "Yes, Daddy."

Rolling my eyes, I never could figure out how our father fell for Betty Sue's act. "You can come in, Dad."

Opening the door, he peeked inside. "I'm about to go to the station. Your mom is already at the feed store. What're your plans, girls?"

"Work, as usual," I said as I looked at my sister to see what she'd come up with.

"Oh, Daddy, I'll be out of town this weekend. A friend from high school has invited me to go with her to Dallas." Betty Sue batted her long, fake eyelashes. "I think her little cousin is having a birthday party. He's turning five. It should be great fun. You know how much I love children."

Dad nodded. "Okay. You be careful and shoot your sister a text when you get where you're going like you always do, Betty Sue." He turned his attention to me. "And you be extra careful tonight at work. You've still got that baseball bat behind the bar, right?"

I'd never had to use the thing my father had given me when I first went to work at The Watering Hole. "It's still right where you put it, Dad. I don't think there's anything to worry about this weekend."

"Still, that's a bar you're working in, missy." He shook his long finger at me. "It would be nice if you'd think about getting a job more like the one your sister has."

Betty Sue smiled at me. "I could ask Miss Cherry if she'd put you on, Bobbi Jo."

While I admired people who worked where my sister did, I couldn't see myself doing it. "Thank you, Betty Sue, but no. I don't think I've got what it takes to work at a nursing home. I like serving drinks and talking to half-drunk people; it entertains me."

Shrugging, Betty Sue said, "I feel like the people I talk too are half-drunk most of the time too. Or maybe it's just the fact most of them have Alzheimer's."

594

I was pretty sure the Alzheimer's had more to do with that than anything else. "Nevertheless, I like my job. And I feel secure there too, Dad."

"You know how I am about my little girls," he said. "You be careful out there. Bye now." He closed the door as I looked at my sister as she went back into the closet to ditch the overcoat.

"He had no clue about you, Betty Sue." I had no idea how my father was so clueless where she was concerned. "He's more worried about *my* job than what *you* do most weekends. Weird."

"I'm just glad it works that way." She stepped into a pair of heels. "Have fun serving drinks, wench. I'll be out with my man for the weekend in fabulous Dallas."

I had high hopes the guy who'd entertained me before would come back in and do it again tonight too.

CASH

Riding one of the horses up the north fence, I saw a Ford truck coming through the pasture on the other side of our fence. As it got closer, I read the sign on the side of the truck: Castle Ranch.

Stopping my horse as the truck pulled to a stop. I got off the horse and went to meet the man who got out.

"Morning," he called out as he came my way.

"Morning." I could tell by the man's age and the way he dressed that this was Richard Castle, the owner of the ranch. The guy at the bar had told me about him. "I think I met your nephew Joey at The Watering Hole last night. You must be Richard Castle." I extended my hand over the barbed-wire fence.

He shook my hand as he smiled. "And you must be one of Collin's grandsons."

"I'm the youngest, Cash. It's nice to meet you, Mr. Castle. Joey told me you knew my grandfather."

Nodding, he shoved his hands into the pockets of his coat. "He and I were the same age. Up until high school, we were pretty good friends. Then he just kind of went on his own. We never were close after that."

"Sorry to hear that." I shrugged. "Or maybe it wasn't so bad that he went his own way. From what I've been told, he was a hard ass, to put it nicely."

Nodding, he agreed. "Yes, Collin was at best a hard ass. But your grandmother wasn't a thing like him. Fiona was a treasure that your grandfather didn't take care of well enough."

"So, my grandmother wasn't as bad as he was?" I had no idea about her. No one had spoken about her at all.

"Fiona was one of Carthage's most upstanding citizens. She worked with many charities here in town. After your father left, she really dove into the community and the church too." His smile told me he'd actually liked my grandmother. "If she hadn't been married to that old cuss, I would've courted her myself."

"And what did your wife think about that?" I had to ask.

He rocked back on the heels of his boots. "I never got me one of those. I kind of pined after Fiona so much that I never did find the right woman for me. I tend to think that's because *she* was the right one for me. I did have a couple of sons out of wedlock though. They lived with their mother in upstate New York. And one day, they will inherit this ranch. It's a shame really."

"Wow." I didn't know what I'd stumbled upon here. "Did you spend much time with my grandmother?"

His smile told me he had. "There were more than a few stolen moments. Your grandfather left her alone most of the time. There was a mistress that took a lot of his time. Fiona banished her for a while. Then the woman came back to Carthage. Her family lives here. She still lives right there in town in the house your grandfather bought for her too. Poor Fiona had to live out the remainder of her years, knowing the woman her husband really loved lived in the same town she did."

"What an ass." I shook my head as I thought how horrible that had to have been for my grandmother. "But my grandmother wasn't exactly a saint. She did agree with our grandfather about my mother not being good enough for my father."

Narrowing his blue eyes, he cocked his head to one side. "What makes you think she agreed about that?"

"Well, because it happened." I thought she had to have agreed with our grandfather about something so big, since it caused my father to take my mother and leave town, never to come back or say another word to his parents.

"Maybe you should ask your parents about that whole thing," he said. "I wasn't privy to all the information on that. Fiona was tight-lipped at times, especially where her son and husband were concerned."

"We're going to go see them soon. I will ask about that." It was obvious that the man had loved my grandmother. "So, I won't tell anyone, but did you and she ever … you know?"

He shook his head. "No. Not that I didn't try. But your grandmother was a good woman—a Godfearing woman too. She wouldn't have done a thing against her marriage vows."

"She didn't live much longer after our father left home."

Richard looked angry as he said, "No, she didn't live much longer after that happened. I know she was heartbroken over your father's leaving, but she was heartbroken over the affair her husband was having as well. Collin didn't waste much time after Fiona's death either. He brought that classless bitch to this ranch before even a month's time had passed."

"That is messed up." That old man had lots of nerve and huge balls to have done such a thing. "I can't understand why he did what he did. All I know is that for some reason, he decided to leave us the ranch and his money. So, what did he leave that woman?"

"All I know is that she still lives in the same house Collin bought her, and she drives the Cadillac he bought her just before he died." He shook his head as if disgusted. "But that woman has never worked a day in her life, so I know he had to have left her some money too."

"Well, I gotta get back. It was nice meeting you, Mr. Castle." I shook his hand again. "Sorry you never got to really get to know my grandmother. You seem like a nice man. I'm sure you would've treated her a hell of a lot better than my grandfather ever did."

"I sure would've. Nice to meet you too, Cash." He went back to his truck but turned to look at me before getting in and waved. "Bye now."

As I climbed back up on the horse, I wondered what kind of life my poor grandmother had lived. It sounded horrible to me.

The rest of the day went by slowly. All I kept thinking about was getting back to that bar and seeing that pretty little bartender again. And as we sat at the dining room table that night, I recalled something Bobbi Jo had said to me.

Ella, our young maid, was refilling our tea glasses. "Hey, Ella, do you think you can make me a plate to go?"

She put her hand on her hip and cocked her head. "Why?"

"Because I want to take dinner to Bobbi Jo." I smiled at her. "So, do you think you could make up a plate nice and pretty for her?"

"Who is Bobbi Jo?" The young maid was full of questions, and I saw my older brother, Tyrell, grinning.

"She's the bartender at The Watering Hole," I said.

"That place is a dive. Why do you want to go there?" she asked. "And what kind of a woman is that for you, Cash? A bartender? Really? You can have any girl you want. She raised her hand and gestured to my brothers too. "Any of you could have any woman you wanted in this town. Even the married ones. So, why do you want to impress a bartender?"

"First of all, I don't even *want* a woman, Ella." I wasn't looking for a relationship. "I'm trying to be nice. This young lady works hard, and she has to eat fast food all the time. I'd like to bring her a homecooked meal now and then. Plus, she'll give me free drinks if I bring her something to eat."

That didn't explain a thing to the young woman. "Cash, that makes no sense. Sure, I can see you wanting to give a girl something good to eat, but don't do it so you can have free drinks. And there are lots better places to find a girl to like than at a bar."

"I don't want to find a girl to like, Ella. You don't get it. And I don't expect you to." I looked to Tyrell for some help.

"Ella," Tyrell said, "Cash is what you would call a player."

"No," I hissed.

Tyrell and Jasper nodded as Tyrell said, "Yes, that is what you are. See, Ella, Cash doesn't want just one girl. He wants them all. So, even you have to be careful where he's concerned."

"She does not!" I looked at the girl who my brother clearly had eyes for. "I think you're cute as hell, Ella. But I don't shit where I eat."

"Gross!" She shook her head.

"I mean that I don't mess with women who I have to see every day." I ran my hand over my face. "So you don't have to worry about me. What you do need to do is go into the kitchen and make me a plate of this magnificent food to go. And please make it look good."

"So you can impress her?" she asked.

I wasn't into impressing anyone. "No. I just don't want it to look unappetizing."

"So, no red rose on the top of it?" She walked out of the room, laughing at her joke.

I looked at Tyrell. "It would be nice if you could get your girl in check, bro."

"She's not my girl, Cash." Tyrell shook his head.

"You've caught her up in your strong arms twice already since we moved in. I think she *is* your girl." I took a drink of the fresh sweet tea Ella had filled my glass with.

"And I think I've never seen you talk so long to a woman before without it ending in the sack," Jasper said as he cocked his head. "You and that bartender never stopped talking. And you didn't even get a goodnight kiss. What's up with that?"

"I didn't ask her for one." I could've gotten one if I wanted one.

"So, you going after that tonight?" Tyrell asked. "Is that why you're bringing her dinner? A little crawfish etouffee in exchange for some tongue action?"

"You are a child, Tyrell." I finished the last of my dinner. "And now if you gentlemen will excuse me, I'm off to hang out at the bar. Maybe I'll play some pool and make some new friends."

"If you can pull yourself away from that pretty little bartender," Jasper teased me.

"She's not so hard to pull myself away from." I got up then stopped and turned to look at them "And she's easy to talk to."

"And look at," Jasper said. "She got a sister?"

"Hell if I know." I turned to leave then stopped again as it hit me that Jasper had said Bobbi Jo was something to look at and it kinda pissed me off. "And I'll have you know that Bobbi Jo is much more than just a pretty face."

"She sure is," Tyrell said with a grin. "She's girlfriend material."

My brothers knew I didn't want a girlfriend. "Don't even joke about that. But I don't think I've got anything to worry about. She's like me in that department. She doesn't want a boyfriend either."

Jasper just laughed. "Yeah, who would want to be the girlfriend of a rich, young, good-looking guy? Certainly not a poor bartender."

"Who said she's poor?" I hadn't said that. "And what do I care how much money she has anyway. We all came from nothing."

Tyrell held his hands up, gesturing to the grand dining room. "Need I remind you that we might not have known it, but we came from this, not nothing. And you will have to watch out for gold diggers, Cash. We all will."

Could Bobbi Jo really be a gold digger?

BOBBI JO

When the door opened, and Cash came walking in alone, I had this feeling he'd come to see me. And I didn't like that at all. "Hi," I said curtly, nodding. "Beer?"

He shook his head as he looked at the pool tables which were full already. "I thought I'd play a game of pool. Looks like everyone thought the same way I did."

Trixie from the Speedy Stop couldn't take her eyes off him, and I watched her get up from the table of girls she sat at. I didn't have much time to save the poor guy. "Why don't you take a seat at the bar while you wait?"

Eyeing the empty barstool in front of me, he looked like he didn't know what to do. "Are there any other bars with pool tables around here?"

Trixie was closing in, and I had to move fast, or he'd be her mark for the night. Cash didn't need that. "Not any as good as this one. And that's not saying much. Come on. Sit down. I'll mix you up a drink if you're not in the beer mood."

Again, he looked at the empty chair as if it had snakes crawling all over it. "I don't know."

There was no time left as the woman with four kids at home

reached out for him. I grabbed his hand, pulling him along with me. "Come on, Cash. Have a drink. It's on the house."

"Hey! I had my eye on him." Trixie shouted as I got him away from her in the nick of time. Thankfully, there was so much other noise in the bar, Cash hadn't realized she was talking about him.

I pretended I didn't hear her either. "So, what're your favorite flavors, Cash?"

He took the seat I'd been offering him as I went around to the other side of the bar. "Depends on what we're talking about. My favorite flavor of cake is strawberry."

"Definitely on the lower scale with that." I reached for a bottle of banana-flavored vodka.

Nodding, he seemed to understand me. "Yeah, no one else in my family likes strawberry anything. And the only candy I like is chocolate."

I pulled out the large bar of dark chocolate and the grater from underneath the bar. "Is there any other kind?"

He shook his head. "Not as far as I'm concerned, there's not." He smiled at me as I took the jar of red maraschino cherries out of the mini fridge. "You know, I wasn't in the best of moods when I came in here."

I'd had that feeling. "No way!" I winked at him.

He just laughed. "Yeah. It showed, huh?"

Holding two of my fingers a small space apart, I said, "Just a little." Then I took out a bottle of vanilla rum. "That's why I'm making you something unique. If you like it, I'm going to call it the Cash Special. Only nine ninety-five."

He looked at what I was doing with interest now. "So what are you making there, Bobbi Jo?"

"First, you tell me what had you all grumpy." I got out the Kahlua and was ready to start building the drink.

He sighed, then looked down at the bar. "This whole having money thing is making life harder than it was."

"I can't see how." I had to laugh. "If it's that bothersome, send it my way. I'll deal with the hardship of being stinking rich to save you the trouble." I was kidding of course.

When his blue eyes met mine, I had the idea he thought I might say something of that nature. "Bobbi Jo, if me and my brothers didn't have any money, would you have treated us to free drinks last night?"

Standing straight up, I had the idea he thought I was after him and his money. "Cash, I give all newcomers—who are new citizens of Carthage—free drinks for one night. And this drink is on the house because I'm using you as a guinea pig. There is no other reason for it."

The way he cocked his head told me he wasn't sure about what I'd said. "My brothers and I were talking at dinner tonight. We talked about how gold diggers might come after us now."

Nodding, I knew he was right. "Yeah, you've got to really watch out for them." I nodded in the direction of Trixie. "See that woman over there?"

He looked back to see her then looked back at me. "The redhead with the toothy grin?"

"Yes, her." I poured the Kahlua into a tall glass. "She's got four kids—all from different men. Now all these men have one thing in common. Money. Not anywhere near what you and your brothers have, but lots of money. And she got pregnant on purpose to get a percentage of their money. And she spotted you quick and in a hurry. I think she must have rich-man radar or something. Not many people know you or your brothers, nor your financial situation. Weird, huh?"

"I'll say." Cash looked back at her, and she waved at him. He didn't wave back as he looked at me. "I think you're right about her. I still haven't bought any new clothes. This jacket is the same one I wore in high school, and so are these cowboy boots."

"I don't think you need to be in a bad mood about those kinds of people, Cash. You'll be able to spot them from a mile away once you get used to it." I poured the other liquors into the glass then topped it with whipped cream, a cherry, and some chocolate curls. "Here you go—the Cash Special." I watched as he took the straw I slid across the bar to him.

One sip led to one long drink, then he sighed. "Ah. It's delicious."

"So, we've got a new drink then." I quickly filled out a recipe

604

card and put it in the book of originals. "I like to come up with something new every now and then."

He smiled as he sipped the drink. "I like being your guinea pig, Bobbi Jo. It's fun."

"Good. I like having someone around who's not afraid to take chances and try new things." I put everything away as he sipped on the drink while looking around the bar. "So, what did your chef make you for dinner tonight?"

"Shit!" Cash put his drink down then got up and ran out the door.

I stood there, watching him and wondering what I'd said to run him off. Another customer waved me down, and I went to take the table some more beers, as Joey was busy. When I got back to the bar, Cash was back in his seat, and a Styrofoam container was in front of him. "For me?"

He nodded as he picked his drink back up. "And it's good too."

Opening the top, a wave of heat came up to meet my face as I took a long sniff. "I love seafood."

"I bet you do." He reached into his pocket and pulled out a plastic fork. "Here ya go. Dig in."

"You really thought of it all, didn't ya?" I was impressed. And when I took a bite, I was in Heaven. "Oh, yeah. Free drinks for a week for this. It's amazing."

He sat there, watching me eat as he sipped on the drink I'd made him. "You know, it wouldn't be considered a date if you came to eat dinner at my place sometime. It would be considered an act of kindness, I think."

"I'd take that act of kindness any day." I thought about it. "Wait, any day that I'm off, which are Sundays and Mondays." I winked at him. "And I wouldn't consider it a date either, so you're safe there, lover boy."

"Tomorrow is Sunday," he pointed out.

I didn't know what to say to that. So I just looked at him.

"So, how about you give me your number, and I'll call you when I'm coming to pick you up?" he asked.

I pulled out my pen and wrote my number down on a napkin.

"How about you give me a call, and I'll come out on my own. We don't want anyone to get the wrong idea about us."

"No, we don't." He took the napkin then pulled out his cell and put my number into his contacts. I felt my cell vibrate in my pocket and took it out. "Is this you?"

He nodded. "Yep. Now you've got my number too. Try your best not to make any midnight drunk calls to me. I'm only human, you know."

"Since I don't drink, that ought to be pretty easy for me." I held up the bottle of water I kept under the bar.

"You work at a bar. You make up your own drinks. But you don't drink?" He looked confused.

"I do taste now and then." I took another bite and hummed with how good it was. "I can't wait for tomorrow. I bet it's gonna be great."

"Me too." He couldn't pull the smile off his face. "I'm glad you're going to come over. The place is so big, and I kind of get lost in it sometimes. It might be nice to check it all out with you."

"I've never been to the ranch, Cash." I had no idea what he thought I could do to help him.

"No, I meant it might be cool to get lost with you." He leaned forward, his breath sweet and warm near my lips as I leaned in close too.

I rested my chin in the palm of my hand. "I do believe my drink has gotten to you, Cash Gentry."

"You think so?" His eyes scanned my whole face. "I like those tiny freckles you've got across the tops of your cheeks. I didn't see them before. I guess you gotta get real close to see them."

I liked him this way; he was sweet and adorable. "I think I'll bring another one of Cash's Specials along when I come tomorrow. They seem to agree with you."

"*You* agree with me, Bobbi Jo." He sat back and looked me up and down. "You don't even try to look good, do you?"

"Huh?" I didn't try to look crappy either.

"I mean, you look good without trying to." He smiled sheepishly.

"Yeah, you're drunk. How about a coffee?" I went to pour him a cup.

"I'm not drunk," he protested. "I'm just pointing out a fact. You look like you just roll out of bed and put anything on and it works for you."

"I do a little more than just that." I put the cup of coffee in front of him. "But thank you?" I wasn't sure if he was complimenting me or not.

"You're welcome." He didn't argue about the coffee as he took a sip. "You even make great coffee, Bobbi Jo. Do you have any faults at all?"

My sister came through the door in her little dress, a tall man at her side, and her eyes on the man who sat in front of me. She left the man in the dust as she came straight to Cash's side. "Hi."

He looked at her, then at me, then at her again. "Has anyone ever told you that you look a hell of a lot like the bartender at The Watering Hole?"

She and I laughed, but I wasn't laughing with ease as she put her arm around Cash's shoulders and grinned at me in a way that made me extremely nervous.

CASH

With a woman hanging on my shoulder who looked a hell of a lot like the one who'd stolen my attention since I first laid eyes on her, I wondered why she wore so damn much makeup. "You know you could do without all that goop on your face, right?"

"Goop?" Her dark blonde brows arched as she looked at Bobbi Jo. "So this is him?"

"Who?" I asked as I looked back at the woman who hung all over me even though she'd come in with a man. A man who stood perfectly still, staring a hole in me.

Bobbi Jo just shook her head. "No. Would you mind getting off my customer, Betty Sue?"

"Betty Sue?" I asked. "Are you two twins?"

"What tipped you off?" the woman I now knew was named Betty Sue asked me with a grin.

"I'm a little tipsy, but I ain't drunk. I can see the similarities." I didn't know why I kept thinking about all the makeup the girl had on, but I did. "Why do you have so much shit on your face, Betty Sue? Look at your sister." I pointed at Bobbi Jo's face. "She's beautiful naturally. You could look like that too."

Grimacing, Betty Sue said, "I like to wear makeup. I feel prettier with some on."

Bobbi Jo's cheeks had gone a shade of pink they hadn't been before.

"Why are you blushing?" I asked.

Shaking her head, she once again turned her attention to her twin sister. "Get off him, Betty Sue. Your date is waiting for you. I thought you two were going to Dallas for the night."

"We are," Betty Sue told her. "He wanted to stop off for a drink first."

"Are you drinking too?" Bobbi Jo asked her sister.

"Yes." Betty Sue finally got off me and went to take the man she'd come in with by the hand. "Lance, what would you like to drink. It's on the house, so order whatever you want."

Bobbi Jo wasn't happy with her sister drinking. "I'll serve him liquor but not you. I'm not letting you drink then drive, Betty Sue. You should know that by now."

The girl's hand went to her slender hip. "And just tell me why not?"

"You've got two DWI's under your belt, and you're only twenty-two." Bobbi Jo put a bottle of water on the bar for her sister. "Here you go. And what will you be having, Lance?"

"Jack on the rocks." He walked up to me, extending his hand. "Lance."

I shook his hand. "Cash. Nice to meet you."

"Same." He took the empty seat next to me. "New in town?"

"I am." I took a sip of the now-warm coffee and made a face at the bitterness.

Bobbi Jo didn't waste a second as she not only poured some more into the cup but tossed in a couple of sugar cubes too. "That ought to fix it up for you, Cash."

I couldn't help but smile at her. "Thoughtful of you. Thanks."

Betty Sue sighed. "Well, Lance, hurry up with your drink. I want to get on the road to Dallas so I can drink too."

Bobbi Jo narrowed her eyes at her twin. "That sounds to me like you plan on grabbing some beer and drinking on the road."

"You can't control me." Betty Sue narrowed her eyes right back at her sister. "I *am* a grown woman."

"Yeah, a grown woman who's spent a week in jail each time you got caught drinking and driving. When will you learn?" Bobbi Jo asked her.

"When will you learn to butt out of people's business?" She looked at the coffee I was drinking. "Did he even order that? Or was he having a little too much fun and you forced him to drink that nasty-ass coffee?"

I held up one finger to stop them. "I can fix this if you want me to, Bobbi Jo."

"This isn't your problem, Cash. Thank you, though." Bobbi Jo turned her attention to her sister once more. "Are you forgetting that it was me who not only had to put up the money to bail your ass out of jail, but I also kept it from Dad as long as I could to help you out? Driving to Dallas to get you out wasn't exactly a thing I had time for, either time you wound up in jail there. And by the looks of things, you're headed to a Dallas jail again tonight. Well, I'm not coming to get you if you end up in jail again; I promise you that."

I felt the need to interject once more. "I can help you out, Bobbi Jo. I really can."

Betty Sue looked at me with a sexy smile. "Tell me how you can help out, Cash."

"Only if your sister wants me to," I told her.

Bobbi Jo huffed as she looked at her sister, then me. "How can you help out, Cash?"

Sitting up a little straighter, I offered my services. "I have a limo and driver at my disposal. I also have a private jet too. I could have the driver come pick them up, take them to the airport here then my pilot would take them to Dallas where they could take a cab to wherever they're going."

"Yes!" Betty Sue said as she jumped up and down, clapping. "Now give me a drink, Bobbi Jo. Cash is taking care of it all." Her blue eyes met mine. "Care to join us, Cash?"

I shook my head. "Nope. I'm gonna hang out here."

Betty Sue shook her head as she looked at her sister. "You're off tomorrow. You hired that new guy. You could come too, Bobbi Jo. I bet if you come, then Cash will too."

She was right. But I didn't really want to go. I wanted to hang out with Bobbi Jo alone. So I gave Bobbi Jo a look that I hoped would telegraph my thoughts to her without me having to say anything.

"I've got plans for tomorrow, Betty Sue. If you want to take Cash up on his offer, I suggest you do so. But leave me out of your plans." She filled a glass with coke and rum then put it in front of her sister. "And so help me, Betty Sue, if you call me telling me that you're in jail, I will wring your neck." Then she smiled at me, and that smile was worth everything. "Thanks, Cash."

"Not a problem at all." I sat back in the tall chair, happy I could help ease the girl's mind. It seemed like a lot of weight was on her shoulders where her sister was concerned.

I pulled out my cell and sent a message to Buddy, asking him about giving a ride to some of my friends. He answered immediately that he'd be right down to the bar to pick them up.

I'd never had the resources to do anything that nice before. Looking up, I silently thanked my grandfather for everything. Without what he'd left us, we'd still be struggling every day just to make a buck.

A short time later, Betty Sue and Lance left. With it being Saturday night, the partygoers stayed until the bar closed. I hadn't had anything else to drink and helped Bobbi Jo clean up and lock up so Joey could go home.

"You don't have to stay, Cash," she told me as she put chairs on top of tables so she could mop.

I'd done my fair share of cleaning in my time. "I'll go make the mop water while you sweep the floor. I don't mind helping you, Bobbi Jo. I even like it. I used to get paid to do things like this. Doing it for fun is kind of cool."

"Fun?" She laughed. "There's nothing fun about cleaning."

All I could do was shrug as I went to make the mop water. To me, it was fun just hanging around with the girl. She was so unlike any of the other girls I'd ever met. She didn't try to act like something she wasn't. She didn't try to flirt with me. She didn't try to make herself as pretty as she could be at every moment just to attract me.

When I came back out with the bucket and the mop, I saw she'd nearly finished sweeping the floor and went to the back to start mopping. "I'm pretty fast at this. Maybe after we're done cleaning, I could give you a lift home."

"I drove my car here." She went to the back to put the broom away.

Hurrying to finish mopping, I tried to think of another way I'd get to spend some more time with her. When she came back out and went to the register to get the money out of it, I came up with another idea. "How about I follow you to your place; you can pack a bag real quick, then I'll take you out to my place? There are tons of empty guest rooms. And you did say you'd come out tomorrow anyway. Why not join me for breakfast. Chef Todd makes some great breakfasts. Ella—that's the maid who my brother Tyrell is sweet on but won't admit it—she said Todd makes Sunday brunches that are to die for. Her actual words, not mine. I rarely say 'to die for.'"

As she put the money into a bank bag, she smiled, and I thought for a moment that she would accept my generous offer. "That's very nice of you, Cash. I like to sleep in on Sundays. That means until two or three in the afternoon. So, you see, I would sleep right through that brunch you're talking about. I meant that I'd come over for dinner tomorrow evening if that's still okay with you."

"Sure." I couldn't hide the disappointment in my voice. "I get it. You work all week, staying up late each night. You need to catch up on your rest sometime. I was just—"

She said, "Thinking you wanted to spend more time together."

Nodding, I smiled at her. "Yeah. Dumb, huh?"

"Wanting to spend more time with me is dumb?" she asked with wide eyes. "I don't think that. I think it's sweet. And I think it sounds like something people who are looking for a relationship do. I want to be perfectly clear with you, Cash. I enjoy your company. I like you. But I like my freedom too."

"Me too." I did like my freedom. "And you're right. I'm asking too much. I'll chill. Maybe it's being in a new town and not knowing many people yet that has me all clinging to you. You're my first friend here, Bobbi Jo."

I liked the way a slow smile traveled over her lips. "That's cool. I think you and I will be great friends, Cash."

612

I'd had it with just being friends. I wanted something a little more too. Not a lot more, just a little. So I pushed the mop across the floor as I made my way to her.

She watched me as I came closer and closer to her. Moving behind the bar, I mopped all the way up to her feet. "Just because we're friends doesn't mean we can't have a little fun. You know what I'm saying?" I laid the mop handle against the bar next to her then put my hands on her narrow shoulders.

She licked her lips. "I think I understand what you're saying."

"Good." Moving my arms around her, I pulled her close as we looked into each other's eyes. Slowly, I moved in until our lips met, and the way lightning zipped through me told me we had what it took to get a hell of a lot more physical with our friendship.

BOBBI JO

Fireworks went off inside my head. That had never happened before, and I had no idea what that even meant. All I knew was that my arms were wrapping around him and my lips parted to let him in.

He lifted me up easily, sitting me on top of the bar. I felt his cock throbbing against my already hot pussy. One of his hands moved to cup one of my tits, and my nipples went hard. I moaned with how amazing it felt to be with him that way.

When he moved his mouth off mine, to trail his hot lips up my neck, I could barely breathe. "You kiss better than most, Bobbi Jo."

"You too." I ran my fingers along his arms. "Maybe it's because your muscles are so damn sexy."

He took my hands and then had me untuck his shirt, then he moved my hands underneath it, pressing them to his muscular abs then pecs. "How do you like these?"

"I like them a lot." He let my hands go, and I moved them all over his tight stomach and chest. "Hills and valleys everywhere."

Reaching behind me, he untied my apron then pulled it off me. His hands moved underneath the back of my shirt, then my bra was unhooked before I knew what was happening.

His hands came around, cupping my tits. "Soft," he whispered.

Even though I hadn't had a thing to drink, I felt drunk. Moving my hands over his, I urged him to caress my tits as I looked into his baby blue eyes. "It's nice being your friend, Cash."

"I like being yours too," he said, then kissed me again. The pure passion that filled me wasn't something I'd ever fully experienced before.

I supposed it was because Cash was the best-looking guy I'd ever kissed. When you added in how well he was built and how much attention he'd paid me in only a couple of days, it all made perfect sense.

He moved one hand down to rub it over my crotch. The heat from it had him groaning, and I knew why. As he pulled his mouth off mine again, I whispered, "It's been awhile. Seems my nether regions are heating up rather rapidly. Please excuse that."

His lips pulled up into a wry grin. "It's been a while for me too. My cock is about to burst through my blue jeans. If you come home with me tonight, I promise to let you sleep as long as you want to. I won't let anyone disturb you, I swear. The beds at my place are kind of amazing. You'll sleep like a baby. Well, afterward, you will."

I acted like I had no idea what he was talking about. "Afterward?"

His eyes danced. "Yeah. After I fuck you like you've never been fucked before."

My breath caught in my throat. No one had ever talked to me that way—raw, purely sexual, and real. Cash left nothing to the imagination. He wanted to fuck me, and I wanted him to.

I suppose the other guys I'd had sex with weren't as passionate, strong, masculine, nor uber-sexy as Cash was. Maybe that was why no one had ever turned me on the way he did. Maybe that was why no one had ever come straight out and told me they wanted to fuck me.

"I don't know about going out to the ranch with you, Cash." I didn't want him to think this was more than what it was—just sex.

"I could go to your place, I guess." He kissed a line along my collarbone.

"No!" I pushed him back as I shook my head. "I live at home. You don't want to meet my parents. Not like that."

He just smiled. "Then come home with me. I'll bring you back to pick up your car whenever you want me to. For now, though, I want you to sit next to me in my truck where I can finger-fuck your hot pussy all the way out to the ranch. I want to feel your hot come all over my fingers."

"Shit," I hissed. No one had ever said anything even remotely like that to me before. "I hope you're as good as your mouth says you are, Cash Gentry."

"I'm better than my mouth says I am, Bobbi Jo Baker." He kissed the soft spot behind my ear. "I asked around about you today and found out a few things—like your last name and the fact that your daddy is the sheriff of this small town. Your mother is a nice lady too. I met her at the feed store this morning."

"How?" I shut up as he sucked a place on my neck that left me speechless.

"You said something to someone about her working there last night. I wanted to meet her. Don't ask me why, because I don't know. But I wanted to see her." His lips brushed across my cheek. "There's something about you, girl. I just want to get all up in you. So, what do you say? Wanna let me?"

My head swirled. My legs shook as he pressed his hard cock against my apex. My hands trembled as I moved them over his shoulders. "When it's over, we'll still just be friends, right? I don't want anything more than that."

"Cool." He kissed my lips softly. "Me neither. Friends with benefits. That's fine with me."

"No sweet names, either. I'm not your baby; you're not my man." I had to make sure we had the rules set. I wasn't going to get involved with anyone. Not yet. I had my life to live first.

I'd seen one friend after another get with a guy, move way too fast, end up in a relationship, which always meant fights. Lots of fights. Arguing over where to go eat dinner, arguing over why some girl said hi to their man, arguing over why he wore a blue shirt when she told him to wear a green one so it would match with her eyes.

Yeah, I'd had a lot of girlfriends in my lifetime who were extra like that. And I didn't want to become one of them. All of them had said I would be just like them when I found myself a man.

I'd be just at bitchy, overbearing, and insecure as they were. I'd be searching through my man's cell every time I got the chance to make sure he wasn't talking to anyone else. I'd be making him dress in a way that made us look like a couple, so no other woman would dare to even speak to him.

I didn't want to turn into that kind of person. I wouldn't do it. No matter what it took.

So sweet names were out.

He pulled the rubber band out of my hair, releasing my ponytail. "Why would I call you sweet names? That's what couples do. We're not a couple."

My heart pounded as he ran his hands up my arms then put them on either side of my face. "We're friends. And as that, we should help each other out at times. Like I helped you clean up after work, right?"

I nodded, barely coherent. "Yeah."

He took my hand then pressed it to the bulge in his pants. "And now you can help me with this little problem, can't you?"

I nodded again. "Yeah."

He let my hand go so he could place his palm on my hot, jean-covered pussy. "And this seems like it's in need of help too. What kind of a friend would I be if I didn't help you out with this?"

"A bad one." I took a deep breath as I looked at his gorgeous face. "So, we can just help each other out then. No need to think it's anything more than a couple of friends helping each other out. Right?"

"Right." He kissed me again, making me even hotter. His hands moved all over my body and mine did the same to his.

I couldn't remember ever wanting anyone so damn much. Every atom in my body wanted this man. Just as that thought came into my mind, he pressed his cock against my aching pussy and pumped a little.

I gasped as our lips parted. "Cash!"

His fingers pulled at the button on my jeans. "Yeah?"

"You'll have to use a condom." I didn't like taking birth control. I didn't have sex enough to warrant doing that.

"I saw a machine in the men's room. I'll be right back." He

617

stepped back, and I could see the size of the hard-on inside his jeans. "I'll get plenty of them. Don't you worry at all."

Sitting on the bar, I nodded as he took off to the bathroom. My breathing was already erratic. My nipples were hard as rocks when I ran my hands over them. That man was about to rock my world, of that I had no doubt.

But would I be able to rock his?

I'd had sex with four guys. I could count on two hands the amount of times I'd even had sex. The sudden onslaught of nerves had me getting off the bar. Pacing, I thought about how stupid I was for thinking I could do this with a man like Cash.

The sound of the bathroom door creaking open had me looking up, and I must've looked a little crazy. "What's wrong? You're not having second thoughts, are you?"

"I'm not sure."

He raced to me, picking me back up and putting me on the bar again. "Don't have second thoughts, Bobbi Jo."

"You're, well, you're better at this than I am." I bit my lower lip as insecurity filled me. "I've had sex less than ten times, Cash. I'm not great at it."

"So." He took me by the chin. "It's up to me to be great. All you've got to do is let me show you what I can do for you. I'm not looking for anything more than that. I'll take on all the work. You just lay back and relax."

He had no idea how sexually useless I was. "I've never given a blow job."

"So." He smiled at me.

"Not a hand job either."

Still, he smiled. "So."

I had one more thing to admit to him that I was truly afraid would have him changing his mind. "I've never had a sexually induced orgasm either. Not one of the four guys I've had sex with has ever been able to make me come."

"I will definitely make you come, Bobbi Jo. That's a promise." He placed his hand on my crotch. "Want me to prove that to you before I take you home and fuck you senseless?"

"How?" My head swooned as the possibilities rose in it.

He slowly unbuttoned my jeans, then unzipped them. Picking me up a bit, he slid my pants and panties down. Then he sat my bare ass back down on the top of the bar.

All I could do was stare at him as he pushed me to lie back. "Feel free to scream when I make you come, Bobbi Jo. Hearing a woman scream my name while in the throes of ecstasy really does it for me."

"K." I fisted my hands as he kissed my intimate lips, then ran his tongue through my folds, before pushing it into me. Gasping, I already felt a twinge of something I'd never felt before. And within a couple of minutes, I was exploding, crashing, and imploding all at once with his name on my lips. "Cash! Cash! Cash!"

CASH

A few days after having sex with Bobbi Jo, all I wanted was to have more of the same. Only she wasn't into coming home with me every night. I got Saturday night and Sunday night too, but after that, I was out of luck.

Hump day was upon us, and I had high hopes of using that fact to get back into her pants. I sat at the bar, nursing a beer as Bobbi Jo put away clean mugs into the freezer. "So, happy hump day, Bobbi Jo." I held up my mug to her.

Laughing, she closed the freezer door then turned to look at me. "Happy hump day to you too, Cash."

"So, on that note."

She shook her head. "Nope."

I had no idea why she didn't want to have sex again. With people in the bar, I didn't want to talk too loudly about it, but I had to say something. "You need my help back there this evening, Bobbi Jo?"

She pointed at Joey. "I've got him to help me. Thanks though."

I decided I wouldn't give up. When Joey came back up to the bar to make some more drinks, I said, "How'd you like to go home early tonight, Joey? I can stay and help the boss clean up after closing time."

"Cool," he said as he jerked his head toward a girl sitting at the far end of the bar. "It's my girl's birthday. I planned on taking her to Whataburger after closing anyway."

Bobbi Jo frowned at him. "Well, why didn't you tell me that, Joey? Hell, take off now. There's no reason for your girlfriend to spend her birthday sitting here at this bar, doing nothing." She went to the register and opened it up, pulling out some money. "Here, take this and take her somewhere better than Whataburger." She pulled a bottle of Texas Crown Royal off the shelf and handed it to him. "Take this too. Have a great night and take tomorrow off too."

"Wow," he said as he looked surprised. "Thanks, boss." He held up the bottle and wad of money in his fist too as he shouted to his girl, "Come on, baby, we're going out!"

The smile that lit her up made me and Bobbi Jo smile too as she ran to him and jumped into his arms. "Oh, Joey!"

As the two left, Bobbi Jo and I looked at each other, then I said, "So, can I help you clean up now?"

She nodded. "Yes. But that's all we're going to do."

"Why?" I put the bottle to my lips as I waited for her answer.

She cleaned off the bar. "I don't want you to get used to doing that."

When she got close enough to me that I could whisper, I asked, "Don't you mean you don't want to get to used to doing that? Screaming my name while you break down into a puddle of pleasure must be terrible for you."

Her cheeks went bright red as she turned to walk away from me. She went straight back to the freezer, opened the door then just stood there. "You're bad."

"You're hot." I took another drink as my cock pulsed.

She closed the freezer door then purposely went to work, arranging the bottles on the shelf, so she didn't have to look at me. "You could stop trying to make me that way."

"What's the fun in that?"

Someone yelled about needing more beer, and she had to come back to face me to get some out of the cooler. "Cash, we're not supposed to be trying to turn each other on all the time."

Nodding, I knew we weren't. But she turned me on all the time anyway. "You could stop being so damn cute," I said.

"I literally got out of bed, took a shower, dressed, then came to work," she said. "My hair is in a damp ponytail, I have on no makeup at all, and I forgot to put on deodorant. Still, think I'm so damn cute?"

I wished I didn't, but that did nothing but make her more appealing to me. "Damn, Bobbi Jo, how do you do it?" I had to move a bit to rearrange myself on the barstool. "You're making me uncomfortable here."

"I didn't mean to." She put the four beers on the bar. "Wanna take those to the guys over there?"

"Um, no." I looked her in the eyes. "You gave me a chubby."

She looked perplexed. "How?"

Shrugging, I didn't know exactly how she'd done it. She wasn't even trying. "All I know is that you could fix it if you'd meet me in the back for a few minutes."

"Forget that." She took the beers off the bar then went to serve them.

I watched her in the mirror; her backside swaying with every step. "Here ya go, boys."

As she walked back toward the bar, she caught my eyes in the mirror and smiled. All I knew was that I would be helping her clean up after closing and we'd be alone. And I wouldn't waste a second getting her on her back.

My cock ached for her. I'd never had such sweet pussy in my life —and I'd had plenty to compare it to. Bobbi Jo did things for me that made no damn sense. She didn't even try to turn me on, yet she still did.

Waking up with her in my arms was a pleasant surprise the two mornings I got to spend with her. I was usually the guy who left way before having to wake up with a girl. But waking up with Bobbi Jo was cool.

We'd brushed our teeth together each morning. And she had pulled the sheet off the bed to cover herself each morning too. I had to yank it off her, toss her over my shoulder, and make her get into the shower with me. We laughed a lot. We kissed a lot. And we connected on a level I didn't know I could with a girl.

The door opened, and group of women came in. They were rowdier than anyone else in the bar and Bobbi Jo clued me in as she hurried to fill up frosted mugs with beer. "Wednesday evening church is out. Have you lost your little problem, Cash? Can you help me out now?"

"I wouldn't call it little." I got up as I had gotten rid of the erection. "What would you like me to do?"

"Grab a tray and take these beers to the ladies over there. Watch out; they can get a little handsy." She winked at me. "But they tip good, so forgive them for their trespasses."

"Sweet." I picked up the tray heavy with mugs of beer then headed to their table. "Evening, ladies. How about some cold suds to make your hump day a little better?"

"Halleluiah!" one of the shouted.

Another added, "Praise, Jesus!"

A third quickly picked up her mug of beer, holding it up high. "Nectar of the gods!"

I thought it a bit funny that these church-going ladies loved their beer so much. "So, what church do you ladies go to?"

"Cowboy Church," one of them told me. "That's why we like our beer so much."

Another pinched me on the ass. "You should come on Sunday and check it out. On Sundays, the men barbeque and we all get drunk after the morning service."

"Okay, thanks for the invitation." I moved one woman's hand off my butt as I tried to walk away.

But another one of them grabbed my hand. "So are you single?"

Another hollered, "What's your name?"

Before I could answer, another shouted, "Do you believe in love at first sight?"

I decided to answer the questions in order, "I am single. My name is Cash Gentry. And I do believe in love at first sight."

"Gentry?" one of them asked. "Like Whisper Ranch, Gentry?"

"Yep." I headed back to the bar, but another one of them caught me by the leg, a bit close to the family jewels.

I looked at her hand as she asked, "Can we have services out there sometime?"

Moving her hand, I shrugged. "I'd have to ask my brothers what they think about that first."

"Are they as gorgeous and single as you are, Cash?" A large, dark-haired lady asked.

"Um, kind of." I made sure to get away this time. "I'll be back with more beer in a bit. And maybe a tray of food too." They seemed like they needed something to eat to make sure the alcohol didn't hit them too hard. The spirit of something had already hit them hard enough.

When I caught the smirk on Bobbi Jo's face, I moved in close next to her. "Very funny."

"I know, right?" She laughed. "I see big bucks in your night, Cash."

All I saw was the end of the night. "I see you waking up in my bed in the morning, Bobbi Jo."

Her cheeks went pink. "Don't get ahead of yourself, lover boy."

"I thought you said we couldn't call each other sweet names." I wasn't going to let her off the hook. "If you get to call me lover boy, I'm going to call you something too. Maybe sexy momma."

"I ain't your momma though." She inched away from me.

I grabbed her by the waist. The bar was tall enough that no one could see what I was doing. "No, but you're my little love slave, aren't you?"

"Nope." She pulled away from me, smiling all the while. "I'm not a slave to anyone or thing."

"Bet you are." She couldn't fool me. I knew she liked—no loved —what I could do for her and to her body. "I'm going to make you beg for it later on tonight, girl. Just wait and see."

A shiver ran through her body, and I watched it tremble. "Hush."

Maybe I was getting too loud. So I got closer. "I think I'll call you cake."

She looked at me with confusion riddling her pretty face. "Cake? And why is that?"

"Because, you are moist, sweet, and I love to eat you." I tickled her tummy, making her squirm.

"Cash!" She stepped away from me as she tried not to laugh. "You're being terrible tonight."

"I'm horny." I didn't see any reason to lie to her.

Putting her hand on her hip, she jerked her head to the table full of women I'd waited on. "Any one of them would be happy to take care of that for you."

"Yeah, I know." I ran my eyes up and down her little body. "But I only want you."

With raised brows, she said, "We're still just friends, you know. If you want one of them, I won't get mad at you. You're a free man— remember that."

"And you're a free woman." I grinned at her. Something about being free to be with anyone I wanted made wanting her that much more appealing. "There's a bar full of eligible men out there. Pick one."

She wagged her finger at me. "First of all, I'm not the horny one here, you are. Second of all, I don't mess with men from the bar. It's bad for business."

"How do you explain me?" I asked.

"I can't." She picked up a bar towel and tossed it to me. "Can you clean up that table the group of guys just left for me?"

Nodding, I said, "Sure. If you can tell me that you'll be waking up in my bed in the morning."

The way her lips quirked to one side made my cock twitch. "You drive a hard bargain."

"I know. I drive other things hard too." Winking, I walked past her, patting her ass as I went by. "My bed, in the morning, waking up in my arms."

"Maybe."

I shook my head. "For sure. You'll see. You'll be begging me later."

She wasn't giving up. "I highly doubt that."

I highly don't doubt it.

BOBBI JO

With my body pressed against the wall, his mouth on my cunt, and my hands fisted in his thick hair, I moaned as he pulled his mouth away from me again. "No, Cash. Don't stop. I was almost there."

"Oh, were you? I didn't know," he said as he kissed a trail inside my thigh.

The smell of bleach water from the mop bucket made my nostrils burn. "I think it's time to go. We've been closed for over an hour. People are going to start thinking we're doing more than cleaning in here."

"So." Cash didn't seem to care what people thought. He moved up my body, then pressed his lips to mine before pulling back. "So, are you ready?"

I'd never planned on going home with him. "Can't you just do me here? Then we can go our separate ways, and no one has to know what we're doing."

"Again, Bobbi Jo, I don't care who knows what we're doing. I don't know why you care either. And if you want more, then you know where you can get that." He nibbled on my ear as he ground his hard cock against my throbbing, bare pussy. He'd taken my jeans off long ago, teasing me relentlessly with oral sex, but leaving me just short of an orgasm.

Taking his face in my hands, I said, "I thought you didn't want a girlfriend."

"I don't." He grinned at me. "And I know you don't want a boyfriend. I'm cool with how things are with us. We have great sex. We get along great too. I see no reason to think beyond that point."

"So, what's this thing with wanting me in your bed all the time and waking up in your arms?" That sounded a lot like a relationship to me.

"I like it." He moved his hands down my waist. "You do too. Your wet pussy each morning tells me that, even if you won't."

My body did love his. "But sleeping together seems too intimate to me. Aren't you afraid of what might happen?"

"Like if we'll fall in love?" he asked, then laughed.

The fact he laughed sort of pissed me off. "Is it that funny to you? You think I'm not a person you could fall in love with?"

"First, I don't fall in love. Second, if I did, you could be a person I would do that with. But for now, I like spending time with you in many ways. I like hanging out at the bar with you. I like talking to you. And I really, really like it when my cock is buried deep in that hot pussy of yours."

"Graphic," I mumbled.

"I like to keep it real." He let me go to pull my jeans up that had been around my ankles. "So, let's get going, cake."

"Don't call me that." I zipped up my jeans, then buttoned them. "I'll drive my car over. I want to leave early so I can get back home and sleep until noon."

Taking my hand, he pulled me back to him, holding me tight. "You'll ride with me, and we will sleep together until noon."

"What's the deal with you, Cash? You want to be around me all the time." I'd never had anyone want to be around me so much.

"So?" He played with my hair after pulling it out of the ponytail. "Are you going to say you don't like being around me?"

"I wouldn't know. Since you came to town, I'm rarely *not* around you." I smiled at him. "But that's because you've made it your goal in life to be where I am most of the time."

"And you want me to stop coming around?" he asked but didn't let me go.

"I didn't say that. I just pointed out that it's you coming around me, and not the other way around."

He gripped me tighter, his voice rough and raspy. "Funny, when we're having sex, it's you coming around me."

"It's always sex with you." I took a deep breath to steady myself as he made me feel weird. Like I wanted to take off all my clothes and just get tangled up with him.

Moving me backward, he danced me to the backdoor. Our cars were parked in back. "Probably because sex with you consumes my thoughts. I just want more and more."

I'd never been a sex object to anyone before. It was kind of mind-blowing that someone like Cash thought of me as one. "Is that all I am to you, Cash?"

"Nope." He opened the door behind my back, then danced me out of it. Letting me go, he pulled the door closed then waited for me to lock it.

After locking the door, I looked at my car, but he grabbed my hand and pulled me to his truck. "I really should take my car, Cash."

"Nope." When he made up his mind, there was no changing it. "You haven't begged enough to suit me yet. I've gotta torment you all the way home. I can't do that if you're not sitting next to me in the truck."

"You're still set on making me beg, huh?" I had to laugh.

He opened the truck door then picked me up and sat me in the driver's seat. "Scoot over, cake."

Moving over, I shook my head. "I hate that nickname, Cash."

"Then make up a new one." He slid in behind the steering wheel. "To be honest, I've had to stop myself from calling you baby."

Shaking my head, I wasn't going to get that started. "No way, Cash. You and I both agreed that we don't want a relationship. I don't want to be your baby."

"But I can be your lover boy?" He started the truck and it roared to life.

"You're not my lover boy," I corrected him. "You are *a* lover boy."

"Okay, so to me you're not my baby, but you *are* a babe." He ran his arm around my shoulders, pulling me tight against his side. "So when I call you baby, I mean that you're a babe. How's that?"

"Not going to fly." I knew using pet names was a bad idea all the way around. "Let's drop the names, other than our real names. It's going to get too complicated if we don't."

"Seems to me that you're afraid you'll fall for me rather easily. I can see that. I mean, I do make you scream my name. And your body melts into mine easily." He moved his hand down in between my legs. "Your pussy is always wet for me."

"In my defense, you have no idea if I get wet for other guys just as easily, Cash." I didn't, but he didn't know that.

"If you did, then you wouldn't have been free tonight." He undid my pants with one hand, then slid that hand into my panties, his fingers sinking into me.

"Oh," I sighed as I gripped his bicep. "Cash. Damn."

Pumping them slowly, he spoke softly, his voice so deep and husky. "You like me inside of you, baby. You want me inside of you. You ache for me just as much as I ache for you. Baby. Baby. Baby."

"Cash," I moaned as he moved his fingers in a way that seemed unreal. "How do you know right where to touch me? How have you found places no other man ever has?"

"Maybe because your body was meant to be pleased by me and me alone." He pumped his fingers a little harder. "Just because we're not in love doesn't mean we weren't meant to please each other."

I didn't want to fall in love. I didn't want all that came with that. But I did want that man to take my body and make it do things only he could make it do. "Please, Cash. Please let me come this time." I didn't want him to stop again. I wanted to feel that rush as my body went over the edge.

Cash could do to me what even a vibrator couldn't do. And I'd tried hard to make it do what he could. I'd been just as horny as he was. At home, I had tried to masturbate, tried to make myself come as hard as he'd made me come. Nothing worked the way he did.

Easing his fingers back and forth, he whispered, "Why should I let you come?"

629

I couldn't help it as my mouth betrayed me. "Because nothing makes me come like you do."

He chuckled sexily. "See, that wasn't so hard to admit, was it? I'll admit something to you too. I've tried jerking off since I've been fucking you and it doesn't work. I need your tight cunt to get me off. I've never needed anyone to get me off until you came along."

I had no idea what that meant. All I knew was I needed him inside of me—and I needed him now. "Pull over." I pulled his shirt; buttons flew all over the cab of the truck as they ripped off from the pressure.

He pulled over, parking the truck then pushing me to lie back on the seat. "You want it now?"

Nodding, I wanted it right then and there. "Please, Cash. Please fuck me like only you can."

He shimmied my jeans the rest of the way off, then pulled a condom out of his pocket before pushing his jeans down just enough to release his massive cock. He held the condom out to me. "You put it on for me, baby." His smile told me that he wasn't going to stop calling me that.

So I decided to mess with his head too. "K, honey bunch."

As I rolled the condom down his long shaft, my heart pounded. He whispered in my ear. "Tonight, I'm going to teach you how to suck me off. That way, when I get too riled up for you, you can take care of me with just your mouth."

I couldn't explain why my mouth began to water with what he'd said. "You want me to learn how to give you head so I can do it almost anywhere?"

"Yep." He lifted my face, holding my chin. "In the bathroom at the bar. In the back room of the bar. In the cab of my truck. Anywhere at all."

"And how will you fix me up?" I wasn't going to be the one doing all the fixing in this thing.

"Are you kidding?" He laughed. "Haven't I shown you that?"

"So, you'd just take me into the back of the bar, drop my jeans, and eat me out?" I felt hot and shocked. "While people are there? Like right in the next room?"

He nodded. "Yep."

No one had ever made me so hot in my life. I gazed into his eyes as he spread my legs apart, then moved in between them, thrusting hard into me. We both grunted with the force. "I suppose we'll have to learn to be quiet if you want to do this in close proximity to others."

"Well, we're alone right now, so feel free to make all the noise you want." He moved harder, knocking the air out of my lungs. "I love it when you say my name."

"Cash," I whispered as I looked into his blue eyes. What I felt scared me a little. I could so easily fall into the man and never come up for air again.

CASH

Bobbi Jo had made some hot nights for me, and I wasn't thinking about anyone else as I walked down the street toward the Dairy King to grab one of their juicy cheeseburgers. Whistling as I walked, I felt a hand run across my back as a saucy female voice whispered, "Miss me, cowboy?"

Spinning around, I found Bobbi Jo wrapped in my arms, her lips pursed for a kiss. Who was I not to oblige the young lady? Leaning in, our lips met, hers parted, and our tongues entwined.

Her breasts felt the tiniest bit smaller as they squished against my chest. Her kiss tasted like cinnamon instead of the usual spearmint. And the way she moved her tongue didn't seem right.

Pulling back, I looked into her eyes. The devilish sparkle told me all I needed to know. "Betty Sue, you little hussy, you." I let her go quickly, then ran my hand over my mouth as if wiping away the kiss.

Her fingers moved over her lips. "What a kisser you are, Cash Gentry." She gave me a sly wink. "No wonder my sister has been keeping late hours since you moved into town. You know, she and I share lots of things. You could be one of them."

I didn't want to be rude, but I wasn't into what she thought I was. "Well, *I'm* not something you two will be sharing."

"Oh?" She looked inquisitive. "You planning on getting serious with my sister?"

I shook my head; seriousness wasn't my intention at all. "Not too serious. But serious enough that I ain't about to start swapping spit on the regular with her twin sister. You shouldn't even play games like that, Betty Sue. Don't you think it might bother your sister at least a little to know that we kissed?"

"I don't see why it would bother her." She licked her lips as if tasting me on them and liking what she'd found. "She and I have been with the same guys, Cash. This town is small. There's only so many girls to go around. The fact is, most of us girls have dated the same guys at one time or another." She looped her arm through mine. "Where are you headed?"

"To get a burger." I started walking that way again. "You're more than welcome to join me." I thought I should lay out some ground rules though. "As long as you understand that I don't wish to date you or do anything else like that with you."

"I see." She pulled the band out of her long blonde hair to shake it out. The sweet scent of honeysuckle eased past my nose. "Well, you can't blame me for trying now, can you?"

I could and would blame her for trying. If any of my brothers had done something that two-timing, I would've whooped their asses right quick and in a hurry. But I really had no idea what the relationship between the two sisters was, so I wasn't about to go making too much of a stink about what she'd pulled. "Just chill, girl. That's all I'm saying."

"I only wanted to convey my thanks for letting me borrow your jet, and the limo rides too." She gave my arm a little squeeze. "I've never even been on a plane before. It was awesome."

"How'd Lance like it?"

"Who?" She smiled at me, knowing exactly who I was talking about.

I opened the door for her as we got to the little café.

"Oh, thank you, Cash. You are such a gentleman." She moved through the door before me then waited for me to be at her side where she once again looped her arm through mine.

I could tell she didn't want to mention Lance. Although I had no idea why that was, I felt it best not to dig too much into her love life. "So, I hear the cheeseburgers here are great. You want one?"

She ran her free hand over her small waist. "Not me. I only eat salads."

Betty Sue wasn't one ounce heavier than her sister who ate whatever she wanted. "You got some weight problem that your twin doesn't?"

"What?" She looked confused and a little horrified.

"Bobbi Jo eats whatever she wants to and it doesn't affect her weight at all. So why do you only eat salads?" I thought about it a second as we took seats across from each other at a booth. "Oh, wait. I know why that is. Hey, look, you eat what you want to. I'm not a romantic prospect anyway. You can think of me like a brother. Brothers don't give a damn what their sisters eat."

"How would you know, Cash?" she asked with a grin. "You only have brothers."

"Well, it's the same with them. We don't care what anyone eats, really. And here's a hint for you. Men do not care if you eat like a rabbit or not. It doesn't make them think any less or more of you. As a matter of fact, if it makes us feel anything, it's sorry for you." I smiled at the waitress who came to us. "Hey, darling. We'll have two of those cheeseburger meals you got up there on the menu. I'll have onion rings and a coke with mine." I nodded at Betty Sue. "And you?"

"A chocolate milkshake and some fries with mine. And no onions or pickles on my burger." She put her hand over her mouth. "They give people bad breath."

"You might as well have them," I said. "You ain't kissing no one anyhow."

She kicked me under the table. "You hush. You don't know what I've got planned for after lunch."

Shrugging, I said, "You're right. Seeing how you like to accost men from behind and smooch away right there on the sidewalk and all."

I got another kick for saying that and a shocked expression from the waitress. Betty Sue growled, "Just leave them off, please." She glared at me. "And you need to learn to watch what you say."

Nodding, I could tell from both their reactions that I did need to learn to do that. "Gotchya."

After the waitress walked away, Betty Sue changed her tone as she said, "So, anyway, what do you think about living at the ranch? Oh, and when are you gonna get around to inviting me out to see it?"

I'd never had any intentions of inviting her out to see the ranch. "After what you just pulled, I don't think it's a real good idea to invite you out to my home."

Rolling her eyes, she huffed. "I told you: my sister and I have kissed lots of the same guys. You're nothing special, Cash Gentry."

"Whoa!" I thought that was a bit uncalled for. "No reason to hit below the belt. And about that kiss … you gonna tell Bobbi Jo or should I do it?"

"I don't see that either one of us needs to tell her anything." She pulled a mirror out of her purse and looked at herself in it. "You could've told me that I needed more lip gloss, Cash." She smiled at me sexily. "You've kissed it all off my lips, you bad boy."

"Okay, so I'll tell her then." I wasn't about to not let Bobbi Jo know what her sister had done.

I'd been through this sort of thing before: kissed a girl while messing with another. Not that we were serious either, but when a third party tells the person you are currently messing with that they saw you locking lips with someone else, people tend to get pissed. And I didn't want Bobbi Jo to get mad at me for something I didn't purposely do.

Not that I thought she'd get mad, but I wanted to play it safe. I liked hanging with the girl. And I particularly liked the sex. I wasn't about to let anyone mess that up for me. Bobbi Jo and I had some pretty serious heat, and there were still plenty of things I would've liked to do with her—and to her. Something like this could throw a monkey wrench in what I had planned for that girl.

Putting on a fresh coat of lip gloss, Betty Sue seemed to be contemplating things. Finally, she put her purse and makeup away, then looked at me. "I'll do it. It wasn't your doing anyway."

"Good girl." I smiled at her as the waitress brought our food.

"And if she asks me anything about it, I'll tell her the truth. So make sure you do the same."

"I will." She looked at the food in her red basket, and I saw the sparkle in her eyes. "This looks great. Fattening, but great."

"Enjoy," the waitress said before leaving us again.

"If you eat it all, I'll give you a dollar." I laughed as I took a bite of my burger.

"One lousy buck?" she asked with a frown. "So, I'm eating lunch with one of the only three billionaires in Carthage, and all I'm offered is a dollar to eat all the food he's already paying for."

"Yep." I picked up one of her fries. "Except this fry." I popped it into my mouth. "This one was calling my name."

She reached over to steal an onion ring. "So, I'll take this to replace it then."

I smiled as I watched her eat it. "I think that's a fair trade." As long as I had someone from Bobbi Jo's family around, I thought I'd ask some questions of the girl. "So, has Bobbi Jo brought many boys home to meet the family?"

"Nope." She took a little nibble of her burger.

"Take a damn bite, Betty Sue," I urged her. "Enjoy the thing."

She took a bigger bite—nothing huge though. "Yum."

"I know." I took a drink of my coke. "So, why hasn't she ever brought anyone to meet the family? She told me about your mother working at the feed store. And from your mom, I learned your father is the sheriff of Carthage. Is that the reason she's never brought anyone home to meet that family?"

She put her finger on her nose as she chewed her food, then nodded as she swallowed. "Yep. You got it, detective. We don't bring home boys to meet our daddy. He's not real receptive if you know what I mean. Mom's nice. Dad's …" She hesitated. "Well, he's just Dad. Gruff, doesn't trust many people, and mostly he's always in a bad mood. I suppose dealing with so many bad people have made him that way. I figure he had to have been okay at least when he met our mom. She's not the type to care for grouches. But she's married to one now. That's for sure."

"So, he's grouchy and doesn't trust people." I didn't think that sounded too good. But then again, I wasn't trying to be Bobbi Jo's boyfriend. "Well, that makes sense then."

"You wanted her to bring you home or what?" she asked with a quizzical expression.

"No." I took another bite of my burger. "She just doesn't talk much about her personal life."

"Yeah," Betty Sue agreed. "My sister is more of a listener than a talker. I guess that's why she makes such a great bartender."

"Yeah, guess you're right." As we sat there eating, both of us got quiet.

Finally, she said, "You know, you're not so bad, Cash. I've never kissed a guy and had them not want more."

Raising my brows, I thought that kind of an odd thing to say. "Even someone who was actively hanging with your sister?"

She nodded. "Yep."

With her answer, I had to wonder just what kind of family Bobbi Jo was from. Sisters kissing the same boys ... what else did they do with them?

BOBBI JO

Cleaning up the bedroom, I looked over at Betty Sue's side of the room we'd shared our whole lives. "Such a pig." I kicked a pair of barely-there underwear of hers that had somehow made it to my side of the floor. "Yuck." They flew to her side of the room, now covered in a pile of dirty clothes, dishes, and bits of paper for some reason.

Hearing the front door to our small, two-bedroom house open, I knew it had to be Betty Sue coming in. "Bobbi Jo? You here?"

My car was in the drive, so she knew I was. "Yep. What tipped you off, Columbo?"

She opened the bedroom door and looked at the heap of crap on her side of the room. "Cleaning, I see. Just once, would it kill you to put my dirty clothes in the washing machine instead of piling them up this way?"

"Have you ever, even once, put my clothes in the wash?" I found one of her many bobby pins on my desk. Picking it up, I tossed it over to her side. "How in the hell do your things end up on my desk? How?" I looked at her for an answer.

All I got was a shrug. "You must use them. That's what I think anyway."

I'd never used a bobby pin in my life. "Sure, Betty Sue."

Moving some things off her bed, covered in stuff, she took a seat. "So, guess who I ate lunch with just a little while ago?"

I had no idea and no care to guess or even to know. "You know I don't care at all, right?"

"You will." She kicked off her shoes then laid back on the filth covering her bed.

"Yuck." I pointed at her and her lack of hygiene. "I can't remember when you last washed your sheets. And you're lying on old food, old clothes, old—God only knows what. Have you no shame?"

She shrugged. "Not really. I think you got all the shame and I was born without any. Thanks a lot for hogging it all, sister." Her lips pulled into a smile. "Guess what I ate today?"

"Don't care." Why she thought I'd care about what she ate, which was most often salads, I had no clue.

"A cheeseburger. And the whole thing too. And I drank all my milkshake and ate all my fries, and I got this dollar for doing it too." She pulled a buck out of her bra. "See." She wiggled it back and forth.

"Whoopee!" I ran my finger in a circle in the air. "Look at you, eating all your junk food. Now, if you'd said you ate a whole plate of green beans, I might be impressed. Chowing down on crap doesn't exactly make me proud of you, Betty Sue."

With a nod, she agreed. "Yeah. I'm not proud I ate all that bad-for-you food either. I did want to order my usual salad, but *he* wouldn't let me."

"He?" I wasn't actually intrigued. I had an idea that she'd gone out to eat lunch with a guy.

"Yes." She smiled as she looked up at the ceiling. "He."

I waited for her to say something else, but she didn't say a word, just stared at the ceiling with that stupid smile on her face. "So, who is he?" I don't even know why I asked. I did not care at all.

"Cash." Her eyes cut to me.

"My Cash?" I felt something cold move through my body, like a river of snakes. My skin began to crawl.

"Yours?" she asked. "I thought you two weren't serious."

"So?" I tried to shake off the terrible feeling I'd gotten. "How did you two end up eating lunch together?"

My sister had always been notorious for not only flirting with the guys I'd been interested in, but she'd done a lot more than that with them too. The way she was smiling filled me with dread.

Have I lost Cash to her too?

"Promise me something first." She sat up, sitting cross-legged on her bed.

"Why?" I wasn't feeling any better about things.

"Because I'm your sister and I'm asking for you to promise me something first. So, please promise me you won't get mad." She looked at me with wide eyes.

Now that I knew I was definitely going to be mad, I crossed my fingers behind my back. "I promise." I didn't say what I promised, just that I did. In my mind, I finished the sentence: *To kick your ass if you did anything more than just eat with Cash.*

"Okay, well, you know how I used to test guys to make sure they really liked you back in high school?" she asked.

Of course I remembered that. Betty Sue would pretend she was me and get the guys who liked me to kiss her. Afterward, she'd admit who she was and that she thought they had a much better connection than what the guy and I had. And the fact that she put-out pretty much made it so that every guy she'd tested went for her, leaving me in the dust.

So, naturally, my blood began to boil. Long gone was the cold river full of snakes that had run through me—now I felt like lava flowed through my veins. But my voice stayed nice and calm as I said, "I remember."

"Yeah, so, anyway, I saw Cash walking down the sidewalk in town." She made a wolf-whistle. "And boy, that cowboy's ass is sure fine."

"I'm aware of that." I bit my tongue so I could wait to hear it all. "And then what happened?"

"Um, well, I really couldn't help myself." She hugged herself. "He's just so hot, you know?"

"Yep." Of course I knew how hot he was. "So what happened?"

All of a sudden, she decided to backtrack. "Okay, anyway, at lunch I was going to order a salad, and he said that I needed to get a burger and that I didn't have a weight problem. And I wasn't sure what that meant. Like, was he looking at my body? I didn't know. And then he went on to say how guys don't actually care if a girl eats salads or not. Like, they just plain don't care what girls eat. You know what I'm saying?"

Of course I knew what she was saying. What I didn't know was what the hell she'd done with my man. "Can you maybe just be specific, Betty Sue?"

"Oh, I can see your eyes are getting a little cloudy." She smiled. "Anyway, so I did get the burger and fries and stuff, and he was all, 'I'll give you a dollar if you eat it all.' Which I was like, 'I don't need your dollar, rich guy.' Or something along that line anyway."

I was starting to lose it. "What happened?" Like I cared about the damn food!

"What happened is that I ate all the food. Like every last bite." She laughed. "Never have I ever eaten that much food. But Cash is so funny and cool that I ate it all without even noticing what I'd done."

"And then?" I clenched my fists as I waited for more. I just knew instinctively that there was more—much more.

"Okay, well then we left, and I came home, and he went—well, he didn't say where he was going." She huffed. "He can be so closed-lipped sometimes. Anyway, what I was asking you to promise me about was what happened before we got to the Dairy King."

I saw her through a shower of sparks as my meltdown was close at hand. "What happened?"

"I don't think you'll care. It's not like it hasn't happened before. And I told him that. I told him we did that sort of thing all the time and it didn't even need to be mentioned." She waved her hand through the air. "But Cash was determined that one of us tell you about it and I said it should be me."

It was imminent; the combustion was going to occur. "What happened?" If I had to ask that again, I would rip her head off.

"So, I saw him and his cute ass," she said, then cocked her head. "He's got a great walk, doesn't he?"

I nodded. "He does."

"Anyway, I saw that ass, that walk, and when I came up behind him, I smelled leather and something smoky, and then I said something cute." She looked up as if trying to remember what she'd said that was so damn cute. "I think I said 'what's up, cowboy?' or something like that."

"That's not so bad." I began to let some of my anger slip back a bit.

"Yeah, it's not, right?" she asked before continuing. "So he turned around. His eyes lit up. He grabbed me, took me into his arms and …" She stopped talking.

"What?" I was already shaking; I might as well hear the rest by that point. "He did what?"

"Kissed me."

My eyes began blinking really fast. My heart stopped beating. My palms felt like knives where being jabbed into them and that's when I realized my fingernails were dug into them. "Kissed you?"

She nodded. "Yeah. He kissed me."

Time stood still, the room began to swim, and I suddenly was flying. Over the pile of her dirty laundry I went. My fist hit her in the chin first. After that, I felt her silky hair in my hand as I yanked it. I think I was trying to yank it all out—make her bald. "You *slut*!"

"Stop!" she shrieked. "Don't make me hurt you, Bobbi Jo!"

I couldn't feel a thing—except super pissed. "You're dead!"

Slapping began, punches followed. My nails dug into her flesh; hers dug into mine. It was a free-for-all.

"Stop!" my sister screamed.

"I hate you!" I was going to do it this time. I was going to kill her.

I'd come close to doing it before, especially when she'd come to the movie theater where John Parker and I were on a date back in tenth grade. I'd gotten up to go use the bathroom, leaving him alone in the dark. That's when my twin sister went to take my place. She took his hand and stuck it in a place I wouldn't have dared stick it. When I came back, they were making out hardcore. I couldn't believe it.

I left without saying a word, without my popcorn, and without the guy I thought really liked me. And I cried all the way home.

Later, I got a phone call from John, telling me how he had thought it was me the whole time. Well, until they walked out into the light and he remembered that I'd had on a red shirt and jeans. Betty Sue had on a blue tank top and shorts.

I thought his apology meant we were back on. But he wasn't finished talking. He went on to let me know that he liked me and all, but he and my sister had more of a connection than he and I did.

There was no physical fight between my sister and me that day. But I did almost kill her. As silently as she'd slipped into my seat next to John at that theater, I'd silently slipped laxatives into her milk that night at dinner.

When she couldn't get off the toilet that night, not even to answer the phone when John called her to see if she'd like to join him for a movie once again that same day, my parents took her to the emergency room. She was severely dehydrated and to hear her say it, had almost died. And I had to admit what I'd done.

We fell off her bed now as we fought like wolves, gouging, slapping, biting, yanking, and even kicking. This time, I would make sure she knew I was mad as hell at her and not taking any more of her crap.

CASH

"Hey, the sign's off, Bobbi Jo." I flipped on the neon open sign on the bar's front window to let everyone know the place was open. "It's dead in here because you forgot to turn this on."

The dim light inside the bar made it difficult to see her clearly, but it looked like she had something held to her face. "Damn. I totally forgot about that. Thanks, Cash."

"It's only fifteen minutes after opening time anyway." I walked over to the bar. The closer I got to her, the more confused I became. "Why are you holding a bag of frozen peas on your eye?"

Pulling the green-and-white bag away from her face, she revealed a swollen, purple-and-black bruised eye. "This is why I've got a bag of frozen peas on my eye, Cash."

Reaching out, I barely touched her swollen lips. "Wanna tell me what the hell happened to you?"

"I got into a fight." She turned away from me as the door opened, letting in a dusty trail of light.

"A fight?"

She nodded then asked the man who'd come in, "What can I get you?" Not that she turned to face him; her back was still to us both.

"Whatever you got on tap," he said as he went to the pool tables in the back.

I walked around to the back of the bar. "I'll take care of him. Have you taken anything for the pain?"

"Pain?" She laughed. "I'm not hurt."

After pulling a frosty mug out of the freezer, I gave Bobbi Jo the once over and what I found told me she was hurting. "So, those bruises on your arms don't hurt at all? And those scratches on your neck don't either?"

"Nope." She leaned over to get something from under the bar and winced.

So now I knew she had some midsection trauma too. "And those ribs of yours are just fine too? No pain there?"

"No pain anywhere. Just some bruises and stuff." She pulled out the cutting board and the knife she used to cut up the various fruits she used for the cocktails.

I took the beer to the guy who'd come in, just as more people began to come into the bar. It was a Friday night; the place would soon be packed. When I came back up to stand at Bobbi Jo's side while she winced with pretty much every move she made, I asked, "Is Joey coming in tonight?"

"He'll be here at eight," she said as she put four bottles of beer on the bar. "I'm okay, Cash. Really. Go sit down. I can handle this. It's not even bad yet."

"You don't look all right. You look like hell, to be honest with you. A little makeup might have been a good idea." I dodged a punch she threw at me.

"Shut up, jack ass." She turned back to look at the door as more people came streaming in. "But I guess I should use your help if you're offering it. Just until Joey comes in."

"You got it, babe." I ignored her frown as I got to work. There was no way I could just sit on my ass and watch her gimping around so slowly and painfully.

Whether she admitted it or not, that girl was feeling some pain. And for some reason, she didn't want me to know who'd done that to her. I couldn't understand why she'd want to keep that a secret.

But I left it alone for now. The place was getting busy, and there wasn't time to talk anyway.

After Joey came in, there was still plenty of work to be done, so I kept on helping them. I liked it. It was a nice change of pace from what I'd been doing all day—riding one of the horses around the ranch, checking the fences to make sure that none of them had holes or openings.

It was crazy how many times I had found places where things had gone through and either broken wires or moved them in a way that a calf could easily get out. I'd seen Mr. Castle while I was out that day and had told him to come to the bar have a cold one on me tonight. So when he came in, all duded up in a pearl-snap, black western shirt and matching cowboy hat, I had to whistle at him. "Hey there, sharp-dressed man." I slid a frosty mug full of beer to him as he took a seat at the bar. "Glad you decided to come by."

"Yeah," he said then took a drink, placing the mug back on the bar. "It's been some time since I've gotten out of the house. I thought I could use a night out." He scanned the loud and crowded bar. "And what a night it is."

"Yep, you picked a good one." I jerked my head toward a table. "We've got a full table of women over there just waiting for some smooth cowboy to ask them to dance."

He smiled. "Maybe after a beer or two. It's been a long time since I've cut a rug."

Bobbi Jo came up to my side. "Oh, hi."

I had to laugh as Mr. Castle couldn't stop the stunned expression that came over his face. "What the hell happened to you?" He cleared his throat then held out his hand. "Richard Castle, by the way."

Bobbi Jo shook his hand. "Bobbi Jo Baker. It's a pleasure to meet you, Mr. Castle. You're legendary around this town. It's a wonder we've never met before." She ran her hand in a circle around her battered face. "And this is just something that happens when siblings disagree on things."

So, she'd gotten into a fight with her sister. I had that much now. "How'd Betty Sue turn out?"

"You don't see her around, do ya?" She smiled, then winced as

646

the action must've hurt her busted lip. "Ow. More frozen peas." She nodded at Mr. Castle. "It's really nice to meet one of Cash's neighbors and Joey's uncle. Thanks for coming. And your drinks are on the house tonight, being that this is your first ever visit to The Watering Hole."

"How nice. Thank you," he said. "I promise not to drink your establishment dry."

"I'm sure you won't." She left to take care of other customers as I watched her hobble away.

Seemed she'd hurt her ankle too. It must've been a pretty tough fight for all the injuries she had. I had to wonder, as the night went on, just why the sisters had fought.

One thought kept coming to mind. The kiss Betty Sue had stolen from me. But why would Bobbi Jo get into a physical altercation over something like that?

We weren't exclusive. She wouldn't even let me call her baby in public and barely in bed. So, why would she care so much about the kiss that she'd get into a fight with her twin sister over it?

Or was it something else altogether and I was just being stupid?

Girls could get into fights over stupid things, that much I knew. Maybe it was because Betty Sue had used her razor or borrowed some clothes and ruined them. That sounded much more reasonable than the two of them getting into a tussle over me and that stolen kiss.

As the night went on, then came to a close, the patrons filtering out a little at a time, I finally found the time to put to the screws to her about what had really happened.

In the back, as I was gathering up a few empty boxes to throw the empty aluminum cans in for recycling, I caught her alone for once. "Hey." I put the boxes down, then went to pin her between me and the wall just as she came out of the walk-in cooler.

"What?" She looked off to one side.

Taking her by her chin, which also had a slight bruise on it, I kissed her swollen and cut lips gently. "Tell me what happened."

"My sister and I got into a fight." She looked me in the eyes.

"*Why* did you get into a fight with her?" I kissed her again, light and easy.

647

She ran her hands up my arms then around my neck. "It doesn't matter."

"It does to me." Moving in, I trailed a line of kisses up her neck, making sure to peck each scratch.

Her chest rose with a heavy sigh. "I really would rather not talk about it, if that's okay with you."

"It's not okay with me. I want to know what had you two fighting like you were in a cage match." It seemed neither of them had even tried to get away.

With a nod, she knew I was on to something. "It was in our little bedroom. There wasn't much room to get away from each other. I think that's why it went on as long as it did."

Kissing the soft spot behind her ear, I whispered, "And why did it start?"

She moaned as I used the tip of my tongue to entice her. "Oh, Cash, what you do to me should be illegal."

"Yep." I didn't let up on her as I ran my hands up into her hair, releasing the ponytail so I could get that silky stuff between my fingers.

The way her hands moved over my back, her nails gently running over my shirt, made me want her right then and there. "Cash, I think I heard Joey walk out the front door. We should really go make sure that's what I heard."

"That would mean that I would have to let you go. And I don't want to let you go." I kissed a line from her neck to her lips.

Moaning softly, she wrapped her legs around my waist and kissed me back. Then the sound of Joey's voice said, "Guys, I'm leaving now."

Pulling my mouth off hers, I called out, "See you tomorrow, Joey!"

Then the sound of the door closing came, and I knew we were all alone. Her eyes searched mine then she asked, "If our fight was kind of about you, would that make you mad at me?"

"Mad?" I shook my head. "But confused, yes."

"She told me, Cash." She looked a bit on the sad side as her legs dropped, her feet going back to the floor. "You guys kissed."

"Not on purpose. Did she make sure you knew that?" I held her tight as I felt her trying to move out of my arms and I wasn't going to let that happen.

"What do you mean, not on purpose?" The way she looked at me told me Betty Sue hadn't been completely honest with her.

"I thought she was you, Bobbi Jo. As soon as I realized she wasn't you, I stopped the kiss and let her know I wasn't into her that way." I couldn't help but smile as she looked relieved. "But what I don't understand is why you would get into a fight with anyone over me. It's not like we're serious. I don't want you getting yourself hurt over me."

Her jaw went tight as her eyes glazed over. "I know we're not serious, Cash. You don't have to remind me."

"I mean, I'm a free agent," I said, trying to rile her up. "As are you, Bobbi Jo."

Her hands moved, coming up between us then landing on my chest. "Yeah, I know that. Look, can you just back up? I've got things to do."

Oops, riled her up too much, it seems.

BOBBI JO

With Cash all up on me, I couldn't think straight. I'd asked him to back up but he hadn't moved, so I had to add, "Please, Cash. Let me go."

"You're mad." He retained his hold on me.

"No." I pushed him gently but firmly on his chest. "I've just got things to do is all."

His hands loosened on my body, he stepped back, and I moved away from him. Even though I knew we weren't exclusive, I didn't like to think about him being with other girls—especially not my sister.

"The kiss wouldn't have ever happened without her sneaking up on me that way, Bobbi Jo. I want you to know that. Our lack of a serious relationship wasn't why I quit kissing her when I realized it wasn't you. I honestly don't like her in a romantic way at all." He leaned back on the wall, placing one foot on it, looking hot as hell as he just stood there.

"Yet, you invited her to eat lunch with you." I hadn't even allowed myself to think about that fact. Why he'd done that was still a mystery to me.

"She *is* your sister, Bobbi Jo." He looked down as if trying to come up with a plausible excuse for taking her to lunch—a thing he and I hadn't even done.

"Yeah, well what about me?" I went to pick up a case of beer to take to the front to put into the cooler. It was a thing I usually did the following day, but I wanted to stay busy so he couldn't wrap me in his arms and stop me from thinking. "My sister has taken a whirlwind trip on your jet. She's ridden in your limo. And now she's eaten a meal with you as your date. I haven't done any of those things."

"Jealousy," he said as he smiled at me. "You're jealous."

"I'm not jealous. I'm just confused. Are you dating my sister but having sex with me?" I knew better than that but had to say it. "And now you've kissed her too. You've held her in your arms, Cash. What if the same thing had happened between me and one of your brothers?"

"It better not ever happen." He moved across the room quickly, taking the heavy case of beer out of my arms. "Let me do that."

"I can handle it." I tried to reach for it, but he was already too far away. I followed him to the bar, watching him as he put the beer into the cooler. "So, how was that kiss?"

"It wasn't you." He put away the last beer then looked at me. "She's not you."

"And *I'm* what you want?" I asked as my heart pounded.

"Am *I* what *you* want?"

I had no idea why I was the way I was, but commitment was a thing I shied away from. "You're what I want for now."

"Ditto." He strolled over to me, put his fingers on my chin lightly. "You're what I want for now too. You know what else I want?"

I shook my head.

"I want you and I to go do something Sunday and Monday while you're off work. I'm thinking something really cool. We can take the limo and the jet and do anything you want." His hands moved slowly until he was wrapped around me. "Maybe out to Maine to get some fresh-off-the-boat lobster."

"That's a bit much." I did like lobster though.

"I know it is." He kissed me. "But what good am I as a billionaire if I don't take my best girl out once in a while?"

I didn't like being called his best girl. "Nope, you can't call me that either."

He nodded. "Okay then. How about the chick I'm currently screwing?"

"Best girl it is." I smiled, and it hurt my busted lip when I did. "Ow." I put my fingers to it. "This was so stupid."

He pressed his lips to the top of my head as he swayed back and forth with me. "If it helps you at all, I thought about what I would've done if one of my brothers had done the same thing to you that your sister did to me."

"And what did you think about that?" I had a pretty good idea he wouldn't be cool with it at all.

"I thought I would most definitely kick some ass if that ever happened." He chuckled. "But I was pretty sure I would be the only one punching if that happened. Why did Betty Sue fight back instead of running away?"

"I have no idea. She really should've run. She was in the wrong after all." I raised my right hand to look at my red and swollen knuckles. "I gave her two black eyes—way worse than this shiner she gave me. Her nose was bleeding, her mouth was too, and she was wheezing something awful when I finally got off her."

He looked a little shocked. "Wow."

"I know."

"I don't know if I'm going to ever want to get on your bad side." He ran his hand over my cheek. "You're kind of a badass."

"No, I'm not." I wasn't proud of myself for beating my sister up. And I knew once my father found out what I'd done, there would be hell to pay. "My father is going to let me have it when he sees my sister in the morning. This is assault. He won't let me forget that fact."

"He won't put you in jail, will he?" he joked.

But what he didn't know was that my father might very well do something like that to me. "Dad doesn't put up with lawbreakers."

"Then I think I had better keep you with me." He ran his hand down my arm, taking my hand. "If he can't find you, then he can't string you up or lock you up."

"You'd hide me out?" I thought that was sweet of him. "Even though I'm a cold-blooded sister-beater?"

Shrugging, he pulled me to go along with him. "Like I said, if the shoe were on the other foot, I would've clocked a man too. Any man. Not just my brothers. But my brothers would definitely get it worse than some stranger."

I held back, digging my feet in to stop him from taking me any further. "Wait. Are you saying that if I told you that any other man had kissed me, you would beat him up?"

Turning to face me, he ran his hand over my cheek again. "I don't know. I do know I would beat the hell out of my brothers for doing it. You girls share a bedroom, huh?"

I nodded. "Yeah. It's not going to be real comfy in there for a while, I guess."

"I'm serious. I want you to come stay with me. At least until things calm down. It's the least I can do for you. Although I can't say this is my fault, I also shouldn't have been so quick to grab and kiss a woman when the woman in my life has an identical twin in the same town." He turned to head toward the door again with me in tow. "It just wasn't a smart thing for me to do."

"Maybe if I told you more about my sister and her penchant for fucking me over where the male species is concerned, you might've been a bit more careful about kissing a girl who looks like me." I knew I hadn't really let him in on how Betty Sue was. "She has not only right out stolen guys I was interested in, but she's given me a bad rep a few times by claiming to actually be me and doing things I wouldn't have ever done."

"Well, if that's the case, then your father shouldn't be too mad at you for finally whopping her ass." He stopped as we got to the door. "This is the first time you've fought her like this, isn't it?"

"It is." We'd had a few smacks between us but nothing this bad. "It got out of hand really quick. I saw red, then black, then nothing at all. I honestly didn't know I was such a savage." I began to feel a tiny bit bad about what I'd done to my twin. "I even pulled a chunk of her hair out."

"Damn, baby." He opened the door and we went out.

I locked the door, then he picked me up, carrying me to his truck. Wrapping my arms around his neck, I gazed into those baby blue eyes of his. "Baby? What did I tell you about that?"

"Right now, I don't care what you've told me about that." He put me down to open the door of his tall, four-wheel-drive truck, then picked me up, sliding me into the driver's seat. I scooted over as he got inside and took the wheel. "Call me a Neanderthal if you want to, but the fact that you got into a fistfight over me is making me hot as hell for you."

I ran my hand in a circle around my battered and bruised face. "Even with this mug of mine?"

The way he smiled made my heart skip a beat. "Even with that mug of yours." He leaned in to kiss me and my breath froze in my lungs.

I'd never been in love before, so I had no idea what that felt like. But what I felt when he kissed me that time was different. It felt deeper somehow. Our mouths didn't open; our tongues didn't entwine. It was a simple kiss on the lips, and yet it felt so sincere, so honest, and so much like what love must be like, that it left me breathless.

When he pulled his lips off mine, he smiled as he looked into my eyes and I caressed his cheek. "You're a very nice guy, Cash Gentry. Most men wouldn't want to kiss lips that are busted and swollen."

"Well, most men haven't had the pleasure of kissing your lips when they're in prime condition. If they had, then they would know, without a doubt, that lips like yours make for good kissing even when they're beat up." He kissed me once more, making my heart feel wiggly.

"Oh, yeah?" came my stupid response. But the fact was, he had me feeling a little drunk on his small kisses.

"Yeah." He ran his finger along my nose, making me feel all cute and adorable as he looked at me. "And I think tonight I'll give you a nice hot bath, a back rub, and some TLC to help ease the pain your body has to be in."

I'd played off the pain the whole night. Now, I didn't feel like I should anymore. He wanted to pamper me—why not let him? "A hot bath sounds great. You getting in too?"

"Hell yes I am." Sliding his arm along the seat behind me, he draped it around my shoulders as he pulled away from the now dark and quiet bar.

I leaned my head on his shoulder as he drove us to his place. "So, I get to spend the night, huh?"

"Get to?" he asked. "No, you have to. I'm not about to let you go back home tonight. And not tomorrow night either. And then we've got our plans for Sunday and Monday, so you'll be with me for those nights too."

"That's four nights." I hadn't ever stayed away from home that long. "And I'll have to go home in the morning to pack."

"I'm loaded, baby. I'll buy you everything you need." He kissed my cheek. "It's the least I can do for my little boxer."

His boxer. His baby. His. I like the way that sounds all of a sudden.

CASH

I'd never had a girl fight over me before. And the way Bobbi Jo looked, she'd fought like a Viking over me. And over just one little kiss too. She had it bad for me. I knew that then.

No matter how much we'd told each other that it wasn't serious, and that we were free agents, it was beginning to sink in with both of us just how much we actually cared about each other.

After parking the truck in the garage, I led Bobbi Jo into the house through the kitchen. "Have you eaten today?" I had my doubts.

"I had an egg sandwich for breakfast, but nothing after that. And by breakfast, I mean around noon." She ran her hand over her stomach. "I could use a bite."

I loved that about the girl. She wasn't afraid to let me know when she was hungry. "Let's see what we've got in the fridge."

She went to take a seat at the island bar as I rummaged through the fridge. "Anything will be fine. I'm not going to be picky."

I pulled out a jar of pickles. "How about a sandwich?"

With a nod, she said, "I said *anything* will be fine, Cash."

"You want some milk with it?" I got out the almond milk as she nodded.

In no time at all, I had a little plate with a couple of turkey sandwiches, pickles, and potato chips, along with two glasses of milk. I sat next to her, then we dug in.

Sitting there in the dim light of the kitchen, the only light on being the one under the cabinets, I liked how we could sit in silence, eating, not thinking about what to say or how to act.

After finishing, she picked up our plates and cleaned things up as I sat there watching her. "We make a good team, Bobbi Jo."

"We do, don't we?" she asked as she put the dirty dishes into the dishwasher. "Maybe you and I should start a business together. You know, do something worthwhile."

"Anything but a bar," I said as I got up when she walked toward me. Putting my arm around her shoulders, I started heading to my room. "These late nights aren't good for us to be doing so much."

"You sound like an old man." She laughed as we went up the stairs.

"What I really mean is that if we ended our nights earlier, then we'd be getting into bed a lot earlier. And once in bed, we could get it on a lot earlier and do it a lot longer." I smiled at her as we topped the stairs.

"Oh, now I get it. It's all about sex to you." She smacked me on the shoulder.

"Of course." I was kidding and she knew that. "And cuddling too. Don't forget cuddling."

"How could I forget the cuddling?" She walked into my bedroom as I opened the door for her. "What a gentleman you are, Cash Gentry."

"I am pretty gentleman-like with you, aren't I?" I'd never been a total ass or anything like that with women before, but with Bobbi Jo, I tended to do a lot more for her.

As I closed the door, she went to toward the bathroom. "I'm going to peel these clothes off while you make me that hot bath you promised. My body is aching."

At least she was finally admitting how much she hurt. "I'm about to fix you all up, Rocky."

She stopped just inside the bathroom door, then turned to look at me as she began pulling off her clothes. "Look, I'm kind of regretting what I did. Maybe lay off the boxer nicknames. I think I

657

need to apologize to my sister. I mean, she deserved a smack or even two, but I gave her a beatdown. I don't know if she needed all that."

"Bet she doesn't try to trick me anymore." I grinned as I moved past her to go start the huge jet tub.

She laughed. "Bet she doesn't try to kiss you anymore, that's for sure. But still, I went overboard."

"I guess you're in love with me," I said, knowing I was pushing it.

"Or, more likely, I'm sick of her doing this to guys I like. It's been years and years. Maybe I finally got fed up with it once and for all. My mind snapped this time." She looked at the half-full tub, standing there naked. "Can I get in yet?"

"I guess so." I started to strip down as she climbed into the tub. "It'll have to get deeper before I can turn on the jets though."

"I don't care." She eased back, her eyes closing. "It's hot and wonderful already. I so needed this." She opened her eyes to look at me as I dropped my jeans. "I so need you."

With the last article of clothing off my body, I got in, sliding in behind her. She leaned back on me, and I ran my hand through her hair. "I like this."

"Me too." She hummed as I rubbed her shoulders.

Feeling relaxed with her, I asked, "Do you ever see yourself settling down?"

"Not for a very long time." She ran her hands down my thighs, leaving them resting on my knees. "I like my life. Well, mostly I do. And now that I have you as a very pleasant distraction, it's even better. Why try to settle down now?"

"I don't know. I just mean that this pace, this working five nights a week is—well, it's not easy." I'd wanted to have a more normal relationship, and with her working at the bar, it wasn't falling into place easily.

"Is that why you ate lunch with my sister today?" she asked as I felt her tense up a bit. "Because I'm not really accessible until after three in the afternoon?"

"I honestly didn't think about that. I asked her to join me so I could get to know more about *you*, if you want the truth." I didn't know a whole hell of a lot about Bobbi Jo. Our time was limited, and usually, lots of people were around. It made it difficult to get to know her on a personal level.

"Well, never think you should get any information about me from her again." She turned her head to one side to look at me from the corner of her eye. "Just ask me anything you want to know."

"Okay then. What's your favorite color? What do you like to do when you have time off? What kind of food is your favorite?" I had a load of questions for her.

She held up one hand. "Stop." A long sigh filled the gap. "Blue, like your eyes. Sleep. And pizza."

I kissed the top of her head as I kept rubbing her shoulders. "Do you want to ask me anything?"

"What is your opinion on mixed vegetables? You know that can of them that you get in the store?" she asked.

I had no idea what to say to that. I had no opinion on something like that at all. "Are you being serious?"

"Very." She turned all the way over, her breasts pressed against my chest, our bodies flush underneath the water. "I need to know if we are really compatible. Now, you may think you have no opinion, but everyone does. If you are served mixed veggies, how does it make you feel? Do you eat them the way they are? Do you separate them into piles of green beans, corn, and carrots? Or do you simply not eat them at all?"

I had to think about it for a moment. The concept had never come to my mind before. But finally, I knew how I felt about the food. "I don't like mixed veggies. If I wanted all of them mixed up, I would mix them up myself. Like, why have one can of them like that when you can get individual cans? What if you like green beans but hate carrots? What if you just want corn? So, I am against mixed vegetables."

Her eyes lit up, as did her body. "I've never been more attracted to you, Cash Gentry."

"So, that's how you feel too?" I asked.

She nodded. "I hate them and I never want to have even a single can of them in my home whenever I get one of my own. My mother has an entire shelf of the nasty things. I could never even think of being serious with a man who has no opinion on mixed vegetables."

"So, I *am* a prospect then?" I had to smile at her as she slid up my body.

Her hand on my hard cock told me she was rather enthused about this find she'd made in me. "Oh, yeah. You're a prospect all right." She moved her body until she had me inside of her. A long moan escaped her as she settled on top of me. "Think we'll make a mess if we do this in the tub?"

"Definitely." I lifted her up then let her slide back down my long, hard cock. "But who the hell cares. Ride me, baby."

She put her hands on my shoulders to hang on. "Buck."

Moving up with sharp thrusts, I had her whimpering with desire as I held her by the waist. "Oh, you're about to get the ride of your life."

"Give it to me, cowboy," she moaned. "Give it to me good. Make me hang on for dear life."

"You had better hang on. I'm about to blow you out of the water." I moved hard and fast, watching her tits bounce as water splashed around us like tidal waves.

She reached behind me to hit the button to make the jets turn on. Water pounded my back as I moved and she squealed with delight. Hearing her sexy laugh as we romped around made me feel something I never had before.

I felt happy just to be with her. If all we were doing was watching television, I had a feeling I'd still be happy. She made me happy in a way no one ever had.

Her body went tight; her nails dug into shoulders. "Cash!" She came all over my hard cock, her walls quaking around me, squeezing me.

I moved us, turning her over, getting behind her, then thrusting into her still pulsing pussy as I pounded into her from behind. My jaw tight, my hands on her waist, holding her steady as I thrusted into her hard, over and over. Water moved in waves, sloshing over the edges, spilling onto the tiled floor.

Everything combined to make it one of the hottest times we'd ever had. When I felt the urge to let it all go, she screamed and came again. "Cash! Damn! Fuck!"

I had no choice; she pulled it from me. I gave it all to her, filling her with my hot seed. "Baby, damn!"

She'd taken me to a whole other place with that orgasm. All I wanted was to go there again and again.

BOBBI JO

Soft snores met my ears as I woke up. Cash's arms around my body made me smile. The wetness between my legs made me stop smiling. "Shit."

Why would there be wetness between my legs when we used a condom?

The activities from the night before came drifting back into my mind. The bath, the bed, the floor, the walk-in closet—and all those times and places had one thing in common.

No condom.

It took me a second to realize I wasn't breathing. When I gasped, the noise made Cash stir a little. I didn't move, didn't take another breath.

I had to get the hell out of there. Maybe I could find a morning-after pill. I had to do something to rectify my reckless behavior.

Sneaking out of the bed, moving his arm a little at a time, I was able to move away from him. Going to the bathroom, with my goal being to find my clothes and put them back on, I went to pee first.

Rubbing my temples, I tried to think about what the right thing to do was. I'd never come out and told Cash that I didn't take any type of birth control. All I had said was that he needed to use a condom. But lots of girls made guys use condoms even if they were on birth control.

They did that to protect themselves from getting STDs. And for all I knew, that was what Cash thought too. He apparently didn't think we *had* to use them, or he would've made sure to use them last night.

And what about last night? What the hell happened to me? Why had I forgotten all about using protection?

Maybe I'd taken a punch to the head that I wasn't aware of. That kind of thing could happen. Maybe I was just out of it and didn't even realize it. And now I'd gone and had sex a whole lot in one night.

I counted the times I could recall on my fingers. Four in all— and none of them with a condom and all had ended with me getting blasted with baby juice.

I'd never wished harder that I had brought my own car so I could just leave. But there was a cab service I could call, so I made that my plan. Only I had no idea what the address to Cash's mansion was.

Just as I got off the toilet and walked over to the sink to use the toothbrush Cash had given me the first night I'd slept over, I heard the sound of the door opening and in came Cash—naked and rubbing his head. "Morning, sweet thing."

"Um, yeah. Hi." I put some toothpaste on my toothbrush then began scrubbing the crap off my teeth as if that would eradicate the abundance of semen that had been squirted at my eggs.

"Hi?" He laughed as he took a piss, still scratching his head with his free hand.

Spitting out the toothpaste, I grabbed the mouthwash. "You know, I was thinking that I could just call a cab and go back home this morning." The idea of stopping at a pharmacy to see about getting that pill to erase the previous night's mistakes was at the top of my mind.

"Nope." He came up behind me, running his arms around my waist, nuzzling my neck. He whispered, "You're staying with me, remember? And for now, we're going to get right back into that warm bed where I'm going to kiss you, hug you, and make love to you until we fall back to sleep."

Him, all up on me like that, made me want to do just what he'd said. Only I knew I had to get to town and to a pharmacy. "That's so sweet sounding."

"Oh, there's not going to be anything sweet about it." He pushed his already hard cock against my bare ass. "See."

"So, right to it, then?" I shook my head. "No, I can't. Sorry."

Being that neither of us had a stitch on, he pulled me toward the shower. "I get it. You feel dirty. We can do it in the shower."

"I've already got quite a bit of love juices on me already, that is true." I would need to, at the very least, rinse off. A full body scrub, inside and out, would've been best, but I had no idea if I had the time for that.

"I'll clean us all up," he said as he pushed the button to start the jets spraying all over the place. Pulling me in with him, he placed me on the tiled seat then grabbed a bar of soap, lathering his hands as his hair became drenched and hung down past his broad shoulders.

I couldn't speak as he moved those soapy hands all over my body. The way he moved around me had me feeling lightheaded again, tipsy even. "I like waking up with you in my arms, Bobbi Jo. I was disappointed when I woke up to find you gone."

"You were?" My head lolled back as he massaged my tits.

I felt his lips on one nipple. "I was very disappointed."

"Maybe you're getting a little too spoiled." I groaned as he sucked on the nipple, licking it as he did.

"Maybe." He kissed a trail down my stomach then pushed my knees apart to spread my legs open. "Let me get you all cleaned up."

I didn't see what his attention to me down there could hurt. There was time after all. I slightly remembered that the pill I'd heard about could be used up to forty-eight hours after intercourse. I had plenty of time. "Please do."

His soapy hands moved all over my pussy that was swollen from all the pounding he'd done to it during our night's activities. "You're so ready for me, baby." His lips pressed against my clit and I gasped with how amazing it felt. "If you think that feels good, wait until I really give you a sweet, long kiss."

I had to grip his shoulders as he kissed me harder down there, his tongue moving all around in ways that seemed impossible. "Cash!"

He didn't stop. He thrust his tongue into me, pushing it in and out until I was screaming his name, a thing he absolutely loved. His fingers dug into my thighs as he couldn't seem to get enough of what I was giving him.

When he pulled back, he looked at me with wild eyes, then I was on my knees on the shower floor as he took me from behind. All I could hear was the sound of the shower jets pouring water over our bodies and the slapping of skin.

I should've said something about protection then. I knew I should've said something. But I didn't want to stop what we were doing. I didn't want to ruin the moment.

When I felt the heat fill me, his cock jerking hard inside of me as he grunted and groaned, I knew I had a whole new batch of baby soup inside of me.

My body sagged as I sighed, then he slapped my ass playfully. "Now that's the right way to start your day. Huh, little momma?"

Little momma?

"Cash, I want to tell you something." He pulled me up and held me tight in his arms, his mouth on mine stopping my words and my train of thought.

The next thing I knew, we weren't in the shower anymore. The bed was under my back when he laid me down on it, then he was on top of me, back inside of me and we were right back at it.

I had no idea what had gotten into the man, but he was letting it all out into me. Over and over. And I couldn't find it in myself to say a word to stop him from doing it either.

For some reason, I was as wrapped up in him as he was in me. And when exhaustion finally took us both over, we crashed on his bed, our bodies all tangled up together, him still inside of me, and we fell asleep.

Somewhere in the deep recesses of my mind, I told myself that I would definitely get up later, go to the pharmacy and get that pill. It would eradicate all we'd done. Everything would be just fine.

Sleep took me over. Hours later, when I felt Cash moving behind me, getting off the bed, I opened my eyes as he said, "Shit. Babe, get up. We've got to get you down to the bar. It's only thirty minutes until it's supposed to open. I'll get Tyrell to see if Ella has something you can borrow to wear to work."

"We slept all day?" I didn't feel like that was possible.

"Apparently. Come on, now. Shake a leg, girl."

Hurrying, I felt dizzy and then realized I hadn't eaten or drank anything all day. "Damn, Cash, I feel like I might pass out."

He nodded as he turned the shower on. "Just get in here and let's not mess around. We've got to get going."

Rushing around, somehow we both got dressed. I found Ella had left me some jeans and a T-shirt on the bed. I'd met her only once and was appreciative of her help. "Remind me to do something nice for Ella for lending me her clothes. It was nice of her."

"Yeah, yeah. Come on." Cash grabbed my hand and away we went. Into the garage where he lifted me up into his truck and then we sped away to the bar.

Being a Saturday night, there were already three cars in the parking lot when we pulled up. I had to get right to work and the night was nothing but chaos for the most part.

When my sister came in the door, her hair in her very made-up face, I took a second. Wiggling my finger, I led her to the back. "Look, I went too far."

Betty Sue pulled her hair back, and I could still see the black around her eyes, the swelling of her nose and mouth, and the chunk of hair that I'd yanked out. "You think?"

"Did Dad see you?" I prayed like hell that she hadn't gone and told on me.

"No. I stayed in bed … claimed I was sick." She sighed. "I shouldn't have done what I did. Although it wasn't exactly planned out for me to get a kiss from Cash, I didn't do anything the right way. None of it. And I am sorry for that."

"And I'm sorry I laid into you so hard. We're adults; we could've handled it like adults." I put my hand on her shoulder. "Let's put this behind us, shall we?"

She nodded. "I've been thinking that this whole time. We need to put all this behind us. All the past years of me doing things to you that have hurt you and you never retaliated. Well, there was that one

666

time you nearly killed me with the laxative. But mostly, you just took what I did and did nothing back to me. I figure that beating you put on me was justified."

I was relieved that she felt that way. But I knew I'd gone too far. "Two wrongs don't make a right. I'll make it up to you, Betty Sue."

She held up her hand, putting it on my chest. "No, you won't. We're even now. Let's move on from here and let all that go. I can see that you really care about Cash. And he must really care about you too. I think he does, anyway. He's a good man, Bobbi Jo. Don't do anything dumb and let him go or let him let you go either."

Before I could say anything, Cash walked into the back room. He smiled as he saw us together. "Good. You two have kissed and made up. That's nice to see." He came up and wrapped his big arms around us both. "We can let bygones be bygones now." When he backed up, taking his arms off us, he looked at my sister. "I'm taking Bobbi Jo out of town tomorrow. We won't be back until Monday night. Think you can tell your parents about that, so they don't have to worry?"

She nodded. "I can do that." Then she looked at me. "He's a good one, sister. Don't lose him."

Before I could say a thing, Cash said, "I won't let her lose me."

All I could do was stare at the man. *What the hell is going on here?*

CASH

The night had been crazy at the bar even with me helping out. But I had managed to find some time to make arrangements for our little getaway.

Even though I hadn't ever done anything like this before, I was smart enough to ask the lady who ran the travel agency in town for help. She'd come in with her husband for a few drinks and a game of pool. With her help, not only did I have all the accommodations taken care of, I had everything Bobbi Jo would need already packed away on the private jet that waited for us at the Carthage Municipal Airport.

"This is silly," Bobbi Jo argued as I drove straight to the airport, passing up the road to her house. "I can just stop by and pack a bag real quick."

"I can see you won't give up, so I'll just go ahead and tell you." I put my arm around her, giving her a squeeze. "I've got everything you need already on the plane. We both do."

She huffed as if she didn't believe me. "And how did you accomplish this, Cash?"

"I had help." I knew she'd be flabbergasted when she saw all I had accomplished while working so hard with her at the bar. "And you and I really should think about starting a business together. Maybe we'll come up with something in the next couple of days."

Her lips quirked up to one side in a lopsided grin. "If you can keep your hands off of me for long enough for our brains to work."

"Well, maybe we won't come up with something." I kissed her cheek. I had no intentions of keeping my hands off her. "We've got nothing but time, girl."

Parking the truck at the airport in the dark of night, I watched Bobbi Jo's eyes light up when the door to the plane's hanger was raised, and the shiny black plane came into view. "Is that it?"

"It has Whisper Ranch written on the side of it," I pointed out. "I think it's a pretty safe bet to think that is it."

I got out of the truck then caught her as she slid out of it too. "It's so beautiful."

"Wait until you see the inside." I had big plans for her inside that plane. "There's a bedroom in there."

She sucked in her breath. "There can't be."

"There is. Right in the back of the plane. And a bathroom too." I took her hand, leading her to the plane where the pilot came out to greet us.

"I hear we're heading to Maine for some lobster." He shook my hand. "Nice to see you again, Cash. And this must be Miss Bobbi Jo Baker. I'm Steven. It's a pleasure to be your pilot this evening." He looked at his watch. "Or rather, this morning. We'll be in Biddeford, Maine in a little over five hours. It's three a.m. now, so that means—"

Bobbi Jo chimed in, "Around ten in the morning. Wait. No, they're ahead of us. Around eleven a.m. we'll be there."

Steven nodded. "Just in time for lunch. And the lobster at Docks Boathouse is off the charts. You'll love it and the atmosphere. Even if it is near freezing."

I hadn't thought about how damn cold it would be in Maine in early February. Texas never had it that damn bad. "Maybe we should go in the other direction."

Steven shook his head. "Nah. We'll be great going that way. And you can't get any better lobster than you can in Maine. So, climb aboard and let's get this party going, shall we? After lunch in Maine, we're going to New York City so you two can stay the night at the Waldorf."

Bobbi Jo's eyes went wide. "Oh, no. Cash, I don't have a clue what to wear. I don't know. This is too much."

"Relax." I tugged her to come with me up the stairs to get on the plane. "I told you: someone else has packed all we'll need for our little trip. It'll be fun. You'll see. But first, you've got to chill, girl."

Taking our seats in the cabin, we put on the seatbelts as Steven got the plane going. Bobbi Jo looked at me with a nervous expression. "I've never been on a plane."

"It's nothing to be worried about." I held her hand then pulled it up to kiss it. "I've got ya. And there are parachutes in the overhead bins."

"Have you ever used one before?" she asked me with a doubtful expression.

"No." But I knew I could do it if I had to. "Believe me: if this plane is going down, I'm going to figure out how to leave it before it hits the ground."

"Cash, I'm going to need to get some sleep with all you've planned." She cut her eyes at the door at the back of the cabin, the one that led to the bedroom. "If we go back there, all we're going to do is sleep. Got me?"

I did have mile-high plans for her. But there was always the trip back home. "I got ya, sweet thing."

With a smile, she closed her eyes. "I've never even dreamt of doing anything like this. It's out of this world amazing."

"And it hasn't even really started yet." I loved the fact that I could do this for her and with her. "Just to let you know, there's never been anyone I've wanted to do something this out of my element with. I must really trust you, Bobbi Jo."

"I must really trust you too, Cash. There isn't anyone else I would've agreed to go with on a trip like this." She sighed. "But I think you're safe enough."

With the plane taking off, we both closed our eyes, and soon we were both sleeping the remainder of the night away. The sun coming up woke us both up and what I saw out the small window took my breath away. "Wow, that's gorgeous."

Bobbi Jo nodded and stretched. "Up here, the way we are, it looks so different—so majestic."

Unbuckling my seatbelt, I thought we should go back to the bedroom and see about getting ready for the day. "Come on; let's go see what we've got back here."

She came along. "So, I have to ask how you managed to get all this done so quickly."

"I'm magic," I said as I opened the door. There were two suitcases on the bed, both open and both empty. "And it seems the person who packed our bags must've unpacked them for us too."

She went to the closet and gasped. "Look at these clothes. There's a black suit for you." Her eyes were big as she read the label. "Are you kidding me?"

"It's some expensive designer, isn't it?" I shook my head as I thought how uncomfortable that was going to be.

"Well, it's just Ralph Lauren, but it looks like something James Bond would wear." She pulled out a dark blue dress. "And look what I'm supposed to wear."

"You will look gorgeous in that dress." I already pictured her wearing it.

"No way." She put it back. "That's so not me."

"Well, the suit is so not me too. But I am going to wear it while we're in New York at that fancy hotel and you will wear the dress. It's beautiful." I went to take her in my arms. "Almost as beautiful as you are."

"But it's so, well, so girly." She frowned. "It's just not me."

"While in New York, one should do what they do. Come on. It'll be like playing dress-up when you were a kid." I kissed her on top of her head. "Now let's shower, then we'll put on something that's casual that I'm sure they've packed for us. For the next two days, you and I are going to be out of our elements, and we're going to see how the other half lives."

She blinked at me a few times. "Only *you* are a part of the other half now, Cash. You're a billionaire."

"And you're with me." I kissed her lips. "Come on. Let's forget about who we really are and be whatever we want to be. At least for a couple of days. I've never been able to do anything like this. I've never even thought to wish for something like this. And I'm damn glad I've got you with me to do it."

She smiled. "I'm glad I'm here with you too. It's weird, but a fun weird."

"If you play your cards right, you'll get to do lots more of this kind of thing with me." I led her to the bathroom where we could shower.

"Who said I'm even playing cards, Cash?" She laughed as I turned to start taking her clothes off.

"Okay, neither of us are playing cards at this time. It's just fun being with each other, don't you think?"

She nodded as I pulled the shirt off over her head. "It is fun being with you, Cash."

"And it's fun being with you, Bobbi Jo." I really did hope we could find something to do together to get her out of that bar. "Maybe we'll find out that we want to open a seafood restaurant in Carthage after eating this lobster."

Her mouth dropped open. "That's actually a great idea. But we might find something even better than that. Running a restaurant is no joke. That takes tons of time."

I thought spending tons of time with her might be a great way to spend time. But she was right. A restaurant would be a lot of hard work, and I figured one would need a fair amount of passion for food to run one anyway.

"Maybe we'll do something a little different, a little less work and a lot more fun." I finished undressing her, kissing her bare shoulder.

"Oh, I know what we could open: a skating rink. My parents use to talk about going to one when they were in their teens. They said it was the local hangout." She began taking my clothes off. "We could do it all old-school—nostalgic, you know."

My lips quirked up to one side. "I like that idea."

"Plus, it won't be open late." She pulled my shirt off, running her hands over my pecs. "And it'll be a good exercise for people too."

I took her hands in mine, holding them to my heart. "That is a great idea, Bobbi Jo." Maybe we would find a way to spend our time together that didn't include nights at a bar.

BOBBI JO

"So this is it—the East Coast." I stared out at the battleship gray water with small white peaks that floated on top. "I always thought the Atlantic Ocean was a bit more—well, majestic."

"This is just a bay," some man said who came up behind Cash and me as we stood on the dock just outside the restaurant. "Believe me—the Atlantic *is* a sight to behold."

"I'm sure it is," Cash said. "Come on, Bobbi Jo. Let's head inside to get something to eat."

By the way he looked at me out of the corner of his eye, I thought he might have been embarrassed by what I'd said. "It's just that I went to the gulf coast once when I was younger, and that water was gorgeous. Like emerald green, clear, and the sand was this really clean light beige color. Now *that* was pretty." I held my arm out in a gesture to our surroundings. "*This*, not so much."

Now Cash had a frown on his face as he looked at me. "Bobbi Jo, can it, will ya?"

I supposed he was worried about offending the locals, so I shut up. The one thing that saved it all were the lobsters. Cash pointed at the mountain of them that sat on a platter on the counter. "Whoa, look at those."

"Now that is a sight to behold." My mouth already watered to taste at least three of them.

With bibs in place, Cash and I began chowing down on the delicious seafood feast that was spread out in front of us. "You want some more butter?" he asked as he pushed a bowl of it toward me.

I dipped a chunk of white lobster into it. "Yes, please." I saw no possible way that we'd be able to walk out of the place. We'd need wheelbarrows to get us back out the door we'd come in through.

An hour and a half later, we waddled outside. The car that had brought us from the airport was still waiting with our suitcases in the trunk to take us to New York. "Here we go, Bobbi Jo." Cash let me get in first.

He and I leaned on one another as the car drove off. Once again, we fell asleep on the ride; it was beginning to be our thing. Get into a moving vehicle—crash out.

The late nights seemed to be catching up with both of us. And the hours and hours of sex probably had a hand in it too.

"We're here," came the driver's voice. "I'll give your baggage to the porter. You two can go in and check in."

I felt like Dorothy in the *Wizard of Oz*. "Where are we?"

"New York," the driver said. "The Waldorf Astoria."

People were everywhere. I could have sworn that there were more people around us than we had in the entire town of Carthage. "I never knew so many people could be in one place at the same time. It seems impossible."

"We're from Texas," Cash let the driver know. "This is like another planet to us."

The door opened, and a man in what looked like a suit one would wear in England at the Queen's palace stood there. "Welcome to the Waldorf Astoria. Please come with me."

Cash and I exchanged nervous glances then got out of the car. Standing up, breathing in the same air as all those around us, felt weird. "Oh, man. I don't know about this, Cash."

"Come on, Bobbi Jo." He pulled me along with him. "It's going to be fun."

"It's going to be something all right. I don't know about fun, but it will be something." I wasn't so sure this place was for me. I wasn't an uptown girl. Not that I was a country bumpkin, but I wasn't a city girl either. "You know, I've never known this about Carthage, but for a town, it's more like the country. I'm way out of my element here, Cash."

He stopped and looked at me with a stern look on his face. "You have got to stop talking like that. If you can't say anything good, just try not to say anything. Please."

For the first time ever, I could feel the difference between Cash and myself. He was rich. He might not have always known he was, but it ran in his veins. He held his head high as we walked up to the front desk. "Gentry—reservation for two."

"Oh, yes. Everything has been taken care of." The woman who stood behind the desk was quick to summon a bellhop. "Take our guests up to room five-thirty-four." She waved at the man who had our luggage on a golden cart. "Give those to him, please. He'll see them up to their suite."

Cash reached into his pocket, pulling out some money, then handed the porter some. "Thank you."

I held onto Cash's other hand, wondering when he had the time to grow sophisticated. I hadn't found that time yet. "You seem like you've done this before."

His lips pressed against the shell of my ear. "Of course I've never done this before. But I have watched movies. Haven't you?"

Shrugging, I had never cared for movies about New York or any other fancy crap. "Not really."

I stayed quiet all the way up to our room. Once inside, I had to put my hand over my mouth as I was afraid my stupid would pour out some more. But after the bellhop left us, a generous tip in his hand, I had to blurt it out, "This place is like something out of a Hemingway novel." I ran to the window and looked out at the buildings, the people, and all the traffic. "It's insanity out there."

When I turned back around, I saw Cash wearing another frown. "Bobbi Jo, what's with you? I never saw this coming. You are acting like—for lack of a better phrase—a country mouse."

Throwing up my hands, I didn't know how he wanted me to act. "Should I be pretending that I've ever seen anything like this?

Should I be acting as if I've always been snobbish, semi-royalty? And why are you acting like this is old hat to you, Cash?"

"Maybe it's because I grew up in Dallas, I don't know." He took a seat on a chair that would've been deemed too fancy to sit on back home. "But this isn't all that out of the ordinary to me. I mean, well, of course, it's different and large, crowded, and even sort of odd-feeling. But the thing is, it's still just a place, Bobbi Jo. You're acting like we've landed on another planet."

He'd hit the nail on the head. "Yes, that's exactly what it feels like to me. And you seem to be acclimating to the atmosphere quite easily while I am having difficulty with it."

His eyes scanned the room, landing on the minibar. "Maybe a drink would chill you out."

"You know I don't drink." I went to sit on the bed and found it hard as a rock. "Ow." I slapped my hand on the mattress. "This thing is so hard."

He came and sat down beside me. "Well, it's not hard, just firm. I suppose people around here like their mattresses firmer than we do in Texas."

"I don't think this trip is turning out the way we'd hoped." I got up then went to look around at the rest of the room.

"You might think about giving it a chance, Bobbi Jo." Cash looked grim. "We could take a nap, I guess. Maybe you've got jetlag."

"Why do you think that?" I put my hands on my hips. "Because I like Texas better than New York, I've got jetlag? Maybe I just happen to like my home better than you do."

His eyes rolled. "Maybe I just shouldn't have brought you here. Maybe a trip to the Dairy King would've been more your speed."

"I didn't ask you to do this, Cash." He was pissing me off by acting like I was some ingrate who'd asked him to do this for me. "You came up with this whole idea. Do you want me to lie? Do you want me to pretend that I love the crowds, the noise, the bone-chilling cold?" I ran my hands up and down my arms. "What is with this cold anyway? It's wet and sticky. And quite frankly, the air smells weird here."

He fell back on the bed, sighing heavily. "I need a nap. Maybe you should take a shower and get yourself ready to go eat later."

"I'm not even remotely hungry yet." I went back to sit in the fancy chair he'd vacated. "Is there anywhere comfortable to sit in this whole room?"

Cash sat back up and looked at me with a bewildered expression. "Do you have any idea how much this room costs?"

I shrugged. "I hope it's not a lot. It's not worth it."

"It *is* a lot. And people come from all over the world to stay here. People feel appreciative of staying here, in this hotel which is known all over the globe." He fell back and sighed again. "How did I not know this about you?"

"How did I not know that you were a closet rich guy?" I got up and went to see what was in the little bar. "I need a Dr. Pepper." When I opened it, I saw many things inside. "There's some type of water in here that I've never seen before. And some club soda too. But guess what there isn't any of?"

"Dr. Pepper," Cash said, sounding weary.

"Yeah. How in the hell do they not have Dr. Pepper?" I was stupefied.

"Can't you just pick something else in there, Bobbi Jo? It's not like you only drink that one soda." He turned over on his side to look at me. "And may I recommend, once again, a real drink. You're kind of being a jackass. Pretty much since we landed, you've had nothing nice to say."

"I beg your pardon." I'd loved the lunch we'd had. "I had only nice things to say about Docks Boathouse. Now that place is one for the books. I have never tasted fresher seafood in my life. I would definitely come back just to eat there. Even if the water wasn't as pretty as I had thought it would be."

"Well, you haven't eaten here yet. Maybe the food here will make this place worth your while." He rolled over, putting his back to me.

As I stood there, looking at him, I thought about how different we were. "You know, my parents haven't ever had a lot of money, Cash."

"Mine neither," he said quietly.

"I suppose I just never thought I would even come to New York or the East Coast." I hadn't ever traveled much at all. "Have you ever been out of Texas?" I went to sit on the bed next to him, running my hand over his back.

"No, I haven't ever been out of Texas, Bobbi Jo." He rolled over to look at me. "This is my first trip out of state. This is my first time to see anything, other than a Texas sky—anything other than a Texas city."

I gulped as I saw something in his eyes I'd never seen before. "You have that thing you see in men's eyes who are wealthy and powerful, Cash. I've never seen it there before, but now I can see it clearly. You're going to outgrow me."

The way he stared into my eyes only cemented that fact in my mind and in my heart too.

CASH

The trip out of town told me more about Bobbi Jo than all our time in the sack. The remainder of our stay in New York wasn't any better than how it had begun.

She hated the meal at the Waldorf. She hated wearing the dress she'd found on the plane. She hated the bed we had to sleep on in the hotel. She hated the breakfast of lox and bagels. She hated the whole thing.

So, when we got back to Carthage, I decided to give it a rest. Maybe she and I didn't have such a great connection after all. I couldn't say I saw it coming, but I had known that she was a small-town girl and, apparently, she wanted to stay that way.

A month had passed since I'd seen her. When I drove through town in the evenings, I saw her car at The Watering Hole. She was still tending bar, which I figured she might do for the rest of her life.

I sat in a booth at the Dairy King one afternoon when my brother's wife came to sit down with me. Tiffany's family owned the small café, and she had been there helping out. "Hey, you. Why do you look so down in the dumps?"

"Do I look that bad?" I hadn't realized I was that transparent.

She nodded. "You've been looking this way for a while now. So,

I'm done waiting to find out why that is. You're going to have to tell me."

"I guess I just don't know what I want in a woman. I mean, I want someone who's down to Earth and stuff like that, but I want someone who wants to see the world too." I didn't know if there was anyone out there like that.

"I don't see what the problem in that is." She looked at me with a puzzled expression. "I thought you and Bobbi Jo from the bar were getting along well. What happened with her?"

"I took her to New York."

When Tiffany nodded as if she understood, I wondered what it was about New York that had Texas women so thrown off. "Well, taking her so far off and to such a different place than Carthage was risky. See, she's been here all her life. I don't know a whole lot about her or her family, but I do know they're from pretty humble beginnings. That might've been way too fancy for her just yet."

"I'm going to want a woman to go places with me. I want to travel the world, Tiff. I want to see it all." I hadn't ever known that about myself, but now I knew it.

"Maybe she's not the right woman for you then, Cash."

Just her saying that made me mad. "But what if she is? What if she's the right woman and I'll just have to suck it up and not get to live my dream?"

Looking confused, she asked, "When did this become your dream, Cash?"

"After that trip." I sighed. "I wanted to really enjoy everything but couldn't because Bobbi Jo had to bitch about it all. The one thing she did like was the lobster place. That was it. Out of everything I took her to do, that was it."

"Okay, see it wasn't a complete bust then." She pulled out her cell. "There are lots of places you can go that might have more of what you both want to do."

"Hell, we haven't even talked in over a month. I doubt she'd give me the time of day anymore." I knew it had bothered her that I hadn't called or come by since we got back to Carthage. I waved at her once when we passed each other in the street, and she'd given me the middle finger wave.

681

"Why haven't you talked, Cash?" Tiffany reached over to put her hand on the back of mine, as I had it lying on the table. "Did she do anything that bad while you were on the trip that warranted you not talking to her?"

"No." *She just didn't have a good time.* "It's just that it was the first trip I've ever taken out of the state. And to be honest, she's the first girl I've ever even taken on a trip anywhere. I thought it would be different. I thought she was more like me."

"But you didn't even know you wanted to travel until recently, right?" she asked.

"Yeah." I looked out the window. "But things are different now. I mean, I just don't know what I want anymore."

"You want that small-town girl, Cash. But you want her to be something she's not. That's not real fair, is it?"

I shook my head. "Nope."

I heard the phone ring up at the counter, and when the girl said Bobbi Jo's name, I knew she was calling in her nightly order. Tiffany did too as she looked over her shoulder at the girl who'd taken the order. "Hey, I'll get that out to Bobbi Jo. Let me know when it's ready." She looked back at me. "And by me, I mean you're taking it to her."

"She might not want to talk to me." I had been thinking it had been kind of shallow of me to just stop talking to her over something kind of dumb. "Dumping her just because she didn't like where we went isn't a good reason, is it?"

"Not really. And you two are young, Cash. She may not be ready to see the world just yet, but maybe one day she will be. You just moved too fast, went too far, you know?" Tiff got up as the girl put the bag of food on the counter and nodded at her. "Come on, Cash. Time to make up. I'm not saying you've got to start seeing her again, but at least make up."

"I don't know." But even as I said that, I got up to follow her. "I do miss talking to her. And kissing her."

Tiffany handed the bag of food to me. "Cash, there's more to a relationship than just the kissing. Maybe you and Bobbi Jo should spend some time doing things that aren't sex-related. Maybe getting to know one another better would be a nice change of pace."

"I wasn't looking to get serious." I walked toward the door. "How did it get serious when I wasn't trying for that?"

She shrugged. "Sometimes things just get out of control. Don't ask her out. Don't try to kiss her. Just give her the food. Tell her you took care of her tab—which I'm going to tear up right now—and then I want you to ask her how her night is going. Ask her how she's been. Let her know you miss her."

"Ugh!" I walked out, then went to get into the truck. "How did things get this way?"

As I drove to the bar, I saw an empty lot, and it caught my eye for the first time. I'd looked up old skating rinks and thought one would fit pretty good right there. But I wasn't going to say a thing about it to Bobbi Jo.

She and I were on different pages of our lives, it seemed. There was no reason to hate each other for that. But there was also no reason to try to make things work when we were so different.

Parking the truck, I wondered how she'd take me coming into the bar. It had been a whole month. It took a fair amount of courage to get my feet to take me inside, but they finally did. I saw Joey behind the bar. "Is Bobbi Jo around?" I held up the bag with Dairy King written on the side of it. "I've got a delivery to make."

"Since when did you start working at the Dairy King, Cash?" he asked with a smile.

"A few minutes ago." I saw Bobbi Jo's little blonde head coming out of the back. When she looked up at me, our eyes locked. "Hey."

She looked off to one side quickly. "Hey."

I put the bag on the bar. "I brought your order."

"Thanks." She walked behind the bar, then grabbed the bag, putting it underneath it.

"You're not hungry?" I asked. "Oh, and I paid off your tab, too."

Her eyes flashed at me, then away. "You didn't need to do that."

"Well, I did it anyway." I drummed my fingers on the bar. "So, how about a beer?"

Joey poured me one. "Have a seat. Stay a while." He put the frosted mug full of beer in front of me.

"That okay with you, Bobbi Jo?"

683

"Sure." She didn't look at me as she began dusting off bottles on the shelves.

I took a seat, then thought about what I could say to make her stop being so uptight. Although I'd had no intentions at all of talking about the skating rink, I had nothing else to talk about, so it popped out. "I think I've found the perfect spot for that thing we talked about."

She stopped dusting to turn and look at me. "The rink?"

I nodded. "Yeah."

She smiled. "That empty lot not too far away from the Dairy King?"

Nodding again, I asked, "You think the same thing?"

"I have." The way she smiled made my heart pound in my chest. But I had to remember what Tiffany had told me. Sex wasn't a thing I was supposed to be thinking about. "Are you still thinking about doing that?"

"Kind of." I had thought a lot about it. The thing was, it was something she and I were going to do together. Without her, there didn't seem to be any reason to get serious about it.

"Well, that would be a prime spot." She pulled out the food I'd brought her and began to get it out of the bag, her appetite back, it seemed.

I chewed on my lower lip as I thought about what to say next. "Maybe we could have a little snack bar there too. You know, corn-chip pies, corn dogs, lobster rolls. You remember those lobster rolls we had? They might be a real big seller here."

"They sure might." She took a bite of her burger. "But it would be a lot of work to get that all going. Do you think you've got that kind of time?"

"I've got nothing but time."

"Yeah, I'm sure you do." She took a sip of her soda. "I think you'll do a great job of it, Cash. I really do."

"Well, I can't do it alone." I hoped I wasn't pushing it too fast.

"I would assume it would be best to get some help." She took a bite of the pickle that had come with it.

"How about you?" I asked then held my breath for her answer.

"Me?" She shook her head and my heart stopped beating. "Not

684

me, Cash. We don't think along the same lines. You'll find someone who thinks like you do. I'm sure you will. And I wish you all the luck in the world with that project. I think I can even make up a recipe for those lobster rolls. I can still taste them sometimes."

"Well, I've got to include you somehow, Bobbi Jo. You were the one who came up with that whole idea." I wasn't about to leave her out of anything.

"Nah." She took another bite of her burger, then walked away as if that was all she needed to say.

But there was a hell of a lot more left to say, and I wasn't about to take no for an answer.

BOBBI JO

I thought it was pretty weird how Cash decided to come in that very day. And with the talk of the skating rink too? Well, it was all a bit too weird.

Cash mentioning the business we'd talked a little about before our breakup—which hadn't been so much a breakup since we hadn't been serious—really threw me. "I can't spread myself out that thin, Cash. I've got my own things going now."

"What kind of things do you have going on now?" he asked as if he didn't believe me.

Joey answered that for me. "Bobbi Jo was gifted this bar on Friday. She's now the new owner of The Watering Hole."

The way Cash sat there, his mouth hanging open, made me laugh. "That surprises you?"

"Well, yeah." He took a drink of his beer. "How did that happen?"

I looked at Joey who went to check on the tables and refill drinks as I went back to the bar, leaning on it. "Mr. and Mrs. Langford have owned the bar for years. They moved to Abilene when I first started working here. I've been managing it for them all these years. Mr. Langford passed away a couple of weeks ago. Mrs. Langford is going to live in Montana with her oldest daughter. She didn't want the trouble of the bar anymore, so she gifted it to me. And along with that, she gave me the sum of fifty-thousand dollars to make it my own. You know, fix it up the way I want it? I've been thinking about what I would like to do to make this place feel like mine."

"I don't know what to say." He looked around the place. "It needs a lot of work, doesn't it?"

"Oh, I don't know." I looked around too. "The locals don't seem to have a problem with it."

"Yeah, but most of them haven't seen much outside of town." He smiled suddenly. "Why not let me be your partner, Bobbi Jo?"

"Um." I didn't know what to say. "I don't know. We think so differently."

He rolled his eyes. "No, we don't. I was wrong, Bobbi Jo. I don't know what I was thinking. I don't know why I wanted to go to New York when we hadn't even talked about what we both liked yet. I rushed it."

"Like you're trying to rush me into partnering with you now?" I wasn't about to rush into anything—especially now.

He took a deep breath then let it out slowly. "I don't know why I'm this way with you—it kind of drives me crazy. Look, I've missed you. And I'm supposed to be saying all sorts of other things, but the main thing is that I have missed you, Bobbi Jo. I miss your smile, your laugh, that dimple on your left ass cheek. I miss it all."

"I would be lying if I said that I haven't missed you, Cash. But things are different. I've got this bar to run now. And some other things have come up too. I'm going to be busy, quite frankly." I didn't know what else to say to the man. "It was fun. It really was. But life is getting busy for me. I can't run off anymore. I can't spend my nights not getting any rest."

"I haven't asked you to do that." He got up and walked away, looking kind of upset, then came right back and sat down. "Look, I want more. Okay, there it is. I want you. I want to do this right this time. I was only fooling myself before. I'm done playing. So, what do you say?"

"What are you asking?" I knew what he was asking, but I wanted him to say it—actually say the words.

"You know what I want." He looked at me with soft eyes. "You know what I'm asking."

I couldn't help but smile. "That means a lot, Cash. I know how hard that was for you to not say." Laughing, I knew he wasn't ready for the real deal. "I've got more to consider now. Playing at love isn't enough for me."

"I'm sorry?" Cash wore a frown. "Playing at love?"

"You don't love me," I stated. "And I don't love you."

"But we do care about each other." He wasn't about to just let things end there. "Love will come. I know it will."

"It could." I shrugged. "But now I'm just not into it. You know what I'm saying? I've got so much to think about now." And I really did have so much to think about. I had no idea how I could possibly fit Cash into my life now.

"Besides this bar, what else do you have going on that would stop you from seeing me?"

But I wasn't going to be spreading news until I was sure there was news to spread. "It's not a good time for me to be getting involved in a romantic relationship. And as far as the business relationship you've expressed interest in, that's out for now too. I want to do *me*, Cash. Can't you understand that?"

"No," came his stoic answer. "I can't see you wanting to just do you, Bobbi Jo. There is no reason to. If you don't want me in your business, then I can respect that. If you don't want me in your bed, I've got to know why that is. Is someone else in it?"

"This town is too small for me to hide a man from you, Cash. I think you know that." I didn't even want another man. "If things weren't so weird right now, I might've taken you up on your generous offer of having a relationship. That is what you've offered, right?"

He nodded. "But if I can be honest, I'm beginning to wish I hadn't even brought it up. I'm kind of feeling a little naked and vulnerable here."

"I bet you are." Boy, I knew that feeling.

"And you're not making it any better." He looked at me as if only I could help him out.

"Look, Cash. I don't know what to do for you. To me, you made the decision that you didn't want to hang with me anymore after our trip to New York." I understood that he liked stuff and I didn't. I didn't think it meant we couldn't still see each other, but apparently he did. "So, why do you want me now? I still hate New York."

"Well, I just realized that I hate it too." He threw his hands up in the air. "There it is. I hated the same things you did. But the difference between me and you is, I gave it a chance before deciding I hated it."

"And I knew I hated it right off the bat." I smiled at him. "What I gave a chance was you. I gave you the chance to see if you liked me or not. And you didn't call or come by to see me, letting me know you didn't like me. I guessed you didn't like me being so honest with you. No matter what it was, you didn't want to talk to me or see me anymore. And guess what, I got over it, Cash."

"No, you did not." He shook his head. "You're not over me."

"I think I am." I picked up a towel to wipe the bar down. "I really do. It hurt that first week when I kept waiting for that call or for you to come in here to see me. But that second week, it got a little easier. The third week, well, I was over it by then."

"The hell you were." He drank down the rest of the beer. "Stop playing. I know I was wrong. I know I was trying to be something I wasn't, and you were just being you. I was wrong, okay? Are you going to make me beg you to come back to me?"

"Most certainly not." I rubbed the bar down as I tried not to get myself in a tizzy over what he was saying.

Did I yearn to feel Cash's strong arms around me again? Sure.

Did I still fall asleep thinking about the man? Well, yes, of course I did.

But was I about to let him back into my heart when he could so easily shut me out? No way in hell.

"It seems like you want me to beg." He looked me in the eyes. "I will beg if that's what you really want."

"Please don't." I didn't want to see him beg. "Really, Cash. You walked away from me for me just being who I am. We never really got to know one another. We got into having sex too soon. It happens. We like the sex we had, and we would like to have more of it. But I can't. Not anymore."

"I do like you."

I shook my head. "No, you don't. I wish I would've taken a picture of your face when I told you I didn't like that hotel. You are exactly the kind of man I guessed you were. You are a rich man who wants the kinds of things rich men want. And I am a woman who is down to earth. I want modest things—simple things. Go get what you want and let me have this little chunk of Heaven I've always had in Carthage."

"So you never want to travel?" he asked me.

"I didn't say that." I did have interest in other places. "There are lots of places I'd love to see and things I'd love to experience. And one day, if we ever get to really know one another, you will find out where those places are."

He tapped the bar. "I don't want you to tell me. I want to figure it out myself. You think I don't know you, but I do. I do know you, Bobbi Jo Baker. You'll see."

"I wouldn't bother if I were you." I put the towel away as I smiled at him. "I really do have my hands too full now to put my heart at risk any longer."

"Your heart?" he asked. "I thought you didn't want to get serious either. I thought you didn't want a boyfriend."

"I didn't. I don't." I had more than I could handle now. Cash would only be in my way. "I had a good time with you for the most part. Let's not ruin it."

"I already have." He looked down. "I don't know why I quit talking to you. I really don't. I was being stupid. Maybe I wanted to be something I wasn't. Maybe I was using you as an excuse. I don't know. All I know is that life isn't fun without you in it." He looked up at me. "Is your life fun without me in it?"

I couldn't lie. "You made it a lot more fun, Cash."

"And you don't want that fun back?"

I did, but then again, I knew I couldn't have things the way they had been. I was pretty damn sure Cash wouldn't be happy with the way I would have to live now. "Cash, it was fun. And now things have to change. I'm not saying fun is completely out, but it's got to take a back burner as life gets going for me."

"What does that even mean, Bobbi Jo?"

In time, he would find out, but for now, I wasn't ready to elaborate on it.

CASH

I'd left the bar confused, a little aggravated, and even a bit hurt. I knew it was all my fault, all my doing, and it was all up to me to put things back together again. But now, Bobbi Jo seemed to be over me —like totally over me. That didn't sit well with me—not even a little bit.

Jasper and Tyrell were in the barn when I drove up. All the outside lights were on, and that meant something was going down. I walked into the barn to find pretty much everyone who lived on the ranch hanging out inside. With a cow on the ground, I pretty much knew why the gathering was going on. "She about to have a calf?"

My brothers nodded.

"Yep," Tyrell said. "She's the oldest cow we've got. We're all pretty interested in how well she does."

The things people on a ranch were interested in boggled my mind at times. Like the day we found a rouge weed in the hayfield. Detailed analysis had to be done to figure out how that weed had even gotten into that hayfield. I swear, I thought the ranch foreman had been about to call in the FBI over that dang weed. And now we had an old cow giving birth. The possibilities of entertainment never seemed to end.

I leaned up against the wall, careful to avoid looking directly at the expectant mother. Staring at them while in labor tended to piss them off. "So, I talked to Bobbi Jo a little while ago."

Jasper made a weird sound. "Finally. Did she give you the time of day after you blew her off the way you did? Because I had my bets that she wouldn't say two words to you, little bro."

"She talked to me." I gave him the stink eye. "I didn't do anything so mean to her to warrant her not speaking to me at all."

Tyrell coughed as if that was ridiculous. "Um, giving her the cold shoulder for a month ain't exactly being nice, Cash."

I knew that. "I meant I didn't talk ugly to her. I didn't talk behind her back. I didn't start seeing anyone else. Other than not talking to her, I didn't do anything wrong. And I wanted to get together with her in a real way this time."

"Did you ask her to get back together with you?" Jasper asked.

"Yeah." I kicked the dirt floor.

"And she must've turned you down," Tyrell said.

I nodded. "And not just for the relationship either. She turned me down as a business partner too."

Jasper laughed quietly so as not to disturb the laboring cow. "Can you blame her? You don't have five minutes of experience running a business, Cash."

"So?" I didn't know what else to say, then thought of something important. "But I do have money and lots of it. I could be a great business partner. Anyone would want me."

"Yeah," Tyrell agreed. "To use your money. What kind of business did you entice Bobbi Jo with anyway?"

"Well, at first it was this old-fashioned skating rink that we'd talked about when we took our trip. But then I found out that she's now the new owner of the bar and I offered to help her out with that." I shoved my hands into my pockets, fisting them with aggravation. "But she politely refused my help. She kept saying how she didn't have time for fun and life had to move on and dumb shit like that."

Jasper and Tyrell looked at each other as Jasper said, "A skating rink sounds fun, doesn't it?"

Tyrell nodded. "Yeah, it does. Maybe we should make one out here."

I had to interject. "No, not out here. In town, where everyone can go and enjoy it."

Tyrell smiled at me. "Yeah, in town. That's a great idea. We should do that. All three of us. We could call it the Whisper Roller Skating Rink. I like it."

Jasper added, "We could use our ranch's brand as the logo. That would be great."

"I had this idea about having a little snack bar in there too," I told them. "Bobbi Jo and I had these killer lobster rolls while we were in Maine. They were served as appetizers at the place we ate at. They were mini hotdog buns filled with lobster that was made a lot like tuna fish salad. But you could make full-size versions of them too."

"A snack bar?" Jasper asked. "That might step on Dairy King's toes a bit, don't ya think?"

"How could it?" I asked. "If we don't sell anything they do, then how could it hurt their business?"

Tyrell shook his head. "The only place I can think of in town where a rink that size could fit is that empty lot not even two blocks away from the Dairy King. If we served any food at all, it would take away from their business. And I ain't about to do that to Tiffany's family."

Jasper agreed. "Yeah, me neither. So, we can have a rink but no snack bar."

"Well, fine." But I didn't even want to do a business with my brothers in the first place. "Then that's your guy's thing. I'll just think of something else." But all I could think of involved Bobbi Jo. But she didn't want to have a business with me either.

I kicked the dirt again, and Jasper put his hand on my shoulder. "Send her some flowers, little bro."

Tyrell came around to stand on the other side of me, putting his hand on my other shoulder. "Send her some chocolates too. Girls love chocolates."

Jasper asked, "Did you tell her how sorry you were?"

Tyrell added, "Did you tell her how stupid you were?"

Jasper went on, "Did you tell her that you were wrong?"

Tyrell had to add one more thing. "Did you tell her how lucky you were to ever have her in the first place?"

"I did apologize. I did tell her that I was wrong. But I didn't tell her how lucky I was." Maybe that would've been the one thing that would've worked. "I'm going to follow your advice, brothers. Operation flowers and candy will begin in the morning. And after that, I'll let her know—without a doubt—that she was the best thing to ever happen to me."

Jasper cocked one brow at me as he asked, "Cash, when did this begin to set into your brain? I mean, yesterday you were still sullen about her and how she acted on that trip. What made today any different than the past month?"

I needed to be honest. "I had this dream early this morning, just before I woke up. It was the first dream I've ever had about Bobbi Jo. She wasn't exactly there, but her voice was. She kept calling out to me, and I kept going toward her voice, but I never could find her."

"Surreal," Jasper said. "A disembodied voice calling to you, using Bobbi Jo's southern twang."

I punched him in the arm. "Come on. You asked me when this came to me, and it was this morning, and that was why. No reason to make fun of me."

Tyrell looked at Jasper with a stern expression. "Yeah, don't make fun of the little dreamer." He patted me on the back. "But I think that dream was a little too faint to be the actual reason you sought her out this evening. You had to have been thinking about her before that."

I got quiet as I knew it was time to admit something. "I've never stopped thinking about her."

Jasper smacked me on the back. "See! Now, that makes more sense. So why did you stop yourself from going to see her or even talking to her in this last month?"

"It was the trip. It was the way she acted on it. She was so comfortable with telling me how she didn't like things." I looked at the ground, trying to make sense out of how that had made me feel.

"Don't you want her to feel comfortable with you, Cash?" Tyrell asked.

"I thought I did, but then I didn't." I looked at him. "Because no girl has ever been that comfortable with me. And to be honest, it makes me feel like she doesn't even like me that much if she's that damn comfortable with me."

Jasper's eyes went big. "Are you shitting me?"

I shook my head. "No." All the girls I've ever had anything to do with walked on eggshells around me. Like they were afraid to show who they really were for fear I'd stop seeing them."

"And then one of them finally *did* show you who she really was and you ghosted her," Tyrell pointed out. "Weird, huh?"

"I think it's time to stop being so immature, Cash," Jasper told me. "Bobbi Jo should be able to be who she is without fear of you dumping her."

It came crashing in on me all at once. Bobbi Jo was a strong, secure woman. She got one whiff of my immaturity and knew she didn't like that one bit. No wonder she didn't seem to be mad at me. She just didn't think that much of me anymore.

"Wow, I'm an ass. I have never wanted to think of myself in that fashion, but that's exactly what I've been all these years. And Bobbi Jo is just woman enough not to want to deal with that crap." I looked at the cow as it let out a loud huffing sound.

Her big brown eyes met mine, and she seemed to be looking right into my soul. For what seemed like forever, that cow and I looked into each other's eyes then she closed hers as the ranch foreman shouted, "We've got a girl!"

"Way to go," I whispered to the cow. "You didn't let age get in your way, did ya, old girl?"

I was the baby of the family—the youngest Gentry brother. Maybe I hadn't thought about growing up much. No, scratch that. I had never thought about growing up.

Somewhere deep inside of me, I liked the fact that women didn't feel comfortable enough with me to be themselves around me. I liked the fact they pretended to like things I did, just to please me. I had been a shallow fool.

I didn't even want to be that kind of guy anymore. I wanted to grow the hell up. I wanted to start maturing. But how?

"Tyrell, how can I stop being so damn immature?"

"Thinking about other people is a start," he told me. "Letting people be who they are, without fear of you judging them or not wanting anything to do with them is also a good idea. Going to Bobbi Jo and admitting everything is also something a mature man would do."

"Maybe you're right." I didn't know if just admitting that I'd been wrong and immature would be enough for Bobbi Jo. She really didn't seem to want me anymore. "Well, I'm going to hit the hay since she's had her baby."

Leaving the barn, I walked through the dark, starry night and wondered why I'd been the way I'd been all my life. Not realizing that you'd been immature was a real drag. Like what else had I not realized about myself through the years?

As I walked up to my room, I took each step slowly. I wasn't in a rush to get into my bed alone that night. Everything felt empty. For the first time in my life, I felt empty.

This feels like crap.

BOBBI JO

The sound of the doorbell ringing woke me up from a deep and restful sleep. I heard Betty Sue shout, "I'll get it. I saw flowers coming up the sidewalk. I'm sure it's for me."

I snuggled back down, sure they were for her too. But then a few minutes later, the bedroom door opened and in came a mountain of flowers. "Surprise, Bobbi Jo. These are for you."

Rubbing my eyes, I sat up. "Huh?"

Betty Sue put the vase full of all kinds of flowers on my desk. "These are for you, Bobbi Jo." She took the card out of them and handed it to me. "I know who they're from. I don't even have to read the card to know that."

The envelope was much bigger than the normal ones that come with flowers. "What is this man doing?" I opened the envelope and out spilled a gift card to Amazon and a thank you card.

"Read it out loud, Bobbi Jo," Betty Sue urged me.

"Okay." I opened the card. "I just wanted to thank you, Bobbi Jo. You gave me more than I could have ever hoped for. I had the chance to see things through your eyes, and I blew it. I know that now. You were right. That bed was hard as a rock. And the city did have a smell to it too. You were right about everything, and I am man enough to admit when he's been wrong. Thanks for opening

698

my eyes to the immature, little jackass I've been my whole life. Sincerely, Cash."

I put the card down to look at the flowers as I noticed Betty Sue's gaping mouth. "Wow. I don't think I've ever had a man say or write anything like that to me before. And I've had quite a few immature jackasses in my time."

"It's not like I even care." I put the card down, making sure to put the gift card in it. "I don't hate Cash. Not even a little. I just have better things to do with my time now." I ran my hand over my still flat stomach.

Betty Sue looked over the massive amount of flowers. "He had to have ordered these online. The delivery driver wasn't from around here. I've never seen these types of flowers in Miss Loretta's shop downtown either."

"What are you still doing home?" I asked, as she should've been at work a long time ago.

"I've been feeling a little under the weather lately. I don't know why but I keep having the dry heaves. It's so weird." She put her hand on her stomach. "My tummy's all wiggly inside sometimes, and then I feel like I'm going to puke. It's so weird. I asked the nurse at work what it might be and she said I might be getting lactose intolerant. So, I cut out drinking milk. But so far that hasn't helped much at all."

Not always, but at times, my twin and I could feel things the other felt. There was this one week back when we first started high school where Betty Sue was having nightmares, and then I began getting them too. And they were identical as well. It was weird, and then it went away.

And I once broke my pinky finger when a friend accidentally slammed it in a car door. Betty Sue had felt that and had actually come home from summer camp, where she'd been. She wanted to go to the hospital, sure she had cancer since there was no reason for her finger to hurt so badly. Our parents were stunned when they found out I'd broken my finger. And the thing that had been even crazier was that as soon as Betty Sue found out what had happened to me, her finger stopped hurting.

I wondered if her illness would stop if I told her why *I* felt sick.

But I wasn't sure about telling anyone just yet. It was so early on, and anything could happen. If things didn't go the way I thought they would, I didn't want a lot of sympathy.

Getting out of bed, I figured I might as well get up. I was thinking about the bar and how I had to make some pretty drastic changes there. And I had a move to think about too. "I should get up. There's lots to be done now."

"With your new ownership of the bar?" she asked.

Nodding, I went to pick out some clothes. "I want to put an ad in the paper for another bartender. I'd like to take a few steps back if I can. Maybe not stay up late anymore. You know, sit back and let others do the hard work while I rake in the dough?"

"That would be smart." Betty Sue put her hand back on her stomach. "Ugh. Maybe I have a bug. It just hits me, then it's gone. It's so weird."

"That is weird," I said. "Anyway, I've gotta get ready to face the day. The sooner I get someone hired, the sooner I can get to doing the real work with the bar. I'm thinking about adding in a grill. That will mean hiring a cook and some prep staff too. And maybe even a waitress or runners or something like that. I want the place to start bringing in more customers, and I want them to spend more of their money at the bar. I'm going to take some online business courses too. I want to make the most out of this opportunity."

"Good." Betty Sue sat on her bed. "Maybe you can finally move out and I can have this room to myself."

With a smile, I nodded. "That is one of my plans. But there's a lot to do first." Time was limited though, so I knew I had to get my butt moving.

After a shower, I got dressed, then headed out. Going to the office where the local newspaper was published, I put an ad in the paper for a bartender. Then I went to the health department to get all the information I would need to put a kitchen into the bar.

Hours later, the need to eat crept up on me just after I'd finished with the health department. I was close to the Dairy King, so I walked over to grab a bite.

Just as I walked in, I saw Cash sitting in a booth. His eyes met mine. I nodded, made my order, then went to say hello and thank him for the flowers. I stood at the end of his table. "Hi. I got the flowers, the card, and the gift card. It was all very nice of you."

"Do you accept my sincere apology?" he asked.

I did accept it. "Cash, it's okay. You are who you are. I know you want someone around who wants to do what you do. And most girls will be more than happy to go along with whatever you want. Just not me."

"Would you like to sit down?" he asked me as he nodded at the empty seat across from him. "I'd like to talk if that's okay with you?"

I had some time to spare. "Okay." I sat.

"My brothers want to make that skating rink." He paused as if waiting for me to say something about that.

"Cool."

He nodded. "Okay. I wasn't sure if you would be mad about that or not."

"Why would I be mad?" He really didn't understand me. "It's a great idea, and if they want to do it, that's great. I don't have the money to make that happen anyway."

"Okay," he said, seeming a little off. "One of the cows had a calf last night when I got home. She was looking at me when she had it. It was weird."

"I bet it was." I smiled at the girl who brought me my order. "Thanks, Bethy."

"You're welcome." She turned to walk away.

But I stopped her. "Hey, Bethy, I'd like to ask you a question if you don't mind."

She stopped and came back. "Sure. What is it?"

"I'm thinking about adding a grill to the bar. Do you think I would need waitresses and do traditional service? Or would an order station and runners make more sense?"

"Def an order station and runners. It's so much easier." Bethy smiled. "And I'd love to work for you, Bobbi Jo. I bet the tips would be great."

"Me too." I gave her a smile. "When I get it going, you'll be on the list of runners for sure. And if there's anyone you know who can work as a bartender, it would be great if you sent them my way. I'm going to stop working nights as soon as I can."

"I'll let you know." She left, and when I looked back at Cash, I found him grinning.

"You're not going to be working nights anymore?"

"Not after I get another bartender. I've got better things to do with my time. Or I will have." I took a drink of my water, then dug into my salad."

His eyes went to the food in front of me. "Salad?"

Nodding, I said, "I'm watching what I eat. It's not about my weight; it's about nutrition. I want to take in only highly nutritious foods and drinks."

He nodded. "Okay. And about the bar. If you're not going to be tending the bar, what are you going to be doing?"

"Just running it." I took another bite as he looked out the window, seeming lost in thought.

"From home or what?" he asked. "There's no office in the bar itself."

"Not yet, there's not." I was still unsure of where I'd make my office. "But I don't know for sure if I'll make one down there or maybe at my place. I'm going to move out of my parents' house."

"And when is that going to happen?" He took a sip of his coke as he looked at me.

"Whenever I find a place that suits me." I wanted something nice. "At least two bedrooms, but it would be best if it had three. I could use one for my office that way."

"And you would use the other bedroom for what?" he asked.

His question pulled me out of my head for a moment. "Huh?"

He smiled. "You said you wanted a three bedroom. One room for you. One room for your office. And one room for what else?"

"Oh," I said as I tried not to seem as if I was making a big deal about it. "You know if something ever came up. You know what I'm saying."

"Nope." He eyed me. "You're looking very pretty today, Bobbi Jo. You have this glow about you." His hands moved over the table toward mine. "I truly am sorry for how I've acted. And I know you might not think that I can change, but I'd like the opportunity to prove it to you."

The sound of my cell buzzing in my pocket had me pulling my

hands away from his. "I need to check this. I've got an ad out in the paper about the bartender. It might be about that." When I looked at the text that had come in, I saw it was from my sister.

My chest filled with air as I took in a deep breath, then held it. She'd done some digging after I'd left the house, it seemed.

She knows.

CASH

"Shit," Bobbi Jo hissed. "Well, it looks like I need to go." She looked over her shoulder. "Bethy, can I get a box for this salad? I need to take it to go."

I saw no reason to hurry away. "What's the rush, Bobbi Jo? What's so important that it can't wait for you to finish eating your salad?"

"I've gotta get down to my dad's office before someone else does." She got up, boxed her salad, then hauled ass out the door.

Her bottle of water still sat on the table, and I stared at it. "What the hell?"

Nothing made sense to me, and I figured nothing would until I got Bobbi Jo to trust me again. I left the Dairy King.

The truck had to stay back at the ranch to get the oil changed by the mechanic, so I'd driven one of the Mercedes to town to grab some lunch. Chef Todd had made a shrimp dish for lunch. I hadn't been able to eat seafood since our trip. It just reminded too much of Bobbi Jo, and I hadn't wanted to be reminded of her. But now, I didn't want to stop thinking about her and how I had to fix things between us.

Just as I got into the car, I heard the sound of sirens filling the air. I had to wait before pulling out as a white car with flashing red

704

and blue lights sped by. That had been the source of all the noise. With it gone, the town went quiet again.

I pulled out, heading home. There wasn't anything else to do in town. I drove around the small town, looking at everything.

The town square was really nice, quaint, and something to be proud of. Small churches dotted the town too. I'd never taken the time to look at the town that would be my new home. It was not only nice, but hospitable, and pretty, too.

Calling Carthage home would be something I might come to even cherish someday. Bobbi Jo had lived her whole life in this place. I could see why she wanted to make her life here, do something here.

World traveling sounded great, but not nearly as great as making Carthage the place we'd live in the rest of our lives. My brothers had different ideas about what to do in the town to make it theirs. Bobbi Jo was going to fix up that bar to make it a place she could be proud to call her own. And what did I have?

Nothing.

I had nothing to call my own. Nothing to leave in this town that would tell future generations that Cash Gentry had once lived in Carthage, Texas.

There had to be something I could give this town. Something that no one else had ever given it.

My cell rang, and I tried to grab it from its place on the passenger seat. But I accidentally stepped on the brake a little too hard and sent it flying off the seat to the floor. When I hit the gas, I accelerated a little too hard and sent the phone sliding underneath the seat. "Well, crap." The pedals proved to be touchy in the beast of a machine.

My cell rang a few times, then went silent. I sighed then took the turn to head out to the ranch. Once I got there, I would fish it out and see whose call I'd missed.

The only person I really wanted to hear from probably wouldn't be the one calling me anyway. Bobbi Jo seemed to be perfectly all right without me. She looked happy even.

It began to sink in that she hadn't really liked me all that much in the first place. Maybe it had been all sex and nothing concrete at all. Maybe she saw through my shiny outer shell to my shallow insides. Maybe she hadn't liked what she'd found.

And who could blame her?

I had to be the richest loser in the world. No one could come close to being as bad as I was.

It might be the best thing for Bobbi Jo if I just left her alone and stopped trying. She deserved better than me. And now that she'd knocked some sense into her evil twin sister, that girl wouldn't get in the middle of Bobbi Jo and whatever new guy she found.

My gut twisted as I thought of my Bobbi Jo being with another man. But I didn't have the right to feel pain over that. *I'd* blown it. I'd had my chance and I'd thrown it away.

And all over the fact that she was just being honest and didn't like where I'd taken her. "Man, if I would've just taken her to Montana to eat steaks, this whole thing could've been avoided."

People in Texas were set in their ways; I had known that. We never ate Mexican food any further north than Austin. Anything after the Austin city limits sign wasn't authentic.

I'd made the mistake of choosing seafood for our first trip together. If she ever gave me the chance, I would never make the same mistakes again. But I highly doubted she'd ever give me another chance. Why would she?

I'd blown it—big time.

My cell went off again and one more time after that. I was beginning to think there was something pretty damn important someone wanted to tell me.

I heard a few text messages come in too. "Man, what the hell is up?"

In just a couple of minutes, I would be able to get the cell out from under the seat. I'd just turned into the ranch and was heading up the driveway. What I saw up ahead confused me.

Blue and red lights flashed in the afternoon sunlight. The white car that I'd seen in town was parked near the front entrance. And there was a tall man, his hand on his holster, his sunglass-covered eyes directed at me.

Tyrell stood at the door, his eyes on me too. He shook his head and moved his arms as if he wanted me to turn around and leave.

And that was when a couple of gunshots were fired; the bullets zipped over the top of the car. I hit the accelerator by accident, as that had totally surprised me. "Fuck!"

Barreling toward the man who'd shot at me, I turned the wheel to miss him and hit the back end of his car. Airbags exploded around me, the sound of metal on metal met my ringing ears, then the car door came open. "You rat bastard! Get the fuck out of the car and put your hands where I can see 'em."

"What did I do?" I felt dizzy from the blow of the airbag. "What's going on?"

A hand came in, then I heard the sound of fabric being sliced with a knife. "Take that seatbelt off and get out!"

"Okay, okay," I muttered as I tried to make my hands work. "I'm kind of freaked out here, man."

"*You're* freaked out?" he hollered. "What about me? What do you think I am?"

"I don't know what or even *who* you are." I hit the button to release the seatbelt, then felt a hand on the back of my neck, jerking me out of the car.

Tyrell shouted, "Hey, you don't know if he's hurt or not! Don't go yanking on him like that!"

"Boy, you better shut up and let me deal with this piece of shit!" the man shouted back at my brother.

"Piece of shit?" I'd been called names a time or two in my life, but a piece of shit hadn't been one of them.

Suddenly, I was pushed to face the wrecked car; my head smacked against the top of the door. That was when my other brother showed up. I heard Jasper shout, "Oh, hell no!"

"You stay out of this!" the man who was roughing me up shouted back.

"You've got one second to get your hands off our little brother or, so help me God, you will never see the light of day again, old man!" Jasper yelled. "Do you know who you're messing with? We're the Gentry boys. We've got more money than God right now. And you won't have a pot to piss in if you don't get your hands off our brother!"

"Who are you?" I asked. "You've got the wrong man. I haven't broken even one law that I can remember in recent history."

"Boy, just shut up and listen to me." The man yanked me back then turned me to face him. "You and I need to talk—man to man. Call your brothers off and we'll settle this shit between us and us alone."

"I'm sorry about this, man, but I ain't about to tell my brothers to stay out of this." I wasn't some idiot. "I have no idea what's going on here. I don't know why you're pissed at me. But I do know that they will kick your ass and sue the shit out of you if you don't let me go."

He looked at his now beat up car and the sigh he let out told me he had no idea what he was going to do next. I had the impression he'd been planning on throwing me into that car and taking me away with him somewhere. "Fuck!"

"Yeah, it's a fucking shame you won't be able to kidnap me." I began to wonder if he'd planned to kidnap me and get ransom from my brothers. I asked him as much.

"What?" He shook his head then finally let go of me. "No. I ain't no kidnapper, you idiot. I was going to take you in. I was going to keep you in a cell while I got answers. I was going to make sure you couldn't run away from me and your responsibilities."

I had no idea what he was talking about. And then I heard my cell going off again. "Look, I need to get that phone and answer it. I'm afraid it might be important. It's been ringing like crazy for a while now."

"Not yet." He put the gun up to my side, the end of it stabbing a spot between my ribs. "If you do so much as try to move, I will put a bullet right in your heart. I can do it. Don't tempt me."

"I don't doubt that you can do it," I told him. "But I would love to know why you *would* do it. Sir," I threw that last part in to try to deescalate the rather dangerous situation.

Tyrell and Jasper moved in, flanking the man on either side as Tyrell said, "Look, mister, we've called the police. You had better let our brother go or there will be hell to pay."

Our driveway was a mile long and already the squeals of tires could be heard as cars turned on it, coming to my rescue. "Come on, man," I said. "We don't have to do this. We can talk. Something is obviously bothering you."

"Put the gun down," Tyrell said. "Come on, now. Things don't have to go like this."

Jasper added, "We don't want anyone to get hurt."

The sound of tires crunching gravel met my ears. Then the tires slid to a stop, followed by the creak of a car door. "Daddy, no!"

I glanced in the direction of the familiar voice. "Bobbi Jo?"

BOBBI JO

I'd never felt more embarrassed. But seeing my daddy with his gun in Cash's ribcage proved to be the most embarrassed I'd ever been. "Daddy, no!"

Cash looked at me out of the corner of his eye. "Bobbi Jo?" He looked at my dad. "This is your father?"

"Yes." I got up next to my father, putting my hand on top of his, pulling the gun back away from Cash. "Daddy, stop. You've got to stop. We need to go. You shouldn't even be here."

I managed to get my father to back up with me as a couple of his deputies pulled up and got out to see what the ruckus was all about. He held up his gun then put it in his holster. "It's okay, boys. You all can go back to the station. I'm calm now."

"You sure you don't want them to stay?" Cash asked. "It might be better if they stayed."

"It's okay, Cash. Daddy won't hurt you," I let him know. "He was just upset." I looked at my father's car that had a Mercedes up its ass. "Wow, what happened here?"

"I hit the car." Cash shrugged. "I wasn't used to the pedals and hit the accelerator instead of the brake. In my defense though, he was shooting at me when I did it."

I couldn't believe my father had done that. "Daddy!"

"Well, he was going to try to make a run for it," he said.

"Was not," Cash retaliated. "There was no reason to try to run. Well, until you went and fired a gun at me, there wasn't."

Jasper cleared his throat. "Maybe we should all go inside and get to the bottom of this."

I didn't want to get to the bottom of anything. "No. That's okay. I'll just take my father and leave you boys alone."

Cash put his hand on my arm to stop me. "No. We need to find out what has your father so upset with me, Bobbi Jo. I would rather not have this happen again."

"Yeah? Well, it won't." I looked at my father who now seemed a lot more settled.

Tyrell wasn't about to let it go either. "No, we're going to get to the bottom of this, Bobbi Jo. We can't just allow things like this to happen."

My father growled. "Just let me deal with him."

"No." I took a deep breath then just came out with it. "Look, my father is worried about some things that he really doesn't need to be worried about. That's all. That's it. So, I'll straighten this out, and we'll get out of your hair." I looked at my father's car. "Do you think your car is drivable, Dad?"

"Not sure." He huffed. "Boy can't even drive right. What kind of a—"

I stopped him from saying what I knew he would say. "Anyway, let's get going. We can see if it'll start." I looked at Tyrell. "My apologies, Tyrell."

Jasper was the next one to stop me from leaving. "Wait a minute, Bobbi Jo. You're acting weird."

"She is," Cash agreed. "What's up, Bobbi Jo?"

"Just tell him," my father said. "Tell him so we can deal with this already."

Cash wouldn't let go of my arm. "Tell me, Bobbi Jo."

I had no intentions of telling anyone anything until things were more written in stone. "My stupid sister is what the problem is."

"I can't imagine what she could've done that would have all this happening," Cash said. "So fill us in."

"Betty Sue called me at work," my father said.

I hurried to add, "To tell him things that really were none of her business *nor* her concern."

Dad sighed then pulled his sunglasses off, looking at Cash. "Boy, you've done gone and got my daughter pregnant." He glared at me. "See, it's out there. Now, what are you gonna do about it?"

Cash stood there, perfectly still. He looked as if his mind was doing somersaults. "Huh?"

Before I could say anything, Dad said, "You're going to be a father, Cash Gentry." He looked at me again. "And I came here to find out what he's going to do about that."

"Well, Daddy, it's up to me what will happen with this baby. Now let's go." I tried to take a step away, but Cash hadn't let me go yet.

His grip on my arm only got tighter. "Wait a second, Bobbi Jo." He took a deep breath as his brothers got behind him.

"It's okay, Cash," Tyrell told him.

"You're going to be fine," Jasper added.

I found it kind of hard to believe they were all so worried about him and not so much about me. "Well, anyway, I am sure you will be fine, Cash. We'll get going now. Come on, Dad."

"Hold on." Cash pulled me to him, his eyes on mine. "Bobbi Jo? Are we having a baby?"

"*I* am having a baby." I had never expected anything out of him. "*Me*, Cash. *I* am having this baby."

My father wasn't about to shut up. "It's his responsibility too, Bobbi Jo. That's what I was trying to tell you, but you wouldn't listen to me."

Cash whispered, "I want it too, Bobbi Jo. It's my baby too."

My father sighed with relief. "Yes. Thank God. He wants it too. Hallelujah!"

"Can we talk about this later, Cash?" I really didn't want to discuss any of this with any of the people who were huddled around us.

"Why not hammer out the details now?" my father asked. "Cash, you up for that?"

"Sure," Cash said. "I'm up for that." He tugged me to go with him. "Let's all go inside and we can talk."

"I don't want to talk right now." I wasn't going to be forced into doing anything.

My father wasn't letting up though. "Cash, I don't know what's going on in my daughter's brain right now, but all I want to know is this: will you be marrying my daughter and doing what's right by her and this baby?"

I dropped my head, feeling heat course through my body as embarrassment overtook me. "Dad, no. We're not going to get—"

Cash interrupted me. "Marry me, Bobbi Jo Baker."

I could not believe what I'd heard him say. Slowly, I pulled my head up to look at him. "You don't mean that."

He nodded. "Yes, I do. Marry me."

My father let out a shout. "Yahoo! Yippee! There's gonna be a wedding! And here I was thinking that I would have to get out my gun again, boy!"

"No need, sir." Cash was all smiles. "I'll gladly marry your daughter."

With all the smiles and high fives going around, no one noticed that I hadn't exactly accepted Cash's proposal. "Um, excuse me. I haven't said yes."

Daddy laughed and picked me up, twirling me around like I was a little girl. "But you will, darlin', you will! Yahoo!"

Cash took me away from my father, planting a kiss on my lips. "We're going to be so happy, Bobbi Jo. I swear we will."

I could hardly speak as my father shouted. "Look at this place. My grandkid is going to live here. What a hell of a deal this kid has gotten, I tell you what."

Jasper put his hand on my shoulder as Cash refused to let me go. "Congratulations, Bobbi Jo. Being a parent is the most rewarding experience in the history of experiences."

Tyrell nodded. "I'm so happy for you, Bobbi Jo."

"But I haven't said yes." No one seemed to hear me. I leaned in close to Cash's ear, hoping he'd listen to me. "Cash, I don't want to marry you."

"Huh?" Cash looked at me, the smile still on his face. "What did you say, baby?"

"I *don't* want to marry you." I put my hands against his chest to show him that I wanted to be let go. "Cash, I want to do this on my own. That's why I didn't rush to tell you. I want to do this my myself."

My father made a sound like a geyser had just blown up. "The hell you say, girl? You can't have a baby all on your own. First of all, it ain't just your baby. Tell her, Cash."

"Yeah, Cash, tell me." I stared him in the eyes, daring him to say the baby wasn't just mine.

It was my body that would carry this baby. Cash saw the look in my eyes. "I want to be here for you and the baby. Don't you want that?"

"I don't know what I want yet. But I know this: I will not be forced into a marriage. I will not be forced into a relationship with you, Cash Gentry. I don't care if you are the father; I will make the choices for this child."

My father huffed. "That's just stupid, Bobbi Jo. This man has lots of money."

"And I don't want any of it. I never have." I wasn't going to go down as the talk of the town. The barmaid who duped poor Cash Gentry into marrying her after getting herself pregnant just to get to his money.

"No one said you did, Bobbi Jo," Cash whispered. "Girl, I *want* to marry you. Do you understand what I am saying to you? I want this. I *want* you and I *want* our baby. And I know you didn't do this on purpose. I also know this a baby deserves both parents."

"This is *my* baby," I let him know. "Until I say any different, this baby is mine and mine alone. You don't know for sure that you're the father."

My father made a whooping sound. "Girl, if you weren't grown and pregnant right now, I would be whooping your hind-end right about now. Now, you know damn good and well that this man is the father of that baby. And I ain't about to let you go making him think anything else."

Cash let me go; he stepped back and looked me in the eyes. "Bobbi Jo, I don't want to make you do anything you don't want to do. I just want you to know that I am here for you and I want to do the right thing. But I will respect your wishes."

"Damn it, Bobbi Jo!" Dad yelled. "Now look at what you've gone and done. He wants to do the right thing. Let him."

I walked toward my car. "I'm leaving, Dad. Get a ride from one of your deputies if your car won't start." I got into my car and turned around, careful not to look at any of the faces that looked at me.

Not one of them knew how I felt. Not one of them knew what it would mean to me if I married a man who not only didn't love me but didn't even like me.

Cash was destined to marry someone else. Some woman was out there who wanted to dine on snails and eat goose liver. Some woman was out there who could find beauty in everything. Even things that stunk and had uncomfortable beds. I wasn't her. I wasn't Cash's dream woman.

My cell rang, and I saw my sister's number on it. So I answered her call. "You little betraying rat. I don't have a sister anymore."

Before I could hang up, she said, "I didn't do it for you or Cash. I did it for that baby. Think about that before you go disowning me, sister."

CASH

After watching her drive away, I stumbled inside. I was going to be a father. Even if Bobbi Jo didn't want to share the kid with me, I was going to be a father.

Ella and Tiffany were talking softly in the next room as I came in to ask them some questions. "Um, I don't mean to interrupt you two, but I've got a question that I think only a woman would understand."

Tiffany smiled at me. "Sure, Cash. Ask Away."

"So, Bobbi Jo just told me she's pregnant, and when I asked her to marry me, she said no. And I'd just really like to understand why she said that." I rocked on my heels as I felt like I might collapse.

Both sets of eyes went wide, then Ella's hand went over her mouth as she squealed. "Wow! Congrats, Cash!"

Tiffany got up and came to hug me. "Oh, my gosh. This is big. Huge!"

"Well, not really." I stepped back, so she had to let me go. "She wants to do this on her own."

Tiffany shook her head. "She has no idea what she's saying right now. Believe me. You can't let her go through this alone, Cash."

"I don't want to let her go through this alone, Tiff. I want her. I want this baby. I don't know what I should do." I was lost and felt like a duck out of water.

"She's in shock," Tiffany told me. "That has to be it."

"See, I would think that too. But she was pretty freaking calm about the whole thing." I got the impression that she'd known about the pregnancy for at least a little while. "Maybe she's had some time to get used to the fact and she just doesn't want anything to do with me. Which is kind of hurtful."

Ella chewed on her bottom lip. "Yeah, but you did dump her after that trip. Maybe she thinks it's best not to marry a man who dumped her."

I had admitted to Bobbi Jo how wrong I'd been about doing that though. "What can I do to prove to her that what I did was stupid and if I could go back and change things, then I would?"

Tiffany shrugged. "Since you can't time travel, you're stuck with what happened. I know it sucks, but even I had to deal with what I'd done and do things to make it right."

"Then tell me how I can make this right." That was all I wanted to do.

Ella shook her head. "Only you will know how to make it right with the girl. You are the one who loves her."

"Oh." I put my finger to my lips. "Love. Hm."

Tiffany nodded knowingly. "They haven't said the words, Ella."

I smiled. She'd hit the nail on the head. "Yeah. We haven't said the words. And to be honest, I'm not sure I can tell her that I love her yet. We haven't gotten to know one another that well."

Ella sighed. "Then what made you think you could ask her to marry you?"

"Yeah, why did I do that?" I felt stupid for jumping the gun. "I should go talk to her."

Tiffany took my hand as I turned to leave. "Give her some space, Cash. Call or, even better, shoot her a text telling her you'd like to talk whenever she's ready. And let her know that you might've asked her to marry you a little too quickly, but that was only because of how excited you are about this baby. Share the baby first and maybe love will follow."

"Maybe you're right." I crossed my fingers as I walked out of the room.

Jasper spotted me as I came out and walked over, taking me in for a big bro-hug. "Come here, you little man, you."

"Jasper, I know you want to joke around with me, but now's not the time. I'm trying to figure out how to fix all this shit."

He let me go, popping me in the shoulder to show me he still cared. "So, now you not only need to win your girl back, you've gotta figure out how to make her marry you too. What a world, huh?"

"I've talked to the girls, and I think I'm going to chill on the marriage thing."

He nodded. "They're probably right. Talk to her and figure out what she wants, bro. Then give her whatever that is."

"I'll try." Bobbi Jo wasn't your typical girl though. "She's a lot like a man at times. I know that sounds odd, but it's true. She's honest. She doesn't try to put on airs or act like someone she's not. And I acted like I was mad at her for being that way. It was a mistake. A huge mistake."

Jasper tapped his chin as he thought. "Okay, then this might be a hell of a lot easier than I thought. If we're dealing with a woman who thinks like a man, we're half-way there. I'm a man. We're not sure what you are yet, but you're coming along nicely."

I punched him in the arm. "Can you be serious for a second, asshole. I've got a baby on the way. I would like to get my life all settled down now."

Tyrell came into the room, a beer in his hand. "I brought you this. Figured it might help you calm down a little. And ease the pain of that harsh refusal of marriage she gave you. Man, I don't know what I would do if I was dissed like that." He took a drink of the beer meant for me.

"Give me that," I barked as I took the tall, dark bottle out of his hand and chugged it. "Man, this sucks ass."

"Totally," my brothers agreed.

We all took seats as they stared at me. "So, she wants to do this all on her own. And she thinks I don't like her. But I do like her. I've messed it all up, and I've got to fix it. And I would guess that

I've got about eight months to do that. So, what am I going
to do?"

Jasper shook his head. "Maybe you should make her a cake."

Tyrell bumped his shoulder to Jasper's. "Or build her a house."

I looked at the idiots I had to say I was related to. "The women
were much more helpful than either of you are. This is serious. I'm
going to be a father. I'd like to get to actually raise my kid. Right
now, that's looking like it might not happen."

"First of all," Tyrell said. "You will get to raise your kid. If
Bobbi Jo wants to play hardball, you've got the harder balls. You get
what I'm saying?"

I kind of understood him. "I've got balls, and she doesn't. Yeah,
I know."

Jasper laughed. "You idiot. You've got enough money to get
great lawyers that would make sure you get to raise your son. Bobbi
Jo wouldn't have any choice in the matter."

As I sat there, chewing on that idea, I began to see things in
Bobbi Jo's eyes. "Do you think she knows that about me?"

"That you can hire lawyers to get your kid?" Tyrell asked. "Um,
hell yes she knows that."

"Do you think that might be a part of what has her saying she
wants to do this alone?" I could understand her being worried about
me being that man who takes his kid away from the woman just
because he can. "She did say something about me being that typical
rich man. She said she saw it in my eyes when we were on that trip."

Jasper nodded. "We all have that, Cash. I don't like it about
myself, but we all have that in us. Like in our genes, man. Our
grandfather passed that shit down. Dad didn't let it affect him. So,
I've got faith that we can do what Dad did too. We can overcome
that asshole, rich-man gene if we want to. Or we can give into it
and become just like old Collin Gentry."

I never wanted to be like that man. "I won't let that happen to
me. I felt it too. I felt aggravated that Bobbi Jo wouldn't like every
damn thing I did for her. I ordered fancy dishes at the Waldorf, and
she took one look at them and shook her head. She wouldn't even
try the things. And I felt mad about her doing that. The thing is that
I don't know why I felt angry about that. When I put that fucking

snail into my mouth to show her how the other half lives, I nearly puked."

Jasper nodded. "I bet you did."

"I did." I'd been so stupid too. "But I chewed that nasty shit up, and I swallowed it. And then you know what I did?"

Tyrell made a gagging face. "You ran to the bathroom and then threw up?"

"No," I said as I shook my head. "I ate three more, just to prove to her that they were good. Which they were not. And then I did the same thing with the goose liver pate. I ate nearly all of it as she looked at me with disgust. Why? I don't know. And that dumbass feeling of anger at her for being true to herself just kept on going. Up until only a week or so ago, I kept thinking that she would never be what I needed in my life. You know, a woman who will do anything I want."

I heard Tiffany's voice as she and Ella came into the room to see what we were doing. "How boring would it be if a woman did everything you wanted her to?"

Tyrell nodded. "Yeah. You looking for a robot wife or what?"

"No." I wasn't looking for a wife at all—at least I hadn't been until today. "I don't know what I was thinking. But I know this. I like Bobbi Jo. I genuinely like her. And that should be enough for now."

I remembered that I'd left my cell out in the car. I jumped up to go out and get it. But I found the car was gone when I opened the front door. Tyrell was right behind me. "They already picked it up to take it to a shop in town to get it fixed."

"My phone was in it." I sagged and leaned against the wall.

Tyrell jerked his head to one side. "Go take another car to the shop to pick it up. Or better yet. Go see Bobbi Jo. She shouldn't be at work yet. And I bet she could stand to hear what you've got to say. Letting her know that you will give her the space she needs, but you will be right here, waiting for her too, ought to help."

"Yeah, it might." I looked at my big brother. "Tyrell, this is really hard for me. I'm jumping up and down inside. I'm so happy about this baby. Not getting to celebrate this with the mother of it isn't sitting well with me."

"You're a good man, Cash." Tyrell patted me on the back. "And you're going to make a great father. She'll see that. Just be yourself and let her see that she's having a baby with the right man."

"I do want to marry her." I didn't know if that was right or not, but I did want that. "But I guess I had better keep that to myself for a while, huh?"

"You might want to, yeah."

Who knew not asking her to marry me would be the best thing to do?

BOBBI JO

My twin might've been the first person to be as close to me as any other human being could get, but now there was my little baby. I knew that person would be even closer to me. And the fact that my sister thought she knew what was best for my baby totally pissed me off.

I slammed into our house and went straight to the bedroom where I knew I would find Betty Sue. Sure enough, she was laid out on her bed, looking at her cell as if she'd done nothing wrong. "Before you say one word, Bobbi Jo, you should know I'm not the least bit sorry for what I did."

"If I weren't pregnant right now, I would do far worse to you than I did that day after you kissed Cash." My fists balled at my sides as they yearned to smack into her.

She put the cell phone down, then sat up to look at me. Not even the slightest bit of remorse was in her expression. "Why don't you take a seat, sis?"

"Why don't you jump off a bridge, sis?" I took a deep breath to try to calm myself down. "Just tell me why you would dig through the bathroom trash to find what you found."

"I was throwing it out. I found it by accident." She smiled. "And let me tell you that what I found made my heart pound and I don't remember ever feeling happier about anything. Nothing, Bobbi Jo. This is great news. Why would you want to hide it anyway?"

I sat on the chair at my desk. "There are the issues with this baby's father to consider, Betty Sue. It's not all black and white; there are a lot of gray areas. And I wanted time to consider everything before I told anyone about this baby. You took that away from me. You stole it, Betty Sue. And you're not even one tiny bit sorry for what you did."

"He deserved to know."

"Betty Sue, you didn't tell *Cash*. You told our *father*. Do you know what he did?"

She shook her head. "I had high hopes he would talk some sense into you."

"Well, your hopes are dashed then." I shook my head as I just couldn't believe how everything went down. "You should know that our father is the hottest of the hot-heads, Betty Sue. He not only pulled a gun on Cash, but he also fired it at him too."

Her eyes went wide. "You're shitting me!"

"I'm not." I put my hand on my belly, a thing I'd done since I found out about my tiny bundle of joy. "You could've gotten this baby's father killed before I even had the time to decide what I was going to do about him."

"So, what are you going to do about Cash?" she asked.

"I don't know," I said. "First of all, he doesn't like me. He doesn't like the person I am. And I will not change things about myself to suit him—or any man, for that matter. I'm okay with who I am. If he doesn't like how straightforward I am, then he doesn't have to be around me. I'm fine with that."

"But that's his baby, Bobbi Jo. He deserves to be a part of that kid's life too."

I understood that. "I never said I was going to leave him out entirely. But I'm only a little over a month pregnant. There's lots of time for me to be alone with this. But now that seems to be gone. It seems I've got to let Cash be with me, even before the baby is born. And I don't really think either of us will be happy with that. The guy thought he had to ask me to marry him. What does that say about him?"

"What does that say about you?" she asked me with a concerned expression.

"That I'm a strong woman who knows that I can have this baby on my own without anyone's help."

She shook her head. "You're delusional."

"Am not," I said. "What about all those mothers out there who have absent fathers for their kids? They do it all on their own. And they have far less resources than I do. I now own my own business. I can make my own hours, and I won't have to even worry about getting a babysitter for my baby. I can take him with me everywhere I go."

She looked upset. "So, you don't plan on even letting us help you out?"

"Who? You, Mom, and Dad?" I asked.

She nodded. "Yeah."

"Well, you can play with him, but I don't *need* you. I don't *need* any of you. Haven't I made that abundantly clear?" I didn't understand why it was so hard for everyone to grasp the fact that I had this covered.

"And what about Cash? Are you going to let *him* play with his own kid too? Or are you going to let him be the *father* he should be?" she asked.

"I don't know yet." I hadn't had time to really think about it. Cash had barely begun talking to me again. How was I to know what the future would bring?

Betty Sue seemed put out with me as she sighed and scratched her head. "Are you oblivious to all the money that man has? Are you unaware that he can get custody of that baby and leave you out of its life?"

"Well, he wouldn't do that. He's not a monster." I knew Cash better than that.

"Oh, so you know how that man will react to you not letting him see his child?" She laughed. "I think you might be underestimating how a parent can react to being kept away from their kid. It can be downright primal, Bobbi Jo. You should start thinking about the reality of this situation and stop thinking about this in your own

724

terms. You really don't have as much power as you think you do over this baby."

"I'm the one carrying this baby. It's inside of me." I knew I had the upper hand.

"You're carrying it for now. Sure, no one can take it from you at this point. But you won't have that baby tucked safely away inside of you forever." She cocked her head to one side. "Only about eight more months is all you have. And then what will you do?"

"I haven't figured that out yet. I will. I mean, I've got to. But for now, I want to be left alone." I wasn't asking for much. I just wanted some time with my baby alone. The kid wasn't even here yet. What was the big damn deal?

A knock sounded on front door and I looked at Betty Sue as she jumped up to go answer it. "I wonder who that could be."

I followed behind her and gasped when she opened the door. Cash stood there. "How did you find out where I live?" I asked him as Betty Sue quickly disappeared.

"I stopped by the sheriff's office and your father was more than happy to give me the address." He stepped inside and closed the door behind him. "I'm not here to pressure you into anything. I want you to know that right off the bat. I feel like you need to hear me out. So, don't say a word, just listen. Okay?"

I stood there with my arms crossed, waiting.

"Okay?" he asked again.

"You said not to say anything. Can I sit down?"

He nodded. "Yeah." He took a seat in my father's recliner as I took one on the sofa. "I just wanted you to know that I'm over the moon about this baby. I felt deflated back there. I wanted to grab you and hug and kiss you. I wanted to celebrate this happy news with you. And when you left, leaving me out, I felt like something was so wrong."

I nodded. "Yeah, I can see that. I didn't think you would be all that happy, to be honest with you."

"It's kind of surprising me too." He smiled and my heart fluttered. "Bobbi Jo, I know my actions in New York made you think I don't like you. But, honey, I do like you. I like you more than I've ever liked anyone. I think we could even fall in love, given time."

I didn't know what to say. But then I thought about the baby. "And if we never do fall in love, then what?"

"Then, we stay friends."

"The way it was before?" I asked. "Friends with benefits?"

He smiled at me. "That wasn't so bad, was it?"

It wouldn't be enough now. "Cash, I liked you too. I don't know if I do anymore. I didn't like the way you acted. For God's sakes, you ate snails and pretended you liked them."

He rubbed his brow and looked grim. "Yeah, I know I did that. I can't explain what I was trying to prove. My brothers and I talked a little about that. We have this philosophy that the genes we've inherited from our grandfather has everything to do with it when we're being assholes."

"I can see that." I couldn't help but smile. "And I can see that you will always have issues with that. And that's okay. You can't help who you are. It's just that I don't want to be a part of that."

His eyes drooped. "You don't want to be a part of me?"

I shook my head. "No, I don't."

I'd never seen that much pain in anyone's eyes before. Cash's chest even caved in as he leaned back in the chair. "Damn."

Something inside of me felt horrible that I'd made him feel that way. "Cash, don't look like that. Just because I don't want to be a part of you doesn't mean that there's not someone out there for you. There has to be some woman who wants to be what you want her to be. I'm me. I'm set in my ways. I have opinions and I don't shy away from them. I don't keep my mouth shut if I do or don't like something."

"I don't want some girl who pretends to like what I like, Bobbi Jo." He looked at me and I saw the pain going clear to his soul. "I know I was wrong for what I thought I wanted from you. I know I was wrong for not talking to you once we got back home. And I know I'm wrong for doing this too. But I will walk away and give you all that you want: your freedom to have this baby all on your own. But I will only do that if that's what you really want."

As I sat there, listening to him give me everything I wanted and knowing he didn't want the same things, I got mad. "Cash, do you think for one second that I want you to be a person who I refuse to be? I'm not some hypocrite. And I don't like you thinking I am. You be you, okay? You say whatever you want to say, all right?"

"So you want me to do what I want to do and not to worry about how you feel about it?" he asked.

I didn't know exactly what I wanted, but I knew I didn't want him or anyone else bending to please me. Not when I wasn't about to bend to please anyone. "Be you, Cash. I'll be me, and you be you."

"Then I want to be here for you and our baby. I'll give you all the space you want, but in the end, I want to be that baby's father, and I want to be your supporter too, Bobbi Jo. I'll support you in any way you need. All you have to do is tell me what it is you need or want, and I'll do it."

"And if I say I just want to be left alone?" I asked because right then, that was all I wanted—at least for a little while.

He got up and walked to the door. "I hear you. You know where I'll be, and you've got my number. You call, text, or just show up. I want you, Bobbi Jo. I like you, Bobbi Jo. And I do believe that I could love you—given time. I think you could love me too if you want to know what I think. But I won't force anything. Well, that's not true. I will force this one thing. I *will* be that child's father. Even if I have to fight you on it; I will not walk away from my kid. I won't ever do it, and there is nothing you can do to make me. I love it already." And then he left.

I sat perfectly still, my hand on my belly. "Did you hear that? He loves you already. So do I, by the way."

Now if we can only find love for each other.

CASH

An entire week passed without Bobbi Jo trying to talk to me. I planned to honor the promise I made her, but something told me to do at least a little something to show her I was thinking of her.

So, my brothers and I hopped on our private jet to head to Maine. "You're going to love the lobster at Docks Boathouse." My mission was to bring back some of that delicious seafood that Bobbi Jo and I had both agreed was fantastic on the trip that had threatened to end it all.

Jasper was a little tired looking as he sprawled out in the chair. "But all the way to Maine, bro? Why so far? Can't you get some great lobster from somewhere nearer to us?"

"Nope." I looked out the window as we flew up high in the sky. "She needs this anyway. This will show her how far I'll go to do things for her; it should help her see there's no reason to shut me out."

Tyrell looked out the window on his side of the plane. "I think it's a great idea. You've got to do something. That girl is just stubborn enough to cut things off with you until she's forced to deal with you."

Jasper sat up; a smile lit up his face. "Oh, I was supposed to tell you this, and I've been forgetting. Tiffany is going to throw Bobbi Jo a surprise baby shower when she's seven months pregnant. She said that's about the official time most baby showers are thrown."

"Ella wanted to know when we could start setting up the baby's bedroom too, Cash," Tyrell said. "You've got to think about all that. No matter what, that baby needs a room in our house too."

I chewed on my lower lip as I thought about that. "I want to offer Bobbi Jo a suite in our house too. Whether she wants to be with me or not, I'd like it if we cohabitated to raise our baby."

"Then invite her to live with us," Tyrell said. "I think it's an awesome idea."

Jasper looked a little like he was on the other side of the fence. "What if you and Bobbi Jo never get back together? What if you want to date someone else? What if *she* wants to date someone else? Living in the same house, in your house, won't be a great idea."

"I don't plan on seeing anyone else." I hoped Bobbi Jo would eventually come around. "I *can* be charming, you know. I think I can win her back if she'll just allow me to be around her for a bit."

Tyrell laughed. "She's a realist, Cash. She's seen through your charming exterior and really knows who you are now."

"How can she know who I really am, when *I* don't even know who I am yet." I wasn't done growing as a person. "I'm not quite finished yet. This isn't the end result."

Jasper shrugged. "Well, what about her? What if she's not into you that way anymore?"

I laughed. "She'll be into me."

"That's a lot of guessing there. And hoping," Tyrell said. "Maybe offer to buy her a house."

"She won't let me." I knew that for a fact. "And that wouldn't help at all, anyway. I want us to be under the same roof. I want us to have equal time with our kid. And I don't want either of us to miss a single thing that goes on with that kid."

"Like waking up in the middle of the night to feed it?" Jasper asked.

I nodded. "Yeah, like that."

"You going to miraculously be able to breastfeed, little brother?" Tyrell asked with a grin.

"You know what I mean." And I had no idea if Bobbi Jo was

going to breastfeed or not. "I can use a bottle even if *she* wants to breastfeed."

Jasper brought up something. "Not all moms want their baby to have a bottle in the beginning. What will you do about that?"

"I'll deal with it when it comes to it." I huffed and crossed my arms over my chest. "She's got to move in. I'll make that a stipulation or something. I want my child in my home and nowhere else."

My brothers looked at each other then they cracked up. They thought I was hilarious. But I did want my baby in my home, and Bobbi Jo would have to get on board with some of the things I wanted.

We spent the last part of the flight in silence as I mulled things over. Bobbi Jo wasn't even a whole two months pregnant yet, and already there was so much to plan for.

When we got to the restaurant, I had an epiphany. "I wonder if the chef will give me the recipe for the lobster rolls. That way I can go back with not only the food but with a recipe she can use in the grill she's opening in the bar."

Tyrell nodded. "That would be a nice gift."

So, I was going back armed with both great food and something that would make her grill stand out. I would make sure her bar and grill were both great successes.

We ate, got an ice chest full of yummy seafood for Bobbi Jo, plus the recipe, then got back on the plane. I was all psyched to see her and sent her a text, asking her if I could pick her up later and bring her to my place. I said I had a surprise for her and me. Since it was Monday, I knew she wasn't working, as she didn't open the bar on those days.

She sent me back a text telling me she'd be waiting for me. I thought that was a pretty great start. Bobbi Jo didn't often want to be without her own car to make sure she could leave whenever she wanted to.

My hopes soared high as we got back to the small municipal airport in Carthage and I put the ice chest in the backseat of my truck, then headed to Bobbi Jo's while my brothers went home.

With all I had armed myself with, I felt like she would fall right into the great plans I had.

Pulling up to her parents' house, I got out of the truck and went to knock on the door. She opened it before I got a chance to knock. "I'm ready."

"Okay." I was kind of caught off guard. "You look pretty today, Bobbi Jo."

"Thanks." She headed to the truck, going to the passenger side.

It was a good ways up to the seat, and there wasn't a step to help her get up. So I walked up behind her as she hopped a couple of times to get herself up into the seat. Placing my hands on either side of her waist, I lifted her. "Here you go."

"Thanks." She closed the door quickly after I helped her up. After I got in, she looked at the ice chest in the backseat, then at me. "Where have you been today?"

"Maine," I said with a grin. "I went to go get you something I knew you would never go and get yourself."

She sighed as she gripped her hands in her lap. "That was thoughtful of you."

"I've done nothing but think about you, Bobbi Jo." I thought I should bring up the fact that she hadn't gotten in touch with me the whole week. "I've missed hearing your voice this last week."

"Oh."

I figured she was just moody with hormones. "Well, how was your week, Bobbi Jo?"

"Full." She sighed heavily. "The health department doesn't want to give me a permit until I make some huge changes to the bar. I called a contractor to see how much the changes would cost me and it's more than what I have. So, I guess the grill part is out."

"It doesn't have to be." I was still willing to go into a partnership with her. "Whether we ever planned on this or not, we're going to be parents together. We might as well be business partners too. We can make that whole bar over if you want to."

She looked out of the corner of her eye at me. "If you did want to come in as a partner, I could only let you put in the same amount of money as I have in it. That would be what the bar is currently worth, plus the money I've got in the bank. I couldn't let you do any more than that. And to make the addition to the structure, plus put in the professional grill, the cost is over three hundred thousand dollars. It's not doable."

"All I see is that some contractor is feeding you a line of shit." I knew that couldn't be right. "I'll find one who will be reasonable. We'll get that grill going, don't you worry. And I've even got a couple of recipes for you to start with. The lobster rolls, for one." I handed her my phone where I put the recipe in my notes. "The chef gave me the recipe and the right to use it. And for the other, we can serve small chunks of steak; we can call them Whisper Bites. The meat for the grill can come from our cattle. We'll make sure to put cattle for the grill in a grass pasture so they'll be only grass fed. That's a thing people like nowadays."

"You've sure been thinking about my business a lot." She turned her head to look at me. "*My* business, Cash."

I nodded. "Am I overstepping my bounds here, Bobbi Jo?"

"You might be. When I tell you what I've got to tell you, you might just want to take your offers back." She ducked her head and wrung her hands in her lap.

I decided to make her feel a hell of a lot more comfortable. "Baby, I don't want to take anything back. As a matter of fact, I want you to know that I want you to live at the ranch too. I want to give you your very own suite. We can make the baby's room right in between ours. And maybe, one day, you'll decide to move into my room, if we ever find ourselves wanting to be romantic again."

"You may not want that at all, Cash." She started to cry, and I pulled the truck over.

"Bobbi Jo, what's wrong?"

She shook her head and kept crying. And I only had one thing on my mind.

Is the baby all right?

BOBBI JO

The morning hadn't gone very well. I kept trying to tell myself that whatever happened was meant to happen. But it wasn't helping me much. No matter how many times I told myself that, it still hurt.

Cash had pulled the truck over; his expression was one of compassion as he asked, "Bobbi Jo, what's wrong?"

I wasn't sure how to say it. And the sobs that had erupted stopped me from being able to say a word. "I …" That was all I got out before a lump got stuck in my throat.

He took off his seatbelt, then slid over to me. His strong arms around me felt good. I buried my face in his chest as he shushed me. "Baby, come on now. You can tell me what's wrong."

Just having him hold me that way had me feeling better. But only a little. "Cash, I'm not sure if I'm still pregnant. I woke up this morning and there was some blood in my panties. When I went to the restroom, there was a little more. I didn't have a pregnancy test at home to take. We may not be having a baby at all. I might've lost it. Or at least be losing it. It's so tiny right now. That's why I didn't even want to tell anyone. I wanted to wait until I was three or four months pregnant before I said anything."

"We're going to the emergency room right now." He kissed me

on top of my head. "You just sit back and don't worry about a damn thing."

"I don't think this is considered an emergency, Cash." I tried to stop crying and opened the glovebox to see if I could find something to dry my tears and blow my nose with.

"It's an emergency to me." He reached into the compartment of his door, then handed me some napkins. "Here you go."

"Thanks." I blew my nose, then wiped my eyes. "Cash, if I'm not pregnant, I don't expect you to stand up to what you've just said."

"I *want* to be your partner." He looked at me as he took a left to go toward the hospital. "And I *want* to see you, Bobbi Jo. I like you. I want you. I don't care if you're carrying my baby or not. I want you."

"Really?" I found that hard to believe. "After how I've kept to myself and not given you any chances? You still want to see me?"

"I do." He reached out and took my hand. "The one thing I've found out about this is that I miss you every single day. I don't want to keep on missing you. I want you with me. I want you with me every day."

Before our breakup, he had come to the bar each night to hang out with me, even when it didn't end up in having sex. "You mean that?"

He nodded. "I mean it. I enjoy your company. And I really meant the apologies I've made to you. And if you will recall, I made them before I knew you were pregnant. This isn't all because of the baby. This is because I want you. And you know what else I can say and mean it?"

"No." I was still reeling from the fact that he wanted to see me even if I wasn't pregnant.

"I went to Maine for you. I can't stop thinking about you. And that means something to me." He squeezed my hand. "It means I love you, Bobbi Jo Baker."

I closed my eyes as I took in his words. "You love me."

"I love you." He pulled up in the parking lot of the emergency room, clicked the tab to release the seatbelt, then pulled me to his side. "Please tell me that no matter what happens with this baby, that you won't keep yourself from me. I don't think I'm the best man I can be if I don't have you. You make me want to be a better man, Bobbi Jo."

My breath caught in my throat. I had no idea what to say at all. And then it slipped out of my mouth. "I love you too, Cash."

The smile he wore went all the way to his eyes. His lips pressed against mine and I felt like the weight of the world had lifted off my shoulders. I'd felt so heavy for so long. Now it was all gone.

He pulled his mouth off mine. "Let's go inside and see what's happening."

So, we got out, went in, and found out that I was still pregnant. The doctor said spotting happened sometimes, and it might even happen more. As long as it wasn't a lot and no cramps accompanied it, then I was fine.

We left knowing we were still having a baby and now, we were in love too. Cash stopped just before lifting me back into his truck. "Don't answer me right now. But one day, I will marry you, Bobbi Jo Baker. I'm going to take you home now. To *our* home."

"Wait." I wasn't ready to do all that. "I want my independence. Living with you will take that all away. I still want to know that I can do this on my own."

His jaw tight, his body tense, he stared at me. "Bobbi Jo, why do you want to make this so hard on yourself?"

"Because I want to know I can handle it." I put my foot down.

"But I'm here and I can help." He didn't seem to be backing down at all.

"Do you love me?" I asked him as I crossed my arms over my chest.

"I do." He put his hands on my shoulders. "And all I want to do is take you home, put your sweet little ass into my bed—a bed that is soon to be known as *ours*—and make sweet love to you."

And that sounded pretty great to me too. "Okay. Let's do that. But then I'll go home. I want to get my own place. I want to go through this alone."

His jaw set, his body tensed up again; he could only stare at me. "You've got to be kidding me. You've got a man with tons of money and you want to do this on your own. You don't make any sense."

"Cash, I've got to know that I can do this without anyone's help."

He picked me up and put me in the truck. "Scoot over. We'll talk about this afterward."

"After what?" I asked as I scooted over, then he slid in behind the wheel.

"After I take you home and we connect in a way that I've only ever connected with you before." He started the truck and off we went. He draped his arm around me, then kissed the side of my head. "I think you need to be reminded of how good we are together. Afterward, if you still want to be all alone, then we'll talk. I want you in my bed or just down the hallway. And I want our baby in our home too. I want to share everything with you."

"Then you'll expect me to share everything with you too." I wasn't sure if I wanted to do that.

"Sharing is what people who love each other do, Bobbi Jo." He wasn't giving up.

And for a moment, I was okay with that. I shut my mouth and rested my head on his shoulder. "Maybe we should have sex. Maybe that would help me make decisions."

"And maybe you might decide to take a backseat and let me make some decisions too." He kissed the side of my head. "I am going to be the head of our family, Bobbi Jo."

I had to laugh. "You had better take a step or two back, big daddy. Little momma here has something to say about how things go too."

He laughed then kissed my cheek. "I'm just messin' with ya, babe. When it comes to our kid and us, we'll make decisions together."

As we rode out to the ranch, I really looked at the scenery as we passed by it. Tall oaks, old mesquite trees, and even some maple trees lined the road. Our kid would call this place home. Our kid would see this road on his way home to the ranch he would grow up on. And nothing could've ever made me happier.

"You know what, Cash?" I asked as we pulled up to the driveway. "We should be business partners too. I really like the idea you had about grass-fed beef. And we could do free-range chickens too. We could even make a big garden so we could have organically grown vegetables." I was getting all kinds of excited.

"Should we change the name of it too?" he asked me. "You know, to incorporate us and the ranch?"

"What if we call it, Whisper Bar and Grill?" I liked the sound of that. "That way the ranch will be known for more than just racehorse semen. I'd like my kids to have a better reputation than just semen ranchers."

"Kids?" he asked, laughing. "More than one?"

"Well, you'll have to marry me if you want to make more kids. I'm done giving you babies out of wedlock. I do have a reputation to uphold, you know. I don't want to be the only one in our little family who doesn't carry the last name of Gentry."

"I hope you brought a ring with you, baby." He pulled up in front of the wood cabin mansion that would be my new home. Then he reached into his pocket and pulled out a huge diamond ring. "But if you don't, that's okay. I happen to have something that will do for now."

I looked at the ring then at him. "Cash Gentry, will you do me the great honor of becoming my husband?"

He smiled. "I will. And Bobbi Jo Baker, will you do me the great honor of becoming my wife?"

"I will." I kissed the man I knew I would struggle with, have tons of fun with, and share all my love with.

Until death do us part.

CASH

Seven months pregnant and the baby shower had begun. My parents had come, as we had the party at a hotel in Dallas. Bobbi Jo's parents and mine were meeting for the first time.

She and I had run off to Vegas to tie the knot after agreeing to get married. We didn't want to wait long to get married and change her name to mine.

As our parents talked quietly in a corner, Bobbi Jo and I sat together as her sister opened the presents. Bobbi Jo hadn't been feeling well in the last week. She had an appointment in a week, so we decided it wasn't anything she needed to make a special appointment about. Until she gasped for air, grabbed my hand, then looked at me with frightened eyes. "Cash!"

"What's wrong?" I looked into her eyes and found pure panic in them.

"Something's wrong." She leaned into me and I felt heat coming off her.

"With the baby?" I asked as everyone gathered around us.

"I don't think so. I think it's just me." She took a shallow breath. "I think you need to get me to a hospital."

When I got up and pulled her to get up too, she collapsed. I caught her just in time, then carried her out.

"You should call an ambulance!" her father shouted.

"I can get her there faster than waiting on them." I got down to the lobby with her in my arms. She'd passed out, but I could tell she was still breathing.

Tyrell hurried to get the valet to bring his car around then we got into the back, and he drove us to the closest hospital. All I could do was keep kissing her on top of the head and praying that everything would be okay. "You're going to be all right. This is just a cold or something." It had to be something that easy; it just had to.

An hour later, with Bobbi Jo in a bed in the emergency room, the attending physician came in with a grim look on her face. "We've got the lab results back. And by what I see here, we're going to have to admit her. Her white blood cell count is very high."

Bobbi Jo looked up at me with frightened eyes. "What does that mean?"

I shook my head. "I don't know."

The doctor added, "We don't know either until we can get more tests done. Bobbi Jo, is there anything that's been happening to your body that's out of the ordinary?"

She chewed on her lower lip. "Well, I don't know if this is out of the ordinary or not for a pregnancy."

The doctor nodded. "Just tell me what it is."

"My left breast has been hurting. And some discharge has been leaking out of it. It smells bad too." Bobbi Jo looked up at me. "It started about five days ago. I didn't say anything to you because I thought it was normal."

I had to hold my tongue, pissed that she'd kept it to herself. "Well, we're here now. We can see if you need some help." I took her hand and held it up to my lips. "But, baby, you really should've told me when it first happened. You wouldn't have gone through so much pain, and this never would've happened if you had just told me."

The doctor nodded, agreeing, "It's important to let your husband know if anything is happening to you, Bobbi Jo. Where your health is concerned, you should always reach out for help."

Bobbi Jo nodded. "Yeah, I can see that now."

An hour later, we were in a private hospital room—along with our parents—when another doctor came in. "I'm Dr. Harvey. I've been brought in to see you. The lab results have been sent to my office and what I saw bothered me. If I could do an examination, that might help us to get to the bottom of things."

I nodded, and our parents left the room as the doctor pulled the hospital gown back to examine Bobbi Jo's left breast. She winced with pain as he pressed on her breast only slightly. And with that small amount of force, a dark liquid came out of her nipple.

He didn't have to say a word. I knew what was going on instinctively. "It's cancer, isn't it?"

"I'm afraid so." The doctor covered Bobbi Jo's breast then looked at me as my wife cried quietly. "We should operate immediately. And then we'll have to do radiation and maybe even chemo."

"No," Bobbi Jo whimpered. "I won't do anything until I have the baby. I won't put poison in my baby's system."

I sat down next to her, holding her hand, trying so hard not to cry myself. "Bobbi Jo, we've got to get you through this. *You're* important here too. Let's hear what the doctor has to say."

"No." She looked at me through the tears. "I won't do anything until the baby is born."

The doctor interjected. "Look, we've got more testing to do. I've ordered an MRI to get to the bottom of everything that is affected by this cancer. We can make decisions after we know more."

Bobbi Jo was being her usual stubborn self as she said, "It doesn't matter. My baby comes first."

The doctor reminded her of an important fact, "Don't you want to be around to see that baby, Bobbi Jo? Cancer moves fast. And the fact that you are pregnant with so many hormones moving through your body is only making this cancer grow even faster. You've got a chance to make it through this. Once it spreads to your lymph nodes, you lose some of the chances you have right now."

"No," she said again.

I hugged her. "Let them do what they need to do, baby."

"No," she whispered. "I won't let them do anything until the baby is born."

I didn't know what to do. I let her go and got up, leaving the room. She'd always been headstrong. But would she die before doing what someone else thought was best for her?

What could I do? Could I make her do what the doctors thought best? Could I demand that they do what I say and ignore her? Where did I stand on this? What rights did I have?

My wife wanted to sit there and do nothing for two months while cancer ravaged her body. And she expected me to sit by and let that happen?

No.

Hell no!

I went back into her room to find the doctor gone and her staring vacantly out the window. "I know you're mad at me, Cash. I can't help that. If I can hold onto this baby for another couple of weeks, then he's got a fighting chance. If I go under the knife, under the anesthesia, then there's a risk that I will die on the operating table. And our son will die with me."

"You don't know that." I hated when she thought she knew something and she really didn't. "You were so sure you were going to have a girl and you were wrong about that. What about that, Bobbi Jo? You're not always right." I didn't want to go into the whole thing, but she'd already begun the thought process, so I had to step into it too. "And if you did die on the table, the baby might not. He might be saved and then what? You're going to leave me alone to take care of a baby who's born two months early. And then you expect me to raise this boy all alone too. Well, no, Bobbi Jo. I want you with me."

She turned her head to face me. The tears had stained her cheeks. "You're Sway's father. You will have to take care of him no matter what. I told you I wanted to do this on my own and God took that out of my hands. But he put it into yours. You may have to do this alone, Cash. It might just have to be that way. But I will not go under the knife and make those chances any greater. I won't do it, so don't ask me to."

I had no idea what to say anymore. But there wasn't anything she could do about assessing the severity of her situation. After the MRI results came in, another doctor came into her room. The expression he wore told me the news wasn't good at all.

"Hey, doc," I said quietly as Bobbi Jo lay in the bed, not speaking, not blinking, not doing a damn thing. "What's going on with my wife?"

He looked at my wife. "You have been in pain for some time, haven't you?"

She didn't nod or say a word. And I couldn't believe she would do this to us. "Bobbi Jo, what have you done?"

The doctor pulled something out of the large envelope he held. "This is the tumor in your wife's left breast." He handed the thing to me. "And all those little circles under her left arm are where the cancer has taken over her lymph nodes. She's known something was wrong for about almost two months. Isn't that right, Mrs. Gentry?"

Bobbi Jo still didn't move or she say a single word in her defense. And I knew she had known something was wrong and she just hadn't told me or even her doctor.

"Is there anything we can do?" I asked him.

"We need to get her into surgery and we need to do it quickly," he said.

"I won't do it until I have the baby. That's why I didn't say anything when I first felt the pain and saw the discharge." Bobbi Jo looked at me with tired eyes. "I'm sorry. I really am. But I won't ever put the baby's life in jeopardy. His life is more important than mine."

I fell to my knees beside the bed. I held her hand and couldn't hold the tears back anymore. "Don't even say that. Please, Bobbi Jo. I love you. I don't want to lose you. I love our baby too, and he's got a chance here." I looked at the doctor. "Get me an obstetrician in here, please. I need to find some things out."

He nodded then left us alone. Bobbi Jo looked away from me again. "I don't know what you think can be done, Cash. I've thought this through. I've looked things up about this. I'll have to wait until the baby can be born safely. I won't agree to do anything else."

"I love you. I want you to keep on remembering that when things happen." I wasn't going to lose either of them. I wouldn't be able to live without either of them.

I won't live without either of them.

BOBBI JO

As my mother and father sat on either side of me, I tried to put on a brave face even as I fell apart inside. "It's going to be okay. You'll see. I'm going to have the baby in a month or so, and after he's born, I'll deal with the cancer."

Cash had left the room so I could talk to my parents. He'd said something about needing to get some facts straight. I knew he was grasping at straws, but I had to let him do something so he didn't feel useless.

Dad got up, wiping his hand over his face. "Bobbi Jo, I don't like this. You've been in pain and haven't told a single soul. Not even your husband. Girl, this isn't right."

Mom ran her hand over my forehead. "You should've told him, honey."

"Why?" I knew what he would've done. "I was only five months pregnant when I felt the first pain. If I would've told him then, he would've made me go to the doctor and stayed on me until I did whatever they wanted me to do. And we would've lost our son."

Mom sighed. "Sweetheart, more children can come to you. But you've got to be alive for that to happen. And Cash would've been right to make you get medical help. And that's why we're behind him with what he's trying to get you to do now."

"I know he means well, but this is *my* body. I want to wait." I knew I could make it long enough to have my baby.

My sister came into my room, her face red, her eyes swollen from crying. "Why, Bobbi Jo? Why did you do this to yourself? I hate you for this. I really do." She fell on her knees, shaking her hands in the air. "Why did you not let me feel her pain this time?"

"I'm glad you can't feel it, Betty Sue. I wouldn't wish this on anyone." I had no idea how much pain a person could live through. I was finding that out though.

Cash came in; a couple of doctors were right behind him. "I've figured it all out, Bobbi Jo. And you're going to like this." He stepped to the side as the doctors came around him. "Tell her what you can do."

"I'm Dr. Janice Prince," the woman introduced herself. "I am a specialist in premature babies. I will be personally taking care of little Sway when he is born."

The man introduced himself. "I am Doctor John Friedman. I am an OB-GYN. We've talked to the oncologist on your case."

I didn't care to hear what they had to say. "Look, I know you mean well, but I've made my decision."

Cash was suddenly at my side, his hand on my shoulder. "Hear them out, Bobbi Jo."

"But I don't—" I had to shut my mouth as my daddy put his hand on my other shoulder.

"Bobbi Jo, you hush up and listen now." He patted my shoulder. "We all love you, and we all love that baby you're carrying. Now, you let these nice doctors tell us all what can be done to help you both. And you just sit back and let us take the reins here, girl. Between your momma, your daddy, and your husband, I think you should feel like you're in good hands."

Betty Sue wiped her eyes and sniffled. "Don't forget about me. You've got your twin sister here too. You know I'm not about to let them do anything to hurt that baby. I can't wait to meet baby Sway."

Looking at all the caring eyes around me, I felt like I had no choice. "I'm not making any promises, but I will hear what you've got to say, doctors."

"Good," Dr, Prince said. "See, we can take this baby by C-section. We can deliver him safely at this time. With the MRI results, we were able to see that everything is looking good with your baby boy. And my team and I will be ready to deal with anything that might happen after the delivery. I can assure you that we have had to deal with worse situations, my dear."

Dr. Friedman took over. "I can have this baby delivered within an hour. With you already under anesthesia, your oncologist will be able to work with the surgeon to do whatever it takes to get you on the road to recovery. And you will go into that knowing your baby is safely out of your womb. That has been your primary concern, has it not?"

I had to nod. "Yeah." I looked at Cash. "You really think this is a good idea?"

He laughed as he looked at everyone else in the room. "I sure do."

"I don't know." I felt like things were moving too fast.

Cash kissed my cheek, then whispered, "*I* do know. Let me make this decision for us. For all of us—*our* family, Bobbi Jo. Like we agreed in our wedding vows, sometimes you would make the big decisions and sometimes I would. It's my turn now. Let me make this decision that affects our family."

"I might not be much help if I'm undergoing all this surgery and chemo and stuff." I knew I would be useless. "Can you handle the baby on your own?"

"If I have to, I will." He looked at my family. "But I think between your family and mine, I'll have all the help I need."

"You bet you will," Dad said. "Let him make this decision, Bobbi Jo. Trust the man. He won't steer you wrong. This man loves you and that baby."

I looked back at Cash. "You do love us, don't you?"

"More than anything else in this entire world." He kissed my lips softly. "So, can you sign the papers and put me in charge of your body for a while? I swear to you that I will only make good decisions where you're concerned."

I took his hand, pulling him close so I could tell him something I didn't want anyone else to hear me say. I didn't need that kind of hassle. "Cash, if my heart gives out while they're working on me, I want you to let me go. I want you to let me die."

He only shook his head. "No way in hell, Mrs. Gentry. I will have them bring you back to me and Sway over and over. So be ready to fight to live. I'll be fighting for that too."

"Well, damn." I didn't know what else to do. "You really do love me, don't you?"

He nodded. "I really do."

I looked at the doctors. "Okay, give me the papers to sign, and I'll put my life in my husband's hands."

After signing the papers, I looked up and talked straight to God. "I sure hope you know what you're doing up there, Lord."

Cash kissed me again. "Don't worry; He does."

As I looked into my husband's eyes, I tried hard not to cry but failed miserably.

Damn, I've got no strength left at all.

EPILOGUE

CASH

Sitting in a rocker in my wife's hospital room, I waited for them to bring her in. "She'll be here soon, Sway. She's out of surgery and is waking up now. That's what they told me. And soon you'll get to meet her face to face. She's very beautiful, so don't be alarmed. And don't worry about it when she cries when she sees you. You're pretty damn adorable yourself. But with a mom like Bobbi Jo, what could you expect, right?"

The door opened, and a whole bed came into the room. "Here she is," a nurse whispered as they brought my wife in. "She's awake, her throat's a little sore, and she's kind of loopy still from the medication. You'll have to hold the baby for her, Mr. Gentry. Don't think she can hold him on her own. That's going to be a while."

"Yeah, I know." I got up, holding my tiny son to my chest. "Can you believe he weighs three pounds?" I looked into Bobbi Jo's eyes. "You ate like a horse for the most part. You would've thought our son would've had some more meat on his bones."

"Sorry," she said with a scratchy voice.

The nurses backed away, leaving us alone. I put our son on the right side of my wife so she could look at him. "Take him all in. He's a keeper, baby."

She nodded as tears filled her eyes. "He's got your hair."

"Yeah." I kissed the top of her blonde head. "Maybe the next one will have your hair."

She looked up at me with big, glassy eyes. "No more."

I only laughed. "We'll see. So, you made it through surgery all right. I knew you would."

"But there's more," she said as she looked back at Sway.

"There is," I agreed. "But you can do it. You've got this little guy to make sure you do. And plus, you love me too. You've got a lot to live for."

She nodded. "Yeah." She ran her right hand over our baby's tiny head. "He's so small."

"He'll be big before you know it." I sat on the right side of her bed. "We'll be looking back at this day and wishing he was still this little. Of course, he'll be swinging from the chandeliers then and we'll be kind of mad at him for doing it."

She shook her head. "No, he won't."

I had my doubts. "Well, maybe he'll be a good boy. You'll have to get better to make sure that happens. I might spoil him rotten if you leave it all up to me."

She smiled. "I guess I'll have to try very hard not to let this cancer kill me, huh? I can't have you spoiling our boy."

"You better try very hard, Mrs. Gentry." I had so many plans for us; she had to stick around so they could come true. "First of all, while you were out and I was in charge, I made an executive decision."

Her eyes rolled. "What is it?"

"You're going to stay home for at least the first year. I've put your sister in charge of the bar and grill." I smiled at her because Bobbi Jo had been grooming her sister to fill in for us while we had the baby anyway.

"Good." She ran her hand over my cheek. "I want to stay home with you and Sway for a long time anyway."

"I want that too." I had no idea when I would be able to let my wife be away from me for any real length of time again. The time she was in surgery was miserable. I didn't know how much more I could take. "I want you right with me as much as I can have you."

"Me too." She leaned her head against me as we looked at our baby, tears in both our eyes.

The sun began to set outside the hospital window and night would soon be upon us. My little family might be starting out on shaky ground, but I had the faith that soon we'd be back at the ranch. One day soon, life wouldn't be like this, so unstable. One day we'd all be laughing again. One day, we'd look back at this time and thank God for all he'd done for us.

It might be at the beginning of our lives as a family, but I knew we'd found what everyone was looking for.

We'd found our happily ever after.

The End

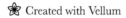 Created with Vellum

CPSIA information can be obtained
at www.ICGtesting.com
Printed in the USA
BVHW051212071221
623416BV00002B/244